Cimarron Jordan
&
El Paso

NOVELS BY MATT BRAUN

Cimarron Jordan
&
El Paso

MATT BRAUN

St. Martin's Paperbacks

Published in the United States by St. Martin's Paperbacks, an imprint of St. Martin's Publishing Group.

CIMARRON JORDAN / EL PASO

Cimarron Jordan copyright © 1975 by Matt Braun.
El Paso copyright © 1972 by Matt Braun.

For information address St. Martin's Publishing Group, 120 Broadway, New York, NY 10271.

www.stmartins.com

ISBN: 978-1-250-25238-8

Our books may be purchased in bulk for promotional, educational, or business use. Please contact your local bookseller or the Macmillan Corporate and Premium Sales Department at 1-800-221-7945, ext. 5442, or by e-mail at MacmillanSpecialMarkets@macmillan.com.

Printed in the United States of America

Cimarron Jordan St. Martin's Paperbacks edition / July 1996
El Paso St. Martin's Paperbacks edition / July 1999

10 9 8 7 6 5 4 3 2 1

Cimarron Jordan

NIGHT FIGHT

Jordan had just passed the last streetlamp when a sharp pain knifed across his thigh. For an instant he thought some wayward bee had stung him, then the crack of gunfire rolled across the flats and he knew different. Hurling himself to the ground, he caught the crimson wink of a muzzle flash out of the corner of his eye. Then another, not more than a couple of yards off to the right of the first in the patch of bushes. Dirt sprayed up right under his nose and he could almost hear the earth shudder as the lead struck home.

Those bastards were shooting at him!

FOR
JOSEPH ELDER
WHO ALSO HEARS
THE CALL OF THE WILD

Author's Note

"Cimarron Jordan" traces a period in western lore un-matched for violent men, shady ladies, and savage death. The extermination of the vast buffalo herds in the 1870s occurred side by side with the birth of the riotous Kansas cowtowns. Brought together in this frenzied decade were forces that would ultimately shape legends larger than life itself. Buffalo hunters, gunfighters, Texas trailhands—all thrown together in a maelstrom of violence, greed, and hu-man frailty.

When the great buffalo slaughter began, it was estimated that sixty to one hundred million of these ponderous, shaggy beasts roamed the western plains. Less than a dec-ade later they were gone, wiped clean from the earth, and along with them a way of life had ended. The Kansas cowtowns survived the buffalo by only a few years, yet their demise was no less certain. After the gunsmoke and dust had settled, all that remained was the empty plains— and the memory of a savage era. But the legend endured, lending a curious immortality to a time when death was the companion of all.

The protagonists brought to life in this tale are not wholly fictional. The character of Cimarron Jordan is drawn chiefly from the life and times of Billy Dixon a plainsman and buffalo-hunter of remarkable courage. Dixon's exploits were recorded by western journalists with something approaching awe; without undue exaggeration it can be said that he had more lives than a cat.

The character of Virge Hollister is patterned on the most ruthless of western lawmen, Wyatt Earp. While ostensibly a peace officer, Earp was a deadly killer whose energies were devoted primarily to political conniving, mining speculation, and assorted swindles. Among the lesser-known truths about this fabled marshal is the fact that some of his family got their start operating two-bit whorehouses in the Kansas cowtowns.

Cimarron Jordan is the story of two men, both fictional, and yet somehow closer to reality than the tinseled myths so widely credited in western folklore. Like the men they lived with, fought, and killed, Sam Jordan and Virge Hollister were flawed, imperfect. But never were they to be counted among those cold and timid souls who lacked the courage to dare greatly.

MATTHEW BRAUN

One

1.

Dodge City was just beginning to stir as the two men crossed the railroad tracks and rode toward Front Street. The dusty plaza was still fairly empty, but several wagons were already drawn up before the row of stores and saloons across the way. Overhead, the merciless prairie sun was climbing steadily, and those with business to conduct had gotten an early start. Plainly, the day was going to be another scorcher.

The riders were covered with grime and had the look of men who had slept lightly, if at all, for some nights past. Their horses were even more jaded, planting each hoof in a weary, shuffling plod. Anyone could tell at a glance that the animals had been pushed hard and without rest over a long stretch of ground. The men, oddly enough, appeared more frazzled than worn—their clothes stiff with an accumulation of dust, sweat, and rancid grease. About them clung a pungent, unsavory odor—the sharp bite of green hides and fresh tallow—so that even a pilgrim just off the noon train would have had no trouble spotting them as buffalo-hunters. Yet, ripe as they were, it was their eyes that told the tale. Bloodshot, veined through with a guarded wariness—the eyes of men grown flaky with looking over their shoulders.

1

Still, the condition of their mounts and the haggard cast to their eyes caused few heads to turn along Front Street. The fight at Adobe Walls was by now common knowledge in Dodge, and folks just couldn't be bothered further. Those that weren't swamped with work were still trying to get their toes uncurled from the Fourth of July. The summer of 1874 had given them much to celebrate, and somehow the fate of a bunch of grubby buffalo-hunters seemed to have lost even passing interest.

Cimarron Jordan reined his roan gelding to a halt before the hitch rack at Rath's Trading Company and dismounted. When his boots hit the ground he just stood there for a moment, looking at the weathered storefront like a man who all of a sudden finds himself in a place he hadn't rightly expected to see again. Beside him, Lon McCabe eased from his saddle with the creaky stiffness of someone too long on horseback. Jordan had the edge on him by twenty years or so, and the ride from Adobe Walls wasn't one McCabe was likely to forget. Not anytime soon, leastways.

Stamping his feet to bring them back to life, the older man let his gaze slew up and down Front Street, as though mildly surprised to discover it still standing. When he had first come here, back in the spring of '71, it was nothing more than a rude collection of dugouts, log shanties, and patched tents. After calculating Dodge's propects at double-ought zero, he had hurried on to Abilene—the rawest no-holds-barred boomtown on the western prairies. Now, barely three years later, Dodge was a bustling little metropolis. Hammered together right out in the middle of nowhere, as if it had sprung overnight from the dusty bowels of the Kansas plains.

The wonder of it never ceased to amaze him.

Granted the fact that Fort Dodge, situated five miles east along the banks of the Arkansas, had played a big part in the town's dizzying growth. But the snowball was only partly the army's doing. It was buffalo-hunters that had made Dodge. Buffalo-hunters, flint hides, and the arrival of the railroad along about cold weather the fall of '72. They went hand in glove—dovetailed in time and place as neatly as fresh snow on frost-hardened ground. Ruminating on it as the numbness slowly faded from his legs, McCabe had to admit that one without the other would have been as useless as tits on a boar hog.

Though he felt he would likely bleed to death if he didn't

2

shut his eyes pretty quick, McCabe couldn't help but marvel at the sprawling, wind-swept hodgepodge of buildings. He was sort of like a snot-nosed kid, all goggled-eyed at the candy counter.

Down at one end of the street was the Dodge House, Zimmerman's Hardware, and the Long Branch, flanked by a mercantile outfit and a couple of greasy spoons. Then up the other way was a scattering of saloons, two trading companies, another mercantile, and the bank. Across the tracks—what folks had taken to calling the South Side—were his two favorite watering holes, the Lady Gay and the Comique. Surrounding them, within easy walking distance drunk or sober, was a regular plague of gambling dives, dance halls, and sporting houses. Wild cards, wicked women, and all the popskull a sane man could want!

Sometimes just thinking about it made him shiver all over.

After a while McCabe got hold of himself and looked around to find Jordan loosening the cinch on his roan. The gelding gave a great sigh of relief and farted loud enough to rattle windows. Jordan shot the old man an amused look, then started slapping dust from his shirt, and mounted the steps to Rath's store. McCabe stared after him for a moment, then tagged along, muttering crossly to himself.

To the best of his recollection, he had been Jordan's chief skinner for better than two years. Long enough to get to know a man's quirks pretty good. But he could sooner stand on his head and piss straight up than predict Jordan's next move. They had just ridden one hundred and fifty miles stirrup to stirrup, and Jordan acted like his jaws were broke the whole time. Now, out of a clear blue, he starts handing out grins just because a horse lets go with a cannon roar.

There wasn't any rhyme or reason to the man. None at all. Sometimes it got downright mortifying trying to figure out which way he was going to jump.

When they walked through the door, Jason Rath came around the counter with a big smile and an outstretched hand. "Sam! My God, boy, you're a sight for sore eyes. I'd about given you up for lost."

"Howdy, Jason," Jordan said, returning the merchant's handshake with a slow grin. "Case you hadn't heard, you're pretty close to right. Whole passel of us came near to losin' everything we had. Topknots included."

"I know," Rath nodded soberly. "Hank Lease killed his

3

horse getting here with word you had been attacked." The storekeeper paused, lifting an eyebrow quizzically. "Wait a minute, now. You mean to say you didn't meet up with the relief column?"

"Can't say as we did." Jordan glanced sideways at McCabe, who just shrugged and shook his head. "Course, that's big country out there, Jason. We left Meyer's tradin' post night before last with twenty-five men. Lon and me came on ahead when we hit Crooked Creek."

"God almighty," Rath blurted. "That bunch headed to Adobe Walls isn't much bigger than the one you brought in. The army turned stone deaf when Lease asked for help, and he could only get about forty volunteers here in town."

"Well, I don't reckon it'll make much difference one way or the other. Injuns sorta got scarce right after we sent Hank for help. We just waited around a few days to make sure they weren't comin' back before headin' in here."

McCabe shifted his quid of tobacco to the off cheek and snorted. "Yeah, but for a while there it was tighter'n a bull's ass in fly season. What Cimarron's not sayin', Mr. Rath, is that them Comanches was half-froze for our scalps."

Jason Rath was neither a brave man nor a coward. He was a merchant. Short and balding, growing stocky with years, he no longer felt a youngster's compulsion to wager against time and life. He left the fighting to those better suited for such things. Sam Jordan—known amongst buffalo men by the *nom de guerre* Cimarron—was a bolder sort. He liked to fight, looked on it as a highly refined sport, and was better at it than most. Sometimes he fought for the same reasons that goaded other men to draw blood. But only sometimes. More often than not he fought for reasons all his own—reasons which few men would have understood had he bothered to explain.

Rath had been fascinated by the young hunter from the start. Though Jordan was twenty years his junior, they had been partners in the trading company since the fall of '73, almost a year now, and the little storekeeper hadn't once regretted it. Each complemented the other, and it had been a profitable arrangement for both of them. But profits weren't everything, not even to a shrewd tradesman like Rath.

There were times Jordan put him in mind of some great

4

carnivorous beast, one that had been housebroken, half-tamed, and allowed to roam unchained through the streets. The curiously addictive part was in not knowing what he would do next—and watching him do it to other men. Sometimes it was even better than profits. Not often, but enough to keep the juices flowing and the nerve ends jangling with anticipation.

Glancing from McCabe back to Jordan, he said, "Sam, exactly what happened out there? Hank Lease was shouting a thousand Indians one minute, and in the next breath he upped it to two thousand. We haven't had the straight of it yet."

Jordan's features tightened, and his gaze again went stony, the look of a hunter remembering what it was to become the hunted. Given to few words, he made it short, cutting a six-day siege to the bare bones. The attack had come at dawn on Sunday. Something over a hundred hunters had gathered at Adobe Walls, after a spate of rumors circulated that the Indians meant to wipe out the men who were methodically exterminating their buffalo herds. The plains tribes were bent on destroying the hated trading post once and for all; they believed the Treaty of Medicine Lodge barred all white men from their ancient hunting grounds in the Texas panhandle.

Jordan had been outside tending his horses when he happened to glance toward a timbered grove to the west. What he saw froze his blood. Thundering forward was a mounted horde of Comanches and Kiowas—later estimated at six hundred strong—and even from a half-mile away their shrill war-cries penetrated right to the marrow. Jordan and a few men forted up in a sod saloon, while most of the hunters took cover in Meyer's trading post. Wave upon wave of Indians surged past the tiny compound, riddling the buildings with rifle fire as they swept forward. Oddly, or so it seemed at the time, the warriors responded with uncanny precision to bugle calls which bore a marked similarity to those used by the U.S. Cavalry. Only afterwards were the defenders to learn that the raiders' chief, Quanah Parker, had drilled his warriors in the disciplined tactics of the Long Knives.

Protected by foot-thick adobe, the hunters blazed away with their heavy buffalo guns. Before long, the toll of Indian dead had mounted alarmingly, and they began falling back in some confusion. By noon the warriors had ceased charging altogether, seemingly content to keep the white

5

men pinned down with sniper fire. The day ended in a stalemate. The buffalo men were trapped, but the Indians clearly had no heart for further frontal attacks. The siege lasted two more days; thereafter the warriors offered only a token show of force, disappearing entirely on the sixth day. When it was over, three hunters, twenty-eight oxen and fifty-six horses had been killed. Though there was no way of being certain, since the Indians carried away their dead, it was speculated that close to a hundred warriors had ridden on their last raid.

Rath listened attentively while Jordan talked, savoring every detail of the bloody fight. Yet some inner recess of the storekeeper's mind was separated, wholly apart, studying the man rather than his words. What he saw was the thing he had pondered from the start—some elusive essential about the young hunter that had intrigued and baffled him from their very first meeting. Unlike so many of his rootless, nomadic breed, Jordan was a man of seemingly inexhaustible contradictions, his character riddled with disparate traits which defied simple explanations.

Though he wasn't a tall man, he was full-spanned through the shoulders, with wrists thick as a singletree, and arms knotted with muscle. Over one eyebrow was an angry, jagged scar, and his nose was a hair off center, marks of saloon brawls long since forgotten. Certainly no one would call him a handsome man, nor one to turn the ladies' heads. Yet women were somehow drawn to him, almost in the manner of a moth to flame. Rath found that strange, very strange indeed. All the more so since Jordan had been keeping company with his daughter for close to a year now.

Perhaps it was the windseamed, burnt-leather features, somehow ruggedly forceful under a thatch of sandy hair and a full, bristling moustache. Or maybe it was his eyes—uncommonly blue, deceptively tranquil—gazing at nothing, yet somehow conveying the impression that he saw everything. *Perhaps, maybe, could be.* It was still a puzzle, for overall there was a formidable quality to Jordan—wide brow, square jaw, cleft chin that seemed to have been split with an ax—something that made others walk lightly in his presence. But it was heaping contradiction upon contradiction, for at the same time, there was nothing cold or intimidating in his manner.

While laconic and hardly a back-slapper, Jordan was amiable as a good-natured bear, the kind of fellow folks

6

went out of their way to cultivate as a friend. Flip the coin, though—trigger whatever it was that lay simmering just beneath the surface—and it was sort of like getting in a fist fight with a real live gorilla. Jordan had cleaned out every saloon and whorehouse on the Kansas plains in his time. Not just once or twice, either. He made it a regular practice. Like clockwork. Only it was Cimarron Jordan who tolled the bell.

Watching him now, Jason Rath felt more perplexed than ever. There were few things he couldn't fathom once he set his mind to it, but this likeable young hellion had him stumped. No two ways about it. Abruptly, the merchant became aware that Jordan was no longer talking. Instead, Lon McCabe was chattering away like a magpie.

"Aw, go on, Cimarron, tell him. Sometimes you get to actin' like a shrinkin' violet."

"Tell me what?" Rath inquired, looking from one to the other.

Jordan didn't answer, and McCabe's eyes crinkled with what passed for a smile. After a couple of seconds the old skinner let go with a wheezy sort of chuckle. "Just look at him, would'ya. Never saw a feller to hide his light under a bushel like this'un."

Lon McCabe was a grizzled, shad-bellied character, all elbows and knobs and bony joints. Though some men claimed they had once seen him smile, he was best known for his flinty stare, an ornery disposition, and a perpetually constipated expression—sort of sour and tight-lipped. His face was covered with a wild, matted beard, so brushy and stickery he looked like a cocklebur with eyes. Yet for all his astringent manner he was a staunch friend, and tagged after Jordan like a grumpy pup.

Still, having him for a sidekick carried its own liabilities. Where a man just naturally wouldn't brag on himself, McCabe was cussed enough to do it for him. Often at the most awkward times. And loudly.

Like many plainsmen, McCabe had a natural flair for storytelling, one which generally held people spellbound. Darting a mischievous glance at Jordan, he began to set the scene. It was the third day of the siege. Since sunup, Indians had been scarce as snake tits. Then, along about noon, a little covey of redsticks appeared on a bluff east of Adobe Creek. Just sitting their horses like a bunch of stuffed owls, watching the trading post. They were so far away they weren't more than specks against the skyline.

7

But that didn't stop Cimarron. No sireee-bob! He laid old Lucretia Borgia—his big Sharps .50—on a windowsill, took a deep breath, and squeezed off. *Boom* went Lucretia, and everybody started waving smoke like mad so they could get a gander.

McCabe slapped Rath on the shoulder and cackled crazily. "Well, sir, I'll kiss your ass and bark like a fox if he didn't drop one of them Injuns. Got him square through the lights, and sent that scutter spinnin' ass over teakettle. Now here's what I was gettin' around to tellin' you. Couple of days later we paced it off, and sure as I'm standin' here, Cimarron made a shot that weren't far shy of a mile. So close it ain't enough to argue about. A mile mind ya! You ever hear tell of such a thing?"

Rath shook his head with just the right touch of amazement, then smiled over at Jordan. Before he could say anything, the younger man took the lead. "Don't pay him any mind, Jason. Lon's so full of hot air he sits around spurtin' like a gassy dog."

"Is that a fact?" McCabe croaked indignantly. "Now I suppose you're gonna tell us you didn't make no such shot. That Injun just died of sunstroke, or old age maybe."

"Well I'll tell you what is a fact. We got the hell out of there and we're not going back." Jordan's steely gaze held for a moment, then he turned back to Rath. "Don't matter how good a shot a man is, there's too many Comanche out there to my way of thinkin'. Besides, it's the hunters that draw 'em, and that country's gettin' too crowded. Soon as the wagons catch up, we're headin' farther south. Somewhere along the Brazos more'n likely."

The storekeeper just nodded, hardly surprised. Jordan had never been a man for crowds, and in that respect, at least, he was running true to form. He was what men called a trailblazer, opening the way, always searching for country that had never heard the hollow roar of a Sharps buffalo gun. Still, even that wasn't as simple as it sounded. There were times he suspected Jordan was searching for something besides virgin hunting ground. Exactly *what* remained unanswered, though. Just another riddle to add to the collection.

Setting the thought aside, he smiled benignly. "Have supper with us tonight. You can tell me all about it then. Besides, if I didn't bring you home, Julia would roast me alive."

Jordan chuckled softly. "She could do it, too. Tell her

to look for me. I'll be there with bells on." Looking around, he caught McCabe's eye. "C'mon, Lon. Let's go get a bath and some new duds. I'm so ripe I'm startin' to wind myself."

McCabe frowned, not exactly partial to water in any form, and they turned to go. Then Rath suddenly recalled an interesting little tidbit. "Say, Sam, I almost forgot to tell you. Virge Hollister killed a couple of cowhands in Wichita a few weeks back. What's that make? Six? Seven? For a lawman, he's getting quite a reputation."

"Beats me. I haven't been keepin' score." Jordan waved and headed for the door. "See you tonight."

But as he hit the boardwalk, Cimarron Jordan's casual manner faded rapidly. Virge Hollister was his oldest friend, and the news disturbed him more than he cared to admit. Killing buffalo for a living was one thing. Killing men for wages was another ball of wax entirely. Even if a fellow did have a star pinned on his shirt.

As Jordan headed toward the Long Branch and a good stiff drink, it came to him that Jason Rath hadn't been far off the mark.

Virgil had come a long way since their early days together.

2.

Sam Jordan had drifted into Abilene the spring of '71 with holes in his clodhoppers and three lonesome dollars to his name. He had worked his way west as a mule skinner, stable hand, and general roustabout. Behind, back home in West Virginia, he had left his folks laid out in the family plot on their barren rock-garden of a farm. With nothing to hold him, he had pulled up stakes and done what every plow jockey on the wrong side of the Mississippi always dreamed of doing.

Come West to make his fortune. Fight Indians. See the elephant.

West, where men were men and women were glad of it. West, where a man's grasp was limited only by his reach. Where a man could stretch and grow and find out just how big his stride actually was.

Naturally, he had come to Abilene. The Sodom and Gomorrah of the plains. The jump-off to nowhere. The first great boomtown to arise on the windswept western prairies.

Slung together out of spit and ripsawed lumber, Abilene had been erected overnight on the banks of the Smoky Hill. As the crow flies, it was about a hundred and fifty miles due west of Kansas City, and farther on there was nothing but buffalo, lots of Indians and a shimmering green sea known only as the Plains. Joseph McCoy had founded the town three years back for the express purpose of luring Texans and their longhorn cattle to the railhead. While America had been a nation of pork-eaters prior to the great war, the eastern public had suddenly developed a taste for beef. McCoy visualized a whole new industry—the business of buying and selling cattle—and he meant to be the kingpin in manipulating supply and demand. Texas beef for Yankee gold made sense to everyone involved. Before long the Chisholm Trail became a thoroughfare of commerce—all of it on the hoof. In the past three years something over a million cattle had been funneled through Abilene.

But that was only a drop in the bucket. The best was yet to come.

There were reportedly ten million longhorns south of the Red River—breeding like flies with each passing spring—and McCoy fully intended that most of them would pass through his stockyards in Abilene.

Curiously, the arrival of the Kansas Pacific on the western plains also coincided with a remarkable discovery in the leather industry. One which was to have vast repercussions across the breadth of the frontier—and serve as a spangly enticement for thousands of men like young Sam Jordan.

Late in 1868, a Philadelphia tannery made a startling announcement. Buffalo hide was superior to steer hide for a whole raft of products. Buggy tops, sledge bodies, book bindings, furniture, wall paneling, industrial belting, carriages, sleighs, even hearses. All the things which required strong, elastic leather that could survive rough treatment. Formerly the market in buffalo had been only for the finest robes, bought solely for their beauty and warmth. Few men had either the skill or the inclination to devote themselves to tanning buffalo hides. It was exacting work, time consuming and dirty, and not especially rewarding.

But harvesting buffalo for commercial leather—just as men had done with steers for centuries—that was a whole new deal. Estimates of the western herds ranged upwards of one hundred million buffalo, and tannery dealers were now paying as high as four dollars a hide. It required only simple arithmetic to see that any fool with a rifle could quickly become a rich man. There were enough buffalo for everyone—forever—and if a man was only a half-decent shot he could make more cash money in one season than he would normally see in a year. Ten years. Perhaps a lifetime.

Within months the slaughter was underway. Whole legions of aspiring hunters swarmed onto the plains, toting everything from muzzle-loading scatterguns to the most expensive European target rifles. As time passed, the killing became more sophisticated—organized, refined, brutally efficient—and each spring another small army of fortune-seekers was disgorged at the western railheads. In 1870 alone, two million hides were shipped east. The Kansas Pacific proudly announced that better than a million pounds of buffalo meat was delivered to the meat-hungry public during the winter. Hundreds of carloads of nothing but tongues were hauled from the railheads, afterwards to be sold in eastern butchers' shops as a delicacy, for twenty-five cents each.

The word spread across the nation. On the prairies of the far west the mother lode had been uncovered. Bonanza. El Dorado. Not in gold, but in the shaggy beasts that roamed the plains in inexhaustible numbers. Men were becoming rich as Midas through the simple act of pulling a trigger, and there was enough for everyone. Even the greedy.

Overnight, Abilene became a seething anthill. Buffalo and longhorns were the money crops, worth millions of dollars to those who had the grit to reach out and take them. But there were other ways to pan gold besides trailing steers or gunning down hump-back monsters. Slyer ways, effortless almost, in a sense skimming the cream from the top of the pail. From the distant border towns and river ports came the purveyors and panderers of a continent—gamblers, whores, bunco steerers, cappers, shills, thimbleriggers—jostling and cursing in a wild scramble for the top of the dungheap.

Sam Jordan had never seen anything like it. Back in West Virginia, vice was something restricted to dark alleyways and sleazy sidestreets. People spoke about it in whispers—except for preachers, who somehow never got down to the really interesting details—and in a way it had forever reminded him of catshit. Somebody always went around covering it up. But there was damn sure nothing hidden about it in Abilene.

That was how he met Virge Hollister. Lollygagging along looking at the painted ladies. Soiled doves, they called them out west.

That first morning in town he was just taking in the sights, strolling along Texas Street eyeballing everything like a real hayseed. For a boy fresh off the farm it was a little hard to believe. Especially coming on it all of a sudden the way he had. The street seemed nothing more than a hurdy-gurdy assortment of saloons, gambling dives, and dance halls. The cathouses had all been moved to a tract east of town called The Devil's Half-acre, but that didn't mean there was no sin for sale along the main thoroughfare. Every joint, from the rawest saloon to the dollar-a-dance palace, had its resident bevy of ruby-lipped charmers. The drinks and a whirl around the dance floor were merely a sampler, something to whet a man's appetite. Once the girls had a buffalo-hunter or trailhand worked up to a full head of steam, he was given a brief, and generally passionless, introduction to the backroom cribs.

Out front of each dive there were usually a couple of real stunners acting as shills. Decked out in spangles and a colorful array of feathers, their faces painted brighter than a new barn, they sweet-talked every man that came down the boardwalk. So long as his pockets jangled, and he could still fog a mirror, he was fair game. Once inside he would be relieved, in short order, of his money, his illusions about a whore's soft heart, and his unshakable faith in the power of his own manhood.

Sam had staked out a spot outside a building where he could watch the action. Two girls in particular had attracted his attention, and he was silently admiring their expertise in gaffing the suckers. He never had any inkling there was somebody behind him till the stranger spoke up.

"Look better'n peaches and cream, don't they? You plannin' to sample the wares?"

Sam turned to find a big, rawboned fellow eying him with a toothy grin. They were about the same age, and one look told him he was standing nose to nose with a brother hayseed. He smiled and shook his head. "Not unless they're cheaper'n they look. My poke's only got a couple of rattles left in it, and I got this bad habit of get-tin' hungry along 'bout sundown."

The newcomer thrust out his hand. "Shake, sport. I'm flatter'n a busted flush myself."

Sam pumped his arm a couple of times and let go. "Might as well get acquainted since we're rowin' the same boat. I'm Sam Jordan."

"Virgil Hollister," the other youngster responded. "Friends call me Virge. Where you from, Sam? If I'm not out of line askin'."

"No harm done. I just got in from West Virginia. How 'about you?"

"Illinois," Virge informed him. "I rode in on a cattle car this mornin', myself. Say, isn't this town the god-damndest place you ever seen? Man alive, I'll bet there ain't a virgin within a hundred miles of here."

"Yeah, I've been thinkin' the same thing myself." Sam's eyes slid back to the two dollies he had been ogling before. "Someday I'm gonna walk in there and buy them two for the whole week. Might even buy the joint and just let 'em take care of me personal."

"Hell, if a man's got that kind of money he don't need whores. Women'd be rubbin' up against him like he was catnip. Know what I mean?"

Out of the corner of his eye Sam took a longer look at his new friend. Somehow he got the idea that Virgil Hol-lister wasn't the kind of fellow who had to pay for it. Ever. There was just something about him. Dark wavy hair, high cheekbones, rugged chin. Sort of a haughty look—like a man accustomed to having his own way. Yet it wasn't his unmarred profile alone, not by a longshot.

There was a certain cast to his eyes unlike anything Sam had ever seen. Piercing somehow, even a little un-nerving if a man was prone to the shakes—downright odd, some folks would have said. The color was strange, too. Kind of gray and frosty, like the cold underbelly of a win-ter cloud. Then there was his height. Hollister was taller than most men, though there was nothing gangling or awkward about him. Sam could see that at a glance. His frame was corded and lean, free of suet, and when he moved it was with the effortless grace of a great, sleek cat. No doubt about it, they raised pretty fair specimens up Il-linois way.

Sam had no more than finished his inspection when shouts broke out down the street behind them. The boys

13

turned toward the commotion about the time two men opened up on one another with pistols. The man farthest away dropped like his legs had been cut off, spread-eagled in the street. The one left standing was obviously a trail-hand, and he looked to be about half crocked. Sam had heard that gunfights were an everyday occurrence in Abilene, and that seemed to be the case.

Wine, women, and a cold deck of cards. The ruination of many a poor boy. Long before his time.

Sam was sort of ruminating to himself about the old bitch called fate—a habit he had picked up traveling light and alone—when a dudish-looking jasper stepped out of the Alamo Saloon and started toward the cowhand. The man had hair that trailed down over his shoulders, and he wore a long frock coat. From a distance it appeared he had some kind of sash around his waist, and the butts of two pearl-handled pistols stuck out over the top. He stopped about twenty feet off from the Texan and said something. The boys couldn't exactly make out the words, but from his gestures it was clear he didn't mean to take any back talk.

"Wild Bill Hickok!" Virge whispered under this breath. "That drover don't have the chance of a snowball in hell."

Just then the Texan made his move. Only it turned out to be the last thing he ever did. Hickok's hand flashed in the sunlight, one of the pearl-handled Colts appeared, and two sharp reports bracketed down the street. The trailhand stumbled backwards, clutching at his gut, then just sort of keeled over and fell spraddled out in the dust. Wild Bill Hickok glanced up and down the street—as though he was ready to accommodate every Texan in town—then turned and sauntered back to the saloon.

Virge Hollister let out his breath in a low whistle, and kept staring at the doors where Abilene's marshal had disappeared. "Jesus Christ! Did you see that? The way he gunned that feller down. Bastard's got more guts than a slaughter house."

"Yeah, he's a cool bird awright," Sam agreed. "C'mon, I'm gonna break loose four bits for a couple of drinks. Seems like my mouth went dry all of a sudden."

"Dry! Hell, that's not the half of it," Virge laughed. "Somebody'd have to prime me before I could work up a decent spit."

They adjourned to one of the cheaper saloons, and found an empty spot at the end of the bar. After a couple of sips of forty-rod, and a rehash of what they had just seen, the boys finally worked around to problems of their own. Namely, money. And how to go about getting some. They were both scraping the bottom of the barrel, and it was either go to work or go hungry.

"Well the way I see it," Virge announced grandly, "there's only one job out here fit for a man. I've sorta got my cap set on being a trailhand. Thought I'd sign on with one of the outfits while they're in town, and go see what all the yellin's about down in Texas."

"I wish you luck," Sam observed, "but punchin' cows isn't my idea of gettin' ahead. Not for thirty a month and found. There's better ways."

"Yeah?" Virge bristled. "Name me one."

"Buffalo huntin'. That's where the real money's being made."

"Sam, you must be pullin' my leg. You ever smelled a buffalo hunter? I've only been in town one day, but I've seen enough to know that's the rottenest job God ever handed out."

"Like as not you're right," Sam conceded. "But that's splittin' hairs too fine for me. I only came out here for one reason. Money. And I don't mind gettin' my hands dirty for eight, maybe ten thousand a year."

Virge gave him a frowning look of disbelief. "Now I know you're funnin' me. Christ almighty, the only people that make that kind of money are whores and gamblers. Maybe bank robbers."

"Well every man to his own poison," Sam noted. "But if you're gonna be a trailhand you might as well crap in one hand and wish in the other. Leastways where money's concerned. Long as somebody'll pay three or four dollars for a buffalo hide, I'm gonna cash in while the gettin' is good. Way I've got it figured, I can shoot as good as the next man. Better'n most. And from what I hear it's not uncommon for a feller to get upwards of two thousand hides a year."

"By damn, you are serious, aren't you?" Virge wasn't bad figuring either, and a crafty look came over his face. "Supposin' a fellow wanted to start out huntin' buffalos. Not that I'm sayin' I would, mind you. But how would he go about it?"

"First thing he'd have to do is hire out to some experienced outfit. Spend about a year learnin' the trade. After that, all he needs is a gun and a half-assed stake and he's

15

his own boss. The buffalo are free. First come, first served."

Virge downed the rest of his drink and mulled it over for a minute. Then he turned and flashed that toothy grin. "You know, I'm not a bad shot myself."

That very afternoon they had signed on as skinners, and departed for the Smoky Hill country west of Fort Hays. They were green and limber and full of juice, and like a couple of young peckerheads, they had hired out to the first hunter they ran across. But they had been lucky. More than they realized till they were off on the western plains, where the only law was what a man made for himself, and even God was a sometimes thing.

Monte Brown, the hunter they skinned for, was an old-timer, weaned on buffalo meat and black powder. What he didn't know about shaggies and Indians and staying alive in the middle of absolute nowhere hadn't been written. They had taken to the plains to become buffalo men, and they couldn't have picked a better teacher.

Still, Sam had always regretted it that they left Abilene so quickly. He never did get around to playing dip the wick with those two gals on Texas Street. Whenever he burrowed down in his robes that first winter, and his tally-whacker went to throbbing like a big, sweet toothache, he often thought of such things.

All night long sometimes.

3.

When Julia Rath opened the door that night, it was as if Sam was seeing her for the first time. It was always that way, or so it seemed to him. Like suddenly stumbling upon a clear, bubbly spring in the parched wilderness, or breaking out into a meadow ablaze with goldenmane and winecups and the gentle scent of bee bush. Somehow, Julia seemed special that way, alive and fragrant, beautiful in a fashion that was generally reserved for wild things.

Though it wasn't a thing he dwelled on, Sam often wondered if it mightn't be the reason he kept coming back.

Julia came up on tiptoe, her eyes sparkling like violets in a bright sun. Softly her lips brushed against his cheek, and she squeezed his arm with an intimate touch that burned all the way through his shirt. "Come into this house, you naughty man." Like a golden butterfly fluttering about his head, she kissed him again. "Oh, it's so good to have you back. I'm just shameless I'm so glad to see you. But honestly, Sam, you don't know how dreadful this town can become when you're off gallivanting around among the heathens and beasties."

Sam never ceased to marvel at the queer way she talked. Julia was an educated woman, and he supposed that accounted for her peculiar choice of words. Grinning, he took her hands and spread her arms off to the side. "Now just look at that, would you. Lady, you're a downright tonic. Never seen anything to beat it."

"Flatterer." She batted her eyes, blushing furiously. But beneath her feigned modesty, a tingling warmth swept through her body, bringing with it a very unladylike sensation in the most curious places. "Sam Jordan, you're an incorrigible flirt. Now you just march yourself into the parlor and talk with Daddy. Otherwise you'll be eating burned steak for supper."

"Supper don't matter," Sam growled in a lowered voice. "It's dessert I'm after."

Giggling wickedly, Julia dug her nails into his meaty paw, then fled to the kitchen. Sam sort of got hold of himself and meandered innocently through the hallway entrance to the parlor. Jason Rath looked up from the *Dodge City Times,* presumably unaware of the little scene that had just been played out in the vestibule. Sam had an idea his business partner wasn't as thick as he acted. The merchant was too astute a man not to tumble to what was happening right under his nose. Still, other than pretending it didn't exist, there wasn't a hell of a lot the old man could do about it. Anyone with a daughter like Julia just naturally had to figure the tomcats would come scratching at the door. From there on out he must rely on Julia's good sense, and her discretion in never permitting the situation to become embarrassing.

"Come in, Sam." Rath gestured toward an easy-chair across from his own. "Make yourself at home. I was just reading the latest reports on the Indian scare. Appears the army has sent troops to chase them back to the Nations. Some fellow named MacKenzie is in charge of the operation."

"Well at least it's not Custer," the plainsman commented, settling himself into the chair. "Near as I can tell, the

17

only thing he's ever done is get 'em riled up more'n they were to start with."

"True. But in a way it's hard to fault the man too much." Rath folded the paper and placed it in his lap. "Washington is where the policy originates, and they're determined to see the Indians pacified. Even if it means killing them to do it."

"Sounds to me like pacified is just a tricky way of sayin' skinned and buried." Then he smiled sheepishly, struck by the absurdity of his own logic. "Not that I've got any love for Injuns, you understand. Nor them for me. Killin' off their buffalo don't exactly make me second fiddle to the army."

"I wouldn't worry about it if I were you, Sam. There will always be buffalo. Long past our lifetime." Selecting a pipe from the rack at his elbow, the storekeeper began packing it with precise care. "By the way, you haven't yet asked how we're doing this season. The way things are going, you know, we might easily become the wealthiest men in Dodge."

Rath began to recount the details in the manner of those who harbor an enduring fondness for black ink and neatly ruled balance sheets. The commerce in buffalo was growing by leaps and bounds. Over the past year, close to a million hides had been shipped from Dodge City alone. More than a fair share of this shaggy cargo had passed through the Rath Trading Company storage sheds.

Needless to say, Jason Rath wryly observed, it had been an extremely profitable arrangement. Nor did this take into account some three million pounds of buffalo meat freighted east during the winter.

Sam listened with only half an ear as his partner droned on. Business talk bored him stiff. Dry statistics, profit and loss, ledgers crammed with figures—it was something beyond his ken, and about as inviting as a toothless crone in a gunny-sack gown. While Rath talked, Sam's gaze drifted to the dining room, where Julia was bustling about with steaming dishes fresh from the kitchen. Now there was something worthy of a man's consideration. Not the food. Christ, hump meat and broiled ribs were better than any vittles ever laid out on a starchy tablecloth. It was the girl that brought the juices to a man's mouth, made his tongue grow thick and cotton sticky. There were morsels aplenty in a man's short fling at life, but none so outright delectable as a pretty woman. Especially none so tempting as the

18

spirited little tease sashaying back and forth in the next room.

Sam had good reason to smack his lips. Since well before reaching womanhood, Julia Rath had been giving everything in pants a severe case of heart palpitation. Though built along dainty lines, she was shapely in all the right places, with a crown of bunched curls sort of flaxen in color, and features that put a man in mind of a delicate cameo come to life. She wasn't tall, maybe shoulder height or a little less, but she carried herself erect and proud, like a high-strung mare full of fire and mettle. When she smiled it was sunrise calm on autumn leaves, all warm and smoky-bright, sending prickly shivers dancing along a man's backbone. She had spunk, too—more than a fellow would rightly ask for if he started out from scratch. Yet there was a disarming quality about her—a sweet, delicate brittleness—as though a harsh word or a hard look might shatter her beyond repair.

She was a rare morsel all right—bright, witty, devastating in the clinches—and it confounded the hell out of Sam as to what she saw in him.

Truth to tell, Julia really wasn't his kind of woman. He was rough, sometimes crude, and nobody would ever accuse him of fancy tastes or mannered ways. His idea of a good time was a roaring drunk, capped off by an eye-gouging brawl and a trip to the nearest cathouse. While decent women weren't exactly immune to his battered charm, he had always been curiously partial to whores. The why of it never really seemed to matter, and he hadn't yet bothered to think it through. In a twisted sort of way, whores just somehow seemed more honest to him; perhaps less of a sham in the open fashion they chose to live. There was something guileful, maybe even fraudulent, about a woman holding out for a wedding band—when all the time she was about to swoon from wanting it so bad.

Puzzling over it as he watched Julia arrange the table, he was more dumbfounded than ever as to why he kept coming back. Something about her drew him back—that much was for certain—and it wasn't just the kisses or the torrid little wrestling matches they had on the porch swing. It was more than that—a kindred link of some kind that as yet remained obscure—or perhaps the attraction of opposites, for never had two people been more different, almost a breed apart.

19

Whatever it was, it left him more disturbed each time he had been here and gone.

Julia Rath wasn't a loose woman, for all the panting and hot embraces she dished out so liberally when they were alone. She wanted a wedding band, church on Sunday, a houseful of kids, and a man who came home to supper every night without having his nose out of joint. She deserved it, too. More than anyone he knew. But—God forbid—not with him. He liked what he was. Cimarron Jordan. Curly wolf of the buffalo hunters. Foot loose and fancy free.

There it was. Plain as a wart on a billygoat's nose. *Free.* He was free as a hawk riding a soft plains breeze. Unfettered. No strings attached or hobbles to shorten his stride. Bound to nothing or no one—save the hungers of the day and the pleasures of the night. He came and went when he wanted and where he chose. There were no obligations, no ties, no one to hold him back. When he got an itch to see what was over the next rise, he went there. If it suited him, he stayed. If it didn't, he came back. Either way, he was his own man—answerable only to the rumble in his gut and the stiffening between his legs. Neither God nor man nor anything in skirts had a claim on him—except for those moments he chose to share. That's the way it had always been—the way he wanted it—and come hell or high water, that's the way it would go right on.

Julia Rath might get married. Might have a dozen runny-nosed kids and a front pew in the local church. Might even have a deacon for a husband, and a union joined in heaven, with life everlasting and a hallelujah choir swinging from the rafters.

But she sure as hell wouldn't have them with Sam Jordan. Not now. Not ever.

Sam had worked himself up so bad just thinking about it, he was ready to bolt from the house and make tracks for the nearest saloon. That scabby old bitch—the one called fate—had other ideas, though. Even as he bunched his muscles to spring from the chair, Julia stepped through the doorway and announced supper was being served. With an acute sense of resignation, he followed the old man into the dining room and took a seat at the table.

Julia heaped his plate with mounds of fluff and whipped air that left a turgid lump down in the pit of his belly. Laughing gaily, chattering on glibly about anything and nothing, she didn't seem to notice that he was stiff as a

20

corpse, and hadn't once managed to look her square in the eye. But Jason Rath was a hair more observant, attuned somehow to the fact that his young partner was floundering like a beached whale. The merchant was also rascal enough to break out his sharp stick and start probing the tenderest spots.

When Julia paused to take a deep breath, he broke in with a guileless smile. "Sam, I don't know if you've taken stock lately, but what with a partnership in the store and the income you derive from hunting, you're getting to be a man of means."

"Yeah, I reckon so," Sam conceded glumly. "Leastways, I've got money in the bank and I don't owe nothin'. There's lots of fellers worse off, I guess."

"Far worse off, my boy. Take it from me. I see them drifting through town every day." Rath piddled around in his mashed potatoes for a moment, as if studying some profound abstraction, then fixed the plainsman with an appraising stare. "Sam, it occurs to me that you ought to start thinking about settling down. You're pushing thirty, and that's long past time for a man to get in harness. Besides, you should begin taking more of an interest in the business end of this operation. I won't be around forever, you know."

Sam gulped, and felt his eyes bulge as he almost choked on a hunk of johnnycake. After an embarrassing silence he managed to swallow, and darted a mortified glance in Julia's direction. She appeared no less astounded by her father's remark, and he decided to skirt the issue lightly.

"Well, I'll tell you, Jason. I've given that a lot of thought here lately. Like you say, I'm not gettin' any younger. Trouble is—well you see, it's like this. There just aren't a whole lot of women that'd put up with a big lout like me. I mean, I'm not exactly what you'd call refined. Some folks might go so far as to say I was sorta short on couth. Guess I'm just not much for churchy ways or citified manners, if you get my drift. But I'm workin' on it. Yessir. Workin' on it steady. One of these days I'll have myself all reformed, and my hair slicked back real nice, and I got an idea things'll take a turnabout for the better. Wouldn't surprise me a bit if it don't work out just that way."

The older man smiled and shook his head skeptically. "Sam, the road to perdition is paved with good intentions. You'd better watch out or you'll end up in some old soldier's home wondering where the years went. Mark my word, it could happen. Frankly, I don't think you're as uncivilized as you make out. Why, if you just opened your eyes—" Rath paused and gave Julia a broad wink, "—I'll wager you wouldn't have any problems at all in finding someone willing to walk down the aisle."

"Daddy! You're just impossible." Julia's face flushed beet red, and her hand darted to her hair like a dying bird. "Now you just quit picking on Sam and let him finish his meal. He didn't come here to be interrogated like some moon-faced schoolboy." With that, she turned to Sam and stopped his fork in mid-air. "Sam, daddy tells me you plan on shifting your hunting farther south in Texas. Have you decided just exactly where you'll headquarter?"

"Close enough, I reckon." Blessing her for changing the subject, he met her gaze levelly for the first time since supper started. "We'll head for Fort Griffin down on the Clear Fork of the Brazos. After that, it's just a matter of scoutin' around for a herd."

Julia nodded thoughtfully, though she hadn't the faintest idea where Fort Griffin was located. "Do you think it will really be safer there than it was in the Panhandle?"

"Well, fair to middlin', I'd say. It sure couldn't be any worse. The Commanche'll have further to go down there, and there's more soldiers out that way, so maybe we'll be rid of 'em for a spell."

What he neglected to say was that the Indians had had little or nothing to do with his decision. Perhaps they had brought his discontent to a head, but hardly more. He was simply fed up with being surrounded by hunters whichever way he turned. The growing army of buffalo men had in turn slaughtered the herds along the Smoky Hill and the Arkansas, and they were now whittling away at the great herd along the South Canadian. Each summer, regular as clockwork, their numbers seemed to drive him farther and farther south in search of untainted hunting grounds. Once he had been able to hunt in peace, without the boom of hungry Sharps encircling him like a nest of swarming hornets. That was the way he wanted to again, and he meant to find it.

Even if he had to trek clean across the Staked Plains.

Jason Rath was all business now, his mind nimbly leap-frogging ahead to a shrewd and very practical move. Before Julia could cut him off again, he casually broached the idea. "Sam, I'm not overly familiar with that part of

22

Texas, but it stands to reason the hunting will gradually shift that way. They always follow your tracks like bloodhounds, and I suspect it'll be the same down there. Why don't we get the jump on competition this time? Open a trading post before Meyer or Wright or any of the rest of them get wind of what's happening. No sense in ignoring added profits, now is there?"

Sam gave him a long, slow look. "Jason, I get a funny feelin' you're tryin' to get me snookered behind a counter. You wouldn't maybe have some fancy notion I'd be runnin' this deal? Or would you?"

"Not at all, my boy. Perish the thought." Rath dismissed the possibility with a wave of his hand. "I can find any number of men to manage a trading post. The essential ingredient is locating it in the right spot. That's where you come in. You know the land and you know the migration habits of the herds. Just find me a good location and I'll take care of the rest in short order."

"Sure, I reckon I could do that." The young hunter flicked a glance towards Julia, then glowered back at the old man. "Just don't get any tomfool schemes worked out for me becomin' a pen-pusher. I'll find you a spot, and I'll even see that it gets built proper. But that's as far as she goes. Understood?"

"Understood and agreed to, Sam. You have my word on it." The merchant hefted his fork and jabbed at a platter in the center of the table. "Julia, pass the boy some more steak. My goodness, you'll send him out of here hungry and then he'll never come calling again. Sam, eat hearty now. You'll not see cooking like this where you're headed."

Julia gave her father a look that could have drawn blood on a rawhide boot. Without a word, she passed the platter and Sam dutifully speared another slice of steak. Even as he cut into it he saw that it was overcooked, and again suffered a vision of tallowed ribs sizzling and crackling over an open fire.

Somehow the mere thought made the charred steak all the harder to swallow.

Later, after a torturous hour of small talk, Sam awkwardly took his leave. Julia walked him to the door and stepped out onto the porch, just as she had done many times over the past year. But tonight Sam wasn't in the mood for fun and games. Back inside, just for a moment, he had come within an inch of being nailed to the cross.

Though it had been a near miss, it had rattled him plenty, and he wasn't about to risk another brush with lady luck. Not tonight, anyway.

Sometimes a fellow hit a losing streak, and if he had the sense God gave a ripe gourd, he just stayed clean away from the tables. The farther the better.

Which was exactly how he meant to handle Julia Rath.

Wisely, Julia didn't try to hold him. She sensed his skittish mood and contented herself with a fleeting kiss. Not that she didn't put everything she had into it. She did. But it was just shorter than usual. Fiery, with a dash of yearning, but not so demanding. After a couple of faltering attempts, he finally said goodbye, and sidled off the porch with an immense feeling of relief.

Turning out of the gate, he took a vote and came to a unanimous decision. Tonight he was going to get crocked clean out of his skull. Then he'd pick a fight with the meanest, dirtiest, nastiest looking son-of-a-bitch he could lay hands on. After that he'd go on down to Ma Smalley's and let one of the girls play God.

Lordy. Lordy. The way them little she-devils went about the resurrection was purely something to behold.

Whistling a tune popular around the buffalo camp, he struck off down the road toward town.

> Cooties and rotgut and wild, naked women
> They'll drive you crazy
> They'll lead you to ruin

4.

Toward the end of the week, Cimarron Jordan had his craw full of civilization. He was wrung out so bad his knees felt like custard, and his head ached fierce enough to make his hair sore. Besides that, he'd only been able to work up one good fight, and even then, it hadn't lasted hardly long enough for him to raise a decent sweat.

There was just no disputing facts. Dodge was getting too confounded civilized for grown men. Especially them that liked their meat raw and sprinkled with a little gunpowder.

Before sunup that morning, Jordan's outfit forded the Arkansas and headed south towards the Nations. Last night he had laid it out for the men. They would stick

24

generally to the Camp Supply road; once past the army post they would set a course for the South Canadian and the Washita. From there they would follow the winding banks of the North Fork of the Red, and cross into Texas where the Pease joined the main stream of the Red itself. After that, it was only a short haul to the Clear Fork of the Brazos and Fort Griffin.

Then, they could get back to the business of hunting— and flush their guts of citified cooking with a feast of hump meat and marrow butter.

Once south of the Arkansas, it was as if a monstrous burden had been lifted from Jordan's shoulders. Behind lay threats to everything he prized and considered of value. The worst kind of threats—creeping, insidious, always slipping up on a man's blind side. Churches and schools, the steady westward movement of reformers and the civilized hordes. Jason Rath, with his cunning little brain working overtime, forever scheming to turn a man into pen-pushing pisswillie. Julia, sweet and tempting, gladly handing out samplers of things to come—all the time contriving to put a ring in his nose. Or worse, her own personal half hitch around his tallywhacker.

Just the thought of it made him wince like a dog passing peach seeds.

Looking around, as the sun burned its way up from the earth's stubborn grasp, he counted himself a lucky man. He had cunning of sorts; he could fight all day and fornicate all night, and he was as fiddlefooted as ordinary man could ever hope to be. Behind him trailed two wagons, four skinners, and enough supplies to last clean into next spring. Ahead lay a land he hadn't seen, buffalo herds that weren't yet hunted out, and the juicy satisfaction of a man doing what it is he does best.

It was something worth fighting for. Or dying, if need be. Then should a man get rubbed out, he would at least cross over knowing he'd seen it all. That he had tasted everything on God's green earth that took his fancy. Bar none.

Leading the wagons away from the Arkansas Bottom, he began ruminating about the first time he had passed this way. Strange, how life had a way of repeating itself. Almost as if a man's days were made up of an endless circle; try as he might, he just kept stumbling across his own tracks whichever way he turned.

Sorting it out in his mind, he recollected it had been

late spring of '73 when he crossed the Arkansas. White men stayed clear of the Nations in those days, leastways if they wanted to keep their hair. Back in the fall of '67, the government had sent peace commissioners to treat with the Southern Plains tribes. They met at Medicine Lodge Creek, close to five thousand Indians and a handful of white men with wagonloads of foofaraws for bribes. When it was over, the Kiowas and Comanches had been ceded lands formerly owned by the Choctaws and Chickasaws. The Cheyennes and Arapahoes got what was then known as the Cherokee outlet. All in all, the commissioners figured they had done a good day's work. Swapped some land in the Nations that they didn't own for some land in Kansas and Colorado that looked pretty interesting.

The only drawback was that the Indians went away with the understanding that white men—especially buffalo hunters—would no longer be allowed to roam south of the Arkansas. Since Texas still retained title of her public lands, and hadn't been a party to the treaty, the whole shebang was suspect right from the start.

But there wasn't an iota of doubt about the newly formed Indian Territory. Anybody fool enough to go wandering in there was courting suicide plain and simple. The only law from the Arkansas in the north to the Red in the south was Indian law, and there was no appealing the verdict.

The fellow that meant to stray over the line and get back with his hair intact had just naturally better be part fox, part grizzly bear, and more than a little hoot owl.

Sam Jordan sort of figured he qualified on all three counts. With Virge Hollister and a crew of skinners, he had just finished a miserable winter up in Smoky Hill country. The herds up that way were all but annihilated, and Hollister had decided buffalo hunting wasn't a fit profession for man or beast. Jordan bought him out and promptly headed for Dodge City. He had heard that the long expanse of plains bordering the Arkansas was teeming with buffalo, and that sounded like just what he was looking for.

But when he got there, he discovered the sound had carried clean across the plains. Every son-of-a-bitch and his dog was out banging away at the Arkansas herd. There had been a financial panic back east and everybody was out of work. Railroad crews, cowhands, raggedy-ass sodbusters. Not to mention the annual drove of pilgrims come to see the wide open spaces. Seemed like everybody had a

26

gun that year, and bright and early every morning it sounded like the battle of Gettysburg had commenced all over again.

Matter of fact, it wasn't far shy of a war at that. Any lamebrain could see that the herds would be stampeded right out of the country. Which was exactly what happened. The shaggies veered off in all directions—south towards the Cimarron, southwest into the Panhandle, and west along the Arkansas, scattering clear to the foothills of the Rockies.

Jordan didn't wait around for the finale. With Lon McCabe and a couple of skinners, he rode south on a dead reckoning for the Cimarron. The army was bound to stop him if they could catch him, so he meant to get far enough below the Arkansas to forestall any interference. That left only the Indians to worry about, which couldn't exactly be considered the lesser of two evils. Still, a buffalo hunter had to go where there were buffalo. It was just that rudimentary.

Since everybody else had gone west, he elected to go south. Given a choice, he preferred taking his chances among the heathens to listening to the monotonous roar of a half-thousand Sharps.

Normally the Cimarron had a shallow channel, and such low banks a man practically stumbled into the water before he saw it. But spring melt-off had come late that year; when Jordan's outfit hit the river it was a mile wide and boiling mad. The current was full of treacherous underflows, and quicksand grabbed hold like a vise with every other step. To stop was to sink.

Jordan had the saddle horses ridden back and forth repeatedly to settle the bottom before any thought was given to crossing. Then the wagons plunged in, one at a time, with the stock doubled up for added power. The teamsters whipped and cursed like madmen, fighting to keep the heads of the mules turned upstream and the wheels moving. Once on the other side, they camped and broke out a bottle.

Not a man among them had any lead left in his pencil.

Standing on the south bank, looking back at what they had just come through, Jordan silently blessed old Monte Brown for teaching him that mules could outshine horses any day of the week. Maybe they were contrary and stubborn as sin, but come a tight situation they almost never went skittish on a man. Where a horse would break out a

27

tongue, or snap off a doubletree, a mule just bowed his neck and went right on digging. But for those long-eared hammerheads, the Cimarron would have claimed his entire outfit that day. With maybe a couple of men to boot.

Turning west along the river, they spent the remainder of that summer in a wildlife paradise. Buffalo were everywhere, more than a man could count, so thick that the hunters sometimes camped in the same spot for as long as a month. With such an abundance of game—unlike anything they had ever seen up north—the men gorged themselves on what seemed exotic fare. Great flocks of turkey swarmed over the southern confluences of the Cimarron, feeding on grasshoppers and prairie seeds during the day. Their squabbling march blackened the land in places, and the whirr of their wings in flight was like the deafening roar of a plains tornado. With dusk, the timber along the creeks was loaded with roosting birds, branches bent and breaking, so bunched together a man could get all he wanted with one shot.

Even deer roamed this land of plenty, like docile cows. Early in the morning, or just at dusk, a man had only to pick a spot and wait. Soon he had his choice from a herd of fat young does, and at times the game was so thick he could have done just as well with a club. The Dutch oven back at camp turned out venison in every known variety, and some newly invented. When the crew finally tired of fancy cooking, they simply went back to spitting it over open coals.

That was quicker and easier, anyway, for hardly a night passed that they didn't have a rack of wildfowl roasting to a golden brown. Grouse and prairie chicken, curlew and plover, pound for pound the most toothsome eating a man would ever hope to find.

In some ways it was like a fairytale, the kind of life all men dream of but few ever really see. Even with constantly being on the alert for Indians—who roved the land in small hunting parties—everyone in the crew agreed that they had never had it so easy. They lacked nothing. Wanted for nothing. Were as free as the wild things about them.

Overlooking a couple of close calls with rabid skunks, they spent a pleasant summer and early fall meandering through the Nations. The whole time they were south of the treaty line, they had only two run-ins with hostiles, and both times it happened when they were carting hides back to Dodge. They had the range on the Indians, though, what with the big Sharps .50, and Jordan peppered them so bad they made dust going away. Lately, the heathens had taken to calling the Sharps the *shoot today-kill tomorrow* gun, and they gave it a wide berth. Which suited Jordan and his crew just fine. Four men against a full war party would have been like spit on a hot stove. Even with the Sharps.

It wasn't a thought they dwelled on overly much—or even talked about amongst themselves—for it kind of gave a man the willies. Every now and then he woke up and discovered he had been damn fool enough to follow Sam Jordan clean down to the Cimarron.

Late fall found them on Beaver Creek, still in Indian Territory, following the herds in their annual pilgrimage southward. So far as anybody could tell, there were three great gatherings of buffalo on the western prairies. The Republican herd, ranging as far north as the Dakotas on the high plains. The Arkansas herd, centralized mainly within the boundaries of Kansas and the Nations. The Texas herd, which roamed from the Staked Plains on down to the upper Pecos. Each spring and winter these three massive gatherings shifted north to south, and back again. Like great furry nomads—sustained by the life-giving sun—they ate their way northward on the spring grasses, then swung about and grazed south in a race against the howling plains blizzards.

After leaving the Cimarron that year, Jordan and his crew had trailed the herd along Beaver Creek, then across Wolf Creek, and finally to the South Canadian. There, they had arrived just in time to get mousetrapped into the siege at Adobe Walls. Neither the fight nor the swarms of buffalo hunters were to Jordan's liking. Especially the hunters. Soon after the Indians disappeared from around the trading post he had set a blistering pace toward Dodge.

But the harm had been done. The story of his trek through the Nations quickly made the rounds. Cimarron Jordan—that's what they had started calling him right away—had moseyed clean through the Nations without so much as a scratch. Took close to six thousand hides in less than a year and came out smelling like a rose!

Thinking about it now, as McCabe and the wagons trundled along behind him on the Camp Supply road, Jordan grunted with disgust. The great herd that once ranged between the Smoky Hill and the Arkansas had been slaughtered in less than three years. Pretty quick now, what was left in the Panhandle would bite the dust. Then, unless he missed his guess, hunters would be swarming south like maggots on ripe meat. That left a man with a choice between the Republican or the Brazos—leastways if he had a notion to be off by himself. Since he wasn't partial to icicles dripping off his nose, that left only Fort Griffin and the Brazos.

But for how long was anybody's guess. Wherever he went—no matter how he dodged and slipped around—the bastards seemed to be forever snapping at his heels.

With a curse, he slammed the gelding in the ribs and put him into a stiff-legged trot toward Camp Supply.

5.

They crossed the Brazos in late August and pulled into Fort Griffin two days later, along about sundown. The fort itself was little more than a log outpost perched on a hill overlooking the river. Back in '67 it had been established smackdab in the middle of nowhere, as a deterrent to marauding Comanches. But the haughty Lords of the Plains were hardly intimidated by a handful of pony soldiers and a crude, weatherbeaten stockade. The western reaches of Texas were part of their ancestral hunting grounds; whenever it suited their purpose, they rode south to steal horses and harass the settlers squatting on their tribal lands.

When the army took to the field in retaliation, the Comanches merrily thumbed their noses and evaporated into the wilds of the Staked Plains. Over the years it had become a game of sorts, with the Indians racking up points right and left. Among those who failed to see the sport in this situation was a crusty old cavalryman, William Tecumseh Sherman. The general had laid it out quite succinctly in a recent speech. *The more Indians we can kill this year, the less will have to be killed the next war.* Farflung outposts had been beefed up with added troops and it appeared that, at last the army was going to get off its duff.

But Cimarron Jordan wasn't fretting about Comanches one way or the other. He had managed to keep his hair this long, and so far as he could recollect, the army hadn't had a damn thing to do with it. What interested him was the land—the vast, uninhibited stretch of plains sweeping west away from the cantonment.

Standing on the hill, looking west by north, he could see that the valley of the Clear Fork was inviting buffalo country. Clean to the horizon the land was bounded by rolling prairies of lush grass, wooded hills, and swift-running streams—the kind of spot any buffalo in his right mind would just naturally cotton to with a vengeance. There was plenty of graze, hardly ever a scarcity of water, and lots of sheltered hollows to break the icy winds howling down out of the north. Unless he was wide of the mark—and he hadn't been yet—there were more shaggies roaming around out there than anybody had every heard tell of.

After giving the fort—such as it was—a cursory inspection, Jordan and his men rode down to have a look at what passed for a town. The village was a squalid, ramshackle affair sprung to life on the flats below the fort. So far it was known as just that, The Flats, since its inhabitants couldn't be bothered with trivialities like naming a town. Even to a buffalo hunter, the place looked to be nothing but a grungy pesthole. The main street consisted of two saloons, a log trading-post, and a tent hostelry that advertised cots for two bits a night. This latter establishment reeked of stale sweat and dirty blankets, and more than likely provided a year's supply of cooties at no extra charge.

Closer to the river, where a grove of pecan trees towered overhead, there was a dingy collection of one-room shanties. Among the townspeople it was known as Naucheville, a local metaphor for the world's oldest, and most enduring, profession. The ladies operating these one-woman brothels were a hardy breed—true advocates of the free enterprise system on a modest scale—and they had something to suit the demands of any man. Whatever his tastes.

There were Mexican putas, Indian breeds, whites, blacks, even one high yellow, and a pink-eyed albino dubbed White Lightning. But they were as scruffy a bunch as a man could hope to find outside a kennel, and it was purely a matter of lust clouding their customer's eyesight that kept them in business.

Considering the town's scarcity of buildings, this thriving industry in nookie had mystified more than one recent

31

arrival. But it soon became apparent that the Flats was a regular anthill of commerce—albeit one of a most unconventional variety. The soldiers from the fort made up only a small part of the trade, squandering their paltry $7 a month in a binge that generally lasted no more than a couple of nights. Freighters, bullwhackers, and an occasional drifter upped the take slightly, but not enough to make any lasting impression. By far the bulk of trade came from two distinct, yet oddly similiar, factions.

Long before Fort Griffin became a frontier waystation, it had served as a hideout for assorted desperadoes and badmen. The Clear Fork of the Brazos was an isolated chunk of wilderness, remote from any railhead, road, or trade route. This backwoods seclusion made it a perfect haven for men riding the owlhoot trail. On any given night, the Flats was crawling with renegades whose chief aim in life was to put distance between themselves and the law. Gunslingers, bandits, cardsharps, common murderers, they all came seeking sanctuary—a fraternity of rogues gathered on common ground.

Then there were the cowhands. Throughout spring and summer great herds of longhorns were driven north from the Pecos valley, then wheeled east at Fort Griffin for an eventual link up with the Chisholm Trail. Cattlemen frequently camped on the banks of the Clear Fork, and it wasn't uncommon to see upwards of a dozen herds scattered about the countryside. Even on slow nights there were as many as fifty trailhands carousing through the Flats, most of them congregated in or around the local watering holes. The rest could be found standing in line waiting their turn down in Naucheville.

Though the cowhands were generally law abiding, they had never been accused of being peaceable. The outlaws, on the other hand, were usually willing to bust loose on either score. Since there was no law on the Flats—save for what a man carried on his hip—brawls were looked upon as a sporting pastime. If a fellow hit town on a really good night, he might even see a shootout. Violence was somehow just taken for granted—part of the local flavor—among men who prided themselves on being rough as a cob and ornery to boot. More often than not, it was bull-of-the-woods squared off against cock-of-the-walk, and blood flowed by the bucketful.

The fainthearts, or anyone afflicted with a queasy stomach, just naturally didn't hang around the Flats too long.

The first thing Jordan noticed as they came down the main drag, was the trading post. Though a crowd of cowhands in front of the nearest saloon paused to stare curiously in his direction, he paid them no attention. He signaled the wagons to a halt, then reined the gelding in at the hitchrack. When he dismounted, the Texans eyed his mule-ear boots and slouch hat with knowing smirks. One of them, decked out in a fancy concho belt and spurs big as a teacup, looked him over with a wiseacre grin and nodded at the roan.

"Say, mister, where d'ya get that goat you're ridin'?"

Jordan smiled crookedly. "Why, sonny, that ain't no goat. That's a sheep. Won him off a busted-down cow puncher shootin' marbles."

There was a moment of dead silence, then somebody started snickering, and they all broke out laughing. Everyone, that is, except the fancy one. His face went bright red and his body tensed all over. Then, just as suddenly, he slacked off. Something in the plainsman's eyes stopped him cold, and after a moment's calculation, he decided the iron strapped to Jordan's side didn't look anything like a watch charm.

Jordan nodded good-naturedly and walked on back to the wagons. Lon McCabe was waiting for him with a sour look. "Cimarron, I'll swear to Christ, if somebody put your brains in a jaybird he'd fly backwards. What was you gonna do, fight all of 'em?"

"Old man, you're so feisty you don't know when a feller's just funnin'." McCabe started sputtering, but he cut him off. "Tell me about it later. Right now I want you to take the boys in there and buy 'em a drink. I'm going across the way and talk to whoever runs that store."

Turning, Jordan walked off and left him standing there. After a moment, McCabe motioned to the other skinners and led them toward the saloon. Over the door was a sign, The Bee Hive, painted in large red letters. Easing through the throng of cowhands out front, he glanced back in time to see Jordan enter the trading post on the opposite side of the street.

Darkness had fallen over the Flats when Jordan came out of the store and crossed to the Bee Hive. The crowd inside was a mixed bag of tricks. Teamsters, slick-haired tinhorns, the usual assortment of cowhands and edgy-looking badmen—and just enough saloon girls to make it interesting. The saloon itself wasn't much to write home about. Log walls, a plank bar supported by barrels, and hardly enough tables to seat a Sunday school class. In the back was a small dance floor, with one lonesome fiddler sawing away; off to one side, at the end of the bar, was a faro layout flanked by a monte spread and a poker table.

Not much. But not bad either, all things considered.

Shouldering in at the bar, he cleared out a place beside McCabe. The old grave robber was already about half pickled, and he clearly wasn't feeling any pain. Jordan nudged him in the ribs. "You buying, Lon?"

"Well, looka here!" McCabe crowed, rearing back to get a better focus. "If it ain't Cimarron Jordan hisself. Now don't tell me! I'll jes' bet'cha been out teachin' them jay-birds how to fly backwards."

Jordan grinned and signaled the barkeep for a glass. "Matter of fact, I've been takin' a few lessons myself." The glass arrived and he paused to pour himself a drink. When he downed it, the whiskey hit bottom and bounced with a molten jolt. He shuddered and shook himself like a wet dog.

McCabe let go with a wheezy chuckle. "Takes a little gettin' used to, don't it? Barkeep calls it Taos lemonade. Grain alcohol, branch water, tabacca juice, and strychnine. Says that last is to keep yer heart beatin'."

"Well, I reckon I've had worse." Jordan studied the bottle a second, then shrugged and poured another shot. "Anyway, what I started to tell you. That feller across the road—name's Clark—has got himself a neat little operation. Tells me he opened up last year and business is boomin'. Now try this on for size. He says there's already some hunters operatin' around here. Mostly Texans. Told me he's got himself appointed agent for Lobenstein and he'll take all the hides we can deliver."

This was significant news. W.C. Lobenstein, operating out of Leavenworth, was the largest hide buyer in the west. Added to the fact that Ed Clark already had a trading post off and running, it meant that Jason Rath's plans must now await a more opportune time. Perhaps of even greater import, it meant that Sam Jordan wasn't the only one who had his eye on the buffalo grounds of West Texas.

The old skinner snorted testily. "You beat anything I ever saw. I knowed all that 'fore I'd been in here five minutes." He jerked his head sideways, pointing with his

34

chin. "See that feller standin' next to you? Name's Frank Lumpkins. Buffalo man. If yer sniffer'd been workin' when you come in here you'd of knowed it right off."

Lumpkins turned at the sound of his name. "What's you say, you old billygoat? I better not catch you bad mouthin' me again."

"Mister, I done said all to you I got to say." McCabe slewed his eyes around and gave the man a corrosive glare. "But just so's you won't die out o' curiosity, I was tellin' my friend here that some dingbat name of Lumpkins is goin' around callin' hisself a buffalo man."

Jordan eased around to find himself faced by a barrel-gutted giant of a man. What Lumpkins lacked in height he made up in girth, built something on the order of a brick church. The weight he packed was solid as a rock, and he had feet the size of nail kegs, with big hairy paws more suited to a lumbering bear. His head was like a weathered chunk of sandstone, grainy and pebbled with deep pockmarks, and he had flat muddy eyes slitted between rolls of flesh. Right now those eyes were zeroed on Lon McCabe, and Jordan could pretty well guess what had happened.

Somehow the viper-tongued old devil had riled Lumpkins, most likely downgrading the man's skills as a hunter. Although he had a glass jaw and the wallop of a cream puff, McCabe fancied himself a barroom brawler when he had a snootful. Curiously, since he generally ended up flat on his back, he never seemed to tire of the game.

"Old man," Lumpkins growled, "you'd better put that rooster to crowin' on another roof, less'n you want me to wring his neck."

Before McCabe could answer, Jordan shifted away from the bar, regarding the beefy Texan with a great calmness. "Friend, I don't know what the problem is, but why don't you just write it off to whiskey talkin' and let it go at that?"

Lumpkins glowered back at him with an owlish frown. "Well first off, we ain't friends, and lastly, it ain't none of your goddamn business. Now why don't you just step out o' the way 'fore I have to walk over you?"

Jordon's eyes hooded and his face went cold. "Swizzle-guts, if I was you, I'd back off. Otherwise somebody's liable to stunt your growth."

Lumpkins grinned like a lard-faced possum and shook his head ruefully. "What'd the old geezer call you? Cimarron Jordan? Well now, looka here, Jordan, there ain't no

35

call for you to get your hackles up. The plain fact of the matter is, he has done insulted me and my crew. Said up beside your outfit we was nothin' but two-bit—"

Jordan was listening attentively, trying to get the drift of the trouble, when Lumpkins hit him. The blow came without warning, out of nowhere, with amazing speed for such a big man. Jordan went down like a polled ox and the whole right side of his head turned numb. Every tooth he owned felt loose as goose-butter, and a brassy taste spread through his mouth as blood leaked down over his chin. He had been hurt worse, but not since the last time somebody whapped him with a sledgehammer.

Lumpkins moved toward him with uncommon agility, lifting his foot as he came. Clearly the big man was a barroom scrapper of considerable experience, and he meant to end the fight right there was a good stomping. Lumpkins' boot looked to be the size of a freight train as it swung toward his ribs, and Jordan knew that if it ever connected, he was done for. The plainsman rolled away, scattering tables and people in every direction as he slithered across the floor. The tactic worked, carrying him well past the reach of Lumpkins' boots. Even as he spun in the last roll, he came to his feet, slinging chairs, bottles, and saloon girls aside.

But his respite was short lived. Lumpkins advanced like an outsized cannonball, snarling a murderous oath as he lumbered forward. The Texan had made his first mistake, though, in letting the younger man gain his feet. Jordan wasn't exactly mild as a sucking dove, but he generally minded his own business and tended to give the other fellow the benefit of the doubt. Until crossed. Or angered. Then something came unhinged back in the dark, brutish regions of his brain, and he turned wild as a mad bull in a spider web. Balancing lightly on the balls of his feet, he waited, coldly inviting the big man to make his move.

Lumpkins took the bait. Cocking his massive fist, he threw a haymaker that would have demolished a stone wall. If it had landed. But it never even came close.

Jordan ducked under the blow, and sunk his fist into the Texan's blubbery paunch clean up to the elbow. Lumpkins' mouth popped open and a roaring whoosh of air burst out, sort of like the pumper letting the wind out of a church organ. He doubled over, clutching his gut in agony, and the plainsman exploded two splintering punches on his chin. Dazed, Lumpkins shook his head, sucking great gasps of air into his starved lungs.

But he didn't fall.

Just for a moment there, Jordan couldn't rightly believe it. Nobody had ever taken those punches and kept their feet. Not in all the years he'd been busting heads. Still, he smelled blood—sensed the kill—and his wonderment was only a fleeting thing.

Shifting, the plainsman kicked Lumpkins square in the kneecap. There was a loud crack, and the Texan let go a whimpering cry of pain. When he grabbed at his knee, Jordan clouted him dead center between the eyes. Lumpkins reeled backwards, his crippled knee collapsing under him, and rocketed through the plank bar. Barrels, boards, and whiskey bottles went flying like a stick of dynamite had been set off. When the debris settled, Lumpkins was flat on his back, blood seeping out of one ear, his nose ballooned like a rotten apple.

But still, he wasn't done for. He shook his head groggily, trying to clear the pinwheeling lights from his head. The shooting stars and swirling dots slacked off just a bit, and he came up on one elbow.

Jordan had seen men take punishment in his time, but never like this. There was something unnatural about it, like fighting a bag of oats that absorbed every blow without lasting harm. Holding off now, though, was out of the question. Lumpkins was dangerous so long as he could move. More than one man had gotten his brains scrambled by backing away before the fight was finished.

Stepping over the clutter, he very methodically kicked Lumpkins in the head.

The blow nearly tore the Texan's jaw off and his skull bounced off the floor like a ripe squash. Then a shudder went through his massive frame and his eyes rolled back in his head like glazed stones. No more than a heartbeat later, his eyes slowly closed, and he settled back in the sawdust.

He was out colder than a wedge.

Jordan steadied himself against the back counter, breathing hard but still full of fight. When he turned, his eyes were like fanned coals, and his glare raked across the men in Lumpkins' crew.

"Any of you buckos want a taste of the same?"

The three men glanced at one another sheepishly, then started looking everywhere but at Jordan. Whether they held no great love for their boss, or they just flat didn't want any part of this young buzzsaw hardly seemed to matter. They plainly had no intention of taking up the fight, and that settled it.

Everyone in the room commenced breathing again, and a ripple of nervous laughter swept over the crowd. Rough and tumble brawls were no novelty to the Bee Hive, not even knife fights and shootings were considered out of the ordinary. The place was a regular bucket of gore, and nightly donnybrooks took star billing as the chief form of entertainment. But as excitement mounted, and everyone started telling everyone else about what they had just seen with their own eyes, there wasn't a doubter among them.

This was no run-of-the-mill knock-down-drag-out. There was nothing common or ordinary about the way this young hunter fought. Not unless a smoky-eyed gorilla was common. Or a snarling, cold-blooded meat eater was to be taken as ordinary. This boy was in a class all by himself—chain lightning in both fists—sudden death let out of its cage.

They swarmed over him, clapping him on the back and calling his name, shouting for drinks, Goddamnit! Give this boy a drink! Glory be to Christ, did you see the way he hauled old Lumpkins' ashes? Set'em up barkeep! See it? God save us, that last punch would've felled a full-growed steer. Weren't never a man hit like that and lived. Not ever!

Suddenly Lon McCabe started shoving men right and left, cackling hoarsely at the top of his lungs. "Give him room, you peckerheads. Whoooiiee!! Stand back and let him stretch. That there's Cimarron Jordan! Half alligator, half curly wolf, and all man! Fightin' him is like pokin' hot butter in a wildcat's ear. Like kickin' a porkypine. Any sane man'd sooner tangle with a boar grizzly when his pecker's stiff. Whoooiiee! Move aside, consarn it. Get back there. Let him have a drink. Barkeep. Dagnabit, barkeep! Let's have some more of that panther juice."

Jordan smiled gamely and accepted all the back slapping and shouting without comment. The way McCabe was carrying on, there wasn't much room left for talk, anyhow. Somebody shoved a water glass of Taos lemonade in his hand and he took a fiery gulp to the delighted shout of the crowd. Out of the corner of his eye he saw Lumpkins being dragged off by his heels, and a mild tingle of satisfaction passed over him.

By Judas, that bloat-gutted hog was still out cold! Maybe he wasn't losing his punch after all.

The plainsman raised his glass to the crowd and flashed a wide grin. Then, just like that, one of his molars fell out.

Laughing wildly, he spit it out in his hand and held it up for everyone to see. The men pointed at it and doubled up in fits of laughter, roaring so hard their eyes welled over with tears.

Goddamn! There wouldn't never be another night like this. Not ever!

Two

> ═══════════════════════════════════════

1.

Virge Hollister came down Main Street and paused at the
corner beside the Keno House. The evening had just
started, but it didn't hurt to let the Texans know he was
on the job. Whenever they saw him out prowling the
streets early like this, they tended to mind their manners a
little better. Not that they were what a man could rightly
call civilized even then. Still, he wouldn't have changed it
for the world. Rowdy trailhands and penny ante badmen
were making his reputation. Just the way he'd planned it.

Several Texans burst out of the Keno House, laughing
and shouting, but their high spirits took a nosedive when
they saw him standing there. Shushing one another drunkenly, like schoolboys playing hooky, they veered off in the
opposite direction. Hollister ignored them. His gaze roved
along the street, lost in a faraway look, and an odd little
smile ticced the corners of his mouth. It was a damn fine
town. His town. And in no small part, he had made it
what it was.

Wichita was still a wide spot in the road when Hollister
and Jordan saw it that first time in the spring of '73. But it
was building fast, a regular ant heap of men, mortar, and
lumber. The hotel—the first brick structure they had seen
since coming west—was still a skeleton. Masons were

40

working by torchlight as beef-buyers and cattlemen were even then converging on town from opposite points of the compass. The New York Store was already erected; saloons were springing up like wildflowers after a prairie shower; the toll bridge was completed, and across the river was a gathering of soiled doves that could have easily serviced an army. It beat anything the two buffalo men had ever seen. Hands down.

Lon McCabe and a couple of skinners were also along, and the little party pitched camp down by the river. Strictly speaking, Virge Hollister was no longer a buffalo-hunter. The winter kill had been about half what they expected, and the spring herds were so sparse they had been content just to hunt their way back to civilization. The Smoky Hill country was shot out—the buffalo slaughtered or driven off—and the only choice left them was to haul south for Dodge City.

But Virge had had his fill. Though they had made money, it was a damn sight less than they expected, particularly since they footed expenses for the whole outfit. Yet, had it been a king's ransom, it wouldn't have been enough for Virge. Not after what they'd seen.

The Cheyenne were on a rampage that year, and along the Saline, just north of Fort Hays, the hunters had stumbled onto a grisly scene. What was left of a government wood-contractor and his men was strewn about a small clearing, and the smell of burned flesh carried downwind a mile away. Apparently the Indians had struck the woodcutters' camp at sunrise, then spent the rest of the day butchering them to death. One man, after being scalped, had been lashed down to a wagon wheel and roasted to a crisp. From the way his brains had fried and burst it was clear the red devils had used a slow fire. Two other men had gone under the hard way. Staked out to the ground, their stomachs had been slashed open and live coals poured into the cavity. Their struggles had worn the earth bare, and there was little doubt that they had lived a long time before the fiery embers sizzled their guts. The fourth man had been lucky. Evidently he was killed outright when the attack took place, and he never knew what happened to him afterwards. The Cheyenne had chopped his head off and stuck it atop a pole. Then they neatly severed his rod and balls and left the whole bloody mess dangling from his mouth.

Virge Hollister had turned away and puked like a buzzard. The other men felt just about as queasy, but somehow they kept it down. After burying the woodcutters in a mass grave, they lugged rocks from the riverbed to stop wolves from getting at the bodies. Then they mounted, and set a fast pace for Fort Hays.

But for Virge, his days as a buffalo-hunter ended right there. Done. Finished with. No more. The dwindling herds had already started him thinking in that direction, and the gory horror along the Saline made it final. Not that he was afraid. There was never any question of that. Virge Hollister feared no man, red or white. But to die like that—hacked to pieces like a butchered hog, whimpering for a death that never comes—the thought shriveled his innards into a cold, hard knot.

After they reached Abilene, and sold their skimpy winter take, Sam had bought him out. Then they started looking around, and discovered that the once great cowtown had turned into a sodbuster's paradise. The railroad had moved farther south, and with it had gone the excitement. Farmers had little time—or money—to squander on whores, gambling dives, and the merry tang of John Barleycorn. The sporting crowd had packed it in and headed for some place called Wichita, down on the Arkansas.

Virge was still undecided as to what he wanted to do next, but he knew damn well he wasn't about to find it in Abilene. Sam never doubted for a minute where he was headed. His mind was settled on Dodge City, and he promptly pointed the wagons south. Virge had tagged along for the ride. Wichita sounded like it might suit his style real well, and if not, then it was as good a place to start as any.

The first night in town, Sam and Virge had gone off to see the elephant one last time together. Sort of a celebration of old friends parting at a fork in the road. The west was a big place—unhealthy in certain ways, too—and it might be that their trails would never again cross. Neither of them really believed that, but one excuse was as good as another to tie on a real whingding. McCabe and the skinners went off on a toot by themselves, leaving the two partners to skin their own wolf.

After taking on a load of popskull—and fighting their way out of the last saloon—Sam and Virge had wandered into the Keno House. Though the interior wasn't yet completed, the place was open for business, and it seemed to be just what the boys were looking for. Bar in front, gambling layout in the back, and lots of pretty girls to keep a man company.

Perfect.

They bellied up to the bar, taking first things first. But before they could even think of a decent toast, a long-legged gal in a peek-a-boo gown wedged in between them and started batting her eyes like a coal oil lamp.

"Evening, boys," she cooed. "Buy a girl a drink?"

Both men gave her a quick once over, and they liked what they saw. She was slim, young, and pretty as a cloudbank at sundown. Fresh somehow. Untainted. Obviously a greenhorn among the frowsy sisters of her trade.

"Little lady," Virge informed her, "you've caught yourself a couple of live ones. This here's Sam and I'm Virge. We've been lost in the wilderness, and we're out to see the elephant."

"Tree the coon," Sam grinned.

"Skin the wolf," Virge hooted.

"Whoa there, nellie," the girl laughed, gracing each of them with a dazzling smile. "Getting treed and skinned is a little out of my line. How about a bottle of bubbly and a few turns around the dance floor instead?"

"Virge," Sam observed, "this gal mightn't be as innocent as she looks."

"I was just thinkin' the same thing myself," Virge nodded, fixing the girl with a sly smirk. "Honey, I like the part about dancin', but I've got an idea the price of champagne might put a dent in us we couldn't stand."

"Just call me Lottie," the girl came right back. "And if whiskey is what you can afford then whiskey is what we'll drink. To be honest with you, I've only been here a couple of nights, and I was trying to make a good impression on my boss." Glancing over at the bartender, she motioned them in closer and her voice dropped to a whisper. "Champagne gives me gas anyway."

Virge roared and gave her a big hug. "See there, Sam. She's innocent after all. Just pure as the driven snow, aren't you, sweetheart?"

"Regular little angel," Lottie simpered, batting her lashes again. "Say, why don't we grab ourselves a table before the rush starts. Just to be real blunt about it my feet are killing me."

Now it was Sam's turn to guffaw. "She's pure awright! Purely tricky. She's just lookin' for a couple of pigeons that'll get her off her feet and let her corns have a breather."

Lottie's eyes flashed indignantly. "What a terrible thing to say. I like you two boys. Honestly. Knew it the minute you walked through the door." Then she sniffed and tossed her head. "Besides, I never had a corn in my life."

The men snorted and grinned across at one another. Sam signaled the bartender for a bottle and tossed a double eagle on the counter. While he was waiting on change, Virge took a half hitch around Lottie's waist and steered her toward a table. Sam joined them with the bottle and poured drinks around. Virge lifted his glass and displayed a set of teeth that looked like he had got them off an ivory trader.

"Here's to old friends parting, new friends meeting, and Lottie's corns that aren't there."

They all busted out laughing again, and when things calmed down, Virge started regaling the girl with stories of their hair-raising exploits on the western plains. Though Sam appeared in the narrative every once in awhile, Virge just naturally gave himself the best of it. Pretty soon Lottie's eyes were round as saucers, and she was watching him like a moonstruck calf. Obviously she had never been around frontiersmen. Or liars either, Sam thought to himself. She was swallowing the whole thing hook, line and sinker.

Virge started another big windy about how he had stood off the whole Cheyenne nation singlehandedly. Well, almost singlehanded, he amended. Sam had gotten in a couple of shots. Sam nodded like it was gospel truth and let Virge have the floor. That was the way it generally worked out, anyhow. Virge had a smoother way with women—all toothy smiles and a glib line of chatter—like a spark somehow ignited him all over whenever he got within range of a skirt. Around men he was usually solemn as a judge, with never much to say. But put him within spitting distance of a woman, and it was like somebody had wound him up and turned him loose.

Sam found it downright curious, yet he had never begrudged Virge his silky manner with the ladies. Truth to tell, he preferred whores, anyway. They didn't have to be talked into anything, generally cost a man a lot less money in the long run, and when a fellow was done, all he had to do was hitch up his pants and be on his way. No tears, no harsh words or fits of temper. Whambam and thank you ma'am, and a fellow could get back to doing whatever suited him.

44

Still, he had to admit that Virge was a caution with the women. Regular ladies man if there ever was one. He had a soft, honeyed way of talking that could have charmed birds right out of the trees, and he purely couldn't resist using it on women. Hell, Sam had even seen him sweet talk a whore one time. After he'd already paid for it, too! Some things just beat all.

But Virge was good, the way he buttered them up. Sam had to hand it to him—he flat knew how to coax them out of their drawers and into bed, and hardly ever pause to take a breath. There had always been a friendly rivalry between them, and Sam had tried to outdo him at first. After a while, though, he gave it up. What Virge had was a natural born talent—like some men are good trackers or skilled hunters. Virge just hunted women, that's all. Sam didn't exactly envy him, and he had never once resented the fact that women sort of turned to putty when Virge started in on them. Matter of fact, he enjoyed watching Virge operate.

Every now and then it put him in mind of a snake hypnotizing a glassy-eyed toad.

Sam's ruminations came to a sudden halt as shots broke out up near the bar. While Virge had been putting a spell over the girl, a trail crew had wandered in and just about taken over the saloon. Two of the Texans, considerably drunker than the others, were firing their six-guns at the ceiling, and whooping it up to beat the band. They hadn't fired more than a couple of shots apiece when the batwing doors slammed open and a fellow sporting a badge churned through. Without a break in stride, he marched up to the cowhands and gave them a frosty scowl.

"You boys are under arrest. Disturbin' the peace. Now hand over your hardware and come along peaceable."

"Hell, we ain't doin' nothin', lawdog," one of the Texans cracked. "Just ventilatin' the roof, that's all."

"Save it for the judge," the deputy snapped. "You boys are going to the lockup. Now pass over them guns."

"Tell you what, shitkicker," the other cowhand grated out, "why don't you try and take 'em."

The deputy just stared at them for a second, like he was sizing them up, then his hand darted to the holster at his side. Even as he did so he knew he had made a mistake. The Texans weren't bluffing, and drunk or sober, they still knew how to use a gun. But he never heard the shots. The big slugs bowled him over and he dropped to the floor like a sack of bricks.

"Hands up! First man that moves is dead."

Sam never did find out why Virge bought into the game. He always suspected that if Lottie hadn't been sitting there Virge wouldn't have opened his mouth. But that didn't necessarily hold. Buffalo men just naturally didn't cotton to cowhands, and that could have been at the root of it. Whatever the reason, there was no doubt that Virge had stepped away from the table and drawn his pistol. He looked cold as ice standing there, almost as if he were enjoying it.

The Texans didn't wait around to argue it one way or the other. They had just gunned down a lawman, which meant they had to start making tracks. Fast.

Both men spun on their heels, ducking sideways as they came around. Virge let fly just like he had been shooting men all his life. The first one he drilled dead center through the brisket even before the Texan got himself straightened out. Then, with no more emotion than an icicle, he nailed the other cowhand with a gut shot. The Texans keeled over in opposite directions, and hit the sawdust no more than a second apart.

Sam, meantime, had shoved Lottie to the floor and brought his own gun to bear on the rest of the crew standing at the bar. Satisfied that the two rowdies were done for, Virge did likewise. The Texans had just about worked up the nerve to make a fight of it when the barkeep thumbed back both hammers on a mule-earred scattergun. Without looking around, the trailhands knew they had a cannon pointed straight at their backs, and they decided to call it quits.

When Marshal Tom Meagher came through the door, he found the Texans disarmed and lined up against the far wall. The barkeep filled him in on the details with no need for exaggeration. The lawman glanced around at the table, where Virge and Sam were again seated with Lottie, but he didn't say anything. When the barkeep finally ran down, Meagher turned and gave the cowhands some stiff advice. *Get out of town and don't come back. Pronto!* After they had filed out the door with their tails between their legs, the marshal holstered his Colt and walked on back to the table.

Nodding to Sam, his gaze went by the girl and settled on Virge. "Understand you're pretty handy with a gun."

46

Virge gave him a wooden look. "Handy enough, I guess."

"You ever worn a badge?" Meagher inquired.

"Nope. Never had any call to."

"I'm shy a deputy. Maybe you ought to give it some thought."

Virge chewed that over for a moment, then he smiled. "You offerin' me a job, marshall?"

"Could be," Meagher said. "Why don't you come round to the jail in the morning and we'll talk about it."

"Might just take you up on that," Virge replied, slewing his gaze around to Sam. "I'm sort of foot loose just at the moment, anyway."

Meagher nodded again, then turned and walked off. They watched him out the door before anybody could get their tongue unhinged.

"Well, I'll declare," Lottie murmured, looking at Virge like he had just sprouted wings. "You just move right in and take over, don't you, honeybunch?"

Virge's mouth split in a pearly grin and he leaned over with his arms around the back of her chair. "Lady, you haven't seen nothin' yet. Wait'll I get you alone, then you'll really start yellin' uncle."

Lottie giggled and squirmed around like soft wax. Virge chuckled and looked over at Sam. "What d'ya think?"

"About what?"

"About the job. Wearin' a badge. You think I ought to take it?"

"I wouldn't exactly match pennies for it," Sam grinned. "Still, the marshal might have a point. You're handy with a gun, right enough."

Virge nodded absently, and went back to sweet talking Lottie. Watching him, Sam figured his mind was more than likely made up. About the job. About Wichita. And about the girl.

Especially about the girl.

2.

Hollister crossed the street, chuckling to himself as he recalled that first night in town. Things had changed a lot since then. More than most folks suspected. And it wasn't over yet. Not by a damnsight.

47

Mounting the boardwalk, he began a leisurely stroll down Douglas Avenue. People had a way of remembering what they saw—as well as the juicier things they heard—and he figured it never did any harm to let the town's big augurs see him out protecting the community. The boneheads had such great respect for the law that the sight of a badge was enough to give them goosebumps. Whenever trouble started they would pop up out of the woodwork—standing well out of range, naturally—and gawk like he was some kind of tent-show freak come to visit the wrath of God on the infidels. Mostly, though, they just stuck to business and tried to concoct some legitimate-sounding way of screwing the trailhands out of one more nickel. Enforcing the law—busting heads, collecting license fees from whores, killing a man on occasion—that wasn't their cup of tea. They paid men to do their dirty work—the double-dealing, godless things they didn't have the stomach for themselves. That way they kept their own hands clean, and could go right on telling the Almighty what a bunch of holyrollers they were.

But that, too was something Virge had counted on.

Smiling pleasantly, he waved to Asa Kuykendall in the New York Store, and knuckled the brim of his hat to Will Davis when he passed the hotel. Farther on, he stopped in at the *Wichita Eagle*, and spent a few minutes chatting with Ed Jackson. The power of the press was a fact of life he had tumbled to early on, and he went out of his way to court the editors of both newspapers. If a man had his eye on the political arena—and Virge wanted power so bad he could taste it—he would have been a fool to do otherwise. Though it was tricky as walking a greased rail—since the *Eagle* and the *Beacon* were violently opposed on every issue imaginable—he had managed to pull it off with a certain flair. They needed good copy to brighten their stodgy rags, and Wichita hadn't seen anything like him since the last twister swept through town.

Thinking about it as he bid Jackson goodnight, it occurred to him that it really hadn't been all that hard. After a fashion he was sort of the local celebrity, what with five men gone to their maker in the name of the law. More to the point—especially in a town founded on avarice, greed, and screw your neighbor—he had milked the Texans for close to $4,000 in fines, and the season not yet half gone. Money was the thing the town fathers had a profound respect for, and anyone who could drum up that kind of revenue was just naturally the fair-haired boy.

Now if he could only get the bastards to take him seriously as a contender in next year's elections.

Not unlike men before him with the lean and hungry look, Virge Hollister was riddled through with ambition. One winter freezing his rump chasing buffalo had convinced him there were easier ways to get ahead. Since he was fast with a gun, and displayed no reluctance to use it, he had drifted into law work. While the pay wasn't much, it opened up a whole grab bag of possibilities for a man who had something besides beeswax between his ears. Especially if he wasn't too persnickity about the methods he used.

Wichita had become the reigning cowtown on the Kansas plains just last year, the summer of '73. When the Santa Fe tracks hit town early that spring, the cattle trade had taken on a whole new outlook. Abilene, Ellsworth, and Newton—the major railheads up till then—withered on the vine overnight. Wichita was farther south, saving the Texans a week on the trail, and it was a natural holding-ground for longhorns. The town was settled on the banks of the Arkansas, just about where the Osage had camped before they were dispossessed back in '68. The river was shallow, easily forded, with a fringe of cottonwoods along the shore and a vast sea of graze in every direction. The Texans took to it like dogs trailing a gut wagon.

That first summer, Wichita had shipped 350,000 head of beef, and estimates for '74 were ranging upwards of a half million. All things considered, somewhere around $15,000,000 would be funneled through the town during the five month trailing season. Though most of it would be carted back to Texas, there was no doubt whatever that a couple of million would rub off on Wichita itself.

It was no game for pikers. The stakes were big, the play was fast, and only the foxy ones got a turn at the trough.

With close to a thousand cowpokes in town on any given night, there was enough action to suit everybody. Of whatever persuasion—crooked, straight, or just slightly bent in the middle. Tradesmen gouged on prices like bandits; the charge of whiskey skyrocketed to an outrageous two-bits a shot; and whores educated the Texans in what it really meant to get a first-class screwing The town fathers even built a toll bridge across the Arkansas, and voted into

49

law a set of ordinances Jesus Christ himself couldn't have upheld.

In a very real sense, the Texans got it socked to them coming and going.

The town had a three-story brick hotel, fifteen saloons and gambling dives, two dance halls, and a row of sporting houses that would have turned the Barbary Coast green with envy. Most of the saloons and gaming parlors were located along Main Street and Douglas Avenue—the town's central thoroughfares. There a man could wet his tonsils with everything from snakehead whiskey to French champagne—and watch the biggest highrollers in the west dealing crooked poker with the aplomb of a Chinese warlord. But to get his pole greased he either had to pay a toll or wet his toes wading the Arkansas. The town council had banished the kingdom of whores to the west bank of the river—and made them pay a stiff license fee for the right to harvest the wages of sin. Still, hardly anyone complained. The string of cathouses was tagged with the sobriquet Delano—for some reason everyone promptly forgot—and the exotic variations offered by its fallen sparrows became a mainstay in Texan folklore.

Virge Hollister had gotten in on the ground floor. When he hit town the boom had just started, and he wasted no time in staking out a plum of his own. Quick as a wink he had wired his three brothers back in Illinois and told them to catch the next train west. When they arrived he had set James, the eldest, to running a sporting house—financed out of his hunting venture with Sam Jordan—and arranged jobs for the other two in gambling dives. Since he was deputy city marshal, he could bring a certain influence to bear where needed, and everything had gone smooth as butter. Under the protection of his badge, the Hollister brothers had quietly cracked a few skulls in Delano, and before long they had a spiffy little protection racket going. James Hollister, unlike his handsome younger brother, was an old hand at the business of vice and the tricky dodges used by gang bosses on Chicago's southside. All they needed was muscle and a bit of clout at city hall, and in no time at all they would *own* the red-light district. Perhaps the whole damn town.

Virge may have been untutored in the ways of vice, but he was nobody's patsy. He had a sharp, cunning mind— the kind that absorbed and improved on whatever it came across—and he was gifted with the moral character of an egg-sucking raccoon. Five months out of every year, money flowed like water in Wichita, and a shrewd man shouldn't have any trouble at all in getting a wad of it to stick to his fingers. But first he had to have power—clout, his elder brother had called it. That meant developing a political base, a springboard to greater things. The most obvious choice was the office of city marshal. Old Tom Meagher was past his prime, and if it weren't for Virge backing his play, the Texans would probably have put him under months ago. Virge had once considered rigging just such an encounter, but quickly discarded the idea. Better to secure the support of the local machine and win the election by popular vote. Then he would have the people behind him—a political base even the big augurs couldn't ignore—and there was no telling where it might lead. Mayor. State senator. Perhaps even governor.

There again, the methods he used in tilting the scales were unimportant, all but meaningless. What was left when the smoke settled and the meek had inherited six feet of dusty earth, was the man who had dared. The one who had grabbed the brass ring and refused to be dislodged. Nothing else mattered. How the game was played—the wailing and gnashing of teeth over rules—didn't mean a hill of beans. It was who picked up the marbles that counted. Just that. Nothing more.

Nearing the toll bridge, he crossed the street and headed back toward the center of town. Later tonight, or perhaps first thing tomorrow, he would have to meet with James and the boys. Put their heads together in a strategy session for the days ahead. The Hollister family would soon control a formidable block of votes over in Delano. In some unmistakable manner that fact must be brought home to the bunch of dimdots running Wichita. But the meeting would have to wait. Right now he was sporting a whole new wardrobe, and he had no intention of wasting it on the likes of whoretown.

Hollister had never forgotten that summer day three years back when he watched Wild Bill Hickok gun down a drunken cowhand. Something about the man's style—both with a gun and in sartorial finery—had left an indelible impression. Throughout the time he had sweated and wallowed in filth working as a buffalo-hunter, he had gone back over the incident a thousand times. Perhaps more. Every last detail could be summoned up in sharp focus, and in his mind's eye he saw it as if it were happening

51

only then. With time he began to pattern himself after Hickok, mastering the Colt .45 with uncanny skill, steeping himself in the guarded cunning that was the gunfighter's edge over lesser men.

When he became a peace officer, it was only natural that he would imitate Hickok's flamboyant mode of dress. Not the sash, or the long frock coat. Even Hollister found that a little bizarre. All the same, he cut a striking picture in a grungy cowtown. His coats were made to order in St. Louis, specially tailored in dark, somber shades to lend him dignity and show off his lean frame. Beneath the coat he wore a brocaded vest, colorful yet properly subdued, and his shirts were of the finest linen. Around his neck was a silk four-in-hand, and peeking from its folds was a stickpin that looked big as a sugarbowl. There were times when some folks—particularly juiced-up Texans—were tempted to call him a dandy. But they didn't, not to his face anyway. For the final item of trappings was the one that marked his calling. Strapped around his waist was a brace of pearl-handled six-guns, the badge of a man who makes his living in a very lonely profession.

People in Wichita had seen him use those guns—seen them appear magically from nowhere—with a suddenness that was hard to credit if a man hadn't witnessed it for himself. That, along with the fact that his guns had killed five times, gave the townspeople mixed feelings about their nattily attired deputy. They liked him, didn't even begrudge him the unsavory antics of his brothers across the river, but they weren't real sure they trusted him. Beneath his pleasant manner they sensed the arrogance of a man who has become too good at what he does. The arrogance of a man who holds himself above common folks, perhaps even the law. That frightened them, and among themselves they spoke of it often. The deputy earned his keep, no argument there. But it would be a mistake to give him too much slack. Like if he tried to run against Tom Meagher in next year's elections.

Tonight, though, Virge Hollister thought he had the world on a downhill slide. The rowdy Texans crowding the street stepped aside to let him pass; the newspapers ballyhooed his growing reputation with reams of praise; not a man alive doubted that it was he and he alone who kept the lid on in Kansas's most rambunctious cowtown. So far as he could see, he had Wichita by the short hairs, and was gaining ground all the time.

52

On the spur of the moment he decided to skip Pryor's Saloon, where his younger brothers, Warren and Morgan, worked as dealers. Instead he headed straight for the Keno House. The outfit he was wearing tonight was a real humdinger, and by all rights, Lottie should be the first to see it.

When he came through the door the band was blaring away on the upper balcony, but it was still too early for a crowd. Mostly townspeople, cattle-buyers, and a handful of drummers. The trailhands would show within a couple of hours, though, and by midnight the place would look like a nest of worms in a hot sun. He spotted Lottie sitting at a table with two other girls, and as he approached, the pair vacated their seats and moved toward the bar.

Glancing after them, he grinned at Lottie. "What's the matter, they afraid John Law is fixing to test their drinks?"

Lottie didn't even hear him. She was inspecting his new duds with a dazzled look. "Virge, I declare. You look like a peacock. Sure you don't want to flap your wings and strut around the room?"

"Thank you, ma'am. I take that as a compliment." Doffing his hat, he dropped it on the table and took a chair. "You girls restin' up for a big night?"

"You bet your sweet life, honeybunch. This joint will be crawling with cowhands before you can shake a stick. My God, I shudder to think what those girls go through over in Delano."

Lottie Siddon had blossomed like a Venus Flytrap in the last year. When a traveling theatrical troupe had gone busted and left her stranded the summer before, she had wangled a job in Whitney Rupp's Keno House. Though prostitution was strictly forbidden in Wichita proper, the Texans never ceased trying, and she had gotten a short but informative education in the woes of a saloon girl's life. The language was salty, the clientele raunchy, and the atmosphere only one step removed from a common brothel.

Still, Lottie hadn't fallen as low as some, and she remained a very pretty girl. Sort of hard around the edges, and a bit cynical about men, but a stunner all the same. Her black upswept hair framed a delicately structured face, with striking, oval eyes and a full, generous mouth. Though hardly buxom, and taller than most girls, she was well rounded in all the right spots, and had the best set of legs ever to come down the Santa Fe tracks. Tonight she didn't have enough on to pad a crutch. Her dress was cut low on top and high on the bottom, and everything she had was displayed so enticingly it could make a man clean forget his supper. Virge was as susceptible as the next fellow, eyeing the merchandise with an appreciative stare.

But there was one essential difference between the lawman and the rest of the gawkers.

Virge Hollister slept with Lottie Siddon. Just about every night. Word had it that she was his woman—private stock, so to speak—and so far no one had seemed disposed to test his claim.

Some people thought it curious that she continued to work in a saloon. Especially if the rumors were true. But there was really nothing strange about it at all. Lottie worked not out of choice but because she had to. Virge Hollister was much too shrewd to support a girl openly—so long as he had political ambitions. The better element in Wichita could be pretty stiffnecked about some things, and oddly enough, they drew the line right about there. Lottie didn't care much for the arrangement, but she understood and went along to keep peace. Since she was sort of sweet on Virge anyway, there really wasn't much else she could do.

Virge ignored Lottie's comment about Delano. With good reason, he always looked a little uncomfortable when anyone mentioned vice. After a moment he brightened, flashing a grin. "Stopped in down at the *Eagle* and had a talk with Ed Jackson."

Lottie was probably the only person within a hundred miles of Wichita with brass enough to mock the young lawman, and she took great delight in bursting his bubble. "Oh, I just knew it. The minute you walked in here I could tell right off. He's going to back you for head dogcatcher."

Virge's eyes crackled fire for a second, but it faded quickly. "You're a real wiseacre to be so little. Matter of fact, he didn't let on one way or another. Just said he thought Tom Meagher was too old to cut the mustard, and he'd think it over."

"Well don't hold your breath, dearie. Half the people in this town could talk out of both sides of their mouths at once."

"Yeah, I know. But that's more'n he's ever said before." Virge mulled it over for a moment in silence, then straightened in his chair. "Say, it plumb slipped my mind. Word came in that Sam Jordan has gone to Texas. Ap-

54

pears he's set on huntin' out of some fort down on the Brazos."

Lottie laughed, her eyes dancing merrily. "That's Sam, all right. I swear, that man has all the instincts of a stray dog." Her gaze settled back on Virge, and a devilish smile played at the corners of her mouth. "You know, lover, I often wonder if I did the right thing. I'll just bet Sam Jordan is a diamond in the rough once a girl breaks through that shell."

"You're just full of zingers tonight, aren't you? Let me tell you something, smart britches. Sam would've had you lookin' like a scarecrow inside of six months. He wears women out so fast they have to keep 'em comin' in relays."

Virge Hollister chuckled to himself, thinking back to all the whorehouses they had demolished together. While he'd had good looks enough for both of them, it was Sam who had always left the girls begging for mercy. Jesus! That stump-necked little bull had a boiler that glowed red hot right around the clock.

Suddenly Virge rocked Lottie back in her chair with a great bellylaugh. One of Sam's dicey sayings had just come back to him.

It ain't what you've got that counts. It's what you've got to drive it with.

3.

Jordan came out of the arroyo and started up a low hill. His heart was hammering against his ribs, and he forced himself to take it slow and easy. Moments before, he had heard the enraged bellowing of bulls squaring off for a fight, and he knew beyond certainty that a herd lay just over the rise. The gelding was tied back down the gully, the wind was in his favor, and it was a hot, lazy day.

Just right. Everything exactly as he liked it to make a good stand.

The grassy knoll was barely two miles from camp. Jordan had ridden out about nine, allowing himself a good hour to get into position. Finding buffalo was no problem—the shaggy brutes encircled the camp like a vast brown sea—the largest gathering he had seen since those early days on the Smoky Hill. Yet, though he still found it

55

hard to believe, this great herd was less than two days ride west of Fort Griffin. That they were so close, and found so effortlessly, somehow boggled his mind. It was almost too easy.

The pattern Jordan followed this sunny morning was one established years back, when he was a greenhorn trailing along behind Monte Brown. Be in position by ten, shoot till the sun was straight overhead, and never kill more than the skinners could handle in an afternoon. Everything had its purpose, according to Monte, and if a man followed the rules he was most times assured of getting a stand.

Never hunt early in the day. The shaggies were restless and easy to spook until they had finished their morning graze. Afterwards, with a full belly and a moist cud to chew on, they settled down for a little siesta. That was the time for a man to sneak up on them. If he moved slow and kept to cover, he might work his way to within a hundred yards of the dumb beasts. The other rule was just as practical. Maybe more so.

Never overkill.

It was a waste of time, powder, and hides. Anything the skinners couldn't get fleshed out by sundown was as good as lost. The wolves were sure to get at the carcasses overnight and spoil the hides. Even if they didn't the skinners would botch it up come morning. Cold meat was hard to skin.

Overkill, though, had never been much of a problem in Smoky Hill country. Not that last year, leastways. The herds had thinned out so bad, a man did well just to find a stand. Never mind worrying about downing too many. Thinking back on it, as he went into a crouch half way up the knoll, Jordan was again filled with a sense of wonder at what he had found in the land west of Fort Griffin.

They had rolled out of the Flats three days back, moving westerly along the Clear Fork. Nearing its headwaters, they had swung north, and within hours began sighting buffalo. At first it was just scattered bunches, but growing thicker the farther they went, and every man in the crew began to get that prickly feeling. The feeling that comes over a man when he had just filled a straight or holds aces full.

The very sharp, savory taste of a sure-fire winner.

Late that afternoon they had topped a rise and came to a slack-jawed halt. Stretched out before them was the greatest single concentration of buffalo they had ever seen.

The high ground afforded them a view ten to fifteen miles in every direction, and as far as the eye could see, the earth was blanketed with a heaving mass of furry brown. Jordan estimated that it would take close to a week for the herd to pass any given point, and near as he could judge, its center was better than twenty miles wide. Any thought of numbers was too staggering to contemplate. Four million. Ten million. Perhaps somewhere in between. Certainly more than a man could count in the span of his days on earth. More than all but a handful of plainsmen had ever seen in a single moment of time.

It was the great Texas herd. Feeding into the wind in its ageless migration across the plains.

Backtracking, they had set up camp on Paint Creek, just below Mockingbird Springs. That night, while the skinners whetted their knives and spoke in awe of what they had seen, Jordan went over his equipment piece by piece.

Lucretia Borgia came first. The big Sharps was a .50-90, throwing a slug nearly a half inch in diameter. With its strong breech, the gun could handle just about any powder charge that suited the man, and Jordan loaded it with 110 grains. The heavy octagonal barrel made it a weighty piece; and it packed the kick of a young mule, but it was deadly accurate up to ranges of six hundred yards. The wallop of the big fifty slug was fearsome to behold, many times knocking a full-grown bull clean off his pins in the blink of an eye. But it wasn't a gun made for boys. It took a man —with a shoulder hard as nails—to keep from flinching when he fired the Sharps steady for a couple of hours at a stretch.

Jordan cleaned Lucretia the way a man fondles a prized mistress, removing every fleck and speck with the utmost care. Next he looked to the shells, sorting an even two hundred into a tanned bull-hide pouch. Then he filled an oversized canteen from the creek, checked to see that he had plenty of swabs, and tested the forked sticks that would support the gun's heavy barrel once he started firing.

Looking it over one last time, he nodded with satisfaction. Everything was ready. Tomorrow he would start the kill. After a pipe, he rolled himself in a blanket and slept sound as a dollar.

That morning, when he rode out of camp, the sun had already burned the damp earth smell off the land. Lazy white butterflies floated on gentle updrafts of air, and shards of light filtered through the cottonwoods overhead in soft golden streamers. It was a good time of day. Maybe even the best. When a man was fresh, full of vim and vigor, raring to lock horns with life. With the hunt before him, the broiling afternoon sun still hours away, and a land not yet filled with the stench of death.

It was as much as a man could ask for. More than most men ever found.

Holding the gelding to a steady trot, he came away from the creek and struck out across the rolling prairie. There was an awesome quality to these plains that never failed to grip him when he rode out of a morning. Almost as if he were intruding on something sacred—something he was never meant to see—a land fashioned solely for dust devils, raging blizzards, and the wild things that had roamed it since the dawning of earth itself. It was as though some brutally magnificent force—call it nature, or God, or the earth-mother—had taken wind and solitude and green grass and molded it into something visible, yet beyond the ken of man. As though the force had purposely created a vast expanse of emptiness where man must walk as an alien. Where, if he intruded, he must wander lost forever. A land of silence and distance, visible yet forever unseen, waiting with eternal patience to claim the bones of those who would violate its harsh serenity.

It was a land of ageless cycles, constant yet forever changing with the throbbing pulse of reborn strength. A still, windswept sea of loneliness that brought man face to face with his own puny insignificance. A hostile, unforgiving moment in space and time that mocked his passage and left no trace of his feeble onslaught.

Yet, small and alien as it made him feel, it was a land that drew a man back again and again. Like a grain of steel that must witlessly succumb to the lure of some earthly magnet. Wherever he went, however far he roamed, it beckoned him back. A temptress, granting nothing while somehow promising all.

Why he came, or what he hoped to find there, was a riddle each man met and solved after his own fashion. Most found barrenness and hunger, suffering and death. The hardy ones—those who endured and withstood the furies about them—sometimes found themselves.

Cimarron Jordan came there as other men before him, drawn by something he felt, but as yet failed to comprehend. He was an outsider—an intruder—yet curiously gripped by a sense of kinship for the very forces that mocked him. The earth. The sky. The grinding solitude that pressed down with relentless ferocity.

As though—should he wander these plains long enough—he would at last come full circle. Face to face with himself.

Then, as Jordan reined the roan gelding down the crumbly banks of a dry wash, his reflections had come to an abrupt halt. The thunderous wroo-wroo-WROO of fighting bulls drifted in on a lazy breeze, and his thoughts snapped back to the business at hand. Once more he became the hunter, the wary predator, letting instinct guide him in the painstaking stalk that lay ahead. When he climbed out of the gully he left behind all reason and thought, his yesterdays and tomorrows.

There was nothing save the moment, and what had brought him here. The kill.

Crawling the last few feet on his belly, Jordan poked his head over the crest of the knoll and uttered a soft, jubilant grunt. Before him the plains were spotted with small, scattered bunches, each comprising anywhere from a hundred to a thousand buffalo. From a distance it would have appeared a yawning carpet of muddy brown stretching to the horizon. But up close, the endless chain of separate herds took form, and closer still, individual buffalo assumed shape, even character.

Some two hundred yards beyond the hill, two ponderous bulls were holding a staring contest, bellowing and pawing dirt with enraged roars. Rutting season lasted from midsummer to dog days, a time when bulls fought bloody duels and courted favor with the cows. The monsters Jordan now watched were clearly working themselves up to a fight for supremacy of the nearest herd.

The bull's guttural roar sounded again, their bloodshot little eyes rolling furiously as they tossed great chunks of earth over their backs. Suddenly their heads lowered almost to the ground, narrow flanks heaving, and they thundered toward one another with churning legs. They came together with an impact that shook the earth and drove both antagonists to their knees. But they scrambled erect in an instant, locking horns with a fearsome clatter as they struggled to gain some advantage. The muscles on their flanks swelled like veined ropes as the sharp hooves strained for footing, and their great shoulders bunched with awesome power. Froth began to drip in long strings from their mouths, and their tongues lolled out as the brutal wrestling match sapped their lungs. Then, with a savage heave, one bull pitched his adversary aside and ripped a bloody furrow the length of his flank. The gored bull began a hasty retreat, breaking into headlong flight as his opponent speared him in the rump just for good measure.

The victor pawed the dusty earth and snorted loudly, striking a grand pose for the benefit of the cows. He had fought and won, and the woolly harem was his alone.

Until the next upstart came along.

Jordan had seen similar struggles duplicated a thousand times over, but his fascination for the crashing battles had never once dimmed. Next to a wild barroom slugfest, it was the best entertainment around. Looking out over the herd of plump cows, it came to him again that the bulls had a good thing for themselves—something worth fighting over.

Not that the cows were anything special to look at right now. Shortly after calving season, buffalo began to shed their winter coats in great, furry patches, leaving them nude as a scalded hog. Raw and tender, covered with scabs, they were pestered by a gluttonous swarm of flies and gnats. The insects deviled them relentlessly, sucking greedily at the raw sores, clustering around their eyes in thick clouds. By midsummer the plains were covered with deep wallows—bowl-shaped mudholes where the buffalo rolled like gigantic pigs, coating their tender hides against the vermin and pests. The wallows worked surprisingly well, but they transformed the buffalo into an ugly, short-tempered brute, covered from head to tail with layers of crusted mud.

What the cows lost in beauty, though, the frisky young calves gained a hundredfold over. Tawny in color, they were fat and adventuresome, and eternally romping off in pursuit of some new discovery. Except when wolves came around, the youngsters were free to explore to their heart's content, and they frisked about the herd in golden innocence. A wild, wobblykneed unknowing, born in equal parts of curiosity and a mad, abandoned exuberance.

Watching them, Jordan chuckled deep in his throat. What mischievous little bastards they were! Always jumping and leaping and butting some old fart square in the ass. They were a mortal wonder, no doubt about it! But that would soon change. Swiftly, and in a way the tawny youngsters least suspected.

The Sharps would roar, lead would splat against muddy

hide, and their mammy cows would drop, kicking, to the ground. Sooner or later the herd would stampede, lumbering away with an ungainly stride that could outdistance even the finest horse. Then, once the hides had been taken and the plains heat did its job, the rotting carcasses would begin to boil and hum with fat, grubby maggots. Instead of frisky calves bounding about, there would be nothing.

Just death.

Jordan blinked, wondering how much time had elapsed while he lay there daydreaming. It was absurd. A grown man going mushy over a bunch of calves. Then a gentle wisp of air brought with it the pungent buffalo smell. The moist gaminess, full of fresh droppings, and sweaty fur, and grassy breath. He filled his lungs with it, liking it. Strong, yet somehow clean and alive. When he let it go, he was himself again.

Easing over the top of the knoll, he slithered down the forward slope and came to rest behind a soapweed. Many hunters swore that the buffalo was a witless brute, dumb as a rock. But Jordan knew better. Though their eyesight wasn't much to rave about, they could spot movement with uncanny skill. Especially a man on foot. Horseback didn't bother them, but put a man upright and they were off in a flash. Like greased lightning, for they were nimble and fast despite their awkward bulk. Still, it was their sniffer a man had to watch out for. They had a keen sense of smell, and if the scent wasn't right, they just walked off and left a fellow looking at a cloud of dust.

Today Jordan didn't have to worry, though. He had the wind in his favor, and he judged the herd to be less than two hundred yards away. No man could ask for better than that.

Scouting around, he got his rump nice and comfortable, set up the sticks, and laid Lucretia over the fork. The shell pouch was handy, ramrod and canteen close by, and the soapweed made a perfect blind. He was ready to start.

Then he paused and began the search for the leader. Every herd had a leader. Generally an old cow. Somehow they were shrewder than the bulls—perhaps more suspicious—and they made the best sentries. Until a man dropped the leader, his chances of getting a stand were practically nil.

The rub came in guessing right the first time. What Jordan sought was a cow that seemed to be unusually watchful, sort of on guard. The leader seldom relaxed: always appeared to be testing the wind and scouting around for signs of danger. Suddenly his eyes stopped.

There she was.

Way back in the middle of the herd, holding herself tight as strung catgut. She was a shrewd old bitch, too. Staring right at him, trying to raise a scent.

Slowly he eared back the hammer and laid the sights a ways behind her shoulder. He centered on the lights—her lungs. Shot anywhere else, she would bolt like a stuck hog and take the herd with her. When the Sharps roared, a steamy gout of blood spurted from the cow's nose and she wobbled unsteadily. Then she took a couple of steps backwards and keeled over. Another cow sniffed the fallen leader, bawling nervously as she started to drift off. Jordan yanked the trigger-guard down, clawed out the spent shell, and threw in a fresh load. When he snapped the lever shut, the cow was gathering speed, ready to break into a terrified run. Quickly he thumbed the hammer back and swung ahead to allow for lead. Lucretia cracked, and the cow collapsed in her tracks, plowing a deep gash in the earth with her nose. Several cows gathered around, looking sort of alarmed, and threw back their heads and bawled. The old bull wandered over, snorting when he smelled the blood, and started pawing the ground.

But they didn't run.

Milling about, they bellowed and hooked at one another, acting bewildered by it all. Some of them kept pawing the dirt and butting the carcasses, trying to goad the dead cows back on their feet. Most went back to chewing their cuds or began cropping grass without apparent concern.

Jordan had his stand.

Working smoothly now, loading and firing in a steady rhythm, he started dropping the skittish ones. Hardly any of the others paid any attention, seemingly undisturbed by the falling bodies or the growing, sickly-sweet stench of blood. Buffalo carcasses dotted the feeding ground now, each report of the Sharps bringing another crashing thud on the prairie below. Ten. Then fifteen. Some thrashing spastically as they drowned in their own blood. Still the herd didn't take alarm, looking on with the disinterested calm of spectators at a shooting match. After every fifth shot Jordan poured water down the Sharps barrel to keep it from overheating. Then he swabbed it out, hurriedly reloaded, and returned to killing. Load, fire, eject. Slow, careful, and steady. The pattern was a part of him—something he did well—and took pride in. Something he enjoyed.

A craftsman working in gunsmoke and blood and death.

Shortly after the sun came overhead, Jordan stopped the kill. By rough count there were eighty carcasses spread over the feeding grounds. Just about what the crew could handle before nightfall. Some minutes later, McCabe led the wagons around the hill and gave him a snappy salute. Jordan grinned and waved back. The old turkey buzzard had probably come running the minute he heard firing—then had to cool his heels waiting for the kill to end.

The herd rumbled off into the distance as the wagons approached, leaving a cloud of dust and a mountain of dead to mark their passing. McCabe and his skinners went to work with brutal efficiency. Each hide meant ten cents bonus, and little time was wasted. The men worked in pairs, first propping the carcass on its back. One man slit the hide beneath the lower jaw, then along the neck and down the belly to the tail. Next he ripped down the inside of each leg and notched through at the hocks, peeling the skin back as his knife slithered across the warm flesh. The second man, using a crescent-shaped blade, then cut clear around the neck, loosening the hide from the carcass. Afterwards, once the buffalo was rolled over, a mule was brought up and a rope snugged tight to the loose wad of skin along the neck. The mule was led forward and the hide peeled off slick as a whistle. Whatever meat the men wanted—tongue, hump, ribs—was rolled inside the hide for safekeeping.

Next came the backbreaking chore. Loading the wagons. Green hides weighed up to a hundred pounds each, sometimes more. When the stack started to mount inside the wagon, a man had all he could do to hoist the next one aboard. But there were no complaints, not even for the crotchety chief skinner.

Every hide meant another ten cents in their pockets, and that was nothing to sneeze at. Many a man had busted a gut for less.

Jordan watched them a while, then lazed back against the side of the hill and lit his pipe. The sun was a fiery ball lodged high in the sky, cooking everything beneath it to a well-sizzled crisp. Still, it wasn't so bad if a man put his mind to it. Matter of fact, upside a hill—with a touch of breeze on a fellow's face—it was a damnsight better than sweating his gonads off skinning shaggies.

The plainsman grunted with satisfaction. It was a good life. Just as good as a man could ask for. Full belly, clear water to drink, and a silky robe to keep him warm at night. All it lacked was a woman.

But then a female was a damn poor substitute for some things. Not that a man had to give up hunting and rotgut and whoring around to get himself a woman.

It just sort of worked out that way. Leastways for those that took the bait.

4.

Julia Rath was an enlightened woman. She didn't hold with the Temperance Leaguers, necessarily, or the radical young suffragettes she had met back east. All the same, she firmly believed that woman was not put on earth to serve as chambermaid, laundress, and shortorder cook to some hairy-handed man. Wife, definitely. Lover, without question. Mistress, perhaps. Depending on circumstance—and the man. But the idea that she was anybody's vassal—a chattel without voice or will of her own—was abhorrent. More than that, it was appalling. Backward. Antiquated. Straight out of a cave with furry little people hunched around a fire gnawing raw bones.

Still, this attitude was perhaps too enlightened for Dodge City. Some folks said it was unladylike. Others called it disgraceful. The more charitable wrote it off as girlish poppycock, witless gibberish from Jason Rath's spoiled, highfalutin' only child. Even the Women's League—comprised in the main of pinched-lipped old biddies with vinegary dispositions—found it downright shocking. Scandalous. Particularly Julia's attitude toward work.

Julia didn't exactly resent keeping house for her father. She just found it boring. Abysmally so. Cooking, dusting, emptying chamber pots—commonly held to be feminine chores—seemed to her little more than a thankless drudge. She had no intention whatever of standing before her Maker on Judgement Day and listening to the Keeper of the Records describe her as just another pot-walloper. Not hardly. There was more to life than baking fluffy biscuits and scouring an endless array of dirty dishes. There just had to be.

As a practical matter, though, opportunities outside the home were a little scarce in Dodge. Limited, in fact. Other than saloons, dance halls, and houses of ill repute, a girl didn't have much of a choice. Since Julia felt herself unsuited for these gamier professions—though they did have a certain wicked appeal that was the least bit disquieting—she took work in the only establishment available. Namely, her father's store. Julia's reasoning was simplicity itself, and for her father, maddeningly irrefutable. He was the one who had educated her in fine schools—given her an appreciation for logic and rational thought—taught her to lift her chin and face the world with backbone firmly anchored in place.

It followed, then, that it was he who must give her a job.

The old man had accepted it with the good grace of a doting father, and Julia had gone to work for Rath and Company as treasurer. While the title was somewhat misleading, since her duties involved little besides bookkeeping, the young woman seemed perfectly content. She had made her point and she was contributing something worthwhile to the family enterprise. If the musty ledgers lacked glamour—and business in its own way was stupefyingly dull—she never once let on. It was a regular circus compared to housework.

The local gossips made much of it, though, in their weekly sewing circles. The scandalous part was not in working. Many women were widowed, or never sly enough to catch a man, and they had to work. That was perfectly respectable. But for a woman to work when she didn't have to—that was mortifying. Sacrilege of a sort. It set a bad example—established a precedent even—and if allowed to go too far, might start to give their own men some disturbing ideas. After all, they clucked angrily while sewing up a storm, a woman didn't waste her youth and beauty snaring a man only to wind up behind a counter. They could have done that on their own. Without some dirty old man pawing around under their gown in the middle of the night.

Julia just ignored their snubs and catty remarks, and calmly went on about her business. Yet, beneath the tranquil facade, she had to admit that everything wasn't as rosy as it appeared. She had a career—of sorts—and a degree of independence that women seldom attained. But she wasn't happy. Just to be candid about it—and with herself—she was downright miserable.

She had gotten her way where work was concerned, but she honestly questioned that it was what she really wanted. Or perhaps she wanted to have her cake and eat it too. The thought wasn't without an element of truth, and lately she had given it serious consideration. She definitely wanted a life of her own, no question about that. But at the same time, she wanted a home. Babies. Fried chicken on Sunday. Flowers in the front, and a little garden out back. Taproots for the days ahead.

Most of all—and this blunt admission came hard—what she really wanted was a man. Not just any man, though. It was a very special man, one who hadn't yet found himself or where he belonged. Rough around the edges perhaps, hardly gentle or easily domesticated, but a man who brought the delicious warmth inside her bubbling to the surface. The only man who had ever made her feel like a woman.

She wanted Sam Jordan.

That was the damnedly frustrating part of it. She wanted *only* Sam Jordan. While many men in Dodge had made overtures——some leaving no doubt whatever that they wished to court her—she just couldn't be bothered. She remained faithful to Sam—though in all candor she had to admit that he had never once urged it on her. Everything she had tried—all the little enticements common to every woman's arsenal of tricks—had failed miserably. So far as she could tell, Sam had no intention of marrying her anytime soon—if ever—and she had the sinking feeling that time was running out. She was fast approaching twenty-five—the age girls ceased being girls and became old maids. Left to his own devices, she had the unnerving presentiment that Sam would wordlessly stand by and watch it happen.

The thought infuriated her. But by the same token, it had made her take a long, calculated look at the man she wanted so badly.

Julia believed very earnestly that women possessed a degree of strength unknown to men. Not in brute force—though a cunning woman could easily overcome that—but in strength of spirit. Strength of character. Strength to endure—the tolerance of pain and suffering. Strength of the nameless inner thing which makes a person morally brave in a world ruled by the precept of might makes right.

Yet for all their formidable array of strengths, women somehow remained at the mercy of men. Just as she—foolishly or otherwise—had allowed herself to become dominated by Sam. Not that he made demands on her—sometimes she wished he would—but in the scheme of things between them, it had evolved that he was the one who must be trapped.

The nature of the beast is to roam free. Unfettered. At one with itself and at odds with all else.

She vaguely recalled the quote from one of her professors back east. How very curious that it seemed so descriptive of Sam Jordan. Particularly when it had been used solely in reference to things of the wild. But, then, Sam couldn't necessarily be classed as tame. Like a wolf cub raised in the home, he was apt to hear the call of the wild at any time. There was a streak of restlessness in him that couldn't be too long held in check. Not by anyone—least of all her—or so it seemed. When the winter snows melted and the soft plains wind came up out of the south, when the trees greened out and the sun went warm, he had to be away and gone. That was the way it had always been with Sam.

It was the nature of the beast.

Julia sat hunched over a ledger in the back office, staring blankly at the neat columns of figures. There it was. Almost as if it had been written across the page in bold red ink. *The nature of the beast.* She shivered, blinking her eyes, willing it to disappear. But it refused to go away, for it was no part of the precise rows in the ledger. Never had been. It lurked in her mind, and had all the while.

Jason Rath cleared his throat from the doorway. "Julia, aren't you feeling well? Your face is white as a sheet."

Only then was she aware that he had been standing there watching her. "I'm fine, daddy. Really I am. It's just a bit close in here, that's all."

"Funny. I thought the days were starting to cool off." The old man cocked his head and gave her an appraising look. "Sure there's not something bothering you?" When she didn't answer right off, he smiled gently. "You know, we used to share a lot of things till you got all ladylike and grown up."

That was true, she thought. After her mother died she had shared everything with her father. Every last girlish

67

secret. Only lately had it changed. "Oh, daddy. I'm really not hiding anything. Honestly. I just got to fretting over Sam again."

Rath nodded, pursing his lips. "Yes, I can see how that would get you a little agitated. Things aren't going according to plan, eh?"

Julia's cheeks flushed and she avoided his gaze. "I didn't know it was obvious. But I suppose it must have been. After Sam was over to supper that night, he never came calling again. Just to say goodbye before he left for Texas."

Jason Rath was tempted to tell her where Jordan had been all those nights she sat home waiting. Still, he knew it would serve no purpose. Instead he came at it from the hind side. "Honey, exactly what do you know about Sam, anyway? I mean, other than the fact that he's my partner and hunts buffalo, what do you really know about the man?"

Now Julia looked at him, and her eyes appeared shot through with chilled green flecks. "You mean that he gets drunk? Chases women? Goes out of his way to pick fights with other men? Daddy, I'm a big girl, and Dodge is a small town. There is very little Sam Jordan does that I don't know about."

The merchant was openly surprised by her admission. "That being the case, I'm a little puzzled as to how you could be interested in him."

His daughter treated him to a shrewd Rath smile. "I haven't noticed you trying to dissolve your partnership with him."

"That's business," the old man bridled.

"In other words, he is honest enough to do business with, but not decent enough to have as a son-in-law."

"Now, Julia, don't try putting words in my mouth. I like Sam. Even admire him in a queer sort of way. That doesn't blind me to his faults, however."

"Don't worry, daddy. I can still see straight." Her smile suddenly dissolved into bemused vulnerability. "It's just that there is so much to Sam that he doesn't know about himself. Things he hasn't discovered yet. I can see it. I know it's there just bursting to get out. Only I don't know if I can wait long enough for it to happen."

Rath's glance was casual, but highly speculative. "There are plenty of fish in the pond, honey. Nobody ever died yet from losing their bait the first try."

"Oh, for goodness sake! You can be so melodramatic

68

sometimes. I'll just wait till he comes home and have it out with him. If it turns out we don't want the same things, then we're both free to go our own way."

The little storekeeper knew his daughter better than that. She was making a brave show, but underneath she was crying real tears. With as much humor as he could muster, he tried to lighten her burden. "I wouldn't fret about it too much, missy. Hound dogs always get tired of roaming and sooner or later they all come home. Sam included."

"Does that hold true for curly wolves also, daddy?"

Rath didn't have any reply for that. He shrugged and smiled reassuringly, then turned back into the store. Walking toward the counter, he was struck by a sudden thought—one of the little ironies of life.

Sam Jordan, who wanted nothing whatsoever to do with business, was rapidly becoming wealthy from his one civilized endeavor.

That would make him just about the most eligible curly wolf on the western plains.

5.

Jordan and his crew had decided to take a day of rest. Nothing religious intended. Just a day to rest their weary bones and catch up on their chores before winter caught them with their pants down and no way to warm their bare fannies. Fall had come to the plains, and in the leafy green of the trees there were splashes of yellow mixed with a wild profusion of red and wine and brownish-golds. Winter wouldn't be long behind, and a smart man found no shame in borrowing a trick or two from the lowly squirrel.

Ducks already clouded the shrunken ponds, and geese were winging their way southward. When morning frost began to whiten the river banks, the buffalo also turned about and started once again for their winter feeding grounds. The bulls had left the cows by now, to spend the grueling months ahead in monastic little bunches, and the great Texas gathering split into thousands of smaller herds as it slowly retreated from the northern ranges. Over the early fall, Jordan's hunting operation had gradually worked its way down the Double Mountain Fork of the

Brazos, then turned due south and come to rest on the Clear Fork some seventy miles west of Fort Griffin.

There, in a grove of cottonwoods on the north bank of the river, Jordan had set the skinners to constructing their winter home. The spot selected was a small hill that formed a natural windbreak, and he had instructed the men to hollow out a chamber twenty by thirty with enough headroom for the tallest of the lot. Along about February, they would be wishing it was twice that size. Dugouts made miserable quarters—rank with the smell of unwashed men, gassy farts, and stale stories that everyone had heard twice over. Living that close together, a crew could be at one another's throats with winter half gone, and he meant to make it as comfortable as possible. The skinners had started work early that morning, and his orders left them facing a real skullduster.

Dig it roomy and shore it up properly with timbers. Then lay a floor of stripped branches, and cover every wall with buffalo hides.

After considerable grumbling, the men started digging in earnest, and Jordan settled down to catch up on his reloading. McCabe had weaseled out of the tunneling operation by promising everyone a real spread of vittles for supper that night. The old rascal wasn't a bad cook when he set his mind to it, and Jordan agreed that the men were overdue for a good bait of innards. They had kept themselves pretty well gorged on the choicest parts—hump and ribs especially—dark, succulent meat which was coarser than beef but much tastier. Marrow was also used unsparingly—shortening for biscuits and fried steaks, and spread liberally like butter on the bread. This simple fare went a long way in keeping their mouths free of sores and heading off the raw, bloody gums that caused a man to lose every tooth in his head.

But a real gut-eater stew every now and then put a man right back on his mettle. The ingredients were nothing much—liver, heart, kidney, small chunks of lights and intestine, a little river water, and a couple of dried peppers. Stewed slowly it came out spicy and tender, and as every plains Indian knew from childhood, it kept a man so healthy he couldn't hardly stand himself.

While he was at it, McCabe had dug himself a brine-vat lined with hides to begin salting hams and tongues for the winter ahead. Later he would throw together a smokehouse of poles and green hides, and further cure the meat over a slow fire. Fried in marrow butter, when the snow was ass deep and fresh meat a dim memory, it made good eating.

McCabe had a habit of talking to himself even around others, and Jordan paid little attention to his muttering. Reloading shells took all the concentration a man could scrape together. Leastways it should, unless he wanted to get the breech-block of a Sharps Fifty straight up his nose.

The bottle-necked shells had already been soaked in vinegar, then washed in warm water and dried thoroughly. After inspecting the three-inch casing for dents or hairline cracks, Jordan thumbed a primer into the butt end of the cartridge and gently pressed it against a wooden block to seat it properly. Next he dipped a tiny horn thimble into a powder keg at his side. The thimble had been painstakingly whittled from buffalo horn, and very precisely measured 110 grains of black powder. Curling his forefinger and thumb around the mouth of the shell, he emptied the thimble without spilling so much as a grain. When done, the brass case had been filled to within a half inch of the top. Next he rammed in a wad, poured a dab of powder on top of that, then seated the big slug. Unlike many hunters, Jordan refused to dip the base of the bullet in beeswax or grease. Instead, he carefully wrapped the hind end of each slug with a paper patch to reduce leading in the Sharps barrel. Once seated, he pressed the ball firmly in place with his thumb and dropped the cartridge into his shell bag. Then he selected another empty casing and started over again.

It was a tedious process, but necessary, and one that he curiously enjoyed. Every time he reloaded a shell he thought of it in terms of a buffalo—could almost see the big hunk of lead mushrooming through hide and tallow—and that somehow took the boredom out of the chore. Besides, there was a lot riding on him and Lucretia. The old girl was a dead center gun—she put a slug right where a man aimed her—and he didn't mean to feed her anything inferior in the way of shells.

McCabe upped the tempo of his muttering, which generally meant he was talking to someone other than himself. "Yessiree-bob! Come supper time, we're gonna be greasin' our chins with some fine fixins. Ain't nothin' like a gut-eater stew to take the kinks out o' a man."

"Puts gristle back in his dauber, too," Jordan agreed

71

casually, sneaking a glance at the skinner. "Leastways if he's not so dried-out it won't get stiff no more."

"There you go again!" McCabe snorted. "All the time talkin' about women. Cimarron, one of these days you'll stick your pecker in some hairy cave and whatever's in there is gonna gobble it up. Right down to the nubbin! You mark my word."

"There's worse ways to go." Jordan paused and let his eyes drift off, as though studying some matter of profound substance. "Come to think of it, I knew a feller once that beat his pud so hard tryin' to get it stiff he just naturally flogged himself to death."

The old skinner shot him a look that could have raised blisters on a rock. "Think you're cute, don't ya? Well lemme tell you somethin', sonny. Ain't no man alive ever caught me doin' that. Nossir. Nary a one. Hell, anybody with a lick of sense knows that kind o' thing'll drive you crazy as a parrot eatin' sticky candy."

"You talkin' about insane?" When McCabe nodded soberly, the plainsman broke out laughing. "Great crippled Christ! If poundin' your pud drove a man crazy, why half the fellers west of the Missouri'd have to be carted off to the loony bin."

McCabe darted a glance toward the men working on the dugout, then lowered his voice. "Cimarron, it's a natural born fact. I saw a feller go daft as a squirrel once. We was trappin' up north that winter, and ever' night he'd flail that thing like he was killin' snakes. Fore spring he went plumb out o' his skull. Attacked me one night and I opened up his gizzard. Poor devil thought I had started lookin' like a female."

Jordan roared so loud he spilled a thimbleful of powder. "Holy jumpin' Judas! That beats anything I ever heard tell of. Lon, that feller wasn't crazy. The sonovabitch was just horny. Probably figured any old hole would do and yours looked handy. That's what you get for winterin' with people of low character."

"Weren't that way at all," McCabe grated out. "Happened just like I said."

"Well, you believe what you want," Jordan grinned. "But I'm tellin' you he just went cabin happy. Locked up all winter that way it can happen to a feller."

McCabe slewed a look over toward the dugout. "I guess we don't have to worry 'bout them boys none. I mean, seein' as we've wintered with 'em before, they're most likely pretty safe. Course, ol' Frenchy is near 'bout as bad as you where women is concerned. Never saw a man to wake up with it stiff so much."

Jordan's gaze settled on the three skinners who were burrowing into the hillside like a trio of badgers. Seth Cook. Dan Huggins. Frenchy Dupre. Men who spent their lives grubbing for nickels and dimes. Willing to tackle any chore that offered a square meal and a dry bed. Stable hand. Pearl diver. Freight loader. Buffalo skinner. Dirty jobs were their stock in trade. The nameless, faceless legion that came west to make a fortune and wound up with a shovel on the dungheap.

Barking broke out, and Jordan turned back to see McCabe's wolf-dog staring downcreek with his hackles on end. The dog didn't bark so much as give out low wolf-like snarls punctuated by hoarse grunts. Being half wolf, he couldn't quite manage a full-fledged bark. The old skinner had bought him as a pup back in Dodge, shortly after the fight at Adobe Walls. Indians being what they are, McCabe had figured it wouldn't do any harm to have a watchdog around camp. Only in this case, it had turned out to be a sort of watch-wolf.

"Reckon he smells somethin' we don't?" McCabe was now staring downstream himself.

"Most likely a wildcat." Jordan went back to reloading shells. "I saw tracks yesterday evenin'."

"I dunno. He's gettin' big enough he'd probably tangle with a wildcat. Stonewall! You ugly mongrel, get on back over here."

The dog trotted over at McCabe's call, and stared up at the old man with bright yellow eyes. Wolf eyes. Though barely a half-year old, he was fed on enough buffalo meat for a whole wolf pack, and he was already the size of a small pony. Clearly he was going to be a monster when he got his full growth.

McCabe kneaded the dog's ruff, still looking off along the tree-fringed river bank. "You know, Cimarron, I've felt a shade uneasy ever since sunup. My game leg's all stove up, and that's a bad sign."

"It's a sign awright," Jordan chuckled. "Means your joints are gettin' old and dried out. Just like I said."

"Now damnit, you know that ain't so. My leg's never failed us before. Has it? You tell me that. Has it ever?"

"Noooo. Can't rightly say it has. But that don't mean

we got to commence huntin' a hole every time your pup goes to barkin'."

"Well I'll tell you somethin' for a fact. My leg and Stonewall can't both be wrong. Just sudden like everything's gone quiet as a gopher with his throat cut. Unnatural, that's what it is. There's somethin' queer goin' on out there, Cimarron."

Jordan felt a chill settle over him, and though it passed quickly, it left a prickly uneasiness. Brushing a fly off his cookie-duster, he carefully inspected the thick stand of cottonwoods downstream. The old man was talking about Indians, and they both knew it. But it wouldn't hold water. Back in September that Colonel Mackenzie had scattered the Comanches at Palo Duro Canyon, and slaughtered better than a thousand of their ponies. Just didn't make sense they would be out raiding after that. Besides, when north winds set in, redskins started hunting winter lodgings the same as white men.

Letting his eyes flick through the cottonwoods, Jordan grunted. Nothing. Just trees. "Lon, you're lettin' that mutt spook you. Kick him in the ass and go on back to work."

Stonewall snarled a savage wolf-like growl and flashed a set of teeth that looked like he had traded them off a shark. But the growl wasn't meant for Jordan. The dog's yellow eyes were fastened on something downstream.

"Jumpin' Jehosephat!" McCabe's face had gone so white his lips had no color, and he was sputtering like a pan of hot grease. "Would you look at all them goddamn Injuns!"

Jordan's head jerked around and his blood went cold as ice water.

Kiowas.

Last time he had looked there had been nothing but trees. Now there were at least twenty mounted Kiowas moving their ponies forward at a slow walk. Sneaky bastards! Meant to walk right up on camp quiet as a bucket of snakes before they opened fire. Catch everybody with their pants down, and the fight would be all over. Real quick.

The plainsman rolled toward the nearest wagon, shouting at the top of his lungs. *"Injuns! Head for the wagons!"*

Jordan scrambled to his feet and pulled a Winchester '73 from beneath the wagon seat. Buffalo guns were all right for long range stuff, but close in like this a man needed to sling a lot of lead in a hurry. McCabe and the other skinners tumbled in beside him and started grabbing whatever gun came to hand. Jordan eased his rifle over the wagon frame just as the head Kiowa let go with a war whoop.

Since their little surprise had been ruined, the Indians weren't playing Sneaky Pete any longer. Moccasined heels slammed up against pony flanks, and the animals came thundering across the clearing at a dead gallop. Jordan brought the Winchester to his shoulder and commenced throwing lead as fast as he could work the lever. Just then he couldn't be bothered with careful aiming. Something had to turn that charge aside or they would have Kiowas swarming over them like smoked bees.

The barrage of .44 slugs went whistling across the glen with telling effect. One brave toppled over backwards stone cold dead, a couple more were nicked, and a horse went down, spilling its rider in a shower of dust. Jordan became aware that his men had joined the fight, even as he saw two warriors swoop in to catch up the dismounted Kiowa. Sighting deliberately now, he shot the Indian on the ground just as the pickup team reached him, then swung ahead and dropped one of the riders as they tore past. McCabe's ancient Henry Repeater cracked about the same time, and the second warrior bounced head over heels when he hit the ground. The balance of the raiding party swerved off and whipped their ponies toward the tree line at the far end of the clearing.

Though a few of the Kiowas had rifles, most were using bows, and Jordan was thankful for that. But he had no illusions about what was coming next. The Indians wanted their saddle horses and weapons. Mules didn't interest them except as something to eat. The thing that really had them slobbering, though, was scalps. Any *Taibo* scalp was good, but a buffalo-hunter's hair was something extra special. They would be back, and chances were they wouldn't make the wait overly long.

"What d'ya think?" McCabe croaked in his ear.

"I think we're in a helluva fix." The plainsman spoke over his shoulder, eyes glued to the distant tree line. "Boys, they're gonna be all over us in a minute. Get loaded, and when you see 'em comin', give it to 'em hot and heavy."

The words were no sooner out of his mouth than the Kiowas exploded from the trees with a chorus of shrill, gobbling whoops. They came again at a full gallop, strung out in a mounted wedge, and it was clear they meant to overrun the wagons by sheer force of numbers. Those with guns had slid over to the opposite flank of their ponies, dangling by a leg as they fired under the horse's neck. The rest bent low and filled the air with a slithery cloud of arrows. Their bodies glistened like greased mahogany in the early morning sun, and as they bore down on the wagons, the head man howled the ancient Kiowa war cry.

Ah-ko! Eeiiooow! Ah-ko!

The white men met them with a hailstorm of lead, working furiously to lever and fire as fast as their hands could move. The fusillade cut through the Indians' ranks like an invisible scythe, sending three braves cartwheeling from their ponies in a flurry of arms and legs. Then another pony went down, dumping its rider to the ground, and both were cut to ribbons under the churning hooves. Jordan's Winchester clicked empty just as the howling pack sheered off toward the east, and his knees went quivery as a bowl of jelly.

For a moment there—just before the charge broke apart—he had felt like a man rolling dice on his own coffin.

Jerking his Colt .44, he laid it over the wagon frame and emptied it into the Kiowas as they gained the shelter of the trees. He saw one rider slump, but no one fell. Cursing, it suddenly came to him that he couldn't hear. His head was filled with the gonging ring of gunfire, as though some giant clapper was bouncing off the inside of his skull. Yet in some curious way he could still hear the feathered whisper of arrows.

Whispered death louder than gunfire.

Knuckling his ear, he looked around to find the other men staring silently at Frenchy Dupre. The little Frenchman lay spread-eagled on the ground with an arrow through his throat. Evidently he had caught one on the last charge. Jordan's mouth went dry and his gorge felt clogged. Good old Frenchy. He would be missed. Every whore from New Orleans to Denver would shed a tear when they heard Frenchy Dupre had gone under.

Suddenly there was a wild screech from the cottonwoods. Glancing back, he saw the head wolf circling his pony in front of the tree line, shouting for all he was worth. But he was as alone as a whore in church. Clearly his braves couldn't be talked into another session and the old boy was roasting them over the coals. Given enough time he might just turn the trick, too.

Which could be damned unpleasant for what white men there were left in this neck of the woods.

Jordan made a quick dive for Lucretia, got her loaded, and took a good arm rest over the top of the wagon. The range was nothing. Less than a hundred yards. Now if that leather-lunged sonovabitch would just stand still.

The Kiowa obligingly brought his pony to a halt, shaking his fist and yelling a string of insults at the silent trees. Lucretia roared, and the clearing all of a sudden went deathly still. Then the head man slowly toppled off his horse and hit the ground with a dusty thud.

Moments later, two warriors galloped out of the trees, leaned down in perfect unison, and snatched up the body of their fallen leader. Then they thundered back into the cottonwoods, and the clearing once more fell hushed.

The Kiowas had called it a day.

Later that evening—after they had rolled Frenchy Dupre in a blanket and planted him—the men gathered around the fire for some gut-eater stew. But it was a sad feast they shared. And the meat somehow had the taste of gall. Spooning out a tallowed chunk of kidney, Jordan could only wonder and curse at the way the chips fell. The Frenchman buried, Dan Huggins with his arm in a sling, and a fresh pot of stew that tasted like batcrap.

The army should feel real proud. They had pacified the hell out of the Indians. Herded them onto reservations. Gave them a cow apiece once a month. Taught them how to make their marks and eat with forks just like white men.

Now all they had to do was break them from killing sheep.

Three

※※※※※※※※※※※※※※※※※※※※※※※※※※

1.

Jordan and his crew rolled into Fort Griffin on a warm spring day with a load of hides that threatened to collapse both wagons. The men were greasy, crawling with lice, and looked like they hadn't had a bath since the last time it rained. Though they had wintered well in the dugout, they were lean, hard, and spoiling for action. They hadn't seen a woman in better than four months and it showed in their faces.

They were loaded for bear. Bushy tailed and bright eyed and wound tighter than an eight-day clock.

One glimpse of the Flats was enough to stop them cold in their tracks. They just sat there gawking, their eyes popped open with astonishment. It wasn't possible, yet unless their eyes deceived them, it was damn sure true.

The grungy village on the banks of the Clear Fork had come of age. All of a sudden.

Over the winter months the crude frontier outpost had been transferred into a regular little metropolis. Word had gone out that Griffin was to be the scene of the next great buffalo slaughter, and from every corner of the plains, the race was on. They all came—hide-hunters, gamblers, cut-throats, and harlots alike—scenting fast money on the freshening spring wind. Sprawling over the flats at the foot of the hill, the town had grown by leaps and bounds as the horde descended on the Clear Fork of the Brazos. Merchants and slick-haired speculators vied with the sporting crowd for choice locations, and whole caravans of lumber were freighted west as buildings shot up at a dizzying pace.

Where before there had been only one store, there were now three—Clark's Trading Post, Frankel's Emporium, and Conrad's Mercantile—each trying to outdo the other in the burgeoning hide business. The Bee Hive also had competition in the form of four new watering holes, and the old tent hotel had been replaced with a grand two-story structure proclaiming itself The Bison House. Even the Naucheville shanties had fallen victim to progress. Along the river bank stood a row of bawdy houses that rivaled anything yet seen on the western plains. Appropriately enough, the red-light district had been rechristened Hunter's Haven.

Griffin even had a newspaper—*The Frontier Echo*—and hardly a day passed that it didn't banner some sensational event in a barrage of Gothic Bold.

Jordan and his men could only look on in spellbound wonder, completely bewitched by the startling change that had taken place. While the street was axle deep in spring mud, it was a cursing, shouting jumble of slab-sided hide wagons and huge Studebaker freighters pulled by triple spans of braying mules. Hitch racks in front of every building were jammed with saddle horses, and the raucous babble from indoors left small doubt that firewater was being sampled in liberal doses—by just about everyone in town. From saloons and dance halls came the strident chords of rinky-dink pianos mixed with the sprightly wail of fiddles and an occasional banjo twanging in the background. Knots of men crowded every corner—hunters and mule-skinners, cowhands and soldiers—and the boardwalks were shoulder to shoulder jostling match as the rowdy throng made its way from one dive to the next.

The Flats was a spangly miracle—a carnival come to life—squalling, blustery, wilder than anything Cimarron Jordan had seen in four years on the western plains. Tailor made, in fact, for men whose appetites ran to fast women, popskull whiskey, and a knuckle-dusting contest open to all comers.

The plainsman tied his gelding to the back of the lead wagon and told McCabe to meet him behind Clark's store.

Then he slogged across the street and entered the trading post just as a group of Tonkawa army scouts came out. Inside he found the place swamped with customers and Ed Clark busily engaged supervising a half-dozen harried clerks. When the merchant caught sight of Jordan he came bustling forward with outstretched hand.

"Cimarron! Long time no see. How d'ya fare the winter?"

"Tolerable, Ed. Just tolerable." The hunter cut his eyes around at the pack of men clamoring to have their orders filled. "Guess I don't have to ask you how you're makin' out."

"Isn't it the goddamnedest thing you ever seen?" Clark's expression was one of mild befuddlement. "They started pouring in here about a month before Christmas. Just after you brought that last load of hides in. Haven't stopped yet."

Jordan nodded glumly, making no attempt to hide his disgust. "There's enough of 'em awright. Most likely killed off everything up north then started headin' south in droves."

"By God, you hit the nail on the head, Cimarron. Droves of 'em. Just droves and droves." Elated by his own good fortune, the storekeeper had failed to detect the bitterness in Jordan's words. "Yessir, Griffin might just turn out to be the biggest goddamn boomtown this country has ever seen."

The plainsman grimaced at the thought and moved to change the subject. "Got a load of hides out back. Two wagons. Pretty close to a thousand all told."

"Good. Good. That's not the lot, though. Couldn't be."

"No, we've got the rest cached. Take us three more trips to bring 'em in. Less you can spare some wagons."

"Sure, we'll work something out. Won't cost you much either." Clark pulled a wide ledger out from underneath the counter and opened it. After studying it a moment he looked up with a grin. "Well, now, you had yourself some year. Case you didn't know it, that's close to seven thousand hides. With what's on the books already, we'll owe you damn near . . . no, wouldn't surprise me if it didn't go over eleven thousand. What're you gonna do with all that money, Cimarron? Not lug it around I hope."

"You can give me three thousand in cash," Jordan said. "Hold another couple of thousand on credit here and let Loberstein forward the rest to my bank in Dodge."

"Then what?" Clark gave him a lewd smirk. "Gonna paint the town red?"

"Red, white, and purple." Jordan smiled for the first time since entering the store. "After payin' my crew off, I figure to get crosseyed, and then have a good fling at screwin' myself to death."

"That's the ticket," the merchant laughed. "Good times and hard work. Keeps a man feisty. Say, be sure and hit Mollie Deno's house. She's got some stuff there you won't believe even after you've had it."

Jordan made a mental note of the name and followed Clark toward the loading dock out back. Pushing through the crowd of men blocking the aisle, his guts went tight as sunbaked flint hide.

The pack had overtaken him again.

Some three hours later, the young plainsman and his crew barged out of the Bee Hive and headed for Hunter's Haven. They had bathed, traded their vermin-ridden clothing for new duds, and consumed just enough Taos lemonade to get a warm glow down around their heels. Cook and Huggins had their minds set on poontang, and had gone light on the juice. But McCabe was already pretty well ossified. Women rarely, if ever, got any of his money and he was tagging along mainly as a heckler. Unless they happened to meet up with a real buxom specimen. Being skinny as a lizard, McCabe was just naturally partial to overplump women.

The three skinners were riding high. They had each made better than $700 since last fall and they had their chests puffed out like strutting cocks. So far as they were concerned—and they were loudly telling it to everyone they passed on the street—Cimarron Jordan was the best goddamn buffalo man that had ever come down the pike. Moreover, they were just about the finest skinners anybody had ever heard tell of. Lumped together, that made Jordan's outfit the best sonofabitchin' crew in the hide business. Bar none.

But Jordan shared little of their exuberance. He had already downed a prodigious ration of forty-rod and there was a mean look in his eye. The look that came over him when something was simmering in his guts, generally a foreshadowing of wrecked saloons, demolished whorehouses, and a whole raft of bloody heads. Since he hadn't said, McCabe and the other skinners weren't exactly sure what was eating at him. They knew him pretty well, though, and one guess between them just about nailed it down. Cimarron Jordan didn't like crowds. Leastways, not when he was hunting shaggies. And as any idjit could plainly see, the Texas herd was about to spend the summer getting chased from hell to breakfast and back again.

The skinners took a vote and agreed to a man. It was going to be an interesting night. Hard on the knuckles maybe. But real interesting.

When they stormed through the door of Mollie Deno's bagnio, Jordan let out a bloodcurdling howl. "Eeeiiioow! Run for your lives. The stud horse is here! I'm gonna fork your shafts and flush the birds. Them that can't take it had better head for the hills. *Urrnnngh!*"

Bellowing like a mad bull he leaped to the middle of the little parlor and swung in a slow circle, inspecting each girl with a hungry leer. The soiled doves stared back in pop-eyed amazement, not quite sure what he was. Most of them had been humped by everything shy of a Bengal tiger, but they had never seen anything like this broad-shouldered fire-eater standing in their midst. After a complete swing around the room Jordan drew himself up and bowed from the waist.

"Ladies, I like you all. Just form a line and gimme a room. First one to yell uncle gets a wart on her nose."

Mollie Deno heaved herself up out of a chair and waddled toward him as the girls started tittering. From the width of her stern she was just about Lon McCabe's speed. She stopped a couple of feet off and let Jordan have a double-whammy with her evil eye. "Buster, this is a respectable house. We don't hold with rough stuff. Now, either behave yourself or get out. That's the rule."

Before he could say anything one of the girls detached herself from the others and strolled over. She wasn't especially pretty, but somehow a man didn't rightly notice. She had a set of knockers that were just short of stupendous, and the way she swished her hips came near creating a draft. Latching on to Jordan's arm, she gave him a big wink.

"Sugartit, don't you worry about a thing. I'm Lulu, and I'm going to do you up so good your ears will melt." Turning to the madam, she arched one eyebrow in an obvious signal. "Now, Mollie, don't you badger this poor boy anymore. He's just lonesome and needs some lovin'."

Tippy-toeing her fingers up Jordan's chest, she gave his brushy souptrainer a gentle tug. "Isn't that right, boopsy?"

Since making his spectacular entrance, Jordan had been having trouble getting a word in edgewise. Now, just as he was about to make a snappy comeback, the door banged open and in trooped a new batch of customers. The young plainsman took one look and felt the hair come up on the back of his neck.

The man in the lead was big as a mountain and had a voice like a bass drum. It was Frank Lumpkins.

"Goddamnit, Mollie, shake the bushes and get to hustlin'! Ol' Frank's back in town!"

Lumpkins spotted Jordan just about then and pulled up so short the men behind him slammed into his back. The smile on his thick lips slacked off and a scowl came over his face. Then a pinpoint of fire kindled in his beady eyes and he swaggered forward another couple of steps.

"Well, just looka here, would ya. If it ain't the terror of the plains hisself."

The big man's nose looked a little flatter than the first time Jordan had seen him, and there was a fresh scar the width of his cheekbone. Jordan suddenly felt so good he wanted to laugh. Jesus Christ and a brass band couldn't have done as much for his sagging spirits.

"Lardgut, you've done wandered into the wrong hog pen. Make tracks or get your plow cleaned. Your choice."

The room went still as a tomb for about three seconds. Lumpkins' face turned red as oxblood, and he was breathing so hard his words came out in a choked rasp. "Mister, I'm gonna stomp all over you and there ain't gonna be nothin' left but a greasy spot."

The Texan started forward, but Mollie Deno jumped in front of him. "Frank Lumpkins! You listen to me, Frank. There'll be no fighting in here. You big bastard *No fighting!*"

Lumpkins flung her aside, delayed only a moment by her struggles. But it was all the edge Jordan needed. Before the big man could get set, the plainsman hit him square on the nose and felt it squash under his fist. Lumpkins didn't even flinch. Out of nowhere he busted the smaller man in the ribs with a blow that knocked him clear across the parlor. Jordan came off the wall on his feet, but he had a funny feeling his spine had come unsnapped. The Texan waded in throwing punches like a windmill. Most of them bounced harmlessly off Jordan's shoulders, except for a clout upside the head that sent a shower of sparks rocketing through his brain.

Jordan could hear furniture breaking and glass shattering all about him, and dimly sensed that his own crew had tied into Lumpkins' men. Just at the moment, though, he couldn't take time out for a look. The Texan had him crowded against the wall, and if he didn't do something damn fast, he was going to wind up in the meatgrinder.

Slipping one punch and ducking the next, he came up under Lumpkins' flailing arms and drove his knuckles into the man's Adam's apple. The Texan's eyes looked like a bolt of lightning had been fired straight up his crotch, and he reeled backward clutching his throat. Like some great blubbery goldfish, his mouth puckered in a thick oval and he retched a gurgled cry for air. His face went red, then purple, and then a dull shade of black, as he choked in a deadly grip of his starved lungs.

Jordan trailed him a couple of steps then moved in quickly and kicked him dead center in the balls.

Frank Lumpkins suddenly learned how to breathe again. He roared like a bull elephant and doubled over, grabbing at his groin as violent spasms of pain knifed through his belly. Jordan shifted, setting his entire weight behind the movement, and launched a blow that caught the Texan flush on the jawbone.

Lumpkins hurtled backwards like he had been shot out of a cannon. When he hit the wall, he kept right on going, taking the front window and six feet of lumber with him. The splintering crash of glass and wood brought everything in the parlor to a standstill, and as quickly as it had begun, the fight was over.

Jordan stepped to the gaping hole in the wall and gazed out at the mountain of flesh lying peacefully in the yard. Then he grinned that old pale-eyed wolf grin, chuckling softly.

"Like they say, lardgut, same song, second verse."

Later that night Jordan and his crew returned to the Bee Hive and found themselves celebrities of a sort. Word of the brawl had already spread through town, and there was much back-slapping and jocular ribbing as the four men squeezed in at the bar. Everyone in the saloon had heard about the hole in Mollie Deno's parlor wall, and they also knew that Jordan had forked over a wad to stop her screeching. That was as it should be, though. Proprietors of sporting houses had to expect damages, and so long as a man paid his freight, they had no squawk coming. The fact was—according to the story circulating along Main Street—Jordan had gone right ahead and humped practically every female in the house except Mollie herself. That alone, everyone in the Bee Hive agreed, showed that Mollie didn't hold any hard feeling. The old catamount had probably enjoyed every minute of it!

But Frank Lumpkins was a horse of a different color. Twice now he had been whipped by the same man, which was no disgrace except to someone like the Texan. Most folks would have thought the better of him for locking horns with a man who had already taken his measure once before. Come tomorrow morning, though, Lumpkins was going to find himself the laughing stock of Griffin. Not for losing the fight. Hell, there wasn't a man in town who could whip young Jordan. But the spectacle of Lumpkins being carted off in a hide wagon like a beached whale was a real knee-slapper. The Texan would probably skin his own skinners when he found out they had used a wagon to haul him away from Mollie Deno's. An even stronger likelihood was that he would try to skin Cimarron Jordan.

There was still no law on the Flats, and every man had to look to his own safety. Jordan gave a pretty fair imitation of a fellow who knew how to do just that, but Frank Lumpkins was known to hold a grudge. Hardly anyone in the Bee Hive doubted that the matter was done with yet. The only real question was whether or not the Texan would choose to raise the ante.

The subject had raised a good deal of idle speculation around the bar, but Jordan just listened and kept working away at his bottle. Despite the gathering army of hide hunters, the night had worked out pretty well after all. Morning was still a long way off and he had already had a doozy of a fight, not to mention shafting that big-titted Lulu till her eyes went glassy. Now it was time for a little serious drinking. Afterwards, once he had his boiler stoked with forty-rod, he might just wander back down to Mollie Deno's. There was a little redhead who had caught his eye—sort of spicy looking. Probably a real chili pepper when a fellow gigged her just right.

Hoarse curses erupted from the back of the saloon and Jordan turned to see a large, florid-faced man clawing at a gun on his hip. The man across from him moved so fast his actions appeared blurred. One moment he was seated and the next he was leaning over the poker table with a gleaming blade in his hand. The knife flicked twice, razoring the big man's brisket on the forward stroke and opening his belly on the return cut. The man's face went white as chalk and he stumbled away from the table, grabbing with both hands to keep his guts from spilling out. He had been eviscerated as neatly as a butchered hog. Without a sound, he dropped to his knees then fell face down in the sawdust.

The second gambler was a cold fish—sallow, ash-blond, so thin and slightly built he seemed almost cadaverous. Jerking a handkerchief, he coughed a couple of times then wiped the blood off the knife and slipped it inside his coat. Gathering his money, he stepped over the dead man and calmly walked from the saloon.

"Jesus Christ!" McCabe muttered as the doors swung shut. "For a little feller he's sort o' sudden, ain't he?"

The barkeep grunted and commenced polishing the counter. "That there's Doc Holliday. Good man to stay clear of."

"No shit?" the old skinner snorted. "Now suppose you just tell me who and what a Doc Holliday is."

"Hell, old timer, Doc Holliday is a gunslinger. Everybody knows that. Came out here when the law back in Dallas got after him."

"Gunslinger?" McCabe cackled. "By God, the way he handles a knife he oughta be a sawbones." Then a sly look came over his face and he gave the barkeep a sour smile. "Most likely that's why they call him Doc. Bet'cha never thought of that, now did'ya?"

Jordan was listening, but with no real interest. Somehow Doc Holliday's barroom surgery brought him round to the thought that he had never personally killed a man. Not a white man, leastways. Though he had whipped many men within an inch of their lives, it had never yet gone the limit. More than once he could have killed if he had wanted to—with just his bare hands. But looking back, it seemed that killing had never been called for, and perhaps that was nearer the truth. Maybe most men were closer to wild things than they knew.

They didn't kill unless they had to.

Jordan took a sip of his drink and rolled it around in his mouth, letting it slowly trickle down his gullet.

It was an interesting thought.

2.

The bender lasted two days. When it was over, folks around the Flats admitted it had been the grandaddy of all drunks. The Jordan outfit had systematically wrecked all four saloons and turned Hunter's Haven into squealing battleground. The high-water mark—duly reported by the *Frontier Echo*—had been Lon McCabe, roaring drunk and buck-ass naked, chasing Mollie Deno along the riverbank in broad daylight. Everyone in town turned out for the event and there was little question that it had been a damn fine race. Though Mollie wasn't built for speed, she had held her own, and the mere mention of her stumpy, pasty-white legs churning across the flats was enough to convulse an entire saloon.

When Jordan and his crew finally came up for air along about noon the third day, they were as mangy a looking foursome as ever drew breath. Their heads thumped with an ungodly hammering, and felt just about the size of watermelons. Merely standing erect had been an ordeal, and when they stumbled out of Mollie Deno's into the blazing sun, walking itself became an exquisite form of torture. From behind their bloodshot eyeballs, the entire town appeared latticed-over with spun fire, and a man had the feeling that if he blinked, the whole top of his head might explode in a puff of smoke.

They weren't so much hungover as just being flat plowed under. Walking dead men couldn't have looked any worse, and the hell of it was, they sort of felt like cadavers.

Strung out in a wobbly line they straggled toward town in a numbed daze. Huggins had lost one boot somewhere in the course of the festivities, and his hobbled pace pretty well suited the whole bunch. Trailing him, Jordan and Cook seemed fairly fit, except for stumbling over rocks and wincing every time a bird chirped. Lon McCabe was nothing short of a walking disaster. Everything he wore belonged to somebody else, and he looked like an underfed scarecrow wearing last year's hand-me-downs. About the only recollection he had of the race with Mollie Deno was that every stitch of clothing he owned had mysteriously disappeared. Even his longjohns. Just vanished without a trace.

The only live one in the whole outfit was Stonewall. Trotting along at his master's side, the wolf-dog seemed so spunky and full of pep McCabe couldn't hardly stand to look at him. For once, though, he was damned grateful Stonewall didn't rightly know how to bark.

McCabe had a very distinct feeling that one loud noise would burst his skull like a ripe grape.

Stiff jointed and sort of queasy in the stomach, they went straight as a string to the Bee Hive. The cool dimness inside was a welcome balm, and their spirits revived slightly as they bellied up to the bar. Except for a couple of cowhands, the saloon was deserted, and Jordan considered it a merciful act of God almighty that the piano player hadn't yet came on duty. So much as a quick toot on a tin whistle would have just about done him in.

The bartender gave them the fisheye and wandered over. "Gents, I don't know what you got in mind. But if you start bustin' up the place again, I got orders to haul out the shotgun."

McCabe clapped both hands over his ears. "Friend, if it ain't too much trouble, would you mind talkin' kind o' slow and quiet like? We come in here to get away from the ruckus out on the street, and you ain't helpin' things none at all."

"I'm just tellin' you what's what. You done wrecked this joint three times in two days, and that's as far as she goes." When nobody answered, the houseman regarded them skeptically for a moment before nodding. "Well, so long as you behave yourselves I guess it's awright. What'll it be?"

"The hair of the dog that bit us," Jordan rasped.

The barkeep went away and came back with glasses and a bottle. After he poured drinks around and Jordan paid him he retreated to the end of the bar. Though they looked harmless enough now, he wasn't taking any chances. He stayed near the scattergun stashed under the counter.

Jordan raised his glass and gave the skinners a wooden smile. "Boys, it's a sorry day and gettin' sorrier all the time. But here's lookin' at you. Hard fists and stiff peckers till they cart us out stone cold dead."

The men knocked down their drinks and shuddered convulsively in a chain reaction. Dan Huggins wiped his mouth and puckered up like he had just bitten into a green persimmon. "Cimarron, I wisht you wouldn't talk no more about poontang. I got a taste in my mouth like I just had breakfast with a buzzard, only that ain't exactly how it come about."

Cook responded with a half-hearted chuckle, but McCabe wasn't in any mood for frivolity. "What'd tickle my gizzard is if you scutters just wouldn't talk at all. My head's so sore my hair hurts, and your jabber ain't helpin' a bit."

Jordan grunted and poured himself another drink. "Listen you ol' chunk of bearbait, you get ornery with me and I'll sic Mollie on you again."

"Yeah, she'd come runnin' quicker'n scat," Huggins snickered. "Never seen a fat lady get so sweet on a man. You boys reckon Lon's got somethin' we don't know about?"

"Hell, even if he's hung like a mule he's done shot his wad." Seth Cook grinned and cut his eyes around at the other men. "Why, just look at him. I calculate a cold glass of water and another hunch would kill him dead as a doornail."

McCabe sputtered curses like a string of firecrackers exploding, lashing out at first one and then the other. The three men doubled over laughing, drawing even greater roars of outrage when they started making obscene gestures about the size of his equipment. Seth Cook was howling so loud he had tears streaming down his face, and Jordan was pounding the bar hard enough to rattle every bottle on the back counter. The two cowhands plastered stupid smiles across their faces, taking care not to laugh outright, but the barkeep wasn't fooled. He figured all hell was about to break loose, and he edged closer to the shotgun.

Just then the door flew open, and Frank Lumpkins strode into the saloon looking like a badly skinned bear. There were fresh scabs all over his head from the glass in Mollie Deno's window, and his nose was purple as a squashed plum. He walked with the pronounced limp of a man who knew what a ballbuster really meant, and there was a bruise about the size of a horseshoe along the slope of his jawbone.

Halting a few feet from the bar, he took a hitch at his pants and cleared his throat with a low rumble. "Jordan, I wanta talk with you."

Jordan turned as the laughter slacked off and regarded the big man's battered features with a wry smile. "Why, sure, Lumpkins. What's on your mind?"

"Your boys have been spreadin' it around town that they whipped the stuffin' out o' my crew. That ain't how it happened and—"

"Now that's queer. Seems to me that's just how it happened."

"—my bunch ain't happy with it at all. They asked me to come up here and put it to you square."

"You mean you're lookin' for a rematch?" The plainsman suddenly had a feeling his day was picking up. "Or did you just want to kiss and make up?"

Lumpkins' jowls quivered and his face went cherry red. "I ain't lookin' for neither. Not today anyhow. But don't think you're runnin' a sandy on me, Jordan. I aim to settle accounts, and you ain't got long to wait."

"Mister, you've got a natural born talent for rubbin' me the wrong way. Now either start something or haul ass out of here. We've got some serious drinkin' to do."

"I'm gonna oblige you sooner'n you think. But my men figure they've got a stake in this too, and they asked me to bring you a challenge."

"Challenge?" Jordan demanded. "Just what the samhill are you talkin' about, Lumpkins?"

"I'm talkin' about a pit fight. My bulldog against that mutt of yours. You name the sidebet, and we'll cover it."

The Texan pointed to Stonewall, who was stretched out at McCabe's feet. Jordan detected something hidden beneath the blubbery mask and a sudden wariness came over him.

"No dice. We'll just keep it between you and me. Besides, that's McCabe's dog, not mine."

"Now hold your horses, Cimarron." McCabe fixed the Texan with a speculative gaze. "Lumpkins, this here bull-dog you're talkin' about. What sort o' critter is he?"

"Oh, he ain't nothin' much," Lumpkins offered. "Most folks use his kind as a catch dog with hogs and cattle. He's not one of them low-slung English jobs, if that's what you're thinkin'."

"Back off, Lon," Jordan cautioned. "He's baitin' it too sweet. Something don't smell right about this deal."

"Aw, quit bein' so jumpy," the old skinner fired back. "I ain't no greenhorn that needs wetnursin'. 'Sides, there ain't a dog this side o' hell that could back Stonewall down."

Jordan's jaw set in hard line and he didn't reply. After a moment he looked around at Huggins and Cook. "You boys got any money left?"

The men exchanged sheepish glances and Huggins spoke up. "Nary a cent, boss. What with the girls and faro, we're flat broke."

Jordan just nodded and turned back to the Texan. "I've got two thousand on credit over at Clark's. All or any part says your dog won't walk away."

"Done!" Lumpkins agreed. "We'll cover the whole thing. Have that fleabiter of yours out back an hour before sundown. Come tonight I got an idea you won't be talkin' so cocky."

The Texan wheeled about and lumbered out of the saloon. When the doors swung shut, Jordan nailed McCabe with a stony expression.

"Old man, I've got a hunch you better feed that mutt of yours a bait of raw meat and gunpowder. He's gonna need all the grit he can muster before the day's out."

Late that afternoon, with the sun retreating slowly westward, men started gathering out behind the Bee Hive. Word had spread through the Flats that there was to be a pit fight, and every man with nothing better to do had come to watch and make a wager. Pitting dogs in a fight to the death was a popular sport, and many were of the opinion that it had cock fighting beat six ways to Sunday. Dogs were stronger, better equipped for killing and they rarely put on a bad show.

The men jostled and shoved for position around an open pit six feet square by three feet deep, and the crowd kept growing larger by the minute. The pit itself had been designed with considerable thought by Chalk Benson, owner of the Bee Hive. It was wide enough to allow plenty of fighting room and just deep enough to discourage a cowardly dog from trying to escape. Especially with a couple of hundred shouting men jammed around the edges. So far, though, Chalk Benson hadn't staged any fights that involved dogs with a yellow stripe. The pit was good for business—blood had a curious way of making men thirsty—and he meant to keep it that way.

Jordan and his crew arrived first, leading Stonewall on a short length of rawhide. The wolf-dog had grown strong and tall over the winter, and he was every bit the monster more commonly seen among his lobo cousins in the wild.

Standing close to three feet at the shoulder, he topped a hundred pounds by a wide margin, and his chest was broad as that of a young bull. His yellow eyes glinted fiercely in the late afternoon sun, and his great wolf fangs looked as though they had been swiped off some ancient adversary. Like maybe a sabre-toothed tiger.

Judged strictly on appearances, Stonewall was a formidable-looking beast.

But was he a killer?

That remained to be seen, and it was a question that swept back over the crowd as Jordan and his men came to a halt at the edge of the pit.

Only moments afterwards, Frank Lumpkins made his way to the opposite side of the arena, and Jordan's worst suspicions were confirmed. Plain to see, the animal at Lumpkins' side was not the garden-variety bulldog fancied by English gentlemen. He was a magnificent, brindle-colored brute, with short hair, clipped ears, and a predatory eye better suited to a hungry lion. Though somewhat shorter than the wolf-dog, he was even wider through the chest, and pound for pound the scales would have tipped out in a dead heat. Inspecting him more closely, Jordan saw that he had the massive, knotted jaws of a killer—jaws that could snap the spine of a yearling buffalo, or lock down with a vise-like hold on the throat that could have only one end.

He was a bulldog well enough—known far and wide as a pit bull. Bred with no other purpose in life but to fight in the pits—used only incidently as a catchdog for livestock—vicious, stubborn, willing to tackle any creature on earth with kill-or-be-killed savagery.

Stonewall had his work cut out for him, and maybe then some.

The dogs had seen one another, and the bulldog was the first to growl, lunging against the heavy rope around his neck. Stonewall got the drift right away, and hit the rawhide lead so hard he almost pulled McCabe into the pit. The crowd roared approval, and everyone started shouting at once as men tried to get down a bet on the outcome. Almost immediately it came clear that the bulldog was heavily favored. Stonewall's remarkable resemblance to a wolf apparently counted for little when the spectators got down to wagering cold cash.

Chalk Benson motioned both owners forward, raising his arms for silence. The leads were let out enough to allow the animals to claw their way into opposite corners of the pit, and a hush fell over the crowd as the slobbering brutes strained to get at one another. When Benson swept his arms downward, the dogs were released, and both sprang forward instantly, crashing head-on in the center of the arena.

Stonewall came near losing the fight in that first bloody exchange. The bulldog was a scarred veteran of the pits, and he hadn't survived this long without a fair degree of cunning. The wolf's opening lunge was bold and instinctive, directed at his adversary's spine, along the base of the neck. But his jaws clanged shut on empty air. The dog dropped low under the charge and came up with teeth firmly embedded in Stonewall's throat. Only the thick, double-coated ruff around his neck saved the wolf. Even the bulldog's massive jaws couldn't get a death grip on a mouthful of fur, and much to his surprise he was unable to force Stonewall to the ground.

The wolf reared back and slung the dog against the side of the pit with a jarring thud, breaking the hold. But they were right back where they had started, for the veteran nimbly kept his feet as he came off the wall. Just for a moment they stared intently at one another, each with a new found respect for what he faced. Then they began circling, wary now, looking for an opening. It was a dance of death—mortal antagonists reverting to an atavistic instinct—kill or be killed. Their eyes veined red with bloodlust; ropy strings of saliva drooled from their jaws; from deep within their chests came the low, rumbling growl of a stalking predator. The spectators scarcely dared to breathe, standing motionless and silent, watching spellbound as the mighty beasts gathered themselves with bared fangs.

Stonewall suddenly launched himself in another assault, driving with sheer brute force. This time he struck lower, jaws working in a maddened rage, and the bulldog went down under his weight. They rolled, snapping and biting, hunks of fur floating skyward, obscured within a tangled thrash of legs and darting heads and a tawny explosion of dust. An instant later they emerged from the shower of grit and dirt, oddly silent as they came apart, and the onlookers loosed a murderous roar. The wolf's muzzle had been laid open to the bone, and bright crimsoned jets spurted down over his snout. Yet, gory as the wound seemed, it was the bulldog who had suffered most. One eyeball hung from its socket, dangling on a silvery thread of tissue, like a glazed marble twirling in the wind.

The blood-splatterèd monsters backed off and again resumed their slow, shuffling dance. They were both hurt, and in some brutish way the pain seemed to fan their rage all the more. The earth puddled red at their feet as they circled the pit with gnashing teeth and threatening growls. Almost as if they had entered into a staring contest, the great brutes watched one another intently, gauging signs of weakness and vulnerability and any momentary lapse of caution. Then with a savage ferocity, the bulldog snarled and leapt to the attack. He was a stubborn beast, and instinctively he sensed that a tactic which had won past fights could be made to work another time around. Feinting, he came in low and again lunged for the throat. Stonewall wasn't exactly a seasoned campaigner, but he was a fast learner. The trick had caught him off guard the first time—now he waited with a cunning of his own. When the dog's head dropped to attack, his nape was exposed for just an instant.

Sliding past the charge, the wolf's mighty jaws chomped down on the brindle neck. When his fangs met flesh he bore down with a brutish snarl, and there was a loud crunch as the bulldog's spine snapped in half. Stonewall lifted the limp body and shook it like a dead mouse, then dropped it disdainfully in the center of the pit.

The crowd went mad, cheering and shouting at the top of their lungs as they surged around the shallow hole. Jordan and McCabe threw their arms around one another and danced a wild, crazy jig. Over the roar of the spectators they yelled soundlessly, aware of nothing save the knowledge they had won.

Stonewall stared out at them from the pit, his yellow eyes glistened brightly with a wolf's amused wonder for the antics of men.

Then he grinned and licked the blood from his muzzle.

3.

Jordan was just drunk enough that he was beginning to dislike the drunks around him. That meant nearly everyone within spitting distance, for the Bee Hive was bursting at the seams with men in search of something to celebrate. Since the fight was as handy an excuse as any, they had spent the last four hours hoisting toasts to Stonewall. The huge wolf-dog was the talk of the town— the sporting crowd was thunderstruck that he had managed to kill a veteran pit bull with such savage ease—and everybody came to stare and shake their heads and offer another toast with ritualistic awe.

Not that they personally had anything to celebrate. Stonewall's victory had cost most of them a pile of money. Still, there was a certain obligation here, for in the sporting man's scheme of things, the vanquished ceased to exist. Only the winner counted, and he must be accorded every honor. Losers were a dime a dozen—to be avoided like smallpox—for there were many who believed that losing itself was a catching sort of a disease.

Jordan liked a winner as much as the next man. He couldn't have been prouder of Stonewall if he had owned the brute himself. But the whole mess had a phony ring to it. Men laughing and swilling whiskey in honor of something they themselves hadn't the guts for. Toasting someone—man or animal seemed to matter little—who had amused and titillated them by spilling blood. Someone who had fought and lived to walk away while the gutless onlookers reveled in the gore and clamored insanely for a quick kill.

It was the same when he fought, surrounded by eager, hungry faces, the crowd chanting madly for blood. Even the ritual that came afterward was the same—backslapping, lusty congratulations, men rushing to buy him a drink—and inevitably he grew bored, perhaps even a little rankled, with the sorry sham it had come to represent.

Ruminating over it as he swigged whiskey and ignored the boisterous throng about him, Jordan was struck by an unsettling thought. *Why did he fight?* Was it the roar of the crowd and the fear his savage brawls kindled in their eyes? Or did he fight for himself alone—unmindful of the crowd—gorging his own bloodlust? Question triggered question, mocking him with a tangled riddle that somehow seemed beyond his grasp. Like everything else, though, there was a beginning even to the fighting.

When he had come west that first summer, he'd been a simple lout with a strong back and a healthy respect for the rights of others. But he quickly discovered that the frontier didn't operate on the Golden Rule. Maybe it wasn't dog eat dog, but it was damn sure devil take the hindmost. Survival was a matter of watching the other fellow closely—knowing that sooner or later someone would come looking for trouble—then doing it to him before he could do it to you. The plains were crawling with rough, hardfisted men, who had been weaned on skinned knuckles and a swift kick to the balls. They fought because they liked to fight—except for the odd ones who simply enjoyed inflicting punishment—and anyone with sense enough to spit played the game by their rules. Or else got the hell back where he came from real fast.

Jordan had taken some bad lickings at first, till he got the hang of rough and tumble fighting. The kick, gouge, claw, and stomp favored in the West—anything goes so long as it wins—which was a far cry from the pantywaist slugfests practiced by easterners. Once he learned the rules, though, the young hunter had become a holy terror. Something hard and brutal simmered within him, and the ruthless climate of the plains had brought it boiling to the surface. Before long he made the startling discovery that he was in his element. He liked to fight. Enjoyed the crunch of his fist upside another man's skull. Savored the taste of blood in his mouth, the cuts and bruises, the little hurts that lingered for days afterwards.

Most of all, he liked the sharp, tingly sensation that swept over him when the other fellow went down and stayed down for keeps.

That first summer he had learned what it was to walk among men. What it meant to take hurt without whimpering, and to inflict it without pity. What juicy sweetmeats there were for the man who could whimper less and administer more hurt than those around him.

Curiously, he found that he thrived on danger—walking the fine line between fear and courage—that it was a tonic more exhilarating than whiskey or women or a mound of gold.

He had come west seeking riches and discovered instead the immense wonder of living among his own kind.

Looking back, it seemed that perhaps he fought—just as all men before him had fought—simply because it was his nature. An urge of some sort. Lacking reason, needful of no justification.

Before he could explore that further, Lon McCabe started cackling in his ear. "Goddamn, Cimarron, I told you, didn't I? You'll listen to me next time. Christ almighty, we could've gotten rich on that fight. Filthy, stink-in' rich."

The old skinner was drunk as a lord, leaning heavily on the bar for support. Huggins and Cook weren't in much better shape, and from the look of things, it was going to be a long night. Jordan had split the afternoon's winning four ways and they were once again in the chips. But their sudden windfall was strictly a passing thing. Easy come, easy go was every skinner's motto, and by morning they would all be busted flatter than a pancake.

"You're right as rain, pardner," Jordan agreed amiably. "Next time we get in a dog fight we'll play it your way right down the line."

"Now yer talkin' sense." McCabe belched and swayed unsteadily. "C'mon, boy. Get to drinkin'. This here's a celebration. Or ain't anyone told you yet?"

The plainsman grunted and took a listless swallow from his glass. "You know something? Either I'm drunk out or they're startin' to serve goat piss in this joint." Slamming the glass down, he pushed away from the bar. "Think I'll take a little walk. How about you?"

"Walk? Who you think you're kiddin'?" McCabe eyed him with a glassy expression. "You got nookie written all over yer face."

"You called it," Jordan admitted. "Thought I'd sashay down and invite that little redhead to a wrestlin' match. What d'ya say? Ready for another round of grab-ass with fat Mollie?"

"Nosiree-bob!" the old man howled. "Further I stay away from that bitch the better I like it. What little pecker I got left, I'm keepin'."

Jordan laughed and headed for the door. When he got outside he turned toward the river, feeling the dark mood slip away as he left the center of town. The night was warm but there was a cool breeze from the west, and he breathed deeply to clear his lungs of whiskey fumes. It was good to be out of that saloon for a while, away from the stale smoke and the drunken gibberish men were so fond of spouting. Thinking about it, he chuckled softly to himself. This was one spree he wasn't likely to forget. Damned if it didn't have a touch of lunacy to it. From the first senseless brawl at Mollie Deno's to the bloodthirsty crowd screaming their fool heads off around the dog pit. The queer part was that nobody thought anything about it.

97

That's just the way the Flats was. Wild, noisy, and a sight less law than a man would find in a wolf pack.

Then he laughed aloud, mocking himself. Maybe he was the one getting queer in the head. Near as he could recollect, that was the first time in close to four years he had found anything odd about ripping a town apart just for the hell of it. Damned strange the way a man's head starts him to thinking funny thoughts.

More than a fellow could rightly figure sometimes.

Jordan had just passed the last streetlamp when a sharp pain knifed across his thigh. For an instant there he thought some wayward bee had stung him, then the crack of gunfire rolled across the flats and he knew different. Hurling himself to the ground, he caught the crimson wink of a muzzle flash out of the corner of his eye. Then another, not more more than a couple of yards off to the right of the first in a patch of bushes. Dirt sprayed up right under his nose and he could almost hear the earth shudder as the lead struck home.

Those bastards were shooting at him!

Clawing the Colt .44 from his holster, he shoved it out in front of him, anchoring it firmly with both hands. Then he waited, gambling that the bushwhackers' aim wouldn't improve. When the slugs started chunking around him, he marked the fiery blasts, judging the distance at about thirty yards. Forcing himself to remain calm and deliberate, he closed his mind to the spitting guns and thumbed off five unhurried shots. Three at the man on the right and two at his partner. With the last shot gone, he rolled sideways a couple of yards and quickly started reloading.

But the gunfire ceased as suddenly as it had begun. Nothing moved and he lay very still, listening intently. Then he heard something off in the darkness. Low and spaced unevenly. Like wind rustling the treetops, or heavy breathing.

Someone moaning.

Jamming a last shell into the Colt, he clicked the loading gate shut and thumbed back the hammer. "Mister, you got three seconds to start walkin' toward me or I'm gonna spray your ass with lead."

From the darkness came a shaky cry. "Goddamn, Jordan! Hold off. I can't walk. You done got me."

The plainsman aimed high and squeezed off a round. "Next one won't be high. If you can't walk then crawl. Tell your partner to get his butt out here, too."

"I'm comin'! I'm comin'. Jesus Christ, don't shoot no more."

"Bring that other sonovabitch with you," Jordan shouted.

"He's dead," the voice called back. "You drilled him clean through the lights."

Jordan knew then that it was a buffalo man even before he emerged from the darkness. Only men in the hide business spoke of the lungs as lights. Shouting broke out behind him and Jordan could hear McCabe's nasal screech as he led the crowd down the street. Just then the bushwhacker appeared in the dim glow thrown out by the streetlamp. One hand was clutching his side and the other was raised overhead. Though clearly wounded, he had managed to walk after all.

Jordan grunted as the man's features came clear in the pale light.

The sorry bastard was one of Lumpkins' skinners.

Coming to his feet, Jordan tested his leg and found that a shallow furrow had been gouged out of his thigh. Then the crowd was around him, jabbering excitedly as everyone tried to question him at once.

"Hold up, Goddamnit!" When they quieted down he jerked a thumb at the wounded man. "Some of you gents take that jaybird on back to the saloon. Just keep him alive till I get back. The rest of you scout those bushes up ahead. Should be a stiff in there somewhere. McCabe, bring Huggins and Cook. We're gonna pay a little call on Mr. Lumpkins."

Trailed by the three skinners, he struck off into the darkness, headed downriver. Vaguely he recalled talk of Lumpkins' camp being close to the bend, and he found himself hurrying despite the dull throb spreading through his leg.

It was high time he settled that lardgut's hash. Once and for all.

When Jordan and his crew returned to the Bee Hive, they found the prisoner bound to a chair and bleeding like a stuck hog. Since he was as good as dead anyway, nobody saw any reason to bother doctoring him. The second backshooter, another of Lumpkins' skinners, had been carried in and unceremoniously dumped in a corner. From the looks of his shirt, he had caught two slugs just below the brisket. For his part, Jordan was forced to announce that Frank Lumpkins had evidently folded his tent and snuck off into the night. They had found the camp well enough, with coals still in the fire, but the place was empty as a graveyard.

Everyone agreed that it was a damn shame, missing a chance to stretch Lumpkins' fat neck. But they still had a bird in hand, and it was the considered opinion of all present it would be a mortal waste to let the mangy son-of-a-bitch bleed to death. Which from the looks of things he might just do if they jawboned about it too long. That being the case, they quickly appointed Chalk Benson to sit as judge, and court was called to order. The prisoner was seated in the center of the room, Benson rapped his pistol on the bar for order, and they set about giving one Jack Pritchard a fair and impartial trial.

"Cimarron Jordan," Chalk Benson intoned, "this court being in session we will now hear what you've got to say about this dirty polecat that calls himself a buffalo man." Cocking an eye in the prisoner's direction, he frowned. "Make it quick, Cimarron. The bastard's leakin' like a sieve."

Jordan stepped forward to a murmur of approval from the spectators. "Your Honor, this feller and his partner—" he paused to jerk a thumb at the body in the corner "—bushwhacked me at the end of the street. Never gave me any warnin' at all. Just let fly out of a clear blue. After they nicked me in the leg I downed both of 'em. Reckon that's about all there is to it. 'Ceptin' I wish their boss hadn't gotten away."

The onlookers grumbled their agreement on that score, but Benson silenced them with another rap on the bar. When things quieted down he turned to the accused. "Pritchard, time's a-wastin'. You got anything to say in your defense?"

Jack Pritchard's face was ashen, as much from the rope he faced as the loss of blood. "Listen, boys. It wasn't me that rigged this. Lumpkins put us up to it. Said it was the only way to settle the score with Jordan. Now why don't you fellers be good sports and let me die peaceful. That's a fair trade for what I just told you about Lumpkins. Ain't that a fair swap?"

The churlish response from the spectators said otherwise, and Benson's tone confirmed it. "No deals. Lumpkins is cold meat if Jordan ever catches him, anyway. You got anything else to say?"

Pritchard shook his head dumbly and slumped against his bonds. Benson saw that he was fading fast and motioned for quiet. "Gentlemen of the jury, you've heard the evidence and the condemned man is leakin' bad. What's your verdict?"

"Hang the sonovabitch!" someone shouted over the roar of the crowd. The vote being unanimous, they lifted the prisoner, chair and all, and headed for the door. Chalk Benson declared court closed and hurried along after them to make sure everything was handled according to Hoyle.

When they reached the grove of trees along the riverbank someone produced a rope and Benson selected a stout limb about ten feet off the ground. The rope whistled over the limb, one of the men made it fast around Pritchard's neck, and a half-dozen others scrambled to grab the loose end. Since the condemned man was too weak to stand, they just cut his bonds and left him sitting in the chair.

Benson halted before him and again motioned for silence. "Jack Pritchard, you have been tried fair and square and sentenced to swing for the crime of bushwhackin'. You got any last words, you better get 'em said."

Pritchard was so near death his voice was a whispered croak. "You're the sorriest bunch of shitheels I ever seen. Hangin' a man this way ain't decent. Praise Jesus Christ and the Lord God Jehovah. Amen."

Benson signaled with his hand and the rope snapped taut. Pritchard shot out of the chair like a rocket and his head cracked against the limb with a loud crunch. The men lowered him a couple of feet and tied the rope around the tree trunk. Then they gathered around to watch him die, but he didn't twitch so much as a little finger. He had gone under even as they jerked him aloft.

Everyone agreed that it was a damned rotten stunt. Cheating them that way right at the last moment.

Walking back to the Bee Hive, Jordan felt his leg stiffening, and he suddenly wondered if Virge Hollister had ever been wounded in a shootout. Knowing Virge's skill with a gun, it wasn't likely. Then his mind drifted back to the ambush and the very deliberate way he had traded lead in pitch blackness. He hadn't flinched—not by a hair—and when it was over he had killed his first white man.

Not with his fists either. In a gunfight, and a damned hairy one at that.

Virge would have been proud of the way he handled himself.

4.

Summer and fall of '72 had been a golden time for buffalo men. The upper Smoky Hill was only then beginning to attract any great number of hunters, and a man could sometimes go for days without hearing the dull roar of another Sharps. Better still, the summer had been unusually wet for the plains, with the grass thick and lush, and buffalo seemed to cover the earth. That fall, as the shaggies ranged northward toward the Republican, the air turned crisp, and the cottonwoods, ash, and willows along the creeks became a small miracle of orangy splendor. It was a grand time to be alive and free, wandering the bountiful plains. One of those brief, unblemished interludes in a man's life which he remembers with vivid warmth all the rest of his days.

Virge and Sam had formed their own outfit just that spring. After a year of apprenticeship under Monte Brown, they felt they had absorbed sufficient lore of the buffalo and his outlandish quirks to strike out on their own. Though hardly greenhorns, they were still a far cry from plainsmen, and Monte had tried every trick in the book to discourage them. Old-timers considered a man a tyro until he had spent many snows among the heathens—and still had his topknot firmly anchored to the roots. But they were young and full of sap, and they weren't to be dissuaded.

They pooled their resources, bought a wagon and team, and hired themselves two skinners. While it became apparent only days afterwards, they had had a rare stroke of luck in stumbling across Lon McCabe. If the old curmudgeon hadn't been blind drunk when they approached him, he would never have signed on with a green outfit. By the time he was sober enough to start screeching, they were north of Fort Hays and up to their armpits in buffalo. McCabe was ever of the opinion that he had been shanghaied, but after a while he cooled off and even took a liking to Sam—in a sour sort of way.

Virge he never cared for, and he was just waspish enough to make no bones about it from the very start.

That summer they had lived in an abandoned stagecoach station on the Smoky Hill trail to Fort Wallace, and hunted mainly along Turkey Creek to the north. They put in long days, short nights, and kept the wagons constantly trundling back and forth to the railhead with cured hides. Virge and Sam rarely missed a day without making a stand, and the prairie around the station-house became a vast carpet of shaggy robes. McCabe started earning his keep with the opening gun, and in his own abrasive way, resumed their education where Monte Brown had left off. The hide yard became his personal domain, and he made good on a boast that amazed the two young partners. After being pegged down and sprinkled with his own arsenic water concoction, not a skin in a hundred was lost to moths. Before summer was out, they had bought a second wagon, hired another skinner, and sold better than three thousand hides for top dollar.

Early fall found them north of the Solomon on Prairie Dog Creek. There they set up camp in a crude dugout and hunted along the southern tributaries of the Republican. The herds had gradually drifted north throughout the summer and would swing about to start their winter migration only toward the latter part of the year. The young hunters planned to stay right on top of the buffalo over the fall months, then trail the larger herds as they scattered southward when cold weather set in.

The Republican was the fall gathering-spot for a vast herd numbering in the millions, and seldom did it take the boys more than an hour between them to kill all the skinners could handle in a full day. Long before the Indians had named the river Kîrârûtâ—loosely translated as Shit Creek—because the immense crowding of buffalo every fall fouled its water with tons of droppings. White men—Virge and Sam among them—weren't nearly so sensitive to the Republican's odorous reputation. Instead of dung, they smelled money—more than ordinary men could grub from life with Herculean labor—and it was free for the taking.

That fall was one they would recall with fondness all the days of their lives. They killed with deadly precision, grew strong on hump meat and tallow butter, and watched their horde of gold swell ever higher with each trip to the railhead.

103

Then, with a suddenness that defied all reason, disaster came to camp on their doorstep.

Overnight, a howling norther struck the plains—the mercury plummeted to twenty below—and the raging wind swept every living thing before its path. The blizzard lasted for eight days, hammering at the tiny dugout with gale force. The men ventured outside only to gather buffalo chips for the fire, and even then, the arctic blast would coat their eyebrows and beards with a solid sheet of ice. They huddled together inside their frigid cave cursing God, fate, and the caprice of nature. But other than venting their anger, the curses accomplished nothing. Blue northers—the kind that iced a man's bones to the very marrow—had a will all their own. They came when they pleased, and they disappeared in exactly the same way. At their leisure.

When it was over, one mule was frozen stiff as a board, and their pegged hides were covered with three feet of snow. Only later were they to discover that they had gotten off very lightly. Elsewhere across the plains, the storm had exacted a grim toll. South of Fort Hays, eight woodcutters froze to death in what was ever afterward known as Freeze-Out Hollow. Worse yet, more than a hundred buffalo men perished in the blizzard, some to be found only after spring thaw uncovered their chilled bones. Frostbitten hunters straggled into the fort fully a week after the norther blew itself out, and the post surgeon performed seventy amputations on the rotted limbs of those who had waited too long. One unfortunate, a green youngster who had come west seeking adventure, lost both arms and both legs, and was shipped back to Ohio in a basket.

Although Virge and Sam, along with their crew, came out of the storm with whole skins, their plans for a winter hung were devastated. When they finally emerged from the dugout they made an appalling discovery.

The buffalo herds had vanished from the face of the earth.

Like a frosty desert, the bleak, snowbound prairie stretched endlessly to the horizon, and not a living thing stirred as far as the eye could see. The buffalo had fled before the blizzard's icy ferocity, scattering across the plains in random flight, and the young hunters suddenly awoke to the fact that there was nothing left to hunt.

Virge was ready to call it quits right there. Already he had had enough of living in a dirty hovel, being constantly filthy, his hair matted and crawling with lice. Eight days of listening to death batter at the door with an icy fist had firmed his resolve even further. The disappearance of the herds was merely the final straw.

The partners discussed it far into the night, and Sam somehow persuaded him to stay on. Virge was like that, quick to act when angered or faced with a disagreeable situation. Yet, oddly enough, he was easily swayed by a stout argument. Sam was just the opposite. Though he sometimes acted on the spur of the moment, he tended to think a lot, and his decisions were seldom as rash as they appeared. Like an owl, he thought slow and acted fast.

It was a gift—the knack of looking ahead and neatly stacking the deck in advance—one that he frequently used on Virge to keep him in line.

But Virge was never the same after the norther. Though he stuck it out that winter, he seemed to have gone sour on the business. Hunting buffalo for a living had lost its tang, and as their outfit criss-crossed the plains searching for the herds, his mind became preoccupied with other things.

He had never quite gotten over the Abilene shoot-out involving Wild Bill Hickok—rehashing it again and again around the fire at night—and now it began to dominate his every waking thought. Seemingly overnight he became fascinated with the old Colt .36 Navy he'd bought last spring. He polished and cleaned till it sparkled like a diamond, and filed away at the sear until the trigger would snap with little more than the fluttered touch of a butterfly. Once he had the pistol revamped, he went to work on the army-issue holster with a skinning knife, painstakingly carving away the excess leather so that the Colt would ride high and clear.

Then he began to practice. Morning and afternoon without fail he would fire twenty rounds. Each shot was judged and analyzed with a thoroughness that left nothing to chance. After every session, he would collect the lead from the bundle of mothy hides he used as a target, and spend most of the evening casting fresh balls. Last thing each night he would spend a solid hour working on his draw. Holding a coin in his hand, he would release it and grab for the gun. The object was to clear leather and snap the trigger before the coin hit the ground. Much to the amazement of Sam and the skinners, he was soon beating the coin four times out of five.

Virge was like a man possessed, driven onward by some grinding compulsion to master the Colt. He was convinced that it was a craft—a skill that could be self-taught—and he devoted himself to it with the fervor of a reformed drunk. Though he rarely shirked his duties to the outfit, he made equally certain that his daily sessions with the pistol were never shunted aside. When they finally located the herds again—after close to a month of wandering the plains—he couldn't have cared less.

He was no longer Virge Hollister, buffalo-hunter. Not in his own mind, at least. Over the course of that month he had become something that suited his style far better. A gunfighter. Slower than he would one day be, perhaps, and with a few rough edges that still had to be honed down. But good. Damned good, in fact.

Fast enough to beat just about anyone. Maybe even the man in the red sash.

While Sam had no overwhelming desire to become a gunman, he slowly found himself being drawn into Virge's compulsive little game. That was really all it meant to Sam—a game. One that Virge was plainly obsessed with, and more for that reason than any other, one which gradually whetted Sam's curiosity. Once they found the herds, and were again back in the buffalo business, he started practicing with Virge late every afternoon. The morning sessions seemed a bit much, and he skipped those. Perhaps the game would come in handy someday—it never hurt to know how to use a pistol—but there was a point past which fun became simple foolishness.

Virge couldn't have been more tickled if somebody had stuck a feather up his nose. Sam had always been better at hunting buffalo—better at most things, in fact, except treeing women—and Virge was delighted to find himself in the position of master instructing pupil. Sam had an ancient Colt .44 Army which Virge promptly overhauled, and he soon had the holster that went with it whittled out just like his own. The next step was to teach Sam what he had discovered about fast versus quick.

As Virge had learned through a marathon of trial and error, it was this single element which separated the quick from the dead.

That first afternoon in front of the bullhide target, Virge had spelled it out plain and simple. "Sam, before you ever fire that blunderbuss, I want you to understand the biggest thing I've found out about shootin' a pistol. Now listen to me close. *Unless you take your time you might as well be chunkin' rocks.* It's just like huntin' buffalo. The only shot that counts is one that hits the vitals. Only if you're shootin' at something that can shoot back, you don't get no second chance. That first shot has got your life ridin' on it, and that's why you have to take your time."

The Navy appeared in Virge's hand as if instinct alone had triggered the movement. Crouching, his arm came level with his shoulder and he slammed five shots into the target. When the smoke cleared, they saw that the shots were grouped in a pattern which could be covered by a man's outstretched hand.

Sam whistled. "That's some shootin', pardner. Damnsight better'n anything I ever saw, and that's a fact."

Virge grinned like a cat with a mouthful of feathers. "Awright, now you try it. And remember what I said. Slow and easy. Take your time."

Sam's draw was good—fast and sure, with no wasted motion—but hardly as smooth as Virge's. Thumbing the hammer, flicking the trigger, he let go with a staccato roar as the big .44 bucked and jumped. Waving aside the thick cloud of smoke created by the black powder, they saw that he had missed three shots out of five.

"No doubt about it," Virge observed dryly. "You're regular chain lightnin'. Only trouble is, you would've been dead right after that first shot. You've got your mind set on speed, and you're just fast enough it'd most likely get you killed."

"C'mon," Sam said. "You're faster'n me. I saw it myself. Speed didn't seem to spoil your aim none."

"There's where you got it wrong," Virge informed him. "I'm quicker'n you on the draw, but if you had watched close you would've seen that I didn't fire near as fast. Now don't get me wrong. When I said take your time I wasn't talkin' about aimin' real steady and squeezin' off every shot. You get the gun out fast as you can, plenty high so you can see the barrel out of the corner of your eye. Then you sorta point it like you would your finger. But that's where speed comes to a screechin' halt."

"Well that don't make a hell of a lot of sense," Sam growled. "You keep sayin' take your time, but I'm a son-ovabitch if there was a gnat's ass worth of time between those shots of yours."

"Goddamnit, that's exactly what I'm tryin' to tell you.

There *was* a gnat's ass between my shots. I don't rightly know how to explain it, but it's like there was something deliberate about it. Just that little split-hair of waitin' till you're goddamn good and sure the gun is pointin' exactly where you mean it to be. Then you fire. More'n likely another man watchin' wouldn't even know you had hesitated. But you know 'cause it's your head tellin' your trigger finger what to do. You follow me?"

Sam mulled it over a moment, then nodded soberly. "I reckon. What it sounds like you're sayin' is that a man has to delay just before he touches off each shot so he'll know right where the ball is headed. Trouble is, how long is long? Meanin', how long does he hold before he lets fly?"

"Don't worry about that," Virge assured him. "You've got the idea. I can tell from the way you said it. Took me near on to a month to learn what I've just taught you in a few minutes. Now all you've got to do is practice. Pretty soon you'll know just exactly how long to wait. Whatever time it is *you* need to make the shot count. I ain't real sure, but I'd just suspect it's different for every last man." He paused and smiled. "Awright, greenhorn, let's get that cannon loaded and try 'er again."

Sam grinned and brought out his loading gear. After tamping the powder and balls down good, he carefully spotted the caps and holstered the big Army. Facing the bullhide bundle, he let his arms hang loose and tried to concentrate the way Virge had told him. Deliberate. Unhurried. No need to rush the. . . .

Sam's arm moved and the Colt came level. The merest fraction of a second elapsed before the gun roared. Then another dot of time slipped by before it bucked again. One by one, spaced evenly and with the fuzz of a gnat's ass between them, he thumbed off all five shots. When the smoke drifted away there were four holes that could be covered by a dinner plate and a fifth about six inches off to the left.

"Jesus H. Christ!" Virge bellowed. "I told you, didn't I? You've got it, Sam! Slicker'n greased owl shit."

They walked up to the bullhide target and Virge flashed his toothy grin. "Now all you have to worry about is if you can do the same thing when somebody's shootin' back at you." Then the smile faded and a funny look came into his eyes. "Come to think of it, that's something we've both got to find out."

Later that winter, Sam and Virge rode out looking for a stand one morning when they happened on to an old bull surrounded by a pack of wolves. The bull was game, but losing ground quick. The skin and flesh on his hocks hung loose in bloody tendrils, and one eye had been torn from his head. Most of the gristle on his nose had been gnawed to the bone, and his tongue was a gory stump, already chewed half off. The wolves were eating him alive, slowly crippling him so they could get at his guts.

The young hunters jerked their pistols and let go with a flurry of shots, dropping wolves right and left for thirty yards. There hadn't been more than a hair's difference between the deadliness of their fire.

Except that Virge held back one shot to finish off the old bull.

Ruminating over it that evening—as was his habit with matters that sparked his interest—Sam figured it was sort of what gave some men the edge in a gunfight.

Throughout the entire ruckus, Virge had known exactly how many loads he had left in his Navy. He had even held back one shot to polish off the bull. Sam hadn't the foggiest where he was at till his gun clicked empty. Yet growing thicker by the hour—muddy wallows, trees used as Virge had fired just as fast—maybe even a little faster— and every shot was dead center.

Four wolves and one bull in a couple of blinks of the eye. With time out to keep track of his loads.

Deliberate was the word for it, well enough. But that didn't hardly do it justice.

It was more like a machine. Cold as a barrelful of eels.

5.

Early in June, some two hundred miles north of Fort Griffin, Jordan reined the gelding to a halt on a rise over-looking the north fork of the Red. Scouting out in front of the wagons since early morning, he had set a course al-most due north into the Panhandle. While they were now less than fifty miles south of the Canadian—which put them infernally close to Adobe Walls—he was already pretty certain the gamble had paid off. Buffalo sign was growing thicker by the hour—muddy wallows, trees used as scratching posts, fairly fresh droppings—and it stood to reason there was a good-sized herd somewhere ahead.

Shaggies were a damnsight brighter than most folks gave them credit for. Simple wasn't the same as stupid. Not by a longshot. The woolly beasts were plenty smart enough to scatter before the cannonade getting underway down around Fort Griffin. Unless he missed his guess, a big batch of the really wily ones had swung north on a beeline for the Panhandle.

The Jordan outfit had rolled out of the Flats barely a fortnight past. There had been a slight delay while he weaned McCabe and the boys off the juice—it always struck him as odd that getting skinners sobered up was a hell of a lot harder than getting them drunk—but afterwards it had taken only a day to get the wagons loaded with adequate supplies to carry them through to fall. Once everything was ready, he had pointed the gelding west and breathed an immense sigh of relief.

The sudden influx of hunters around Fort Griffin had left him cross as a sore-tailed bear. There was nothing for it but to try and outrun the bastards again. Somewhere he would find a place where a man could hunt in peace—without being up to his bellybutton in a swarm of pesky hide-hunters. The land was just too goddamn big, and buffalo too plentiful, for a man to waste his days trying to outgun the army fast gathering on the Clear Fork of the Brazos.

His first thought had been to head straight into the Staked Plains. *Llano Estacado*. Home of the rattlesnake, gila monster, and buffalo. Ancient summer hunting-grounds of the Comanche. Broiling sun, searing desert winds, and long thirsty stretches between water holes. Harsh and uninviting, a land few men dared to challenge. The one place on earth he could probably have all to himself.

But the Staked Plains were a last resort. Even for him. After considerable speculation, he decided to try the Panhandle. The battle at Adobe Walls had sent most of the hide-hunters packing out of there, and Colonel Mackenzie's scrap with the Comanches at Palo Duro Canyon had presumably solved that problem. Leastways to hear the army tell it. It might just be that if a man didn't tell anyone where he was headed—especially a flannel-mouthed old geezer named McCabe—he could sneak off and stake out a spot all his own.

After traveling west along the Clear Fork for a day—just to sucker everyone into thinking he was sticking around for the summer—he made a ninety-degree turn and led the befuddled skinners due north. Over the next two weeks they crossed the Pease, the Prairie Dog Fork of the Red, then the Salt Fork, and continued straight as a string toward the valley of the North Fork. The plan he had in mind was to simply vanish in a small cloud of dust. The likelihood of anyone figuring out where he had gone was damn near nil. Which suited him right down to his boot heels.

Not that he wasn't likely to happen across somebody in the Panhandle. There was always some hair in the butter a fellow hadn't counted on. It was just that he didn't expect to see any *white men* up that way. But that didn't unsettle him much one way or the other.

Right about then, Indians sounded like pretty good company.

Leaving McCabe in charge of the wagons, he had spent most of each day scouting ahead for signs of a herd. Like most plainsmen, he had long since acquired the knack of allowing his mind to operate independently of his senses. Instinct, along with keen ears and constantly roving eyes, revealed every secret of the land around him. Buzzards circling in the distance, a bobwhite scolding its chicks, wolves skulking off over a far rise. The prairie held no mysteries, so long as a man kept his senses attuned to the things about him. Once it became habit—and a man soon mastered the trick if he wanted to keep his hair—it left a fellow lots of time for thinking.

Since the whingding back at the Flats, he had been unable to get Julia Rath out of his mind. Something about the little redhead he humped that last night had reminded him of Julia. Maybe it was her green eyes. Or the fact that she had just a smidgen of what passed for gentility. Whatever it was, it had set him to thinking. Remembering. Puzzling again over the strange bond that wouldn't let him forget the girl back in Dodge. A weird, cryptic sort of fascination that attracted and repelled him in the same moment. Twisted as a cork-screw was how he thought of it. Like a man that had got his brains scrambled and didn't rightly know his ass from his elbow. That was the way he felt. Part of him wanted her and part of him was repulsed by the whole idea.

Worse, still, he couldn't seem to decipher which part of him wanted what. Was it his pecker sending signals to his brain, or the other way round? Had she actually aroused something within him that he didn't fully understand, or was he just after another roll in the hay? Perhaps that was why he always took off running when things got too sticky. Maybe he really didn't want to know the answer. Or maybe there wasn't any answer. Maybe he was just a square-headed coo-coo who couldn't tell a case of hots from the real article.

It was goddamn baffling. Whichever way the dice fell.

One thing was for damn sure, though. Chasing whores and getting drunk with the boys made life a hell of a lot simpler. Nothing worrisome there. None of this wondering and pondering and wracking the brain to come up with answers that probably didn't even exist to start with. Just lay your money down and take your chances. What you get is what you pay for. Even-steven. A winner every time and no bellyaches afterwards.

Jordan was still brooding over Julia Rath when he topped a little tree-studded knoll and jerked the roan clean back on its haunches. Jaw agape, eyes popping, he thought for a moment he had gone stark raving mad.

Below him, on a wide swale of grassland bordered by a creek, were close to three hundred soldiers and better than a hundred wagons. Unless the sun was playing tricks on him, the bastards were actually building a fort.

Jesus H. Christ. A fort! Smack dab in the middle of absolutely nowhere.

It didn't make sense, yet there it was. The army made plenty of mistakes, but fort building didn't happen to be among them. Just sure as God made little green apples, some general had taken a stab at a map and said he wanted a fort built. Right there! Porbably nobody knew where it was or even cared for that matter. An order was an order, so the boys in blue had loaded up their play pretties and hauled ass. Now they were actually building the goddamned thing.

Right in the middle of his hunting grounds!

Jordan kicked the gelding into a lope and went scrambling down the hill. When he came to the first group of soldiers he stopped to inquire directions to the commanding officer. They pointed toward a field tent, set off by itself near the creek, and he rode in that direction. Skirting the work detail busy erecting a cluster of buildings, he presently reined up before what was clearly temporary headquarters. The sentry out front gave him a cold look and sniffed like he had smelled something bad.

112

Just as he dismounted, a thin, stoop-shouldered man wearing captain's insignia stepped from the tent. The sentry started toward Jordan, but the officer waved him away. "Afternoon. Welcome to the Sweetwater Cantonment. You're the first visitor we've had since construction started."

"Howdy." Jordan gave his hand a perfunctory shake and let go. "Cap'n, I don't mean to sound short, but what the hell are you people doing out here, anyway?"

The officer smiled wryly, glancing around the prairie. "It is rather godforsaken, isn't it? The truth of the matter is. . . . I'm sorry, I don't believe I know your name."

"Jordan. Sam Jordan. Buffalo-hunter."

The captain's eye flickered over his grimy clothes. "Yes, I had deduced that much. Well the truth of the matter is, Mr. Jordan, we have been ordered to build a fort as protection against Indian depredations."

Jordan grunted, smothering a laugh. "Just what did you have in mind protectin'?"

"Why, the. . . ." The officer stopped and fixed him with an appraising look. "Little attempt at humor, eh? Very amusing. Although I'll have to admit you've got a point. Still, ours is not to reason why, Mr. Jordan. The army moves in mysterious ways, its wonders to perform."

"Cap'n, between the spot you're standin' on and Dodge City—that's about a hundred-fifty miles as the crow flies—there's nothin' but red Injuns and buffalo. Did somebody neglect to tell you fellers that?"

"I daresay the army is aware of that fact, Mr. Jordan. My understanding is that this fort will serve to contain the Indians on their reservations. Something of a western roadblock, if you care to think of it in those terms."

The plainsman snorted skeptically. "I just suspect the Comanche'll die laughin' when they hear that. All they've got to do is circle around you and go on about their business. Cap'n, lemme ask you something. You got the least idea where you're standin' right this minute?"

The officer's mouth lifted in a patronizing smirk. "Certainly I know where we are. This is Sweetwater Creek. The Texas Panhandle. To the north lies the Canadian and to the south the Red."

"No sir, that's not exactly what I meant. Where you're standin' at right now is in shaky boots. If the Comanche and Kiowa and Cheyenne ever decide to get together and

113

come pay you a visit, folks are gonna start callin' this Dead Soldier Creek."

The captain's smirk evaporated and his eyes turned steely. Before he could say anything, Jordan resumed. "One more question and I'll be on my way. You know if anybody's got plans to build a tradin' post around this fort of yours?"

"Not to my knowledge," the officer informed him stiffly. "I suspect most merchants are of an opinion similar to the one you just expressed. Why do you ask?"

"No reason. Nice chattin' with you, cap'n. Watch your hair."

Jordan mounted and rode off, leaving the officer staring after him with a bemused expression. When he crested the knoll south of the creek, he halted and looked back. Then he chuckled sardonically as one of Jason Rath's little homilies flitted through his mind. Something about even an ill wind blowing up some good.

Later that evening, camped a few miles west on the Sweetwater, the plainsman laid it out for McCabe. "No need pissin' and moanin', Lon. They're here and there's not a goddamn thing we can do about it."

"Hell's fire, Cimarron, you just beat all." The old skinner screwed up his face in a tight knot. "Buildin' a fort this close to the Nations is gonna draw Injuns like flies to honey. You know how them red varmints loves to play hide and seek with the army."

Jordan's gaze shifted to the fire, and for a moment he didn't say anything. "It's not the Injuns I'm worried about. What that fort will draw is buffalo men. Before cold weather they'll be crawlin' over this country like lice."

"Well it had to happen sometime anyway," McCabe said. "Always does. Sooner or late don't make a hell of a lot of difference. Hadn't been this year it would've been next. You know that well as I do."

"Lon, I'm damned if I don't think you're right." Jordan's face had a look of profound revelation written across it. "Matter of fact, you just made me own up to something I've been tryin' to duck ever since I saw them soldiers."

Jordan rose and moved quickly to the wagon where he started stuffing gear in his warbag. "Old man, you're finally gonna get your chance to quit skinnin'. Come first light I'm headed for Dodge. While I'm gone you try your hand at huntin'. You always said shootin 'em was the easy part, so let's see you put your money where your mouth is."

"Cimarron, you are the most scatterbrained sonofagun I ever run across. Goddamn me if you ain't. Now just what in the billy blue hell are you fixin' to do, anyway? You just tell me that, if it ain't too much trouble."

"Lon, if you can't beat 'em, join 'em. I'm fixin' to start skinnin' me a new kind of critter. The two legged kind."

The faint light of false dawn had barely shown next morning when Jordan kicked the roan into a lope headed east. Lon McCabe watched him ride off, then went back and squatted down beside the fire. After pouring himself a cup of coffee he stared into the flames with a look of abject resignation. Then he snorted, struck by the awful truth that life was an endless string of shitty little riddles.

First and foremost being the squirrely sonovabitch that had just rode off with a burr up his ass.

Four

%%

1.

Dodge City had grown considerably in the past year, but for some reason it didn't look as active as when he last saw it. The thing that caught his eye right off was the railroad yards. Where before there had been racks of flint hides stretching for a half-mile along the tracks, there was now a bare spot. Thinking about it as he crossed over from the South Side, his surprise faded on the moment.

There weren't any hides because there weren't any buffalo.

The great Arkansas herd had been exterminated—or scattered south before the army of hunters—and so far as anyone knew there wasn't a decent day's hunting within three hundred miles of Dodge. Once the Comanche had driven the hide men from Adobe Walls the action just naturally shifted to Brazos country, which meant that Fort Worth was the closest railhead to the new killing grounds.

That left Dodge high and dry. Sucking hind tit, as Lon McCabe would have put it.

Jordan crossed the plaza and reined in at the hitch rack in front of the store. But as he dismounted he decided to have a drink before calling on Jason Rath. It was sure to be a lengthy session once the merchant learned of events on the Sweetwater. After three days on the trail, his throat was so dry he couldn't hardly work up a good spit, and right now a drink sounded better than talk. The Alhambra was closest, and while it wasn't exactly his favorite hangout, he was just thirsty enough that it didn't matter.

When he came through the door, he commenced wishing he had stopped instead at one of the dives on the South Side. Seated at a table was the ruling clique of Dodge—Jason Rath's cronies to a man—the big augurs who ran the town pretty much to suit themselves. Dog Kelly, owner of the Alhambra and the city's mayor. George Hoover, the town's leading banker. Judge Homer Beverley, magistrate of the local court. Deacon Cox, proprietor of the Dodge House and perhaps the largest landowner in town. Though he had always been on good terms with them, Jordan never really felt comfortable in their presence. They accepted him because he was Rath's partner—an alliance fraught with paradox in their views—but they didn't approve of his unsavory profession or his reputation as a confirmed brawler.

Not that they had anything against buffalo men. Or hellraisers, for that matter. So long as they kept to their own kind over on the South Side.

North of the tracks—the civilized part of Dodge—was a different ball of wax entirely. It was owned, operated, and presided over by a select little club. Buffalo hunters, whores, and other common types weren't considered eligible for membership.

Jordan nodded pleasantly to the men and crossed to the bar, ordering a whiskey. He could feel their eyes on his back, and he had a pretty good idea their muttered conversation had turned to buffalo hunters. One in particular. After knocking down a shot he sipped the second more slowly, letting the sharp bite of the whiskey wash the grit from his throat. Finished, he tossed a coin on the bar and turned to leave. There was a nice warm glow down around his bellybutton, and he felt just about right for a little confab with his partner.

More to the point, perhaps, the liquor had nerved him up for a few words with the other half of the firm. Julia Rath.

When he came away from the bar, Dog Kelly caught his eye and signaled. "Jordan, if you've got a minute, how about having a drink with us?"

The plainsman kept his surprise well hidden and walked toward the table. They had never offered to buy him a drink in the past, which meant that today's invitation probably had strings attached to it. Wary now, he pulled up before the group and nodded to each man in turn. "Dog. Gents. What can I do for you?"

Kelly smiled amiably and gestured toward an empty chair. "Sit a spell. Take a load off your feet. Tell you the truth, we were hoping you might be able to give us a bit of information."

Jordan took a seat, saying nothing. Whatever they wanted he felt just ornery enough to make them work for it. After a moment George Hoover poured him a drink and favored him with an oily grin. "Sam—if I can call you that—we understand you know the Nations just about as well as any man living. Fact is, I seem to recall they nicknamed you Cimarron when you broke the treaty and spent a season hunting down there."

Jordan sipped at the whiskey and took his time before answering. "I reckon I could find my way there and back if I had to."

"That's rich, eh, boys?" Kelly chortled out loud. "Jordan, the way I heard it, you know that country like the back of your hand. No need to hide your light under a bushel. You're among friends."

Dog Kelly had a casual way of putting a man at ease and Jordan wasn't unaware of the fact. The saloonkeeper used a pack of blooded hounds for antelope hunting—which was where he had gotten his unusual moniker—and of the four men seated around the table, Jordan found him the easiest to take. Strictly in short doses, though.

"Let's just say I know the Nations and deal the next card."

Judge Beverley gave him a patronizing nod. "Well put, young man. Now, Dog, why don't you cut out the chitter-chatter and get down to brass tacks?"

"Homer, that's just what I was about to do." Kelly leaned forward with his elbows on the table. "Jordan, I don't have to tell you that the hide business is a thing of the past here in Dodge. More than likely you saw it coming before we did. Be that as it may, this town is in bad shape. Economically, I mean. We're hurting, and every business on both sides of the tracks is feeling the pinch. We've got to do something fast or Dodge City will go back to being a wide spot in the road."

"I'm listenin'," the plainsman remarked, "But I still don't see what it's got to do with me."

"Just this," Kelly informed him. "We're set to organize the damnedest campaign you ever saw to get the Texans to trail their herds into Dodge. This town needs money pumped into it if it's going to grow. Lots of money. And the cattle trade is the place to get it."

"That's right, if you don't mind havin' your town hurrahed seven nights a week." Deacon Cox wasn't a talkative man, but every now and then he got in his two cents worth. "Maybe it would take a year or so, but I still say we ought to try and attract farmers instead of those crazy Texans."

Silence fell over the group and it was clear to Jordan that they had argued the matter at some length. After a moment he glanced around the table. "Guess it's sort of like the fella that couldn't decide whether to shit or go blind. Time he made up his mind, it turned out he'd done both. Way I heard it, the shock killed him dead as a doornail."

"By God, Jordan, you're right!" Kelly slapped the table with his open palm. "We're in a predicament that calls for action. That's exactly why I called you over. Now, putting the cards on the table, what we've got to know is this. Is there a way for the Texans to drive their cattle to Dodge that *bypasses* Wichita? I figured you would be the man to know if anybody does."

Jordan didn't answer right away, seeing again in his mind's eye the vast uncharted wilderness of the Nations. Slowly the land and its stepladder of rivers came into focus. The storehouse of knowledge he had accumulated in his months below the treaty line clicked and calculated, measuring time, distance, and the topography of the land itself. After a moment he nodded to himself, thought a moment longer, then grunted as his brain spewed out the answer.

"There's a spot where the Chisholm Trail crosses the Cimarron. From right there, it's the same distance to Dodge as it is to Witchita. What a man could do is trail up the Cimarron till it makes a sharp bend to the west. Then he'd turn due north and come straight into Dodge. Matter of fact, it'd be easier trailin' that way than it would to Wichita anyway. I'd judge a man would save himself fordin' at least a half-dozen streams."

Kelly slammed the table again, grinning widely. "Boys, do you hear that? We're in business. Damned if we're not!" Looking back at the plainsman, his eyes brightened with excitement. "Jordan, if it works, you've just done this town one hell of a service. How would you like to earn a pile of money laying that trail out for us?"

Jordan shoved the chair back and came to his feet. "Sorry, Dog, 'fraid I can't oblige you. Got things of my own that need tendin' to. Thanks for the drink."

Before they had a chance to argue it further he turned and walked from the saloon. The men watched him through the door and then began congratulating one another on their good fortune. With Jordan along to show the way it would have been easier, but they weren't concerned. Simply knowing that such a route existed was half the battle. Perhaps more.

Something over an hour later Jordan started to get the feeling he should have accepted Dog Kelly's offer. Jason Rath had been delighted to see him and the plainsman felt about the same way himself—especially when he found that Julia had taken the day off to help organize a church social. That allowed him a few more hours grace before he had to face her—although why it had him rattled he couldn't rightly say—and he immediately launched into a description of what he had seen on the Sweetwater. Much to his bewilderment, Rath had received the news without the slightest sign of interest.

Upon learning exactly where the Sweetwater Cantonment was situated, the little merchant had voiced strong reservations about building a trading post there. The Panhandle was a risky proposition, he noted, even with an army garrison right next door. Should the Indians ever decide to come boiling out of the Nations, such a small outpost wouldn't stand in their way. The battle of Adobe Walls had proved that the savages could gather in formidable strength without the army being the wiser. Perhaps it would never happen again. That remained to be seen. But if it did, then any trading post that stood in their path would be levelled to the ground, and an investment of many thousands of dollars scattered to the winds.

Jordan had argued till he was blue in the face, but to no avail. Rath could be as stubborn as a goat on occasion and this seemed to be one of his off days. The stalemate was all the more annoying to the plainsman simply because he had ridden long and hard to deliver the news. After some harsh words, they stood around not looking at one another for a few minutes. Finally Jordan's exasperation got the better of him.

"Well it sure beats the hell out of me what you had in mind. You know, this whole thing about a tradin' post was your idea to start with. Now that I find a spot we can sew up tighter'n a drum, you say it's too risky. Judas Priest, there's not a square inch of ground out there that's not risky. Sweetwater or the Brazos, it's all the same. That's why it pays good. The stakes are high and a man stands to win big."

"What you say is true, Sam," Rath conceded. "But a man could also lose big. Frankly I would rather invest in something with less risk attached and be satisfied with a smaller return."

"Shootin' for chalkies ain't exactly my style," Jordan said coolly. "I gambled on you pretty heavy if you recollect. Damned if I ever thought I was backing a piker, though."

Rath's face colored and his voice went up a couple of octaves. "Sam, I dislike reminding you of this, but your investment bought only a one-third interest in this store. That gives you one vote to my two, and I'm turning thumbs down on this Sweetwater idea. You know very well that I enjoy a good gamble, but I also like to play the odds. Fort Griffin was a good bet, and I would have gone along with that. The Panhandle is like raising on a pair when you have a flush staring down your throat. Think about it. You'll see I'm right."

"Goddamnit, I have been thinkin' about it," Jordan growled. "I've had my butt in the saddle for three days, and there wasn't much else to do but think. You're the one that put the idea of a tradin' post in my head in the first place, and now that I'm hot for it you're tryin' to crawfish."

Muttering angrily to himself, he marched to the door, then abruptly turned back. "Jason, how much you reckon it would take to get a store like that started up?"

The merchant regarded him with an appraising stare for a moment. "Twenty thousand more or less. That is if a man meant to do it right."

Jordan pursed his lips and took a tug at his cookieduster. "I've got pretty close to that in the bank, and I figure George Hoover would loan me the rest on my one-third of this place. Maybe I'll just open up my own tradin' post. Might be better like that all the way round, anyhow."

Rath looked like somebody had just hit him on the toe with a hammer. "Now don't be hasty, Sam. If you sink all your money in a trading post and it goes under, that means I would wind up with Hoover as a partner."

"Could be," Jordan allowed. "Like you said, it's a risk."

The storekeeper's eyes narrowed as comprehension seeped through. "That's very shrewd, Sam. You're a better businessman than I gave you credit for." Then he smiled and shook his head. "All right. You have yourself a deal. We'll open a store on the Sweetwater and start saying prayers that the dice fall right."

"Well, now, that's mighty white of you, Jason. Sort of makes a feller think you'd rather have me as a partner than Hoover. And all the time I thought you two were such bosom buddies."

"Sam, as I suspect you're well aware, bankers make wonderful friends but damn poor partners. They're never content with a slice of the pie. Besides, they're not gamblers. Not like us at all."

"Yeah, I see what you mean." Jordan chuckled and started out the door. "Say, tell Julia I'll be over tonight. Got lots of things to tell her about my little jaunt down south."

Jason Rath just nodded and stood there at the desk with a funny look in his eye. After a moment he laughed softly. More at himself than the way the discussion had worked out. That young squirt had just nailed his hide to the wall, employing some damned crafty moves in the process.

Perhaps there was more to Sam Jordan than met the eye. Considerably more.

That evening after supper Sam came around with a hired buggy. Tonight he meant to find out something about Julia, and whatever kind of skirmish developed, he wanted it held on neutral ground. The Rath household was hardly that—he had been outflanked there more times than he cared to remember—and the buggy suited what he had in mind right down to the nubbin.

It would just be them and the horse. Under a great big sky with lots of stars and a big yellow moon. Short of sneaking her into the Dodge House, that was about the best he could rig on the spur of the moment.

Julia was waiting, seemingly unchanged, just the way he had imagined her all those months in Texas. She bubbled over the minute he walked in the door and kissed him as though they had been holding hands every day for the last year. When he suggested a buggy ride she agreed without any pretense or hesitation, and they sailed out the door arm in arm. Jason Rath barely got two words in edgewise, and had to content himself with peeking out the curtains as they pulled off. Afterwards he grumped around the empty house for a while, then returned to his newspaper—and thoughts of ruination on the Sweetwater.

Sam kept to the river road for a couple of miles, letting the horse shuffle along at its own pace. Julia was full of questions about Texas and Fort Griffin and the buffalo herds, flitting from one subject to another like a hummingbird. When he started to run dry on answers she switched with great finesse, and began chattering about happenings in Dodge. That didn't cover much territory, but she gussied it up till it sounded almost interesting.

Watching her in the pale moonlight, Sam was again struck by the way her mood and expression could vary so greatly, almost as if she became a different person from moment to moment. One second her wide green eyes would be touched with mischief and her face mock serious in a way that would have fooled anyone. Then she would become amusing and wholesomely beautiful, only to appear a naughty, calculating little vixen with the flicker of an eyelash. Sometimes, in rare moments, there would be a look around her mouth that was at once vulnerable and tender, in the way of all helpless things. Yet there was a resilience and strength to her that came through whatever her mood.

She was a strange girl. Different from anyone Sam had ever known. Certainly more complicated and harder to hang a tag on. But she was also the prettiest and the ripest looking—thoughts that had nagged him all the way to Texas and back—and before the night was out he meant to have an answer to one question at least.

When they had gone a few miles out of town, Sam reined the horse into a grove of trees overlooking the river and brought the buggy to a halt. Before Julia could get his head spinning with another barrage of words, he pulled her to him and kissed her the way no man kisses a nice girl.

Just for a second she stiffened beneath his hand, then she melted and came into his embrace, seeking his mouth hungrily. After a moment he cupped her breast, rubbing it gently, and she moaned with a soft yearning cry. When his hand dropped to her thigh and began exploring deeper, she surged against him, squirming and clutching at him tighter with her arms. He could feel her hot breath and the flush of her face next to his own, and she thrust herself at him in a demand that was wanton yet somehow innocently eager.

Then, without the slightest warning, tears spilled over in her eyes and she began struggling to break free. Once out of his arms she retreated to the far corner of the seat, sobbing in muffled little gasps. "I can't, Sam. You know I want to, but I can't. I just can't." Then she turned her face into the corner and beat her fist senselessly against the seat frame. "Oh, damn, damn, damn! Sometimes I loathe what I am."

Sam slouched down in the opposite corner and mumbled a few curses of his own. Their near miss had shown him two things quite clearly. He would, if she let him. That was revealing in itself, though he wasn't exactly sure what it revealed. The second thing was, she wouldn't let him. That required no examination. It was a fact all by its lonesome. Without church bells and a preacher, he would die horny before she gave in.

"Sam, do you hate me?" Her voice sounded small and trembly.

"No, I don't hate you. I'm just sorry you can't loosen up. Or maybe I'm not. Hell, I don't know. I'm just sorry the whole thing happened."

There was a long silence and her tears seemed to have stopped. "Do you love me?"

Sam didn't say a word. Without moving he shifted his eyes and started trying to figure how he could back the buggy out on the road.

When he didn't say anything she sat up and blew her nose in a hanky. "Sam, I have a confession to make to you. I've been seeing other men."

"Yeah?" He was afraid to say more. It was the best news he'd had all night, and he didn't trust his voice not to give him away.

"Yes I have," Julia admitted firmly. "When you didn't come back after all those months or even bother to write I decided you couldn't care very much. So I started encouraging gentlemen callers. They've been trying ever since I came to Dodge, you know."

"Well that figures. Pretty girls are sort of scarce out here." He paused, wondering what the hell to say next.

124

"You did the right thing, I reckon. I mean it's just natural a girl wants to go places and have men tell her how sweet she is. Most natural thing on earth."

"Oh, damn you, Sam Jordan. Damn you. Damn you." Julia's backbone stiffened like a poker, and her green eyes flashed murderously in the moonlight. "You sit there like a big lump and tell me it's all right to see other men when you know very well it's—" Catching herself, she bit her tongue and regained a measure of composure. Then she smoothed her skirts and gave him a frosty look. "Sam, tell me something truthfully. You never meant to marry me, did you?"

"Marry you!" Sam blurted the words in a hoarse croak and he felt a cold sweat break out on his forehead. "Well now, that's a little sudden, isn't it? I mean we've hardly got to know—"

"Thank you, Sam, for being so honest. Now I think we can go home. I still have a cobbler to bake for the church social, and I'm sure you have other friends to see while you're in town."

Sam got the buggy straightened out and popped the horse a good one across the rump once they hit the road. They didn't say a word all the way back to the house, and when Sam helped her down her hands were cold as ice. Their parting was strained and awkward. Julia started off then turned back.

"Goodbye, Sam. I hope you find whatever it is you're looking for. If you should get to Dodge again please come by and say hello."

Smiling, she walked off up the path and disappeared through the door. Sam crawled into the buggy and cracked the reins so hard the old horse farted in his face and took out at a dead lope. Barreling down the road toward town, he tried to focus his thoughts on whiskey and sloe-eyed girls, all the good times that awaited him on the South Side.

Then he saw Julia again. Helpless as a crippled bird, green eyes glistening brightly in the soft moonglow, yet game clear through. Walking away proud and full of grit, getting stronger with every step she took.

Goddamn women to hell anyway! Nothing was ever enough. They always had to keep messing around in a man's mind.

2.

Winter came early to Sweetwater that year. The herds had drifted as far south as the Salt Fork of the Red, but they seemed to be holding there. Though there had been a fair amount of snow, it was light flaky stuff, covering the ground with a fine powdery crust. Unlike cattle, the shaggies weren't bothered in the least by this minor inconvenience. They simply pawed the snow aside and grazed on the cured bluestem that lay beneath. Until the real blizzards came sweeping down across the plains, it seemed unlikely that they would start a full-scale migration to the southern feeding grounds.

Sam Jordan was no less content than the buffalo. While he never cared much for plains winters, this was one year he was glad to see an end to warm weather. Summer and fall had been a hectic time, with never enough hours in any given day to accomplish all the tasks at hand. Jason Rath had been as good as his word, supplying the know-how and half the funds to establish a trading post on the Sweetwater. The rest had been up to Jordan, and it had proved a grueling experience.

The plainsman had returned from Dodge with twenty laborers and a wagonload of equipment. Though he had never before built a trading post—much less a town—he chose the site for a village with an eye to the future. Already he had contracted with a saloonkeeper and a dance-hall impresario to provide the essentials of his burgeoning venture. Buffalo men demanded certain things of a town—high on the list were women and whiskey—and they had been known to haul their hides a hundred miles out of the way just to visit a favorite whorehouse. Jordan's deal—which he financed out of his own pocket—had been shrewd and quite simple. For a nominal cut of the action, he would construct the saloon and dance hall. The flesh merchant and the saloonkeeper had only to supply a proper sampling of soiled doves and plenty of snakehead whiskey. Once the hide-hunters got wind of a new town, Mother Nature would take care of the rest.

Thereafter, Jordan had spent the better part of the summer loping back and forth between the hunting grounds and the construction site, which was located on a flat stretch of prairie below the garrison. After appointing a burly Irishman as foreman of the work crew, he was able to ride out at dawn and reach the herds in plenty of time to provide a day's kill for McCabe and the skinners. Then, just as quickly as he downed the last shaggy, he hit the saddle and flew back to Sweetwater City. The raw beginnings of a frontier outpost hardly deserved such a grand name, but it was slowly taking shape.

Much too slowly to suit the harried young plainsman. What with supervising construction on into full darkness every night—and galloping west at the first crack of light each morning—there was little room left for much else besides a couple of quick meals and a few hours sleep. Dark hollows began forming beneath his eyes, and his muscular frame stripped down to the lean hardness of spring steel. Still, he had never felt more alive or galvanized with energy.

It was just that along about dusk every evening—when the work was done and he started to unwind—he suddenly discovered his tail was dragging the ground.

But Sweetwater City was gradually taking form just as he had envisioned it. The work crew had first felled trees along the creek bank and snaked them back to the construction site using double mule teams. After the logs had been barked and allowed to cure, the men started erecting buildings. The trading post headed the list, rising log by log in dimensions of thirty by a hundred feet. Jordan had even brought along a couple of carpenters, and as the walls went up, the flooring, two long counters, and a jumble of shelves were being hammered in place. The back end of the store was partitioned off into a cookhouse and bunkroom, and out behind was an enormous pole shed for storing hides. By the time the roof and the stone chimney were completed, the place was ready for business, and not a day too soon as it worked out.

Twenty-six wagons loomed over the horizon late one afternoon, each drawn by four spans of mules. Once Jason Rath decided to take a hand in a game he didn't fool around. The wagons were loaded to the gunnels with powder and lead, clothing and fancy tinned goods, and enough foofaraws and assorted paraphernalia to warm the cockles of any buffalo-hunter's heart. The little merchant had also sent along a four-eyed adding machine by the name of Hiram Greene to run the trading post. Greene was humorless as a lizard, and wore glasses that would have pickled an eagle with fits of envy. But his mind was faster than an abacus in the hands of a Chinese silk merchant. Rath had hired him away from a Wichita emporium, and Jordan had never been so happy to see anyone in his life. Greene took over management of the trading post like a whirling dervish, and the plainsman returned to building his town.

When it was finished—along about the end of August—Jordan had every reason to be proud of his handiwork. Across the street from the store stood a stout log saloon flanked by a larger, and equally sturdy, dance hall. South of the hide shed, closer to the creek, was a roomy bunkhouse for freighters and visiting hunters, and just beyond that was a large pole corral for their livestock. Jordan had even built a laundry house, staffed by a fawning Chinese bandit, to serve the army post. Since buffalo men seldom washed—either themselves or their clothes—the laundry was a complete loss where they were concerned. The soldier boys were a different breed of cat, though, and the gibbering washerman soon had enough business to keep his lamp burning far into the night.

The new post commander, Major Anthony Cogswell, was rather pleased to have a laundry close at hand. He was a stickler for spit and polish, and it bothered him not a whit that a soldier might have to spend a quarter of his month's pay to ransom his uniforms back from the Chinaman. But the major's good will toward Sweetwater City stopped at the front door of the laundry. The rest of the village he viewed with a jaundiced eye, and not without some justification.

Word of the garrison—now being called Fort Elliott—and Rath's Trading Post had spread across the southern plains like wildfire. The Panhandle was safe again, protected by the army itself, and even its proximity to the Nations no longer quickened the dread men had felt since the fight at Adobe Walls. More significant still, the herds being driven north by the slaughter around Fort Griffin could now be pursued in relative safety. After all, that spanking new army post had to have something to protect, and it might as well be hide-hunters as rattlesnakes.

Like Hays and Dodge and Griffin before it, the tiny outpost on the Sweetwater was soon deluged by parasites scenting easy money. The buffalo hunters came first; it wasn't uncommon to see as many as twenty wagons a day clustered around the trading post. Hard on their trail arrived the human wolf pack—gamblers, whores, and a steady trickle of outlaws, drawn inevitably to the newest sanctuary. One even more remote than the hellhole below Fort Griffin.

By late fall the town had mushroomed, sprouting sod huts and split-log shanties all along the grassy swale bordering the creek. Another saloon and a second dance hall opened, and whores set up shop in everything from hide hutch to a pocket-sized parlor house. On any given day there were upwards of two hundred men roaming the dusty street, and the volatile mix of bad whiskey, wild women, and pistol-toting rowdies boiled over into violence regular as clockwork. Hide-hunters detested the muleskinners, the sporting crowd looked on both those groups as dimwitted hooligans, and everyone joined ranks in reviling the soldiers. Sweetwater City shortly became a lawless zoo of meateaters—home to a gathering of the frontier's crudest element—and a man's sole assurance of living to see another dawn rested squarely on his hip.

Cimarron Jordan liked it, though. In a queer sort of way he could almost imagine how God must have felt on the seventh day. When it was all finished—the buildings up, the dance halls blaring away, men cursing and drinking and killing one another—he sat back and rested, and was as pleased as punch with the whole goddamn shebang. Sweetwater City was as tough as any town on the plains. A wide open fleshpot where a man could bite off anything he was big enough to chew. Jordan was damned proud of his handiwork. He had started with an idea and a patch of ground, and built himself a town. Walking through it of a warm evening, listening to the hurdy-gurdy pulsebeat that rocked the very earth itself, he couldn't have been more tickled if he had fathered a two-headed billygoat with a gold plated bunghole.

Still, Jordan could only take towns in limited doses. The fact that Sweetwater City was his own creation didn't change that one iota. It was still a town, and by its very nature suffocating to a man who craved warm prairie breezes and the vast star-speckled umbrella of the plains sky. Perhaps being his town made it even more stifling, for there was a nagging sense of responsibility that went hand in glove with the pride he felt. Shortly after cold weather set in, he promoted Hiram Greene to official overseer of his little backwoods kingdom. Greene had proved himself trustworthy, as sharp as a tack, and Jordan had no misgivings whatever that he would exact every cent due from the various enterprises.

After shaking Hiram Greene's bony hand, Jordan had piled aboard his gelding and disappeared like a scalded goose for parts unknown.

Oncoming winter found the plainsman and his skinners camped below the Salt Ford of the Red. Fresh snow had fallen overnight, and the horizon lay bleak and gray. Bad weather was building, perhaps the first real norther of the year, and it was only a matter of time before the herds retreated southward to await spring. The cows were alone now with their calves, long since deserted by the lordly bulls, and their thick bluish-black coats was simply another sign that winter had come to the plains.

That morning, when they crawled out of their blankets, McCabe had ducked through the door of the hide hut and stood peering at the sky. "Cimarron, if I was you, I'd get me a stand early and shoot 'till I was out of shells. Come night, I got a hunch there ain't gonna be a solitary cow within ridin' distance of here."

Jordan stretched and took a deep breath, then gave him a wry smile. "What's the matter, old man? You been seein' owls in your sleep?"

Though McCabe believed strongly in certain Indian superstitions, he denied it hotly when pressed. "No, I ain't seen no owls! Don't need to see none neither. Even a blind man could smell what's blowin' itself together up north. 'Sides, my leg is achin' somethin' fierce, and you know what that means."

"Well why didn't you say so?" Jordan grinned. "That leg of yours is a sure fire cinch. Better'n owls any day."

"Go ahead and bray, you young jackass! Laugh your balls off. 'Fore dark you'll be freezin' them off anyway. Just hang around and wait. You'll see."

While he would never have admitted it to the old skinner, Jordan placed a good deal of faith in McCabe's leg. He had seen it foretell trouble—especially Indians—too often for him to remain even slightly skeptical. Without being too apparent about it, he had gathered his equipment and ridden out early. McCabe hadn't said another word, but he knew the old man was patting himself on the back for having had the last laugh.

Less than a mile out of camp, Jordan found a fair-sized herd blowing snorty puffs of steam as they pawed snow

130

from the grass. They hadn't had their morning feed yet, and they would most likely be skittish, but the old man had called the tune. Today might be the last stand they saw for quite a spell.

After tying the gelding in a dry wash, Jordan kept downwind and made his way to a spot some two hundred yards from the herd. He much preferred to shoot from an elevation, but beggars couldn't be choosers. Today he would take what he could get, and glad to get it. Climbing to the top of the gully, he scooped out a seat for himself, then arranged his gear and laid Lucretia over the forked sticks. On a level like this it was damned hard to spot the leader, and he knew already he had his work cut out to hold this herd long enough to make a stand.

Suddenly he jerked bolt upright. Then he rubbed his eyes hard and took another look. There was no doubt about it.

Smack dab in the middle of that herd stood a white buffalo.

Just for a moment he still couldn't believe what he was seeing. Any second now he could wake up back in the hide hut and start telling Lon of the strange sight that had come to him in a dream. Not one man in a million had ever seen a white buffalo. Like albino humans, they were an oddity—a freak of nature—something that came along so rarely there were many hunters who refused to credit the existence of such a creature.

The Indians knew better, though, and over the centuries had evolved a whole raft of superstitions about the strange ones. The white robes were thought to possess supernatural powers, and medicine men of every tribe used them in ritual cures over the desperately ill. One Cheyenne chief had even worn such a robe into battle, calling on its magic to shield him from harm. It was said among his people that he died a very old man, unscarred from a lifetime of warring upon their enemies. Some tribes gave the robes a much broader spiritual significance. After being decorated elaborately, the coat of a strange one would be taken to the top of a high hill and left as an offering of thanksgiving to the Buffalo Woman. There were none who could deny the power of such things, for the red man had survived beyond memory on the generosity of his brother, the buffalo.

Jordan's mind was crowded with such thoughts as he watched the white one graze in the center of the herd.

Overhead, an eagle soared in great circles and snowbirds fluffed and fluttered across the plains. But he saw none of this. His eyes were fastened on the strange creature before him, as though an apparition had risen in a trance and he dared not blink for fear it would vanish in a tiny wisp of smoke.

Then he shook himself and sucked in a deep draught of cold air to steady his nerves. Adjusting the sights, he laid the Sharps over the sticks and took a fine bead. When the rifle jumped against his shoulder, he saw the white buffalo go down, snorting a bright fountain of blood from her nostrils over the fresh snow. Other cows gathered around the strange one, bellowing a low, mournful sound as they scented blood. Within moments the white cow was completely surrounded and a number of buffalo had taken posts on the edge of the herd. Just as they would when guarding against wolves! Jordan again stared in disbelief, hardly able to credit what he was seeing with his own eyes.

The herd had closed ranks to protect the white one. Shielding her with their own bodies.

The plainsman jacked the spent shell out and reloaded. He had his stand. No question about it. That herd would stand there till hell froze over. But somehow their blind loyalty to the fallen cow had taken the zing out of it. There was something spooky about the whole thing. Unnatural. They should have panicked and run. Yet there they stood. Immobilized by an overpowering urge to protect the one different from themselves. An urge stronger than the instinct for survival itself.

It was a chilling spectacle. Even worse, it had ceased being a sporting proposition. Like shooting fish in a barrel.

Still, a stand was a stand, and hunting for a living was no game. It was a business. One with no room for simpering rules and jellied guts. Jordan fired and quickly reloaded without even bothering to watch the hit. Today was one of those days. He sensed it somehow, strong and pulsing.

There was no way he could miss. Not now.

Three hours later, Lucretia Borgia fell silent. Jordan climbed stiffly to his feet, and walked toward the steaming carcasses. The center of the open prairie had become a circle of death, turned darkly crimson where blood had spewed out over the powdery snow. The herd had stood and died to the last cow. Then the last calf. Moaning and pawing like mourners gathered at some ungodly wake. Unable to move even as death stalked among them.

The plainsman came to a halt before the white cow. Perhaps in all the world the one he stared upon now was the last.

The last white buffalo on the face of the earth.

It was a sobering thought.

Only once before had he seen such a robe. But that didn't hardly count.

Not the way he recollected it anyhow.

3.

When Sam Jordan had stepped off the train in Wichita late one afternoon back in the fall of '73, he had to restrain himself from gawking like a country bumpkin. The bustling metropolis before him bore scant resemblance to the budding cowtown where he had parted company with Virge only four months earlier. It was bigger and brassier. Infused with a carnival atmosphere of loose money, fast women, and bold, nervy men. The stark contrast between buffalo town and cowtown set him back on his heels for a moment. The more he stared, the brighter it glittered, and he wasn't quite sure but what he hadn't stepped off at the wrong station. Kansas City, maybe. Or St. Louis.

Summer and fall had transformed Wichita into the premier boomtown on the Kansas plains. Better than three thousand longhorns were being shipped east daily, and the odor of cow dung from the holding grounds hung so thick it saturated the air for miles around. But the people of Wichita rarely seemed to notice, or care. They were drunk on the heady fumes of a far sweeter smell. The balmy, ambrosial scent of greenbacks and gold. Their town was bursting at the seams—the population had rocketed to more than 2,000 within the past five months—and a welter of new buildings seemed to materialize every time a man blinked his eyes.

Longhorns and Texans were the name of the game. One to be skinned and the other to be fleeced. Wichita was eager to accommodate on both counts, and like witless vagabonds answering the siren's lure, the trailhands showered the town with a golden flood of bright, shiny coins.

133

Only that morning Sam had left Dodge with the thought to pay Virge a quick overnight visit. Wichita and back was only a day's train ride, and his crew needed a couple of nights to let off steam anyway. They had been down in the Nations for three months—gradually hunting their way toward the headwaters of the Cimarron—and had finally decided to bring a load of hides into Dodge. Once there, he had found plenty of reason to stay. Old Man Rath's daughter for one. He had taken quite a shine to the girl, and after she got over her stuffy eastern ways, she hadn't found him hard to look at either. Not that he was stuck on her, far from it. She was just different—wholesome and fresh, unlike the dance hall girls and whores he generally bedded—and something about her aroused him in a way he couldn't quite put his finger on.

Girls aside, though, he had found it even harder to slip away from the hide-hunters. When the word got out that he had been hunting below the treaty line—right in amongst all the red savages—he became a celebrity in no time flat. Every buffalo man in town wanted to buy him a drink, and they lined up three deep to listen whenever he spoke of the Nations. Not that he said much. Mostly he left the talk to McCabe, and the old reprobate was so smooth at spinning windies he had them goggle-eyed in a couple of shakes. Before Sam knew what hit him, somebody had christened him with a new handle—Cimarron Jordan—and the drinking pace picked up speed right away. Sam ducked out when nobody was looking, and boarded the morning train for Wichita. The way they were belting it down, he wouldn't be missed, and there wasn't much chance of the meeting being adjourned before he got back.

But the girl sort of bothered him. Damned if she hadn't looked a little pouty when he went by the store that morning to say goodbye. All the same, Virge was his oldest friend, and every once in a while a man was obliged to go see how the other fellow was doing.

Virge was eating high off the hog, as he soon found out. Sam caught up with him in the marshal's office about sundown, and damned if his former partner hadn't changed just about as much as Wichita itself. Virge was dressed fit to kill, and the brace of pearl-handled Colts he now sported were real knockouts. When he spotted Sam coming through the door he let out a wild whoop and started shaking hands like he had a job pumping water.

134

After they had brought one another up to date over a drink, nothing would do but what he took Sam on the fifty-cent tour. They hit every dive along Main Street and Douglas Avenue before the night had hardly commenced, and the way Virge carried on, a man would have thought he owned the whole shebang. Plain to see, he looked upon Wichita as *his town,* and Sam got a sneaky hunch he might just have his sights set on becoming the he-wolf of this glittery circus. When they crossed the toll bridge to Delano and started a whirlwind excursion of the sporting houses, Sam's hunch slowly ripened to downright certainty.

Virge talked sort of like he held first mortgage on every cathouse they saw, and the way the madams groveled and licked his hands, it was easy to believe. Watching it, Sam got the message in big bold letters.

Virge already owned the red-light district. Now he had his eyes trained across the river. On Wichita itself.

When they finally got around to meeting Virge's older brother, any lingering doubt went by the boards. Sam took an immediate dislike to James Hollister, the way one dog will sidle up to another with raised hackles. Being the eldest, he had a patronizing manner, even with Virge, and Sam pegged him right off as the kind of fellow who got a kick out of beating women. Which damn sure put him in the right line of work.

Both brothers talked openly of the lock they had on whoretown, and they made no bones about the fact that it took considerable muscle to keep everyone in line. There were certain factions—like Rowdy Joe Lowe and Mag Woods—who were always looking to overthrow them. Control of the vice district paid handsomely, and blood sometimes flowed when folks got too big for their britches. If it hadn't been for James's gang of hooligans, and Virge's star to back their play, they would have been out on their ear in short order. The way James told it, that was about the gist of it. But it didn't take much savvy to see that both the Hollister brothers had their sights set on bigger game.

Walking back to the bridge, Sam couldn't help but marvel at the remarkable change in his friend. *King of Whoretown.* Much as he enjoyed the company of shady ladies, it was a distinction he wouldn't have cared for himself.

Virge next took him to Pryor's Saloon, where they had a short snort with the younger members of the Hollister clan, Warren and Morgan. Afterwards they staked out a table in a back corner and got down to some serious jawboning.

The young lawman was proud as a peacock, and quite clearly wanted to talk about his own affairs. But he had acquired an element of tact over the months, and sort of backed into it in an offhand way. "Sam, you're a sight for sore eyes. No foolin'. Now c'mon, give me the lowdown. You haven't hardly opened your mouth, except to say you've been down in the Nations. Hell, man I want details. How many Injuns did you kill? How much money did you make? You know, the goodies."

"None and lots," Sam answered with a grin. "We saw some Injuns, but Lucretia sort of made them stay clear of us. Or maybe they just weren't spoilin' for a fight. Hard tellin' what a gut-eater's got on his mind. Tell you the truth, we had more trouble with skunks than anything else. Guess you heard about that, though." When Virge just nodded, he went on. "Now as to money, I reckon I'd have to say we did pretty well. After this and that, I figure to clear two big ones for the summer."

"Two thousand!" Virge whistled softly, but his eyes said he wasn't impressed. "Not bad. Not bad at all. What d'ya aim to do with it?"

"Get drunk and screw myself to death."

They busted out laughing, and after a moment Virge busied himself filling their glasses again. When he didn't say anything, Sam could tell he was waiting for the questions to start coming the other way. This was a new side to Virge, and he wasn't sure he liked it. Men who became overly proud of themselves often got arrogant, and along with it he saw a mean streak coming to light in his friend. Even down in Dodge he had heard of Virge's growing reputation as a gunman. While he hadn't killed anybody since becoming a lawdog, he had shot up two Texans pretty bad and split the heads of more rowdy cowhands than anyone could count. Word had it that he was tough as nails and wouldn't think twice about gunning down anybody who gave him a hard way to go. Maybe the mean streak had been there all the time, but Sam sure as hell couldn't recollect seeing it before. Still, a friend was a friend. You took them the way they were, and didn't pay much mind to what they weren't. Besides, he didn't have much room to be chucking rocks, anyway. Not the way he lived.

Sam took a pull on his drink and smiled slyly. "You're

not doing so bad yourself. What is it now—four months you've been here—and you already own half the town. Way I calculate it, that is what's called comin' up in the world."

Virge flashed a toothy grin and held back from preening too openly. "Yeah, I guess I have come a ways since we met last." Dusting an invisible speck off his vest, his hand drifted to the diamond stickpin. "Not bad for a fellow that rode into town smellin' like a goat, is it? But hell, Sam, I haven't even scratched the surface. There's bigger and better things in the wind for old Virge. Mark it down. I've got a smart piece to go, but I'm gettin' there real fast."

"Well, exactly where is it you're headed?" Sam felt like a man teasing a big diamondback. Even knowing what it would do, you still wanted to hear it rattle. "I mean, from what your brother says, you've already got the sporting houses sewed up. What's left?"

Virge's eyes came alive like fanned coals. "Wichita. The whole goddamned town! I mean to own it lock, stock, and barrel, Sam."

The plainsman shrugged and shook his head. "That's a pretty tall order. Folks have sort of gotten out of the habit of rollin' over and playin' dead. Or did you just mean to step out in the street and declare yourself King of the Hill?"

Virge threw back his head and let go a great bellywhopper. "Goddamn your hide! You've got a tongue like a pointed stick." After a couple of seconds the laugh subsided and he leaned forward intently. "Sam, come election time I'm gonna be marshal of this burg. That's less than two years off. Longer'n I care for, but it gives me plenty of time to get the big augurs thinkin' my shit don't stink. Once I'm elected I'll appoint my brothers as deputies, and we'll run this town to suit ourselves. Folks hereabouts don't know it yet, but they're fixin' to become sharecroppers for the Hollister Family."

Sam wasn't exactly surprised, more like disappointed. Not in Virge's ambition, or even his greed. Those were traits common enough to the best of men. It was the underhanded way Virge had chosen to pull it off. That went against the grain. Clean through.

Still, he couldn't lay the goad aside. "What then?"

"Why, old pardner, I'm gonna skim off the cream with one hand and scoop up the gravy with the other. No tellin' where it'll end. Hell, I might even wind up makin' speeches in Topeka."

Governor. Sam blinked on that. Virge was hungrier than he suspected. "You make it sound easy as fallin' off a log. Wonder if it is, though. I mean, don't you reckon folks might put up a fight before they start handin' over all that cream?"

"Sam, being a lawman is an education that can really open a fella's eyes. The first thing you learn is what makes this world go round. It's real simple. Foolproof, too. The strong take it away from the weak and the smart take it away from the strong. Works everytime. Always has. Always will."

"Trouble is, you might run up against somebody smart er'n you. It's like being fast with a gun. You live long enough and you'll always cross trails with some jasper who's just a shade faster."

That touched a nerve. But Virge didn't let on. "You're barkin' up the wrong tree. Think back. I taught you that being fast with a gun is a good way to get yourself killed. The fella that walks away from a shootout is the one that plays it cagey. Uses his head. And let me tell you something, sport. I'm just about the cagiest sonofabitch you ever run across. Now you take this money scare back east—"

"What the samhill has that got to do with anything?"

"—that's got folks wettin' their drawers. Everybody starts runnin' scared just because a few banks close their doors. Callin' it Black Friday and moanin' like the devil has got them by the short hairs. But look around you. Are the saloons closed? Have the whorehouses shut down? Not on your tintype. There's plenty of money around for them that knows how to get it. That's what I meant a minute ago. Fast ain't the same as smart."

Sam digested that and had to concede the point. "Yeah, I can't argue with you there."

"But that's not the half of it, Sam. Smart is being where the other fella don't expect you to be. Doing what he didn't count on, or wasn't cagey enough to figure out for himself." Virge edged closer and lowered his voice to a conspiratorial whisper. "Everyone in this town is scared shitless the cattle trade is gonna fall off because of tight money. They're sellin' property on the sly for whatever they can get, figurin' there won't be any trail drives next year. Christ, how stupid can you get?"

138

"Meanin', you think the Texans will trail north next year?"

"Why, hell yes. Those bastards didn't have two coppers to rub together after the war, and they were still trailin' cows all over creation. People back east want beef, and come spring you'll see more longhorns pushed up that trail than you've ever heard tell of."

Virge paused and glanced around, leaning even closer. "Now this is what I was gettin' around to tellin' you. Me and my brothers are in the right business. Hard times don't never come knockin' on a whorehouse door. We've got lots of money. Not in banks either. Cold cash. Every time somebody gets an itch to sell a piece of property, we buy it. No dickering. Just hand over the deed and we pay off. What folks don't know is that when this money scare's over, the Hollisters might just own about half of Wichita. That's what I just got through tellin' you. Smart is doing what the other fella don't expect, when he least expects it."

Sam had to admit that Virge made quite a package. Tough. Resourceful. Smart as hell. And cold-blooded enough to play dirty pool whenever fair and square wouldn't work. But he wasn't the same Virge who had ridden west with him to the buffalo grounds. That was a different Virge—one who had been swallowed whole by ambition and a thirst for power.

In his place sat a stranger.

When Sam's thoughts came full circle, he noticed that Virge was staring over his shoulder. The young lawman's pale eyes were fixed on something toward the front of the room. Turning in his chair, Sam saw a bunch of Texans ganged around a portly little man standing at the bar.

Then he started, almost rising from his chair. They were examining something he had thought existed only in legend, Indian mumbo-jumbo. The robe of a white buffalo.

The stout man at the bar, who later proved to be a drummer from St. Louis, had bought the robe off a hunter in Dodge for $500. Back home he could sell it for easily twice that amount, and so far it had bought him all the free drinks he could hold in half the saloons in Wichita. But he finally wandered into the wrong dive.

The Texans had had just enough to drink to make them ornery. When the drummer refused to sell that robe they started throwing their weight around, trying to scare him into a deal. Sam saw Virge heading toward them, and came out of his own chair in the next moment, but they were too late.

Virge froze as one of the cowhands snatched the hide from the drummer's hands and flung it in the air like a furry white cloud. Quick as a flash, the Texan jerked his six-gun and put three shots through the robe before it hit the floor. Turning back to the drummer, he laughed drunkenly.

"There ya go, dude. Now ya can tell all them rubbernecks back east ya shot it for yourself."

"Hands up!" Virge shouted.

Sam could have sworn the trailhand turned more out of surprise than with any intention of making a fight. But they never found out. When he came around Virge put two slugs through his chest with about the same emotion he would display in shooting a tin can. Covering the remaining Texans, he wiggled the barrel of his Colt at the dead man.

"Drag that dog meat out of here and bury him. Pass the word around. Anybody that burns powder in Wichita don't walk away."

After Virge escorted the cowpokes to their horses, Sam joined him on the boardwalk. They stood there watching till the Texans disappeared around the corner and the lawman still hadn't spoken. Gave no sign whatever that Sam was even there. Finally Sam couldn't hold his peace any longer.

"Did you have to kill him, Virge? He was just drunk and cuttin' up."

"Sport, if a man's worth shootin' he's worth killin'. You ever get in that fix, don't go squeamish. Second prize is a box."

Later that night they dropped around to see Lottie and had a few laughs about old times. But it wasn't the same somehow. The Virge Hollister he knew from the Smoky Hill days had been laid to rest. The stranger who had emerged was an icy sonofabitch he didn't care for. Not even a little bit.

When he boarded the train for Dodge next morning, he didn't even look back. Virge was still standing on the platform when the train pulled away, but Sam wasn't thinking about him anymore.

He was wondering if the poor bastards who thought they owned Wichita knew that they had a man-eating shark masquerading as a peace officer.

140

4.

Virge Hollister was mad enough to spit nails. After nearly two years of scheming and conniving and political skulduggery, he was right back where he had started. On the outside looking in. The mealy-mouth bunch who called the shots in Wichita had spoken—loud and unmistakably clear—leaving no doubt whatever as to the stand they had taken. Their announcement, as reported in the *Eagle*, had in one breath consigned him to political oblivion.

We endorse and wholeheartedly support Mr. Jediah Smith for the office of city marshal.

The worm had turned—with a vengeance—and Hollister's guts were afire with malice and outrage. Two years down the drain, with nothing to show for it but a pile of money and a polite kiss my ass from the town fathers. It wasn't enough. Not nearly enough. Somebody was going to pay through the nose, and soon. They might wield the big stick, but they would goddamn sure know they had been in a fight.

Only last summer Hollister would have bet his last nickel that he had a sure-fire lock on the marshal's job. Since the financial panic back in '73, the Hollister family had acquired considerable property in Wichita. Though they continued to operate the vice district as if it were their own personal fiefdom, the mere fact that they were landowners had lent them a semblance of respectability. Most of the property they had bought was situated in the center of town—two saloons, a mercantile emporium, and a livery stable—which gave them a voice in the business affairs of the community. Hollister had used this lever for all it was worth in his campaign to win the backing of the town's high and mighty.

While he hadn't been invited to join the inner circle, it had opened doors that were formerly closed altogether, and little by little the barriers began to crumble. Men who in the past had treated him with aloof courtesy—judges, business leaders, even a couple of bankers—thawed noticeably once it became known that he had worked a minor coup during the tight-money scare. Perhaps they didn't approve of his shadier enterprises, or sanction the tactics employed by his brother across the river, but they respected a man who was clever enough to take advantage of an economic crisis. Astute, they called it. The shrewd type of gambit they understood and appreciated with the savor of those addicted to fast, shifty deals. The young lawman remained something of an outsider, but he had at last engineered a first-name acquaintance with many of the town's more influential citizens. Hollister's confidence swelled by leaps and bounds, and with each passing month he became convinced that his plan was proceeding right on schedule.

What he wouldn't learn until later—much too late as it turned out—was that Wichita's movers and shakers were playing with marked cards.

Still, it was the only game in town, and he would have played regardless. Though he'd have played more cautiously, had he known the deck was stacked from the outset.

The big break came the night he got the goods on Tom Meagher. Through sheer happenstance he had discovered that the marshal was taking bribes from three crooked gambling dives, two on Main Street and the third across the river in Delano. Though hardly guileless in such matters, the revelation came as something of a shock to Hollister. The old lawdog was a pillar of the community—deacon in the church, city marshal since the town was chartered back in '69, an outspoken leader in the fight for law and order. Should it become common knowledge that he was up to his eyeballs in graft and corruption, it would rock Wichita to its very foundation.

Thinking back on it, Hollister could see that he had been duped himself. More than once he had suspected that certain games in town were rigged, particularly during trailing season when Texans stood in line to buck the tiger. But Meagher had always diverted his attention to more pressing matters—brawls, shootouts, collecting license fees from the sporting houses—saying that he personally would look into the situation. Understandably, the marshal had never been able to unearth evidence of trickery. Hollister wasn't so much rankled at being strung along as he was for being hornswoggled out of a share of the loot.

All the same, his discovery couldn't have come at a better time. It was a windfall of profound dimensions, the stroke of luck he needed to cinch down the marshal's job.

Cornering Meagher in the office next morning, he had elaborated in some detail on the evidence already accumu-

142

lated. The old man went paler by the minute, and when he had been shaken to the quick, Hollister outlined his deal. The price for his silence would be painless and direct. Meagher would first appoint him to the post of chief deputy marshal, followed by an announcement to the newspapers that the position had been created in long overdue recognition of Hollister's valiant service to the community. Then, along about the middle of trailing season, Meagher would let it be known that for reasons of ill health he was retiring at the end of his term. That, too, would be followed by an announcement to the press. The man he would support for marshal in the forthcoming elections that fall was none other than his chief deputy, Virgil Hollister.

Meagher could then retire with honor and live out his days basking in the heartfelt admiration of a grateful community. With no one the wiser that he was crooked as a dog's hind leg.

One more thing, Hollister had added. Meagher was to go right on collecting payoffs from the gambling dives. Only in the future he would trot on back to the office and deliver the proceeds to his new chief deputy. The pecking order had changed, and with it the distribution of wealth.

Meagher had caved in like a sack of feathers, and over the next few months things had gone strictly according to plan. Hollister had got himself a shiny new badge, the old man announced his retirement, and in a stirring speech declared his chief deputy the only man worthy of replacing him. The young peace officer tossed his hat into the ring and was off and running.

But Virge Hollister wasn't the only one that worked in the dark. Behind the scenes—in the privacy of smoke filled rooms—there was a movement afoot to axe young Mr. Hollister like a Christmas goose. The political apparatus of Wichita operated like a well-oiled machine, and the grease-can was jealously guarded by a very small group of men. They were the original settlers—merchants, bankers, professional men—not at all like the johnny-come-lately Hollisters. While their first concern was for themselves and their own murky schemes, they had a profound regard for the well-being of the town itself. A good part of their lives had been devoted to building Wichita, and whatever they hoped to attain in the future was tied directly to a prosperous and growing community.

Among them there was common accord. They had no intention of relinquishing one iota of political power to a young upstart. Particularly one whose only visible qualifications were a fast gun and a weasel-like cunning.

More to the point, the thought of Virge Hollister as city marshal sent shivers right down to their toenails. Should he ever take office, Wichita would be subjected to a reign of intimidation, shakedowns, and outright plunder. The force of the gun was persuasive—as Hollister had demonstrated with chilling ruthlessness—and what had happened in Delano could just as easily come to pass in Wichita itself. Worse yet, were the young lawman to be elected, he would surely deputize his brothers, and the thought of four Hollisters wearing badges was a horror none of them cared to contemplate.

They bided their time, though, allowing Hollister to court them with all the zeal he could muster. While they never said they wouldn't support his bid for office, they were equally careful never to intimate that they would. They implied many things, but promised nothing. It was the dangling carrot routine—always just out of reach but never wholly unattainable—and it would have been vastly amusing if it weren't for the fact that they were toying with a human bombshell. They recognized the risk of leading Hollister on, well enough, but they were also quick to grasp the even greater risk of allowing him to become the law in Wichita.

It was the lesser of two evils. The frying pan or the fire. A calculated risk taken in the belief that even Virge Hollister wouldn't have the nerve to call out unarmed men.

Then, just a month before elections, they blew the lid off. Their full page endorsement of Jed Smith in the *Eagle* was the opening blow. But hardly the most telling. That same morning rumors began circulating through town that, if elected, Hollister would immediately appoint his brothers as deputies. Everyone knew what that meant. James Hollister would organize a protection racket for saloons and gambling dens the same as he had done with whorehouses in Delano. Soon it was being bandied about that the Hollisters might even move in on legitimate businesses.

While Jed Smith had never fired a gun in anger in his life, he was a solid citizen, with the plodding, amiable nature of a tame bear, and a good family man to boot. All of a sudden—especially since everyone was scared to death of Virge Hollister anyway—good old Jed sounded like a damn fine choice. Just the man Wichita needed for marshal. Someone more like Tom Meagher. Not so pushy. Or quick with a gun.

When Smith started drifting around town that morning, casually jawboning with folks on streetcorners, they came away even more convinced. There was nothing flashy or tinhorn about him. He was simple folks, honest as the day is long, and as any fool could plainly see, he didn't have a mean bone in his body. What he had to say about the Hollisters made sense, too. Matter of fact, it was the same thing everybody else was saying. Only not quite so openly.

Hollister caught up with Smith in the Keno House shortly before noon. After reading the endorsement in the paper that morning he had gone straight to the office, sus·pecting Meagher had had a hand in the doublecross somewhere. But the marshal hadn't backed down, insisting he had kept their bargain right to the letter. The long argument that ensued came to nothing, and Hollister finally stormed out of the office even more frustrated than before.

Grudgingly, he had to admit that he had been flimflammed by the politicos themselves. They had given him the bait, and after he had swallowed it whole, they simply let him run with the line. Now, with perfect timing, they had sunk the hook and gaffed him all in one stroke. Prehaps there was little he could do to them—the bastards always made a big show of not going armed—but there was damn sure something he could do to their candidate.

There it was. The very touch he needed to regain lost ground.

Show Smith up for a gutless pisswillie. Pick a fight and send him packing with his tail between his legs. If the sonofabitch was stupid enough to go for his gun, then so much the better.

When he came through the door of the Keno House, Smith was standing at the bar. Several men were crowded around listening to him deliver a homespun lecture on law and order. Then someone noticed Hollister bearing down on them, and the loafers scattered like quail. The lawman stopped a couple of paces from Smith and glowered at him through slitted eyes.

"Smith, I understand you've been bad-mouthin' me and my brothers around town."

"I wouldn't exactly say that." Smith was no coward, but he wasn't a fool either. Diplomacy looked to be the way out.

145

"Then what would you say, peckerhead?" Hollister's gaze was pale as frosted milk.

"I guess I'd say . . ." Over Hollister's shoulder Smith saw Tom Meagher and Deputy Jack Barnes come through the door. The worried expression faded from his face, and he suddenly felt a surge of confidence. "I guess I'd say that if the shoe fits you ought to wear it. I haven't said nothin' that wasn't the truth. Everybody in town knows it, too."

"Smith, you're a goddamn liar."

"You're entitled to your opinion. I reckon we'll see who's lyin' when election day rolls around."

"You egg-suckin' sonofabitch," Hollister snarled. "I just called you a liar. You too yellow to do something about it?"

Smith's features went red as beet juice, but he didn't look away. "I'm not carrying a gun, Hollister. Even if I was I wouldn't fight you. It's your kind I mean to post out of town, and then men won't have to carry—"

Hollister produced a Colt out of nowhere and thunked the candidate upside the head. Before Smith went down he clobbered him twice more, breaking his nose and laying open a deep gash along one cheek. Suddenly footsteps sounded behind him and he ducked, whirling blindly in the same movement, and slammed the pistol barrel over somebody's skull. Only as the man went limp and started to fall did he see that it was Tom Meagher.

"Freeze, Hollister! You're dead if you don't."

Hollister looked up to find Jack Barnes staring down the twin barrels of a sawed-off shotgun. He froze very still. Barnes had always resented him being appointed chief deputy, and he knew the bastard was just itching for an excuse to pull both triggers.

"Drop the gun and turn around. Spread your hands out flat on top of the bar."

Hollister did as he was told. Things had suddenly gone from bad to worse, and under his breath he dredged up every curse he had ever heard.

There seemed no end to this flaky nightmare.

Less than an hour later, Virge Hollister was on the wrong side of a jail door for the first time in his life. Standing outside in the corridor were Mayor Dan Harris and Judge Percy Atwood. They hadn't said anything yet, having only just arrived, but there was a smug, very satisfied look about them. Like a cat with his head in a cream pitcher.

The two men exchanged glances, and the mayor cleared his voice. "Hollister, I suppose you know you're in serious trouble."

"Go to hell," Hollister grated out. "You sorry bastards are the reason I'm in here. If you hadn't ditched me for that clown none of this would've—"

"Young man," Judge Atwood informed him, "you keep a civil tongue in your head. Otherwise you will get a lesson you didn't bargain for."

"And let's don't hear any more about who promised what," Harris added. "You've done a lot of wheedling and coaxing in the last six months, but nobody ever promised you a thing."

"Awright, so you're a couple of straight-arrow saints," Hollister rasped. "Say whatever's on your mind before I get sick and start pukin'."

Harris shook his head, as if confronted by a testy child. "As I started to say, you're in deep trouble. Luckily both Meagher and Smith will recover. But as it stands now, you are charged with two counts of assault with intent to kill."

"*Kill?*" Hollister slammed up against the bars. "Listen you broken down old fart, when I set out to kill someone I don't do it halfway. That'll never stand up in court and you know it."

"I wouldn't be too sure of that," the judge observed. "You seem to forget that it's my court, and it sounds like a very reasonable charge to me."

Hollister glared back at him, but he didn't say anything. The mess he was in seemed to speak for itself.

After a moment, the mayor made a game effort at smiling. "Now, Virgil, we're not hard men. You know that. We're willing to strike a bargain with you. Something fair for everyone concerned."

Hollister felt a vague uneasiness creep over him. "Yeah. What kind of bargain?"

"Quite simple really," Harris assured him. "You clear out of Wichita, and all charges will be dropped. The alternative is that you will spend five to ten years behind bars."

Hollister didn't flare up as they expected. He saw the handwriting on the wall now, and an icy calmness settled over him. "You're trying to frame me, aren't you?"

Judge Atwood chuckled slyly. "Son, I'm afraid framed isn't quite the word for it. We're going to have you stuffed and mounted if you don't talk sense. That's straight from the horse's mouth, and you better take it as gospel."

Hollister's jaw clenched and his eyes went smoky with rage. "You rotten shitheels. You've had it in for me from the start, haven't you? Never could stand the thought of a lawman runnin' the sporting houses. That's it, isn't it?"

"My boy," the judge snapped, "I wouldn't care if you had carnal knowledge of a pickel barrel. The fact is, you are a menace to this town and we mean to be rid of you. One way or another. Now let's quit beating around the bush. Just give us a simple yes or no."

Hollister drew himself up straight and looked them square in the eye. "Why, judge, I'd be happy to oblige. I couldn't shake the dust of this goddamn place fast enough. That suit you?"

"One other thing," Mayor Harris noted. "We'll require that you sell all your property in town. Naturally, we will see to it that you don't lose on the deal."

"Naturally," Hollister cracked. "You being so honest and above board and all that."

"We'll have the papers drawn up and expect you to be on the evening train." Judge Atwood paused and stared at him for a long moment. "Virgil, you're a likeable man in a peculiar sort of way, so I'm going to give you some advice. Don't ever come back. Without that badge the Texans would eat you alive."

The politicians turned without another word and walked off down the corridor. When Hollister heard the cell-block door slam behind them he sat down on the cot and covered his face with his hands. Just for a moment he felt light headed, and a brackish filth puddled in his gorge.

Jesus Christ. What a way to go. Like some tinhorn cardsharp being hustled out of town.

Then he grunted to himself.

One thing was for sure. It beat the hell out of tar and feathers and riding a rail.

Just barely, though. Just barely.

5.

They came to the Washita in the Moon When the Ponies Shed. The great bend in the river, some twenty miles east of Antelope Hills, was their meeting ground. Where

148

they would council and decide what must be done about the *taibo* dogs, the killers of buffalo.

Little Bull came first, with a small band of Comanches. This was as it should be, for it was he who had sent runners during the Snow Thaws Moon to call a council meeting. With him came Sky Walker, the foremost *Do-ha* on the Southern Plains. Like skulking dogs they had left their reservation in the Wichita Mountains two sleeps past, traveling only at night. Should the Great Father's agent discover their absence, it would be said that they had gone only on a short hunt. That their people needed meat and they would return before the sun faded on the fourth day. While he was a *pawsa*, a crazy man, the agent would know that not even a Comanche could raid the *Tejanos* in so short a time.

Stone Calf and his party of Cheyenne rode in from the north shortly afterwards. They, too, had slipped away in the night, but there was less likelihood they would be found out. This place was but a quick ride from the hated lands ceded them about the Canadian, and they had little fear that the pony soldier chief at Camp Supply would miss them. Not as long as firewater kept his eyes red and left him clumsy as a newborn child. Stone Calf had suggested they meet on the Washita for that very reason. Though in his message to Little Bull the reason given was of a broader nature. The Comanches and Kiowas—while allies for generations beyond counting—were bitter rivals in all things. Better that the council should be held on neutral ground, where all came equally, without thought to rank or tribal jealousies.

Lone Wolf, fearsome warrior chief of the Kiowa, was the last to reach the Washita. This surprised no one, least of all Little Bull. The Kiowas were mighty fighters—not even the Comanches could claim more *Tejano* scalps—but they were lazy and shiftless, moving only as a slow breeze on a warm day. They were a people of moods and whims, governed by childish superstitions. Little Bull and Stone Calf were in accord on that point at least. Anyone who believed that the flesh of the bear was bad medicine deserved whatever ridicule came his way. Though the Kiowa were of the True People, their words were of small value around the council fire. They were hardy warriors, fearless and skilled in matters of battle. But they were not wise men.

Still, each of the three leaders who met on the Washita

149

that crisp spring morning was an *on-de*, a man of honor and courage. Through years of making war on the *taibos* they had all earned the right to be called chief. While they and their people had been herded onto reservations, these three had never taken the white man's road. They had watched the old leaders die off—most killed by the pony soldiers, the remainder left to rot in the dank holes the white-eyes called prison. Yet they never weakened, or allowed themselves to be intimidated by the blue-coated army which encircled their lands. Their hatred remained strong, eating corrosively at their insides, and the need to strike back had diminished not at all with the passing of time.

They sought a return to the old ways, to the way it had been before the coming of the *taibos*. When a man rode free on the prairie, making the long hunt, killing buffalo and stealing horses from the Pawnee. The time of dancing with the young women and coming in the dusky evening to a warm lodge to spend the dark hours with a favorite *paraibvo*. They remembered and dreamed back to a time when to be a man was to be alive, with each dawning full of excitement and things of great goodness. That long ago time when the wide plains and silty rivers were theirs. When the lodge fires rang with laughter and the high blue skies looked only upon the red man. When there was warmth in a man's heart and the love flutes called softly on the night winds.

The love flutes had long been silent now, and in that there was a message for all who would follow the white man's road.

Seated around a small fire, there on the banks of the Washita, they came quickly to this business of the white-eyed killers. *Tai-me* in his great generosity had given the buffalo to the red man. Made them brothers so that one might nourish the other through all his days. Beyond the memory of even the ancient ones it had been so. Dark, juicy meat to make the people strong, furry robes to warm them against winter storms, and sewn hides to cover the poles of their lodges. Bones to provide tools and ornaments and even toys, and thick bull hides for shields to deflect the arrows of their enemies. The buffalo had been there for all time, giving the People life and strength and the freedom to roam their father's lands, and now the *taibo* butchers would take that away. Forever.

The warriors who had escorted these men to the

Washita seated themselves behind their leaders and waited. It was the Comanche who must open the council talk, for he had brought it about. Each *on-de* would have his say, but only after Little Bull had spoken. When the onlookers at last fell still, the Comanche leader rose. He was a tall man, with a square chin and broad cheek bones, and his black eyes glistened in the early-morning sun. Though there was a sharp bite to the air, he wore only a loin-cloth and moccasins. Around his neck was a medicine bag of wolfskin, and snake rattles dangled from each ear. Stuck upright in his hair was a single hawk feather tipped with red.

He had come to the council as a warrior, and it was of war he would speak.

"Long ago this land belonged to our fathers. Even as a child I remember this as being so. I was born on the prairie where the wind blew free and there was nothing to break the light of the sun. I was born where there were no walls, where all things breathed free. I know every stream and wood of this land, for I have hunted and lived over it throughout my days. I lived as my fathers before me, and, like them, I lived happily. That is how I will die, and on the land of my fathers is where I choose to die."

Little Bull paused and looked around the gathering. A murmur of agreement swept over the warriors, and across their faces was a look of great expectation. This man was famed not for courage alone, but for the wisdom of his thoughts. When he spoke of dying it was not something to be taken lightly. They leaned closer as he resumed.

"Our old leaders are all gone. Rubbed out by the *taibos*. Santana, Satank, Black Kettle. No more will they ride with us. Now the white-eyes say we must build tree lodges and scratch in the ground like squaws. They herd us like cattle and rob us of our wealth. Does any man here not recall two snows past in the canyon to the west? The pony soldiers came from out of the night when it was dark and still, and they fired our lodges. Instead of hunting game they killed our horses and brought sorrow to our camps. We went out like buffalo bulls when the cows are attacked by wolves, and they scattered us to the winds. Can one among you forget the suffering of our people as they drove us back to this place?"

The goad cut deep, and there were shouts of anger from the braves. Little Bull waited a moment, then silenced them with a quick chopping motion of his hand.

"Whose voice first sounded on this land? Was it the *taibo*? Or was it the voice of the True People? Yet the white-eyed killers come into our country and leave a trail of blood and bones behind them. They have destroyed our homes, and the graves of our dead, and everything we held sacred. The very land given us by *Tai-me*. Now they would destroy the buffalo. Rob us of the tomorrows of our children's children. I say, never. *Never!* From where the sun now stands I will run no more. I ride against the killers of buffalo. Those of you who heed my words are welcome to follow. I have spoken."

The challenge was thrown out with quiet arrogance, as befitted a Comanche chief. They spoke of themselves as Lords of the Plains, and Little Bull could have uttered the call to war in no other way. Not if he was to save face among his own people.

For perhaps ten heartbeats, a strained stillness fell over the Indians. Then, with all the dignity he could command, Lone Wolf came to his feet and stared about the curious faces. Though squat and heavily featured, as were most Kiowas, he was still an imposing figure. It was said that he had personally killed more *Tejanos* than any man living. Those gazing upon his cruel mouth and cold, ugly eyes found it easy to believe.

Without so much as a flicker of recognition for Little Bull, his raspy voice floated over the clearing. "The earth and myself are of one mind. The measure of the land and the measure of my body is the same. Do not misunderstand me, but understand me fully in my love of the land. I never said it was mine to do with as I choose. The one who has the right to dispose of it at will is the one who created it. *Tai-me*. I claim only the right to live on my land. Yet the *taibo* swarms over the land like maggots on a rotting carcass. When I go up the river I see camps of white-eyed buffalo hunters on its banks."

Lone Wolf stopped, and his hands flashed in the sun. Both palms went up, fingers and thumbs extended. Then his hands came erect, fingers and thumbs joined, and he made a circular motion to the left.

One thousand buffalo-hunters.

"They kill our buffalo and take only the robes, and when I see that my heart feels like bursting. Have they become children that they kill so recklessly and not eat? When the People slay game they do so that they may live and not starve. Should I lay aside my bow and shield and

152

let the white-eyes destroy our brother, the buffalo? Would I then feel safe shut up in the strange lodges forced on us by the *taibos?* Would my children grow fat and strong on *taibo* cattle as they have done on buffalo? I do not believe it is so. We would grow pale and die, as many have done already. If I am to die, then let it be as a warrior."

Again his hands spoke with deadly eloquence. Holding them wide apart, with fingers extended, he brought them together in a rapid jabbing motion. Then he put his palms together and erased them for the rubbed out sign.

"War on the killers of buffalo until they are no more! Only then, my brothers, can the True People look one another in the eye again. The Kiowas have killed more *Tejanos* than any among the People. That is not an idle boast. It is a truth. We, too, shall ride against the *taibo* killers. I say now, for all to hear, that none who ride west will take more scalps than the Kiowa *T'ai-peko.*"

With this parting shot at Little Bull, he took his seat beside the fire. The two chiefs looked neither to the right nor to the left—certainly not at one another—and a husky muttering rippled back over the assembled warriors. The Kiowas were pleased that Lone Wolf had thrown the challenge back in Little Bull's face. Their warrior societies— the *T'ai-peko*—would teach the haughty Comanches a lesson in warfare that would be spoken of around camp fires for many snows to come.

But the Comanche braves were angered by Lone Wolf's insolent words. That a lowly Kiowa would presume to address them in such a boastful manner was an affront to their dignity. The matter had now become an affair of honor. They must humble these stump-legged braggarts by taking more scalps from the killers of buffalo than the Kiowas could dare imagine. Granted the Kiowas were their brothers, but an unruly child must be taught his place from time to time.

Stone Calf looked on with detached amusement, concealing it well beneath a wooden composure. The Cheyennes, as any reasonable man would agree, were greater warriors at their worst than these buffoons had ever been. Still, it was an interesting diversion to watch the Comanche leader manipulate Lone Wolf's feeble mind. Little Bull had purposely scorned the Kiowas, knowing they would rise to the bait. Now, not only had they agreed to join the raid, they would outdo even their normal ferocity in the fighting to come. Once word of the Comanche challenge swept through the Kiowa villages, every man able to mount a pony would ride out seeking the killers of buffalo. Which was exactly as Little Bull had planned it. He was a shrewd judge of character, this imperious Comanche, never to be underestimated.

After a suitable period of time had elapsed, Stone Calf came erect and waited for the muttering to subside. Taller than Little Bull, he was a magnificent specimen of a man. Lithe and broad-shouldered, his features were as if carved from bronzed granite. The high cheek bones and wide, slitted mouth were set off by a flat, stoic gaze that seemed to penetrate everything it touched. He was dressed simply: fringed buckskin shirt and leggings with a bear-claw necklace around his thick corded neck. Yet none among those present were fooled by his unadorned appearance. This hawk-eyed Cheyenne was known across the plains for his supreme courage in battle, and even the ancient ones considered him a sage of the highest order. When he spoke, other men listened, for his was the voice of reason.

"The Comanche and Kiowa leaders have spoken bravely and with wisdom. But there are things that must be said which they have left unsaid." Stone Calf paused to let his words take effect, and was rewarded with absolute silence from the upturned faces. After a moment he swept his hand out from his breast. The sign that he would speak from the heart. "When I was a young *ho-ta-min-tanio* I rode this land with my brother Dog Soldiers and saw none other than the True People. After many summers I rode again and found that people had come to take it away from us. We never did those first *taibos* any harm. We were willing to be friends with them. Yet their greed was as the plains and sky, unending. Now, after they have taken all else we possess, they would take our buffalo. When the buffalo is no more, our bellies will grow tight, and out of hunger the white-eyes will force us to their ways. Those who can see the road ahead know that this is how the *taibo* dogs have planned it. They mean to starve us into submission."

An angry grumbling arose from the warriors, forcing him to halt. What he said had the ring of truth—never had they considered it in just that light—and it struck home. There was no end to the white-men's treachery. They fought without honor, lowering themselves as a pack of dogs snarling over a bone. Who else would think to win the land by slaughtering the buffalo brother? Before their

154

anger got out of hand, Stone Calf motioned them into silence.

"Once each of us here was a great nation—strong, with warriors aplenty—but now we are few. Yet the white-eyes are as leaves on the trees. Their numbers never cease, and they grow stronger around us with each passing moon. What I have come here to say is that we are as helpless as young spring calves encircled by wolves. For us there is nothing left but the choice of how we shall lose."

One of the Comanche braves leaped to his feet and shook his fist at Stone Calf. "Go back to the squaws, old man! This talk of defeat is not the talk of a warrior." Little Bull spun around and gave him a withering stare. His action had shamed the Comanches, for it was the law that a council speaker had the right to be heard in full. Unable to meet Little Bull's furious glare, the man sank to the ground and lowered his eyes in disgrace.

Stone Calf nodded with a benign expression and resumed. "Brothers, I come here to talk of war, not of peace. The True People wait to die—that is a truth only the foolhardy could dispute—we carry our lives on our fingernails. But how a man chooses to die—there is the thing we must decide this day! The Cheyenne bowed to the will of the Great Father and came south to this land, and I would have held my word until the stones melted. But I will not be driven to the mountains, no more to see the plains or ride free with the wind. I will not honor a treaty that the *taibo* killers of buffalo spit on as a man would spit on filth. Even our raid of two summers past on the adobe fort to the west has not stopped them. Nothing will stop them until they are rubbed out. The thing we must all consider is that by taking the war trail we speed our own death. We are free men, and this is a thing that must not be left unsaid, for each of us has the right to choose his own path. For myself, there is no choice. Better to die fighting than to perish like a whimpering pup along the white man's road. Let it be said when men speak of this thing in days to come, that the Cheyenne died as they had lived. Like warriors."

Stone Calf remained standing a moment, then sat down. Briefly the three chiefs discussed what must be done and it was decided among them. Each would return to his people and raise a war party of those who wished to die as their fathers and their fathers' fathers before them had died. They would meet again at this place on the Washita with the coming of the Bud Moon. Once assembled, they would ride west and strike the killers of buffalo along the Sweetwater. Because of the rivalry between the Kiowas and the Comanches, they would not select a *To-yop-ke* to act as leader of the combined forces. Instead each chief would lead his own warriors, and the raid would be carried out by three fast-striking columns. Afterwards they would scatter south across the Prairie Dog Fork of the Red and regroup at Yellow House Canyon. From there they would raid throughout the land of the Brazos—and wait for the pony soldiers to come. Whatever day they came, that would be a good day to die.

When it was decided, Little Bull signaled to the prophet, Sky Walker. They must have the sign, an omen of good medicine, so that they might return to their people with encouraging words for the success of the raid. Without good medicine there would be no raid, for none would follow a fool who went into battle against the sign.

Sky Walker climbed stiffly to his feet and walked toward the fire. He was an old man, stooped and short of breath, but age had not eroded his fame as a prophet. Long ago, in the earliest days of his manhood, he had fallen into a trance and followed the dead man's road. When he had crossed over to that land beyond, he came to a green valley with a sparkling stream, and there he met again all who had once walked the earth. The dead. They gave him great powers and returned him to the living so that he might do good among the People. The greatest power they gave him was that of an owl, who saw all things past and present. Through the sacred owl the dead would speak to the People, warning them of bad medicine and foretelling good. Such power had never before been given to any man, and because he had been returned from the land of the dead, the youngster was given a new name. Sky Walker. His fame had spread across the plains to every tribe, and in the decades that passed there were none to equal the influence he possessed among the True People.

The aged prophet stopped before the fire and held a beaded medicine pouch aloft. With a look of profound omniscience, he stuck his hand in the bag and withdrew it to reveal an owl perched on the end of his arm. Though it was clearly a superbly skinned owl, the great horned bird seemed somehow the embodiment of all things living and dead. It ruffled its wings and cocked its head from side to side, gazing out over the warriors with godly disdain. Then the owl's yellowed eyes blinked, flashing ominously in the early morning sun, and across the clearing came the twittering screech of a great bird of prey.

Sky Walker stared at the owl for a moment with a look of awed homage, then carefully returned it to the medicine pouch. When he withdrew his hand it was as if it were in no way connected with the godlike creature. Turning, he walked from the fire and resumed his seat.

The sacred owl had spoken. Their raid would bring great victory.

Little Bull signaled for a pipe, and when it was brought he lit it with a smoldering stick. This was the final act. All who smoked would be obliged to take the war trail against the *taibo* buffalo killers. The Comanche held the pipe to the sun, the earth, the four winds—honoring all things. After puffing and letting the smoke roll slowly toward the sky, he hesitated a moment, as if undecided. Then he passed the pipe to Stone Calf.

Lone Wolf could wait his turn. The Kiowa's brazen manner of speaking was a vulgarity not easily overlooked. Perhaps waiting would teach him to be more civil when he addressed a Comanche.

Even so, it would hardly make him less a barbarian. Not even *Tai-me* had been able to do much toward curbing the Kiowas.

Five

1.

Skillet Thompson and Spotted Jack Dean could hear the steady thump of Sewall's Big Fifty in the distance. After listening for the better part of an hour they knew he had a stand, and they set about hitching the wagon. The skinners had worked for Marshal Sewall since last fall, and they were of one mind that he was the best damn boss on the plains. Easygoing, rarely failing to make a stand, he paid well and never asked more of another man than he demanded of himself. Most evenings he would read aloud from leather-bound volumes of plays and poetry—*Don Juan, The Taming of the Shrew, Othello*—acting out each part so lifelike a man could almost see the characters there before the fire. Skillet and Spotted Jack didn't always get the drift of what was being said, but they understood tomfoolery and death when they heard it, and whenever Sewall read it was a warm fascination that held them spellbound. They wouldn't have skinned for another hunter for twice the money. Some things—like those little leather-backed books—a man just couldn't put a price on.

When they were about a half-mile from the killing ground, the big Sharps went silent. There was a low rise directly ahead, and they couldn't be sure, but it sounded like Sewall had ended the stand. That or the herd had finally stampeded. Then, very suddenly, they heard the faint bark of a pistol and the answering crack of repeating rifles. Spotted Jack popped the reins and put the team into a dead gallop toward the gunfire. Both skinners had a pretty fair idea of what they would find, but Marshall Sewall wasn't the kind of man a fellow deserted when things got dicey.

Spotted Jack slewed the wagon to a halt atop the little knoll just in time to see Sewall go under. The hunter had somehow made it to a buffalo wallow and was putting up a stiff fight until his pistol ran dry. When he switched back to the slow-loading Sharps, the Indians simply overran him, and he went down under a snarling pack of red savages. From the hilltop Spotted Jack and Skillet could see the knives flashing in the sun, and they knew very well what was happening down in the wallow. There wouldn't be enough left of Marshall Sewall to draw buzzards. Something more than fifty Indians were racing their ponies back and forth around the wallow, shrieking the wild, gobbling war-cry. Kiowas from the looks of them.

Just then one of the Indians sighted the wagon and howled at the top of his lungs, kneeing his pony into a lope toward the hill. The rest of the war party wasn't far behind, and all of a sudden the skinners found themselves in a very hairy predicament. Skillet sent the lead brave tumbling with a shot from his Winchester right about the time Spotted Jack decided to get the hell out of there. Even as the wagon careened back down the hill, with the mules going flat out, Skillet couldn't help but think about the buffalo carcasses he had spotted around the wallow. Fifty, maybe more, that would never get skinned. And one damn fine white man that had been.

Spotted Jack was cursing a blue streak at the mules, but they weren't built for speed. Already the bloodcurdling yelps behind them were getting louder and it looked to be a damned uneven race. Maybe no race at all. Abruptly it dawned on the skinner that there was no way in hell they could outrun the gut-eaters. The wagon was about to become their tomb unless they did something fast. Goddamn fast.

All of a sudden he remembered a brush-choked gully they had passed on the way out from camp. The thought no sooner popped into his mind than he reined the mules in that direction and gave them another crack across the rump. Just thinking about what he meant to do gave him

159

the shivers, but this was no time to get fainthearted. The only other choice was right behind them, and that made it no choice at all. Glancing around at Skillet, he shouted over the thundering din of hoofbeats.

"Get ready to jump! Take to the brush!"

Skillet couldn't really believe his partner would do it. But before he could get a word out, Spotted Jack drove the team straight off into the gully. Both men leaped at the last instant and went hurtling through the tangled overgrowth of brushy limbs. Behind them came a splintering crash and the terrified bawl of the mules as they were crushed beneath the wagon. But the skinners had thought for nothing save their own hides just at the moment. Cut and bleeding from their explosive encounter with the brambled thicket overhead, they jumped to their feet and took off running in opposite directions along the gully. The Kiowas went into a frenzy at being outwitted so easily, and raced their ponies along the rim of the arroyo trying to spot the white men. After a fruitless ten minutes they gave it up as a lost cause and pounded off in a dusty gallop headed west.

They couldn't be bothered with two miserable *taibos*. There was game aplenty all around them. Just waiting to be rubbed out.

Marshal Sewall was the first man to die in the raid that morning. But hardly the last. Buffalo men from the Sweetwater to the Prairie Dog Fork of the Red went to meet their maker before the sun was hardly an hour old. The plains were swarming with painted savages, and their bloody scalp-cry sounded again across the land.

Death had come to pay another call on the killers of buffalo.

The vast stretch of prairie south and west of Fort Elliott had been divided into three parcels by the Indians. The Kiowas were to attack along the North Fork of the Red, avoiding Fort Elliott and the Sweetwater settlement. Even Lone Wolf had agreed that there was nothing to be gained in engaging the pony soldiers until absolutely necessary. The Cheyenne war party, something over fifty strong, was to raid along the Salt Fork of the Red, then turn southwest and hit Palo Duro Creek. Little Bull had claimed the Prairie Dog Fork of the Red for the Comanche. With the Bud Moon nearly gone, that was where most of the buffalo killers would be congregated. Since the Comanche party numbered well over a hundred warriors, it was only fair that they take the choice raiding ground for themselves.

Lone Wolf and his Kiowas had objected, but not too strenuously. There was a certain logic to Little Bull's argument that could not be denied. The main point being that the Comanche had the Kiowa outnumbered. Once that was settled, the chiefs agreed to leave their meeting place on the Washita one day apart. The Comanche had the greatest distance to ride, so they left first. The Cheyenne had departed the next day, and the Kiowa the day after. The raid was set for sunrise of the fourth day, and it was understood that the separate columns would join up again two days later at Yellow House Canyon.

Shrewd tactician that he was, Little Bull had split his Comanches into five raiding parties. The morning of the attack, with the sun at their backs, they struck five buffalo camps almost simultaneously. Once they had finished with the killing and looting, each party rode west along the river in search of new game, always forcing the *taibo* dogs to fight with the sun in their eyes. The Comanches *Toyop-ke*'s orders were brutally simple. Strike fast and hard and leave nothing alive. Not even the mules. Saddle horses could be taken prize, if it in no way slowed the raid. Otherwise, everything left behind must be suitable only for the carrion eaters.

They were to kill and butcher and burn. The killers of buffalo must be taught for all time that the price of their greed was death itself.

Cimarron Jordan and his men were luckier than most that morning. Their camp was situated far to the west, along the headwaters of the Prairie Dog Fork. When the raids broke out, they could hear gunfire from downstream, and it didn't take any fancy guesswork to figure out what was afoot. The firecracker burst of shooting could mean only one thing. Somebody was swapping lead with somebody else, and it was a pretty safe bet that the second somebody rode mustang ponies and had bungholes red as cherry pits.

Jordan was still studying it when McCabe came around the corner of the wagon jamming loads into his old Henry Repeater. "Cimarron, are you just gonna stand there scratchin' your ass 'til they're right on top of us?"

"Slow down, Lon, and put your noodle to work." The

161

plainsman paused and cocked his head as a fresh outburst of gunfire erupted. "Few minutes with our thinkin' caps on might just save our hair."

McCabe looked at him like he had gone simple. "Sometimes I think you must sneak off at night and eat loco weed. Time's awastin', boy. We gotta get the hell out o' here. *Muy pronto!*"

The shooting swelled in volume, from the sound of it not more than a couple of miles downstream. Jordan nodded to himself, as though something profound had suddenly come quite clear. Listening a moment longer, he turned to McCabe and the skinners, who had armed themselves and hurried forward. "Now shut up and pay attention. Time's short and we've got lots to do. They're movin' straight upstream, raidin' the camps as they come to them. That means they'll hit three maybe four camps before they get to us. Injuns generally get their fill of fightin' pretty quick, and I figure they're gonna have a bellyfull by the time they hit us."

"Jesus Goddamn!" McCabe groaned. "You aim to stay here and fight 'em? Cimarron, we gotta make a run for it while there's time. Use your ears. There's a whole passel of Injuns down there, and in case you ain't counted, there's only four of us."

"Old man, I told you to keep your trap shut. I don't have time to argue." Jordan's eyes got the steely look that meant he wasn't fooling. "If we run and they catch us out in the open, we're the same as dog-meat. What we've got to do is fort up and make it hot for 'em. I've got an idea they'll be pretty well tuckered out by the time they scent us. Now everybody get it straight and don't make me tell you twice."

The camp was in a clearing close beside the north bank of the river. Though it was shaded by a grove of cottonwoods, trees grew sparse this far west, and the open timber made it possible to see well beyond a quarter-mile downstream. Whatever a man could see he could shoot—particularly with Lucretia—and Jordan was staking everything on a single judgement. After three or four stiff fights, the Indians wouldn't be feeling tricky. They would attack head-on rather than make a wide circle and come in from the rear. Since there hadn't been any gunfire from behind them, he felt reasonably confident that there were no hostiles to the west of camp.

If he had calculated right, they could start potshooting

redskins long before the bastards got anywhere near camp. But there wasn't a hell of a lot of margin for error, and he didn't especially dwell on what would happen if he was wrong.

Working quickly, according to the plan Jordan hurriedly sketched for them, the men hitched the mules and backed the wagons side by side. They left a six foot gap between the wagons, and blocked off the wheels with large rocks. Next they tied two mules and a saddle horse at each end in the opening between the vehicles, then stacked cured hides on the ground underneath the wagon beds. When they were finished, they had a sealed space between the wagons that protected them on all sides, yet allowed them to shoot in any direction. The livestock was fastened securely to the wheels, and even if they were killed, their bodies would still block the gap at each end.

Finished, they sat back to wait and listen to the battle raging downstream. Shortly the gunfire slacked off, and there was a lull that lasted the better part of a half-hour. Then it started up again with renewed intensity, and the shooting was closer this time. Much closer. While no one said much, it was obvious how things stood.

They were next on the list.

Jordan kept his eyes glued on the treeline downstream, with an occasional glance at Stonewall and the mules. For some reason, mules had a positive terror of Indian smell, and they made damn good sentries. Stonewall had already proved himself a born Indian-hater, and if the wind was right he would set up a ruckus even before the mules got skittish. Just looking at the huge wolf-dog gave Jordan an added sense of well-being. If the gut-eaters ever got over the wagons and it came down to knives, the yellow-eyed brute would be worth two extra men.

Stonewall let out a low growl just about the time one of the mules whickered and laid back his ears. Jordan saw them then, close to twenty warriors riding through the trees on the other side of the river. They were still too far away to make out what tribe they belonged to, but right at the moment, their pedigree didn't seem to matter much. The bastards were hostile, and that was all a man needed to know. They were taking it easy, looking for sign, and near as he could tell they hadn't spotted the camp yet. But they would, just any moment now. Especially if the mules started acting up.

"Awright, boys," he said in the next thing to a whisper,

163

"time to go to work." When the skinners crowded around he nodded at a cottonwood about two hundred yards off that had been struck by lightning. "See that burnt out tree just back from where the bank curves? When they get there I'll bust the one in the lead. I want all you fellas to draw a bead on the next man in line. If we can down two of 'em right off, they might just hightail it out of here. If they keep comin', then pick your shots and shoot 'em as you see 'em."

Jordan laid Lucretia over the wagon frame and sighted on the blackened stump in the distance. When the lead scout passed the tree, he picked him up in the sights and waited a moment to let the second warrior come into view. When the Sharps slammed back against his shoulder, the forward scout flew off his pony like he had been hit by a thunderbolt. The Winchesters and McCabe's old Henry went off in his ear in the next instant, and he saw the Indian just behind crumple over and pitch to the ground. The rest of the war party started playing hide and seek among the trees, gobbling to one another like a flock of turkeys.

But they weren't running, and Jordan grunted with disgust. Chalk up one mistake for the big bad Indian fighter. And hope to hell he hadn't misjudged anything else.

"Get set, boys. They're gonna rush us sure as hell."

The words were no sooner out of his mouth than the war party split up in two bunches. The first forded the shallow stream and started filtering through the trees on the north bank. The rest stuck to the scattered cottonwoods on the other side and rode forward at a steady clip. The Indians were using timber to best advantage, knowing that a moving target passing through a stand of trees is hard to sight on. Clearly they meant to hit both flanks in a concerted attack and swarm all over the white men.

Jordan and his men triggered a few shots as the braves drew steadily closer, but it was like trying to hit a fast moving duck in a crooked shooting gallery. The plainsman switched to his Winchester and loosened the Colt in its holster when the range dropped to a hundred yards. Things were about to get hot and he wanted to sling all the lead he could in that first minute.

That's about what it boiled down to. One minute. If they hadn't stopped the bastards by then they probably never would.

Someone in the bunch on the north bank let out a shrill

cry and the braves put their ponies into a gallop, dodging in and out of the trees like overgrown hornets. The warriors on the south side of the stream broke clear of the cottonwoods and came splashing through the water in a massed knot of horses and glistening red bodies. Jordan saw right away that they were Comanches. But fewer than he had calculated. Maybe fifteen all told.

After that he didn't think anymore. He just worked the lever as fast as his arm would move and concentrated on catching a piece of red hide in his sights. The Comanches made it about half way across the clearing before their charge fell apart. Three braves and a couple of horses had gone down under the storm of lead spewed out by the repeaters, and the remainder evidently decided it was no longer a good day to die. They whirled their ponies and thundered south across the stream in headlong flight. When they hit the treeline, they just kept right on going.

Fighting *taibos* who forted up behind wagons wasn't their style. Especially when they had lost five braves in as many minutes. Besides, they had all the plunder they could carry, and it wasn't worth getting themselves rubbed out for four buffalo killers more or less. Little Bull would never know the difference anyway. Not when they showed him all the scalps they had taken downriver.

Jordan and his crew waited for an hour, just to make sure the Comanches hadn't crawled off to get their second wind. Then McCabe and the plainsman scrambled over the wagons and walked toward the fallen warriors. Huggins and Cook covered them from behind the bullet-riddled vehicles. Though Huggins had had his brow laid open by a flying splinter and one mule was down, the outfit had come through otherwise intact.

The hunter had just finished toeing over the second brave when McCabe called to him. When he came over, the old skinner pointed with his rifle barrel at one of the dead Comanches. Dangling from a thong around the warrior's waist was a blood-crusted scalp unusually amber in color and streaked through with gray.

" 'Pears like ol' Monte Brown done went under."

"Damned if it don't." Jordan stared at the scalp for a moment with a mildly puzzled frown. "Funny the way things work out. I didn't even know Monte was down this way. Not that it'd make much difference one way or the other, I guess. When a man's string runs out, he don't much care who's standin' beside him."

165

Jordan took first watch that night. Not that there was much to worry about except guarding the livestock. Indians didn't like to fight at night. Had some damnfool notion that their spirit would get itself lost if they got themselves killed in the dark. That suited him just fine, though. He'd had enough fighting for one day. Especially after seeing Monte's scalplock that way. It was a damn strange way to run across an old friend—hanging off some gut-eater's belt like a watch charm.

Life took some mighty queer turns, and a man never rightly knew when he was apt to run up on Old Scratch. Most likely when he least expected it. Wherever he was, old Monte was probably shaking his head and wondering why the hell he hadn't gone north instead of south. Or anywhere besides the Prairie Dog Fork of the Red in late April.

Thinking about it, Jordan became aware that the night was absolutely still. Soundless. Not even a katydid tuning up for a screechy lullaby.

Somehow that seemed damned fitting. The dead needed all the quiet they could manage in order to get wherever they were headed. Especially before first light.

Come morning the magpies would be eating eyeballs for breakfast. Which wasn't the kind of thing a fellow wanted to hang around and watch happen to himself. Not if he could help it, leastways.

Ruminating over it, he hoped Old Monte had already managed to cross over. Maybe the other side really was the way the Indians believed. If so, Monte was going to see more damn buffalo than any white man ever thought existed.

Little ghosty looking, maybe. But lots of them. A whole sky full.

2.

Hide-hunters and their skinners started straggling into Sweetwater City late that night. Hardly an outfit among them had escaped unscathed, and the tales they told had a gruesome sameness. Indians, hairless corpses, and men hacked to pieces like butchered hogs. By late afternoon of the next day, close to three hundred men had gathered in the tiny settlement, and they were in an ugly mood. The toll of dead and wounded had mounted steadily throughout the day—not to mention the loss in livestock—and they wanted revenge. Somebody had to teach the gut-eaters a lesson they would never forget. The only kind of lesson they understood. The kind written in blood.

Jordan and his crew rode in about sundown. They had left the wagons on the Prairie Dog Fork and covered the sixty miles to Sweetwater by circling west along the upper tributaries of the North Fork. Huggins and Cook were riding mules bareback, and their rumps were sore as boils, but that was soon forgotten when they came through the door of The Bucket of Blood. The saloon was packed to the rafters, and when the hunters sighted Jordan the whole place went into an uproar. They mobbed around him, each one trying to outshout the other as they described their hair-raising ordeals of the day before. The concensus seemed to be that Jordan had built Sweetwater, and lured them back into the Panhandle, so it was up to him to map out some plan of action. They wanted blood. The pure red kind. And one way or another they meant to get it.

Word of Jordan's arrival had spread through town, and more men were pouring in the door by the minute. When the railing and ranting started to get out of hand, the plainsman finally jumped up on top the bar. Holding out his hands for silence, he slowly got them under control. Looking down on their sullen faces, his mouth set in a grim line.

"Boys, there's not a man here that wants Injun hide more'n me. I lost the oldest friend I had in the world. Monte Brown. Some of you most likely remember him from the Smoky Hill country."

"Goddamnit, Jordan," one of the hunters shouted, "we all lost friends. What we wanna know is what the hell's gonna be done about it."

"That's right!" another man yelled, casting a glance around the room. "We're all of one mind here. Am I right, boys? We wanna skin some red meat!"

The crowd roared their approval and surged forward. Their bloodlust was aroused, and if something wasn't done quickly they might just start by taking the town apart. After a hectic couple of minutes, Jordan again motioned them into silence.

"Listen, any sonovabitch here that thinks I don't feel the same way just step right up. C'mon, goddamnit! Who's gonna be first?"

Nobody stepped forward and a hush fell over the entire saloon. "Awright, that's better. Now let's take first things first. Has anybody been to see the major up at the fort?"

Someone at the back of the room hollered over the heads of the others. "Screw the army! What'd they do after the raid at Adobe Walls? Went out and shot a bunch of Injun ponies, that's all."

"By God, he's right," a bearded skinner chimed in. "They didn't kill enough redsticks to fill a gnat's eye. Just herded 'em back to the reservation like they was a bunch of kids playing hooky. Fat lot of good that did us."

Jordan broke in before the crowd had a chance to get unruly. "You'll get no argument from me on that score. Most of you know there's not any love lost between me and the army. But we damn sure haven't got nothin' to lose by trying to get 'em to put a couple of troops of cavalry in the field. Hell, boys, who knows? They might accidentally back into some Injuns and *have* to fight!"

The men started laughing and cutting their eyes around at one another. *That Jordan was a real stemwinder, sure enough! The tin soldiers didn't have him fooled. Nosireebob! Not even a little bit.* Slowly they talked themselves into the idea and came around to wondering if maybe he didn't have a point after all.

They discussed it some more, wrangling back and forth about how it should be handled. Dirty Face Jones and Hi Bickerdyke almost came to blows, but cooler heads got them separated, and somebody finally called for a vote. Sol Rees shouted them down and made a motion of his own. Cimarron Jordan was the man to brace the army. It was his idea, and by damn, he was the one that ought to see how the bluebellies' stick floats! The crowd seconded that at the top of their lungs and the issue was decided. But no backing off, they thundered. With or without the army they intended to start hunting redskins come morning. Jordan crawled down off the bar and agreed to have a powwow with the brass.

When the plainsman walked out the door, everybody was telling everybody else how smart they were, and admitting to one another that ol' Cimarron was the trickiest sonofabitch in the whole lot.

Twenty minutes later, Jordan was escorted into the post commander's office by a burly Irishman with stripes the length of his sleeve. Major Cogswell was shuffling papers from one side of his desk to the other, doing his damnedest to look busy. When the door shut he glanced up with a chessycat smile, then went back to his paper sorting.

"A soldier's work is never done, Mr. Jordan. You buffalo-hunters are fortunate you don't have all this red tape to contend with. What brings you calling at such a late hour?"

Jordan stifled an impulse to say what he was really thinking. "Major, I don't suppose you've heard about the little Injun scare we had yesterday?"

"Why, yes, as a matter of fact. My patrols brought in a report just last night." The officer shook his head ruefully. "Terrible thing. Your people have my profound sympathy. Only wish there was something I could do to correct the matter."

Jordan blinked and a small frown puckered his brow. "You mean you're not going after the hostiles?"

Anthony Cogswell was one of those professional soldiers who were sort of frayed at the corners and spongy in the spine. He had served without distinction in the late war and was now marking time in fond anticipation of his retirement pension. Hopefully without any blemish to mar his spotless, if somewhat lackluster, record. The last thing he wanted right now was to mount a campaign against the Comanche and their heathen cohorts. Nobody won any prizes fighting Indians. Neither glory nor promotion. Custer had proved that on the Washita against the Cheyenne. Cogswell had thought it out with the utmost care; he was quite content to rest on his tattered laurels and retire a lowly major.

"Mr. Jordan, I regret to say, I am helpless. Naturally, I have apprised General Miles on the situation by telegraph. But until I receive orders directing me to take the field, I simply haven't the authority to go off chasing a few wayward Indians."

"Few and wayward don't hardly cut it," the plainsman glowered back at him. "Near as we can calculate, there's better'n a hundred hostiles on the loose. They've already killed close to thirty men and wounded another fifty. Now do you mean to tell me you're gonna sit on your duff and just do nothin'?"

"Sir, I repeat, I am powerless to act." Squaring his bony shoulders, Cogswell added lamely, "But, of course, the moment I receive orders, my men will be on their trail in full force."

"Well, major, that'll be a mortal comfort to the fellas that got scalped yesterday. Yessir, they'll rest easier knowin' the army's passin' the buck back and forth. Course, I guess it don't make a good goddamn that the Injuns'll be scattered to hell and gone before the army ever gets off its ass."

"Come now, Mr. Jordan. Don't lose your temper. The army works at its own pace, and it generally gets the job done. Perhaps not quickly enough to suit you or your friends, but that is no reason to get testy."

"Soldier boy, where I come from there's an old sayin': 'Don't get mad. Get even.'" Starting for the door, the plainsman turned back with a scowl. "Something else you can pass along to your general. Tell him that just sure as hell don't freeze over there'll be a whole passel of dead Injuns before the week's out. You can send your boys along to bury 'em."

"Mr. Jordan, I warn you. Don't attempt taking matters into your own—"

The door slammed shut with a force that almost tore it off its hinges. Anthony Cogswell sat watching it a moment, then let his breath out in a long sigh.

With any luck at all, the headquarters staff would debate his report for days before submitting a recommendation to the general. Perhaps by that time the Comanches and these filthy hunters would have killed one another off.

Which would solve his problem very neatly. Very neatly indeed.

Jordan stopped by the trading post on the way back for a talk with Hiram Greene. He found the storekeeper still skinny as a beanpole and frightened half out of his wits. When the plainsman came through the door Greene ran around the counter with a look of quaking relief spread over his features.

"Mr. Jordan! I've never been so glad to see anyone in my life. I heard you were in town, but believe you me, yesterday aged me ten years. When you hadn't shown up this morning I was sure the savages had gotten you."

"Well, you can rest easy, Hiram. I've still got my hair." He gave the store a quick once over, noting the full shelves and crowded aisles. "How's business?"

"Couldn't be better, Mr. Jordan. We've been moving

more and more merchandise every week." Suddenly his smile faded and his angular face creased with worry. "Up until yesterday, that is. I certainly hope the Indian scare doesn't affect our profits. I mean, everything had been doing so well till this happened."

Jordan had always been slightly amazed by what he thought of as the merchant mentality. Jason Rath was like that, too. More concerned with money than men. Profits over people every time. Close to thirty men dead and Greene was worried about business falling off. It beat the hell out of him what men like that ever got out of life. They were juiceless, like prunes. Probably spent their nights dreaming of neatly ruled ledgers filled with black ink. God forbid that it be red!

Still, he let it pass. Some folks just ticked different from others, and there was no changing them. "Hiram, that's why I came by, after a fashion. To talk to you about business. The way all these hunters are talkin', this raid might just scare some of 'em back into another line of work."

"Precisely my thought, Mr. Jordan." The worry lines on Greene's forehead deepened. "The hide men are our largest source of trade. If they were to ever depart the Sweetwater area, I'm afraid our concern would be in serious difficulty."

The plainsman liked the way Hiram Greene talked. Sort of scholarly and refined. Sometimes he even made good sense. "Hiram, you took the words right out of my mouth. Without the hide business we'd have ourselves a case of the cold sweats. That's why I thought I ought to let you know we're gonna form sort of a militia and go after the red boogers. Figured it would ease your mind some."

"We?" Greene had the sinking feeling he was somehow being included in the venture.

"Yeah. The hide men. We'll pull out first thing in the mornin' and start trackin' them down."

"Well now, that's splendid, Mr. Jordan. Really first rate. I'm sure that once you have settled the problem, business will go back to normal in no time."

"Thought you might see it that way." Jordan grinned and laid his arm around the storekeeper's shoulders as he started toward the door. "Hiram, in a little bit I'm gonna send over some fellas to give you a hand. I want you to lay out enough food to last fifty men pretty close to a week. Oh, and plenty of cartridges, too. We'll be needin' them when we catch up with them Injuns. Don't get stingy neither. Men need to eat good when they're headin' into a fight."

Greene halted, aghast at what he thought he had just heard. Behind the thick glasses his eyes blinked furiously. "Mr. Jordan, you can't be serious. Why that would cost a—a fortune! Believe me, Mr. Rath would never sanction such an expenditure, and I feel dutybound to protect his interests. Just as I do yours, of course. Frankly I don't see how we could possibly justify equipping this militia you speak of. Not gratis, at any rate."

The plainsman gave him a jaundiced look. "Let's you and me get something straight, Hiram. I wasn't askin' you, I was tellin' you. And you'd best do it just the way I said." Then he smiled and chucked the storekeeper lightly under the chin. " 'Cause if you don't, I'll come back over there and wring your scrawny neck."

Striding through the door, he called back over his shoulder. "Don't worry about Rath. If he bellyaches too loud, we'll take it out of my share of the kitty."

Hiram Greene stood there in a state of shock, appalled by the sudden turn of events. Slowly his hand crept up to his thin neck and his Adam's apple bobbed convulsively. In his mind's eye came an image of a chicken with its neck wrung, thrashing about on the ground, and a shiver went up his spine.

That great bushy-headed ape might just do it. And not to a chicken either.

When Jordan got back to the Bucket of Blood, things didn't seem quite the same somehow. While about half the hide men had already floated their eyeballs in rotgut, the rest stood around looking like a bunch of scalded owls. Plain to see, there had been some sort of rhubarb while he was gone, and not everybody was happy with the way things had worked out. McCabe caught him just as he came through the door and pulled him off to one side.

"Cimarron, the boys had a little set-to right after you left. Turns out some of 'em ain't so keen to go off chasin' Injuns as they let on. Fact of the matter is, there's a right smart of 'em got their peabrains set on headin' back to civilization. Said they figured they'd had enough buffalo huntin' to last them a spell."

Jordan's grin was so wide it was almost a laugh. "Lon, that's the best news I've had tonight. This country could

172

stand a little thinnin' out. Separate the men from the boys and there'll be more shaggies for them that's left."

Moving to the bar, he cleared an opening and vaulted onto the counter. "Awright, everybody. Let's gather round and get our heads together." When the crowd quieted down, he gave them a sardonic grin. "You boys called the shot. The army's got their thumb up their ass and they can't get it unplugged. Just to make sure he won't get himself in dutch, that major has even got his head up his ass."

This was met with a great roar of laughter, but when it slacked off, Sol Rees took the floor. "Cimarron, we didn't figure it would work, but we allowed it only fair that you have your chance. Now what do you aim to do?"

"Sol, I sort of thought I'd take a little sashay down south and see if I couldn't skin me some of that red meat you were talkin' about."

The men crowded around the bar broke out in lusty cheers, but those off against the back wall still looked like somebody had doused them with hot grease. Jordan waved his arms around till he got the commotion calmed down, then he pointed a thorny finger at the glum-faced bunch.

"How about you boys? You game for a little target practice?"

The hold-outs darted sheepish glances at one another, and for a moment nobody said anything. Then a man that looked to be the runt of the litter edged forward a couple of steps. "Mister, I don't know about these fellers, but I ain't lost no Injuns, so I don't reckon I'll go huntin' none."

The crowd at the bar hooted him down, but Jordan shouted them into silence. "Now boys, there's no need to get yourselves in a swivet. This here's a free country, and every man's got a right to call 'em as he sees 'em. The way I see it is pretty simple. Them that wants to go huntin' can march on over to the tradin' post and get themselves outfitted with food and cannon fodder. On the house! I like the idea of fightin' Comanches so much I'm gonna finance this deal out of my own pocket. Anybody needs a better reason than that, let's call it a last testament to old Monte Brown."

That called for another round of drinks. Most every man in the saloon could have paid his own freight, but they agreed it was damned sporting of Jordan to foot the bill. Some of the more cynical allowed that his generous nature might not be all that charitable. What with his having the most to gain by keeping Sweetwater City afloat. But they didn't say it very loud.

After a while talk got started about the need to organize this expedition, and before long they had worked themselves around to voting on leaders. Deacon Jim Harvey grabbed the floor and proposed Cimarron Jordan as captain. The plainsman tried to protest—hollering that he would rather fight than lead—but the motion carried unanimously and they wouldn't take no for an answer. Next they picked Limpy Joe Freed as lieutenant and the Cherokee breed, Lou Keyes, as chief scout. Then someone shouted for a speech and the crowd immediately went into a clamoring chant, demanding that Jordan say a few words to the troops.

He took their ribbing with a big grin and waited till the horseplay died down. "Boys, I haven't got a hell of a lot to say. You picked me and that's the way she'll be. But don't anybody start bitchin' when I go to bustin' heads if you don't take orders. I might not be much of a soldier, but I'm purely hell on givin' orders."

They all laughed about that, not quite sure whether he was funning them or not. Quicker than anyone expected, they got their answer.

"Just so's you won't think I'm pullin' your leg, here's my first order. Only fifty of you are going on this little jaunt." The catcalls came hard and fast, but he waved them down. "That's all we need and that's all we're takin'. Any more'n that and we'd be stumblin' over each other. We'll draw lots to see who the lucky ones are, and the rest'll stay here to guard the whiskey barrels. Way I see it, that sort of divvies out even all the way round. Time we get back half of you will have sore butts and the other half'll have sore heads."

Everybody started chuckling over that, and even the grumpy ones had to admit that Jordan might pan out to be a good captain. He had a way of giving orders that wasn't all that bad. Sort of slipping it in sideways so that a fellow didn't find it all that hard to swallow. Whether a man went or stayed, this deal looked to be more fun than a barrel of snakes.

Jordan had one final order for the night. "Boys, you can drink till the well runs dry if you want. Makes no nevermind to me. But we're pullin' out at first light, and them that can't ride gets left behind."

With that he leaped from the bar and poured himself a

drink. After the second one he grew reflective and started chuckling to himself.

Hell, there wasn't nothing to this leader business. All a fellow had to do was shout louder than anybody else.

Course, when the shooting commenced he'd damn sure better have some tricks up his sleeve.

Or else grow eyes in the back of his head.

3.

The Comanches came first to Yellow House Canyon. They had ridden throughout the night and all the next day, pausing only to eat and rest a few hours before dawn. Their women and children had joined them the second day on an isolated creek above the River of Running Water. The pony herd was intact and growing sleek on spring grasses, and the older boys were filled with pride that they had lost not so much as a single colt on the long journey. It had been a reunion of great joy and much laughing. They had escaped the *taibos* hated reservation, captured many fine horses, and from their scalp sticks hung the gory trophies of their victory over the killers of buffalo.

Tai-me had smiled on them, and their hearts were filled with gladness as they rode southward toward the sacred land. *Llano Estacado.*

The Staked Plains was a land that only a red man could view with reverence. High on a wind swept plateau, it stretched farther than the eye could see in every direction, farther than a man could ride in many sleeps with even the finest pony. It was a desolate land, parched by constant hot winds and barren of growth, beautiful only to those who could match its harshness with a spartan tolerance of their own. Yet for a man who knew its ways and respected its awesome malevolence *Llano Estacado* was a land of warm days and cool nights, sparkling water and full bellies. A sanctuary where his enemies dared not venture. The holy place where he could live in peace with the sweet smell of the earth all to himself.

For the Comanches it was more than the sacred land. It was home.

Little Bull's band came through the steep ravine leading to Yellow House Canyon some two hours after the sun had passed overhead. There was a great outpouring of

175

happiness as they entered the canyon itself and saw again the inviting solitude that had been much on their minds these past days. Before them was a slight knoll, and beyond that stretched a vast meadowland not unlike a shimmering emerald sea. *Casa Amarilla*, an icy, spring-fed stream, flowed gently the length of the canyon near the south wall, and its banks were lined with shady cottonwoods which rustled softly in the breeze. Here a man had everything he could ask of life. Buffalo on the high tableland to fill his belly and provide him with warm robes. Grass and water for his ponies, so that they might grow strong and fleet for the hunt. Shelter from storms that ravaged the plateau above, and escape from the brutal plains winds that left a man scorched and his tongue thick with thirst. Trees in a treeless land where he could raise his lodge and watch his giggling *paraibvos* grow fat and his sons grow tall. The bountiful refuge where the True People would never know want or hunger throughout all their days.

Tai-me had indeed been generous.

Yet there was more to the canyon than mere shelter and shady trees and full bellies. Little Bull also saw it through the eyes of a warrior, and what he beheld was a remote fastness which shielded his people from the hand of those who would do them harm.

Yellow House Canyon was situated below the headwaters of the Double Mountain Fork of the Brazos, a hard day's ride south and west of Palo Duro Canyon. There, two snows past in the Middle of the Summer Moon, Three Finger Mackenzie and his pony soldiers had taken them by surprise. Slaughtered their horse herds, put them to flight, driven them like whipped dogs back to the accursed reservation. But such a thing could not happen here. There was an entrance into the canyon and several smaller passages out, each of which could be defended by a mere handful of warriors when attack came.

That it would one day become necessary to defend this place, Little Bull never doubted for a moment. The white-eyed soldier chiefs would not allow the Sweetwater raid to go unavenged. When the Comanche and their allies began raiding along the Brazos, the *taibos'* outrage would mount even higher. Pursuit would come, of that he was sure. Columns of bluecoats would ride out from the many forts built on land stolen from the True People and they would find nothing, for even their *Kia-hi-piago* scouts, the flesh-eater Tonkawas, were miserable trackers. But sooner or later, their Bearded God would smile on them and they would stumble upon the secret of how the Comanche vanished so easily.

It was always so. If not one day, then perhaps another. For it was a certainty which any *To-yop-ke* must harden himself to accept. The gods were capricious, almost as if they decided the fate of a people on a cast of the bones. They caused the winds of war to blow first this way and then that; a leader could do little except attack when he was favored and flee when he was not.

So it had always been, and so it would remain. One day the *eks-a-panas* would come with their sabers rattling, the steel hooves of their fat horses throwing sparks from the rocks, and they would find this place. But they would leave wishing they were blind pups who had not the sight to trail Comanches. For to enter this canyon uninvited was to enter the house of death.

Little Bull had chosen Yellow House Canyon as his final refuge for that reason alone. He would run no more, neither from the caprice of *Tai-me* nor from the guns of the pony soldiers. Here he would die, fighting as a *ko-eet-senko* was meant to die, and when he went under he would take with him every bluecoat within reach.

Shortly before sundown, the Cheyenne entered the canyon, and as dusk spread over the grassy meadow, the Kiowa arrived. The Comanche *To-yop-ke* resented even their presence in his stronghold, but he needed the warriors of Stone Calf and Lone Wolf. Too many Comanches had taken the white man's road, setting aside the old ways, and he had been unable to raise a force of sufficient strength among his own people. The five bands comprising the Comanche tribe, once united in their war on the whites, were now humbled and broken. They were warriors no longer—like toothless old men they had resigned themselves to a life on the *taibo* reservation—and the mere thought of it made him want to vomit.

They had called him renegade and crazyman—a *pawsa* who would break the peace and bring the wrath of the Great White Father down on their heads. Yet one day, when he had crossed over in that last fight, they would honor him and paint word pictures on the skins to record his deeds.

Among all the chiefs, they would recall, it was he alone

who had kept his warrior vows and cursed the whites with his final breath.

But tomorrow had not yet come; it was today he must reckon with for the moment. Allies were needed if he was to rid the plains of buffalo killers, and for that reason alone he had left warriors to guide the Cheyenne and Kiowa to his canyon. When others heard of his fight perhaps they, too, would come to join him. Should he live long enough there might come a day when he could command a force of sufficient strength to drive even the pony soldiers from the sacred lands.

There was much left to do before that day arrived, though. Tonight, when they celebrated their victory, he would speak of such things and prepare the way.

When the Cheyennes and Kiowas had raised their lodges along the creek bank, Little Bull sent a herald through the village announcing a feast and victory dance to be held that night. Comanche braves had killed many fat buffalo cows and there was to be fresh meat for all, with slices of raw liver as tribute for each warrior. There would be speeches and recounting of brave deeds in battle; the people should empty their stomachs in preparation for the feast. It would be a long night, for they had much to celebrate. The first of many victories over the killers of buffalo!

After a huge fire had been lighted in the center of the meeting ground, the people began to gather. The warriors came painted as if for battle and proudly drove their lances into the ground so that all might see the dangling scalps they had taken below the Sweetwater. Those who had not been so fortunate brought along older trophies, crusted with age and losing the hair in spots, but grizzly symbols nonetheless of their prowess in battle. The women wore their finest gowns, decorated with shiny beads and porcupine quills, and the children stared on, round-eyed with awe at the pageant unfolding before them. Hump meat and ribs and large mounds of viscera were spread out, and the canyon rang with the laughter of the True People as they waited for their host to signal the beginning of the feast.

Once all was in readiness, Little Bull stepped from his lodge and strode to the fire with the stiff hauteur befitting a Comanche *To-yop-ke*. Folding his arms across his chest, he waited until the people had fallen silent. Then he spoke, in a clear strong voice that echoed across the breadth of the canyon.

178

"When we rode out from the Washita we were of one mind, united in the path we would follow. We turned our backs on the white man's road for all time. This we did with full knowledge that our ranks were few, and that before snow flies we will certainly face the pony soldiers in battle. They will pursue us. None here doubt that now, just as none doubted it even before we left the Washita. They must drive us back to the *taibo*'s reservation, for if they fail in that, others among the True People will follow us here. Just as surely as spring grass follows warm rain. Yet there is a thing I would say to you. Among the ancient ones it is taught that while a fool can catch a bear, only a wise man has the sense to let go. When the *eks-a-panas* come to this place with their long knives and big guns they will have caught themselves a bear. But on that day it is the bear who will not let go."

This brought smiles and grunts of approval from the throng of warriors. That was a good thing to think on, the pony soldiers caught in a trap of their own making. When the ripple of laughter subsided Little Bull went on.

"There are those in the days ahead who will say that each of us here is a *pawsa*. They will nod wisely and agree among themselves that only crazy men would take a path which must certainly lead to death." Pausing, he touched his tongue with his forefinger, then thrust his hand into the air with two fingers forked erect. "Yet it is they who speak false words. For they are the ones who will follow a road more bitter than death itself. A road of shame and dishonor. The white man's road."

With that he stepped forward and pulled from the earth a lance festooned with scalps, holding it aloft for all to see. "There is the honor for men who would call themselves *ko-eet-senko*. The hair of buffalo killers! Enemies of the True People we are sworn to destroy. Each time we ride from this place there will be fewer such men, and there will come a time when across our hunting grounds they will be no more. One day, not too far distant, all among the True People will turn and point to this place, and they will say 'there live the men who have honored their fathers and their fathers' fathers before them. *There live the warriors!*' "

Shaking the scalps overhead in a gory thrash of hair, he uttered the ancient war cry. *"Ah-ko!"*

The canyon trembled as the warriors responded with a mighty chant. *"Ah-ko! Ah-ko! Ah-ko!"* Bodies glistening in the light of the flames, they surged forward and began a mad, writhing dance around the fire. Wolves high on the mesa above slunk away at the sound of their savage howls, and the steady throb of drums filled the canyon with the beat of their victorious war-cries. Eerie contorted shadows played across the sheer walls of their fortress meadow, and the very earth seemed to quake beneath the force of their pounding feet. They were *ko-et-senkos!* Fiercest of all warriors! *Ai-ee-ee! Ahhhhhh-ko!*

The Comanche *To-yop-ke* walked from the fire and stood for a moment before the place reserved for chiefs. Then, as though it had been ordained long ago, he took a seat between Lone Wolf and Stone Calf.

The place of honor.

None of them so much as blinked, and not a word was said. Though each was an *on-de* in his own right, they knew that the order of things had changed. The Comanche had asserted his will, and never again would it be the same so long as they rode the same path.

Little Bull kept his eyes fastened on the warriors, holding his great laughter inside. Hidden from the two stone-faced owls who flanked him.

The Kiowa on his right and the Cheyenne on his left. Just as it should be.

Exactly as he intended it all along.

4.

It took them three days of hard riding to find the Indian camp. Their breed scout had found the trail easily enough, for on the open prairie it was difficult to hide the tracks of many ponies. But from that point on, their march became a grueling test of endurance for man and animal alike.

Jordan had elected to follow the Comanches, since from all reports their band seemed to be the largest of the three raiding parties. The trail led west and south, toward the Staked Plains. Some miles below the Prairie Dog Fork, Lou Keyes halted at a jumble of tracks where the Comanches had regrouped forces, and the hunters were startled to find themselves trailing nearly a hundred hostiles. Lumped together with the Cheyenne and Kiowa parties that meant they were on the track of better than two hundred warriors. While nothing was said about turning back, the men rode in grim silence afterwards. They were in for a stiffer fight than anyone had expected, and the hunt no longer seemed the lark it had appeared upon leaving Sweetwater.

Quickly it became apparent that the Comanche had anticipated pursuit of some kind. The war party had followed the tracks of a buffalo herd for some miles in an effort to disguise their own trail. When the hoofprints of the ponies finally broke clear and again angled off to the southwest the hunters got another surprise. Travois marks in the dusty soil indicated that the warriors had been joined by women and children. This was no band of hostiles down out of the Nations on a lightning raid. It was a well-organized, carefully planned flight from the reservations. Hatched by some cunning and farsighted booger who had decided to declare war on the buffalo-hunters.

The deal got dicier by the moment, and some of the men began to wonder aloud if they hadn't bitten off more than they could chew.

The second day out they came to the escarpment that guarded the high tableland of the Staked Plains. The single wagon they had brought along to haul supplies had to be triple-teamed up the steep, winding trail, with a half-dozen grunting men shoving from the rear. When they emerged on the plateau above, it was flatter than even the sweeping prairies of Kansas. A land of sun and solitude, far horizons stretching endlessly to nowhere, covered with a thick mat of curly mesquite grass. Hardly a tree or bush was to be seen in the vast emptiness of *Llano Estacado*, yet the eastern rim of the high plateau was broken by a latticework of wooded canyons. From a distance these rocky gorges were all but invisible to the eye, and a man could sometimes find himself standing at the edge of a sheer precipice where only moments before there had been nothing but miles of solitary space.

The Comanche trail ran straight as a string toward the far canyons. Only now it had converged with the tracks of the Cheyenne and Kiowas, and the breed scout estimated the village would number better than a hundred lodges—close to five hundred Indians.

The Sweetwater men should have turned back right there. They were in over their heads and everyone knew it. But not a man among them had the stomach for facing the derisive jeers awaiting them if they returned with their tails between their legs. Jordan put it to a vote, stating flat

181

out that there was no shame in backing off when the odds went sky high against a man.

Recklessly perhaps, but with a grit that marked them as a breed apart, they voted to go on.

Toward sundown on the third day, Lou Keyes came racing back to the column with a wide grin plastered across his face. Ahead, not more than three miles away, was a deep canyon. The Indian encampment was beside a stream on the canyon floor.

Jordan quickly dismounted the men and told them to see to their equipment. With Limpy Joe Freed and the scout, he then rode off to have a look at the enemy stronghold.

Which was exactly what it turned out to be.

Leaving their horses tied to a stunted bush some distance back, the three men crawled on their bellies to the rim of the canyon. When Jordan saw it, he grunted with a mixture of disgust and admiration.

The foxy bastard who rode at the head of those heathens knew his business. He had chosen a spot that wasn't exactly impregnable to attack, but it would damn sure discourage anybody who wasn't willing to get his nose bloodied in the effort.

The main part of the canyon looked to be about a half mile across and perhaps two miles in length. The Indian lodges had been thrown up along a shallow stream which meandered through the broad gorge. Groves of cottonwood trees were spotted along the stream, and the entire canyon floor appeared to be a lush grassland. Twisty curls of blue smoke arose from cooking fires in the dusky light, and there was considerable activity around the lodges.

Studying it, Jordan saw that Keyes's estimate had been right on the button. There were well over a hundred lodges down below, which meant better than two hundred warriors and at least that many women and children. Glancing off toward the far end of the canyon, he saw a pony herd numbering upwards of five hundred head—two or three horses for every warrior—and this again confirmed the odds they would face when it came to a showdown.

But it wasn't the warriors that had him bothered right at the moment. It was the canyon itself.

While there appeared to be several smaller corridors leading out at the far end, the main entrance was a narrow ravine barely fifty yards in width. This rocky defile sloped downward at a sharp pitch from the plateau above and afforded about as much concealment as a plucked chicken. Since the walls of the canyon were sheer drop-offs, the only practical means of attack was through th cramped ravine. Sentries were more than likely posted at the mouth of the ravine where it fed into the canyon, and it didn't require much imagination to see what would happen if the warning was ever sounded. Ten well-armed warriors at the mouth of the ravine could hold off an army, and any force that let itself get trapped in there would be picked off like sitting ducks. Attacking from the far end appeared even riskier. The corridors there were just wide enough for a horse, and one rifleman at each hole would have the same affect as popping a cork in a bottle.

Whoever led this pack of savages was one fine general. He had himself a regular little fortress, and trying to enter it was sort of like sticking your head in a mousetrap.

Limpy Joe Freed clucked his tongue and darted a glance at the plainsman. "What d'ya think, Cimarron?"

Jordan snorted. "I think anybody that tries to go in there is soft in the head."

"Them's my feelin's exactly," Limpy Joe said. " 'Ceptin', I got a hunch the boys won't buy it. Seein' as they rode all this way, they're liable to get hardnosed if we try to back off now."

"Yeah," Jordan noted sourly, "that's about the size of it awright."

Limpy Joe gave him a sideways look. "You gonna pull out? Don't rightly see how anybody'd blame you."

Jordan didn't say anything for quite awhile, and the other men could tell he was wrestling with a tough decision. Then he chuckled softly. "Hell, you only live once, I guess. The boys elected me, and I reckon I'll take 'em down there if that's what they want."

"Thought so." Limpy Joe grinned, as though it was the answer he expected all along. "Got any idea how you're gonna do it?"

"Well, you know, I've been studyin' on that while we was talkin'." The plainsman shifted to get a better look at the ravine below them. "Seems to me the only way to come out of this with our hair is to borrow a trick from the Injuns. Sort of give 'em a taste of their own medicine."

Limpy Joe's eyes scrunched up quizzically. "I ain't right sure I follow that."

"What I'm sayin' is, hit 'em fast and hard. Then get the hell out. Same way they do when they raid us."

"Yeah, that oughter work. Course, the boys won't like it much. I mean, they'll probably figure the thing to do is go in there and stay 'til we got the redsticks wiped out."

"Joe, only a goddamn fool raises when he's lookin' at a pat hand. You've been around long enough to know that. I'll take 'em in there and anybody that wants to stay can. I'm comin' back out. Pronto."

When Limpy Joe just nodded, Jordan looked over at the breed scout. "How about it, Lou? Sound like it'll work?"

"Go in fast. Come out the same way," the breed observed. "Then ride like a sonovabitch. Anybody stays, he gonna stay long time."

"Damned if that ain't a fact," Jordan chortled. "Next thing he'd likely hear is old Gabe tootin' the bugle. C'mon, let's get on back and break the bad news to the boys."

The meeting back at the wagon was sort of short and bittersweet. The men didn't care much for Jordan's plan, but since it was the only way he agreed to lead them they finally gave in. Once that was settled, he laid it out for them fast and simple. Lou Keyes and Al Waite would enter the ravine an hour before first light and take care of any sentries. The rest of them would follow along and come charging out of the ravine the minute there was enough light to shoot by. Joe Freed would take half the men along the south side of the creek and Jordan himself would take the other half down the north bank. One sweep down the canyon and one sweep back. If they could manage it they would stampede the pony herd ahead of them on the sweep back. Then they got the hell out. Any man that chose to hang around was on his own hook.

The plainsman next advised them to eat something and get some sleep. It might be a spell before they saw much of either again. When the men started to drift off he called them back with an afterthought. Whoever was caught shooting women and children would answer to him personal. And they wouldn't like the way he asked questions.

The truth was, they didn't like the way he was handling the whole deal. Spoiling their fun after they had busted their tails riding halfway to hell. Besides, he was starting to talk like a regular little general, the way he spouted orders right and left.

But they kept their grumbling to themselves. Leastways, till they got out of earshot.

Little Bull was restive that night. Uneasy in a way he couldn't quite put into words. Not that he would have spoken of it to anyone even if the words came. The *To-yop-ke* of the Comanche kept his own counsel. It was better that way. Warriors respected a man who spoke little and thought much. So long as he led them boldly and kept their scalp sticks weighted with fresh hair.

Perhaps that was the thing bothering him. Earlier he had heard a wolf howl. That in itself was nothing; the sacred plains were alive with wolves trailing the buffalo herds. But this wolf had given the sign. Four mournful howls one after the other. Then repeated the second time without pause. Four was the Comanches' magic number, as even a *pawsa* knew, and a good sign under certain circumstances. Yet it could be a bad sign. Particularly from a wolf in the sequence he had heard tonight. The meaning was well known, a truth handed down by the ancients. The wolf's call was a warning that a warrior's medicine had turned bad. Disaster impended. Something no reasonable man would ignore or dare to test. Certainly a sign that the *To-yop-ke*, who carried the lives of all in the palm of his hand, could not fail to heed.

Before the Bud Moon ended he had planned to resume the raids. Since their great success against the killers of buffalo below the Sweetwater he had a strong hold over Lone Wolf and Spotted Calf. It had been his plan and his cunning and his foresight which had brought them so many scalps with such ease. Those things again would be the telling factor in the raids to come. The Cheyenne and Kiowa *on-des* were painfully aware of that truth now— they believed his medicine to be very strong. But that had been before the wolf sign. Others had heard it—knew its significance as well as he—and it was reasonable to believe that they would begin to wonder. Even grow suspect. For if his medicine lacked power, and he led them into battle, they would each carry their lives on their fingernails.

Perhaps it would be better to postpone the raids. Make offerings. Restore his medicine as favorable signs revealed themselves. Then in the Moon of Red Cherries they would strike the buffalo killers along the Brazos. How he wished Sky Walker were here. If only the owl could speak—making known the wisdom of the Dead Ones—then he would know exactly what must be done.

But Sky Walker was not here. Nor the owl. Only the wolf and his evil howl.

185

Turning in his robes, Little Bull moved closer to the soft warmth of his *paraibvo* and clasped her breast in his hand. Obediently she rolled around, offering herself to his will, and for a moment he no longer thought of the wolf.

The first streaks of false dawn were lighting the sky when shots sounded from the mouth of the ravine.

Jordan caught a sharp intake of breath from the men behind him, and no one needed to ask what it meant. Keyes and Waite had missed one sentry, perhaps more, and the shots were certain to arouse the encampment. The element of surprise had been a decisive factor in his planning, and the plainsman cursed the breed and his partner for their sloppy handling of a vital task.

Still, there was no use crying over spilt milk. They had come here to fight, and with or without the advantage of surprise, they were too far out on the limb to turn back now.

Turning in the saddle, he shouted back up the ravine. "Boys, the cat's out of the bag! Follow my lead and give 'em hell!"

With that, he put the big roan into a gallop and tore off at breakneck speed down the rocky path. Behind him the hoofbeats of nearly fifty horses reverberated off the gorge walls like the clatterwheels of hell, and he could hear Squirrel Eye Smith shrieking a hoarse Rebel yell. Then the column rounded a slight bend, and he could see the mouth of the ravine a few hundred yards ahead. Drawing nearer, he could make out the bodies of Waite and an Indian lying off to one side of the trail. Lou Keyes was hunkered down behind some rocks on the opposite side popping away with his six-gun. From the way dust and rock chips were flying all around him somebody was returning considerably more lead than he was throwing.

Just for an instant Jordan debated halting right there. Common sense told him that to go beyond that point was lunacy, sheer madness in the face of what he saw before him. Then the urge to fight—the old bloodlust—exerted its grip on him, and he slammed his heels into the gelding's ribs. He had never won yet by holding back, and now didn't seem the time to start.

When they roared out of the ravine into the canyon, he knew immediately that he had made the biggest mistake of his life.

Perhaps the last.

Directly to the front some two hundred yards away was a low rise, commanding a perfect field of fire into the mouth of the ravine. Dozens of warriors were flopped down on their bellies atop the knoll, and scores of reinforcements were scurrying from their lodges along the creek. Though he could see smoke from the Indians' rifles, the rattle of gunfire seemed somehow faint and vaguely distant. But suddenly he became aware of lead whistling around his ears like angry hornets, and mixed with it were the screams of the dead and the dying behind him. Ahead lay certain death, and there was no mistaking it now. The heathens held the high ground, with more guns coming into action every moment, and he saw all too clearly that the charge had been doomed before it ever started.

Whirling the gelding, he leaned low in the saddle and pounded back the way he had come. Behind him the ragged line of horsemen had already broken and was fleeing in disorder toward the ravine. As the roan stretched out in a dead lope, he saw the bodies of downed men. A half-dozen, perhaps more. Joe Jackson. Lee Grimes. Billy Devins. Some whose faces he couldn't make out as they flashed by. Then, as if by a miracle that surpassed understanding, he was in the ravine and safe again.

Shouting over the din of gunfire, he called off men to act as horse-handlers, and drove the rest by threat and brute force back into the rocks at the head of the gorge. Retreat was impossible and escape was out of the question until they somehow eliminated the threat to their rear. Dismounting, he flung himself down behind a rock and began slinging lead at the distant hilltop. Within moments he became aware that the buffalo men had gotten their second wind. They were firing steadily, picking their shots with care, raking the little knoll with a deadly barrage.

For the first time since he came thundering out of the ravine like a madman, he had a feeling they might just leave this gorge with their hair attached.

The firing grew more sporadic over the next hour, and by full sunrise it had turned into a long-range sniping contest. The buffalo men had no equal at that game, though. Their Sharps had the Indians outgunned, and before long the warriors were showing hardly more than a rifle barrel when they got off a shot. Toward mid-morning, Jordan sensed that something was brewing over behind the hill. The hostiles' fire had slacked off to nothing, and he knew damn well they weren't giving up the ghost that easily.

Then, with startling swiftness, fifty mounted braves came tearing around the left side of the knoll, and the gut-eaters on top again started peppering the ravine with lead. But there was something phony about the deal. There weren't more than a handful of Indians firing from the high ground. Which left a hell of a lot of heathens unaccounted for!

"Hold your fire, boys!" Jordan bellowed. "It's a trick."

The words were hardly out of his mouth when close to a hundred warriors erupted from a defile which ran the length of the canyon along the north wall. While they were advancing on foot, they were only a long stone's throw from the mouth of the ravine when they suddenly materialized out of the earth. The mounted braves hung back, covering them with diversionary fire as they charged toward the hunters. Jordan's warning had come just in the nick of time, and now the buffalo men turned their guns on the howling pack racing across the open space. When they cut loose, Indians were knocked sprawling in every direction, and before most of the hunters had time to get off two or three shots the charge had been broken. The warriors turned tail and dived back into their hole, and the mounted party disappeared just as quickly around the side of the hill.

After that everything stayed quiet for a while, and then the sniping contest broke out with much the same result as earlier. The day passed with interminable slowness, hot and gritty, without a breath of air stirring in the ravine. Sometimes an entire hour would pass without a shot being fired, then with no apparent reason a storm of lead would come sailing across from the hilltop. Afterwards would come another lull, and more waiting. Late that afternoon, as the sun cast lengthening shadows over the canyon walls, Jordan got a sneaky hunch that something was afoot in the Indian encampment. Crawling to the forward edge of the rocky gorge, he took a quick peek around the corner. Then he took a longer look, and for the first time since sunrise the little ball of fire in the pit of his gut faded away.

The cottonwood groves along the creek were empty. The hostiles had struck their lodges and hauled freight.

When Lou Keyes returned from a scout an hour later, it became official. From the tracks in the canyon it seemed apparent that the Indians had spent the afternoon moving the women and children, and finally the horse herd, through the narrow corridors along the east wall. The sniping and occasional burst of sustained fire from the hills were meant solely to keep the buffalo men pinned down until the escape could be made good.

Yellow House Canyon was empty.

Later that night, after the hunters had retreated from the ravine and pulled back onto the high plateau, Jordan stretched out on his blanket, and gazed up at the starry sky. His mind was a spinning top, full of gunfire and screams and the stench of death. Almost as if his head was gorged with the sights and sounds and smells of men doing their damnedest to kill one another.

But to what purpose? Buffalo? Land? Because one was white and the other red? Somehow, after what he had seen today, none of those seemed reason enough at all.

Then his thoughts drifted back to the canyon as it had been when the hunters pulled out about sundown. Empty and still. Lifeless. As though nothing had ever walked there, and never would.

The idea somehow stopped his mind from whirling, and he slowly drifted into an uneasy sleep. But just before his eyes closed, a wry little smile touched the corners of his mouth.

Folks down around the Pecos had a name for it. A Mexican standoff.

Chalk up one for the gut-eaters.

5.

The Sweetwater Militia made a sorry spectacle when it rode into town. They were haggard, covered with grime, and sour-tempered as a herd of turpentined bears. Many of them had wounds bound up with bloody rags, and behind on the high plains they had left eight of their number buried in shallow graves. Not a man among them had anything to brag about.

While they had killed some Indians, and driven the gut-eaters from their encampment, it was victory by default. The Comanche and their allies had quit the fight not because they were beaten, but only out of concern for the safety of their women and children. The whole sorry mess had about it the taste of ashes, and the hunters would have preferred to let it drop right there.

189

Jordan was perhaps the most shame-faced of the lot. They had elected him captain, and in his own mind he had failed them miserably. Though none of the men faulted him—for he had warned them that the canyon was a deathtrap—he was thoroughly disgusted with himself. Looking back, he knew that he could have stopped them if he had really tried—made them turn about the night before the attack and get the hell out of there. But he had been spoiling for a scrap—allowed it to cloud his judgement—given in to the ungovernable force that drove him to fight for the sheer joy of fighting itself.

Because of it eight men had died.

The fact that the others found no fault with his conduct meant little. He knew what he had done—and failed to do—and the knowledge left him embittered with his own sorry performance.

Jordan left the men as they dismounted in front of the saloons, and rode on up to the fort. Though he was in no way obligated to keep the military informed, he somehow felt bound to make a report. An atonement perhaps for the arrogant manner he had taken with the post commander a week back.

Riding into the compound, it occurred to him that only seven days had passed since he was last here. Somehow it seemed the better part of a lifetime.

When he was ushered into the office, Cogswell was still shuffling papers. Looking up, the officer's face was reserved and stiffly formal. "Well, Mr. Jordan, I see you have returned. From your expression I take it the Indians gave you the slip."

"No, we found 'em well enough," Jordan replied. "Down south of the Double Mountain Fork of the Brazos."

Cogswell stopped shuffling papers. "Really? Well out with it man. What happened?"

The plainsman met Cogswell's eyes, but the words came hard. "We got about twenty of them and they got eight of us. Sort of a draw, I guess you'd call it."

"Your brevity is commendable, Mr. Jordan, but hardly appropriate. I need details. This information could be of great value to the army. Now, sir. Exactly where did you find them and how many were there? Which tribes?"

Halting at first, Jordan began to relate the particulars of their expedition onto the Staked Plains. Then, as he warmed to the task, he felt a growing indifference to

Cogswell's opinion of the outcome. Hell, the Indians had been running circles around the army for years, and so far as he could see, the bluecoats weren't the least bit embarrassed about it. When he came to the fight itself he carefully described the canyon, noting that they had been opposed by Comanche, Kiowa, and Cheyenne. Next he outlined the Indian's unexpected withdrawal and the grueling journey back to Sweetwater.

When he finished, Cogswell came out of his chair and moved to a large map hung on the wall. "Mr. Jordan, if you would be so kind. Please locate the hostiles' exact position on this map."

Jordan came around the desk and stood looking at the map for a moment. Across the western reaches of Texas there was a wide blank spot marked *Llano Estacado*. While the headwaters of various rivers were indicated, the topography of the land and the string of canyons along the eastern rim were noticeably absent. As a map, it was a joke. There were a hundred buffalo men who could have done better with a pencil and a piece of butcher's paper.

"Major, it appears the army don't know a hell of a lot about the Staked Plains. There's not much I can show you on a blank map."

Cogswell arched one eyebrow and sort of looked down his nose. "For your information, Mr. Jordan, hardly anyone except Indians and a few like yourself know anything about that area. Now do the best you can. You mentioned something about the Double Mountain Fork of the Brazos."

The plainsman nodded and studied the map a bit more closely. "Well it's sort of like spittin' at the sky, but I'd say that canyon was right about here." He stabbed at a spot on the map with his finger. "Looks to be maybe fifty miles due southeast of the headwaters. That's not gonna help you much, though. There's so many canyons in there, it'd be like huntin' for a needle in a haystack. Besides, the gut-eaters have done vamoosed." He waved his hand across the broad region encompassing the Staked Plains. "They could be anywhere in there. If I was you, major, I wouldn't go down there without a damn good scout. Water's sort of scarce out that way, and the Comanche are just tricky enough to lead you straight into a furnace."

"Oh I have no intention of going after them." The officer returned to his chair and favored Jordan with a patronizing smile. "It may interest you to know that a troop of the Tenth Cavalry left Fort Griffin yesterday. Headed in exactly the direction you indicated. You see, Mr. Jordan, the army is not wholly unschooled in such matters. Naturally, I will forward your report on to Fort Griffin, but I dare say the Indians will get their comeuppance very shortly. Very shortly indeed."

"Well I hope you have better luck than we did," Jordan commented. "The boys'll be glad to hear the army's on the job, anyway."

Cogswell's eyes narrowed, and a tiny smirk appeared at the corners of his mouth. "Mr. Jordan, I believe you are operating under a misapprehension. The army hasn't taken the field because of the raid made on you and your friends."

Jordan's chin came up and his mouth set in a hard line. "No? What for then?"

The soldier's smirk widened into a smug grin. "Why, because the hostiles left their reservation. What else?"

"How about better 'n thirty white men being killed? Wouldn't you say that's a pretty fair reason, major?"

"Buffalo-hunters? Oh, I hardly think so, Mr. Jordan. You seem to forget the Treaty of Medicine Lodge. According to the most common interpretation, that treaty explicity forbids white men to hunt below the Arkansas. That would seem to include the Sweetwater country as well, wouldn't it?"

"Then why do you let us hunt? If the army's so allfired concerned with treaties, how come they haven't run us off?"

"Well now, I should think that would be obvious. General Sheridan has certainly made no secret of the fact that he considers elimination of the buffalo herds the first step toward pacifying the Indians. After all, without buffalo to sustain them, their roaming days are over. They will have no choice but to stay on their reservations."

Jordan grunted sharply. "So you're willin' to let us do your dirty work, but you're not willin' to protect us while we're at it."

"Mr. Jordan, I'm afraid you overlook the salient issue." Cogswell shook his head with a condescending air. "The army could hardly place itself in the position of aiding those who are flagrantly violating a treaty made by the United States government. General Sheridan's statements notwithstanding, it would be very impolitic of the army to openly sanction such a move. Does a ray of light begin to seep through?"

The plainsman's jaws clenched so tight his lips barely moved. "Cogswell, so far as I can tell, about the only difference between the army and a bucket of horseshit is the bucket. Matter of fact, the horseshit might smell a little better."

Spinning on his heel, he stormed out of the office, slamming the door so hard this time, the top hinge busted loose. Anthony Cogswell congratulated himself on his extraordinary repartee and went back to shuffling papers.

Dusk was settling over Sweetwater when Jordan hitched the gelding outside the trading post and went inside. He wanted a drink so bad his teeth hurt, but he figured Hiram Greene might go into a foaming tissy if he didn't put in an appearance fairly quickly. Besides, once he got started drinking he wasn't going to have time for Greene or anyone else. It was going to be a stormy night, and anybody that looked at him crosswise might wind up wearing store-bought choppers come morning.

When he came through the door there were a half-dozen hide men crowded around the counter, and Greene was writing furiously as they called off their orders.

Sol Rees, who was standing toward the back, spotted him and came forward. "Say Cimarron, Lon McCabe was in here a while back lookin' for you. Acted sorta fidgety, like somethin' was troublin' him."

"He didn't say what he wanted?" Jordan asked.

"Nope, just danced around like he had ants in his pants and went sailin' out. Said he'd been huntin' you all over town."

"Well, I'll catch up with him later most likely." Looking over Rees's shoulder, he jerked his chin at the crowd. "You boys headed somewhere?"

"Damned right," Rees informed him. "We gotta get back to huntin'. This Injun-chasin' business don't pay worth a crap."

Jordan couldn't argue with that. "Sounds like you figure the gut-eaters to lay low for a while."

Hi Bickerdyke overheard the remark and turned. "Don't much matter whether they do or don't. We got hides cached out there that's got to be brung back. Damned if I'm gonna lose money just 'cause there's Injuns around."

"Them's my sentiments persactly," Rees agreed. "Man

193

can't diddle away the summer sittin' in town. Leastways, not if he means to eat regular. How 'bout you, Cimarron? You stayin' or goin'?"

"Reckon I'll head out, too," Jordan admitted. "Now that the army finally got off it's duff, maybe the redskins won't have time to worry about us?"

"The army?" Bickerdyke's whoop brought the others away from the counter. "Goddamn, that's the best news I've had in a coon's age."

"Now that's funny, Hi," Rees grinned. "I seem to recollect you sayin' the army couldn't catch its ass if they was tied in a towsack."

"Christ a'mighty, I don't care if they catch the heathens," Bickerdyke snapped. "Just so they keep the bastards on the run. It's like Cimarron said, if the army keeps them thinkin' about their own hides they won't come botherin' us."

Jordan's face twisted in a mocking scowl. "Boys, I don't mean to prick your bubble, but the army don't give a good goddamn whether the Injuns eat us alive or not. I just got that from the horse's ass himself."

Everybody commenced talking at once, but John Godey was the loudest. "What're you talkin' about, Cimarron? The army might be slow as molasses, but they ain't gonna sit back and watch white men get butchered."

"Godey, if that's how your stick floats, then power to you. I'm just tellin' you what that peckerhead major told me. He says the army is all for us killin' off the herds, but they're not gonna play nursemaid while we do it. Said it wouldn't look right, since accordin' to the law we're huntin' below the treaty line. The only reason they put troops in the field was to get them gut-eaters back on the reservation. That and nothin' else."

"Well I'll be dipped in shit," Sol Rees exclaimed. "That's the beatenest thing I ever heard of."

Bickerdyke scoffed at the whole affair. "Who gives a crap *why* they're out there? The fact is, they're in the field, and that'll keep the redskins hoppin'. Which means we can get back to huntin'. Hell, that's all I cared about, anyway."

There was a general murmur of agreement from the others, and Rees lost his frown. "Y'know, Cimarron, he's got a point there. And I got a hunch most of the boys'll see it just that way, too. Wouldn't surprise me none if this town emptied out like a goose come mornin'."

Jordan glanced over at Hiram Greene, who had been

following the discussion closely from behind the counter. "Hiram, you heard what the man said. Sharpen your pencil and get out your order book. Looks like we're gonna have a landslide business any minute now."

Before Greene could frame an answer, Lon McCabe came bustling through the door, screeching at the top of his lungs. "Cimarron! Goddamn, I turned this town upside down lookin' for you." His face was flushed and his eyes were round as cartwheels. "Listen, son, you ain't gonna believe it when I tell you who's over in the saloon."

Over in the Bucket of Blood, Limpy Joe Freed had taken just about all he could stand of the big-mouthed Texan. But he had seen Frank Lumpkins in action down at Griffin once, and he knew damn well he didn't want to tangle with the man rough and tumble. Still, something would have to give pretty quick. He couldn't put up with much more of the blowhard's guff.

Lumpkins was bellied up to the bar with his crew, but his remarks were addressed to the saloon at large. "Yessir, boys, that's what I call real Injun fightin'. Three days out and three days back and one day to get their ass shot off. Whooooeeee! That beats anything I ever heard tell of."

The big Texan had soaked up enough whiskey that he was feeling mean, and he figured he had just about treed himself a whole saloon. Grinning arrogantly, he turned to face the room and hooked his elbows over the bar.

"Say now, any of you fellers belong to this here militiaer outfit I been hearin' about? C'mon, don't be 'shamed to speak up. Hell, there ain't nothin' wrong with lettin' a bunch of half-assed Injuns shoot your balls off. Not much there ain't!"

His great belly shook and he roared with laughter, elbowing one of his skinners in the ribs. The man grinned weakly and darted a nervous glance around the room. The hunters gathered in the saloon weren't amused, and it was only a matter of time until someone worked up the gumption to take Lumpkins on. Many of them remembered him from the Flats below Griffin, a swaggering loudmouth who was always looking for trouble. They also recalled that Cimarron Jordan had cleaned his plow twice and killed a couple of his skinners in a gunfight. Right now, though, they had just about had a bellyful of listening to his jeering insults. Granted their little foray against the Indians

195

was nothing to brag about, but this big blowhard of a Texan had no business rubbing their noses in it.

Bill Spivey, one of those who had fought at Yellow House Canyon, decided it was time somebody took a stand. Without moving from his seat, he gave Lumpkins a sour look. "Mister, there was some good men died in that fight, and we'd sorta appreciate it if you'd just pull in your horns."

Lumpkins' grin widened. "Well now, looka here. We got ourselves a feisty one. Sonny, why don't you just walk on over here and have a try at clippin' my horns?"

Spivey's face went chalky, and for some reason he felt naked as a jaybird. "Maybe you wouldn't talk so big if Cimarron Jordan walked through that door. I seem to recollect he's hauled your ashes a couple of times."

The Texan slowly came off the bar. "Now, boy, why d'ya think I been standin' here runnin' my tongue? Sure Jordan'll come walkin' through the door, 'cause he was captain of your outfit, and when he hears what I been sayin' he'll beat a path over here. If you was still around when he got here, you'd see me break his back in ten different places. But you ain't gonna be around, 'cause I'm gonna bust your head right now."

When Lumpkins started toward Spivey a hush fell over the room. Just then Limpy Joe Freed stepped clear of the bar and faced him. "Lumpkins, right there's where I draw the line. I got no intention of fightin' you barehanded, but you move another step and I'll dust you on both sides with a hunk of lead. Just as sure as Christ—"

The Texan pulled a gun and shot him before he could finish the threat. Like many men, Limpy Joe had never learned when to stop talking and when to commence fighting. He sort of wilted in the middle when the slug slammed through his ribcage and then slumped to the floor flat on his face.

Lumpkins not only knew when to start a fight, he also had savvy enough to recognize the time for a judicious retreat. Every man in the room was on his feet, and with only four rounds left in his gun, the Texan damn sure couldn't take on a crowd. Waving the pistol in a menacing arc, he slowly backed out of the saloon and eased through the door. Not one of his skinners moved out of their tracks; so far as they were concerned the surly bastard was on his own. The room suddenly came alive as part of the crowd unlimbered their guns and headed for the door while others gathered around Limpy Joe Freed.

Jordan was crossing the road from the trading post when the shot sounded and he saw Lumpkins back out the door. The glint of light on metal told him that the Texan had a gun in his hand, and it was reasonable to assume that he had just used it on somebody inside the Bucket of Blood. Still, the plainsman had never been one to back-shoot a man and he couldn't start now.

"Lumpkins!"

The Texan's reaction was instantaneous. He rolled and dropped, snapping a shot at Jordan in the same motion. Jordan hit the ground in time to see the big man roll to a stop behind a parked wagon, then leap to his feet and take off down the street. When Lumpkins passed the lighted windows of a cathouse, the plainsman came to one knee and triggered a fast shot. Splinters flew from the corner of the building, and in the next moment the Texan disappeared into the darkness.

Jordan jumped to his feet and started at a dead lope toward the creek. Most men were creatures of habit, and thinking back to Fort Griffin, he figured he had Lumpkins' number. The Texan liked to camp near water, and more than likely he was headed there now to get a horse. Since there was a row of crib shanties downstream, that meant he was almost certainly moving upstream. Quartering off to the southwest, Jordan sprinted as fast as his legs would pump, and moments later skidded to a halt in a grove of cottonwoods along the bank. Breathing deeply, he got his wind back and felt his nerves steady to somewhere near normal. Then he waited.

Only seconds later he heard approaching footsteps and knew that he had calculated it just right. Lumpkins couldn't chance missing his camp in the dark and had stuck to the road till he hit the ford. Now he had turned upstream and was headed directly toward the trees.

The plainsman never gave him a chance. He stepped from behind the cottonwood, levelled his Colt, and when it came to bear on the hulking body, he fired. The slug jolted the Texan offstride and he stumbled toward the creek, thumbing two hurried shots as he slid down the bank. Jordan didn't move, even as the lead thunked into the tree beside him. Steeling himself to wait, he fired again just as Lumpkins regained his feet at the edge of the water. The impact of the bullet buckled Lumpkins' knees, and he slowly toppled backwards into the stream.

Jordan moved cautiously to the creek bank and looked down. In the pale starlight from overhead he could see the Texan struggling to rise. The vitality was fast draining from his massive frame, but Lumpkins still had his gun, and through sheer force of will he was bringing that strength to bear with agonizing slowness.

The plainsman very deliberately raised his pistol and shot him in the head.

The slug caught Lumpkins over the right eye and blew out the back of his skull. Like some great ponderous beast he settled into the water with a crash, and the current carried away a frothy glob of brains and bone matter. His legs twitched once, then again, and at last he lay still.

Jordan holstered his gun and turned back toward town. That last shot had been the easiest shot of his life. Easier than shooting a buffalo. No emotion. No sensation. Just something that had to be done, and being necessary, then best done quickly.

The thought bothered him, though. The way he had levelled the Colt so precisely, with a cold unhurried sense of detachment. Like administering the mercy shot to a crippled bull. Only this time it had been a man.

Still, there was no denying that the world in general, and Sweetwater in particular, was a far better place with Lumpkins dead.

Whistling softly, he strode off into the dark, suddenly wanting a drink to wash away the pasty taste in his mouth.

Then a crooked little grin spread over his face.

For a day that had started out so sorry, it had turned out fair to middling after all.

Six

▰▰▰▰▰▰▰▰▰▰▰▰▰▰▰▰▰▰▰▰▰▰▰▰▰▰▰▰

1.

Jordan left the Sweetwater in early June, bearing due
northeast over the Canadian and Wolf Creek. Upon
reaching Camp Supply, he turned the gelding north along
the road to Dodge. While he had seen plenty of Indians
above Antelope Hills, they all appeared to be of the tame
variety. Reservation Indians, folks were calling them these
days, as opposed to the renegades who were still raiding
down south. There were rumors afoot that the Cheyenne
had become increasingly restive, demanding to be returned
to their ancestral lands above the Republican. But the government was holding firm, and as yet there had been no
general outbreak of violence. The real trouble, according
to scraps of information Major Cogswell chose to share
with lowly civilians, was the Sioux. The mightiest tribe on
the western plains had taken the war trail, and there was
widespread fear along the frontier that it might spark an
uprising among the hostiles in Indian Territory.

The country was awash with speculation, but one thing
was for damn sure. Jordan was almighty thankful he had
never been tempted to hunt on the northern plains. The
Sioux made the Comanche and Kiowa look like a bunch
of amateurs.

The long solitary ride to Dodge gave him plenty of time

to think. Not just about Indians, either. The purpose of his trip was a business confab with Jason Rath. Or perhaps it was merely an excuse. The plainsman hadn't quite made up his mind on that score. He knew that some part of his journey was prompted by a need to see Julia again, but just how big a part he wasn't exactly certain. As with most things concerning Julia, it remained confused and hard to pin down. Like trying to catch a butterfly with a fruit jar. `

Back on the Sweetwater he had suddenly awakened to the fact that almost a year had passed since he last visited Dodge. Time had somehow gotten lost in the shuffle, overlooked or ignored, or maybe just buried beneath the press of greater urgencies. Building a town and operating a hide outfit, not to mention playing blindman's bluff with the hostiles, had a way of focusing a man's mind on events instead of dates. His calendar became the day Sweetwater City was completed, the morning he had shot the white buffalo, and a bloody dawn in a canyon to the west. Time itself was merely a silent hourglass, passing unnoticed, something a man lost track of in the rush of building and killing and staying alive.

Though letters had passed back and forth between Dodge and Sweetwater by way of the supply trains, Jordan had never been much at expressing himself on paper. Hiram Greene made long, scrupulously detailed business reports anyway, so he really couldn't see the need to waste time laboring with pen and ink just to pass along idle chit-chat. Rath's letters had been filled with praise for the roaring success of the trading post and glowingly optimistic about prospects in Dodge. It seemed the town fathers had followed Jordan's advice to the letter and laid out a route connecting Dodge directly with the Chisholm Trail. Overnight the former buffalo capital had become a cowtown, and boom times had again come to roost on the banks of the Arkansas.

Curiously, it irked Jordan that Julia Rath had never once bothered to pen so much as a note. Nor had the old man mentioned her name, except to observe in passing that she was well and staying busy.

The plainsman could have said much the same for himself, in spades. The trading post commenced doing a landslide business once the army took the field against the hostiles, and it showed no signs of slackening off. Jordan had even hired himself a hunter and three additional skinners. Bob Judd, an old-timer in the hide business, had been burned out by the Cheyenne in the April raid and had agreed to work for wages until he had a stake saved. With two outfits working the herds, Jordan figured he would take close to eight thousand hides before first snow. The proceeds from the hunting operation, added to the enormous profits from the trading post and his interest in the Dodge store, came out to a figure that left him staggered. Unless the bottom dropped out, he stood to clear better than $20,000 for his first year on the Sweetwater.

Five years ago he had been scratching his butt and wondering where his next meal was coming from. Now he had so much money he couldn't even think of a way to spend it, and damned if he wasn't beginning to fret about making more.

While it couldn't be classed as greed, his newly acquired ambition had given him some sleepless nights all the same. He had always viewed merchants and tradesmen as necessary evils, regarding them with the mild contempt a hunter reserves for housebroken city folk. Yet it seemed he was becoming more like them with each passing day. Especially with the new scheme he had dreamt up to lay before Jason Rath.

Oddly enough, the end result of the Indian raids had been to attract even more hunters to the Panhandle. Troops were marching and countermarching from every fort across the plains; orders had come down that the savages must be contained on their reservations at all costs. Even if it meant killing them off. With the army swarming across the frontier, anybody who owned a gun felt it safe to have a fling at buffalo-hunting. But the boom wouldn't last long. Jordan could foresee that as clearly as he could read storm clouds on the horizon. Perhaps another two years, three at the most, and then the Panhandle would go bust.

The herds were being driven ever westward by pressure from hunters along the Brazos and the Panhandle. The day must ultimately come that whatever buffalo were left would take to the Staked Plains. When they did, the hunters would be right behind them, which meant that anyone with a nickel's worth of horse sense would commence planning ahead for the westward shift in the hide business.

Jordan had in mind a trading post along the Double Mountain Fork of the Brazos, some hundred miles west of Fort Griffin. The location was ideally situated to the

Staked Plains, and would save the hunters upwards of two weeks travel back and forth with each load of hides. Whoever got there first would virtually monopolize the business: it would be foolhardy for another trading company to take the risks involved on the off-chance they could beat out a going concern. That the risks would be heavy, Jordan never questioned for a moment. The trading post would most certainly invite attack from the hostiles roaming *Llano Estacado*, while at the same time being a two-day forced march from the nearest army garrison. That made the odds stiff and the investment something beyond mere speculation.

Yet that was exactly why the venture appealed to him.

Where the risks were high—even higher than those he had faced on the Sweetwater—the returns were certain to be enormously fat. Barring any major setback—such as getting burned to the ground by the Comanches—he would need a caravan of wagons just to haul the money to the bank.

That was the kind of gamble he liked. The kind that made other men sweat. Everything riding on a single roll of the dice. Winner take all.

Not that he didn't expect one hell of a rhubarb with Jason Rath. The little merchant would doubtless wet his drawers when he heard what Jordan had concocted this time. The Sweetwater had been merely risky. The Double Mountain Fork of the Brazos would be downright hazardous. Still, there were ways and there were ways. Even around someone like his partner, who was always looking to copper his bet.

When the plainsman hit the South Side he knew right away that Dodge City was back in the chips. Saloons, whorehouses, and gambling dives had sprung up like weeds in a berry patch, and if the vice district had been rowdy before, it was just plain woolly-booger wild now. The streets were jammed with Texans, which really didn't surprise him since he had spotted vast herds of longhorns on the holding grounds along the river. The trailhands were just about as he remembered them from Abilene and Wichita—loud-mouthed, cocky, and quick to empty their six-guns at the sky the moment they got a load on. In the way of men who pride themselves on their skill with weapons, Jordan had always been amused by the Texans' great fondness for Sam Colt's equalizer. Cowpokes were notoriously bad shots—often worse sober than they were

202

drunk—which he supposed was why they liked to shoot at ceilings or the sky. Something big like that, they couldn't hardly miss. Anything smaller than a full-grown elephant, though, and the target was an odds-on favorite to escape unperforated.

From the looks of things, Jason Rath's letters hadn't exaggerated even a little bit. Dodge was wide open and running wild, the same as any other railhead he had ever seen. Every business in town—on both sides of the tracks—was probably using a number three scoop to sack up the money they gouged out of the Texans. Matter of fact, that was the whole idea. To send the cowhands back down the trail with sore heads and empty pockets.

For some reason the dumb bastards thrived on such treatment, and always came back for more. Maybe it was working with cows so much that scrambled their brains, or perhaps being out in the sun too long at a stretch. Whatever it was, Texans were a queer breed. Seven days a week.

The moment he crossed the tracks Jordan sensed a remarkable change in the flavor of things. It was like passing from a battlefield into a churchyard. There were no drunks, no pistol shots, in fact, damn near no Texans. Those that were around seemed to be conducting themselves in an orderly fashion, and while the plaza was crowded with wagons and horsemen, the only disturbance came from cursing muleskinners. North of the tracks everybody appeared to have their minds on business, and for some reason the rowdies were keeping to themselves on the South Side.

That was something he would have to remember and ask Jason about. It was damned curious. Sort of eerie in a way.

When Jordan stepped down off the roan in front of the store, his jaw came near popping out of socket. Standing there with his hand outstretched was Virge Hollister.

Just for a moment he felt like a harelip kid trying to recite poetry. After a couple of false starts, he mumbled, "Well goddamn, Virge, you sure know how to surprise a fella."

"Howdy, sport." Hollister flashed his old grin. "Long time no see."

Jordan returned the smile and let go his hand. "Two years, near as I recollect. What the samhill brings you out this way?"

Hollister peeled back his coat and a shiny star winked in the sunlight. "City marshal. Started work the first of last month. Guess next to seein' me here that'd be about the last thing you expected."

"Damn if I know which bumfoozles me more." Just seeing Hollister had been surprise enough, but the plainsman was clearly thunderstruck by the badge. "Last time we crossed trails I sort of thought you had Wichita with a knot in its tail."

Something funny happened to Hollister's grin and his eyes went smoky. "Much as it galls me to admit it, I reckon it turned out the other way round. C'mon, I'll buy you a drink and we'll swap stories. Rath tells me you've got your own little kingdom down there."

"Well I wouldn't exactly call it that. But it pays good." They started toward the Alhambra and Jordan was struck by a sudden thought. "Say, if you know Jason how come he never wrote me about you being made marshal?"

"Said he did," Hollister replied as he went through the door. "Letter's probably on the last supply train that went out."

"Likely I missed it on the way up. The wagons stay clear of the Nations."

"Can't say as I blame 'em. Not after what you boys went through this spring. Hey, that reminds me. Weren't you captain of that bunch that chased the redskins down to the Staked Plains? Rath was braggin' all over town about it."

"Wasn't much to brag about. Especially from where I sat."

They took a table at the back of the saloon, and before they were even settled good the barkeep came hustling up with a bottle and glasses. Evidently Hollister rated first-class service in the Alhambra. Which spoke for itself since the joint was owned by the mayor.

Hollister poured and then raised his glass. "Here's to old times. And better days ahead."

"I'll drink to that," Jordan said, tossing the first one down neat.

The lawman poured again and insisted on hearing about the Battle of Yellow House Canyon, as the fight had been dubbed by the Dodge City *Times*. Apparently Cimarron Jordan had become something of a local hero, and the newspapers had run big spreads on his exploits in the Panhandle. The way they wrote it, Hollister noted wryly, he had founded a town and whipped the sass out of the Indians. All singlehandedly. Not to mention being the man responsible for discovering the trail that had brought the Texas herds to Dodge. Like it or not, he was going to find himself something of a celebrity among the townspeople.

Under Hollister's prompting, the plainsman related highlights from his year on the Sweetwater. Some things he was proud of—building the town and trading post, fashioning a raw, tough-as-nails community out of the wilderness—and he talked at length regarding how it had all come about. Even the Indian raid he dwelled on extensively, describing in detail how they had outfoxed the Comanches. But the fight at Yellow House Canyon was another ball of wax entirely. The only thing noteworthy, he observed, was that they had gotten out alive. Otherwise it had been a fiasco from start to finish. Hollister didn't press him, and after revealing the bare bones of the story Jordan let it drop.

Sipping his third drink, he reversed the tables. "What about you? Hell, I've been runnin' my tongue at both ends and you haven't said boo. Now c'mon, spill it. What happened in Wichita?"

Hollister grunted and downed the rest of his drink. "Sam, the sonsabitches sold me down the river, plain and simple. Just flat nailed my hide to the wall and hung me out to dry."

Jordan wanted the full story, but he came at it obliquely. "Well that sure beats the hell out of me. When I was there I would've bet my saddle you had that town by the short hairs."

The frustration and hate ate at Hollister's guts like a nest full of worms, and the plainsman's comment brought it boiling to the surface. Swiftly he told of the political chicanery and the slick way he had been hoodwinked, ending with a blow by blow account of how he was framed and forced to leave town. Once freed from jail, he and his brothers had taken the first train west and come to roost at Dodge. They were rolling in money, and shortly after arriving they had bought a saloon-gambling dive on the South Side. This time they weren't going to get mixed up in the shady lady business. People could respect a gambler, but they had nothing but contempt for a whoremonger. That was one pitfall Hollister fully intended to avoid in the future. After things settled down he had sent for Lottie, and she was working in the Lone Star, their dive on the other side of the tracks.

While he talked, Jordan noted that he hadn't changed much. Not on the outside at any rate. He still sported the brace of pearl-handled Colts and was as nattily attired as ever. Even had the same diamond stickpin. But that didn't mean much one way or the other. What he really wanted to know was whether Hollister was still the same on the inside.

"Sounds like they gave you a raw deal awright," he agreed when the lawman wound down. "But there's something I don't savvy. After gettin' locked up in Wichita how the hell did you land a job as marshal here?"

Hollister brightened at that. "Sam, talk about fallin' in slop and comin' up smellin' like a rose. This takes the cake over anything you ever heard."

Some five months after the Hollisters hit town, Dodge suddenly found itself without any law. Bill Brooks, the city marshal, had gone after a drunken buffalo man and ended up cowering behind a water trough while the hide-hunter sprayed him with a Sharps Fifty. Overnight, Brooks lit out for parts unknown. That left the town fathers staring straight into the teeth of a trailing season with nothing but a couple of rum-dum deputies on the payroll. Unless they came up with something quick, the Texans would take Dodge apart board by board. Everyone knew that Hollister was in town, just as they knew of his reputation as a fast gun back in Wichita. Since the job of marshal was an appointed position in Dodge, and the town council didn't have time to shop around, they had closed one ear to the more unsavory stories circulating about the Hollisters. They had hired Virge with only two stipulations. That he keep the cowhands south of the tracks, and that his family not engage in the flesh game. Other than that he had a free hand.

Jordan poured another round of drinks as he finished. "Well, Virge, I'll have to hand it to you. The Texans are damn sure stayin' on the South Side. Saw it myself when I rode through. Offhand I'd say the town council is gettin' their money's worth."

"Aw, that was the easiest part, Sam. I just renamed the tracks. We call it the Deadline now. Anybody that comes across tryin' to hurrah the north side is dead. That's the rule I laid down and so far nobody's seen fit to test it."

Jordan could understand that. Hollister's reputation with

206

a gun was common knowledge among cattlemen who had trailed to Wichita. "You say that was the easy part. Next to that I'd damn sure like to know what you consider hard."

The lawman frowned and sloshed the liquor around in his glass. "Sam, it's the same old story. The toughest part is gettin' yourself accepted by the big augurs. They've got the political machine workin' for them, and they don't want any outside help. Maybe this time I'll work it a little smarter, though. Hell, if a man don't learn by his mistakes he ought to cash in his chips and go on home."

Hollister paused, plainly groping for the right words to say what was in his mind. "Sam, I learned a real important lesson in Wichita. Power isn't a toy they hand out to good children. It's a weapon folks guard real close for their own use. The man that wants it has to figure out a way to take it off 'em before they tumble to what it is he's after. Otherwise they'll put the skids to him. Just like they did in Wichita."

Jordan had his answer. Hollister hadn't changed. Not by a hair. The plainsman glued a smile on his face and listened as Hollister rambled on about the headway he had made in Dodge to date. The more he heard, the less he thought of Hollister as a friend. There was something sinister about the man's obsessive ambition—his fixation with power for power's sake. Jordan didn't understand it fully, but he knew he didn't like it. Worse yet, he sensed that it offered nothing but trouble and hard times for the people of Dodge.

Clearly, Hollister had already made a name for himself in town. He was maintaining law and order and had the Texans behaving themselves. Leastways, when they came north of the Deadline. Dog Kelly and his political cronies probably figured they had just bought themselves a fast gun for the trailing season and weren't even thinking beyond that. But Hollister was. From the little he had said it was clear he meant to keep his nose clean, play his cards close to the vest, and sneak in through the backdoor. How, he hadn't revealed, but that wasn't important right now.

What mattered was that he meant to take over Dodge. Just as he had tried to take over Wichita.

Jordan had noticed something else about Hollister while they were talking. The lawman now kept his back to the wall and his eyes were never still.

Like an old wolf who only lays up where nothing can

get around behind him. Otherwise he never lives to be an old wolf.

Perhaps Virge had learned that in Wichita, too.

2.

Jason Rath was firmly convinced his young partner had gone soft in the head. They had argued it backwards and forwards, examining it from every angle, and so far as the little merchant was concerned it came out the same every time. A trading post on the Double Mountain Fork of the Brazos wasn't harebrained, it was absolute madness.

"Sam, I really don't know what else to say to you." Rath shrugged and threw his hands up in exasperation. "I like a challenge as much as the next man, and I'm gratified that some of my business sense has rubbed off on you. The mere fact that you're thinking ahead and planning alternatives shows that you have a knack for business. But frankly, my boy, you're incorrigibly reckless."

Jordan smiled, not at all offended. "C'mon, Jason, don't try to beat me down with four-bit words. Last year you were pawin' the ground and bellowin' the same way when I started talkin' about the Sweetwater. I didn't steer you wrong there, did I? Or aren't you happy with the reports your stooge has been sendin' back?"

"Hiram is not my stooge." Rath drew himself up like a bantam cock. "Furthermore, he has done a commendable job out there. You know, Sam, there's more to making profits than just building a trading post. Granted it was your vision that brought it about, but without someone like Hiram Greene it might well have been a miserable failure."

"There you go, beatin' around the bushes again." Jordan had the storekeeper in a corner and he knew it. "Did I steer you wrong or not?"

Rath opened his mouth to say something, then his teeth clicked shut with a snap. Finally he took a deep breath and exhaled slowly. "No, you didn't steer me wrong. But that doesn't mean this new scheme of yours won't go busted. You're trying to compare apples and oranges. The headwaters of the Brazos isn't even remotely similar to the Sweetwater. My god, we would have to hire our own army just to protect the place from Indians. You said it yourself. There isn't a fort within a hundred miles of there."

"So? We'll build our own fort. Hell, ever since I came west I've heard about some fella named Lisa that did it up in Crow country, and the Bents built their own fort in Colorado before it was even a territory. Trouble with you is, you've got Injun on the brain. Lemme tell you something, Jason, gut-eaters have to hold onto it when they take a leak just like everybody else. They can be snookered easy as the next man."

"Perhaps. Since I have never dealt with them you have me at a disadvantage there. But I have a very bad feeling about this deal, and as I recall you once told me that a man should always play his hunches. Something about instinct being superior to intelligence was the way you put it. Not in just those words, but that was the thought all the same."

Jordan grinned, almost as though he were enjoying baiting the older man. "There's times instinct'll get you through where thinkin' will get you dead. That's for damn sure." Hesitating, he studied the merchant for a moment. "Tell you what. You think it over and decide what you want to do. No hard feelin's either way. I've got more'n enough stashed away to do it on my own. But I'd like to have you in on it. Gotten to where I sort of look on you as my lucky charm."

"Well, I'm flattered you feel that way, Sam. I really am." Rath smiled and shook his head. "Give me a couple of days to consider it. We'll test your theory of instinct versus logic."

With business out of the way, Jordan's mood seemed to change on the instant. The smile faded from his face and his eyes became grimly serious. "Jason, you're gonna think this sounds funny comin' from me, but I'm wonderin' how much you know about Virge Hollister."

The storekeeper regarded him with mild surprise. "You're right. That is an odd question coming from you. Why do you ask?"

There was a moment's silence while Jordan debated something within himself. Conflicting loyalties tore at him, but presently he got everything sorted out. "Virge is about the oldest friend I've got, and I expect I know him better'n anyone else. Maybe that's why I was a mite puzzled to find him wearin' a badge when I rode in today."

"Sam, that statement is a little too cryptic for me." Rath

was alert now, sensing that the plainsman was trying to tell him something in a roundabout way. "You'll have to spell it out."

Jordan selected a cigar from a box on the merchant's desk and took his time about lighting it. "How much do you know about what happened in Wichita?"

"If you mean do we know he was fired for beating a rival candidate, the answer is yes. That story even made the papers here."

"Did it say anything about him gettin' thrown in jail or why he was turned loose?"

"Yes and no. From all we could gather he was probably released on condition that he got out of Wichita."

Jordan pondered the ash on his cigar for a second. "Got any idea why they wanted him out of town so bad?"

"Nothing more than speculation," Rath admitted. "We presumed the fact that he pistol whipped their marshal and a political rival was sufficient reason in itself."

"Could be, I guess," Jordan observed. "Then you don't know anything about what him and his brothers were mixed up in?"

"You're talking about the sporting houses. Yes, we knew about that, too. But that won't happen here. We thrashed all that out with him before he was hired."

"What about him runnin' for marshal in Wichita? You hear anything about that?"

"Sam, you're the one that's beating around the bush now. Whatever you have to say, why not just lay your cards on the table?"

The plainsman couldn't bring himself to come at it straight out. The misgiving he had about Virge Hollister was like a barb that had worked deep and festered with poison. But the lawman had been his friend—still trusted him enough to reveal what had really happened in Wichita—and it was hard to discount such things entirely. Though he knew exactly what Hollister had in mind, he couldn't force himself to openly state the accusation.

"Y'know, Jason, ambition is a queer sort of thing. Sometimes it feeds on itself like green rot once it gets started. When it gets hold of a certain kind of man it'll eat him alive. Just being marshal might not be enough. Next thing you know he wants to be sheriff or mayor or—well whatever it is he's got his mind set on. I guess I'm not makin' a hell of a lot of sense, but maybe you get my drift."

The little merchant stared at him for quite a while, then

nodded at last. "What you're trying to tell me is that Dog Kelly and the city council had better watch their step. That your friend Hollister has designs on greater things. Like taking over the South Side. Or perhaps even Dodge itself. Will that do for openers?"

Rath had articulated what was deepest in his mind, the thing he couldn't bring himself to bluntly reveal. Stubbing out the cigar in an ashtray, he looked up. "I reckon I'll have to leave it up to you and your pals to check or bet. I mean, Dodge is just another town to me, so its not rightly my game."

"Sam, I'm not sure you really believe that. If Dodge was just another town, then I suspect you would have gone on about your business and kept your thoughts to yourself."

"That's why you've never been able to understand me, Jason. Places don't mean nothin'. It's people that counts."

When Jordan left the office after they had talked a while longer the storekeeper had much to think about. Not all of it concerning Virge Hollister, either. There were many facets to his young partner, but perhaps not as complex as he had once thought. The hunter had sounded a warning which could have won him the gratitude of many people in high places. Instead he chose to do it in a manner that left him out of it entirely, eliminating any possibility that he might profit from the disclosure.

That dovetailed nicely with what Rath had suspected all along. Despite the rough life he led, Jordan was both an honorable man and one who retained the freedom of a wild thing by never incurring the obligations of others. It was one of the little perversities of life that once a man made someone obligated to him for a favor he soon found himself responsible for them in many ways. While it should have worked the other way round, it rarely did. The young plainsman knew that somehow, and he very studiously avoided such entanglements.

Yet something had come to light in the conversation which intrigued the merchant even more.

Beneath the flinty, hard-as-nails exterior, Sam Jordan had a weak spot.

People. Or more precisely, certain people.

That from a man who seemed impervious to even the simplest emotion was a revelation in itself.

After a long, steamy bath and a trip to the barbershop,

211

the plainsman got himself decked out in some new duds and paid a call on Julia. The old man had told him that she showed signs of becoming bored with business and now spent only two days a week in the store. That was an interesting development, although Sam couldn't rightly say why he attached any significance to it. Nor, for that matter, was he able to see why it should even interest him.

As he yanked the pull bell he was still wondering what the hell he was doing there in the first place.

The door opened and he was no longer in a quandary about much of anything. She was wearing a starchy, tight fitting dress and its bright pattern was a ray of cheerfulness in what had otherwise been a pretty drab day. The question of why he was there had now been answered. It was standing right before him.

Julia extended her hand and smiled. "Sam, it's so good to see you again. I didn't even know you were in town."

He was so accustomed to being kissed every time he walked through her door that for a moment he didn't quite know what to do with her hand. Then his wits returned and he simply let go. "Well I only got in this mornin'. Just a fast trip to have a little powwow with your dad."

Julia led him into the parlor, and they sat across from one another. Right away he saw that this wasn't going to be like the old days. No more hugging and kissing and cooing like a couple of turtle doves. This was damn near like calling on a stranger. Suddenly he was sorry he had come. The situation was intolerable, both for him and Julia. Perched there on the sofa, he felt like a jackass in the wrong stall.

Whatever he expected to find, it wasn't here. Probably never had been. Otherwise he wouldn't have stayed away so long.

Then, much to his wonder, it dawned on him that Julia appeared wholly unchanged. Except for the fact that she wasn't swarming all over him with kisses, she was still as vivacious and charming as he remembered her. She seemed genuinely happy to see him, and there was nothing the least bit artificial about her smile or the warmth in her eyes. Even the teasing lilt to her voice was the same.

"Sam, you had better watch yourself or daddy's going to corrupt you. He swore a long time ago he would turn you into a businessman. Or maybe you don't remember that?"

"Yeah, I do. He said it plenty of times." Sam unbent a

little and even managed a weak smile. "Course, the shoe's on the other foot now. He's sort of got the idea I'm tryin' to corrupt him."

Julia giggled softly. "Corrupt daddy? Oh, I hope you can, Sam. He's so stiff and scratchy, sometimes I think an old-fashioned binge would do him worlds of good."

The thought of Jason Rath stumbling drunk made her laugh, and she clapped her hands together like an exuberant child. Watching her, Sam noted that she had gone back to some of her eastern ways. Talking as though she was almost out of breath and flinging her hair around like it would somehow accentuate her words. Evidently she wasn't as unchanged as he had first thought.

"Guess I'll have to disappoint you there," he said, cutting short her laughter. "The kind of corruption I meant has to do with business instead of booze. I've been tryin' to talk him into buildin' another tradin' post farther west."

"See!" She exclaimed with delight. "Just what I said a minute ago. He has already turned you into a businessman. Now it's you out searching for new ventures. Sam, I hate to say it, but I'm afraid Daddy Rath has made a convert out of you."

Sam had had some thoughts along the same lines himself, and it made him uncomfortable to hear it put into words. Before he could frame a reply she clapped her hands again and her green eyes sparkled brilliantly.

"Oh, Sam, I just thought of something. Has anyone told you that your old friend Virge Hollister is our new marshal?"

"Yeah. Matter of fact, Virge was the first one I run into when I stepped off my horse. Gave me a fright there for a minute. Thought I was seein' things."

Julia fairly bubbled now. "Weren't we fortunate to get so good a lawman on such short notice? Why, I just don't know what this town would have done if it weren't for him. Can you imagine all those horrible Texans over on the north side? It makes me shudder to think of it."

"Well you don't need to worry about that none." Sam chuckled, thinking back to another time. "Course, Virge is a holy terror now, but I recollect a time when a ten-year-old kid could have laid him away."

"Really?" Julia's eyes got big and round. "Why, it's hard to imagine him ever being anything but the way he is now."

Sam grinned widely, remembering how it had been.

"Naw, when he started out he was like a gangly colt that hasn't got his legs under him yet. That second winter we was together up on the Smoky Hill was a bad one, and he started messin' around with a pistol. Y'know, teachin' himself to be another Wild Bill Hickok. Well, he'd been practicin' his draw for about a week and one mornin' he finally decided to try it with real cartridges. Me and the skinners acted like we wasn't watchin', but we saw the whole thing. When he pulled that gun out he got the sight caught on the holster and it went off quicker'n he expected. Drilled a hole clean through the holster and took a chunk out of his boot heel. You never saw a man so mortified in your life, 'especially when he looked around and caught us laughin'."

Julia smiled politely, but she didn't seem too amused. "Well, I would think so. Now, Sam, you just keep that story to yourself. Don't go spreading it around town. If something like that got out Virge would be so embarrassed he couldn't show his face."

Sam caught an inflection in her words that brought him up short. "What makes you so worried about Virge Hollister?"

Julia's cheeks colored slightly, and for the first time since he had known her she appeared at a loss for words. After a moment she looked up and something defiant had come into her gaze. "Virgil has been calling on me, Sam. When you said you had talked with him I just took it for granted he had told you."

The plainsman felt a rush of anger, both at Virge Hollister and Jason Rath. Neither of them had mentioned it, and they'd sure as hell had opportunity enough to do so. Then, in a sudden flash of understanding, it occurred to him that they'd had no reason to mention it. Julia Rath damn sure didn't belong to Sam Jordan. Never had, as a matter of fact.

"Guess Virge didn't have any reason to bring it up. We were talkin' about other things." The words seemed to jog his senses and a picture of Lottie Siddons flitted through his mind. Then another thought came, triggered by the first. Virge trotting back and forth between Julia on the right side of the tracks and Lottie over in whoresville. "I don't suppose anybody told you about. . . ."

He couldn't do it. Not even to someone as sneaky as Virge. When he didn't elaborate, Julia left well enough alone. Recalling the lawman's oily charm with the ladies,

214

Sam's guts went tight as he thought of it being used on Julia. Clearly Virge meant to use her as a wedge in opening all the right doors in Dodge. Then he caught himself before he could say anything stupid. She would just have to find out for herself. He had no hold over her, and certainly no right to start getting bossy. But there was one thing he could say.

"Julia, do you know what business Virge and his family made all their money in?"

"Why, of course. They own a saloon on the South Side. There is nothing disgraceful about that."

"No, not here. I mean back in Wichita. That's where they made their money."

"I'm not quite sure I understand what it is you're trying to say."

Then she didn't know. Sam tried another tack. "Suppose their family business wasn't so *decent*, as you put it. Would that shed some light on the subject?"

"Sam Jordan, I won't hear another word!" Julia jumped to her feet and fiery green sparks shot out of her eyes. "Virgil Hollister is a good man and Dodge City can thank its lucky stars he happened along. I refuse to listen to any back-fence gossip about him or his family."

Sam came off the sofa and started looking around for his hat. "Guess I'd better be movin' on. Just a little word of advice, though. Sort of one old friend to another. Keep your eyes open and don't go doing anything silly. Virge fights dirty in the clinches."

Julia just stood there looking pop-eyed, and she hadn't moved when the door closed behind him. Once on the road headed toward town he let off steam with a few pungent curses and it made him feel a little better. But not much. Virge was slick as an eel, all right, and this time he was going to use every trick in the book to get on the good side of the big augurs. Even to conning a girl into breaking the ice for him.

Striding along, Sam decided the hell with the whole sorry bunch of them. He wasn't his brother's keeper. Or his sister's either. And he damn sure hadn't had much luck walking on water lately. So that sort of left them on their own hook. He had warned them and that was just about as far as he cared to go.

Then he chortled, mocking himself with sardonic bitterness. All that year out in the Sweetwater country he had remembered the look on her face that time she mentioned

215

marriage. Even got himself to thinking she might not be so bad to come home to. What a crock! Like the fellow said, distance goddamn sure lends enchantment. But that could be fixed real easy.

This time he'd go so far it would take a mirage to get her face in focus. Besides, he must have had rocks in his head to have commenced thinking of settling down. There was still too much country out there he hadn't yet seen. Too many women he hadn't yet bedded. Too much to do.

Like building that fort on the Double Mountain Fork.

Everybody else could eat beans and bark at the moon if they wanted to, but he was headed home. To the plains.

Still, try as he might, he couldn't rid his mind entirely of Julia's image. There was something different about her now. Stronger, more poised, possessing a confidence he hadn't seen before. Yet in a way she was still that spoiled little schoolgirl who came west expecting to find Indians and road agents hiding behind every bush.

The thought jarred something in him—a wish almost that they could go back and start fresh. But maybe it was like the Indians said, after all.

Nothing lives forever.

3.

After leaving the Rath home, Jordan spent the rest of the afternoon trying to avoid Virge Hollister. The way he felt right then, just about anything would have set a match to his temper, and he had never before coldcocked a lawman. Were they to meet, words would be exchanged. One thing would lead to another and sure as hell he'd wind up slugging Virge. Which probably wouldn't accomplish a damn thing except to land him in the hoosegow.

Returning to the Dodge House, he went up to his room and stretched out on the bed. While he kept telling himself that the whole mess was none of his business, he couldn't quite swallow his own argument. Sometimes a man got involved whether he wanted to or not. The simple act of accepting another person's friendship obligated him. Jason Rath. Julia. Even Virge Hollister. Along the way he had shared things with them—laughter and sweat, hard times and good—and like it or lump it, he somehow felt responsible for their well-being.

It was stupid. Asinine. Ever since his folks died and he came west, he had gone out of his way to avoid getting entangled in other people's lives. Somewhere along the line people always disappointed a fellow if he let them get close to him. They died or got themselves killed. Went broke or lost their marbles. Got themselves into bone-headed jams and came whimpering for help. When all the time the thing they needed most was a swift boot in the can. The misery they caused a man just wasn't worth the infrequent moments of comfort they gave in return.

Take Lon McCabe. The cantankerous old scissorbill had attached himself to Jordan like a blood tick on a fat hound. Not that he didn't pull his own weight. Hell, he did his share and more. But it was like he couldn't fend for himself if Jordan were to suddenly cut him adrift. McCabe made it known in little ways, the things he did on the sly that were meant to please Jordan without being obvious. The bossiness and his eternal bitching were only an act, a cover-up for the puppy-dog feelings just beneath the skin. Truth was, he got skittery every time Jordan rode out. Like he was afraid the hunter might just keep right on riding one day and never come back. Jordan had seen it coming way back on the Smoky Hill—from their very first days together—and like a damn fool had gone along. What had started as a simple arrangement between hunter and skinner became something else. Friendship.

But it wasn't the sort of friendship Jordan liked or wanted. The kind where a man was free to pack his war-bag and say *adios* whenever it suited him. It was the graspy kind that got a man all entwined and made him feel suffocated with. . . .

With that? It was always there, that question, and no matter how a fellow dodged and twisted, it always came back to the same word.

Obligation.

That was what he felt now toward Juna and her father. Despite his own arguments to the contrary, he couldn't shake the feeling, either. In a quirky sort of way he even ' felt obligated toward Virge. Like there was something he could do—or hadn't done—that might straighten the law-man out. When all the time he knew there wasn't a god-damn thing short of killing him that would ever change Virge Hollister.

Maybe, though—just maybe—there was still a spark of decency left in Virge. Perhaps he had judged him too

217

quickly. Or too harshly. There was just an outside chance that he was playing it straight with Julia. That he wasn't hosing Lottie on the side while courting Rath's daughter to further his political schemes.

The likelihood was damn slim, though. Jordan wasn't kidding himself there. But slim or not, it was sure as hell worth investigating. Just this once Virge might have fooled him. Played it by the rules instead of getting cagey.

Shortly after sundown, Jordan left the hotel and had supper in a greasy spoon up the street. Afterwards he strolled into the Long Branch and killed some time over a couple of drinks. When he came out the door and headed across the plaza he figured he had timed it just about right. The South Side was already crawling with cowhands, and even if he met Virge on the street they wouldn't have a chance for more than a few words. Not this early in the night, anyway. There were too many Texans roaming around looking for a place to light. Until they did, the marshal wouldn't have a minute to spare—even for an old friend. Which suited Jordan just fine.

When the plainsman came through the door of the Lone Star, the first thing he saw was James Hollister. The eldest member of the clan was standing near the gaming tables where he could keep an eye on the action. Except for having grown heavier, he looked just about the same as he did in Wichita. Sort of cross and tight-lipped, like his bowels had been locked for a couple of days. Jordan had a feeling the bastard wouldn't have trusted his own mother any farther than he could see her. Which seemed to hold up under scrutiny. The younger brothers, Morgan and Warren, were doing the dealing, and James was watching them like a hawk.

Just about then, the elder Hollister looked up and spotted Jordan watching him. They nodded, but neither man made a move toward the other. They didn't like one another and they both knew it, so there was no need for pretense. Jordan respected him for that, if nothing else.

The saloon was a regular antheap, with Texans standing three deep at the bar and more crowding through the door every minute. But the one thing that caught a man's attention was the dazzling array of girls. They were all over the place, a giggly, undulating mass of fluffy curls and heaving breasts and teasing eyes. Waves of cheap perfume hung over the room like a thick mist, but for all their numbers there was a certain sameness about the girls. Like somebody in the backroom was molding kewpie dolls put together with jangly bracelets and spangled dresses and a heavy dose of clown red for the cheeks.

One thing about James Hollister. He purely knew what made the world go round. From the looks of the Lone Star, he had brought about half the chippies in Wichita along to Dodge.

Jordan saw Lottie standing by the piano with a bunch of trailhands and headed in that direction. Waving her arms like a choir director, she was leading them in a bellowed rendition of "The Yellow Rose of Texas." Waiting until the song came to a grinding halt, he moved in behind her.

"Lottie."

Glancing around, her face brightened with a wide smile. "Sam! Where in the world did you spring from?"

"Nowhere in particular." Smiling, he cut his eyes at the Texans. "Reckon you could ditch them for a while? I'd like to buy you a drink."

"Bet your boots! That's the best offer I've had tonight." Turning, she gave the cowhands a devastating smile. "Boys, you hold the fort. I'll be back in a couple of shakes."

They groaned loudly, but she waved them off and took Jordan's arm, steering him towards a table in the back. Once they were seated the plainsman got his first good look at her, and it was about what he had expected. She was still pretty, with upswept raven hair and a delicate face. Even her curves had held firm in all the right places. But the life of a saloon girl had taken its toll. There were tiny crow's feet at the corners of her eyes, and she somehow appeared wiser, harder almost. As though the grab bag had long since ceased to hold any surprises for her.

"Sam, you just don't know how good it is to see you again." She placed her hand over his and gave it a soft squeeze. "What are you doing in Dodge? I've been reading about you in the papers, and I mean to tell you, folks around here think you're a hot ticket."

A waiter materialized out of nowhere with a couple of drinks, and Jordan paid him. Looking back at Lottie, he grinned. "Don't believe everything you read. Most of the stuff is just hogwash. Sells papers, that's all."

"Now look at that, would you. A blushing violet." She laughed and tickled him under the chin. "Mr. Modesty himself. Of course, I should be peeved at you, Sam Jordan. Been in town all day and I'm the last on the list to get a look at your ugly puss."

"Oh, Virge told you I was in town?" The question sounded innocent enough, but it was an opening shot.

Lottie gave him a pouty look. "Why, of course, he told me, silly. You're my best friend, too, you know. He came over right after you two had a drink this morning. Talk about excited. Well! You'd have thought he just laid an egg. He thinks the world of you, Sam. Maybe he doesn't say much, but I can tell."

Jordan nodded and took a sip of his drink. "We don't talk about it much, so I'll take your word for it. Reckon you know him better'n anybody else anyhow."

"Well I should hope so!" Lottie giggled at her racy admission. "You know, sometimes I get to thinking about it and I just can't believe we've been together going on three years. I mean, I'm not hard to look at, but you'll have to admit Virge is a handsome devil. He could have had his pick of anything in skirts. Anytime he wanted it. You know that as well as I do."

Jordan couldn't help but feel sorry for her. So bright and gay, and so damnably pathetic. She was stuck on Virge so bad she couldn't see straight—blinded herself to what he really was—and there was something very sad about that. Just for a moment he debated carrying it any further. She had given him the answer he needed, and there wasn't much to be gained by putting her through the wringer. Still, he had to be sure.

"Listen to the lady brag, for chrissakes!" Leaning closer, he gave her a jesting smile, with just a hint of mockery in his eyes. "Lottie, if you hadn't started tootin' your own horn I wouldn't have said nothin'. But it appears to me you're gettin' too big for your britches." Glancing around, his voice dropped to a conspiratorial whisper. "Keep it to yourself where you heard it, but a little bird told me Virge boy has been keepin' company with some filly over on the north side."

"Oh, fiddlesticks!" Lottie admonished him. "I thought you had something really spicy to tell me. You're talking about that Rath girl. I know all about her."

"You do?" Jordan's jaw dropped a couple of inches. "How the hell did you find out?"

"Virge told me, dopey." Grinning, she gave his cookie-duster a playful tug. "Nobody but you would dare carry

220

tales on him. They're all scared to death he'll snort fire and start spinning his pistols."

The plainsman looked even more baffled. "Virge told you himself that he's been seeing this Rath girl?"

"Well, of course, he told me, Sam. There's nothing between them. He's just buttering her up so he can make the right connections on the north side. You know how Virge is. Always playing the angle."

There it was. Exactly as he had figured it. The only difference being that Virge was shrewder than he had thought. By telling Lottie he had completely disarmed her, eliminating any possibility that she might get jealous and spill the beans. They were still shacking up and probably had been since the night Lottie hit town. Nothing had changed from Wichita except they weren't being so open about it. Otherwise he couldn't use the little dumbbell across the tracks to give him an air of respectability.

The bastard was going to have his cake and eat it too.

Lottie was eyeing him quizzically, but before he could reply James Hollister pulled up before the table. He nodded at Jordan and give the girl a dirty look.

"Lottie, we're sort of swamped tonight. Maybe you and Jordan could have a chat on your own time."

The plainsman felt like clobbering the surly-mouthed sonofabitch right where he stood. Yet it would only have made matters worse for Lottie. She might sleep with Virge, but in the Lone Star she had to jump rope to the tune played by the maestro whoremonger.

Jordan came to his feet, ignoring Hollister completely. "I've got to be runnin' along anyway, Lottie. I'll catch up with you before I leave town and we'll have ourselves a real gabfest."

"Please do, Sam." Her eyes thanked him for not making a fuss. "Come back one afternoon and we'll talk all day. Promise?"

"It's a deal." Walking away from the table, he didn't even look at Hollister. Something about the man curried him the wrong way. Every time. Luckily the bastard had left well enough alone and hadn't said anything else.

Jordan came through the door just as a volley of shots rattled across the South Side. Out in the middle of the street, close to a dozen Texans were moving towards the tracks, whooping Rebel yells and firing their pistols in the air as they lurched along. Plainly they were well oiled and bent on causing some devilment. The hunter followed along simply because he was headed in that direction, his mind absorbed with the tidbits Lottie had unknowingly revealed. Abruptly his thoughts were jarred back to the present as a familiar voice rang out.

"That's as far as you go! Just turn it around and make tracks the other way."

Up ahead, through the fuzzy glare of the street lamps, Jordan saw Virge Hollister standing astride the railroad tracks with a sawed-off shotgun cradled over his arm. The cowhands ran up on one another as they came to a halt facing the lawman, then broke off and formed a thin line. One of the Texans, sporting a brace of fancy six-guns and a huge cream-colored Stetson, stepped forward.

"Lawdog, you'd best step aside. Lessen you want us to walk right over you."

"Kennedy, I understand you've been braggin' around you mean to hurrah Front Street tonight. Let's just see how much guts you've got." Hollister kicked the railroad track with the toe of his boot. "That's the Deadline. Anybody that steps across won't walk back. Who's gonna be first?"

The challenge was met by angry muttering from the trailhands, but the one named Kennedy let go a cackling laugh. "You got yourself figured for a regular bearcat, ain't you? Trouble is, you're standin' there all by your lonesome. Or didn't your mama teach you how to count?"

"I've got all the help I need right here." Hollister patted the scattergun. "There's a double load of buckshot that says you boys never make it across the tracks."

The Texan took a hitch at his fancy gunbelt and started forward. "Mister, let's just see what kinda sand you got in your craw."

"Freeze!" Jordan shouted from behind them. "First man that twitches gets drilled."

The threat from their rear turned the cowhands to stone. Not one of them batted so much as an eyelash. Except the man named Kennedy.

The Colt in his hand moved, and he opened his mouth to yell something. But no one ever found out what it was he meant to say. Hollister swung the shotgun around at waist level and let fly with one barrel. The blinding roar lighted the street, and in the same instant Kennedy was almost cut in half as the buckshot struck him just above the belt buckle. The Texans on either side of him also fell, caught in the spreading pattern of lead. But they suffered only superficial wounds. Kennedy was stone cold dead.

"Drop your guns!" Hollister commanded, watching closely as they shucked their hardware. "Now get your hands up."

When the trailhands had complied, he let the sawed-off cannon rove over them. "Boys, we're gonna march down to the jailhouse. First one that looks back gets his eye shot out. Now some of you carry those wounded men and let's get movin'."

Jordan came forward and fell in beside Hollister as the Texans shuffled off toward the lockup. The lawman flashed his old grin. "Thanks, Sam. I owe you one."

"Virge, why the hell didn't you have any deputies backin' your play?"

"Didn't need 'em. Soon's I got Kennedy they would've backed down. He's been blowin' all over town how he was gonna make me eat crow."

Jordan grunted to himself, understanding it now. Kennedy hadn't known it, but he was a dead man the minute he started toward those tracks. Hollister had simply used him as an object lesson for the rest of the Texans in town. Even the absence of deputies made sense in a very cold, calculating fashion. The marshal meant to rout the Kennedy outfit single-handed and get his name splashed all over the front page of both newspapers. The queer part was, a man couldn't help admiring him. The bastard was double-wolf on guts.

As they neared the jailhouse Jordan decided to go whole hog. "Virge, a minute ago you said you owed me one. How about payin' off right now?"

Hollister's milky eyes swung around, just the least bit wary. "Name it."

"Take it easy on Julia Rath."

"You mean stay clear of her?"

Jordan chewed on it for just a second. "No. I reckon she wouldn't want it that way. I'm just sayin' take it easy on her."

The lawman nodded, his jaw set in a grim line. "You got yourself a deal."

Jordan turned and started to walk away as the Texans crowded through the jailhouse door. Hollister's voice brought him up short. "Sam, we've been friends a long time, so I'm gonna ask you instead of tellin' you. Don't monkey in my business again. I got plans for Dodge, and I won't stand for nobody messin' with 'em. You just called a debt and I paid up. I'll watch my step wtih Julia. But that's as far as it goes. Savvy?"

"Virge, you stick to our deal and I don't give a damn what you do to this town. But if you don't I'll cut your balls off and stuff 'em down your throat. You know I can do it, too."

Jordan walked off and left him standing there. About halfway back to the tracks a wayward thought brought a low chuckle from him. Without even thinking, instinct again, he had touched the right nerve.

Virge was very skittish about his balls.

Had been since that time back in '73 when they saw what the Cheyenne had done to them woodcutters.

Now that he thought about it, the plainsman had a sudden notion that Virge more than likely quit the hide business for that very reason.

Facing drunk Texans with a gun was easy. Losing your balls, though, that touched Virge Hollister right where he lived.

Without a stiff pecker he would be nothing. Less than nothing. Double-ought zero.

4.

Clouds of white and orange butterflies fluttered in the warm sun, and the fragrance of chokecherry blossoms filled the air as Jordan rode into Camp Supply. He had allowed two leisurely days for the trip down from Dodge, letting the roan set its own pace while he sifted through a jumble of nettlesome thoughts. There was much on his mind this hazy June morning—none of it calculated to ease a man's sullen temper—and as he sighted the cantonment it occurred to him that his brief stay in Dodge City had been a fool's errand.

Then, with a surly grunt, he revised the thought. Fool was too mild a word. Jackass was more like it.

Before he arrived in Dodge, everybody had been pleased as punch with themselves and their lives. But when he rode out, they were disgruntled and only slightly less grumpy than a bunch of molting owls. The only thing he had accomplished was to get everybody sore as a boil. Mostly at a fellow named Sam Jordan.

Jason Rath was worried sick about his daughter running with a common mankiller. Not to mention the fact that the gunslinger in question also had designs on Dodge City itself. Caught on the horns of this dilemma, the little merchant had been unable to make a decision about the proposed trading post on the Double Mountain Fork. Which left Jordan hanging fire unless he wanted to foot the bill out of his own pocket.

Still, that didn't bother him nearly as much as what he had done to Julia. Where before she had been bright and witty and gay, now she was grouchy as an old sow grizzly hung in a rusty bear trap. After their set-to over Virge, she had stuck her nose in the air and acted like something smelled bad every time he came around. Which wasn't often. They hadn't exchanged a dozen words his last day in town, even though she knew he had saved Virge's hash the night before.

Then there was good old Virge. He was just plain ticked off. Especially when he found out Jordan had been around pumping Lottie. But that was sort of a last straw, and a feather-weight at that. Virge was scalded mainly over the showdown with Kennedy and his Texans. The newspapers had given Jordan almost as much credit as they did the lawman, and that really stung. Virge had planned on stealing that show himself. Instead he ended up sort of second fiddle. The deal they made about Julia hadn't galled him nearly as much as losing the spotlight in the newspapers. Though the two men had avoided one another the day after the shootout, Jordan had seen Lottie again and she seemed genuinely perplexed that hard feelings now existed between the former partners.

Thinking about it as he rode south, Jordan had glumly admitted to himself that Sweetwater was looking better all the time. His chief regret was that he had ever left there in the first place.

Dismounting in front of headquarters, the plainsman noted the lack of activity around the post. There were few Indians about, and those he saw appeared to be tame enough. Since being herded onto reservations they had become pretty much dependent on government handouts, which would tend to take the starch out of damn near anyone. Even a savage.

Still, the gut-eaters were an unpredictable lot. The raid below the Sweetwater had proved that to everybody's satisfaction. They could go on another rampage just about any

225

time they pleased, and from what he'd seen, there wasn't a hell of a lot standing in their way. The army wasn't bad at catching Indians, but they weren't worth a crap at herding them.

Which was the purpose of his stopover at Camp Supply. There were rumors the heathens meant to bust out again, and it stood to reason the post commander might know something worth hearing.

Once inside the orderly room it took a stiff argument to get past the sergeant major, who had the voice of a foghorn and breath like he'd just had breakfast with a vulture. They exchanged a few pungent comments on one another's ancestry, and after Jordan raised enough hell the old trooper finally relented. Knocking lightly, he eased into the commander's office and returned moments later with a dour expression stamped across his mug. Holding the door ajar, he waved the plainsman through, mumbling something under his breath that sounded vaguely insulting.

Colonel Roger North was nothing more nor less than Jordan expected. West Pointer, going paunchy around the middle, and a nose veined red from an intimate acquaintance with John Barleycorn. Seated behind a massive desk, with a cigar jutting from his mouth, the officer waved toward a chair.

"Let's make this quick, young man, Sergeant · Major Quincannon said you wanted to talk to me about Indians."

Something about the man troubled Jordan, and for a moment he couldn't put his finger on it. Then, quite suddenly, it came to him. The sonofabitch was trying to ape Ulysses S. Grant! Right down to the bulldog scowl and the mushy cigar. Trouble was, it appeared he couldn't handle the firewater as well as old U. S. had reportedly done when he was still in uniform.

"Colonel, my name is Sam Jordan." The plainsman ignored the chair. He didn't figure to be there that long. "I own the trading post and most of the town over at Sweetwater."

"Is that a fact?" North replied, staring him up and down. "From the looks of you I would have guessed something more on the order of a buffalo-hunter."

"You're gettin' warm," Jordan allowed. "I've got a man that manages the store and I generally spend most of my time huntin'."

"Hold on now, Jordan!" The officer blinked furiously and started munching his cigar. "You're the one who led

226

that mob on a wild goose chase after the hostiles. I had a full report on you from Major Cogswell at Fort Elliott."

"Well it wasn't exactly a wild goose chase, colonel. Or maybe Old Spit and Polish didn't happen to mention that we caught the gut-eaters down on the Staked Plains."

"Who's that? Old Spit and Polish. Are you referring to Major Cogswell?"

"Yeah, that's the name he's got around Sweetwater. He's so keen on keepin' his troopers all spiffed up that the boys figured he needed a new handle."

North smothered a chuckle behind a polite smile. "Yes, I see what you mean. Well then, Mr. Jordan, it won't offend you if I mention that Major Cogswell made some rather inflammatory remarks about you in his reports."

"Just like pourin' water off a duck's back," Jordan grinned. "The major and me don't see eye to eye on a hell of a lot."

"That's understandable. As I recall, Tony Cogswell has never held buffalo-hunters in high regard."

"I sort of got that impression myself. Not that he said anything outright insultin'. Being a gentleman, he just hinted around that we were a couple of notches below a cow pod so far as the army was concerned."

"Be that as it may, Mr. Jordan, it might interest you to know that General Sheridan is fighting tooth and nail on behalf of you hunters." When he noted the blank look on Jordan's face he leaned forward and tapped a dog-eared newspaper lying on the desk. "Or weren't you aware that the Texas legislature is considering a law which would ban all further slaughter of the buffalo herds?"

The plainsman was too dumbfounded to say anything for a moment. He had visions of Sweetwater City and his idea for the Double Mountain Fork going up in a puff of legislative smoke. When his voice returned it came in a gargled rattle. "What the hell would they do a thing like that for?"

"Why, the world is full of bleeding hearts, my boy. If they had their way the buffalo and Indians would come first, and white men would have to content themselves with leftovers."

"Well what's happenin'? I mean, do you think there's any chance of them passin' a damnfool law like that?"

"I would venture to say it's nothing more than a tempest in a teapot." The officer picked up the newspaper and propped reading spectacles across his nose. "Here, let me

227

quote from excerpts of Sheridan's speech before the Texas legislature. 'These men have done more in the last two years to settle the Indian question than the regular army has done in the last thirty years. They are destroying the Indians' commissary. Send them powder and lead, and a hearty vote of thanks. For the sake of lasting peace, let them kill, skin, and sell until the buffaloes are exterminated.'"

North removed his glasses and tossed the newspaper on the desk. "I can't say that I appreciate the general's comment with respect to the army's fighting ability. But he's right about the buffalo. Once they are exterminated the Indian is done for. The filthy beggars will have no choice but to accept life on the reservations. Which is exactly where they belong anyway. Animals should be penned. Even the two-legged variety."

Jordan passed on that one. "Colonel, what's all this talk about extermination? Hell, it'd take a man a couple of lifetimes to count all the buffalo south of the Canadian."

"Perhaps you're right, Mr. Jordan. However, it won't require nearly that long to slaughter them. The latest government reports indicate that close to thirty million buffalo have been killed in the last seven or eight years. The demand for hides is as great as ever, and there is certainly no scarcity of hunters, so I believe it is reasonable to assume that the buffalo will become as extinct as the mastodon in a few more years."

Jordan decided to sit down after all. "Colonel, I came in wonderin' if the Injuns was gonna put me out of business and now you tell me I'm gonna put myself out of business. That sort of makes a fella suck wind."

North's brow lifted in little furrows of puzzlement. "I'm afraid I don't follow you. How could the Indians put you out of business?"

"I don't know how much Cogswell told you in his report, colonel, but we lost better'n thirty men in that raid. The bunch that hit us wasn't all that big, either. Just a couple of hundred renegades that got together from the different tribes. Now supposin' the gut-eaters really got wound up and came boilin' out of the Nations in droves. You tell me what would happen."

The officer smiled and shook his head with mild amusement. "That is a very interesting theory. Farfetched, but interesting. Would you mind telling me how you arrived at such a conclusion?"

228

Jordan's backbone stiffened a little. "You're pokin' fun at me, colonel, and I'm dead serious. Everybody knows the Sioux are on the warpath, and there's talk it might get things stirred up here in the Nations. Where there's smoke there's generally fire, and it looks to me like anybody with a lick of sense would take to sleepin' light. I've seen lots of good men lose their hair 'cause they underestimated Injuns. I don't aim to be one of 'em."

Roger North decided on the spur of the moment that he rather liked this crude-mannered frontiersman. Unlike other hide-hunters the soldier had known, Jordan appeared to be a man of considerable intelligence, with a knack for looking ahead and weighing alternatives. Perhaps a trifle overimaginative, but not without a certain native shrewdness. A rarity among the riffraff more commonly associated with the genus Buffalo-hunter. Something of a diamond in the rough.

"Mr. Jordan, it occurs to me that you are a man who appreciates a libation on occasions. May I offer you a drink?"

Jordan's pugnacious scowl evaporated on the instant, replaced by a small grin. "Colonel, I reckon you wouldn't have to twist my arm none. After two days in the saddle a fella can work up a pretty good thirst."

The plainsman reminded North of an amiable bear, brutish in temperament and undoubtedly dangerous when angered, but amusing to have around nonetheless. Moving to a wall cabinet, he selected a bottle of French cognac and returned to the desk with a couple of glasses. Glancing up as he poured the drink, he smiled dryly.

"I take it, Mr. Jordan, that you are thirsty as a mud hen on a tin roof." When the hunter's face registered surprise, North laughed. "Oh, I'm quite conversant with western colloquialisms. Something of a hobby, you might say." Raising his glass, he arched one eyebrow. "I believe you will find this an improvement over rotgut and popskull, Mr. Jordan. Happy days."

Jordan failed to observe that the officer merely sipped his drink. The delicately stemmed brandy glass appeared to be nothing more than a fancy jigger, and he tossed it off in one gulp. The cognac hit bottom and exploded through his innards like a roman candle. Just for a moment he expected to see smoke pour from his nostrils and a queer thought passed through his mind. Maybe this was

229

the stuff those fireeater fellows in the circus used. If it wasn't they were damn sure missing a good bet.

North was watching him with what bordered on clinical interest, smiling faintly. "Care for another, Mr. Jordan?"

"Don't mind if I do," the plainsman replied, extending his glass. "That's pretty tasty stuff, colonel. Has a nice bite. What d'ya call it, anyway?"

"Cognac. It's a form of brandy. Comes all the way from France. Terribly expensive, I'm afraid. But then, a man shouldn't deprive himself of life's smaller pleasures. Don't you agree, Mr. Jordan?"

"Yessir, I do. Fella only goes around once and he's a damn fool if he don't make the most of it while he's got the chance." Studying the amber liquid a moment, he took a cautious sip and smacked his lips. "Ummmm. Little bit goes a long ways, don't it? Maybe I'll order me some of this next time I'm in Dodge."

"Excellent idea, my boy. Once you acquire a taste for it you'll find that all else pales by comparison." The officer's shiny nose stood as mute testament to his expertise in such matters. "Now, to return to the question of Indians."

North resumed his seat behind the desk and made a steeple with his fingers, peering over it at the plainsman. "Let me begin by saying that the hostiles who raided your men have been run to earth by the Tenth Cavalry. They will shortly be returned to the reservation, and according to communiqués received from Fort Sill, their leaders will be sentenced to life in prison. Which amounts to the same thing as a death sentence. That observation is based on experience we have had with Santana and Satank and other renegade chiefs. Once in prison, the smelly beggars somehow will themselves to die. Rather extraordinary when you stop to think about it."

The officer took a sip of cognac and rolled it around on his tongue, impressed by the profundity of his own statement. "Be that as it may, I think you can rest easy about the future, Mr. Jordan. The Indians, in a very real sense, are much like the buffalo. Except that they have been given an alternative to annihilation. Those who refuse to be pacified will, of course, be dealt with harshly. Measures have already been taken to insure that there is no repetition of this last outbreak."

Jordan didn't ask what was meant by *measures*. Somehow he would just as soon not know. "Colonel, I'm not doubtin' your word, but the army has been makin' promises like that as far back as I can remember. What about the Sioux? Are you sayin' them going on the rampage won't get the tribes down here all hot under the collar?"

Tilting back in his chair toward a large wall map, North took a pointer and circumscribed an arc around the mountain ranges of the northern plains. "See that area? It is the Powder River and Big Horn country. Last refuge of the Sioux and the Northern Cheyenne. While it isn't public knowledge as yet, Generals Crook and Terry have mounted a campaign into the very heart of that stronghold. Their columns will perform a classic pincer movement—much the same as Grant used in Richmond—and once the jaws of the trap are locked shut the hostiles will be destroyed. Take my word for it, young man, the Indian wars will shortly become a thing of the past."

"General Terry?" Jordan scratched his jaw thoughtfully "Seems like I recollect hearin' that Custer had something to do with this fella Terry."

"That's correct. Custer commands the Seventh Cavalry, which is part of General Terry's force. From what we gather, Custer's regiment is to be deployed to the front as a reconnaissance screen for the main body. Standard maneuver in actions of this nature. Elementary, one might almost say. Even Custer should be able to handle that without any great problem."

North's none-too-subtle observation on Custer was an opinion widely shared among army men. Jordan made no comment one way or the other, but he had a small inkling that the expedition against the Sioux wasn't going to be the cakewalk everyone expected. The army had a natural gift for gathering a pretty good bunch of fighting men together and then putting a jackass in command. From what he had heard about Custer, it stood to reason that General Terry was in for some rough sledding once his outfit came nose to nose with the Sioux.

Roger North lectured for another half hour, becoming increasingly garrulous as he dispensed brandy with a free hand. But for Jordan the talk provided little else besides more of the same. The army would soon have the Indians performing like trained bears. Their chiefs were either in prison, or dead, or shortly would be. Without leaders the young hostiles would quickly come to heel, and life on the reservation would have them tamed in no time.

According to the colonel, the frontier was secure at last.

Now all the hide-hunters had to do was polish off the remaining buffalo herds, and the Indians' most visible symbol of freedom would have disappeared forever.

Jordan finally took his leave, hoisting one for the road with his slightly ossified host. Not that the plainsman was feeling any pain himself. With the load he was carrying he figured he was safe from snakebite, ague, and every form of rheumatism known to medical quackery. When he swung aboard the gelding he made a mental note to stick to popskull in the future. Maybe it wasn't as tasty, but at least it grabbed hold of a man fair and square. That goddamn cognac was straight Sneaky Pete, with a wallop like a mule.

Along about dark he stopped on Wolf Creek to camp for the night. After hobbling the roan and washing down some jerky with creek water, he lay back on his blanket and gazed for a long while at the starry sky. His head was clear now, and his mind started drifting back over the conversation with Colonel North. What was it the old alky had said?

The Indians are much like the buffalo.

Their days of roaming free and untethered across the plains were numbered. All but gone. One to be locked in a cage like a wild beast and the other to be exterminated for a variety of reasons, all having to do with greed. The colonel had called it extinct. Which was just a polite word for being wiped out.

Still, it was a term that applied not just to buffalo. As far as the gut-eaters' old ways were concerned, they would be goddamn near extinct themselves.

When a man looked at it from the hind side it was a damned shame. Maybe they were heathens, and holy murder when they caught a white man with his pants down, but a fellow couldn't help admiring them. They had lived free as the wind, answerable only to themselves and the ancient rhythm of the seasons. What they'd had was the thing every man searched for and few found. The very thing he had yet to find for himself.

Somehow the thought troubled him in a way he couldn't quite fathom. Mocked him even in its very elusiveness.

Like a shadowed portent of things to come.

Seven

1.

It had been a dry summer, hobbling on toward autumn like some wounded, thirsting animal. The plains had shriveled under the brutal mace of the sun, slowly converting the parched grassland into a vast tinderbox. Creeks became mere trickles of moisture, and even the mighty rivers shrunk to half normal size, leaving barren, rock-strewn shorelines which glistened in the sun like ribbons of bone. The land contracted and burst, strangling on its own dust, and gigantic cracks snaked across the prairie as the sod turned its withered bowels to the sky.

But the hide business blossomed as never before. Not unlike carrion eaters growing plump and content amidst the workings of death, buffalo men swarmed across the Southern Plains. Some estimates ranged upwards of two thousand hunters, and twice again as many skinners. Though prices dropped as the market became glutted with hides, there was no letup in the killing. Hunters simply shot longer hours and downed more shaggies, compensating for lowered prices with an ever-growing volume of hides. It became a vicious circle of death. With each slump in the market the killing accelerated in pace, and the heedless slaughter drove prices into an even sharper nosedive. Before summer had ended, buyers were paying as little as $1.50 for prime robes.

Still, nothing seemed to discourage the buffalo men. Despite drought, dwindling herds, and rock-bottom prices they flocked to the plains without respite. The threat of losing their scalps to the Comanches and Kiowas had been removed—or so the government said, at any rate—and the rush was on. Everybody wanted a piece of the bonanza while it lasted, and now there was nothing to stop them. With the hostiles driven to the reservations, fainthearts and pilgrims alike swarmed west.

Sweetwater City became a flourishing little community over the summer, waxing fat on the buffalo trade. Though there was still no law, and it remained a haven for those riding the owlhoot trail, the town had doubled in size. Whorehouses, saloons, and gaming dens sprouted along the creek like mushrooms in a dark cellar; whatever his appetites, a man could find anything he was looking for in blustery Sweetwater. Even old-timers agreed that it was the equal of the Flats below Fort Griffin. Maybe better. Hell, in Sweetwater they didn't even have vigilantes! The only law was what a man made for himself, and that dispensed by Cimarron Jordan whenever things commenced to get out of hand.

But then, Jordan wasn't in town very often, and most times whatever a man was big enough to do, he did. Which was just the way the hide-hunters liked it. Tough as nails and salty as hell.

Jordan didn't care much for his town anymore. Like Hays and Dodge and Griffin on the Flats, it had grown too big to suit his tastes. While hide-hunting wasn't especially profitable these days—not unless a man shot from morning till dusk—he spent more time then ever on the plains. The trading post, and his various enterprises in Sweetwater, were making him wealthy, but the constant ebb and flow of activity in the town left him uncomfortable. He took it in short doses, if at all, and generally just stayed the hell away.

With Hiram Greene to handle things in Sweetwater and Bob Judd still on the payroll as a hunter, he really didn't have to do anything but sit back and count the money. Every month his bank account in Dodge ballooned another couple of thousand, but try as he might, he couldn't think of anything to spend it on. Women and whiskey were around whenever he wanted them, yet a man could get jaded on both real quick if he wasn't careful. Fancy clothes and a grand tour back east—which was what most fellows did when they struck it big—held no appeal for him. Business bored him stiff, perhaps more so than ever. Even poker had lost its zing. Whenever he took a chair he invariably won, no matter how recklessly he played. It was as if he had acquired the magic touch in whatever he tried. Uncaring, not particularly concerned with whether he won or lost, everything he did seemed to wind up smelling of gold. Like some mad alchemist had doused him with a special brand of holy water, and regardless of the odds, he just couldn't lose. Not anymore.

Sometimes he even wondered why he bothered to continue hunting. Certainly it wasn't the money, not with hide prices scraping the bottom of the barrel. What he made out of the trading post more than doubled what he cleared from hunting, so money itself was no longer a factor. Once it might have been the thrill of the hunt, but now he had to chalk that off as well. He had killed better than thirty thousand shaggies since coming west, and making a stand had long since lost even a twinge of challenge. There were times he thought the feeling got its start with the white buffalo he had downed last winter. Afterwards, when the hoopla died down in the newspapers and men stopped buying him drinks, hunting somehow lost its savor. It was as though he had seen it all, done everything there was to do, and hide-hunting had become little more than a habit. Like some men were addicted to tobacco and others to alcohol, he had become hooked on killing buffalo.

Or maybe the buffalo were just an excuse.

Whenever he had had his fill of towns and people, he returned to the herds. They were there, always waiting, and killing them in a businesslike way justified his existence as a buffalo-hunter. Lately, though, he had commenced wondering if the buffalo hadn't always represented more than just money and a certain independence to live as he pleased.

As long as there were buffalo he could wander the plains at will, living off the bounty of the land as did all wild things. For in his mind it was the wild things that were free. Not men.

But what happened when the buffalo were gone?

Throughout the summer, as he roamed the length and breadth of the Panhandle, it had been a question much on his mind. What would be left for men like himself when

235

the herds were wiped out? Would freedom disappear in the very instant that the last buffalo crumpled to the earth? Perhaps it would work out just that way, as it had with the mountain men thirty years back when the fur trade played out. Maybe, like them, he would wind up running a trading post, or sitting on the porch of some lonely cabin wondering where the hell it had all gone. It was a disquieting thought, more so than he cared to admit.

Yet one that could hardly be shunted aside.

The herds this year were thinner than ever before. He had seen it happen on the Smoky Hill and the Arkansas in exactly the same fashion. Buffalo roving the land in scattered bands one year and simply vanishing the next. Annihilated as if a giant eraser had wiped them clean from a thinly penciled drawing. Either that or driven ever westward as they fled before the encircling roar of gunpowder and lead.

The telltale signs he had seen so often in the past were all there. Rotted carcasses and bleached bones marring the plains as far as a man could see. Green flies buzzing and humming in dense clouds as the stench of death hung in tainted layers over the killing grounds. Packs of wolves and coyotes prowling the land while overhead buzzards circled in the hot sky.

Carrion-eaters gathering from far and wide to share in the feast of death.

There remained only one last step. The final kill. Then, as it had been along the hunting grounds farther north, the Panhandle would grow silent. Wiped clean of the shaggy beasts that had grazed there for untold centuries.

Early in September, Jordan had led his outfit toward the headwaters of the South Canadian in an attempt to escape the constant roar of Sharps buffalo guns. Even that far west there was no scarcity of hunters. But at least he wasn't in the midst of a battlefield, and the smell of rotted flesh had lessened enough that a man could again breathe in comfort. McCabe and the skinners took a day to set up camp along the south bank while Jordan scouted the countryside. There were small herds dotting the plains—the remnants of what they had seen along the Prairie Dog Fork that spring—but enough to keep them in business for a fortnight. Perhaps longer, if the army behind them didn't advance too swiftly.

That night after supper the men were swapping yarns when Huggins noticed a peculiar orangy glow in the sky to the north. They moved a little higher up the bank to get a better look, and stood there watching it for some moments in silence. Every man in the outfit knew what it was. Not one of them, though, knew where it was. Or where it would be before night fell again.

McCabe finally glanced around at Jordan and posed the question on everyone's mind. "You think it'll get this far?"

The plainsman tested the wind and studied the sky a while longer. "Hard tellin'. The wind's carryin' it south right now, but that could change anytime. We'll just have to wait and see."

"Then you're aimin' to stay here?" McCabe said.

"Unless you want to chance gettin' roasted alive. Them flames look to be a good ten miles across. Maybe more. If we head south and get caught out in the open, we'll wind up sort of crispy."

"I reckon you're right. Sure gets at a man's innards, though, to just sit and watch the thing come at you."

Jordan grunted, never taking his eyes off the distant sky-line. "Runnin' away from things usually gets a man in a sight more trouble than holdin' his ground. That goes especially for prairie fires. This time tomorrow we might be damn glad we've got a river to squat in."

With dawn the northern horizon was fiery red and the air had become stifling. The wind hadn't changed, and the men could detect faint traces of smoke in the air. Jordan had them strike camp and hitch the mules, certain now that it was only a matter of time until they were forced into the river. Toward mid-morning the prairie around them turned dusky as the smoke grew heavier, and the sun became a thin, glowing disk, all but hidden in the blackened sky. Then, distant at first but swelling to a thunderous clatter, they heard the hoofbeats.

Jordan ordered the wagons into the streambed side by side, then had all the livestock lashed securely to the rear wheels. This final precaution was accomplished not a moment too soon. The air suddenly filled with ashes as the wind came up strong, and before it fled the wild things. The antelope and deer came first, bounding down the north bank and across the river to disappear over the prairie in headlong flight. Only moments later the ground began to rumble with a deafening roar, and buffalo started spilling over the far shore by the hundreds, then in the thousands, as a gust of hot air swept in from the north.

The herd came in a solid wall of fur and hooves almost a hundred yards wide and strung out nearly a mile in depth. The hide men could only stare in awed wonder as the hump-backed beasts splashed through the water barely twenty yards upstream and lumbered up the south bank.

Though none of them said anything, they each knew what would have happened had the herd barreled head-on into the wagons.

The wolves came next, pausing to look back from the south bank, then scampering off with their tails between their legs. Close behind appeared rabbits and skunks and badgers and a dozen different prairie creatures, all scurrying madly to escape the inferno at their heels.

Even before the last animal could quit the far shore a great wave of crackling flame, spitting and leaping high in the air like fiery thunderclouds, burst off the plains on the shoulders of a scalding wind. The flames came to a sizzling halt as vegetation petered out near the water's edge, but the air bore ashes and sparks across the riverbed in a churning whirlwind of heat. One instant a wall of flame stretching miles in each direction went dead on the north bank, and in the next instant the inferno was reborn with added ferocity on the south bank. Then, with a blinding flash, it gained strength and roared southward across the plains.

Choking, their eyes blinded with smoke, the men threw themselves in the water to drown the fiery ashes that had settled over their clothing. Within moments they were on their feet, using their hats to toss water on the terrified livestock. Sparks had ignited the animal's hair, and the crew worked frantically to douse the patches of wispy smoke. Next they went through the wagons, beating out little tendrils of flame wherever some piece of gear had caught fire. Satisfied that the livestock and their equipment were safe, the men then looked to themselves. Though they had covered their faces with wet bandanas, every man in the crew had had his eyebrows singed off, and most of them had burns around the forehead and neck. They made a sorry spectacle, ludicrous almost, with steam lifting off their clothing in tiny puffs and their brows shorn clean of hair.

But nobody laughed. Old Scratch had come much too close for it to be a jesting matter. Later perhaps they could joke and have a few chuckles, but not now.

Jordan walked to the north bank and stood staring out

over the devastated land. The air was brisk and cooler here, but still filled with the strong odor of burnt things. Streaks of bluish smoke drifted along the ground from buffalo chips and clumps of bunchgrass left smoldering on the blackened prairie. As far as his eye would carry he saw nothing but death. Turning, he looked southward, and miles away, on a dead reckoning for the Prairie Dog Fork, he saw a towering wall of flame and smoke racing across the plains.

Watching the smoke billow and roil in the distance, it came to him that death had had itself one fine summer. Monte Brown and many good men like him rubbed out back in the spring. More lost at the fight at Yellow House Canyon. Then Custer and his bunch getting wiped out on the Little Big Horn. Even Bill Hickok, the toughest old bird of them all, had gone under some place up in the Dakotas. The way things shaped up, it didn't look to be much of a year for old hands.

Grunting, he shook his head and breathed deep to clear his lungs. Damned if he wasn't getting as superstitious as McCabe. Looking for signs where none existed. Trying to make something out of fools getting themselves killed and a prairie fire that just happened to sweep through the buffalo herds. Rot and nonsense, that's all it was. Men die and fires start, and it doesn't mean a hill of beans as far as what ticks around next on the clock.

Scrambling down the bank, he headed back to the wagons. Instead of hunting for bad signs, he ought to look on the bright side. That fire hadn't gone anywhere near Sweetwater, which meant that his town had escaped unharmed. That was something to crow about right there. Few men would have as much to laugh about this day.

Still, Sweetwater was only about halfway between nothing and something. It wasn't everything, and never would be.

Not by a damnsight.

2.

Virge Hollister came through the door of the Lone Star and stood for a moment observing the sky. The sun was bright and warm, but there was a crisp bite to the air and a brittle stillness had settled over the land. Winter wasn't far off. Before long the winds would come howling down out of the north, and on their tail would follow the blizzards. Within a month, perhaps sooner, Dodge City would become a tiny snowbound island in a frozen wasteland.

But Hollister wasn't going anywhere. Not this winter. Stepping off the boardwalk, he filled his lungs with the fresh morning air and walked toward the plaza. Much had been accomplished during the trailing season, and he had ample reason to look back on the past five months with a warm glow of satisfaction. Still, everything to date had been merely an opening gambit. The bait. Today he would make the second move in the very carefully engineered plan he and James had worked out. The step which would ultimately consolidate his position among the uptown crowds who ran Dodge.

Thinking about it as he strode along at a brisk pace, he gave himself a small pat on the back. For someone who had stepped off the train with egg on his face just ten months back, he had come a long way. Considerably farther than anyone suspected. Particularly the hayseeds who thought they had a hammerlock on Dodge politics.

While the trailing season had ended with the first snap of cold weather, everybody in town was congratulating themselves on the haul they had made off the Texans. Yet the past summer had been only a sampler. There were great things in the offing, and the citizens of Dodge City shared a mounting confidence about what lay just around the corner. The former buffalo capital, facing ruin and economic collapse only a year back, was now on the brink of becoming the queen of cowtowns.

Quite unexpectedly, the Kansas legislature had become Dodge's newest ally in the campaign to lure the Texas cattlemen away from Wichita. The lawmakers had commenced making noises about passing an embargo act which would ban longhorns from the eastern half of the state. Their concern stemmed from the fact that most of their constituents were farmers, whose livestock had suffered grievously from an outbreak of Spanish fever. This virulent disease, which often proved fatal to domestic cattle, was spread by a small tick that came north each summer, firmly attached to the longhorns. Unfortunately, it had the disturbing habit of dropping off along the trail and finding a new home among the less hardy breed that had been imported from the east. The farmers were justly outraged, and their indignant howls had fallen on receptive ears at the state capitol. In Kansas the farm vote generally decided an election, and the politicians were quick to get the message.

The Texans weren't exactly slow themselves. They had been barred from Abilene a few years back, and now a movement was afoot to block them from trailing to Wichita. The handwriting was on the wall, plain for everybody to see, and contrary to common gossip there were many Texans who actually knew how to read. Already there was talk of blazing a new trail north through the Nations, one which would by-pass the old Chisholm Trail completely. Called the Western Trail by those who had a passable knowledge of the land, it would run due north from Fort Worth and across the Red at Doan's Store. From there it would pass about fifty miles east of the settlement at Sweetwater, then skirt Antelope Hills and connect with the road north out of Camp Supply. After that it was only a short haul into Dodge.

Everybody readily agreed that crossing the lands of the Comanches and Kiowas was a bit dicier than dealing with the Five Civilized Tribes to the east. But it didn't worry the Texans enough to sour them on the idea of a new trail. The army had the hostiles pretty well whipped into line, and the cattlemen figured they were willing to risk it. Some of the more farsighted among them couldn't see that they had much choice, anyway. Not with the Kansas legislators breathing down their necks.

Virge Hollister had played an important role in bringing to fruition this love affair between Dodge City and the Texans. Though he would hardly have considered himself a matchmaker, it was exactly this function he had performed. The lawman had learned much about the peculiar nature of Texans during his time in Wichita; while he didn't respect them, he was pragmatic enough to admit that without the trailhands' rowdy antics there would be no need for men like himself. From his viewpoint, he had as much at stake as the business community in making Dodge the premier cowtown on the western plains. Bearing that thought uppermost in mind, he had acted as something of a lightning rod between the townspeople and the rambunctious Texans.

The first step had been in convincing the town council that the cowhands should be allowed to carry guns, as long as they stayed south of the tracks. There was strong opposition to this at first, for the town fathers were determined that Dodge would not be turned into a shooting gallery. But Hollister finally persuaded them with a very simple argument. Ban the Texans from carrying guns openly and they would commence carrying them secretly. Texans were a stubborn breed, and an ordinance against firearms would be like a red flag in front of a bull. More to the point, it would mean that every time a cowhand wandered across the tracks to Front Street he would like as not have a gun under his shirt. The wisest course was to restrict carrying of weapons only north of the tracks. Leave the South Side wide open.

The Deadline had come next. Hollister posted notices all around town before the first herd arrived, and much to the town council's surprise, the Texans thought it was a pretty fair idea. As long as they could carry their guns south of the tracks, they didn't mind taking them off when they crossed to the plaza. Since the saloons and cathouses were on the South Side, they didn't figure to be spending much time north of the tracks, anyway. The only challenge had come in June from Ned Kennedy and his crew. Thereafter, the Deadline had been observed religiously. Once the Texans saw what a quart of buckshot could do to a man's gizzard, they decided to stick to the rules.

The rest of the summer had passed uneventfully, at least for the townspeople north of the tracks. On the South Side the cowhands had killed and wounded a number of fellow Texans, but only one local man had fallen victim to their guns. Since he was a tinhorn gambler, caught with a holdout clip up his sleeve, the town gave him a quick burial and let the matter drop right there. Otherwise, an average night in the vice district sounded like any normal Fourth of July, and the Texans adopted as their favorite target the street lamps spotted along the boardwalk. Since Hollister and his deputies made enough arrests to generate close to $7,000 in fines, the town council was happy to replace the lamps as quickly as they were shot out. All the more so since one of the council members was the contractor who supplied the city with street lighting.

But it was the townspeople themselves who began singing the praises of Virge Hollister. His tough, yet seemingly fair, attitude toward Texans had given Dodge more law and order than it had had any time since its incorporation back in '69. Marshals had come and gone throughout the years, but none had displayed his knack for holding the rougher element in line. Better yet, he had done it without giving the cowhands a sour taste about Dodge. They thought the South Side was the greatest thing since apple pie, and had gone back to Texas raving about it the way little boys will carry on over a three ring circus.

There was one other factor at work here, too. Perhaps more important than even law and order to the citizens of Dodge. The Texans had pumped close to $500,000 into the town's economy over the trailing season, providing new lifeblood for future growth. Hollister had performed the rather nifty high-wire act of holding the cowhands in check while the townspeople skinned them out of their last nickel.

That took a rare kind of talent, and the people of Dodge had applauded heartily once the season drew to a close.

The town council had no choice but to extend Hollister's contract and offer him a raise in pay. Forewarned by Jason Rath, they would have preferred to let him go when the season ended. Regardless of how adept he might be at enforcing the law, they had no intention of sharing their power with a common gunslinger. But the voice of the people had spoken and the politicos were forced to go along. Less than a year hence they themselves must stand for election, and they could ill afford to tell their fellow townsmen that they feared Hollister's ambition. That might set folks to wondering if they, too, weren't uncommonly ambitious. Or even worse, that there was something besides civic pride which prompted them to serve on the town council.

Hollister got a new contract, with a clause awarding him one-fourth of all future court fines and a vote of congratulations from the town fathers. Yet the bonus he really wanted—and needed—wasn't forthcoming. Jason Rath continued to give him the cold shoulder.

Not that the little merchant was unfriendly. That wasn't his way. He was civil, courteous, and never too busy to pass the time of day with the marshal. But he remained politely aloof. Hollister could sense the storekeeper's wariness whenever they were together, and he suspected that Sam Jordan was behind it somehow. Still, it wasn't something he could broach openly with Rath, for he couldn't risk offending the man. While the merchant wasn't actively engaged in politics, he was a long standing crony of those who were, and it was through him that Hollister meant to gain membership in the club.

Sometimes he wondered if Rath had any inkling that this was his real reason for courting Julia. Back when they were looking for a way to breach the power structure, James had once likened it to a series of padlocks. Julia was the key to Rath, who in turn was the key to the town fathers. It was merely a matter of picking the locks with a delicate touch and opening the doors when the timing seemed right. Despite his guarded attitude, Rath had never attempted to stop the lawman from calling on Julia. At first this had puzzled Hollister, for it seemed inconsistent with the merchant's obvious distrust. But gradually he had come to understand how it was between Rath and his daughter. Julia was a headstrong, impulsive girl, governed by strong emotions despite her witty chatter about logic and intellect. Rath knew his daughter, and he had appraised the situation with uncommon shrewdness. Were he to forbid Hollister to call on her, Julia would become defiant and wind up doing something foolish. Instead the merchant kept hands off, wagering that with time she would come to the right conclusion all by herself.

Only within the last year had Virge Hollister become perceptive enough about men and their motives to see beneath Rath's little game. After getting his ears pinned back in Wichita, he had lost some of his arrogance. Facing five to ten years in prison has a way of pulling a man up short and forcing him to take a long, hard look at himself. Hollister had done that, retracing step by step the reasons for his downfall in Wichita. Somewhere in the process he had come to a couple of very startling conclusions, both of which had great effect on his outlook regarding the Dodge venture.

Just for openers, he had violated his own rule by resorting to violence in Wichita. The situation had clearly called for cunning and stealth, but in the heat of the moment he had forgotten that the smart take it away from the strong. It wasn't something he would overlook again.

The second relevation had been stronger medicine still. While it came hard, he had to admit that there were any number of men who were as smart, perhaps even smarter, than Virge Hollister. Some of them he had met in Wichita. They had outfoxed him at every turn and pegged his hide to the wall before he knew what hit him. With this newly won pragmatism, Hollister could even admit that some of the politicos in Dodge probably had him shaded in the brains department. Which meant that he would have to be

244

trickier, quicker, and infinitely more clever to outwit them.

Bloodied, but wiser, he had departed Wichita a far more dangerous foe than the swaggering young hothead who had ridden in off the plains two years previously. Now he wasn't so quick to display his mental agility. It served his purpose to let people think he was a fast gun who coincidentally had enough brains to come in out of the rain. Over the long haul they would relax, let their guard down, telling themselves and each other that they could outmaneuver Virge Hollister with both eyes closed. Ever so slowly, one step at a time over a period of months, he would convince them that they had nothing to fear from him. That he was just bright enough to be valuable, but not so smart that he would ever pose a threat. Then, when they saw the townspeople behind him—with Julia on his arm and old man Rath giving him the nod at last—the big augurs would invite him to join the club.

Their reasoning would be faultless. Here was a personable, good-looking young chap who had a way with the voters. Better yet, he was the kind of a man they could run for office—mayor perhaps, or state legislator—and still control from behind the scenes. Just sharp enough to fool the voters but ever responsive to the strings being pulled by those who put him in office.

Right about then, they would discover a fly in the butter. Instead of controlling a wooden dummy—who burped up whatever words were fed into him—the politicos would awaken one morning and find that their young protégé had taken command of the ship. But by the time the flaw in their maneuvering became evident, it would be too late. The power would rest in his hands, and with it he could sway the voters in whatever direction he chose. The blockheads who had put him in office would find themselves neatly snookered. The only choice left them would be to jump on the bandwagon—and start taking orders like everyone else.

The entire plan, from winning Julia Rath to taking over the political apparatus of Ford County, had been Hollister's own design. James had contributed, but not all that greatly. For the lawman had learned a third, and perhaps equally important, lesson in Wichita. His older brother was a sadistic malcontent who enjoyed inflicting punishment more than he did winning. Somewhat like a pugilist who was content to lose the fight if only he could bloody his opponent's nose. That didn't make a hell of a lot of

245

sense to Hollister. Whatever the game—politics, mumbly-peg, or a gunfight—the object was to win. Consolation prizes were strictly for suckers.

Looking back, he could see quirks in James's character that had been a liability from the start. The gang of hooligans kept on the payroll solely to administer beatings, and those freaky sessions with some of the girls after hours. Hollister had stayed clear of the whole mess, never once trying to interfere. But the stories he heard were enough to make a man's skin crawl. Yet, only lately he had put it all together and come up with a rather unsettling conclusion.

His elder brother wasn't all there.

Curiously, though, James was a pretty good businessman, and did all right operating the Lone Star. But the lawman would just as soon he stayed on the South Side and kept his nose out of Dodge politics. The less the uptown crowd saw of James the better. It sure as hell wouldn't do for them to get wind of the oddball pastimes practiced by the elder Hollister. Not unless everybody in the family wanted to stay saloonkeepers and whoremongers the rest of their lives.

Walking through the deserted vice district, Hollister found it strange not to hear gunshots and drunken shouts. With trailing season over, there wasn't a Texan left in town. Shortly after the cowhands had departed, the South Side had shut down tighter than a drum. The gamblers, whores, and saloonkeepers had made their money, and now they were off to spend the winter enjoying it. Most of them headed for St. Louis or Chicago. Some even went as far as New York City. That had always amused Hollister in a perverse sort of way. The sporting crowd spent the summer skinning the Texans then headed back east where the real sharpers spent the winter skinning them. Chuckling to himself as he crossed the tracks, he figured there must be a moral in that somewhere if a man had the time to dig it out.

Striding along in the brisk morning sunlight, he headed straight for the Long Branch Saloon. Shortly after being appointed marshal he had started scouting around for a new frontman. With James put out to pasture, that left him no choice but to select someone local. Morgan and Warren were still too inexperienced for political skulduggery, and he really didn't want them involved anyway. What he had searched for over the months was a man who had connections both uptown and on the South Side.

246

Along about next fall, when election time rolled around, he was going to need money for bribes and someone to handle the payoffs. Should it become necessary, the man might even have to throw his weight around to get the sporting crowd to cough up contributions. After studying Dodge for the better part of six months he had settled on Luke Short, the owner of the Long Branch.

Short was a gambler who ran highroller games for the Texas herd owners as well as local businessmen who liked to plunge. He was well liked, respected for running straight games, and had connections with everyone who counted along Front Street. That, added to the fact that he had reputedly killed four men in gunfights, made him welcome in the dives on the South Side as well. From where Hollister stood, he suited the ticket just fine. Connections with the big augurs. Fast with a gun. Access to every cash box in town. That was a hard combination to beat, and for that very reason Luke Short had been nominated.

Today he would get the message.

The Long Branch was still empty when Hollister came through the door. Nodding to the barkeep, he skirted the gaming room and rapped a couple of times on the door of Short's office. Without waiting for a reply he twisted the knob and went on in.

Short was seated at a desk working on some ledgers and he didn't rise. Curiously, considering his name, he wasn't a tall man. But he had the grit of a bantam cock, and was reportedly fast as a snake with a gun. Right now his eyes held a mixture of surprise and mild irritation.

"Marshal, you ought to try waiting for an invite before you start opening doors. Never know what you might find waiting for you on the other side."

Hollister stopped before the desk and smiled crookedly at the little gambler. Then his hand moved, and without hardly seeing it happen, Luke Short found the muzzle of a Colt jammed up against his nose. The lawman slowly thumbed the hammer back and the metallic clicks brought a bead of sweat to the gambler's forehead.

"Luke, I hear you're fast with a gun. Now, let's have a straight answer. Think you can beat that?"

Short's head didn't move, but his eyes lifted from the gun barrel. "Tell you the truth, I wouldn't want to try. It'd be so close, I'd get drilled either way."

Hollister eased the hammer down and holstered the gun.

247

"I wanted you to see my hole card before I said my piece. I came over here this mornin' to offer you a deal. You can turn me down and no hard feelin's. But if you pass and I ever hear you talked out of school, I'll come lookin' for you. Fair enough?"

"You're dealing," Short observed. "Whatever you say stops right here."

The lawman noted that Short's hand was steady and his eye firm. The pint-sized gambler was used to playing for high stakes and Hollister had a hunch he had tapped the right man for the job. "Come election time there's going to be some changes in Dodge. What I'm aimin' for is mayor. I'll need a frontman to collect a war chest and handle payoffs. Most of the support we need I can get legitimate, but there's always somebody that'll have to be bought. You've got contacts on both sides of the tracks and you can put a bee in the right ear. The job's yours if you want it."

Short didn't even take a deep breath. "What's in it for me?"

Hollister pulled a chair up beside the desk and took a seat. "If I have to tell you how many ways there are to milk a town once a fellow gets to be mayor then you're the wrong man for the job. Whatever we rake in you'll get a share right off the top. Startin' next year or the year after there'll be a couple of million dollars dumped on Dodge every trail season. I figure the absolute worst we could do is about ten percent."

"Well, you know how to sweeten a pot, that's for sure." The little gambler mulled it over a minute, then cocked his head quizzically. "Why come to me now? With the South Side closed down I couldn't start building a slush fund until next spring."

"That's right, but you're going to be playin' plenty of poker with Kelly and his bunch between now and then. They talk around you and I want to hear what they've got to say. I've got some plans in the mill and you'll be able to tell me how it strikes them. Course, here and there you might even put in a few zingers for everybody's favorite candidate. Good old Virge Hollister."

Short didn't say anything, and the lawman waited a while to let him sort it all out. Finally he came out of his chair and moved back around in front of the desk. "Luke, I'd like to give you a couple of days to think it over, but it's not that kind of game. So I guess it's sort of up to you. Check or bet."

The gambler's wooden expression cracked with a slight smile. "Marshal, I like the way you deal. Where do we start?"

Hollister chuckled and flashed a wide grin. "We've already started. About six months ago. I'll let you know when something's ready to pop. Meantime, keep your ears open." Striding to the door, he turned the knob then looked back. "Luke, I've got a hunch we'll make a pretty good team. You just hold up your end and we'll both come out smellin' like roses."

When the door closed, Luke Short leaned back in his chair and clasped his hands behind his head. That last statement sounded innocent as hell, but he had been around long enough to recognize a threat when it was dropped in his lap.

Virge Hollister hadn't said it outright, but the message was plain to read. Hold up your end or else. The *or else* needed no explanation.

The little gambler's mouth lifted in a tight grin. All of a sudden he decided he was going to like this game.

The stakes were just about his speed. High card take all.

3.

When Jordan came out of the dugout that morning the sky was metallic, almost colorless, the air murky. He stood for some moments scanning the horizon in every direction, noting that the sun was hidden behind a thick overcast which hung suspended across the land. There was a raw, blustery wind out of the northwest, but the skyline appeared clear. Not a storm cloud in sight.

Just another winter day. Colder than most and gloomy as a graveyard. But a good day for hunting.

The plainsman was dressed warmly, for the weather had been unseasonably cold and the ground was covered with a foot of hard, crusted snow. His furry buffalo coat, along with a full beard, gave him the appearance of a great, shaggy bear standing upright. The bull-hide pacs, extending to just below his knees, made for clumsy walking, and when he started toward the livestock shed he looked like a waddling ball of fur.

Huggins had already watered the mules and horses, and Cook was busy forking out a ration of cured bluestem to each of the animals. Moving behind the roan, who had been given the warmest spot in the shed, Jordan saw that the load of grass they had collected and stored in late fall was running dangerously low. Early snows and intense cold had forced them to keep the stock under cover more than normal, and the animals hadn't been able to forage for themselves. When the grass was gone it would be a steady diet of cottonwood bark for horse and mule alike. Still, they were a sturdy bunch, and he had no doubt they would come through the winter in good shape.

McCabe was standing in the doorway peering at the sky when Jordan came around the corner of the dugout. The old man slewed a glance at him then went back to watching the dingy overcast. "I was out early this mornin', 'fore you and the boys had your peepers open."

McCabe liked to build a mystery around things whenever he had something important to say, and he always came at it in a roundabout fashion. The plainsman had long since grown accustomed to his peculiar ways and was generally able to play the game with a straight face. "Well you could've fooled me, Lon. I thought it was pack rats raidin' us again."

The skinner shot him a sour look and spat a wad of tobacco juice toward the river bank. "Saw a white owl perched in them trees just after dawn. Biggun, too."

Jordan's gaze flicked through the cottonwoods, finding nothing. "What happened to him?"

"He took off 'fore it was plumb light." McCabe's head swiveled around, and he waited just long enough to lend emphasis to his words. "Headed south."

"Maybe he was just gettin' an early start." Jordan again searched the northern horizon, but the sky remained washed out and still. "Near as I can tell, there's nothin' blowin' up. Not anytime soon, leastways."

"Christ a'mighty, you got the hardest head of any man I ever met. Even a greenhorn ain't so dimwitted he don't know what it means when you see a snow owl. Them birds just don't come this far south less'n there's somethin' goddamn fierce right behind 'em."

"Old man, I can't rightly argue it one way or the other. First off, I've never seen a snow owl. For all I know, the critter don't even exist. And lastly, I got a sneakin' hunch all that Injun mumbo-jumbo is pure hogwash anyway. Hell, gut-eaters got so many superstitions it's a wonder they don't walk backwards."

"Then you aim to go lookin' for a stand regardless?"

"Reckon so. We're not gonna make any money with me layin' around camp on my backsides."

"What if I told you my leg was all stove up? Wouldn't that convince you?"

"Lon, that leg of yours is pretty good sign on Injuns, but it's nothin' to brag about when it comes to weather." The pained expression on McCabe's face brought a chuckle from the plainsman. "Now c'mon, you old fart. Quit your frettin'. More'n likely you was seein' things anyhow."

"Cimarron, you're a gol'danged fool!" McCabe snorted and limped off toward the shed. "I seen plenty of snow owls when I was in the mountains, and I ain't forgot what they look like neither. But you just go on and be a smartass. See if I give a damn."

Jordan watched him stump off around the corner, still cursing a blue streak. Cook and Huggins were in for a good half-hour's lecture on the ignoramus ways of buffalo-hunters. Especially the pigheaded kind. Ducking low through the door, the plainsman entered the dugout and started gathering his gear. McCabe meant well, but sometimes he was just a natural-born pain in the neck. Jesus! White owls. Next he would be seeing visions like some bare-assed Comanche witch doctor.

Then Jordan laughed. Hell, why not? After a man had seen a white owl he could conjure up just about anything that took his fancy.

Outside, McCabe was busily delivering a tirade to Huggins and Cook as they commenced their morning chores in the hide yard. The hides dried slowly in the chill winter air and had to be turned several times before they were cured. Afterwards they were sorted, bulls in one pile and cows in another, and stacked eight feet high. The young stuff went into a kip stack. Then they were cinched down tight with whangs of green rawhide to await the day Jordan decided it was time for another trip to Sweetwater.

The ways things had been going lately, though, that wouldn't be anytime soon.

The prairie fire earlier that fall had driven the herds south in search of graze long before they would have normally started for the winter feeding grounds. Jordan and his crew had trailed them across a burned-out swath some twenty miles wide stretching clear to the Prairie Dog Fork of the Red. Along the way they had seen the blackened hulks of thousands of buffalo and smaller animals that had perished in the fiery holocaust. The plains reeked with the sickly-sweet stench of charred flesh, and it was only after crossing the Middle Pease that they left the smell behind. Though they had seen herds days before, Jordan refused to stop until they had outdistanced the regiment of hunters also driven south by the fire. Through late fall and early winter they had followed a twisting course over the Tongue and the Washita River, finally coming to rest on the Salt Fork of the Brazos some miles east of where it joined the White River. There they had burrowed and shored in a small knoll back away from the stream and settled down in their dugout for the winter.

The herds were scattered over a wide area, and it was the worst hunting any of them could recall since their last winter on the Smoky Hill. Jordan was often forced to scout miles away from camp before sighting buffalo; even when he made a stand the herds were so thinned out that he rarely killed enough to keep McCabe and the skinners busy for more than a few hours. The way things were shaping up it would be the skimpiest payday any of them had had since coming west. The men bitched and belly-ached constantly around camp, but it did little good. The buffalo simply weren't to be found, not in the numbers they were accustomed to seeing, and no amount of complaint would change that. Their bewilderment mounted as hard winter set in, and many a night they gathered around the fire to discuss the shaggies' strange disappearance. But their speculations and theories were little more than idle conversation.

Nobody had the answer. Except the one that none of them cared to voice. Or face outright.

This particular morning Jordan had decided to circle west in a gradual swing toward the Double Mountain Fork, which lay some ten miles to the south. Over the past few weeks he had hunted west along the White and east toward Kiowa Peak, then made a sashay across the northern strip in between. While hunters were thick as fleas, the buffalo had seemingly scattered to the winds, and by his calculations the crew had barely made wages. Last night, after crawling beneath his robes, he had tossed and turned for hours, working himself into a foul temper as he stewed over their predicament.

Something had to change, and damned quick. Otherwise

they might as well go on back to Sweetwater and spend the winter in a warm saloon.

Jordan's scouts had come to cover such distances, generally wandering erratically over the countryside, that the skinners no longer trailed him to the killing ground. Since his stands these days rarely accounted for more than twenty buffalo, there was plenty of time to return for the crew and lead them back. Only once in the past month had they failed to skin out all the carcasses before sundown. Even then it wasn't due to the number of hides they took, but rather because they had had so far to travel to the kill.

After saddling the gelding, Jordan briefed McCabe on the general direction he meant to scout and then rode out. The old skinner hadn't said anything more about the white owl, and Jordan figured it was just as well. While it had seemed funny earlier, the humor escaped him now. They needed a stand—in the worst way—and all this spooky nonsense about bad signs didn't help matters even a little bit.

Some time around noon, the plainsman stopped to give his horse a breather. The crusted snow made it rough going on the roan, and Jordan was kicking himself for not having ridden one of the mules instead. The best he could figure, they had made less than five miles in close to three hours without sighting a goddamned thing. Unless they got lucky pretty quick he would be forced to turn back. Though he didn't have the slightest notion of how cold it was, he knew the temperature had dropped rapidly just within the last hour. Near as he could judge, it was the kind of day brass monkeys got their gonads froze off, which was cold enough for man or beast. Matter of fact, he was having a little trouble keeping his own pizzle warm, and unless he kept moving, the bull hide pacs didn't do a hell of a lot for his feet either. While the gelding's winter coat had come in shaggy and long he didn't look to be doing much better, if as good. All things considered, it appeared to be one of those days when everybody should have stayed in bed.

Jordan had his foot in the stirrup when he saw the frost cloud. Some three hundred yards to the front there was a stunted ridge, and from behind it vaporous gray pockets were drifting skyward. Even from that far away he knew it was caused by the steamy breath of a buffalo herd.

Judging from the amount of smoke they were putting up, it looked to be a fair sized bunch.

Quickly he tied the roan to a withered chokecherry bush, slung Lucretia over his shoulder, and unstrapped the rest of his shooting gear. The wind was still out of the northwest, and he circled off to the east to make damn sure the herd didn't raise his scent. The snow was firm enough that he didn't break through, and less than a quarter-hour later he inched up the backside of the ridge on his belly. When he poked his head over the top it was like old times again. Upwards of three hundred buffalo were spread out on a wide swale below, pawing at the frosted snow as they dug for the grass underneath.

More goddamn shaggies than he had seen in a month of Sundays!

The ridge was bare of cover, offering nothing whatever in the way of concealment, and he decided to shoot prone. Spreading his gear within easy reach, he commenced scanning the herd for the leader. Presently he spotted her, an old cow, standing with her nose straight into the wind. Scooting around, he set the sights for two hundred yards and fumbled a shell into the breech. His mittens made for awkward loading, but he didn't dare take them off. Snapping the lever shut, he brought the Sharps to his shoulder and sighted on the cow. But the end of the barrel was wobbling so badly he couldn't begin to draw a decent bead. Right about then he decided it was a damnsight colder than he'd suspected. True, he hadn't seen a herd this big in quite a while, but he had been at the game too long to start getting buck fever now. So it had to be the cold.

Tensing his body against the chill, he managed to hold the barrel fairly still and sighted again on the cow. Even as the Sharps slammed up against his shoulder, he knew the shot had gone wild. The big slug struck the cow above the knee, breaking her leg. Flinging blood in every direction, she plunged into the herd and went hopping across the snow with one leg dangling crookedly. Working frantically, Jordan threw another shell into the rifle and steadied himself with a deep breath. When Lucretia roared the second time the cow went down as if struck by lightning. The buffaloes who had tagged after her stopped and commenced bellowing as they scented fresh blood. Several cows rushed over and started hooking the dead one, pawing snow as they grunted and shoved. Most of the others just stood around looking alert but bewildered, like they couldn't quite make up their minds.

Jordan's blood was running hot now, impervious to the cold. Loading and firing with deadly precision, he dropped seven cows closest to the leader before halting to cool the barrel. While he worked he kept one eye on the herd, just in case somebody spooked and he had to make a fast shot. But the scare had run its course.

Solemn as a bunch of judges, the shaggies bowed their massive foreheads and went back to pawing for grass. Undisturbed by the steaming mound of carcasses in their midst, they could think only of the rumbling hunger in their stomachs.

The plainsman had his stand.

Holding himself to a measured pace, he began dropping cows at the edge of the herd, those that appeared to be drifting off. Load, fire, eject. Ten shots, then halt to cool the rifle. The cold was so intense that he could fire ten times without overheating the barrel, and it made the job of keeping the herd bunched much easier. Even so, it wouldn't have been that much of a chore on a bright summer day. What was happening below was a drama of death and tragedy he had seen unfold a hundred times over in the past five years. Seemingly insensible to the slaughter around them, the dimwitted beasts had concern for nothing save the patch of graze directly under their noses. Almost as if the instinct for survival had been shunted aside by the more immediate need deep within their guts. Even those who had finished grazing and started chewing their cuds seemed contentedly indifferent to the systematic butchering of their fellow creatures.

It surpassed understanding, but then Jordan had long since given over trying to fathom why buffalo accepted death so placidly. He merely took advantage of it, dispatching them as quickly and painlessly as his skill allowed.

The movement of firing and loading fought off the chill from his body, and by the time fifty cows were down he had eased into the methodic rhythm so necessary to sustaining a long kill. He was operating on reflex and instinct now, hardly thinking, concentrating fully on the next shot, then the next, and the next. Somehow it was as if nothing existed on the face of the earth except the buffalo and Sam Jordan. Every fiber and sinew of his being focused solely on the herd, and within him grew a fixated obsession that he must kill them all. Sparing none.

This would be his greatest stand. One men would talk about for years to come whenever they gathered to swap tales of the old days. A story to rival the one they now told about his white buffalo.

Had the plainsman's thoughts centered less on the herd, he would have noted a stark change in the weather. Great dark storm clouds had rolled in from the northwest and the wind had risen with demonic force, blasting across the plains with a mournful whine. The temperature plummeted below zero, then lower still, coating everything it touched with an icy fire. Snow began to fall, lightly at first, then heavier and wetter, until a thick flaky blanket seemed to have enveloped the land. What some called a norther and others a blue howler had struck the southern plains. Yet by any name, it was gathering within itself, building slowly and with merciless ferocity into a ranging blizzard.

Still Jordan continued to load and fire, wholly separated from anything save his complusion to finish off the shaggy beasts below him. He was counting now, mumbling a frosty number with each shot, and only as he reached 186 did he become aware of a concerted movement within the herd. The buffaloes had winded the brewing storm, and as one they turned and lumbered toward a sheltered ravine along the southern corner of their grazing land. The plainsman began firing feverishly as they shuffled off, killing some, crippling others, missing almost as often as he hit. When the last furry rump disappeared into the ravine he jumped to his feet with a fresh load in the rifle, unable to believe that they had gone. That he had been robbed of his great stand.

Moments passed as he stood there, eyes fixed on the distant ravine, certain somehow that they would return. Then, as the spell slowly passed and his head cleared, he saw for the first time the results of his handiwork.

A circle of death, soaked in blood, littered with close to two hundred carcasses. Steaming and stiffening as the cold set its jaws to warm flesh.

But as he watched he became aware of something else. The furry black carcasses were slowly turning white. Becoming mounds of snow. Only then did his mind awaken to what his body had known for some time. He was numbed and shivering, standing atop a ridge in tbe middle of nowhere with spitting snow flurries and a howling wind buffeting him from every direction. Whirling about, he gasped as pain knifed through his joints and his teeth began chattering. The cold had pentrated his body, reamed out all suppleness and warmth, like oozing marrow sucked clean from a bone.

Unknowing, mindless, he had lain there and very nearly frozen to death.

The plainsman reacted instinctively. Unless he moved and kept moving he would be a dead man within a matter of minutes. When the wind came down out of the north like that, it was gathering itself to kill. Man. Beast. Whatever stood in its path.

Gathering his rifle and the shell pouch, he struck off at a stiff-legged lope toward the spot where he had tied the gelding. Every muscle in his body was gripped with searing agony for the first hundred yards, but slowly his blood began to warm and circulation restored itself to his hands and feet. Within minutes he felt perspiration form beneath his shirt and he slowed to a walk, knowing that if he sweated too heavily it would turn to ice inside his clothes. More than one man, fearful of the outward cold, had become a well insulated icicle by pushing himself too fast, too hard.

Shortly he stood looking at a snowy chokecherry bush. But just that. Nothing more. The gelding was gone.

He grunted, finding grim humor in the absurdity of what his eyes made real. The goddamn horse had been smarter than his master. Like the buffalo, he hadn't waited around for the storm to kill him. He had tucked tail and headed for home.

Just for a moment Jordan was struck with the idea of following the roan's tracks back to camp. Then he took a closer look and saw that he was fresh out of luck. Snow had covered the tracks long before he reached the chokecherry bush. If he was to reach camp it would be on his own hook. Astride shank's mare.

Shielding his eyes from the blinding snow flurries, he sucked up his gut and steeled himself to what lay ahead. Camp was on a dead reckoning to the north some five miles from where he stood. The only other thing he knew for certain was that the wind had been out of the northwest all day and more than likely hadn't changed. But knowing that much, he might just make it.

Unless he met Old Scratch along the way.

Quartering into the wind, keeping it always off his left shoulder, he struck out at a slow walk through the flaky blackness.

Six hours later the plainsman stumbled to a halt. For what seemed a small eternity he had wandered aimlessly, losing track of the wind and all sense of direction. Though he had no idea how far he had come, he knew he would never go a step farther. The will to live still burned fiercely, but try as he might, he couldn't budge his legs from the snow drift blocking his path. There was no feeling from his knees down, and even as he stood there, a tingling numbness spread over the rest of his body.

The blizzard tore at him with fiery claws, raking him with stinging blasts of sleet and snow, sapping his body of all will to resist. His eyelashes were frozen in narrow slits and a thick coat of ice covered his beard. Even his jaw felt locked in a vise. The lockjaw that comes shortly before the final sleep. Unless he moved he would die, of that he had not the slightest doubt. Yet will alone wasn't enough. The body must function as well, and his head already embraced the icy-fingered drowsiness that beckoned with a gentle touch.

Judgement Day was here. Now. The witless stupor that gripped him as he stood alone in the swirling white death.

Jordan dropped to his knees and knelt there for a moment staring at the rifle in one hand and the shell pouch in the other. Whatever hope he had left was there in his hands. Slim at best, but better than no chance at all.

Stiff and fumbling, his hands nearly frozen, he worked a shell into the rifle and fired it overhead. Against the howling wind the Sharps sounded like a firecracker, and if his jaw hadn't been locked shut he would have laughed. But he didn't quit. While fingers still worked he fired again and again. And once more. Then he stopped. The shell pouch was empty.

Now he wished he could laugh. The whole goddamn day had been sheer lunacy from start to finish. McCabe and his white owl. Him sitting on his butt in a snowbank popping off shots nobody would ever hear. What a way to go under. It deserved a laugh. Better yet, a horselaugh.

Then he blinked and blinked again, trying to get his eyelashes unstuck. Somewhere out there, through the spitting flurries, he had seen an orange flash of light. Or maybe he hadn't. Maybe he had already gone off his rocker and his mind was just playing cute tricks.

There is was again!

This time it was closer and he heard it. A gunshot! Twisting around, he dug underneath the buffalo coat and clawed the Colt from its holster. Thrusting the pistol overhead, he started thumbing off shots, working the hammer over and over until finally it clicked on an empty cylinder.

But by then the answering shots were even closer and he could hear voices. Men shouting. He couldn't make out the words, yet in some curious way it didn't seem to matter. They were there. Whoever they were. He had pulled it off. Cheated the blizzard and Old Scratch and that goddamned owl. Just him against the three of them.

Sinking back, he fell over in the snow. The voices were almost upon him now, but he wasn't listening. He was back on that ridge, gazing out over the biggest stand he had ever made.

Then, with a great effort, he finally laughed.

That goddamned owl had beaten him after all. Snatched the day's kill right out from under his nose. But the sonovabitch had needed a blizzard to do it.

Still, there was something fitting about it. Maybe even just, in a queer sort of way. Right at the moment, though, he was a little too bushed to think it through.

Settling back in the snow, he closed his eyes and felt a velvety darkness blanket him in warmth.

4.

Jordan's recovery was something more like a coming back to life. Slowly, and with enough pain to make even the strongest of men grit his teeth. When McCabe and the others had found him lying in the snow he was stiff as a board. They thought at first that he was a goner, for frostbite had already taken hold of his hands, feet, and the exposed parts of his face. Back in the '72 blizzard, up around Fort Hays, they had seen men only slightly worse off whittled to pieces under the post surgeon's scalpel. The lucky ones had come out of it with one leg and a stump, and a good many of them had to commence learning to eat with their elbows.

With McCabe barking orders like a drill sergeant, they

had lugged the plainsman back to the dugout and built a roaring fire. Working feverishly, they had stripped him naked, and while Huggins carted in buckets of snow, the other two gave him a frosty massage. They were old hands at this business, and they knew that if he was to be saved he must be thawed out gradually. Otherwise green rot would set in and his flesh would begin to mortify in a matter of days.

The snow rub seemed to turn the trick, and along toward midnight Jordan's color began to return. While he was never fully conscious, they managed to get a quart of scalding coffee down his gullet, and moved him closer to the fire. McCabe never left his side throughout the night, covering him with a stack of buffalo robes and periodically dosing him with a jigger of trade whiskey. The plainsman was delirious off and on, thrashing about under his covers and wildly raving something about an owl spoiling his stand. The words were muddled, crazy gibberish that didn't seem to make any sense. Except to McCabe. Though the old skinner didn't know exactly what had happened on the stormy plains south of camp, he had a pretty fair idea the snow owl had made a convert out of Jordan.

The hard way.

Once Jordan become so violent it took all three men to restrain him, and the spell lasted so long everybody was bathed in sweat by the time they finally got him calmed down. Then, shortly before dawn, the plainsman's delirium passed and he drifted off into a peaceful sleep. McCabe relaxed his vigil long enough to grab a few winks himself, but with sunrise he was up and had the skinners hustling around like a couple of chambermaids.

Later that morning, when Jordan awakened, the first thing he heard was the howling wind battering at the door. Just for a moment he thought he was again stumbling blindly through the snowy hell, and an icy claw of fear told hold of his spine. Then he felt the warmth of the fire, heard whispered voices, and slowly became aware of where he was.

When McCabe saw his eyes open he started fussing around like a mother hen. The old man had fashioned a broth of sorts out of finely chopped hump meat, bone marrow, and water. Before the plainsman could get a word out, McCabe was spooning the concoction down his throat and grinning from ear to ear. In all their years together Jordan couldn't recall seeing the skinner grin in just that way. Though he was still in a daze, he spotted a misty look around the old rascal's eyes, and it brought a lump to his throat so hard he could barely swallow the broth.

McCabe jabbered like a magpie while he wielded the spoon, spouting any nonsense that came into his head. But by the time he got the second cup of broth down Jordan he appeared to have gotten hold of himself. Sitting back, he gave the patient an astringent frown. "Well, I reckon you're gonna live. Not that I would've bet much on it the shape you was in when we found you."

Jordan smiled weakly, his voice hardly more than a whispered croak. "Did the roan make it back?"

"Jesus H. Christ! Boys, would you listen to that." McCabe threw up his hands and rolled his eyes around at Huggins and Cook. "This big lunkhead damn near froze his pecker off and he's layin' here worryin' about a horse. I'll kiss your ass and bark like a fox if I ever heard anything to beat it."

"You still didn't tell me," Jordan insisted.

"Tell you what?"

"About the roan."

"Why hell yes he made it back," the old skinner snorted. "Just goes to prove what I've always said. Horses've got more sense than people any day of the week. How in tarnation did he get away from you, anyway? You must've been lollygaggin' around like some pilgrim to get yourself set afoot."

"I had a stand going when the storm came up." Jordan's words were raspy and so low the men had to bend closer to hear. "Guess he got spooked and decided to make tracks for home."

McCabe scrunched his eyes tight, and glowered back at him. "You had a stand, d'ya? Well, now, ain't that a fine kettle of fish? The goddamnedest norther anybody ever heard tell of, and you're sittin' out there burnin' powder. Sonovabitch. That's one for the books, ain't it, boys?"

Huggins ignored the testy remarks and smiled at the plainsman. "Was it a good stand, Cimarron? Must've been or you wouldn't have stayed out there."

"Dan, it was the sweetest thing you've ever seen in your life."

Halting at first, then with growing excitement as his voice gained strength, Jordan told them of finding the herd. When he mentioned the size of the kill, their eyes went round and there was considerable cursing about the storm robbing them of a decent payday. After they quieted down, he commenced describing the trek back to camp, but the story got a little sketchy in spots. He recalled heading north upon finding the roan had bolted, and he vaguely remembered voices and gunshots toward the very end. Everything in between was fuzzy and blurred, like a nightmare that comes back only in snatches. Blinding snow. Winds that sliced through a man like a knife. Lurching from one snowdrift to the next. Falling, rising to fall again, stumbling on in a white hell that had no end.

And cold. The most ungodly, searing cold he had ever known. Like being buried alive in a vat of ice and slowly becoming so paralyzed that even the pain ceased to exist. Just numb and cold. Terribly cold.

Jordan had never in his life known fear. Even as a boy he wasn't afraid of the dark, or spooks, or any of the things that frightened other children. Since coming west he had battled Indians, fought other men with guns and knives and fists, even broken whiskey bottles. But never once had he felt fear.

Not until now.

The thing that raged outside, buffeting the dugout with its icy malevolence, wasn't flesh and blood. There was no way a man could grapple with it, outwit it, pit his strength against the force of its blow. There was an inhuman ferocity about it—something pitiless and malignant—that mortal man could never hope to match. Or dare to challenge. Just listening to it made him shiver, and he broke out in a cold sweat remembering the ease with which it had nearly killed him.

Ruminating on it after McCabe and the men had crawled into their robes for a well deserved nap, he suddenly recalled the legend of The Cold Maker. Some grizzled old plainsman had told the story at Fort Hays back in '72 when buffalo men had gathered there seeking shelter from the arctic winds. The tale had spread among hide-hunters across the plains, and being a superstitious lot, many of them came to accept it as gospel.

Long ago, so the legend went, a warrior who had grown old and feeble died during a bitter winter-storm. Though he was an ancient, a fearless Dog Soldier who had won much glory for his tribe in days gone by, the people couldn't be bothered with a ritual burial. Not with the howling winds and stinging flurries raging around their

262

own lodges looking for fresh victims. Instead of constructing a proper scaffold out on the plains, they had buried him hastily and without ceremoney in the lower branches of a cottonwood tree. That night a pack of wolves pulled the body to the ground, but finding it frozen solid and too tough to eat, they abandoned it. The old warrior's spirit had not yet crossed over, and seeing this great indignity occur, it reentered his body. Rising from the dead, he called back the cold north wind and led it to the tribal camp, to punish the people for their mistreatment of one who had served them with honor. According to legend, the wolves came to represent hunger and starvation; the wind, cold, desolation, and death. Retribution brought down on the people by The Cold Maker.

Whatever it was howling outside, Jordan wanted no part of it. Not anymore. Whoever sent it—whether the white man's God or the red man's Cold Maker—seemed a matter of small consequence. What counted was that it had tried to kill him, and nearly succeeded. Only a fool would refuse to acknowledge that he had met his match.

While he was still unable to accept superstition as fact, the plainsman was now imbued with a healthy respect for snow owls and other legends. Whether hogwash or holy scripture, he was willing to concede that there were some things a man just shouldn't mess with.

This hard-won enlightenment became all the more clear when he thought back to how miserably close he had come to cashing in. From the way McCabe and the boys told it, he was only twenty yards from the dugout when they found him. Just a few steps from warmth and safety, and he had been ready to call it quits. Had it not been for the booming roar of his Sharps Fifty, they would never have known he was there. Even now he would be lying in that snowbank.

Frozen stiff as a slab of ice. Just him and the owl and The Cold Maker.

It was something to reflect on. Carefully. A none-too-gentle reminder that it didn't pay to scoff at another fellow's beliefs.

His gods might be listening.

The blizzard lasted five days. Jordan's face peeled and scabbed, and his nose swelled to the size of a purple onion. Though his hands and feet remained sore as a ruptured boil, he was able to hobble around by the third day.

Except that there was no place to hobble to. They were trapped in the dugout, venturing outside only to care for the livestock and lug in another armload of buffalo chips for the fire. Luckily, they had plenty of fuel on hand. Even in their well-insulated cave the cold was so bitter that throwing dried chips in the fire was like tossing sparrows down the throat of a hungry lion.

While it had been an unpleasant chore back in late fall, they were thankful now that they had spent days carting in wagonloads of plattershaped buffalo dung. When dry it gave off an intense heat, with little smoke, and in time a man even got to where he liked the pungent odor emitted by the flames. They were no less thankful that they had set back a large cache of cured hams, hump meat, and tongues. Not even wolves would have attempted hunting in the snowbound, frozen wasteland outside. Drifts around the dugout were a foot or more over a man's head, and they had tunneled paths to the livestock shed as well as to their stores of fuel and food. The wind blew constantly with gale force, moaning a sorrowful whine like a bereaved woman. Not a day passed without the spitting flurries whistling down across the plains, and the tiny camp became merely a mound of snow in a vast white sea. The men were marooned as surely as if they had been cast ashore on some barren atoll, cut off from earth, sky, and every living creature.

Though the horses and mules suffered the most, subsisting wholly now on cottonwood bark, the men of Jordan's outfit shortly discovered that an enemy of a different sort had come to pay a call. Boredom.

Full bellies and a snug cave comforted a man only so far, and as the days passed, monotony began to exert an oppressive hold over the entire crew. With little to occupy their time, locked together in the dugout like caged animals, they began to feel bordom grate on their nerves. Talk ran dry, and minor differences flared into full-fledged arguments. The men grew testy, quick to take offense or find fault, and by the fifth day anyone who opened his mouth was likely to get flayed with a waspish rejoinder.

Jordan had no way of forecasting how much longer the storm would last, but he sensed that the men would goddamned well be at one another's throats before another night passed. The mood in the dugout was downright acrimonious, and something had to be done to clear the air. After considering and rejecting a number of ideas, he finally hit on what seemed a sure-fire purgative for a case of the doldrums.

Shortly after the noonday meal he announced that come nightfall they were going to have a party. With a tall-tale contest thrown in for good measure. McCabe was appointed chef, with instructions to concoct a spread of choice morsels. Huggins was placed in charge of liquid refreshments, and Cook got the job of decorating their drab abode. While they were working, each man was to sort through his storehouse of whoopers and dust off a real lulu for the contest. They would be allowed only one story apiece, so he warned them to consider at length and take their best shots. Jordan himself would act as judge, and first-prize winner got to sit on his backside for a full day while the losers attended to all camp chores. Stonewall was assigned to supervise the whole operation, and the wolf-dog got so excited by all the activity he promptly started cold-nosing anybody who didn't keep moving.

With sundown, Seth Cook had the dugout spic and span, and Dan Huggins had hatched a formidable brew consisting of trade whiskey, chewing tobacco, dried peppers, black molasses, and a pinch of gunpowder. McCabe topped it off with a feast of son-of-a-bitch stew, sourdough biscuits, hot marrow butter, and prune pie for desert. The men gathered around the banquet and ate like four shoats being larded up for a trip to market. Afterwards, stomachs distended and belching appreciatively, they commenced sampling Huggins' secret recipe. Everyone smacked their lips a lot and kept swiping at the tears it brought to their eyes, but they agreed unanimously that it was mighty tasty. Little hard on the innards, maybe, but damn good drinking. Besides, they figured McCabe's prune pie would have everybody cleaned out come morning, so there was no real harm done.

Once the crew was about half zonked, Jordan concluded the time was ripe and announced that the tall-tale contest was now in session. Huggins first. Cook next. McCabe last. Each man could take all the time he wanted, but the stories would be judged on originality, not length. The winner would be the man who spun the biggest windy, and somehow kept it within the realm of believability.

Curiously, Cook and Huggins had chosen the same topic for their yarns. Rattlesnakes. Huggins' tale had to do with a rattler so fast it could catch bullets in midair. While wonders were possible, it sounded just a bit farfetched, and drew groans from the other men. If anything, Cook's story was even more outrageous. It had to do with a musical sidewinder, whose specialty was hissing "The Battle Hymn of the Republic." The audience hissed Cook and quickly booed him off stage.

When Jordan gave McCabe the cue, he climbed to his feet and stood before the fire. The old skinner had both jaws loaded with Climax and could hardly get his mouth open. After gumming it around for a minute he turned and let go with a stream that came near putting the fire out. The chips hissed and sent up a steamy cloud; it had the strangely pleasant odor of tobacco juice and buffalo dung. McCabe waited for everything to settle down, then swung into his tale with the glib, honey-tongued orchestration of a medicine show quack pitching the rubes.

It was a whopper about his prospecting days. Though rambling at times, it told of a winter in the high mountains. The winter he and his sidekick, Jethro, had holed up in a cabin to sit out the storms. With the scene set, the old skinner upped the tempo just a bit.

"Yessir, things had commenced to look mighty bleak. We was down to our last pot of beans, and that night the grandaddy of all northers jumped us. Boys, it was the goddamndest blue howler anybody ever heard tell of. So cold spit would've froze on the stove. Course, after we'd et, there wasn't nothin' to do but curl up in our blankets and hold tight. But right about then Jethro asks me what day it is.

"Well, says I, near as I can figger it must be nigh on to Christmas. Jethro thinks that over a minute and then sorta gloomy like, he allows as how St. Nick ain't likely to pay this place a visit. Jethro was sentimental that way. Seen him cry at a funeral one time.

"Anyways, we're snoozin' along when there comes a poundin' on the door that rattles the whole cabin. Jethro leaps up, smilin' kind o' foggy like, and he yells. 'It's Santy!' Before I got time to holler, he runs over and throws the door open. 'Stead of the jolly old gent, though, there stands the biggest, meanest goddamn grizzle b'ar you ever seen in your life.

"Well, sir, Ol' Ephraim walks right in and commences to dispense peace on earth and good-will toward men. Cuffs Jethro upside the head—laid him out cold as a wedge—and starts makin' a feast on the last of our beans. I grabs my rifle in one hand and Jethro's scalplock in the

266

other and hauls him through the door. Licketysplit, we're outside freezin' our butts off in a snowbank. And Ol' Eph is inside greasin' his chin on our beans.

"Now, the upshot of it was, it turned out to be a merry Christmas after all. When that grizzle b'ar come out of the cabin I filled him full of holes and he was so big we et off him clean into spring. 'Cept for him, we might've starved to death."

McCabe paused, and just for a minute his eyes took on a peculiar glaze. Then he blinked and looked around. "Funny thing, though. When that silvertip crashed over dead, we heard jingle bells high up in the sky and a big, hearty laugh. The kind you'd expect a fat man to let loose. Lookin' back on it, me and Jethro sorta figgered Santy had done right good by us. B'ar steak and all the trimmin's. And the finest rug you mortally ever seen."

Spraying the fire once more for good measure, he resumed his seat with a studied nonchalance. The other men appeared in a bit of a quandary. The old man's yarn sounded just plausible enough to be the truth. Yet this was supposed to be a tall-tale contest. Huggins and Cook had a sneaking hunch he had slipped in a ringer, but the trouble was a man never rightly knew when the old devil was lying and when he was preaching the straight goods.

The one thing that none of them doubted though, was that his grizzle bear had just whipped the living bejesus out of a couple of rattlesnakes. Jordan got no argument when he tapped McCabe the winner and relieved him of all camp chores for a day. The other two men weren't exactly sore losers, but they were pretty sure they'd been greased down the chute. Still, they weren't the type to hold a grudge, and in a manner of speaking, Huggins' secret recipe seemed consolation enough for anyone.

That being the case, everybody proceeded to get gloriously drunk.

Later Huggins and Cook started harmonizing in a duet that sounded a little like a bulldog and a wildcat thrown in the same gunny sack. Jordan leaned across to the old skinner and gave him an appraising look. "Lon, I never knew you'd been a gold prospector. When did all that happen?"

McCabe's glassy-eyed stare revealed nothing. "There's lots you don't know. Ask me no questions an' I'll tell you no lies. Savvy?"

The plainsman wasn't sure he did. McCabe had just told him something, or on the other hand, maybe he hadn't.

But all things considered, it didn't matter much one way or the other. The skinner's bear story was a dandy, and the boys would be rehashing it for days to come.

Leaning back in his robes, he took a swig of the recipe and winced as it sluiced down through his innards. Damned tasty stuff. Just the thing to take a man's mind off his troubles. Howling furies. Frostbite. Buffalo. Snow owls.

And green-eyed women.

5.

Conversation at the table had proved sparse and somewhat strained. Jason Rath was displeased with his daughter, and it showed in his gruff manner. While it rankled him that Virge Hollister often spent an evening in the parlor courting Julia, he had been wise enough not to interfere. There were some things a strongminded girl had to find out for herself. Particularly when it came to Dodge's illustrious city marshal.

But to find the man breaking bread at his own table was just too much. Damned if it wasn't!

The girl had stepped out of bounds by inviting Hollister to supper, and she was going to hear about it later. In no uncertain terms, too. Though Julia seemed captivated by the lawman's daring and his tricky charm, Rath labored under no such misapprehensions. He considered Hollister nothing more than a common killer. One who coincidently wore a star. Not to mention the underhanded plot he had organized to take over Dodge. That alone made him unwelcome at the Rath table. The fact that he was coldblooded as a weasel into the bargain simply added insult to injury. Every forkful the little merchant put in his mouth tasted bitter as gall, and it was only with the greatest effort that he had remained civil throughout the meal.

Immersed in his own thoughts, he slowly became aware that Hollister had asked him something. "I'm sorry. My mind was occupied with other matters. What was it you said?"

Hollister smiled understandingly. "Nothing earth shattering. I just asked what you thought the prospects are for next summer."

"Whose prospects? Yours or the town's?" Rath cursed

268

himself the instant it slipped out. Bluntness just wouldn't do. The mayor had made him promise to stay on good terms with Hollister. There was always an outside chance the scurvy rascal would somehow tip his hand trying to impress Julia.

"I'm not sure I follow you," the lawman replied, still smiling but wary now.

"My question was unnecessarily cryptic, I'm afraid." Rath was suddenly delighted with himself. Any day in the week he could give this young pup a lesson in mental agility. "Let me restate it. Are you asking about business prospects, or do you mean your chances of standing off the Texans for another season?"

Hollister grinned, thoroughly at ease once more. "I meant business. Just between you and me, I don't lose much sleep worryin' over Texans. Most of them would assay out to about twelve ounces of hot air to the pound."

"Daddy, in case you haven't realized it, Virge is a very competent peace officer." Julia graced Hollister with a dazzling smile and gave her father a sniffy look. She wasn't at all happy with his grumpy behavior tonight. "Just think back. Until Virge came along, Dodge City certainly wasn't what a person would think of as a safe, law abiding town."

Rath could have enlightened her about a deeper, more insidious threat to the town, but he passed on that. "Young lady, a Front Street merchant has ample reason to appreciate restricting drunkenness and disorder to the South Side. You shouldn't have to be told that. Now, marshal, as to your question. I suspect this summer will be the greatest boom in the town's short history. In my judgement, it will exceed even the peak years of the buffalo trade."

"Mr. Rath, I'm glad to hear you say that. It bears out what I've been thinkin' all along. Sort of brings us around to something I've been wantin' to talk to you about, too. Now when this town starts growin'—and it will, with all that cattle money being spread around—I've got a feelin' we're—"

"Excuse me, marshal." Rath dropped his napkin on the table and shoved his chair back. "Perhaps we can save this discussion for another time. We're involved in annual inventory just now, and I'm afraid the clerks expect me back at the store."

269

Stepping away from the table, he glanced at Julia. "Very nice meal, my dear. Sorry I can't stay for dessert." Then he nodded to Hollister. "Marshal, drop around to the store sometime and we'll have that talk. Always interested in new ideas."

The merchant walked from the dining room through the parlor, and a moment later they heard the front door close. Julia tried to cover her father's abrupt departure with a bright little smile. "Virge, why don't we have coffee in the parlor? That way you can smoke if you like."

"Never seen it fail." Hollister gave her a sly look as she started for the parlor carrying their cups and saucers. "A woman can't stand to have her cookin' aromas spoiled by the smell of tobacco. Bet if the truth was known, you females are just scared of the competition."

"Oh, a lot you know, Virge Hollister." Julia glided to the settee and placed the cups on a low table. "The truth, if you really want to hear it, is that cigars have a repugnant odor. In the parlor some of the smoke at least goes up the chimney."

Hollister took a seat beside her, but his jesting manner seemed to have disappeared. "Talkin' about odors. The way your pa's been actin' lately you'd think I didn't bathe regular or something."

"Why Virge, that's nonsense." She admonished him with a shocked look, trying to disguise feelings she harbored of a similar nature. "He's just reserved with anyone who calls on me. You know, fathers never believe that any man is good enough for their daughters."

Julia very discreetly changed the subject. Her father had some peculiar aversion to the lawman—something he refused to discuss with her—and she felt it wiser to avoid the matter entirely. Besides, there weren't any callers except Virge. Not since Sam Jordan left town.

Chattering on with a gaiety she hardly felt, the girl steered Hollister into a discussion of the recent blizzard that had dumped tons of snow on Dodge. When that topic went dry she switched to church affairs, and was off and running before he had time to mention her father again.

While Hollister listened attentively, throwing in an occasional comment, his mind was still on Jason Rath. Lately the storekeeper had shown signs of increasing hostility, and if allowed to go too far it might put the quietus on his well-laid plans. With Luke Short in his corner he had made good headway over the past few months. All that remained was to get Julia in front of a preacher. Once the knot was tied her daddy would come around. Julia would see to that.

Rath might be a stubborn old goat, but the girl would never stand still for him refusing to support a son-in-law. It would become a matter of family then, and when Hollister threw his hat in the ring for mayor the merchant would have to back him.

Or chance losing a daughter.

But the way things were shaping up, Rath might botch the whole deal before it got started. Especially if he somehow persuaded the girl that a Rath had no business getting hitched to a Hollister. No, the time to move was now. Before the storekeeper had a chance to dust the moonglow out of his daughter's eyes.

That she was sweet on him, Hollister never doubted for a moment. Most women went gooney with a couple of kisses, and he had been nuzzling her for close to eight months now. Not that she was what a man might call cooperative, but that would change. She was just the kind that needed a wedding ring before she could turn loose.

Very abruptly, Hollister decided the time would never be riper than right now. He had planned to talk to the old man first, but after tonight he could see how that would be a huge mistake. The thing to do was pop the question and get her committed. Then Rath would be snookered and he'd have no choice but to go along.

When Julia finally came up for a deep breath he grabbed the lead. "Not meanin' to get you off the track, but you remember at supper when I mentioned wantin' to talk to your pa?"

"Why, yes, Virge. You said something about the town growing and an idea you had. I think that's wonderful. You should talk to daddy."

"Well, I was being a little sneaky there. That was really just an excuse to get him out in the parlor while you cleared the table. You see, there's something I've been wantin' to ask you and I figured to do it proper by speakin' to him first."

Julia blinked a couple of times and got busy messing with the coffee cups. "Oh?"

When she didn't say anything else he cleared his throat and waded in. "Well, Julia, it's like this. I'm not much for words, but I think you know how I feel about you. Man like me finds it tough to talk about love and stuff like that,

271

but that don't mean he doesn't feel things. Guess I'm comin' at this pretty clumsy, but what I'm gettin' around to sayin' is that I'd be proud to have you as my wife. I'm not a regular Christian, and I've knocked around a little, but I think we'd make a pretty good team once we got spliced. If you'll have me, that is."

Julia appeared flustered, and it was a moment before she could bring herself to look at him. "Virge, I don't quite know what to say. You've taken me a bit by surprise. Please don't misunderstand. I think it's the nicest compliment I've ever had in my life. But you will have to give me a little time. Marriage is very serious to me and it isn't something I would rush into."

Hollister didn't care for that idea at all. Delay could spell disaster. Holding back his annoyance, he smiled affectionately. "Well, we've been seein' each other going on eight months now. Seems to me you'd have a pretty good idea whether or not I'm the fellow you're lookin' for. Wouldn't you say?"

"Virge, I'm sorry. Really I am."

"Sorry! What the hell's sorry got to do with it?" The anger spilled over with indignant harshness. It was no longer a matter of political conniving. This uppity little tease was the same as turning him down. "I suppose the next thing you'll tell me is that there's someone else."

Just for a moment Julia stared right through him, eyes wide and blank. Then she blinked, as though somewhere within herself a long festering question had been resolved. "Yes, Virge. I'm afraid there is."

"Don't tell me. Let me guess. Among those high-class types he runs with he's known as Cimarron. Short for Sam Jordan."

"Virge, please don't be bitter. You knew I was seeing Sam long before you came along. Somehow the feeling just didn't die. I don't know why, but it's still there."

"Hell, I'm not bitter. If I had to lose out I'd sooner it be Sam than anybody I know." But the look on his face belied his words. Virge Hollister didn't like to lose. Especially where women were concerned. It touched a nerve that was wired straight to his vanity. And he particularly didn't like getting beat out by a greasy buffalo-hunter. "Tell you the truth, if I'd have known Sam was still in the race I wouldn't even have bothered. Sam Jordan's about the only man on earth I don't care to tangle with. Especially over a woman."

272

"I believe that is what people call a backhanded compliment." Julia laughed, relieved to see the lawman taking it so gracefully. "The likelihood of you two coming to blows is rather remote, though. As much as I hate to admit it, Sam isn't fighting too hard for my hand. Being very candid about the whole thing, he's proving damnably hard to catch."

That was the first time Hollister had ever heard her use a curse word, and more than anything else it convinced him that she had her sights set for just one man. His old partner. To pursue the matter further would be whipping a dead horse, and he wasn't one to waste time or energy on lost causes. After a few minutes of banal platitudes about remaining friends and still seeing one another on occasion, he took his leave. Her turndown was a blow to his plans, but nothing he couldn't overcome. There were ways around anything, and he still had an ace or two up his sleeve.

Besides, in a way he was just as glad it hadn't worked out. Lottie probably knew more about keeping a man happy than Miss Priss Rath would learn if she spent the rest of her life in a first-rate cathouse.

When Jason Rath came home late that evening he found Julia still sitting on the settee. She was gazing into space with a hollow stare and wasn't even aware of his presence until he sat down beside her. "Oh, hello, daddy. Did you finish with inventory?"

"Honey, are you all right? You look a bit peaked around the gills."

"Yes, daddy, I'm just fine. Better than I've been in months. Virge asked me to marry him tonight."

"Is that so?" The merchant's tone was flat and guarded. "And what was your answer?"

"Oh, I thanked him but I had to refuse." Looking at him, her eyes sparkled mischievously. "Daddy, I've decided that come hell or high water I'm going to marry Sam Jordan. Even if I have to lure him into a shotgun wedding. I hope that doesn't shock you, but he's the right man and I'm just getting too old to wait around till he gets through sowing wild oats."

"Doesn't shock me in the least, daughter. In your shoes I probably would have sprung the trap a long time ago." Rath favored her with a warm smile, but after a couple of moments his face went solemn. "Julia, I'm a very proud

273

father tonight. Not because you chose Sam. I had hoped you would all along. I'm proud because you displayed the good sense to give Hollister the gate. There were things I wouldn't discuss with you for fear you might rebel and do something foolish. I wanted it to be your own decision. Now I'm going to tell you the truth about Virge Hollister."

Jason Rath leaned forward and began to talk with a frankness that both fascinated and repulsed her. He told her many things about the Hollister family—and Virge Hollister in particular—that were common knowledge among the sporting crowd in Dodge. Yet some of what he told her had been made privvy only to a select few. Threats and intimidation. Bribes and shady deals. Bawdy houses and whispers of aberrations that went on late at night. Senseless, cold-blooded killings cloaked behind the legality of a badge, merely to promote the name and image of a diabolically ambitious man.

Then, when he had spoken on these things and more, he told her in straightforward, unvarnished words the tale of Lottie Siddons.

Eight

1.

Shortly after the winter snows melted off that spring, drought came again to the plains. Grass shoots withered even as they sprouted, sucked dry by the searing winds; the prairies, once ablaze with wild flowers, lay fallow and parched under the merciless ball of fire lodged in the sky. Lacking rain, the silty rivers crested with the early spring thaw, then bottomed out to sand and bedrock as the mighty waters receded to a muddy trickle.

Fleeing westward from the smell of rotted carcasses, the last remnants of the great southern herd converged on the farthest headwaters of the arid streams. The shaggy beasts marched steadily on, forced into a shambling, dust-choked retreat in their quest for water. The scorching heat shadowed them relentlessly, draining the earth of moisture, and even as they gathered along the upper tributaries, the stream beds turned powdery as crushed bone beneath their hooves.

Beyond this lay *Llano Estacado*. The Staked Plains. A land where nothing, not even wild things, ventured of its own accord.

Then one morning a light breeze from the west brought with it a hint of something more than dust and sand. The smell of water. High on the distant tableland a dark cloudbank had passed over, leaving in its path the sparkling shimmer of a reborn lake.

Slowly, cow leaders of the scattered herds lifted their heads, testing the wind with flared nostrils. Deliberately, they turned and commenced to move westward at a determined pace. One after another the little bunches came, joining shoulder to shoulder in a furry crush, until a long, unbroken line wound through the breaks leading to the plateau above. There, in a land beyond all headwaters, they marched into the wind once more. Just as the great herds had done since the beginning of time.

Throughout the night and on into the heat of the next day they trudged westward, swelling in number as more hurried along from the lowlands behind. The herd grew wild with thirst as they scented moisture on the freshening wind. Young calves lagged back as the pace increased, only to be urged along by impatient cows. The shuffling walk became a trot, then a frenzied run as the great mass spread over the land, their black tongues swollen and hanging from their mouths. The earth trembled from the clatter of their hooves, and a towering plume of dust lifted skyward as they thundered across the open plain.

Then, just as the weaker ones began to falter, a blue lake suddenly appeared on the burnt prairie. The herd pounded forward in a dark wall and hit the water with a geysering crash. Those in the lead were trampled underfoot by the squealing thirst-crazed horde, and within moments the shoreline was ringed by a solid mass as the hump-backed beasts swizzled greedily from the clear waters.

Gradually the smaller creatures frightened off by the racketing din crept back to the lake. Wolves and coyotes eased in as the buffaloes slaked their thirst and moved away. Even a small band of mustangs appeared, switching flies with their bushy tails and crowding in to nuzzle the clear surface. Snipes, curlews, shitepokes, and loons settled down from the sky, while dragonflies hovered aloft on the soft, hot breeze. Where only days before nothing had existed but lizards and rattlesnakes, the wild things had come to take their fill and rest from the blazing fireball overhead.

The shaggies spread over the prairie to graze on the curly mesquite grass, and the predators crawled off to await the coming darkness. For while it was a harsh, uncompromising land during the day—a limitless inferno

276

without echoes or trees—the Staked Plains changed at night. The winds cooled and became alive with the sharp desert smells. Stars cluttered the inky sky, cold silver mixed with ice blue, and for a few brief hours it became a place of gentleness and comfort.

Still, with the dawning of each new day, it returned to what it had always been—a hostile, uninviting land—a land of refuge precisely because only the most hardy could survive there. Which made it perfect sanctuary for the tattered relic of what was left from the great southern herd. Grazing contentedly on the grassy plain surrounding the lake, they were but a wavering reflection of the majestic host that had once roamed the lowland prairies.

One man, given adequate powder and lead, could have killed them all within the span of a single year. Perhaps sooner.

Across the southern plains, better than a thousand hide-hunters waited for the herds to appear. Just as they had returned last spring, and the spring before that, and each spring farther back than even the ancient ones among the Indians were able to count. The hunters waited throughout April, then May, and on into June, awakening each morning with renewed certainty that the herds would come lumbering over the prairie at any moment. Many chalked it off to the hard winter, saying the blizzards had forced the shaggies farther south than usual. Others blamed it on the drought and struck off for the distant headwaters, confident they would find the herds gathered there. Some didn't know what to make of it—they only knew that sooner or later the herds always returned. And so, with mounting apprehension, they sat and waited, ever certain that tomorrow would be the big day.

But the buffalo had come for the last time. They would return no more.

Jordan and his crew waited like the others, postponing the trip back to Sweetwater day by day, in the hope that the herd would appear and they could follow it north. The winter kill had been scant, earning them little more than butter and bread money, and they hung on looking for a payday that was long overdue. Yet, while he hadn't discouraged the skinners in their determination to stick it out, the plainsman likewise hadn't deluded himself.

The buffalo weren't coming back, he could see that now. Perhaps more clearly than anything he had ever faced in his life. Through the winter, after recuperating from his bout with frostbite, he had gradually widened his scouts to the headwaters of the Salt Fork, nearly forty miles west by north. Always he noted that the shaggies were retreating ever westward, fleeing before the dense cloud of gunsmoke and lead laid down by their relentless pursuers. Exactly as he had predicted to Jason Rath back in Dodge last June.

Just as sure as Christ was spiked to a cross, the herds were being driven to the Staked Plains. Even a damn fool buffalo preferred *Llano Estacado* to the gun-crazy mob swarming across the prairie.

But skittish herds, grown wary as lowland deer, weren't the only thing Jordan had observed in his solitary rides west. While hunters he talked with blamed heavy snows and spring draught for the shaggies' curious disappearance, he saw that as a factor of small consequence. Granted the herds had been scared into flight—for a variety of reasons—but that hardly accounted for their dwindling numbers. The simple truth, if a man was willing to face it squarely, was that the buffalo hadn't pulled some tricky vanishing act.

They had been exterminated. Wiped out.

Looking back, he could see now that the old colonel at Camp Supply had been right all along. While he had used a fancier word for it—annihilated—it came up snake-eyes either way. The great southern herd had been rubbed out. Like wiping over a schoolroom slate with a wet eraser.

Talking with Rath in Dodge last summer, he had estimated that it would take two, maybe even three years for the herds to be driven onto the Staked Plains. What a joke!

It hadn't taken even half that long to kill them off completely.

Sure, a likely number had escaped to the Staked Plains. But every sonofabitch and his dog would be headed up there with gun in hand. Before the summer was out the slaughter would be finished once and for all. There wouldn't be any buffalo. Not on the Canadian or the Red or the Brazos.

Or on the Staked Plains.

The thought of building a trading post on the Double Mountain Fork was now so absurd it was almost laughable. Just almost, though. The way things were shaping up it would take something uncommonly funny to raise a laugh out of a man these days.

Come to think of it, Sweetwater didn't look to fare any better. Once the hide-hunters lit out for parts unknown, there wouldn't be enough business left to support two whores and a plank saloon. The soldier boys might generate some business, enough maybe to keep a couple of the dives operating. But the trading post was a dead duck. Hiram Greene didn't know it yet, but he was only a hop and a skip away from presiding over a wake.

The thought brought him full circle. The biggest wake of all had already been held. Out on the plains, where rotting carcasses and bleached bones stretched as far as a man could see. Or ride. There had been no sermonizing, of course, and no one had shed any tears, so maybe it didn't rightly qualify to be called a wake. Still, with that many dead it damned sure deserved the full treatment. Dirge, death knell, candles, and all.

Then a curious thought flitted through his mind. How many was *that many*? Ten million? Twenty million? Outside of a half-assed guess, no one knew. Probably never would know. The only thing a man could say for certain was that in less than four years the great southern herd had been wiped clean from the face of the earth.

However many *that many* was, it was a hell of a lot of buffalo. More than anyone realized when everybody kept yammering that the shaggies would last forever. Damn sure more than a fellow would have killed had he known the end would come so quickly.

Jordan wasn't fooling himself on that score. The shaggies meant nothing to him in a personal sense. Maybe the Indians looked upon the buffalo as their brother, and cloaked the ponderous beast in all sorts of mystic rigamarole, but to the plainsman it had been a business. Nothing more. Yet he might have killed less—and fought to stop others from killing so many—had he suspected the herds would vanish with such abruptness.

The hell of it was he couldn't quite get his thoughts sorted out on the whole sorry mess. While he kept telling himself that hide hunting was nothing but a business, he felt a queer sense of loss knowing it was over and done with. Something ill-defined had withered and died in him over the winter, washed away in the same bloodbath that had exterminated the herds. Maybe getting himself half-froze in that blizzard had brought him to his senses, or jarred his brain off the trolley one. Whichever, it didn't seem to matter much, for the cards read the same up or down.

Buffalo had been a way of life with him, yet only in looking back could he see that the herds had represented a living symbol of the freedom he coveted so greatly. Dead, they were only so much putrid meat, and by sharing in their slaughter, he had killed the very thing that meant the most to him. His freedom.

What he had searched for wandering across the plains—the thing that seemed forever to elude him—had been right there before him all the time. The freedom to roam, to subsist at will, to want for nothing and remain answerable to nobody. Like the fellow too close to the forest to see the trees, he had been unable to recognize it when he was staring straight at it. Shaggy. Hump-back. Ugly as sin. It was there all along except he had never bothered to look.

Now, Lucretia Borgia and a thousand more like her had stilled it forever.

When he rode into camp late one afternoon, it was this single thought which gave muscle to his resolve. Tonight he would do what he should have done weeks ago. What he had been comtemplating for nearly a month. There was a time to ruminate—maybe even a time to weep and moan—and there was a time when a fellow had to get off his duff and go on with the business of living. Maybe it was more bitter than sweet, and hard as a gourd to swallow, but playing hide and seek inside his own head didn't accomplish a goddamned thing. Like a leg gone foul with green rot—the sooner off, the sooner better.

After supper that evening he called the boys around the fire and gave it to them bluntly, without the least attempt at sugar-coating. "Boys, I've decided to call it quits. I'm finished with huntin'."

The skinners looked at one another slack-jawed, never more astonished in their lives. McCabe popped his teeth and started to screech, but the plainsman cut him short. "Now before you get yourselves bent out of shape let me tell you why I'm callin' it a day. Might be it'll help you sift out a few things, too."

Jordan took out his knife and traced a map of the upper Brazos country on the dirt floor. "What I've been doing the last week or so was scoutin' the headwaters of the Salt Fork and the Double Mountain Fork. I didn't say nothin' about it because I didn't want to get you fellas in a swivet. But I've got the straight goods now, and I figure it's time to give you the lowdown." Pausing, he scratched a line in the dirt across the watersheds of both streams. "There's not a buffalo between there and here. Not a cow or calf, not even an old castout bull. They're gone, and they're not comin' back."

"What d'ya mean, gone?" McCabe barked. "Gone where?"

Jordan jabbed his knife in the ground west of the river tracings. "The Staked Plains. The tracks are there for any fool to read. Every last one of 'em has gone there straight as an arrow."

"Aw, Cimarron, that won't hold water and you know it." McCabe's eyes slewed around, glinting hotly. "There's two hunnert miles easy between the Canadian and the Brazos. Them goddamn woolies could be hid off anywhere in there. Few tracks leadin' to the high country don't mean they've all skeedaddled."

The plainsman grimaced and shook his head, wanting to make it clear. "Lon, I've talked with hide men comin' from every direction. North, south, and east. They were trailin' west to the last man. There's buffalo in only one spot now, and everybody knows it." Again he jabbed with the knife. "Right out in the middle of that furnace."

The old skinner commenced to sputter, but Cook beat him to the punch. "What you're really sayin' is that you don't want no part of the Staked Plains."

"Seth, that's a good part of it. Livin' with horny toads and rattlers isn't exactly my style."

McCabe cocked his head, appraising Jordan with a crafty look. "What d'ya mean, that's a good part of it? I got an idea there's more to this than you're lettin' on. We're full growed, y'know. Why don't you just spill the beans and be done with it?"

"Guess I might as well at that." Jordan took a deep breath and let it out slowly, studying each man's face for a moment. "You're not gonna believe this right off, but before summer's gone you'll see it for a fact. The southern herd is gone. Wiped out. The only part that's left is what's up on the Staked Plains. And there's so many outfits headed up there, it won't take more'n a few months before that bunch is finished off. Come first snow you won't find a shaggy south of the Yellowstone."

Just for a moment the men couldn't hardly comprehend

the enormity of his words. Yellowstone country lay seven hundred miles to the north as the crow flies, with millions of square miles between. That there could be no buffalo in that vast wilderness strained belief. Left a man staggered right down to the bootheels. Which is exactly how the three skinners looked.

"You're not funnin', are you?" Huggins asked softly. "You're tellin' us the straight article."

"Dan, much as I hate to admit it, that's the way she lays. You saw the Republican herd get wiped out. Then the Smoky Hill and the Arkansas. The same thing has happened here. That leaves the herd up on the northern plains. Wouldn't surprise me none if that wasn't gone in a couple of years, too."

The men didn't say anything. Couldn't. They were too stunned by the sheer magnitude of the thought. *No more buffalo. Gone. Sent up the flume like so many cords of firewood.*

After a while the plainsman snapped them out of their funk. "The way I hear it, the Yellowstone country is colder'n a witch's tit, so I don't reckon I'll be headin' north. But I've got a hunch most of the outfits down here will be, just as quick as they've cleaned out the Staked Plains. I'm gonna give you boys a bill of sale for the wagons and teams and all the equipment. You've been with me a long time and I feel like I owe you. That way you can get a head start on the rest of the pack and stake yourselves out some good huntin' ground. With you ownin' the outfit you can hire yourselves a hunter and come out of it smellin' like a rose when the shootin's all over."

Cook and Huggins brightened a bit at that, but McCabe's face got even longer. They discussed the Yellowstone country at some length, but as the hour grew late the two skinners called it a night and crawled off to their robes. Left alone, McCabe and Jordan sat staring into the orangey glow cast off by the fire. Finally, the old man sighed listlessly and let go a jet of tobacco juice.

"I don't reckon you'd change your mind?"

"No, guess not."

"Which way's your stick floatin' then? I mean, if you've given up huntin'."

"Lon, I don't rightly know, and that's a fact. It's sort of crap in one hand and wish in the other. About the only thing I'm sure of is that I'll have to close down most of the Sweetwater operation sometime this fall."

There was a long silence and McCabe squirted the fire a couple of times before he worked up the nerve to speak out. "I reckon you'll be playin' a lone hand, but if you got use for a partner, I'm sorta at loose ends."

"Goddamn, I thought I was gonna have to sit up half the night waitin' for you to ask." Jordan grinned and glanced at the old skinner out of the corner of his eye. "I'm not real sure where the trail's headed, but I'd be right proud to have you ride along."

McCabe looked away and got busy wiping his nose. After a moment he snorted and started off towards his robes. "Figured you might be needin' some company. 'Specially since you never learned how to cook worth a damn nohow."

Jordan chuckled in his throat and let the old rascal have the last word. Though he was sleepy, he didn't feel much like bed. His mind wouldn't seem to rest, and there was something soothing about watching the fire die down to cherry red coals. Strangely, though, what he saw in his mind's eye was neither flame nor coals, but a shaggy sea of brown that in some curious way he had loved even as he was killing it.

Watching the tawny calves romp around and the bulls slinging dirt as they pawed and bellowed and thundered toward one another, he smiled. That was the way he would remember them. Shaggy wild things covering the land with their pungent smell. Just the way he had first seen it back on the Smoky Hill.

2.

The riders skirted south of Antelope Hills, but they stuck fairly close to the Canadian. It was the only stream they had seen in the last two days that had enough water to wet a man's socks. Both the Sweetwater and the Washita were dry as a bone, and their horses hadn't had a decent drink since they rode off from the trading post. Come morning, when they turned north toward Dodge, the animals would have to be watered good. Unless it had rained up ahead somewhere, this was likely the last swig they would get before reaching Camp Supply.

Jordan was looking forward to seeing Colonel North again. The officer wasn't as stiff-necked as some he knew, like that dimdot back at Fort Elliott. When North got himself dosed with French brandy he really came unwound. The plainsman had to chuckle remembering their last conversation. Both glassy-eyed as owls and nowhere near as wise. Jordan wasn't especially anxious to tangle with that brandy again—he had brought along two quarts of popskull just to even things out—but he was plenty curious to hear what the colonel had to say about Custer losing his hair on the Little Big Horn. From the cutting remarks he had made last time, it figured that North would have some juicy tidbits to relate about the boy wonder getting himself plowed under.

The more he thought on it, the better Jordan felt about spending an evening with the colonel. He could goddamn sure use a few laughs. Particularly after the stopover at Sweetwater. There was something unreal about the town now. Ghostly almost. Like the haunts had moved in after all the people had moved out.

Curiously, though, Hiram Greene hadn't been as downhearted as Jordan expected. The storekeeper hadn't had any good news to report, that was for damn sure. The town was deserted, sales were off better than fifty percent, and they had taken in less than twenty thousand hides from the winter season. Compared to the half-million they had bought and resold last year, it made for slim pickings. Practically all the saloonkeepers and whores had packed it in and headed for greener pasture. They hadn't seen enough buffalo-hunters since spring thaw to fill an outhouse, and the soldier boys at the fort weren't exactly the last of the big spenders. Whiskey and women were always in demand somewhere, and the sporting crowd had departed without a backward glance.

Boomtowns went bust sooner or later—they had seen it happen a hundred times over in mining camps and cowtowns—and it was the wise apple who knew when to pick up his marbles and call it a game.

But Hiram Greene hadn't gotten the least bit twitchy about Sweetwater's sudden demise. That was the thing that floored the plainsman. Though he was concerned over slipping profits, he felt that the town was entering a period of transition that came eventually to all frontier outposts. The lag of time which came between the departure of the trailblazers and the arrival of civilization. Even when Jordan informed him that the hide business was on its last legs, the storekeeper had taken it with surprising equanimity. Over the winter he had given it considerable thought, and he was convinced that Sweetwater's prospects for the future were anything but dim.

While he hadn't expected the hide business to collapse so abruptly, he had known all along that it must ultimately end. Such things always died out—fur trapping, gold mines, even the demand for buffalo hides—it was simply a matter of economics and the historic encroachment of civilization on wilderness areas. Being a student of both economics and history, he had felt reasonably confident from the outset that Sweetwater's reign as a boomtown would be brief. Highly profitable, but brief.

Still, he wasn't overly apprehensive about the future. With the Indians pacified and the buffalo cleared from the plains, it was logical to anticipate a gradual influx of settlers. The land was rich and well watered—drought, so he had learned, was fairly uncommon to the Panhandle—and it stood to reason that such country would attract farmers and ranchers. Lush grasslands which had fattened millions of buffalo could do the same for cattle, and from the little he knew about soil, the rich earth of the Panhandle would lure sodbusters westward by the droves. Citing a case in point, he reminded Jordan of the rapid expansion of farming in Kansas. Already the eastern half of the state was overcrowded, and settlers were pouring into the western end by the hundreds. The Homestead Act was the magnet that drew them west, and it would entice them into the Panhandle just as it had in Kansas, Oregon, Nebraska, and many other territories.

Granted, operating a trading post for farmers and ranchers wouldn't make a man wealthy overnight. Not the way it had with buffalo-hunters. But it would be a solid business, more substantial in the long run. Less vulnerable to the caprice of nature and the whimsy of eastern tanneries. Something a man could build his life around and be assured of a modest return on his investment year in and year out.

Having lectured at length on Sweetwater's finer points, Greene then rocked the plainsman back on his heels. Assuming Rath and Company was receptive to the idea, he would like to buy the trading post. Lock, stock, and barrel. Though he wasn't a monied man, he could raise some capital, and he would gladly sign a long-term note for the balance. Since the only alternative open to Jordan and

Rath was to close down the operation completely, he considered it a fair proposition for everyone concerned.

Jordan had agreed to discuss the offer with Jason Rath and present their answer within the month. But as he rode away from the trading post he was filled with mounting respect for Hiram Greene. The storekeeper was gutsy in a way he had never suspected. Not to mention being shrewd as hell to boot. He had thought it out from every angle—quite clearly using the expansion in Kansas as a yardstick—and come to the conclusion that there were brighter days ahead for Sweetwater. While success of the venture hinged on certain assumptions—peaceful Indians and a growing demand for land—a man would be hard put to think of any business that didn't involve an element of risk. Greene had calculated the risks in orderly fashion, weighing each factor with precise care, and he was willing to bet the limit.

Jordan admired a man who was willing to put his money where his mouth was. The world was full of blowhards who were brave with other people's money and spent their lives riding on the next fellow's coattails. There was something refreshing, maybe even reassuring, about a squint-eyed stringbean who was willing to root hog or die. All things considered, there might be hope for the human race after all.

Thinking about it as he and McCabe rounded the eastern slopes of Antelope Hills, the plainsman slowly arrived at another deduction. He liked Hiram Greene. Maybe he wasn't much for whiskey and women, and he damn sure couldn't fight his way out of a wet paper bag, but he had sand in his craw. The kind that lasted over the long haul.

"Judas Priest!" McCabe's blurted remark brought him up short. "Would you look at all them goddamn cows."

Jordan did just that. There was no way he could have missed them anyhow. Below, in a swelter of dust and bawling cattle and cursing cowhands, was a herd of longhorns that looked to number upwards of two thousand. Conditioned by years of reading sign and keeping a sharp lookout for his hair, the plainsman's eye also noted something else. Those weren't the first cows to come this way. There was a well-beaten track stretching north and south that had been churned to dust by countless hooves.

"Lon, I've got an idea somebody's found themselves a shorter trail to Dodge. Let's pay 'em a visit and find out."

Jordan kneed the roan into trot and started down out of the hills. McCabe and Stonewall weren't far behind, and as they rode closer it became clear that the thirsty herd was being watered then turned back onto a grassy meadow which bordered the trail. Cowhands were circling the longhorns, bunching them on what was apparently intended as their bedground for the night. From the looks of things, the Texans meant to graze the herd overnight then water them again in the morning before fording the Canadian.

Sighting smoke in a stand of Cottonwoods along the river bank, Jordan reined the gelding in that direction and moments later spotted a chuck wagon. When they rode up, a slim hawk-faced Texan was having what appeared to be a heated discussion with the cook. Both men fell silent, and the taller one walked forward.

"Light and tie," he greeted the hidemen. "We got plenty of java, and if you ain't in any rush we'd be proud to have you stay for supper."

"That's right neighborly of you," Jordan replied as he piled off the roan. "Sure it wouldn't be puttin' you out none?"

"Hell no! Us boys been together so long we're sick to death of one another. Always glad to see a new face. My name's Slim Jeeter, foreman of this outfit."

The plainsman took his hand and gave it a couple of pumps. "I'm Sam Jordan. This here's my sidekick, Lon McCabe."

McCabe just nodded, intrigued by all the activity over around the fire. The cook was flinging flour and beefsteak and assorted foodstuffs in every direction as he got the evening meal started. Observing them as the old skinner edged closer, Jordan had a hunch his partner had found a talking buddy. The cook had the same constipated look around the mouth, and from the way he was cussing to himself, he was most likely ornery enough to hit it off with McCabe.

Jeeter was giving the plainsman the once over. "Didn't figure to see many buffalo men this far east."

"Ex-buffalo man," Jordan smiled. "Case the word hasn't spread yet, the Texas herd has just about cashed in. What's left has taken to the Staked Plains."

"Well now, that's good news, sure enough," Jeeter offered a plug of tobacco, and when Jordan declined he bit off a large chaw. "With them woolie boogers gone that

287

means there's gonna be lots more grazin' land for cattle-men."

"Queer you bringin' that up. Friend of mine, store-keeper no less, was sayin' the same thing a couple of days back." The plainsman jerked his head back at the longhorns. "When d'ya start trailin' cows through this neck of the woods?"

Jeeter had his wad working good, and he spat, drowning a fly in midair. "First herd come up this spring. They're callin' it the Western Trail, and I wan'cha to know I'm glad to see it. We're Bar Double X, from down around Uvalde way, and this beats the livin' shit out o' swingin' east to catch the Chisholm."

"Shorter, huh?"

"Man, I hope to tell you. When a feller eats cow dust for two months, he'd pretten near kiss a pig's ass to save himself a week."

They passed the time of day for a while, then Jeeter rode off to assign night guards and make sure the herd was settled down. Cowhands commenced drifting in shortly afterwards, making hungry noises and drawing a volley of snippy curses in return from the cook. Jordan could tell from the way McCabe grinned and kept tossing little asides to the old potwalloper that the two of them had struck up a fast acquaintance. More than likely they were comparing notes on their repartee of vinegary cracks. The plainsman had an idea the trailhands were about to get scalded with a whole raft of insults they hadn't heard before.

The men slouched around the camp ground waiting for their supper, standing stoop shouldered and hipshot in a stance that seemed to be characteristic of Texans. When Jeeter returned, the cook, who was addressed simply as Slick, called them to come and get it and started dishing out great gobs of food as the hands filed by with their tin plates. Talking with the ramrod as they ate, Jordan learned that the cook had picked up the moniker Slick'n Greasy because every dish he cooked was swimming in lard. The name had eventually been shortened to the sim-pler handle Slick. The plainsman also discovered that cow-hands ate like ravenous wolves because they were generally fed only twice a day. Breakfast was before first light and supper at sundown, with a good fourteen hours in the saddle between meals. Evidently trailing cows wasn't all it was cracked up to be.

288

McCabe was tickled pink with his new friend. Squatting down beside Jordan, he grinned like a bear in a honeytree. "Cimarron, ol' Slick there has been showin' me some of his secrets. Now that steak you're eatin' is rolled in flour 'fore it's fried. Tasty, ain't it? The way it looks, we ain't gonna be gettin' much hump meat anymore, so I thought I'd best get some tips on cookin' beef. That other stuff is called spotted pup. Ain't that a riot? Rice, raisins, and brown sugar. Slick showed me how to fix it, too. Easiest thing in the world."

Jordan sort of liked the spotted pup, but he didn't care much for the beefsteak. Compared to hump meat it was bland as shoe leather, and just about as tough. Still, it was like McCabe said: buffalo wasn't on the bill of fare anymore. That being the case, a man would just have to get used to stringy beef. That thought sparked another, and he grunted to himself. With the shaggies gone there were lots of things he'd have to start getting used to. Which brought him around to something that had been in the back of his head ever since his talk with Hiram Greene two days past.

Sluicing a hunk of steak down with a swig of coffee, he turned back to Jeeter. "You said something about being from Uvalde. Guess it's pretty warm down that way?"

"Well fair to middlin'," the foreman allowed. "We get a cold spell ever' now and then, but mostly it stays sorta toasty. Why, you lookin' for a place to light now that all the buffers is gone?"

Jordan smiled and shook his head. "Nope. Just curious, that's all. I've been thinkin' about them cows of yours and wonderin' what would happen to 'em if they ever got caught in a norther."

"Why, wouldn't nothin' happen to 'em," Jeeter laughed. "Mister, the toughest sonovabitch on the face of this earth is a longhorn cow. The bastard is about equal parts o' catamount, tornado, and bull elephant. There ain't nothin' God ever whipped together that could punch their ticket. Northers included."

The plainsman had heard Texans brag before, and he wasn't to be put off so easily. "Well now, you know cows, I'll grant you that. But folks down your way aren't exactly on a first name basis with blizzards. You take this past winter. It was so goddamn cold out on the Salt Fork I saw buffalo bulls shiverin' hard enough to make their hocks rattle. Now you mean to tell me one of them skinny cows

289

could go through that? Hell, they don't even have any fur."

"Lord God a'mighty, man, it ain't fur that counts. It's gristle. There ain't nothin' on four legs that'll fight to stay alive like a longhorn. I've seen 'em tie into panthers, bears, wolves. Hell, you name it and I've seen 'em whip it. Snow? Christ a'mighty, snow don't mean no more to a longhorn than it does a hoot owl. Many's the time I've seen them cantankerous bastards standin' in snow right up to the bungholes, and you wanna know somethin' that's a fact? They didn't flinch. Not even a pucker."

"Where was this? I recollect your sayin' the winters aren't that bad down your way."

"They're not," Jeeter admitted. "But back in '68 I was a hand with Print Oliver when he drove a herd up north to Platte country. The army couldn't use all we had and there was quite a bunch we held over til' the next spring. Say, you talk about cold. And snow! You ain't seen nothin' til' you get a peek at them blue howlers they got up north. Holy Christ, it makes what we get down here look like a Sunday school picnic."

McCabe elbowed Jordan in the ribs. "He's right, Cimarron. You disremember I wintered up there a few times myself. If them cows could take that, they could walk through hell barefoot."

With support from an unexpected quarter, Jeeter pressed home his argument. "Well it don't exactly need provin' anyway. Case you ain't heard, there's plenty of Texans that's already started spreads up in Nebraska and Wyoming. If cows couldn't get through a blizzard, you can bet'cha boots they wouldn't have tried it. Fact of the matter is, 'bout ever' second herd that comes up the trail now is breeder stock to be sold to them northern spreads. Hell, they're even drivin' mustangs up. The biggest goddamn horse auction you ever seen in your life is right in Dodge City."

Jordan thought it over a little, convinced now that he had heard the straight goods. "What do they get for them breeder cows? I mean, do they sell 'em by the head or by the herd?"

The ramrod chuckled, making a note to tell the hands about that one later. "Why, I reckon for cash money in hand they'd sell 'em anyway you want 'em. Course, usually a man just buys hisself a herd. One cow's pretty much like another. Sorta the same as buffalo, if you see what I mean. Price depends on how good a man can dicker. Generally starts at about thirty a head."

Across the fire one of the Texans suddenly let out a whoop and started banging his spoon against the tin plate. "Hey, Slick! There's somethin' crawlin' around in my spotted pup."

The old cook raised up from the Dutch oven and gave the man a withering scowl. "Well you can talk to it if you're of mind, but don't play with it. Else everybody'll want one and I ain't got enough to go around."

The whole crew started bellowing at the red-faced cowhand, but none laughed harder than Lon McCabe. That Slick was a hot ticket. Goddamned if he wasn't! Set that loudmouth right back on his heels and made him eat crow. Swabbing the gravy out of his plate with a sourdough biscuit, McCabe crammed it in his mouth and climbed to his feet. There were lots of things a fellow could learn from someone like ol' Slick, and not all of them about cooking either. Only slightly more devious than usual, he decided he would help Slick wash up. Then they could really get down to swapping some zingers.

Jordan and McCabe were far up the trail by sunrise. They had breakfasted with Jeeter's crew and ridden out shortly before the stars faded into false dawn. The plainsman wanted to arrive at Camp Supply well before dark so he could have a long gabfest with Colonel North. But as they rode through the blackjack-studded countryside his thoughts kept returning to the conversation with the Bar Double X ramrod. They had talked far into the night, and while he had really only scratched the surface, he knew a hell of a lot more about cows than he had this time yesterday.

Still, there was a lot left to learn. More than he had any idea of, probably. But that didn't bother him a whit. Anybody who could figure out a buffalo shouldn't have any trouble boning up on cows.

McCabe had been watching him cogitate all morning, and he finally couldn't hold his peace any longer. "You're gettin' yourself worked up to go in the cow business, ain't you?"

Holding back a grin, Jordan looked straight ahead. "What makes you think that?"

"Hell, I ain't deef, dumb, or blind," the old Skinner

291

snorted. "Any idjut could've seen why you was pumpin' Jeeter."

"Well, I reckon I'll just have to 'fess up then. That little talk I had with Greene set me to thinkin'. There's plenty of land out in the Panhandle and it's all free. Fella got himself a few cows and a nice chunk of land he could make a good thing of it. Fact is, a man could do lots worse without hardly tryin'."

"What would you call a few cows?"

"Oh, I dunno. Maybe five hundred to start off."

They rode along in silence for a while before McCabe got himself situated for a flank attack. "Why cows? What about mustangs? Jeeter said there's a big demand for horses in Dodge. We could just as easy go wild horse huntin'."

Jordan had given that some thought even before they met up with Jeeter. Not every man could play the wind just right and use his head enough to make a stand among the shaggies every day for years running. Even fewer could outwit the wily mustang. With only hooves to protect themselves, the wild horses had learned to depend on fleetness of foot, keen instincts, and the best set of ears in the business. Mustangs weren't to be stalked as easily as buffalo, and even a smart man could figure it might be a long dry spell between paydays. Still, that wasn't the reason he had discarded the idea.

"No, Lon, I guess mustangin' isn't for me. Too much dust and sweat involved. Not to mention work."

"I suppose cows ain't no work at all?"

Can't rightly say, never havin' herded any. But hell's bells, there couldn't be much to it. Not if Texans are smart enough to turn the trick."

McCabe again fell silent, but his mind was a regular cyclone of ideas. Some better than others. Some worth nothing. Then he hit on one that struck sparks in every direction. "What about wolfin'? I hear tell there's fellers makin' lots of money takin' pelts. The bounty's real good and there ain't a hell of a lot of work to it. Lots less'n cows."

The plainsman couldn't argue with that. The big prairie wolves had been an ace in the hole for lots of men when the buffalo herds started to dwindle off. All a fellow had to do was plant strychnine in bloated carcasses and sit back and wait. With shaggies being scarce, wolves got hungrier and less cautious about the man smell. Even

292

snowbirds made good bait. Couple of loads from a scatter-gun into a flock and a man had enough bait for fifty wolves. In a way it was even better than using buffalo hulks. With all those bones and feathers, it was a lot harder for a wolf to puke up a snowbird. Once be swallowed it he was done for. But Jordan wasn't tempted by the thought of becoming a wolfer.

"Tell you, old man. That wolfin' is dirty business. Shootin' an animal is one thing, but using poison sort of curries me the wrong way."

"Cimarron, lemme ask you somethin' straight out." McCabe's eyes twinkled in the early morning sunlight. "Why are you goin' to Dodge?"

The plainsman saw the trap, but there was no way to avoid it. "I've got business with Rath. Before I can start thinkin' on cows, something's got to be decided about the Sweetwater operation."

"That's it then? Just Rath. You wouldn't be thinkin' about his daughter, now would you?"

"Maybe. What makes you ask?"

McCabe gummed his chaw around and spit a couple of times before he decided to come at it from the hindside. "Y'know, one time I run acrost this feller that went plumb cross-eyed over the way his gal smiled."

"I ought know better'n to ask, but go on and tell me. What happened?"

"Well sir, he sorta slipped up. 'Stead of marryin' the smile he married the girl. Time he found out what happened when she stopped smilin', it was too late. Feller was so mortified he shot hisself."

Jordan busted out laughing. "You old fart. You're about as hard to see through as a windowglass. Suppose I got myself married? What the hell does that change? We're still partners. When I asked you to ride along I didn't say nothin' about halfway. I meant right down the line."

McCabe screwed his face up in a whiskery scowl. "Got it all worked out, don't ya? Little woman in the house and a bunch of cows out in the pasture. What happens when you get an itch to travel or go bust up a saloon? What're you gonna do then?"

Now it was the plainsman's turn to go silent, and he took his time about answering. When he did, his voice had an unusual timbre, different from anything McCabe could ever recall from the past. "Lon, I've been losin' a lot of sleep puzzlin' on this, and I finally woke up to something.

So long as a fella's his own man, what difference does it make if he hunts buffalo or chases mustangs or raises cattle? The fact is, he's his own boss and he comes and goes as he pleases. Now as to settlin' down, there's never been a woman born that could put a ring in my nose. Happen I ever got hold of one that couldn't see it that way, then I reckon we'd quit pullin' double right about there." Cocking his head, he grinned the old wolf grin. "Listen, you old coot, we're gonna be wreckin' saloons and bustin' heads till our twigs go limber. Hell, life wouldn't be no fun if a man had to give up sportin' events like that. You just quit your frettin' and leave the details to me."

McCabe let it drop, and Jordan was just as glad he did. Without knowing quite how it came about, he had charted some course for himself. Stated things as certainties that up until minutes ago had been only idle speculations in the back of his head. Still and all, they must have been pretty well firmed or even McCabe couldn't have goaded him into saying it. What was it the old rascal had called it? *Little woman in the house and a bunch of cows out in the pasture.*

Damnation, maybe it was like folks said after all. That a fellow changed after he`got enough knots on his head. Somehow the whole blessed thing—woman, cows, and all—sounded pretty damn good.

Even the house struck him as a fine idea. Though it would have to be a cabin. After sleeping so long on the ground and in dugouts, he would have to work up to the real article sort of gradual like.

Thinking about it, he suddenly remembered a spot back on the Sweetwater where they had once camped. Grove of cottonwoods on a little knoll overlooking the stream. Shady in the summer and protected from northers in the winter. Lots of grass, plenty of water, and all the sky a man could ask for.

That was a damn fine spot all right. None better. Just the place he'd pick if it ever came down to brass tacks.

Which in an uncertain world was no certainty at all.

3.

The plainsman rode into Dodge with his decision made. Cimarron Jordan had been laid to rest and the man that remained must now accomplish two things. Before his resolve had time to fade. The first had to do with Jason Rath. The second depended largely on some questions he meant to ask the little merchant.

McCabe declared himself for drinks first and business afterwards, but Jordan couldn't be sidetracked. When the old skinner's arguments fell on deaf ears, he peeled off with Stonewall at his side, huffily announcing that when and if anybody needed him he could be found on the South Side. The streets were teeming with cowhands, even though it was just past the noon hour, and McCabe was quickly lost in the crowd.

Jordan was too absorbed in his own thoughts to bother with McCabe's sulky mood, and he headed directly for the store. Crossing the plaza, he saw that a number of new buildings had been erected and even the older establishments seemed to have undergone a facelift. Front Street was a regular beehive as masses of people and wagons bustled back and forth; it appeared that boomtimes had taken up permanent residence along the banks of the Arkansas. Which all seemed to confirm something Roger North had said to him a couple of days back at Camp Supply.

The colonel had received him warmly, and they had spent the better part of a night talking and drinking. Jordan had insisted that they temper the officer's cognac with equal doses of popskull, and the combination had proved potent. Halfway through the evening they were both crocked, and the plainsman's recollection of what was said afterwards remained a bit hazy. But the earlier part of their discussion was still vivid, and the older man had made some astute observations.

Times had changed, North asserted. The frontier as they had known it was on a collision course with oblivion. The buffalo were gone, railroads were laying tracks all over kingdom come, and a wave of settlers that had yet to crest was pushing westward in search of land. The Southern Plains tribes had grown tame as lap dogs, and even the warlike Sioux had been whipped into submission and driven to reservations. Simply stated, an era had passed. For better or for worse, civilization had come to the west. Law and order had replaced anarchy. Ballots instead of bullets. Peace and harmony had come to a land where once dwelled bloodshed and death. Men no longer lay wakeful and guarded during a Comanche moon. They could get on

295

about the business of building homes, raising families, planting roots in a land that had moved swiftly from raw frontier to an orderly society structured on live and let live.

Perhaps it wasn't as civilized as back east—might never be for that matter—but the wilderness had been tamed and brought to heel.

The rugged loners, men who had fled from restraints imposed by the will of the majority, had become anachronisms, throwbacks who had outlived both their time and their usefulness. They had no place left to run. The day had come when they must, however reluctantly, again join the human race. Or be weeded out. Like the buffalo, and more red men who had ended up *good* Indians than anyone cared to admit.

Jordan's idea to establish a ranch on the Sweetwater met with the colonel's hearty approval. Unlike the loners—that throwback breed he had spoken of with such eloquence—this hard-faced plainsman appealed to North. Some spark of rapport had been generated between them, and it would have saddened him greatly to see Jordan waste his life pursuing some will-o'-the-wisp dream that had ceased to exist. Earnestly and at considerable length he had encouraged the younger man to take root and focus his energies on the even greater challenges that lay ahead. In the course of their discussion, the plainsman mentioned Hiram Greene's evaluation of future prospects in the Panhandle, and he found North in complete accord.

Land was the key, the colonel had advised him. God wasn't making any more of it, and the men who controlled it could write their own ticket in the years to come. All men were free, masters of their own destiny, he announced with brandy-inspired magniloquence. But some more so than others. None quite so much as the man who owned the land. What Jordan should strive for, he declared, was a kingdom of his own. Baron of the Sweetwater.

Then he would not only possess freedom, but he would have the wherewithal to defend it as well.

The more they sipped, the better it sounded. Baron of the Sweetwater. Had a nice ring. Big and unhobbled. Before the night was over they had resolved with drunken solemnity that the ex-buffalo-hunter and skirtchaser supreme would found a new dynasty. Landed gentry of the Texan Panhandle. The Jordan empire.

The two day ride from Camp Supply had cleared his head of whiskey fumes, but the plainsman remained fascinated by the idea all the same. When he walked through the doors of Rath and Company he knew exactly where he was headed and precisely how he meant to get there.

The store was swamped with customers, and clerks were running around like harried mice. But Jason Rath was calmly munching a sandwich in his office while scanning a sheaf of invoices, and it was there Jordan found him.

Standing in the doorway, he shook his head disdainfully. "Christ a'mighty! Times must be good when the boss can sit on his backsides and let the peons do all the shovelin'."

"Sam!" Rath dropped his sandwich and bounded out of his chair, grabbing the younger man's hand. "My boy, you're a sight for sore eyes. We had about given you up for lost after Hiram's last report arrived. He said he hadn't seen hide nor hair of you since last fall."

"Yeah, we sort of got ourselves snowbound down on the Salt Fork." Jordan knuckled a livid scar which ran the length of his jawbone. "Frostbite had a way of slowin' a fella down."

"I knew it!" The little merchant was still clasping Jordan's hand. "That's exactly what I told Julia. When you hadn't shown up by late spring I said, 'Sam's in trouble.' Just sure as God made green apples."

"Well it wasn't that especially. I spent a while scoutin' the upper Brazos before we came in." Letting go of Rath's pudgy fist, he tried to sound casual. "How's Julia gettin' along?"

"Fine. Fine. Still bossing me around as bad as ever."

"That's good. How about Virge Hollister? What's the word on him these days?"

Rath shot him a quick glance, detecting something hidden beneath the question. "Sam, I'm happy to report that Hollister's star has passed it's zenith. He and Luke Short have a little conspiracy in the works, but the powers that be haven't been idle. I can safely predict that he'll never rise above the post of city marshal. Not in Dodge at least." Motioning Jordan to a chair, he returned to the desk. "Seems as though it just hasn't been Hollister's year. Even Julia put him to the skids. They haven't seen each other for some months now."

"Is that a fact?" The plainsman's tone betrayed nothing, but the kinks in his stomach started to come unraveled.

"Say, Dodge is really growin'. Looks like cows're doing a lot more for it than buffalo ever did."

The storekeeper was disappointed that Julia's name fell by the wayside so quickly, but he didn't let it show. "That, my boy, is perhaps the understatement of the year. In the event you haven't dropped by the bank yet, you'll be interested to know that your balance has increased by another eleven thousand since your last visit."

"Well, now, that tickles my fancy right nice. Tell you the truth, it couldn't have come at a better time. I'm gonna be needin' it."

"Oh, still determined to open that trading post on the Double Mountain Fork?"

"Nope. The buffalo're all shot out down that way. Since I'm not partial to the winters up north I sort of thought I'd put myself in the cow business."

"*Cows?*" Rath's mouth popped open and he just sat there gaping at his young partner.

"Yeah. Y'know, ranchin'. Got to lookin' things over and talkin' to a few Texans, and I decided that if them nitwits could do it anybody could."

"But my God, Sam. Cows?" The very thought seemed abhorrent to the merchant. "Why not come into the business with me? You know that's what I've always wanted. We could do worlds together."

"No, my mind's pretty well set. Even got a place picked out down on the Sweetwater." Jordan eyed him a moment, then let go with both barrels. "Fact is, Jason, I came in mainly to talk to you about sellin' out. I figure to buy me a whole heap of land, and cows don't come cheap neither. The way it shapes up, I'll be needin' a pile of money."

"Now wait a minute. How can you buy land? That's all public domain out in the Panhandle. The best you could do is homestead a hundred-sixty acres."

"There's ways. Fella named Jeeter told me how the cattlemen are doing it up in Nebraska and Wyoming. You just round up a bunch of men and have 'em file homestead papers on the spread you want. Then you pay 'em off and they give you a quitclaim deed to the land. Figure I'm gonna get myself twenty, maybe thirty thousand acres just like that. More, if I can swing the cash as I go along."

"So you want me to buy you out? Just like that?"

"Not all the way. I'm only talkin' about the store here in Dodge. Greene's got some notion of buyin' the Sweetwater operation off us, but I'm not in favor of that. Looks to me like there's gonna be plenty of farmin' and ranchin' going on out there before long, and I think we ought to hold on to it. Course, we'll have to make Greene a partner to keep him happy. Offhand, I wouldn't feel right about anybody but him runnin' it."

"Lord God, you're a pistol, aren't you?" Rath slumped back in his chair and tried to collect his wits. "You come sailing out of the blue wanting to sell this and buy that and make people partners. Sam, I sometimes regret having schooled you in the fine art of manipulation."

Jordan chuckled and patted his cookie-duster with a show of modesty. "Well hell, Jason, a fella don't get anywhere sittin' on his duff. Gotta keep movin'. Speakin' of which, let's get down to talkin' turkey about my one-third of this money machine you're operatin'. How much you figure it's worth?"

The storekeeper studied him for a long while before answering. "Sam, let's hold off on that for a minute. There's something I want to ask you first."

"Shoot."

"You're talking about a big operation. Twenty thousand acres, you said. That means settling down. Does Julia figure in that anywhere?"

Jordan's poker face held for only a moment, then he smiled. "That's sort of up to her. I've fiddlefooted around so long it's probably too late now. But I'm gonna ask her all the same."

Rath grinned and bounced erect in his chair, suddenly infused with life. "That's capital, my boy. First rate. However, that being the case I'm afraid I can't buy your stock in Rath and Company."

The plainsman's smile evaporated and he came up on the edge of his seat. "Why the hell not?"

"Very simple really. I plan on keeping everything in the family. Assuming Julia doesn't give you another case of frostbite. Now let me tell you what I'm driving at."

Without preamble, Jason Rath launched into a dissertation on the future as he saw it. Not only was the cattle trade growing by leaps and bounds, but homesteaders were pouring into western Kansas by the trainload daily. Those homesteaders would be the farmers of tomorrow, the solid bedrock upon which the future of Kansas rested. When the cattle business began to bottom out—as ultimately it must when the railroads stretched south and made trail-driving unnecessary—the slack would be taken up by farm trade. That meant the boom had only just begun. Good times were here to stay.

There was even added gravy to consider, the merchant noted. A whole new industry had sprung up around buffalo bones. Jordan should know better than most that the plains were covered with the skeletons of millions upon millions of rotted carcasses. Back east a huge bone market had come into being virtually overnight. Pulverized, the skeletons went into bone china, carbon needed by sugar refineries, industrial phosphorus, and fertilizer for soil crops around the nation. Bones had become legal tender. Already more than a million pounds had been shipped from Dodge, and that was just for openers. Traders, such as Rath & Company, bought them at $8 a ton delivered to the railhead and resold them at $14. Six dollars profit on every ton for the middleman! Moreover, a really shrewd man—and he was organizing this operation right now— could buy them from bone pickers out on the prairie for $2.50 a ton. Even with overhead, that jumped the margin to about $9 on the ton.

For that matter, Rath observed, the Sweetwater was no different from Dodge. While Hiram Greene was waiting for the homesteaders to hit the Panhandle, he could hire crews and begin scavenging the Southern Plains. With buffalo-hunters going hungry he could probably hire a whole army for next to nothing and keep a steady caravan of wagons on the road to Dodge. Across the prairie there were millions of tons of bones to be collected—first come, first served—and with the wide profit margin involved it was the traders who would reap the harvest. The little storekeeper intended that Rath and Company would get its fair share. Perhaps more if they moved fast.

Jordan grasped the potential immediately. "Jason, that's a hell of an idea. Matter of fact, I've even got the man to handle the Sweetwater operation. Lon McCabe. Maybe he's cantankerous and stubborn as a mule, but he knows the plains better'n any man alive. Better yet, he knows all the hidemen and he could get 'em organized quicker'n you can say scat."

Rath jiggled around in his chair he got so excited. "Sam, you're a man after my own heart. We'll let Greene handle the details and put McCabe to scouring the countryside. We'll make a fortune!"

"Hold on now. That's all well and good, and I don't mind gettin' it organized. But that's money down the line.

I need a payday right now. Like another twenty thousand to go with what I've got in the bank. You did a lot of talkin' but you still haven't said why you won't buy back my one-third of this place."

Rath grinned more exuberantly and got busy fussing with a cigar. "My boy, let me put it to you this way. If Julia turns you down, I'll buy you out. But if she accepts, then I will personally loan you the twenty thousand. More if you need it. Since you won't come into business with me, then I believe you have made a wise choice in selecting the cattle industry. This has become a nation of beef-eaters, and I foresee great things ahead for ranchers. Particularly one with a head on his shoulders. As you so aptly commented, if the Texans can make money at it, there's no limit to what a smart man could do."

Jordan mulled it over a moment, finally nodding, "Awright, it's a deal. Like you say, assumin' Julia don't give me the evil eye. But we've got to have it understood right off. The money's a loan. I don't mind being partners in a store, but what I build down on the Sweetwater's gonna be just for me." After a brief reflection he amended that. "And Julia, of course."

"Of course, my boy. And let's not forget my grandchildren. Between the two of us we'll leave them a legacy second to none. Stores, land, real estate, cattle. Damn me for a greedy old goat, but it makes my skin tingle just to think about it."

Neither of them said anything for a couple of seconds, and when Rath looked up again his eyes were clouded with a fine mist. "Hurry, Sam. I'm getting on in years and I want to see that first grandson." Then he brightened, smiling widely. "And I'll lay you eight to five he'll be more Rath than Jordan. By God, we'll have another merchant in this family yet. You just wait and see."

After the plainsman had left, Rath leaned back in his chair and mused on the tenuous fibers of life. Because of a poker game one desperate night he had gained a friend, a partner, and great wealth. The gods willing, even a son-in-law.

Perhaps that was enough. All a man should ask for. But he would give that and more to see his grandson.

To know that it wouldn't die with him.

Jordan had stopped over at the Dodge House many times in the past. There, in a scalding tub, he peeled off months of accumulated grime and rid himself of the rank tallow smell. While he was at it he scrubbed away any little varmints that might have hitched a ride to town, and scraped his face clear of whiskery stubble. Only his moustache was left intact, except for a careful trimming, for the soup-strainer had become as much a part of him as his ears or nose.

But never before had he bathed so thoroughly, shaved so closely, or barbered so neatly. Even his clothes were a step above ordinary this time. Though he always bought new duds when he came to town, he had never gone whole hog. Today he sported not only a floppy tie, but new boots and a somber jacket of imported wool. The best money could buy.

When he stepped through the door of the Dodge House he looked like a spiffy advertisement straight out of a mail order catalog.

The quarter-mile hike to the Rath house was perhaps the longest walk of his life. There were some things that came hard to a man, but perhaps the cruelest of all was admitting to himself that he had been a fool. Still, there was no other word for it. Julia had the Indian sign on him, and he had finally owned up to it. Though he had fought it every step of the way, she had drawn him back like a lodestone time and again. She jitterated his juices in a way no other woman had ever come close to touching, and even a thickheaded jackass was smart enough to know there were some things a fellow just couldn't fight.

When he turned in at the gate, a tranquil quietude settled over him. Somewhere between a blizzard on the Salt Fork of the Brazos and a steamy bath in the Dodge House he had come to understand that freedom was in a man's head. Circumstances couldn't change that. Neither could shackles. Nor people. When a man's mind soared high on an updraft with the eagles, and the wild things lived on inside him, there was nothing on earth that could bring him to his knees. His freedom was a thing of the spirit—immune to external forces—and wandering as a nomad all the rest of his days would prove nothing.

Except that he was a goddamn fool.

Before he could yank the pull bell, the door flew open and Julia rushed into his arms. She planted a big one right on his mouth and squeezed his neck so hard he thought something was sure to snap. Just for a moment he was too bowled over to react, then his wits came untangled and he gave her a bear hug that made her gasp.

When they finally came up for air she put her lips close to his ear and whispered, "Yes."

"How's that?"

"I said, yes."

Holding her back a step, he gave her a scrutinizing look. "Yes what?"

Her green eyes clung to him as though caught in something sweet and sticky. "Yes I'll marry you—you big lummox."

His jaw went slack and for a second he thought somebody had taken a half hitch on his tongue. "How the hell did you know I was gonna ask?"

"Daddy was so excited he came home the minute you left the store. He told me everything. The ranch, how you've settled down, that you meant to call on me. He also told me that if I said no I'd be out on the street begging for my supper before sundown."

"Well, he's got a hell of a nerve, I'll say that for him. Least he could do is let a man do his own proposin'."

"Oh, don't be grouchy with him. He loves you almost as much as I do." Throwing herself around his neck again, she hugged him fiercely. "That's not true. Nobody could ever come close to loving that much."

Julia had had most of the afternoon to think about it, and she knew that even loving so much, it wouldn't be easy with Sam. Something in a woman's nature made her want to delve into the farthest reaches of her man's mind and soul. She had seen other women make themselves and their husbands miserable with this constant probing. Yet she would have to stop short of that with Sam. There were parts of him—hidden, inner things—that he would share with no one. Her included. While love might move mountains, she knew in her heart that there was a distant corner of Sam's mind that could never be penetrated.

He was his own man first and hers second. That she must learn to accept. Not to smother him, either with love or the compulsion to share his darkest secrets. Otherwise she would destroy the thing she loved most. The wild, unfettered spirit which had never known bondage.

Sam held her off, searching her face. "You sure you can take livin' on the plains? There's nothin' much out there but sun and sky and grass. It won't be easy."

303

She gave him a bright little nod, hardly able to speak for a moment. "I can take it. Just as long as you're there."

"Now that's something else you should consider. I'm not gonna be the easiest man in the world to live with. There for a while, y'know, it'll be like an old bear gettin' his cave mussed around. Leastways till I get used to your ways. Or vice versa."

"Land sakes, Sam Jordan, you sound like you're trying to talk me out of it. Don't you think I know you're an old sober-puss? But don't get too comfy on your high horse. I've got a few tricks of my own. Just wait, you'll see."

Chuckling deep in his throat, he reached for her. "You bet your life I'll see. I've been waitin' a long time. Too long."

Spinning out of his grasp, she darted through the door, clapping her hands with the greedy savor of a little girl. "Sam, you're a naughty, wicked man. Now you come into this house right this instant. I've made cookies and hot chocolate and we are going to have ourselves a nice long talk. I want to hear all about the Sweetwater."

Taking his arm, she nestled up close and steered him toward the parlor. "Oh, Sam, that's such a lovely name. Sweetwater. I just know we'll be happy there. Is it an Indian name? And the soil, Sam. Is it right for flowers? Can I take my potted things?"

Sam grinned and nodded like a stuffed owl, bursting he wanted to laugh so bad. She was talking a mile a minute and working up to a full head of steam. But goddamn, she was some handful of woman. Cute as a button and spirited as a young filly. They were going to make some pair.

Bull o' the woods and the fairy princess.

All of a sudden he felt like shouting. Tearing off down to the South Side and spreading the word. Wouldn't that make them perk up their ears, though.

Goddamn, boys, did you hear the latest?
Cimarron Jordan's gettin' himself hitched!

4.

Virge Hollister wasn't exactly frothing at the mouth when he came out of the office, but he was mad enough that nobody said a word to him as he stalked through the Long Branch. When he slammed through the batwing doors and hit the boardwalk he headed straight across the plaza, back to the South Side. His stride was long, shoulders squared back, and he didn't step aside for man, woman, or beast. Everybody got the hell out of his way, for it was plain to see that the marshal was in no mood to be crossed.

Hollister had been holed up with Luke Short for the better part of two hours, and their heated exchange had left his teeth on edge. There seemed to be no end to the abuse and outright humiliation a man was forced to suffer. Somehow, no matter which way he stacked the deck, the cards came up the same way everytime. A busted flush.

Short had tried to soften the blow, but it was difficult to cushion a sledgehammer upside the head. Last night the little gambler had played poker with George Hoover and Judge Beverley. While a couple of well-heeled Texans had also sat in, it came clear as the evening progressed that the politician and his banker crony weren't there so much to play cards as to deliver a message. Relying heavily on innuendo and glossed-over insinuations, they had been able to speak their piece with the cattlemen none the wiser. The message, with all the double talk boiled clear, was quite simple. The town fathers had tumbled to Hollister's little plot. Working quietly, they had already formed the tradesmen and townspeople in a united front to support Dog Kelly for mayor in the forthcoming election. Hollister could remain on as marshal as long as he minded his manners. The minute he commenced to get too big for his britches he would be out on the street looking for a job.

The big augurs had spoken. Like tossing a bone to a dog, they had offered him a Mexican standoff. Should he refuse, they would simply fire him and spread word around town that he had been collecting graft from the South Side dives.

Which wasn't too far from the truth. Luke Short had made the rounds just as quickly as the sporting crowd hit town to refurbish their joints for the summer trailing season. What he told them had been understated, low key. But madams and saloonkeepers were past masters at reading between the lines. They got the drift in big bold print. Either they kicked in something every week to build Hollister's war chest or they would find the law occupied elsewhere whenever rowdy Texans started busting up their establishments.

The sporting crowd had grumbled a bit, but they

weren't all that adverse to the idea. They didn't care much
for the high and mighty muckety-mucks on the north side
of the tracks. Never had. The political clique that ran
Dodge had always tolerated them with cavalier snobbish-
ness. Allowed them to operate their gambling dives and
watering holes and brothels because it was the bait which
brought the cattle trade to Dodge. But the South Side
bunch was held in scorn by the uptown crowd, and no one
made any bones of the fact that they were welcome only
in the summer. Worse yet, the town council taxed them
unmercifully for the privilege of skinning the cowhands.
Every saloon, gaming den, and whorehouse paid through
the nose for a license to operate, then kept right on paying
in the form of hefty taxes. Yet the business establishments
along Front Street—even the saloons—were taxed at a
lower rate.

The hypocritical bastards turned their noses up at sin,
but they damn sure didn't find anything tainted about the
money. Fact was, they were always first in line when it
came time to be paid off.

Far from being angered by the marshal tapping them
for a contribution, the sporting crowd jumped aboard the
bandwagon with great relish. Virge Hollister for mayor
just tickled them pink. Then the old fogies uptown could
stand around and scratch while the South Side showed
them just how wide open Dodge could get. Hollister and
his family were one of their own, and with him running
the town they saw nothing ahead but happy days and rose
petals.

With a lowered tax rate, naturally.

Looking back, Hollister could see that his first mistake
had been Luke Short. Word had gotten out that the sawed-
off runt was the marshal's bag man. Before long everybody in town knew that Short didn't unbutton his fly
unless Hollister gave him the high sign. After that the uptown crowd wouldn't give Short the time of day, and any
influence he had once had with them went by the boards.
Worse still, the gambler's efforts at bribing various council
members and lesser politicians had been rebuffed at every
turn. Everybody seemed to be watching everybody else,
and any of them that might have sold out were shaky
about getting caught with their hands under the table. The
party would have dumped them on their ear if it ever
came to light, and that risk far outweighed the money involved. Since there wasn't a soul north of the tracks who

gave Hollister a Chinaman's chance of getting elected, the scheme was stillborn from the outset.

Luke Short notwithstanding, Hollister was frank to admit that his biggest mistake had been the Rath girl. Perhaps he had pushed too fast and frightened her off. On the other hand, maybe he should have treated her more like a woman and less like a porcelain doll. The whole sorry affair still had him baffled. From a day long ago, when he had first discovered that sweet talk could turn women to whimpering jelly, Julia Rath was the *only* girl he hadn't nailed. While missing out with her had been bad enough, it was the loss of her old man's support that really grated on the bone. With Jason Rath's backing he might have made it, despite Luke Short's bumbling. Without it, the whole goddamn mess was a washout.

Yet, in a way that only now came clear, he had been whipped before he started. Sam Jordan had seen to that. While he couldn't prove it, Hollister would have bet his last nickel that it was Sam Jordan who had put the bee in old man Rath's ear. Then the storekeeper had passed it along to his chums on the town council and the cat was out of the bag even as Hollister pussyfooted around trying to slip in the backdoor.

The sonsabitches had sat back all those months and laughed themselves silly watching him make a horse's ass out of himself.

The lawman even laid the blame squarely on Jordan for his failure to score with Julia Rath. Not that Jordan had been actively courting the girl. Hell, he hadn't even been in town—and that really made a man eat humble pie. The little bitch had told him straight out. She preferred a grimy buffalo-hunter to someone with his style and class.

That stuck in his craw worse than anything. He could overlook Jordan meddling in politics, but for the ugly bastard to beat him out with a girl!

There was one I.O.U. he wouldn't soon forget.

Crossing the tracks, he clenched his jaw against the blinding headache that had suddenly set hammers to pounding inside his skull. He had worked himself into a faunching rage just thinking about all the crow he'd have to eat when word got out on the South Side. They wouldn't say it out loud, but before nightfall they would be whispering and snickering behind their hands.

The uptown crowd has nailed Hollister to the wall!

Striding along he began glaring at the Texans thronging

307

the street. Just let one of the sonsabitches get out of line. Just one! He'd show them something.

Something so goddamned fast they'd never even see it.

Lon McCabe and Stonewall had just about taken over the Lone Star. James Hollister had tried to eject them once, arguing that dogs weren't allowed on the premises, but Stonewall had backed him down with a gleaming snarl. The saloonkeeper wasn't alone on that score. McCabe and his wolfdog had hurrahed half the dives on the South Side that afternoon, and the old skinner figured he was just getting his second wind.

Actually he had taken aboard enough rotgut to pickle a full-grown steer, and he was only a couple of snorts away from falling flat on his keester. But he was getting meaner by the minute. While he wouldn't admit it to himself, he was thoroughly ticked off with Cimarron Jordan, and had decided to tree the town as a substitute of sorts.

Over the past few days, a deep bitterness had been festering within him about the way things were shaping up. When he and Jordan rode north from the Salt Fork a week or so back he had just naturally assumed they were off on some new kind of lark. Though it was a damn shame that the shaggies were gone—and even worse that Jordan wouldn't consider taking the outfit to Yellowstone country—he figured they could always find some mischief to keep themselves amused. Christ a'mighty, wolfers and mustangers made out real good, and in a way it wasn't hardly different at all from hunting buffalo.

Then the young squirt had come up with some damnfool notion about cows. Great crucified Christ! Didn't that make some pretty picture, though? Lon McCabe, supreme buffalo skinner of all time, prodding a bunch of bawling cows around. Jesus! The very thought was enough to make a man puke. Texans prodded cows. Kindeygarten games like that were right up their alley. Grown men hunted buffalo or wolves or mustangs. Or any goddamn thing that ran wild and kept a man on his mettle if he wanted to go on eating regular.

But cows! Holy jumpin' Moses! It was enough to curdle a feller's innards.

Then there was the little matter of Cimarron's girl. Now wasn't that a fine kettle of fish? Bad enough that he meant to turn himself into a cow herder, but now he was all primed to get in harness with a woman. Not just a com-

mon garden variety, run-of-the-mill woman either. One of
them snooty eastern hussies, with fancy airs and no more
starch than a bunny rabbit. Judas Priest, down on the
Sweetwater she would wilt like soft lard on a hot rock.
What Cimarron needed was a squaw, not a wife. Get himself a hot-blooded little squaw and he'd really have himself
something. Wouldn't be any trouble either. She could cook
and make buckskins and shoot and ride and go anywhere
a man could. Just what Cimarron needed.

Not some mousy little citified piece of fluff that would
most likely cave in the minute they crossed paths with
hard times.

The thought alone made him boiling mad. Goddamnit
to hell anyway! The fix he had got himself in he'd wind up
taking orders from some skirt that didn't know beans from
buckshot about nothing.

Standing at the bar, he grunted morosely and downed
another shot. Stonewall was sitting at his feet, sort of
keeping an eye on things, and the crowd had edged away
on either side of them. Since their little ruckus with the
elder Hollister, everybody in the place had given them a
wide berth. But McCabe had been brooding silently for
some time now, and a couple of cowhands down the bar
decided the smelly old booger might be good for a few
laughs.

The one closest, a freckle-faced towhead, started it off.
"Say, granpaw, what kinda dog is that there, anyway?"

McCabe's head swung around and he gave the boy a
corrosive stare. "Sonny, that's a wolf-dog. Would you like
to know what I feed him for breakfast?"

The cowhand cut his eyes around at his partner and
bobbed his chin. "I sure would. Lessen it's a secret."

"Ain't no secret to it," the old skinner snorted. "First off
I round me up about a half-dozen Texans. Then after I
get through stompin' all the bullshit out of 'em, what I got
left over just about fills him up. That satisfy you?"

The towhead's face went red as oxblood. "You got a
smart mouth, don't ya old-timer? You oughta watch it,
else somebody's liable to trim your wick."

"Why don't you try, you litle dingbat?" McCabe was
pretty well oiled but he knew what he was doing. "I ain't
so old I can't send you suckin' back to mama."

The freckle-faced one came off the bar and moved forward, his eyes gone smoky. "Old man, I'm gonna teach
you some manners." Over his shoulder he called back to

his partner. "Bud, keep a watch on that dog. If he moves, drill him."

McCabe very casually poured himself a drink and lifted the glass to his lips. But as the cowhand closed in, his wrist flicked sideways and the fiery liquor splattered in the boy's face. Blinded, he let go a roar of pain, then stumbled closer, clutching wildly for the old skinner. McCabe grabbed the whiskey bottle and swung it in a high arc, shattering it over the boy's head. The youngster went down without a sound, out cold. Behind him, the second Texan came up with a pistol, but he barely got it out of the holster. Stonewall had him around the wrist in one leap, and when the wolf-dog closed his jaws, the crunch of bone sounded like a gunshot. The boy screamed in agony, kicking and pounding at Stonewall with his free hand as he tried to break loose.

McCabe called the dog off as he saw trailhands along the bar jerk their six-guns and begin edging around for a clear shot. Quick as a wink, he whipped out a wicked-looking knife with a long, curved blade and backed against the bar with Stonewall at his side.

"C'mon, you lousy scutters! Who's got the balls to fight like a man. That's it. Keep comin'. Keep comin'. I'll gut you open clean to your eyeballs." Throwing back his head, the old man did a little jig and howled madly. "I'm half alligator and half mule. Full of fleas and never been curried above the knees! Step in you shitkickers and lock horns with the curly wolf. Whoooooiiiiieeeee!"

The crowd suddenly parted and Virge Hollister stepped into the crescent-shaped opening wedged around McCabe. Directly behind the lawman was James Hollister, who shook his fist at the old skinner. "Virge, you get that son-ovabitch out of here. Lock him up and throw away the key. Him and that dog have been causin' trouble ever since they walked in here."

The marshal's gaze flicked over the unconscious cowhand, then to the one holding his mangled wrist, and finally back to the skinner. "McCabe, I want you to drop that knife. Right now."

"Well looky here, if it ain't the law God a'mighty his-self."

McCabe didn't drop the knife, but he thrust it back in the scabbard at his belt. "What's the matter, you fresh out of drunks? Gonna tackle a full-grown man for a change?"

"Don't give my any lip, McCabe. Just drop that gunbelt

and come along peaceable. Otherwise you'll get more than you bargained for."

"Listen to the rooster crow, would ya? Why you young pup I had your number the first day I ever seen you, and I still got it."

Hollister's pale eyes glinted coldly. "I'll tell you once more. We're not playin' games back on the Smoky Hill, McCabe. I'm the law here. Now shuck that gunbelt."

McCabe glared back and gritted his teeth, making knots in his jaws. "You Fancy Dan pissant. You just wade on in here and see who walks away."

Hollister started forward, figuring he could get close enough to bend a gun barrel over the old man's head. Stonewall snarled ferociously, reacting out of brute instinct, and moved in front of his master. Before McCabe could call him off, the wild-dog sprang at the lawman. Hollister's hand seemed to move not at all, but a Colt appeared out of nowhere and spat a sheet of flame. Stonewall took the slug full in the chest and dropped dead at the lawman's feet.

McCabe's response was one of blind fury. Tears spilling over in his eyes, he clawed at the gun on his hip.

Hollister gut-shot him without an instant's hesitation, and as the old man struggled to remain erect, he thumbed off a second round. The slug caught McCabe in the chest and drove him back against the bar, then his body went slack and he toppled to the floor.

Hollister stared down at the old skinner for a moment, as though inspecting a side of beef. "Somebody close his eyes."

Turning, he holstered his pistol and walked from the saloon. When he went through the door there was a faint smile playing at the corners of his mouth.

Sam Jordan must be in town. Otherwise his viper-tongued sidekick wouldn't be stretched out back in the Lone Star.

It made for interesting speculation.

5.

McCabe's death was the hardest blow of Sam Jordan's life. Coming as it did, suddenly and wholly unexpectedly, it rocked him to the very core of his being. The shock

311

numbed him into insensibility at first, like a man who had chopped his toes off but had yet to feel the pain. Then the glaze slowly passed from his eyes and the anger set in. Savage, virulent anger—twisting his guts with sharp, fiery spasms, sending a rage born of spleen and hate coursing through his veins. Just for a moment something blind and instinctive gripped him—the brutish fury of a wounded animal lashing out—and his hands shook with the urge to tear and shred and kill, unlike anything he had ever known.

But that too passed, even more slowly and not without the loss of whatever compassion he might once have possessed. The anger went dry, his rage was snuffed out, and in its place came a cold, hard deadliness. From deep within him spread a malevolent serenity, remorseless and implacable, like a wild thing stalking its supper.

Jason Rath had brought the news of McCabe's death, bursting through the door even as Julia peppered Jordan with questions about the Sweetwater. With him was Dog Kelly, looking solemn and uncomfortable, as witness to the plainsman's shuddering grief. Rath had hauled him along despite heavy protest, knowing he would need support in what was to come. The mayor was a persuasive talker, and with his voice to bolster the merchant's hastily constructed arguments, there was an outside chance they could stop Jordan from getting himself killed.

But reason and logic had no visible effect on the plainsman. It was like chipping at granite with an icepick. Their words were blunted on his stony composure, and they might well have saved their breath. Only when Dog Kelly described the scene in the Lone Star did Jordan seem to perk up. His eyes lost their hollow look, and he listened with quiet intensity while the mayor reconstructed the story as he had gathered it from James Hollister and the two trailhands. Virge Hollister had been very matter-of-fact about the whole affair, stating that McCabe was simply another drunk who had started to buck the law. Kelly had left him at the jailhouse, calmly swigging coffee as he thumbed through the latest batch of wanted circulars.

Jordan grunted dourly at that, but he seemed mollified when the mayor explained that he had ordered the old skinner's body to be laid out in style at Hackenberry's Funeral Parlor. Kelly was somewhat startled when the plainsman inquired about the dog. He was even more astonished when Jordan asked him to arrange for McCabe and the dog to be buried together. Though Kelly was partial to canines himself, the request struck him as just the least bit odd. Jordan didn't notice the look, though, for he was momentarily preoccupied. The thought was warmly satisfying in a grim sort of way.

McCabe would have liked his arrangement. The old rascal and his dog had been inseparable right up to the very last. Stonewall would make good company, even in death.

After that, Jordan's mood hardened to indrawn bleakness, focusing on the task ahead. He dismissed their arguments with brittle indifference, and nothing they could say seemed to dissuade him. They could talk till they were blue in the face and it wouldn't change a thing.

He was going to kill Virge Hollister.

Julia sat through it all, tight-lipped and pale, knowing that nothing could touch him now. Neither words nor tears nor love. That distant corner of his mind—the dark, atavistic side to his nature—was impervious to any appeal. Inviolate. He had withdrawn into himself, and whatever they might say wouldn't extinguish the furies that had been unleashed by an old man's brutal slaying.

Curiously, though she had never met McCabe, she understood why the plainsman felt obligated to settle the score. But comprehension alone failed to lessen the numbing dread which had settled over her.

When Kelly and Rath both ran dry of arguments, Jordan came out of his shell long enough to ask a couple of favors of the mayor. The first was to have the hotel clerk send over his pistol and gunbelt. The other request was what he had been mulling over while they showered him with unheard entreaties.

Inform Virge Hollister that he would come for him before sundown. Whatever spot the lawman picked would suit him just fine.

Jordan would find him.

Kelly reluctantly agreed, looking more unnerved than ever, and when he had gone, a pervasive stillness fell over the parlor like a shroud. Jason Rath slumped down in a chair with head bowed, racking his brain for some choice bit of logic that had escaped him up till now. The plainsman's gaze was focused on something beyond the ken of anyone but himself. So absorbed was he in his own thoughts that he remained wholly unaware of what effect his decision was having on the girl who had accepted his proposal only an hour past. Julia was engaged in a solitary walk through an anguished hell, and was fighting a losing battle to hold back her tears.

Some minutes passed before the merchant sighed and roused himself for one more try. "Why must you be in such a rush to die, Sam? Eternity awaits us all, and it comes soon enough without foolishly tempting it beyond safe limits."

The plainsman said nothing, didn't even look around. But he heard, and somewhere in the darkest region of his mind a disembodied chuckle lifted in ironic amusement. The gods waited all right. Slobbering, intoxicated with their own power, laughing fit to be tied, as they piddled around in men's lives. But hell, why shouldn't they laugh. They were fickle as a two-bit whore and about as trustworthy as a rattlesnake, and they still had the world eating out of their hands. It was the biggest goddamn joke ever thought up.

Eternity awaited, there was no doubt about that whatever. But it wasn't gods or spooks or any other ghosty things that would decide what happened here today.

It was just between Virge and him, and who shot the fastest. Or maybe the straightest.

When he didn't answer, Rath's brow furrowed even deeper. "My boy, I want you to listen to me for a moment. Not as a friend or a business acquaintance or even as one of the family. But as one who has lived longer than you and seen more. The fruit of a man's years, Sam, is wisdom. And it is on the basis of that alone that I ask you to heed what I say. What you intend doing will accomplish nothing. Killing never does. It's merely revenge, a renegade's substitute for the law. Hollister will get his comeuppance. Sooner or later his kind always does. But let the law do it in it's own time and place. Why wager your life to kill a man who isn't worth the dirt under your fingernails?"

Jordan's gaze swung about, scornful and remote. "Jason, you wise men always think you've got the other fella figured out. The way you see it, everybody ticks alike. But they don't, and that's where you make your mistake. The law is a playtoy that people like Kelly and his cronies monkey with till it arranges things the way they see 'em. That don't mean I see it the same way, or that I have to live with it just to suit them. There's a better law. The kind we had down in Sweetwater and Griffin. Protect what's yours and your own. If a man needs killin', then kill

314

him. Don't pussyfoot around waitin' for God or the law or some natural disaster to do the job for you. There's no satisfaction in that, Jason. When you set out to kill a man it's because something inside you wants him. Wants him bad."

Rath heard him out, then just nodded wearily. It was plain to both men that further discussion was futile. Julia's eyes were glistening wetly, and her voice quavered, but she blinked back the tears. "Sam, would it make any difference if I asked you not to do it? For no other reason than that. Just my asking."

The plainsman saw the tears start to form in her eyes and he had to look away. "If anything could stop me, that would. But I guess there's just some things a man feels called on to do and there's no settin' them aside. Lon McCabe was more than a friend to me. He was like family, and I let him down. When we rode in this mornin' he was ticked off and I knew it. If I'd been thinkin' I would've seen he was headed for trouble. That's the way he was when he got singed. Always lookin' to pick a fight. But I had my mind on business and I let him go off on his own."

Something caught in his voice, and he swallowed around a hard lump. "He was a good old man. Best I ever met. If I had stuck with him he'd still be alive. I reckon I owe him one. It's as simple as that."

Tears finally spilled over in Julia's eyes, and she dabbed at them with a hankie, trying all the while to smile. To let him know that she understood. Jason Rath slumped lower in his chair, intrigued by a thought so elemental that it was downright profound.

Indeed, it was as simple as Jordan stated. The oldest, simplest laws of them all. An eye for an eye. Kill or be killed.

There were none simpler. Perhaps none as good. Ancient and outmoded, granted. Yet somehow they never seemed to disappear from the scheme of things.

Man in his wisdom had seen to that.

The sun sank lower, smothering in a bed of copper, as Jordan eased around the corner of the livery stable and stood looking down Front Street. The orangey ball of fire would be at his back as he moved along the street, which was exactly as he had planned it. Whatever edge he could get he would need when it came to the showdown with Virge. He had no illusions about his chances against the lawman. Virge had always been faster and a better shot to boot. That was an unavoidable fact.

The question right now, though, was of a different nature. Maybe of greater bearing then even speed and accuracy when it came down to the wire.

Was he smarter?

Jordan was neither chivalrous nor a fool. When one man set out to kill another, he did it in the most expedient manner that came to hand. Dead heroes were a dime a dozen, and forgotten before the first shovel-load of sod hit their caskets. Virge had always said that it was the smart man who walked away from a gunfight, not necessarily the speed-demon or the sure-shot.

That's what it worked down to here. Now. Which of them was the smartest.

Wherever he found Virge, the plainsman meant to take him off guard. Get him talking. Distract him. Blind him with the sun. Somehow get the edge and kill him before he had a chance to react. Perhaps it wasn't sportsmanlike, but this wasn't a game. Virge would be playing it the same way. Looking for the angle. Fairness had nothing to do with it.

It was a matter of who did what to who first.

But for it to work he must catch Virge on the street. Stand back away from him and use the sun. Otherwise his chances were practically nil. In a saloon, at close range, he would be running neck and neck with a snowball in hell.

Then he saw Virge.

Just where he wanted him, too. Standing in front of the Long Branch. It couldn't have been better if he had put a hex on the sonovabitch.

Now if he just put his noodle to work he might walk away from this deal in one piece.

There were few people on the street at suppertime, but those about scattered and rushed indoors. Word of the impending shootout had spread through town like wildfire, and while there were plenty of spectators peeking through doors and windows, nobody was especially anxious to get caught in the line of fire.

When Jordan drew closer, he saw Luke Short standing in the doorway of the Long Branch, and it crossed his mind that he might be facing double trouble. But as he approached, the lawman flung some words over his shoulder and the gambler ducked back inside the saloon. The

316

plainsman halted about thirty yards off, just far enough to dull the edge of Virge's blinding speed.

Hollister appeared calm and collected, smiling even. "Real smart using the sun that way, Sam. But it won't get you much."

Jordan's nerve ends were jangling like chain lightning now that he was face to face with his ex-partner. What seemed shrewd as hell a moment ago suddenly looked to be as full of holes as a sieve. The palms of his hands were moist with sweat and he took a deep breath to steady himself.

"I don't need much, Virge. You taught me. Remember?"

"Sam, you're north of the Deadline and wearin' a gun. You know the law, so unbuckle that belt and let it drop. You're under arrest."

Jordan couldn't help but admire the cagey sonovabitch. One way or another he was going to make it appear legal. "Still hidin' behind that badge, aren't you? Was it the law that gave you the right to kill Lon?"

"Not that it makes any difference," Hollister observed, "but I had to shoot him. He pulled a gun on me."

The plainsman's voice was gritty as ground glass. "Virge, you're a goddamned liar. McCabe's pistol was still in the holster. Dog Kelly told me so himself. You could have buffaloed the old man and you know it."

"Maybe. That's water under the bridge, though." Hollister shifted slightly, tilting his hat-brim against the glare of the sun. "Listen, why don't we call it quits for old time's sake? Shake hands and back off while there's still time."

The lawman started forward, but Jordan's growl brought him up short. "Don't come any closer. I like the range just the way it is."

"Sam, I don't especially want to kill you, but I guess you won't have it any other way." Hollister flashed a wide grin, thoroughly confident of the outcome. "I always told you it was different shootin' at something that could shoot back. Your hands startin' to sweat a little?"

"You're not runnin' a sandy on me, Virge. You've never killed anyone in your life but drunks and amateurs."

"You took on the real toughnuts, I suppose?"

"The ones I've killed got the first shot. From what I've seen, you gun 'em down before they even get started."

That stung, and the lawman recoiled at the insult. "Well I tell you what, sport. I'll give you first crack out of the

317

box. But take a deep breath before you pull. It'll have to last a long time."

Jordan had the edge he was looking for.

Not as big as he wanted, perhaps, but enough. Sunlight reflected off Hollister's gaze, turning his eyes pale as clabbered milk. The plainsman gathered himself, taking a tight rein on his nerves. There would never be a better time.

Jordan's hand darted to his side, but even as it closed around the butt of his six-gun, he heard the whirr of a Colt's hammer being eared back. Somehow Virge Hollister was standing there looking at him down the barrel of a shiny pistol.

"You blinked, Sam. Dead giveaway."

The lawman sighted coolly and shot him in the thigh. Jordan felt the femur bone shatter, and a gout of blood splattered down over his pants. Then his leg went dead beneath him and he fell, landing on his rump in the dusty street. There was no pain, though, not yet, and he clawed at the gun on his hip.

It couldn't end like this. The bastard had to die. Had to!

"Don't make me kill you, Sam!" Hollister yelled.

Jordan had the pistol clear now, thumbing the hammer back, and his arm came level. Hollister had delayed too long for a deliberate shot, but he snapped off a hurried round and the Colt bucked in his hand. The heavy slug slammed Jordan backward pounding him into the dirt, and a bright red dot appeared on his shirt front. Just for a moment he stiffened, then his body went slack and the pistol dropped from his hand.

Hollister just stood there, blinking in the deepening sunset as people began pouring out of the buildings. Jason Rath and his daughter ran from the livery stable where they had been watching, and the girl went to her knees at Jordan's side. The merchant knelt down and placed his hand over the plainsman's chest, then whirled back to the crowd.

"He's alive! Somebody get the doctor. Quick!"

Dry eyed, biting her lip, Julia started shredding her petticoat to staunch the blood spurting from Jordan's chest. Rath jerked his belt off and slipped it around the wounded man's leg, tightened it into a simple tourniquet. Moments later the doctor came loping up, and after a brief inspection of the wounds, ordered Jordan carried to his office. Several men stepped forward and lifted him gently, carrying him off down the street. Julia trailed along in

318

their wake, her hands smeared with blood and the front of her dress gone crimson.

After they had disappeared into the doctor's office, Jason Rath drew himself up to his full height and faced the lawman. "Hollister, you're through in Dodge. I personally guarantee it. If you don't believe me, just look around. These people wouldn't support you for dog-catcher."

There was a hoarse rumble of approval from the crowd surrounding them, and Hollister suddenly started wishing for eyes in the back of his head. Dog Kelly pushed in beside the merchant and stuck out his hand. "Hollister, I'll trouble you for that badge. As of right now you're suspended as city marshal. The town council will meet within the hour, and I believe you can safely consider yourself fired."

Hollister ripped the badge from his shirt without a word and flung it at Kelly's feet. Before he could move, the mayor unloaded another sally. "Mister, if I were you I'd get out of Dodge City the fastest way possible. When the Texans find out you don't have the law backing your play any longer, they'll be looking you up in bunches. Right about then I suspect you'll begin wishing your name weren't Hollister."

Whirling about, Hollister gave the packed throng a murderous glare, then shouldered his way through the crowd. Luke Short waited on the boardwalk in front of the Long Branch, covering his back until he slammed through the batwing doors. Then the little gambler turned and followed him inside.

Jason Rath and Dog Kelly hurried off toward the doctor's office and about half the crowd tagged along behind them. The rest commenced drifting off in little knots, talking excitedly, and a good many headed toward the Alhambra for a much-needed drink.

But not one among them made a move in the direction of the Long Branch. The general consensus was that nobody wanted to be around when the Texans caught up with Virge Hollister.

They'd sure as hell drink to Cimarron Jordan, though. Even flat on his back he had shown men what real grit looks like. Thrashing it over in a dozen different versions—how he had sat there in the dust and jerked that six-gun—they agreed to a man.

319

It'd be a cold day in hell before his kind showed again. Maybe not ever.

He was the last of a breed.

The curly wolves.

Epilogue

The towering cottonwood rustled softly in the evening breeze, and the flowers around the headstone shimmered vividly in the faint light. The washed blue of the plains sky had gone smoky with dusk, and across the stream an emerald carpet of bluestem and buffalo grass brought a whispered fragrance on the gentle wind. Jordan leaned back against the trunk of the tree, puffing meditatively on his pipe as he watched sparkly ripples rise and fall over the Sweetwater.

He liked to come here this time of evening, when the day's work was done and supper finished and darkness starting to settle over the land. There was something special about this place, unlike any other along the stream. Solitude and peace seemed to abide here, demanding nothing of a man, yet willing to share their serenity with blissful generosity. Here he could ponder and muse on the things that touched his mind, and in some queer way he always felt a shadowy communion with McCabe.

The headstone was simple, very plain really, but the old man would have liked it. Jordan had sensed somehow the first time he saw this place that McCabe could rest comfortably here. The graveyard back in Dodge wasn't right, never had been. It was a spot like this—wild and undisturbed, the rich smell of earth and the sky overhead—where the skinner could find whatever comfort was to be had from eternity. Just the kind of place the old rascal would have picked for a camp ground back in their buffalo days.

After the cabin was built, and things settled down around the ranch, Jordan had sent for McCabe and Stonewall. Had them dug up and carted all the way from Dodge, so they could rest easy in a place that better suited their style. Jason Rath had damned it as sheer lunacy. Expensive lunacy, at that. But Jordan had his mind set, and it was done just the way he wanted, even down to the rough, unadorned headstone. There was a certain contentment he felt at having McCabe near—nothing he could put into words exactly—just a sense of things being the way they should, so long as the old skinner was close by.

Not that McCabe would have liked the ranch itself. Jordan had to chuckle whenever he thought about it. Sometimes it was like he could hear the old chunk of bear-bait cussing and snorting about the way grown men let themselves get weaned away from the wild life. There was always Sweetwater City, of course, and every couple of months Jordan went in for a few snorts and generally wound up beating the shellac out of some loudmouth. But it wasn't like the old days. None of those knock-down-drag-out bloodbaths. Wherever he was, him and Stonewall, McCabe doubtless did a few jig steps every time he saw the plainsman swing back into action again.

Just in case they drew the shutters, though—wherever a fellow went when he crossed over—Jordan always came to sit by the headstone and give the old man a blow-by-blow account of how the fight had gone. Folks would have thought he'd lost his marbles if they ever saw him squatted down talking to a headstone, but it didn't bother him one way or the other.

McCabe could hear him somehow—he felt sure of that—and in itself, that was enough.

Even with the wild days gone forever, life had been pretty damned good. Not anyone, McCabe included, could deny him that. Truth to tell, there were times when he couldn't hardly recollect the wild days at all. As though something wouldn't focus right anymore. Like there had never been anything but the ranch and him and Julia.

Still, it hadn't been easy. Except for that sawbones back in Dodge, he would have been dog-meat long ago. While it had been touch and go for a time, with the kind of pain a man didn't like to reflect on too much, he had been infernally lucky. Come out of it with a gimpy leg and a patch of scar tissue the size of a cartwheel on his chest. Not bad considering what a couple of .45 slugs could do to a man's insides.

The part he regretted most, though, was Virge Hollister. Till the day he went to his grave he'd still be wishing he had killed the sorry bastard. But time has a way of healing all wounds, as the womenfolk were fond of saying, and after he was back on his feet he couldn't quite see the sense of pushing it further. Especially since he would have had to murder the sonovabitch. Bushwhack him or backshoot him one. Which wasn't exactly his style.

Virge was just too damn fast for him, and there was no fooling on the score. Not after that little sideshow out in front of the Long Branch.

Hollister had made tracks by the time he was up and around anyway. So he had left well enough alone, and chalked it off to unfinished business. Later he heard that the whole clan, with Lottie and Luke Short in tow, had shown up in Deadwood, Dakota Territory. From reports that drifted back, Virge was up to his old tricks again. Trying to muscle his way to the top of the heap, just as he had in Wichita and Dodge. Some people never learned. Almost like each new dawning found them no farther along—or much brighter—than they had the day before.

But maybe it was like Jason Rath said. Somewhere, when the time and place seemed right, the old bitch they called a lady would skewer his rump on a bolt of lightning. The only thing that grated on the plainsman was that he wouldn't be there to see it when Hollister's string ran out.

All the same, he had plenty to keep him occupied without fretting overmuch on the likes of Virge Hollister. The ranch was taking shape just the way he had envisioned it more than a year back. Though he had only five thousand acres nailed down so far, the plan was working well, and every month he added another half-dozen parcels or so. Given another couple of years, with the beef market holding firm, he felt reasonably assured that the Circle J would wind up with a spread of twenty thousand acres or more.

Not that he had any ambitions to become Baron of the Sweetwater. That had had a damn sweet ring to it one drunken night back at Camp Supply, but sober and a year older he wasn't so keen any longer to be some kind of backwoods kingpin. Jason Rath would have called it a year wiser, and perhaps he had something at that. The stores at Dodge and Sweetwater City gave him a hefty income, which he plowed right back into the ranch, and so long as he had room to stretch his wings it was enough.

There was something mortally satisfying about having his own brand, though. Circle J. Every time he saw it stamped on a cow's rump it sent a warm glow through him, and he was seeing it plenty these days. The spring calf crop had been better than he expected, and most of them heifers, too. Looking back, he saw that it had been a smart move to sink his extra cash in some fine bulls. After trailing the breeder herd in from Dodge and hiring some experienced cowhands who had gone busted seeing the elephant, he had just let nature takes its course. Bulls being what they were, everything seemed to have worked out just fine.

Now if he could just get Julia to thinking along the same lines. He wanted a son in the worst way, and it galled him no end that she was so stubborn. Some men had another kid every time they shook their overalls at their wives. But not Julia. Swore and bedamned that she would hold off getting in a family way until he had this operation off the ground and running strong. The little hussy hadn't made any bones about it either. Just flat out told him she wanted to make certain he was settled down before she went to the bother.

Held it over him, too. Like dangling a carrot in front of a mule.

Christ, that woman was a caution. Sure enough. She had more wiles and guiles and tricky dodges than a whole barrelful of eels.

Sitting out here in the evening, puffing his pipe, he thought about it a lot. What it would be like to have a son. Julia was the best and finest thing that had ever happened to him in his life, and he had a hunch that kids were going to make it even better. Especially if they looked anything like their mother. God, she was easy on the eyes. Made a fellow forget he had ever seen another woman.

Except for one or two. Way back when.

Sometimes, especially when he'd been on a toot and had one of those little talks with McCabe, his thoughts were a kaleidoscope of the past. Drifting back over the old days, remembering, relishing how it had been. Those were great times, none better. The wild drunken sprees, and the fights. Judas, how he missed those fights! But curiously, his thoughts never dwelled much on the women. They were easy enough to recollect all right—hell, they'd all been as much alike as nickel cigars—but he just couldn't seem to concentrate on them overly long. Another face kept popping into his mind, sort of delicate, with mischievous green eyes, and it had a way of pushing everything else aside.

Climbing to his feet, he tamped his pipe out and headed back toward the cabin. Julia would likely have the supper dishes done and they could talk for a while. He liked that, talking with her around the fire in the evenings. She was smart as a whip, educated, and he had learned a lot listening to her carry on about a world he had never known. She could purely carry on, too. Lord, she could bend a man's ear till his head was just buzzing with words. But he liked it. Even encouraged it. There was something about watching a beautiful woman talk that made a man get feisty, made him feel his oats.

Knowing what would come later. When the talk ran dry.

Nearing the cabin he could smell the flowers and honeysuckle she had planted. Even out in God's own wilderness she was determined to have things nice. Just a touch of refinement, she called it. Something to hold them over until they built a real house. Knowing the way she had of working her little tricks, he suspected that wouldn't be far off either.

When he came through the door the cabin was dark and nobody in sight. Which was damn queer with the sun barely down. "Julia?"

There was no answer, and for a moment he thought she might have made a trip to the outhouse. Then he spotted a crack of light under the bedroom door.

"Julia?"

Still no answer. Striding across the room he pushed the door open and froze solid as a rock. Except that his jaw came near popping out of its socket.

Snuggled down in bed, Julia had the covers pulled up to her chin, and her green eyes sparkled devilishly in the cider glow from the lamp. She batted her lashes and smiled, then flicked a glance at the lamp.

"Make a wish and blow out the candle."

Sam Jordan got busy doing just that. The light was no

sooner out than he had his boots off and working fast on his pants. Then, as he hopped into bed and reached for Julia, a thought skittered through his head. Suddenly a throaty chuckle rumbled up out of his chest and he nuzzled her close in a warm embrace.

If it was a boy, they'd name him after Jason Rath.

El Paso

SUDDENLY THE night was split by an ungodly scream of sheer, animal terror. Then just as quickly all went still, and the lawman could feel a vagrant breeze cooling the sweat on his forehead. Wondering if Bajeca had met his match, Stoudenmire scrambled up the hill, trying to make as little noise as possible. Within moments he topped the rise and plowed down the other side, cocking both hammers on the shotgun as he skidded through the dusty soil. Moving cautiously now, he eased through another stand of juniper and tangled underbrush, gliding silently from tree to tree. Abruptly he broke out into a small clearing and froze dead in his tracks.

Beside a crackling little fire sat Bajeca, calmly wiping his knife clean on Kale's shirt. Glancing up, he grinned like a playful wolf and lifted Kale's severed head from the ground.

"A gift for *el patrón*. One *gringo pistolero* who will kill no more."

AUTHOR'S NOTE

—◄━▥▮▥━►—

El Paso is essentially the story of one man, Dallas Stoudenmire. Lawman, gunfighter, mankiller, he was all these and
more. Yet unlike the cotton-candy heroes of Western folklore, Stoudenmire was imperfect, flawed; a man who lived
by his own code in a land where it was often difficult to
separate evil from good.

Born to German parents who had immigrated to the Lone
Star State, Stoudenmire was named after George Mifflin
Dallas, a Texan who served briefly as vice-president of the
United States. After four bloody years fighting for the Confederacy, Stoudenmire returned home a trained killer; cold,
impersonal, something of a loner. Over the next decade he
became a lawman of formidable persuasion, killing an unre-
corded number of badmen with the precision and stoic disinterest that was to remain his trademark. Along the way, he
served variously as a Texas Ranger, deputy sheriff, and city
marshal, evincing little concern for titles so long as he had a
star pinned on his chest.

When the call came to tame El Paso, Stoudenmire was
ready. Everything past, from the killing ground of the Civil
War through the deadly years as a Ranger, had been but a

preliminary to this main event. Like some intricate jigsaw puzzle of destiny, the toughest bordertown on the frontier and the lone-wolf lawman were brought together in a clash that reshaped western legend.

Although the events depicted in *El Paso* are based on documented records, certain liberties have been taken with time, place, and various names. The fact remains, however, that what is written here was essentially what occurred along the banks of the Rio Grande during that desperate summer of 1881.

Dallas Stoudenmire left his mark on El Paso, as well as on the era of the gunfighter. Yet, in passing, it must be noted that he bore small resemblance to the mythical lawmen of folklore. He was simply a man doing the job for which he had been trained, perhaps colder and more deadly than most, but fairly typical of his breed. Resourceful, honest to a fault, brave beyond the measure of other men; a mankiller who coincidentally happened to wear a star.

Matthew Braun

CHAPTER ONE

1

Lieutenant John Tays found himself at a slight tactical disadvantage. He was leading a force of eighteen Texas Rangers, and his orders were to safeguard the journey of three American businessmen. But at the moment, he was standing eyeball to eyeball with close to a thousand Mexican insurgents, and whoever blinked first would very likely wind up cold meat. Somewhat like a man who has a bear by the tail, Lieutenant Tays had developed a sudden liking for far away places.

That morning, as false dawn had given way to first light, the besieged Americans saw that all hope of escape was gone. Under cover of darkness the villagers of San Elizario had encircled with hastily dug rifle pits the adobe hut in which the Americans were trapped, and the sun's brilliant streamers glinted off a solid ring of blued steel. Rangers and civilians alike gazed at the fortifications in dull apathy. After seven days of intermittent fighting, any hope that the army would lift the siege had long since faded. Time had run out, and to a man they knew full well that the Mexicans would exact a grim price for the misery inflicted on them in the last few months.

Waiting for the final attack, Charles Howard could only reflect on the vicious bitch called fate. Earlier that year he had formed a combine with various El Paso businessmen for the sole purpose of cornering the Rio Grande salt trade. East of town, across a hundred miles of barren desert, lay a small chain of salt lakes. Though only recently arrived in Texas, Howard was a man of considerable ambition; an opportunist not above an unsavory deal if enough money were involved. And he was quick to grasp that whoever held a monopoly on the salt lakes could name his own price for that precious commodity.

Though Howard bore a remarkable resemblance to a well-fed hog, he was an affable, persuasive talker. Political skulduggery was a game he understood well, and within a short time, his combine had been allowed to file a claim on the distant lakes. While such grants were normally restricted on public service lands, the burgeoning salt cartel had in effect been given a license to steal. With legal possession of the lakes, they could collect a fee on every *fanega* of salt hauled away, and there were none to prevent them from raising the price to whatever the traffic would bear.

But Howard and his cronies had miscalculated the temper of the people. Throughout the memory of many generations, natives from both sides of the Rio Grande had driven their oxcarts to the dry lakes, braving a fortnight in the waterless desert so that their families might have salt. Moreover, they also bartered salt in the interior regions of Chihuahua, and the gummy cakes they gouged from the earth represented the primary money crop of every village along the border. The El Paso combine posed a threat not only to the natives' own humble needs, but more significantly to the meager livelihood they had been able to glean from the salt trade itself. Reaction was swift and violent.

Under the leadership of Don Luis Cardis, the insurgents had captured Charles Howard at San Elizario, the village closest to the salt lakes. There they forced him to relinquish all claim to the disputed lands, presumably squelching his salt racket in the bud. Then, in exchange for his life, they extracted his promise never to return and sent him packing down the road. Though Howard was built along the lines of a whale, he was hardly a jovial fat man accustomed to turning the other cheek. Ten days later, he caught Don Luis alone in El Paso and gave him an overdose of buckshot, leaving the Mexicans leaderless, if not wholly defanged.

Public officials immediately set the telegraph wires humming, urging the governor to request assistance from troops stationed at nearby Ft. Bliss. Of the fifteen thousand souls along the upper Rio Grande, roughly a thousand were *norteamericanos*. Should a race war erupt, they would be doomed by the sheer weight of numbers. More distressing still, El Paso was isolated by an arid waste of some five hundred miles from the nearest American settlement. With visions of the entire community being wiped out overnight, local politicians demanded forceful action from the government in Austin.

Characteristically, the governor disdained the use of federal troops and sent instead a company of Texas Rangers, commanded by Lieutenant John Tays. Never wanting for a glib argument, Howard somehow convinced Lieutenant Tays that the Mexicans were in open revolt. *After all, fewer than five decades had passed since Texans defeated Santa Anna at San Jacinto. Only a fool would doubt that the greasers remained loyal to Mexico!* Accompanied by the Rangers, Howard and his cohorts had returned to San Elizario, determined to recover what was theirs by right of connivance and political clout.

But natives along both sides of the border were also marching on the sleepy village. Chico Barela had emerged as their new leader, and his call to arms drew upwards of a thousand fighting men even as Howard prepared to reclaim the salt lakes. No sooner had the businessmen arrived in San Elizario than they found themselves confronted by an ugly mob. The cry went up for blood, retribution for the murder of Don Luis Cardis, and the Rangers were barely able to hold them off. Retreating to an adobe hut on the south side of the plaza, the hated *gringos* quickly found themselves under siege by the frenzied Mexicans.

The next week proved a hellish nightmare for the Americans. They ate horse meat, rationed their water, and waited anxiously for federal troops that never came. Instead of attacking directly, the Mexicans pinned them down with sniper fire night and day, certain they couldn't hold out longer than the dwindling water supply in their canteens. Then, as the seventh morning dawned, the natives waited in their newly dug rifle pits, ready for an all-out charge should the *gringos* prove unreasonable.

Shortly after sunrise Chico Barela called for a parley under a white flag. Lieutenant Tays stepped from the adobe, and the Mexican leader's conditions were heard clearly by everyone in the hut. The Rangers would be allowed to depart in peace, but Howard and his partners, John McBride and John Atkinson, would remain as hostages in the village. The *gringos* had one hour to consider the offer, and if they refused, then their company would be killed to the last man. With that, the Mexican flashed an arrogant grin and strode back to the rifle pits.

Turning, Tays moved through the door of the hut, only to be greeted by a deadly silence. None of the Rangers could bring themselves to look at the three businessmen. While they were sworn to uphold the law, they had families to think about, not to mention their own skins. *And besides, hadn't the greaser promised that the three men would simply be held as hostages? Like as not, they'd be released just as soon as things calmed down. Probably no more'n a day or two at the most.*

Charles Howard was many things, but above all else he was a man who believed in hedging his bet. Even if the Rangers agreed to fight, which seemed highly unlikely, he would surely be killed. That was a foregone conclusion. No, the wiser move was to surrender. Although he wouldn't trust a greaser's word any further than he could spit, it made sense to get the Rangers clear and hope they could return in time with a cavalry troop. Briskly confident, he outlined the plan to Lieutenant Tays and saw the strain wash out of the Rangers' faces. McBride and Atkinson weren't too happy with his decision, but then they didn't have a hell of a lot of a choice. Come to think of it, none of them did.

Thirty minutes later Tays and his Rangers pounded out of the village, spurring their horses for El Paso. Behind they left Howard and his partners the featured attraction amidst a howling mob. Some years would pass before even the strongest of them could erase the scene from his memory.

Chico Barela was no less pragmatic than Charles Howard. He remained a leader only so long as he served the will of his people, and right now, his ragtag army was calling for blood. *Gringo* blood! With the Rangers hardly out of sight, the hostages' arms were bound behind them, and they were marched across the plaza to an adobe wall beside the ancient mission. While McBride and Atkinson seemed numb with shock, Charles Howard allowed his captors nothing more than a tight smile. He had gambled and lost. And where he was headed, he had best enjoy the fresh air while he could.

Without benefit of prayer or even a blindfold, the prisoners were shoved against the wall as a firing squad was hurriedly formed. Lacking a sword, Barela borrowed a *machete* and raised it overhead. When it fell, the roar of gunfire thundered across the plaza, instantly followed by the maddened shout of the onlookers. Atkinson and McBride dropped lifelessly in the dust, but Howard had been gut-shot, and he staggered forward, knees buckling.

"*¡Más arriba, cabrones!*" he moaned through clenched teeth. "Higher, you stinking goats!"

"*¡Acábenlos!*" roared the delighted mob. "Finish him!"

Chico Barela marched solemnly to the wounded man. Deliberating a moment, he gauged the blow, then swung the *machete*. Charles Howard's head toppled to the ground, ending his brief moment as salt baron of the Rio Grande. Spurting bright fountains of blood, his body simply collapsed, and the crowd went mad with a spasm of sheer joy.

"*¡Hecho!*" cried Chico Barela. "It is done! Don Cardis is avenged. The salt lakes belong again to the people!"

2

Shortly after suppertime, the men began drifting into the compound. Spread along the banks of the Rio Grande just west of town, Hart's Mill was an imposing structure. The river had been channeled and damned so that it flowed through a high stone arch erected on one side of the mill-house. Locally, it was said that the sluggish river was a mile wide and a foot deep; too thin to plow and too thick to drink. But as it tumbled from the towering arch, sufficient force was generated to turn a huge creaking waterwheel. Seth Hart had copied it directly from those he remembered as a boy in New England, and along the upper Rio Grande, his was the only gristmill. Somewhat like its owner, the mill seemed formidable, unrelenting as it ground inexorably on; one of a kind in a land where industry and determination often fell victim to the drowsy pace of the natives.

Near the mill stood Seth Hart's home. Overlooking the river, it was built of foot-thick adobe and surrounded by tall shade trees. And it was here that various El Paso business-men who shared Hart's political persuasion met once a week for a bruising, heads-up poker game. The house rules were table stakes, check and raise, and a good stiff jolt of rotgut for those left sucking hind tit. As in his business and political endeavors, Seth Hart played poker to win.

After being greeted by their host, the men took their usual seats and settled down for a long, spirited night. They were old friends, each having come to El Paso when it was still a stopover to somewhere else, and there were few secrets among them. They loved whiskey and cards, shared a long standing dream to make El Paso the hub of power in west Texas, and considered themselves ethical businessmen as well as adept politicians. They saw no contradiction in this latter belief, for they readily agreed that a man of substance must play many roles. While there were no saints among them, neither were there any scoundrels, and on this bedrock, their friendship had taken root and grown.

With drinks served and small talk out of the way, the men sat back to await the first deal. But Seth Hart absently riffled the cards, as if pursuing some elusive thought that resisted words. His thatch of white hair spilled over his head like an unkept mane, and the soft, cider glow of the lamp gave his face the flat sheen of weathered rawhide. Were these men his sons, or had this been a land of clans, he would have ruled as patriarch, the venerable elder to whom all others looked for guidance. Although neither condition existed, Hart was still a man of considerable influence, and his four friends seldom made a move without seeking the miller's counsel. Curiosity whetted, they waited in deepening silence as he sifted the chaff from what it was he had to say.

Hart cleared his throat and spat a wad of phlegm at a cuspidor beside the chair. When he spoke his voice was gravelly, as if he had spent too many years swallowing the dust from his own gristmill. "Boys, before we get side-tracked on poker, I'd like to get your ideas on this hornet's nest Charlie Howard stirred up. We're looking down a long, hard road, and if somebody doesn't calm the Mexicans pretty quick it's liable to be a bloody one." He paused, mulling the thought further. "One thing's for certain. Just as sure as we're sitting here, Ed Banning and his bunch aren't going to do a damn thing except keep right on lining their pockets."

"Maybe the greasers'll ventilate Banning the same way they did ol' Charlie." Doc Cummings, owner of the local mercantile emporium, chuckled softly at his own wit. "After all, Charlie was a spoon-fed piker compared to the Banning boys."

Horace Adair reared back in his chair. Noted for his hair-trigger temper, the Irishman was general manager of a mine north of town. "Jesus Christ, Doc! You made your point and missed it, all in the same breath. Granted Ed Banning would skin a flea for its hide and tallow, but he only steals from poor folks indirectly. Political corruption and cattle rustling rarely matter one way or the other to *peones*. Come to think of it, they might even admire him."

Curiously, Horace Adair was closer to the truth than he realized. There were many in El Paso who openly admired the Banning brothers, and their ranks weren't limited to saloonkeepers, madams, and cardsharps. Ed and Sam Banning had hit town in the spring of '79, shortly after word leaked out that three railroads were laying track toward the border. At the time, El Paso was little more than a crossroads. The trail from Santa Fe to Mexico City ran directly through the center of town, while the stage route connecting San Antonio with the Pacific Coast meandered off in the opposite direction. And El Paso's chief claim to fame lay in the fact that the Butterworth stage stopped there twice a day.

But with the arrival of Southern Pacific's first train only last month, the little border town had undergone some startling changes. Trains were daily disgorging a horde of mercenaries who smelled loose money on the freshening wind. For those with a strong stomach, there were fortunes to be made, and whores, tinhorn gamblers, thimbleriggers, and gunslicks had descended on El Paso like swarming locusts. Hardly to anyone's surprise, the Banning brothers were running strong at the head of the pack, welcoming outlaw and harlot alike with open arms. With liberal doses of bribery, intimidation, and outright murder, they had taken over city hall and virtually dominated the city council. Although it saddened early settlers like Seth Hart and his friends, there was no denying that in only two short years Ed Banning had become the power to be reckoned with in El Paso.

"Horace, as usual, your logic is devastating." Doc Cummings cast a mischievous smile around the table, amused by the Irishman's pugnacious manner. "But I'll tell you one thing. Ed Banning's day is coming. He's got his finger in everything else, and he'll probably get around to trying to steal the salt lakes just like Charlie Howard did. Maybe if we wait long enough, the greasers'll settle his hash for us."

Before Adair could frame a reply, Seth Hart broke in sharply. "Doc, you and Horace are both missing the point. Howard trying to grab the salt lakes only aggravated a sore that's been festering for years. And mark my words, the Bannings' rustling operation across the river will one day force the *patrones* to lead their people against us. So far they've sat back and watched, but if their ranches keep getting raided, they'll organize those *peones*, and God help us then."

The men silently glanced at one another, weighing Hart's words. Nate Hobart, proprietor of the Alhambra Hotel, sucked nervously at his drink and tried to think of something profound to add. But his natural reticence won out, and he merely waited for the shaggy-haired miller to resume.

When the stillness thickened without anyone venturing a solution, Hart tossed out another firecracker. "Boys, what I've been leading up to is simply stated. El Paso is just facing too goddamned many problems all at one time. Ed Banning is stealing the town blind, and when you get right down to cases, his political shenanigans are one of the big causes of our Mexican problems. Appears to me that, if we solve one, we'll have gone a long way toward solving the other. What I'm suggesting is that we put Banning to the skids and send him packing."

"Well, we could always have George Campbell run him out of town," Cummings observed dryly. The comment was greeted with grunts and snorts by the other men, for it was common knowledge that City Marshal Campbell was one of Banning's political flunkeys.

"Shit fire," Adair remarked acidly. "George Campbell couldn't catch his ass if he was tied hand and foot in a tow sack."

"By God, what we need is a *town tamer!*" John Simmons, owner of the livery stable and feed store, suddenly came alive. His eyes glittered with comprehension, as if the answer had been revealed to him alone. "Someone like Wild Bill Hickok, or Bear River Tom Smith. A real head-cracker!"

"There's only one problem with that, Johnny. They're both dead." Horace Adair's sardonic comment brought chuckles from the other men, and a withering look from Simmons.

Doc Cummings abruptly came up on the edge of his chair. "Maybe so. But by Jesus Christ, I know one that's not dead! He's a deputy sheriff up in Colorado County, and, gents, he's the meanest sonovabitch that ever got up and walked on his hind legs. Name's Dallas Stoudenmire, and lemme tell you, he eats knotheads like Ed Banning for breakfast."

"Is that a fact?" Adair inquired innocently, glancing about the table. "And how is it you know so much about a Dutchy gunslinger?"

"Horace, he just happens to be German. Or at least his folks were. And for your information, he's gonna marry my sister later this month."

"Doc, we're not playing for chalkies, you know." Seth Hart gave him a searching look. "This is serious business. You sure you want to get your brother-in-law hooked up in a deal like this?"

"Hell, Seth, I can't see how it'd hurt to ask," Cummings replied. "He's full grown, and I reckon he knows how to say no. Besides, he's been a lawman of one kind or another since the end of the war, and even if he don't want the job, he could sure as hell give us some powerful advice. Offhand, I'd say it's as good a place to start as any."

Hart pondered this for a moment, then nodded. "All right, send him a wire. But don't let the cat out of the bag. Just say you'd like to see him on a matter of some importance."

"And what will we accomplish, even if he's as tough as Doc says?" Adair's bulldog jowls set in an obstinate scowl. "You don't seriously think the city council will fire Campbell and hire a new marshal?"

Hart smiled patiently. "Horace, let's take 'em as we come to 'em. Don't forget that Doc and me both have a vote on that same council. And if we want to play dirty pool, we might just figure a way to ram it through."

The miller ran callused hands through his white mane, then picked up the deck of cards. The discussion had ended. "Boys, let's get down to some serious poker playin'. The name of the game is stud. Ante five dollars and take your licks like real white men."

3

Dallas Stoudenmire wasn't what folks would call a handsome man, but he looked like he had been built to last. Rangy and lean, he was hewed somewhat on the order of an oak door, standing six feet four and weighing in at a gristled two hundred twenty. Few men knew his full strength, and those who had tested it rarely came back for seconds. His very presence was enough to halt most troublemakers in their tracks, and his fearsome impact wasn't lessened by the craggy features, the jut of a heavy brow, and a shock of hair like burnished wheat. His face looked as though it had been hurriedly chiseled from a hunk of granite, and above the hollow cheeks his eyes touched lightly on all about him. As if it concealed some shallowly buried danger, his gaze seemed pale and depthless in its constant movement, like mountain water beneath freshly frozen ice. All in all, he was a solitary sort, a man best left to himself. And most people took him just as they found him. At a distance, in short doses.

When Stoudenmire stepped from the train at the Southern Pacific depot, he felt the stares of those crowding the platform. While he was used to it, the gaping looks never ceased to nettle him, like farmers gawking at some oddity in a tent show. He knew he was different from most men, colder, quicker to strike, drained of remorse once it was done. But it didn't bother him; he accepted it for what it was, wasting little thought on the compassion and gentleness that preachers rated so highly. Time lays scars on a man, bloody welts tracing a path from where he stands back to where he started. In the overall scheme of things, there were some men who needed killing, and it stood to reason that there had to be a few who were hardened to wield the instrument of destruction. Why he had been tapped for the job, or how it had come about, seemed unimportant, lost in the haze of long-ago, faraway things. Somehow it had started, leading him step by step from a wild young hellion to a man with a star on his chest. He was good at it, perhaps the best. And for now, being best at what he did was all that mattered.

Ignoring the stares, Stoudenmire turned his broad back, on the train station and strode off down Main Street. Though he knew little of El Paso, he had heard that it was nestled in the Tularosa Basin and was thus unprepared for the pervasive sense of being encircled by mountains. The *Conquistadores* had named it El Paso del Norte, for it formed a natural pass to the north over the mountains that now joined Texas, New Mexico, and Mexico. The bare, craggy slopes of the Franklin Mountains dropped off from a high rim to the north, and the town itself lay in the shadow of Comanche Peak. To the east lay the arid plains he had crossed by train, broken only by the flat desert mesas, jutting unevenly from the parched earth. Beyond the tablelands, he could see the Hueco Mountains, with the sheer cliffs of El Capitán thrusting skyward as if to escape the desolation and heat.

Turning, he studied the land to the southwest, across the river. In the distance, he saw the Sierra Madre range, forming a backdrop for El Paso's twin sister on the opposite border, Paso del Norte. Even though the towns appeared similar in every respect, he had heard on the train that Paso del Norte was strictly for Mexicans, a place where a *gringo* wandered at his own risk. The thought brought his mind back to the reason for being here, and he crossed the plaza in search of Doc Cummings. The cryptic telegram in his coat pocket said little, and perhaps that was what made him curious enough to travel six hundred miles. Most times the things men left unsaid were what counted in a pinch, and knowing Doc, he had no doubt there was considerable yet to tell.

Later that night, Stoudenmire and Cummings met with Seth Hart and his poker cronies. Although the five businessmen were the only ones who knew the purpose behind the lawman's visit, Stoudenmire's presence in El Paso was hardly a secret. Earlier in the evening, Cummings had taken him on a tour of the town's gamier dives, and there was considerable talk in the red-light district about the solemn-faced jasper with the frosty eyes. But the brief walk through the southside had served its purpose. Within an hour's time the lawman had counted close to thirty saloons, an equal number of dancehalls, and a rash of whorehouses unlike anything he had ever seen. Moreover, he had observed two saloon brawls, a knifing, and a somewhat amateurish gunfight, all within the space of two blocks. Yet not once had he seen a man wearing a badge. Any lingering doubt in Stoudenmire's mind had fast been dispelled. El Paso was in desperate need of a responsible peace officer.

Once introductions were out of the way and the men seated in Hart's study, the miller briefed Stoudenmire on the extent of the problem they faced. Without need of exaggeration, he detailed events leading to the salt war, the general hostility that existed between whites and Mexicans, and the stranglehold the Bannings had secured on the political apparatus of the town. While he spoke, Seth Hart had been sizing Stoudenmire up, and he liked what he saw. But there was more to a man than what met the eye, and that's what they had to find out before the evening was finished.

"Frankly, Mr. Stoudenmire," Hart concluded, "if I were in your boots, I wouldn't touch this job with a ten-foot pole. Course, you're a lawman, and I'm not, so I suppose you know what you're gettin' into." Then he paused, letting the silence mount as he appraised the other man. "Well, no sense beatin' around the bush. What about it? Do you think you're man enough to cut the mustard?"

Stoudenmire's eyes narrowed at the outright challenge, and the room went still as the men waited to see how he would answer. "Mr. Hart, it sort of looks to me like you've got the saddle on backwards. I didn't come here begging a job. You sent for me, near as I recollect. Whether or not I can pull your bacon out of the fire is something you'll have to decide for yourself. My record as a peace officer isn't hard to track down, and if I'm any judge, you've already put out feelers in the right direction."

Doc Cummings couldn't restrain himself from butting in. "Dallas, don't be so infernal high and mighty. He's only tryin' to get your opinion of our predicament. Christ, I've already told them how you fought for the Confederacy and served as a Ranger before you took the deputy job. They know you can clean up El Paso. They're just tryin' to get you to say it."

The lawman just nodded, smiling tightly. "Well, I'll tell

you, Doc. I'm not right sure I want the job. Leastways not until we come to an understanding about a few things."

"If you want my two cents worth," Horace Adair snorted, "I'm not convinced he can handle it. Running the Bannings out of town is gonna be like tryin' to pour hot butter in a wildcat's ear. All this bullshit about him being a gunslinger might impress the folks back home, but goddamnit, this is the border. If he starts playing the big, tough *hombre* on the southside, those boys are just liable to whittle him down to size."

Stoudenmire's flinty gaze swung around, and he looked at Adair as if he were something hairy that had just crawled out of the gravy. "Mister, I never had much use for little men with loud mouths. Now if you pop off once more, I'll be forced to forget you're Doc's friend. Savvy?"

"Hold it!" Hart's gruff command came just as the Irishman's jowls swelled with rage. "Horace, sometimes I'd swear you don't have sense enough to carry guts to a bear. Granted Mr. Stoudenmire might be young in years, but it seems you aren't able to see beyond that. There are other ways of measuring time, you know. Offhand, I'd say that anyone who has killed six men upholding the law doesn't need a wet nurse, even on the border." The startled looks from his friends brought a benign smile to the miller's face. "Why the surprise? You boys know I don't bet without peeking at the hole card. Like Mr. Stoudenmire surmised, I've already gone to the trouble of having him checked out."

Horace Adair glued a sheepish smile on his face and got busy sipping his whiskey. The big sonovabitch was for real after all! Silently, he wondered what went on inside a man's head who killed so easily, and for pay at that. The cold-eyed bastard probably pissed ice water and slept on nails.

"Well goddamn," Cummings crowed. "Are we gonna sit around on our thumbs or do we offer the man a job? How about it, Dallas? Want to try cutting El Paso down to size?"

"Trying won't get it. Not by half," Hart interjected. "He'll have to bet the limit and back every play to the hilt. Otherwise, he'll be cold meat inside of a week. But before we go too far with that, I'd like to hear more about those conditions Mr. Stoudenmire wants us to meet."

The lawman glanced around the room, studying each man in turn before responding. "Gentlemen, with the exception of Doc, I don't know any more about you than I do Adam's goat. You say you want your town cleaned up, and until you prove different, I'll take you at your word. But if I'm going to kick over a shithouse, it'll have to be done my way. That means no interference, no deals, and no special treatment for friends. Whoever gets in the way gets hurt. If you can't swallow that, then let's just shake hands, and I'll see about catching the next train out."

The men stared at Stoudenmire as if hypnotized, certain he meant every word he said. Whoever got in his way wouldn't just get hurt. They would get killed. And in his own way, the lawman was warning them that it could happen. Still, they didn't have a hell of a lot of choice. It was either suffer along under the Bannings or take a chance on a killer who just happened to wear a star. The one bled you dry with political corruption, and the other might just chase the whole damn town up a tree. But you paid your money and you took your chances. The odds came out the same no matter how the nut was cracked.

"Boys, it looks like we've got ourselves a new marshal." Seth Hart's tone left no doubt that the decision had been made. "Now we'd better get down to figuring strategy. I've got an idea the city council is gonna wet down their legs when we spring Dallas on them."

Stoudenmire leaned back in his chair and lit a cigar. As the men began talking, he sipped at his drink for the first time. Good whiskey. Damned good, in fact. And he had to admit that he was impressed with the company, too. Still, he'd seen sure-fire winners turn to busted flushes more than once. Better to bank on himself and forget about handouts. Storekeepers were generally soft in the guts anyway. Besides, when the shooting started, a man did well to forget he had friends.

4

El Paso's city hall fronted Oregon Street on the west side of
the plaza. Once a month, Mayor Isaac Porter convened the
city council in an upstairs meeting hall. There they met to
consider the bagful of problems generated by the town's
mushrooming growth.

Since the mayor, as well as two of the councilmen, Simeon
Ogleby and Pud Brown, danced to whatever tune the Banning
brothers happened to favor, the monthly meetings were generally cut-and-dried affairs. Occasionally, the irascible Doc
Cummings would liven up what he called "The puppet show,"
but more often than not, the meetings made for a dull, frequently wasted, evening. The sole ambition of Mayor Porter
and his two henchmen centered on milking the town dry with
corrupt schemes, and even Seth Hart in his tenacious, probing
way had been unable to get the goods on them to date.

The June council meeting promised to be little different
from those in the past. After reviewing progress on current projects, which included a public waterworks contract
awarded to Pud Brown's brother, the mayor opened the floor
to new business. Hart and Cummings sat back to watch the
show. While the council's shenanigans sometimes curdled
their stomachs, there was a perverse fascination about the
rogues' devious methods; as if a primer in civic malfeasance
was being acted out right before their very eyes. Still, tonight
might prove more interesting than anyone suspected, for Seth
Hart planned to drop a bomb right in the mayor's lap. Just as
soon as the four-flushers finished ramming through their
latest swindle.

Isaac Porter was a beefy little man, whose spongy face
was deeply pocked from a childhood bout with smallpox.
Careful grooming did little to improve his chunky figure, and
he had the disconcerting habit of peering at a man like some
wise, inquisitive bird. The role of charlatan suited him perfectly, and as he faced the council, none doubted that he had
few peers in the art of slick manipulation.

"Gentlemen, before the night's over I have every intention of breaking the faro bank at the Monte Carlo, so what do you say we get down to brass tacks? The floor's open, first come, first served."

Simeon Ogleby's hand shot skyward, and the mayor recognized him with a benevolent nod. "Mr. Mayor, I'd like to propose that the council entertain a motion to build a bridge over the Rio Grande. It's a public disgrace for a town of this size not to have a fine, substantial bridge joinin' us with our neighbors across the river. Besides that, now that the railroad has reached us, we should provide some civilized way of importing and exporting goods with Mexico. Trade is the backbone of commerce, and if this town's gonna grow, we've got to start thinkin' *progress*."

Hart and Cummings exchanged glances, never ceasing to be amazed by the sheer audacity of these rascals. Though he knew it was futile, Doc couldn't resist a bit of heckling. "Simeon, what the hell are you gonna do with a bridge? You could wade that goddamn mudhole without gettin' your toes wet."

"Commerce, Doc. Commerce. The backbone of trade." Ogleby floundered, trying to remember if he had his terms in the right order. "And vice versa, of course."

Isaac Porter gave him a devastating look and jumped into the breach. "Gentlemen, I personally find great merit in this proposal. Why, just think of it! El Paso would be the only town on the border with a bridge connecting it to Mexico. The possibilities for international trade are enormous. I might even say, unlimited. As a matter of fact, the idea has such merit that I suggest we broaden the discussion to consideration of selecting a contractor to build this fine bridge."

"Hell, why not give it to Pud's brother?" Doc cackled. "He knows all about working in water."

Pud Brown shot a nervous glance at the mayor and smiled apologetically, like he expected someone to kick him in the ass. Porter studiously ignored Doc's wisecrack and went right on with the meeting. To no one's surprise, a building outfit resting in Ed Banning's hip pocket was selected, and an allocation of twenty-five thousand dollars earmarked for construction. The motion was quickly brought to vote and passed three to two. Hart and Cummings voting *nay* had somewhat the same effect as spitting into the wind.

As the mayor and his two cronies were congratulating themselves on their slippery footwork, Seth Hart decided it was time to rock the boat. But it would have to be done skillfully, in a roundabout manner. For if the Bannings ever tumbled to his real purpose, then no amount of pressure, deftly applied or otherwise, could force them to oust George Campbell.

"Mr. Mayor, I would like to bring a matter of some importance to the council's attention. Just now you made the point that our town is growing by leaps and bounds. And I agree wholeheartedly. Our first bank has just opened, we've got two newspapers, and before the summer's out, another railroad will reach us. All in all, I'd say we're about to become the biggest thing that ever hit West Texas. But if we're ever going to equal the likes of Austin or San Antonio, we've got to bring about some changes. To use your term, Isaac, we've got to get down to the brass tacks of civilizing a town that thinks it's still a frontier outpost."

Hart had their attention, though it was obvious they were waiting for the ax to fall. Looking around the table, he let the suspense build for only a moment, then pushed on. "We're faced with two problems that aren't about to solve themselves. First, there's the Mexicans. The army proved they're unwilling to take a hand in civilian matters when they let Charlie Howard get sliced to ribbons. And Austin isn't gonna keep sending a detachment of Rangers everytime we yell wolf. Which means we must solve it ourselves. As long as there's a threat of violence, El Paso won't be anything more than a jerkwater whistle-stop.

"Now the second problem is just as bad, from a standpoint of the town growing and attracting more business enterprises. Any night of the week you wanna go down to the southside, you can see at least one gunfight and probably stumble across two or three cadavers without even trying. And every last one of you knows it's true. Brawls, shootings, knife fights. The kind of violence people expect from a cowtown, but certainly not a progressive community. And to my way of thinking, gentlemen, the blame falls on our shoulders, not on the townspeople. Calling a spade a spade, I'm talking about the man we appointed to protect the citizens of El Paso. George Campbell is worthless as tits on a boar hog. He not only isn't man enough for the job, he doesn't even try. I can guarantee you he's sacked up in some whorehouse swilling whiskey at this very moment. And with my own eyes, I've seen him make a beeline in the opposite direction whenever trouble starts."

Mayor Porter chuckled softly, then broke in before Hart could catch his breath. "Now, Seth, it's not all that bad. George isn't the best peace officer, I grant you. But he's certainly not the worst. Good Lord, this town's still got growing pains, and you can't expect any man to civilize it overnight."

"Well, by God, somebody better," Cummings snorted. "Otherwise, we're gonna have greasers crawlin' over us like flies on a manure pile. That is, if the rowdies don't kill everybody in town first."

The mayor and his cohorts suddenly began squirming in their chairs. Huddled together at the end of the table, they peered blankly at Hart and Cummings, like a trio of owls caught in a chicken coop. Apparently, the businessmen were in dead earnest, and the Banning underlings had no desire to create a row over such an insignificant post as city marshal. Their crooked little empire was running under full sail, and anyone who made waves would have to answer to Ed Banning personally.

Porter blinked first, unwilling to start a fight without Banning's approval. Then in his oily, politician's voice, he began probing for a weak spot. "Now Doc, don't get yourself in a swivet. We're all reasonable men here. And I'm sure Seth will agree that we can come up with some way to get George Campbell back on the straight and narrow. Think about it calmly for a moment and then tell me where you think the marshal has gone astray."

Cummings regarded him with a brash, amused insolence.

"Isaac, you're slick. Real slick. Remind me of a tomcat I heard about once. Seems like he got the hots for a little skunk pussy and started humpin' a female polecat. Well, sir, after a couple of whacks, he had to call it quits. Hadn't had all he wanted, you understand, just all he could stomach. What I'm gettin' around to saying, Isaac, is that unless you put a damper on the southside and the greasers, the voters of this town might start figuring they've had all of you they can stand."

"Doc's right, Mayor." Seth Hart grabbed the lead before Porter could gather his wits. "The marshal was appointed because you supported him, and everyone knows it, and as any fool can see, George Campbell wilted when the going got rough. He's your responsibility, Isaac, and if you don't do something about it, the decent people of El Paso are going to start having second thoughts about their mayor."

Porter glared at him across the table, trying desperately to muster some reasonable argument. But Hart's words had the ring of truth, and everyone in the room knew it. Ogleby and Brown simply held their breath, like something rancid had been smeared on their upper lips. Yet the silence deepened, and their faces went taut as they waited on the mayor to offer a snappy rebuttal.

Watching them, Doc Cummings couldn't resist the temptation. "Blessed are those who have nothing to say and cannot be persuaded to say it."

The sarcasm brought Porter out of his funk. He shot Cummings a stinging glance, then looked back at Hart. "Exactly what is it you're suggesting, Seth?"

"Not much, really. Just that Campbell be replaced with a man who can make El Paso a safe place to live."

"And I suppose you've got his replacement all picked out?"

"You might say that. We've been talking to a fellow named Stoudenmire. Got a fine record as a peace officer in East Texas. We think he's got the backbone the job calls for."

"And if I refuse to consider a change?"

"Why, Isaac, I suppose I'd be forced to call in the newspapers and tell 'em the mayor got skittish when we started talking about cleaning up El Paso. You know, elections are only a year or so away, and lots of people are just achin' to stir up a reform movement."

Porter mulled it over for a moment, desperately aware of the need to talk with Ed Banning. "Tell you what. We'll take it under advisement and come to a decision at next month's meeting."

"Sorry, Mayor, but that won't cut it." Hart's eyes hardened, and his jaw set in a stubborn cast. "I'll agree to twenty-four hours, which means we meet again tomorrow night. Otherwise I sic the newshounds on you."

Isaac Porter merely nodded, his face flushed with indignation and worry. Rising, he stalked from the room, trailed closely by Brown and Ogleby. Breaking the bank at the Monte Carlo was now the furthest thought from his mind. It had been a rough night, and right at the moment, he needed a good, stiff drink.

Observing their hasty departure, Cummings heard the warm, moist chuckle of a fat man laughing and turned to find Seth Hart thoroughly amused by the new order of things.

"Doc, just offhand, I'd say we've got 'em on the run. Goddamn me if they didn't look like three little shoats that just come out of the cuttin' pen."

The two men shook hands heartily and strode from the meeting hall with new zest to their step. Things were looking up, and if the Bannings weren't careful, they might just wind up snookered in their own game.

5

Some two hours after the council meeting, Isaac Porter wandered into the Coliseum Saloon. His step was slightly unsteady, and his eyes had taken on a glassy sheen, but otherwise, there was no outward sign that he was carrying a load. Since leaving city hall, he had belted down the better part of a quart, and at the moment he was feeling no pain. Still, he was in command of himself, and his confidence had risen sharply as he moved from saloon to saloon along San Antonio Street. Tipping his hat to the bartender, greeting his

constituents with an expansive smile, the mayor eased
through the boisterous crowd and headed for the Coliseum's
back room.

Like most watering holes in town, the Coliseum had a long
mahogany bar with a smattering of nude paintings and French
mirrors hung on the walls. But the similarity ended there, for
the Coliseum was owned by the Banning brothers, and it was
hardly an accident that their establishment was the showplace
of El Paso. On one side of the large hall, there was a row of
gaming tables, offering faro, chuck-a-luck, roulette, and other
pleasant devices for separating the sucker from his poke. Toward the rear of the room, angled across one entire corner,
was a small stage where dancing girls, Irish tenors, and
stuttering comedians took turns competing with the roar of
the crowd. Taken at a glance, it was quite a place, and for
most men, owning the Coliseum would have represented the
end of the rainbow. But Ed Banning had never considered
himself molded from common clay; what was enough for the
average pilgrim was merely a sampler for El Paso's political
kingpin.

After threading his way through the packed house, Mayor
Porter halted before a door at the rear, adjusted his coat, and
knocked lightly. From inside came a muffled command,
barely audible over the hubbub from the saloon. Sucking up
his paunch, Porter twisted the doorknob and entered Ed
Banning's office.

The first thing he saw was Sam Banning. The younger of
the Banning brothers had a way of drawing attention, even
in a crowd. For a big man, he was uncommonly handsome,
and the fact that his nose had been broken on occasion somehow lent character to his broad, rough-hewn features. But
after fashioning his face, the gods in their perverse way had
played a cruel joke on Sam. His wide, heavily muscled shoulders gave way to long dangling arms, and his hands looked
as if they could crush coconuts if the need arose. Still, the
crowning touch was that Sam had grown to manhood almost
as thick through the head as he was through the shoulders.

All in all, the young Mr. Banning seemed only one step removed from walking on his knuckles.

Porter nodded to Sam, then turned to his brother who was seated behind a massive, ornately carved desk. "Ed, how's tricks? Looked like you're making money hand over fist out there." The mayor jerked his head back toward the door, and his hat tilted askew, cocked rakishly over one eyebrow.

Ed Banning regarded the dumpy politician with a speculative gaze. Isaac Porter had achieved minor fame as a boozer in earlier days, and Banning had a sneaking hunch he was on the firewater again. "Mayor, what brings you down to this neck of the woods? Thought you had a council meeting tonight."

"Oh, we did, we did," Porter assured him. "Passed that bridge deal one, two, three, and awarded the contract to our sterling partner in illusion, Ab Roberts."

El Paso's political boss just nodded, observing him closely, certain now that Porter's euphoric mood was about nine parts alcohol. Banning's frowning eyes slanted upward, two cold, ashen sockets in a long, bony face. Unlike Sam, he was a spare man, with a chalky, pallid look, almost as if he had been sickly as a child. Somewhat withdrawn by nature, he was an astringent sort, who usually spoke through clenched teeth, as if his jaws had been broken and wired shut. But the most disturbing thing about him was his eyes, menacing yet somehow lifeless, tinted a strange, dispassionate shade of gray, curiously suggestive of a cold winter cloud in a dead sky.

With the exception of his brother, Ed Banning had little use for other men; cynical of their motives, sharply aware of the imperfections that flawed their character. Remote, purposely holding himself aloof from the crowd, he played on other men's frailties and, with reasoned audacity, brought them to their knees in the crunch. Now, irritated by Porter's weakness for the bottle, he decided to whittle his political front-man down a notch or two.

"Isaac, you're soused. And the only thing lower in my book than a drunk is a reformed drunk. Now, suppose you pull up your pants and tell me what happened at the council meeting to set you off."

The mayor's bonhomie wilted under the biting sarcasm, and his motley features dissolved beneath a mask of outright alarm. "Ed, it wasn't my fault, honest to Christ it wasn't. That bastard Seth Hart has got it in his head that we need a new marshal. And he's threatened to blow the lid off unless we appoint some John Law he's scrounged up. I swear to you, Ed, I didn't have a thing to do with it. Absolutely nothing."

"All right, Isaac, keep your dauber up. There's a difference between having your tit in a wringer and losing all the marbles. Now just start at the beginning and tell me exactly what happened."

"Goddamn, Ed, you ain't gonna get nothin' out of him that makes sense." Sam's eyes flashed like coals of black ice as he gestured comtemptuously toward Porter. His normal disposition was something akin to a boar grizzly with its paw in a rusty bear trap, and right now he regarded the stubby little politician with a hungry glare. "Lemme take old swizzle-guts out and dump him in a horse trough. That'll bring him up talkin' a blue streak."

"Sam, try not to be so rash. Isaac's not that bad off. Are you, Isaac?" Ed Banning paused and Porter nodded dumbly, darting a nervous glance in Sam's direction. "See, what did I tell you, Sam? Isaac's got it all sorted out, and he's going to pony up just like he had balls. Now you go right ahead, Mayor, we're all ears."

Fumbling the words, Porter tried to flush the whiskey fumes from his spinning brain. Haltingly at first, he started to relate the gist of what had happened at the council meeting. Warming to his subject, the old warrior then launched into a vitriolic, damning tirade against Seth Hart and Doc Cummings. Gaining confidence as his grasp for the trenchant phrase returned, the mayor swept into the home stretch with a dire warning that all was lost unless the two businessmen were somehow thwarted in their underhanded conspiracy.

When he finished, standing spent and slightly breathless, the brothers simply stared at him with disgust. Ed Banning finally shook his head with a patronizing smile. "Isaac, if anybody ever takes the trouble to kick all the bullshit out of you, they could bury you in a matchbox."

Sam's hoarse grunt cut him off. "Forget him, Ed. We got to worry about them smart-aleck sonsabitches uptown. I say get 'em in a dark alley and split their heads with a bungstarter. Teach 'em they can't get away with muckin' up the water. Let everybody in this whole goddamn fleabag know who's callin' the shots in El Paso."

"You know, Sam, sometimes I think our old man's oats must've been thinned out when he get around to you. Killin' Hart and Cummings wouldn't do anything but get the reformers out on the street pounding their drums." When the younger Banning gave him a baleful frown, Ed chuckled lightly. "Now don't get all bent out of shape. Lemme have a minute to think this out."

Unlike his brother, who operated solely on raw instinct, Ed Banning was coldly phlegmatic when crossed; a calculating, passionless instrument even with his back to the wall. Leaning back in the chair, his eyes clouded over and fixed on the ceiling, as if the answer lay hidden in the broad crossbeam. Slowly, piece by piece, he took the puzzle apart and put it back together again, examining each possibility with precise care before discarding it. Then, as he stood back and looked at the situation as a whole, the jumbled parts abruptly fell into place, no longer obscured or muddied but suddenly clear and shiny bright.

With the solution now in hand, his eyes focused again, and he found Sam watching him intently. "Brother, it occurs to me that dogs don't lie down just one way. And I think this is one of those times when we're gonna let Mr. Seth Hart go away figurin' he's bluffed us out."

When Sam's forehead wrinkled in protest, Ed held up his hand. "Let me finish. We're gonna let them have this hayseed as marshal. Stoudenmire, is that his name? Well they can have him, and welcome to him. It's no sweat off our balls. So long as we control the courts and city hall it doesn't make a good goddamn who wears that tin star. Without the mayor or the judges to back him up, Stoudenmire is gonna be flounderin' around like a hamstrung calf. And the dandy part of it is that we have absolutely nothing to lose, whichever way the dice fall. If he does get the greasers calmed down and clamps a lid on the southside, then we'll take credit for appointing the man who cleaned up El Paso. Lookin' at it the other way, if he falls on his ass or gets himself killed, then we'll dump the blame right back on Hart's doorstep. Like I said, there's no way for us to lose. It's like playing with a stacked deck."

"By God, Ed, you've done it again!" Isaac Porter grinned broadly, nodding his head with a great show of awe. "I'll just walk into that meeting tomorrow night and tell Hart to bring on his horses."

"You do that, Mayor. Only make damn sure Hart and Cummings believe that their threats worked. Otherwise, they might shy off and start kicking over more rocks."

Later, after Porter had wandered back into the saloon, the Bannings broke out a bottle of their own. Downing a shot, Sam smacked his lips, like a dog sniffing horse apples. Then he started, as if the whiskey had jarred his dim wits, and peered quizzically at his brother.

"Say, Ed, I just thought of somethin'. What the hell kind of excuse are we gonna give George Campbell?"

"Don't worry about it, I'll think of something. Course, we could send him on a raid across the river. Maybe somebody'd put a hole through him and let a little of that rotgut leak out." Lazing back in the chair, he sipped the whiskey, savoring its pleasant bite as his eyes drifted off. "Sam, if you're ever gonna amount to anything in this game, you've got to get one thing through your head. Men are the cheapest commodity on God's green earth. You buy 'em like pig's knuckles. By the pound or by the keg. And even then, you've got to figure you've been robbed. No matter what you paid."

Sam Banning's thick brow wrinkled, and he dimly wondered what the hell his brother was talking about. Then he decided it wasn't worth the effort, and went back to the more inviting certainty of the bottle.

CHAPTER TWO

—◆—

1

"Doc! Doc!" Kate Stoudenmire rushed forward and threw herself into the storekeeper's arms. She hadn't seen her brother in almost a year, and she sorely missed the eldest of the Cummings brood.

"Lordy, Kate girl, just look at you." After a mighty hug Doc held her at arm's length, mumbling appreciatively as he made a slow appraisal. "Yessir, gal, you are purely somethin'. Can't rightly call you my baby sister anymore. All growed up and married. Say, speakin' of husbands, where's Dallas?"

Glancing around, they saw Stoudenmire threading his way through the crowd gathered about the train station. Behind him came two Mexican youngsters who had all they could do to handle Kate's assortment of luggage. Trailing at his heels was the biggest dog Doc Cummings had ever laid eyes on.

As the two men shook hands, Doc saw the dog give him a long, speculative stare. He was easily the most ferocious-looking beast Doc could recall having stumbled across, including a couple of brief encounters with grizzlies. Built along the lines of a mastiff, he had a deep bull-chest, an enormous furrowed head, and a jawful of teeth that looked like he'd traded them off a shark. And like his master's, the dog's eyes were cold, somehow menacing, constantly shifting as he noted the movement of all about him with a wary scowl. In the background, Doc overheard the little Mexicans talking about *el lobo hambre*. The hungry wolf! Somehow it fitted the dog perfectly, and he idly wondered what the hell Stoudenmire fed the brute.

"Dallas, it's good to see you," Cummings said, tearing his thoughts away from the dog. "How's it feel to be an old married man? And what have you done to Kate? Man, she looks like someone just handed her the keys to the goody factory."

Stoudenmire's face cracked in a rare grin. Kate was his one weakness, the only soft spot in some thirty years of steeling himself to toe the mark in an uncompromising land. "Doc, near as I can see, I haven't done a thing for Kate. She's just a natural looker, that's all. Trouble is, you've been sittin' out here remembering your baby sister, and all the time she was studying to be a real eyeful."

Kate was a stunner, no question about it, and a man needed only one look to work up a fit of envy toward the lawman. Standing about even with Stoudenmire's shoulder, she was what people back home called dainty. But unlike many delicate women, she hadn't been shorted when the sweetmeats were handed out. Her oval face was framed by hair black as obsidian, and her eyes shot sparks of fiery green, like some ancient feline goddess. She had a devastatingly winsome smile and a bewitching manner that was both seductive and impish in the same breath. Yet Kate somehow created the illusion of being one of those fragile, gentle things that would vanish in a wisp of smoke unless handled gingerly. And beneath these more obvious features was a sense of refinement and gentility that left even rawboned Texans gulping for pretty words and mushy phrases.

Although one man's eye for beauty might easily leave another man doubting his judgment, there were few who wouldn't agree that Dallas Stoudenmire had snared a rare prize indeed when he got himself spliced to this toothsome young piece.

Cummings slapped Stoudenmire on the shoulder and crowed with laughter. "Maybe I remember her in pigtails, like you say. But I bet I wouldn't be wide of the mark thinkin' you got more than you bargained for too." Rolling his eyes, he chortled and nudged the lawman in the ribs, glancing slyly at Kate. "You're lookin' sort of peaked, son. Not lettin' Katie girl work you overtime, are you?"

"Honestly! Men are so crude." Kate blushed up to her hairline, eyes flashing with mock indignation. "You two act like you're in a stable discussing some high-stepping brood mare. Well you'd better take care, mark my words. I know enough about the both of you that, if I ever started talking, this whole town would roll over on its back."

"God save us, she'd do it too!" Grabbing his sister around the waist, Cummings struck off toward a horse and buggy hitched near the end of the depot. "C'mon, Dallas. Let's take your bride on a tour of the town before she ups and spills the beans." Over his shoulder he darted a quick glance at the dog. "That grizzly bear of yours can ride in the caboose. What's his name, anyway?"

"Tige. And you'd better take care what you call him." The dog's ears perked up at the sound of his name, and Stoudenmire knuckled his wrinkled brow. "He's sort of proud of being a dog, and he don't take kindly to most folks."

"Man or beast?" Cummings called back in jest.

"Both." The lawman chuckled softly, and Tige licked his hand, sensing in some distant way that his master had had the last word.

Shortly, luggage and dog had been loaded on the buggy, and they headed uptown. Chattering like a magpie, Doc Cummings enlightened them on the points of interest, allowing small room for questions. San Jacinto Plaza, renamed for the battleground where Texas had won its independence. The Notice Tree, an ancient shadetree on which proclamations and death warrants had been tacked in times past. The State National Bank, first of its breed on the upper Rio

Grande. And its partner in commerce, the Parker House
Hotel, even then rising from the dust in a whirlwind of mor-
tice and wood.

Pausing at the native market, the storekeeper explained
that the countryside abounded with Mexican *granjeros*, small
farmers who spent their lives coaxing raisins, grapes, and
various fruits from the hostile soil. Centuries ago, hard on
the heels of the *Conquistadores*, Franciscan monks had
planted vineyards across the basin, and Paso wine, along with
a fiery *aguardiente*, were now relished throughout the Southwest and Mexico. While the natives were far from prosperous, they seldom experienced the famines of old, and with
the coming of the railroad, their produce could be marketed
on an even vaster scale.

Kate was all eyes as the buggy trundled through El Paso.
Her life had been spent in the backwoods village of Columbus,
and she had always dreamed of living in a city. While a bit
disappointed, with the monotonous adobe buildings, she
was enthralled with the bright costumes and gentle gaiety of
the people. There were few Mexicans in East Texas, and by
contrast, the border town seemed very colorful and exciting,
almost quaint. Maybe it wasn't Austin or San Antonio, but it
wasn't the sticks either. Besides, she was seeing it all for the
first time with the man who had rescued her from a shabby
life in the backwaters of nowhere.

Dallas Stoudenmire was her savior, sometimes gruff, often
inscrutable, but a man of intense passion and hidden
warmth. He had snatched her from the jaws of marrying some
farmer with one cow and a boil on his rump. Had that happened, she would have ended up like her mother, old and
worn before her time, having another baby every-time someone shook a pair of overalls at her. Now she was somebody,
the wife of a man selected for an important civic post, a
celebrity after a fashion. And while he had never suspected,
she would have gladly kissed her husband's feet on their wedding day.

Thinking about it, she made a tiny gurgling sound deep
in her throat, half wonder, half pure joy. With the excitement

of the moment, it was a heady mixture, and her head spun with the sheer exhilaration of just being alive. Then the moment of reverie passed, and Doc's voice once again intruded on that highly personal little world of her private thoughts.

"Yessir, we're a community that's going places. Agriculture, ranching, mines up north in the mountains. And the railroad just puts frosting on the cake. Everything a town needs to thrive and grow, make something of itself. Wouldn't be surprised but what El Paso becomes a real force in this state's economy before we're through."

"Doc, I think the word you're hunting for is boomtown," Stoudenmire noted soberly. "But from what I've seen so far the biggest business in El Paso is vice. Least-ways most of the *dinero* spent in this town finds its way back to the southside in one fashion or another. Course, I could be all wet. I'm sort of Johnny-come-lately around here, so I reckon I'll have to wait till I see the full show."

"No, you're right as rain, Dallas. Hit it dead center, as a matter of fact." The storekeeper's face twisted with disgust, and he spat over the side of the buggy. "Sometimes I get wrapped up in what this town *could be*, and I lose sight of what we've got to overcome to get there. Ed Banning and his gang are the nerviest bunch of cutthroats along the border, and they've got to be sent packin' before El Paso will ever amount to anything. That's why we hired you. And being plain-spoken about it, most of the townspeople don't care whether you run 'em out or kill 'em. Just so they're gotten rid of."

"We'll see, Doc," the lawman said. "I don't believe in callin' my hand till all of the cards have showed."

"Perfectly understandable. Anyway, you're the marshal as of tomorrow morning, and you can run it however you see fit." Doc's face suddenly brightened, and he leaned across to swat Stoudenmire on the knee. "Damnation, I clean forgot. Seth Hart pulled a few strings back East while you were gone. Might say he called some political debts. Anyway, he got a pipeline into James Garfield and had you appointed a deputy US marshal. What with wearin' two stars, I'd say you oughta be able to cover just about any play the Bannings make. Course, you might do best to keep that under your hat. Seth figures it's an ace in the hole you shouldn't play till your back's against the wall."

Stoudenmire just nodded, reserving comment one way or the other. "Likely it'll come in handy, but tell Hart I don't want any more favors. I took this job with the understandin' I wouldn't be beholden to anyone. I meant just that, Doc."

"Pull in your horns, boy. Nobody's tryin' to get you obligated. Seth just wants what's best for the town, and he figured you could use all the muscle we could muster."

"Doc, I've got no more use for a politician than a hog does a sidesaddle. Just keep your cronies clear of me and let me do my job. If gettin' the Bannings' ashes hauled is what they're really after, I reckon they won't have long to wait."

Doc Cummings hunched forward and gave the horses a good swat with the reins. Damned if his brother-in-law wasn't as contrary as an old mule about certain things. Stubborn as a Dutchman, people always said, and by God, these Germans sure fitted the ticket.

Seated between them, Kate had remained silent throughout the discussion. Dallas had told her little of what lay behind his appointment, and for the first time she became aware of the task he had undertaken. Deputy sheriff of a settled county was one thing, but marshal of an untamed border town was more than she had bargained for. As they drew up before the house Doc had rented for them, Kate decided that something would have to be done about finding her husband a safer line of work.

2

The dim light of a quarter-moon cast a faint glow over Paso del Norte. Along the main street, soft music drifted from a scattering of *cantinas*, and in a large building to the west, the lively tunes of a *fandango* floated across the plaza. Horses lined the hitchrails, standing hip-shot in the warm, sleepy night, yet the street was nearly deserted. The festivities had only just begun, and those not attending the dance had settled in for a night at their favorite saloon.

But the sleepy tranquillity of the village was abruptly shattered by coarse laughter and drunken shouts that were unmistakably American. The doors of a *cantina* burst open and four men stumbled into the street, steadying each other as they lurched to a halt. They reeked of *tequila*, and as they wobbled about, their eyes searched the night for some devilment worthy of their rowdy mood.

"For Chrissakes, boys," roared one with a thatch of red hair, "I still say we oughta slip on down to that *fandango* and find us some little chili peppers."

"That's the ticket!" another agreed drunkenly. "I'm a man that needs to get his log sapped, and them Mex gals purely know how to jitterate your juices. Whooeee! They is somethin', ain't they, Red?"

Before Red could answer the oldest member of the crew cut him off. "Listen you goddamn nitwits, you go down to that dance and you're gonna end up shootin' marbles with your balls. Them greaser bastards don't like whites messin' with their women."

With a wild screech a runty, bowlegged little man reeled away from them, violently flapping his arms to keep from falling. "Yellow sonsabitches! Yer nothin' but a bunch of gutless shitkickers. Gonna let them greasers run it over you? Bullshit! There ain't a man alive that can make me back up."

With that, he stumbled backwards and sat heavily in the dusty street. The other men regarded him solemnly for a moment, dimly attempting to sift out the gist of his angry tirade.

"Goddammit, boys, he's right," Red growled. "Them greaser pricks ain't gonna brace us. Long as we stick together and keep our guns handy, they'd let us hump their mammy right in the middle of that dancehall."

The horny one perked up at that, and the older man merely mumbled sourly to himself. The decision made, they ambled forward and clumsily lifted their sidekick from the dirt. Just then, an obscure figure materialized from the darkness and silently glided past them, hugging the shadows near the adobe buildings.

Glancing up, Red batted his eyes and squinted hard, not sure he was seeing right. "Boys, if these old peepers ain't playin' tricks on me, that there is a livin', breathin' chili pepper."

The men's heads swung around, and for a moment they stared drunkenly into the shadows. Then their eyes came uncrossed, and without a word, they moved toward the dim figure. Fanning out, they formed a half-circle, bringing their ghostly quarry to bay against a wall.

"*¿Quien es?*" a small, quivering voice implored. "What is it you want, *señores?* I was only on my way to the *baile.* I meant no harm."

Trapped between them stood a young girl, hardly more than a child. Her eyes went wide with terror, glistening in the soft moonlight as she cowered against the building. She pressed herself flatter against the cool adobe, paralyzed with fear, whimpering as the men advanced on her. Then they leapt forward like a pack of wolves on a bleating calf, dragging her to the earth in a silent rush. Beneath her simple cotton dress they could feel the ripe young breasts, the warm thighs, the gentle swell of her girlish hips. Suddenly their tongues went thick, and the brassy taste of lust flooded their mouths. Red clamped his hand over her face, and they wordlessly lifted her. Gripped with shock, the girl stiffened under their hands like some frozen little bird with a broken wing. Moving swiftly, they ducked through the alley and faded into the darkness.

Less than a quarter-hour later the men reappeared from the alleyway, brushing dirt from their clothes. The edge had been blunted on their drunken mood, and their words came in terse, surly grunts.

"Shit, boys, I've had better poontang'n that screwin' a knothole. Come to think of it, Mother Thumb and her four daughters has got that gal beat."

"Goddamn right! That little bitch just laid there like a

board. I'll bet she didn't wiggle her ass once the whole time I was humpin'."

"Quit pissin' and moanin', will ya? It was free, and that's likely the first time you ain't paid for it since you quit jerkin' your pud."

"Listen, you little turdknocker, I've had about enough of your lip for one night. Keep it up and you're gonna get . . ."

The four men came to a halt as they emerged onto the street, falling silent as they blundered into the path of several horsemen. Riding past were seven *vaqueros* mounted on their best cow ponies, clearly dressed for the *fandango*. The Mexicans eyed the men haughtily, their gaze wavering between curiosity and outright contempt. Then, just as they drew even with the Americans, the girl stepped from the darkness at the *gringos'* backs. Blood streamed down her legs, staining her torn skirt the color of burnt ochre; the bodice of her dress had been ripped apart, revealing the delicate bud of her childish breasts. Her eyes seemed wide as saucers in the pale light, and beneath them lay the dull gaze of one who has just walked barefoot through the coals of hell.

The *vaqueros* reined their horses viciously, wheeling toward the Americans. Startled, the four men turned to see what had attracted the Mexicans and found themselves face to face with their own handiwork. The specter advancing toward them froze the Americans in their tracks, like the sightless dead come to exact some nameless vengeance. Suddenly the feisty little man with the bowlegs snarled and spun about, clawing at his six-gun as he turned. But before he could clear leather, the *vaqueros* cut loose with a ragged volley, and pockets of dust spurted from his shirtfront. As he slammed backwards, his legs folded beneath him, and he dropped to the earth with a dusty thud. His partners briefly considered making a run for the darkness, then discarded the thought. They had no more chance than a flea on a wet hog; any sudden movement would leave them as dead as the sawed-off runt lying at their feet. Slowly they raised their hands, halfway expecting to get it in the back even as they did so.

Within the hour, the villagers of Paso del Norte had gathered before the local *calabozo*. Inside the jail, Pedro Vazquez, their *alcalde*, was attempting to piece together the story. As mayor, it was his responsiblity to determine the charges and hold these men for the *rurales*. Quite by chance, his nephew, Ramón Vazquez, was the leader of the *vaqueros* who had captured the Americans.

Listening to Ramón recount what had happened, the *alcalde* sensed that the temper of the crowd was better suited to a quick hanging. But these were his people, and they would never go against his wishes. Quite clearly, the *norteamericanos* were guilty, and they would be executed without doubt. But all according to law. So long as he was *jefe* of Paso del Norte, there would be none of the senseless violence that went on across the river.

As his nephew finished speaking, Pedro Vazquez heard a sullen muttering erupt from the crowd and turned to see people easing away from the door. Then a man and a woman appeared in the doorway, shielding the girl between them. With great dignity, they moved across the room and stopped before the *alcalde*, looking neither right nor left. The girl simply stared at the floor, unable to look at anyone.

"*Mi niña*, I would spare you this if it were within my power." Pedro Vazquez lifted her chin and kissed her gently on the cheek. "But we must know who did this terrible thing. So you must be brave and force yourself to look upon these men. If they are the ones, then it is your duty to make this known. Have no fear. Just look and tell what you see."

The girl slowly turned her head and stared for a heartbeat at the three men, now securely locked in cells at the end of the room. Huge tears welled up in her eyes, rolling down over her cheeks, and she nodded. Just once, almost shyly. Then her gaze went dull, and a merciful darkness swept over her eyes.

When the girl had been led away by her parents, the *alcalde* turned back to the prisoners, speaking in broken English. "You have been identified as the men who did this horrible thing. Were it up to me, I would hand you over to the people. Instead, you will be tried by law and executed before a firing squad."

"Listen, you tub of guts," Red shouted, "we didn't do nothin' to that bitch that ain't been done before. She's a whore. You understand, a *puta?* Just come right out and offered it to us."

Ramón Vazquez advanced on the cell, his face twisted with rage. "*Gringo bastardo.* Only filth like you would do that to a young girl. She was an *inocente*, a virgin!"

Red swallowed hard, but he didn't back off. "You're not spookin' us, greaser. We're Americans and we know our rights. Besides, we work for Ed Banning, the big *hombre* across the river. If you do anything to us, he'll burn this goddamn pigsty down around your ears."

"*Tien cuidado, bárbaro!*" The *alcalde*'s warning sounded with all the finality of a death knell. "Take care, barbarian! Do not offend your God. You will have need of him where you are going."

"*Sí*, my uncle advises you well," Ramón Vazquez added. "Look to your God for *absolución*. You will find none from Señor Banning. Scorpions like him eat their young when the road grows hard."

The prisoners' faces took on a wooden look. They understood, even halfway believed it. But they didn't like what they heard. The horny one slammed up against the bars and shook his fist in Ramón's face. "You greaser sonovabitch! Your day's comin'. You just wait. We'll get out of here, and when we do, I'm gonna cut your nuts off and feed 'em to the pigs."

The *alcalde* turned and walked to the door, pausing before the jailer. "*Alguacil*, if these *gringo* dogs so much as rattle the bars on their cages, you are to shoot them without hesitation."

Pedro Vazquez stepped into the night, followed closely by Ramón and his *vaqúeros*. The jailer closed and barred the door, then pulled an ancient Colt from its holster. Cocking it, he eased himself onto a stool and regarded the Americans like a fat snake.

Right about then, Red got to wishing he had a stump between his legs. Damned if it wouldn't make life a hell of a
lot simpler.

3

Stoudenmire crossed the plaza with Tige hard on his heels.
The morning sun was barely two hours old, but already the
broad square was a beehive of activity. Everyone in El Paso
got an early start, for as midday approached, the heat became
oppressive, downright unbearable for some. While greenhorns were known to laugh at the town's casual pace, they
quickly learned that the afternoon siesta was a touch of ge-
nius born of sheer necessity. Those who didn't heed the message like as not ended up with sunstroke.

Walking north across the plaza, Stoudenmire reflected on
the unsettling bit of news Doc Cummings had passed along
only moments before. When he had stopped in at Doc's store,
the tale of last night's trouble in Paso del Norte was already
making the rounds. Bad news travels fast, and the young girl's
rape along with the killing that followed had spread alarm
among the townspeople. Something like this could trigger a
shooting war with the greasers, and most everyone agreed
that El Paso was sitting on a powder keg with a short fuse.
The new marshal was of a similar opinion, for it was well
known that the Mexicans thought highly of their women. And
deflowering a virgin was damn near the last straw for anybody! Whichever side of the river they happened to call home.
Thinking about it, Stoudenmire decided he hadn't come to
town any too soon.

But at the moment, he had a more immediate problem.
Namely George Campbell and his deputy, Bill Johnson.
Against his better judgment, Stoudenmire had agreed to keep
them on as deputies. Somehow he was skeptical of any man
who meekly accepted demotion from marshal to deputy, and
it occurred to him that George Campbell would likely try to
undermine his efforts at policing the town. Seth Hart had
termed it good politics, but it had left a bad taste in Stouden-

mire's mouth from the very start. Still he had agreed, and like it or not, he would have to go through the motions.

Entering the office, he found Campbell seated behind the desk and Johnson stretched out on a rickety bunk. One glance was all he needed to catalog this pair. Throughout the war and almost ten years as a peace officer, he had dealt with their breed more often than he cared to remember. Shiftless, slovenly men without roots; warped in mind and filthy by choice; willing to cut their own mother's throat for a decent meal or a shot of cheap whiskey.

The men returned his look with casual indifference, neither stirring from their indolent pose. Plainly they had every intention of giving him a hard way to go, right from the start. Their attitude made it clear that taming El Paso was his ball of wax, and they were merely paid observers. They figured to lay up on their backsides and wait for him to get his nose bloodied. Chuckling to himself, Stoudenmire recalled he'd played this same game before, and he had picked up a few dodges that even these sharpies hadn't seen.

"Off your ass and on your feet, gents. The reins just changed hands, and we're gonna operate a little different around here from now on. In case you hadn't heard, my name's Stoudenmire, and that's my desk you're sittin' behind."

This last remark was aimed at Campbell, who blinked like a horny toad that had just stepped on a rattler's tail. He was a thin, stringy sort of fellow, who looked as if he had been stretched out to dry and left in the sun too long. As he unfolded from the chair and came to his feet, his beady eyes glinted with outright hatred. "Sure thing, Dallas. You just set right down and take over the ship. And if it gets a mite leaky, why Bill and me'll be real proud to give you a hand bailin'. Won't we, Billy boy?"

Johnson mumbled something under his breath and heaved himself off the bunk with considerable effort. From the look of his eyes, he might bleed to death at any moment, and anyone who doubted he was a confirmed rummy just couldn't read sign. Twenty years of beans and sowbelly and green rotgut were starting to show at his beltline, and from all appearances, he couldn't have fought his way out of a rotten gunnysack.

Stoudenmire merely glanced at him, then leveled a flinty gaze on the former marshal. "Campbell, let's get something straight from the outset. When you speak to me, it's Mister Stoudenmire, or Marshal. I'm sorta particular that way, and you'd do well not to make me tell you twice."

"Well, yessir. Marshal, sir. You play the fiddle and we'll do the dancin'. And Billy, let's not forget to salute when *Mister Stoudenmire* starts barkin' orders.

"Gents, I've got a feeling that ridin' double with you two is gonna be more than I could stomach." His pale eyes settled briefly on the rummy, then shifted back to Campbell. "There's two things I never had much use for. Tin-horns with a flannel-mouth, and a swizzelguts that can't wean himself off the juice."

Campbell's face blanched, and his Adam's apple bobbed like a fishcork. "Lemme tell you somethin', *Marshal*. We been around a long time before this town ever heard of you, and we're gonna be around a long time after you're gone. There's more'n one way to skin a cat, you know. And I got an idea somebody's gonna nail your hide to the wall before you even get started real good."

"Is that a threat, sonny?" Stoudenmire deliberately goaded the man, enjoying himself immensely now that it was out in the open. "Or are you just makin' promises you can't keep?"

"Mister, you're walkin' on eggshells, and you don't even know it. If I was you, I'd take to avoidin' dark alleys and lonely places."

"Campbell, you just tied a can to your own tail." Stoudenmire's glare raked the other man. "You and Johnson pick up your gear and clear out. You can collect your wages at city hall."

Campbell took a step forward, his fists clenched. "Listen, you overgrown sack of shit, you can't fire me. I don't take orders from anybody. . . ."

A pistol suddenly appeared in Stoudenmire's hand, and he laid it upside Campbell's jaw like a sledgehammer. Fiery sparks erupted inside the skinny man's brain, and the whole left side of his head went numb. Without a sound he crumpled to the floor as if his backbone had been snatched clean.

Across the room, Johnson's hand edged slowly toward his gun, almost as though he wanted someone to stop him before he worked up the guts to make a try for it. Snarling, Tige padded forward with hackles raised, baring his fangs. Johnson froze, eyes bright with fear, as if he had been turned to stone. One wrong move and he knew the ferocious-looking bastard would start at his boot tops and eat him alive.

Once he saw that Tige had Johnson cornered, Stoudenmire hefted Campbell, lugged him to the door, and tossed him into the street. Returning, he grabbed Johnson by the collar, waltzed him across the floor and planted his boot straight up the rummy's tailbone. Johnson shot through the door as though propelled from a cannon and came to a shaky halt beside his fallen partner.

Massaging the seat of his pants, he tried to suck up the nerve to stand and fight. "Marshal, you're a real stem-winder. But you ain't as big as you think. Things are gonna get plenty sticky around here, and it might just be I'll take a hand in it personal."

Leaning against the doorjamb, Stoudenmire smiled sardonically. "Johnson, find yourself another trough to swill at. You mess around with me and you'll get hurt."

Unable to stand up under the lawman's cold stare, Johnson turned and helped Campbell to his feet. Bleeding freely from a wide gash in his head, Campbell moaned something that didn't make much sense and slumped against his cohort. Supporting him, Johnson started off at a slow walk across the plaza. Every few steps, he turned to peek back over his shoulder, like a jowly old rooster twisting his neck to hunt for lice.

Stepping back inside, Stoudenmire took a seat behind the desk and waited for the explosion. Twenty minutes later it came. Mayor Isaac Porter stormed through the door in a faunching rage. Before the lawman could open his mouth,

Porter launched into a frothing tirade that would have turned a faith healer green as pickle juice.

"By all that's holy, Mr. Stoudenmire, you are a very temperamental sort of man. You can't just go around whipping the bejesus out of your own deputies and dumping them into the street. Something like that creates a bad example for the rest of the town. Sets law and order back on its ear. Gives it a black eye, if you see what I mean. This is a civilized town, Mr. Stoudenmire, and we can't have the law fighting among themselves. It just won't do. By glory, it won't do at all!"

Porter's overbearing manner left the marshal thoroughly unimpressed. "Mayor, you might as well save your breath. What's done is done, and that's the end of it."

"Not by a damnsight it's not, Marshal. When you appeared before the city council to discuss this job, we took you to be a reasonable man. It was agreed that Campbell and Johnson would be retained as your deputies, and I'm just afraid we'll have to hold you to it." Porter's voice had risen sharply as he spoke, but he suddenly lost wind as he noticed Tige eyeing him with a strange look. "And if you don't mind, please call your dog off. I don't care for the way he's staring at me."

Stoudenmire rubbed behind the dog's ears, smiling faintly. "You can relax, Mayor. Politicians are a little rancid for his tastes. But that's neither here nor there. I've given your stooges the gate, and that's how it stands. If you or the city council try to interfere, then you can start hunting for a new marshal. Now, I haven't got all day to stand around listening to you preach, so fish or cut bait."

Porter was on the verge of blowing his cork when he thought better of it. Banning had ordered him to let the German have his head. And by God, that's just what he'd do. *He'd let the arrogant sonovabitch hang himself!* "All right, Marshal. Don't do anything rash. There's no need to get riled up over such an insignificant matter. We hired you, and we'll back you to the hilt. Even if we don't fully agree. But I feel duty bound to warn you that this isn't a town that can be policed by one man alone."

Stoudenmire grinned cockily. "Don't get yourself in a

lather over that, Mr. Mayor. Just happens there's a fellow on his way here that I've already signed on as deputy. Name's Jim Gillette. He's not much to look at, but he's tougher'n most. Found that out when we rode together in the Rangers."

Mayor Isaac Porter just nodded and plastered an assy smile across his face. Someone had just been feinted into position and given a first class screwing. And he had the very distinct feeling that it was Mother Porter's youngest son. The slow one.

4

Ramón Vazquez had awakened earlier than usual that morning. There was a taste of ashes in his mouth, and it occurred to him that what lay suppurating in a man's mind often surfaced in his gorge. Dressing slowly, his thoughts returned again to last night, and he silently offered a prayer that it had been his bullet that killed the *gringo cerdo*. Since squeezing the trigger that once, he had cursed himself a thousand times for not continuing to fire until all the filthy beasts were dead. *Muerte!* That is what they each deserved, quickly and simply, without the mercy one shows even a dumb animal.

But then, a man could not easily escape the lessons of his youth. And a Vazquez would never lower himself to act in the manner of the barbarians across the river. Especially one who had risen to the position of *caporal* over the largest ranch in the district. After all, Don Miguel Salazar expected him to set the example! *El patrón* would hardly bestow his blessings on a foreman who taught *vaqueros* to shoot men down in cold blood.

Somehow the thought filled him with disgust. Mercy and aristocratic conduct were for the *hidalgos*, the ruling class. Perhaps compassion was a luxury the common people, the *peones*, could no longer afford. The time for civilized behavior was when one faced an honorable enemy, not when the *gringo* jackals were snapping at the heels of the poor and the defenseless. While he had been revolted by the brutal executions of the *norteamericano* businessmen at San Elizario, it came to Ramón that there was much to be said for dealing harshly with such scavengers. *¡Madre de Dios!* What he wouldn't give to be an Apache for a short time. There was a form of moral conduct the *gringo bárbaros* could understand. And never forget!

Leaving the bedroom, Ramón walked toward the center of the house. Though this was the *casa* of his uncle, he thought of it as his own, for he had grown to manhood within these walls. And it was good to have spent such a night in the place of his youth. Somehow he seemed stronger for having slept in his old bed again. Moments later, he entered the dining room to find Pedro Vazquez already seated at the head of the table.

"*Buenos días, mi tio,*" he greeted the older man. "*¿Como está usted?*"

"*Bueno*, Ramón." The *alcalde* paused just long enough to note the hollow cast to his nephew's eyes. "*¿Y tu?*"

Ramón merely shrugged, sliding listlessly into a chair. After pouring a cup of hot chocolate, he idly stirred it with a spoon, clearly absorbed with his own worrisome thoughts.

"*A quien madruga, Dios le ayuda,*" Pedro Vazquez observed. "God favors those who rise with the dawn. Are the circles beneath your eyes from early prayer, *mi hijo?*"

Ramón shook his head, then gestured heavenward. "Does He also favor those who cannot sleep for want of destroying their enemies?"

"My son, God overlooks much, but he would be displeased to see your hatred so quickly aroused." The older man examined the dregs in his cup thoughtfully, as if seeking some further enlightenment. "Ramón, no rational man could deny that the situation worsens between the *yanquis* and our people. I, too, spent a restless night considering this very thing. But if those to whom the people look for guidance were to sanction violence, then the Rio Grande would run red with blood. *¡La jugo de muerte!* The juice of death."

"*¡Bueno!*" Ramón's dark gaze crackled with sudden ferocity. "So long as it is *gringo* blood, then I would gladly cut the first throat. We have lived too long under the oppression of this filth. It must end. *¡Pronto!*"

The *alcalde* flinched, his face gone tight with shock. "And is spilling blood the only way it can be ended? Are we not reasonable men who can employ persuasion with our enemies? Have we learned nothing from the suffering of our *antepasados* under the Spaniards?"

"You talk in riddles, *mi tio*. The yoke of oppression was lifted from our people only after Juarez led them to war. It would seem that the way of our ancestors contradicts your cry for reason."

"So you would have our people take up the sword and march on El Paso. Slaughter the *norteamericanos* as if they were hogs in a charnel house. Is this what you are telling me, Ramón?"

The younger man flushed and looked away, shamed by his uncle's heated rebuff. "You twist my words, *padrino*. I meant only that we should defend ourselves and have no mercy on these jackals when they swim the river to violate our lands and our women. How could anyone who values his manhood do less? Can you look inside yourself and state with certainty that the *gringos* would ever be swayed by reason? Even if they were, what would be gained besides a moment in time? We have seen them break faith again and again with the *indios* of the north. Are we *ingeui niños* to believe that they will treat Mexicans with greater honor than they have shown the red men?"

The *alcalde* nodded, more in understanding than agreement, as though weighing the younger man's words before he spoke. "Since your mother and father died and you came to live with me, I have tried to raise you as a son. *¡Mi hijo!* And now I will repeat a blasphemy to you that a man would dare whisper to none but his own flesh. I have lived long and seen much of the evil men practice among themselves, most of it so terrible it is best forgotten. As *jefe* of this village, I have learned that brotherhood is merely a word employed by priests, for if God smiles on a man, then he must afterward hold himself beware of his neighbors.

"But wisdom such as this often makes a man *cinico*, and we are confronted by problems, Ramón, that will never yield before cynicism alone. Certainly we can open our eyes to the *gringos'* treachery, but to fight them is to do battle with the wind. There is no end to it. A man must ultimately tire, and when he does, he will be blown away, as chaff from wheat. Somehow we must seek out men of reason among the *yanquis* and deal with them not so much from trust as from necessity. Until then, we must not provoke our people to foolhardy acts. Among the old ones it is well known that even the bravest *toro* can thrash himself to death in a spider web."

Ramón heeded the wisdom of his uncle's counsel, but it did nothing to lessen his hatred of *gringos*. Nor did it have much effect on his fear that even then the *norte-americanos* were planning reprisals against their village. Although it was true that the cloud of rage no longer blinded his thinking, he still saw the situation for what it was.

Last night's tragedy was but a quirt to the hostility that existed between the two races. Perhaps the last in a dreary chronicle of injustice and duplicity that would soon drive his people beyond the point of reason. Regardless of his uncle's belief that decades of humiliation could be resolved with pretty words and unstinting faith.

Long before his time, it had started with the Treaty of Guadelupe Hidalgo. That infamous document, which had allowed a river to split a city in half, leaving thousands of their people to suffer under the rule of arrogant *tejanos*. While it had never touched him personally, he had seen with his own eyes the degradation of those who lived north of the Rio Grande. It was not a sight easily forgotten.

Yet that was only the beginning. Wherever a man turned, he seemed to find *gringos* blocking his path, scheming and clawing to satisfy their monstrous greed. There was the constant rustling of cattle from Mexican *ranchos*, an indignity that *patrones* and *vaqueros* alike had suffered for much too long. The *yanqui* mining interests were burrowing like moles throughout Chihuahua, sapping the strength and the spirit of *peones* enslaved in those dungeon pits. Even the salt war had been the *norteamericanos'* fault, for it was they who sought to rob the poor by withholding the very substance of life itself.

Now they had committed the unforgivable indecency. Despoiled a young girl of her virtue. And he had no doubt that those across the river were at that very moment planning to rescue the three barbarians held prisoner in Paso del Norte.

The *alcalde* had waited patiently while his nephew sorted out his thoughts. When Ramón finally looked around, he smiled and clasped the younger man's arm. "It occurs to me that you are a good man, *mi hijo*. Never had I heard you speak out against the *gringos* with such anger until the ordeal of this young girl. Compassion for the weak is a commendable thing, particularly in a man. But never should it be allowed to cloud your judgment. The people look up to you, and in time, you could become their *jefe*. Yet I would caution you that there is more to being a leader than making impassioned speeches and provoking men to spill blood. A fool often regrets his words, but a wise man seldom regrets his silence. You would do well to think on this in days to come."

Ramón stared at the old man for a long time, wondering if wisdom and reason could, after all, bring about justice for their people. Troubled beyond measure, he had allowed himself to be persuaded that nothing should be done to incite violence. And for the moment, he would respect his uncle's wishes. But persuaded or not, he fully intended that the *cabrones* in jail would never again cross the Rio Grande. Except as dead men.

5

Jim Gillette arrived on the afternoon train. While he was glad to get his feet on solid earth once more, he didn't waste any time gawking at the sights. Like the man, his gear was honed to essentials, and he came straightaway to the office. When he stepped through the door, he carried a warbag, a mule-eared sawed-off shotgun, and a Colt .44 cinched high on his hip.

Stoudenmire came around the desk, and the two men shook hands. Though they hadn't seen each other in over a year, they had kept in touch, and there was little need for small talk. They liked each other, respected one another's skills as a peace officer, and felt confident enough in their friendship that there was no need to prime it with meaningless words.

With greetings out of the way, they had gotten down to business. Gillette hitched a chair over beside the desk, and Stoudenmire proceeded to brief him on what they faced. In a detached, unemotional voice, he related each incident in the long chain of bloodlettings leading to the present tensions between Mexicans and Yankees. Then he covered the Banning Brothers in similar detail, stressing their political stranglehold on the town and their dominance of the vice district. Much as an afterthought, he next outlined the support they could expect from Seth Hart and the council of businessmen, noting wryly that it was something on the order of a fresh water spring in an alkali desert: just when you needed it most, it would more than likely go bone dry.

Gillette toyed with his mustache and asked few questions, occasionally snorting like an old plow horse when a particularly juicy item was ticked off. In one form or another, he had seen this pathetic little drama repeated almost endlessly across the frontier. After twenty years, he had become a jaded warrior in a land where every dusty, ramshackle crossroads had both an arena and its own version of the Christians and the lions. Only the names and faces changed. And sometimes the death list.

Observing his calm, unruffled manner, Stoudenmire was again reminded that the former Ranger wasn't much to look at, coming or going. Gillette was whipcord lean, gaunt as a skinned lizard, and his washboard ribs gave the impression he hadn't had a decent meal since he quit the farm. Beneath a mop of shaggy hair, his narrow face was set in a woebegone, saturnine mold, as though he toted the troubles of the world on his bony shoulders. While he wasn't a jolly man, occasionally he would grin like a horse eating briars, and at the oddest times. Like at a funeral or when he was headed into a gunfight. His watery eyes were uncommonly tranquil, like a pool of maize pudding, and to all outward appearances he seemed mild as a sucking dove. But a man's looks could be curiously deceptive. Stoudenmire had seen this long drink of water in action. When push came to shove, he was fast as a snake, and what he could do with that old Colt .44 made greased lightning look like molasses at twenty below.

The rest of the afternoon had been spent in war council, with the two men discussing how best to approach the double-barreled dilemma confronting El Paso. Stoudenmire's disposition improved markedly just knowing Gillette was on hand to back his play. Having the gloomy-faced deputy around was much like pulling on an old pair of boots, comfortable and somehow reassuring. Along toward sundown, they had mapped out their opening strategy, leaving plenty of room for fancy footwork in the clinches. Once they started booting asses, there was small likelihood of predicting which way the worm would turn, and neither man tried to fool himself on that score. Looking ahead, they were agreed that, after a certain point, they would just have to play the cards as dealt.

Stoudenmire invited Gillette home for supper and positively glowed under the old lawdog's praise of Kate and her cooking. Afterward, they strolled downtown and began a systematic tour of the southside dives. Much to the marshal's amusement, Gillette's doleful features took on a spark of liveliness as they inspected row after row of whorehouses, saloons, and gambling dives. Never had he seen so much vice crammed into so little space, and he noted that, heathen for heathen, the sporting crowd of El Paso more than likely topped Dodge City in its heyday. Then the pensive look returned to his face, and the deputy observed that it was a shame to put the skids under such a testament to man's moral blight. After all, it was the nature of the beast to wallow in fornication and sin, and who were they to upset the Good Lord's grand design. Stoudenmire just chuckled, never quite sure whether the old fox was pulling his leg or actually making some profound comment on the shaky state of men's affairs.

Later in the evening, they swung back toward the plaza and decided to have a look at the Coliseum Saloon. So far, they hadn't seen anything they couldn't handle, and the only unknown factor remaining was the Banning brothers themselves.

"Just might as well let 'em know we're in town," Stoudenmire remarked. "Sooner we put a bad taste in their mouth, the quicker we'll get 'em to come out in the open."

"Dallas, you're a natural wonder. Back 'em into a corner, twist their tail, and make 'em howl! Yessir, there's more'n one way to make a dog shit peach seeds. Present company excepted, of course."

Gillette glanced down at Tige, who was trotting along at Stoudenmire's side. The dog returned the stare with a kindly light in his eyes, and even gave his tail a patronizing wag. The new deputy was one of the few men Tige tolerated as an equal, and Gillette considered it an honor that he had been accepted into the dog's select circle of friends.

Together, the three of them marched through the swinging doors of the Coliseum and halted to give the place the once-over. Other than the fact that the room was jammed to the rafters, there wasn't anything noteworthy going on, and after a few moments they took up positions at the end of the bar. But even in the mad swirl of roughly dressed men and spangled saloon girls, their arrival hadn't gone unnoticed. As they bellied up to the bar, an undercurrent swept through the crowd, and within moments everyone in the room knew that the town's new marshal had paid an unofficial visit on El Paso's political kingpin.

Before Stoudenmire and Gillette appeared out of the night, conversation at the bar had centered around the three men being held in Paso del Norte. Sam Banning had been right in the thick of the discussion, occasionally prodding the crowd on with a bitter comment about the uppity greasers. Talk had slackened momentarily with the arrival of the lawmen, but hard whiskey makes for loose tongues, and before long the angry shouts began anew.

"Boys, you can say whatever you damn well please," barked a chunky man built along the lines of a beer keg. "But I'm here to tell you that there ain't a man-jack among us that's safe once them Mexicans get the idea they can jail a white man."

"Goddamn right!" growled a beefy miner with hands like ore crushers. "We oughta go over there and wipe out the whole fuckin' village. Just like the Indians." He slammed his fist on the bar, and bottles rattled its entire length. "Nits and lice, by Christ!"

Sam Banning's bullish roar drowned out the crowd's response. "Now wait a minute, boys. You're going off half-cocked. There's no need to start a war. The way to teach them greasers a lesson is to show 'em we won't stand still for white men being arrested. Ride over there a couple of hundred strong and just flat-ass free them three men. Show them *cholo* bastards who's boss around here, and by God I'm layin' money our troubles are ended."

"Sam, you're all wet," the big miner shot back. "There's only one thing them sonsabitches understand, and its name is Judge Colt. What we gotta do is make a lead mine out of a few of them greasers. That'll take the kinks out of their tails once and for all."

While the men were arguing, Ed Banning had eased through the crowd and now stood beside his brother. Word had reached the backroom that Stoudenmire was on the premises, and the boss decided to have a look for himself. What he saw left him thoroughly unimpressed, and it occurred to him that the crowd would enjoy a little sport at the marshal's expense. *Might as well put the big bastard in his place right from the start!*

"Marshal Stoudenmire, we'd like to hear your opinion about all this." The crowd went silent, sensing that Banning was out to gig the new lawdog. "We know you haven't had time to get your feet on the ground just yet, but we'd be interested in hearing how you'd go about freeing those poor boys."

Everyone at the bar turned to look at Stoudenmire. Although they had heard of him, few had seen him before tonight, and they were openly curious as to where the new marshal stood. Stories were already circulating that the city council had been blackjacked into hiring the German, but as yet no one had figured out to what purpose.

Stoudenmire's flinty gaze rested on Banning for a moment, then swung around the crowd. "Gents, if you want some good advice, you'll stay on this side of the river. Mexicans are about as fair as anyone else unless they're curried the wrong way. If those three fellows really did gang up on a young girl, then I reckon they deserve whatever they get."

A murmur of resentment swept through the crowd, ending with hoarse muttering from those nearest the lawman. Then the one built like a beer keg spoke out. "Shit, I always heard that rapin' a Mexican gal was no more a crime than humpin' a nanny goat."

The men laughed good naturedly, turning back to the marshal for his reaction. But the miner with the fearsome hands wouldn't let it drop. "You know, I've heard of nigger-lovers. But I'm a sonovabitch if I ever heard of a greaser-lover. Marshal, you're wearin' a badge on the wrong side of the river. Why, over there, I'll bet your shit wouldn't even stink."

In one stride, Stoudenmire was on him, pistol barrel flashing in the dull glint of the overhead lamps. The Colt landed with a mushy thud, and the miner's eyes rolled back in his head like glazed stones, flat and unseeing. With a great sigh, he simply collapsed and sank to the floor.

Stoudenmire spun on the crowd, his eyes cold as chilled glass, every fiber of his body prickly and tensed. This was the part he enjoyed, the moment that made all the drudgery and routine bearable. Meeting the bullyboys and hard-cases head-on, cracking their skulls with the old buffalo trick, or forcing their hand until they did something even more foolish. Like going for their guns.

"Anybody else got something on his mind?"

The crowd remained curiously still, stunned by the speed with which Stoudenmire had floored the ruffian. They were also distinctly aware that Gillette was covering the marshal's back, which meant that whoever got brave would be caught in a cross fire. To make matters worse, Tige had materialized beside his master, showing a row of teeth like a shark. Between the guns and being chewed on by a snarling brute, the men just held their breath and waited it out.

Then the blood pounding against his temples eased off and Stoudenmire relaxed. "Gents, in case someone forgot to mention it, the Bannings are playing you for fools. The men being held over in El Paso del Norte are on their payroll. They were just setting you up to do the dirty work for them. If I were you, I'd think it over before I risked my neck to pull someone else's fat out of the fire."

Casually reholstering his gun, Stoudenmire turned his gaze on Ed Banning and waited. But the political boss wasn't about to face another man at his own game, especially with the deck stacked against the house. Smiling tightly, he just nodded. This was only the opening gambit, and until the odds suited him better, he wasn't going to be pushed into anything hasty.

After a moment Stoudenmire turned and walked leisurely from the saloon, trailed by Gillette and Tige. As the batwing doors swung shut, the crowd let out a huge sigh, and everyone started talking at once.

El Paso had a new marshal, and he gave every indication of being man enough to handle the job. But anyone who had seen the look of evil stamped on Ed Banning's face would have laid odds that Dallas Stoudenmire was a walking dead-man.

CHAPTER THREE

―――⟋⟍―――

1

Sam Banning kept a loose rein on the high stepping bays, letting them pick their own way over the rutted, twisting trail that led eastward from El Paso. Beside him, Ed sat lost in contemplation, stewing on the way Stoudenmire had jackassed him the night before. The political boss was a man easily affronted, and he wasn't about to overlook outright contempt from anybody. Especially a two-bit lawman set on making a name for himself. Stoudenmire had called the tune last night, but there were ways of bringing the big German to earth.

Their buggy raised a rooster-tail of dust as they traversed the desolate country east and north of the Rio Grande. It was an arid, hostile land, filled with sand, rattlesnakes, and thorny chaparral. Yet it wasn't a barren land, not if a man knew where to look. There were vast, hidden stretches of buffalo and grama grasses, generally sharing the soil with yuccas that sprouted stalks of brilliant, white blossoms. Scattered waterholes seldom went dry even in late summer, and spring rains usually brought the countryside alive with Tahoka daisies, buttercups, and fiery paintbrush. Stands of lacy mesquite and barbed cat's-claw fought for the earth's moisture, but somehow the sparse grasslands survived, mocking the fallow plains that dominated the cardinal points of the compass. And curiously enough, that remote, seemingly ravaged land provided a bountiful life for great herds of longhorn cows.

But while the arid flatlands offered bounty of sort for the mossyhorns, they held forth even greater lure for the Banning brothers and their night riders. Within such desolate country was to be found the isolation and secrecy so highly prized by those who prey on other men's possessions. Especially the four-footed variety.

Shortly after arriving in El Paso two years earlier, Ed Banning had undertaken a search for ranchlands far removed from the settlements along the Rio Grande. After crisscrossing the countryside for nearly a month, he finally found exactly what he had in mind: a rundown spread so far back in the wastelands that a man needed a map to find it. The next step had been to hire a crew and flush out the half-wild longhorns inhabiting the brush and thorn patches dotting the land. Once he had a going concern, Banning began greasing the right palms, and before long his outfit was awarded the beef contract at Fort Bliss. With a legitimate front firmly established, he then branched out, regularly ordering his crew into Chihuahua and Sonora to raid the wealthy Mexican *ranchos*. The rustled cattle were herded back to the ranch, given a brief introduction to a running iron, then either sold to the army or trailed to Fort Worth. With the coming of the railroad, the operation was simplified even further, and the gratifying part was that hardly anyone cared how or under what circumstances the cattle came to be north of the Rio Grande.

The ranch itself was little more than a wilderness outpost, consisting of two adobe buildings, a cookshack, and a log corral west of the compound. Northeast of the ranch, the terrain lifted gradually to a chain of stunted mesas, and in the distance hung the towering peak of Cerro Alto. Beneath the sheer cliffs of this great mountain, the adobe structures looked small and insignificant, dwarfed by the immensity of rock and sky that dominated the landscape for twenty miles in every direction. All things considered, it made for a foreboding, uninviting scene. The kind that people normally went out of their way to avoid.

When the Bannings pulled up before the main house, Tom Kale stepped through the doorway and ambled toward the buggy. Kale had worked for Banning from the beginning, ramrodding the ranch, organizing and leading forays into Mexico; in general, contributing greatly to the devious schemes of his boss. He was a leathery man, tightlipped and unsmiling, as if the merciless sun had long ago melted both the suet and the humor from his lean frame. Weathered by a lifetime in the saddle, his features looked as though whittled from some dark, resisting wood, and his nose jutted from between sharp cheekbones like a jagged outcropping of rock. There was no sign of warmth in his long, dour face, just as flaked stone seems all the more cold for its lack of expression.

Those who best knew Tom Kale seldom let their guard down whenever he was near. For like the land itself, the Banning foreman was a brutal, often murderously savage man who derived some queer satisfaction in watching both man and beast suffer at his hand.

After alighting from the buggy, Ed Banning led the way toward the house without uttering so much as a word. Kale knew a thundercloud building when he saw it, and rightly suspected that a storm was about to break. Once inside, out of sight of the bunkhouse, Banning turned on him like a sore-tailed bear in fly season.

"Kale, you've got my ass between a rock and a hard spot, and something has to change or else you're gonna be looking for a new meal ticket. I've told you till I was blue in the face that our men aren't to be allowed in Paso del Norte. Yet you just go your own way and let 'em do as they damn please."

Kale opened his mouth to speak but Banning cut him off with a dismissive gesture. "Now don't give me any of that horseshit about having to play nursemaid. You're paid to ramrod this outfit, and that includes seeing to it that they follow orders. Well, by Christ, crossing the line and raping a Mexican girl right in the middle of the village isn't my idea of sticking to business."

In a cold, metallic voice, Banning related the gist of what had happened in Paso del Norte the night before last. Sparing no detail, he then recounted Stoudenmire's visit to the Coliseum and the duel of wits that had subsequently ensued. When he came to the part about the marshal's outright challenge, Banning's face blanched. As he remembered how he had been ridiculed before the townspeople, his voice went shaky with rage, and for a moment, Kale thought he was going to come unglued. But Banning quickly got hold of himself and resumed in the flat, menacing tone he normally employed.

"I blame you for this whole goddamned mess, Kale. If you'd been minding the store none of it would've happened. And just in case you've got any doubts, *you're* the one that's gonna get it straightened out. We've got too much at stake to let things get out of hand now."

Tom Kale got busy rolling a cigarette and made a stab at changing the subject. "Boss, I've never let you down yet, even if them knuckleheads did sneak across the river. But the thing that's got me bumfoolzled is this new marshal. What the hell's he doin' in El Paso anyway? Some of the boys say they heard of him when he was a Ranger, and the way they tell it, he's just about as good with a gun as he makes out. You reckon we've done bit off more than we can chew?"

"That big crock of shit?" Sam blurted angrily. "Listen, when Ed gives the word, I'm gonna tie a knot in his tail so hard he'll never sit down. Near as I can tell, the only thing he's good at is makin' fools out of other people."

Ed glanced sourly at his brother. "You don't need to keep harping on it. But you're right about one thing. We've got to act fast to save face in town. Stoudenmire has rigged it so that everyone is waitin' to see if we're gonna let those boys go up against the wall. If we leave 'em to a greaser firing squad, we're gonna be the laughingstock of West Texas."

Kale peered at him owlishly through a haze of smoke. "You mean you want us to raid that Mex jail?"

"Kale, if you had dynamite for brains, you couldn't blow yourself off a jonny pot." Banning shook his head sadly, as if reprimanding a backward child. "Now pay attention, just like you had good sense. Tonight I want you to raid one of the big *ranchos* south of Paso del Norte. Make it worthwhile in terms of cattle, but the important thing is to shoot up the *hacienda* and the Mex crew. That'll scare the bejesus out of every greaser in the district, and tomorrow night they'll all be home with their doors barred."

"Then we raid the jail!" Kale laughed, slapping his thigh.

"No, you goddamn nitwit! You're not to go anywhere near that jail. I wouldn't trust your boys to piss on a dead dog. What I'm gonna do is send a buggy over there about an hour after suppertime. Three of my girls will be decked out like housewives, and they'll say those boys are their husbands. Only they're gonna have guns under their dresses, and when they leave, those boys won't be so helpless anymore. Later, they can make a break and swim the river. If nobody shits and steps in it, I figure we can get 'em free and make an ass out of Stoudenmire all in one stroke."

"Boss, that's slick," Kale snorted, shaking his head with admiration. "We'll have them boys back over here before anybody even tumbles to 'em being gone."

Banning's eyes leveled down on the foreman, fixing him with a malevolent glare. "And once you get 'em back here, I want you to march them over to the bunkhouse and shoot 'em right in the doorway. It's time you and the rest of these bastards learned that when I give an order I expect it to be followed. Savvy?"

Tom Kale wasn't easily frightened, yet he swallowed nervously under Banning's harsh scrutiny. Killing was his stock in trade, and adding three more to the list was all in a day's work. But the death sentence he had just heard pronounced indirectly included him. Should he foul Banning's nest again, his life wouldn't be worth a plug nickel. Kale's mouth suddenly turned dry as a gourd, and his guts went stone cold. Working for this ruthless scutter was like being harnessed shoulder to shoulder with Lucifer himself, and he had the very distinct feeling that he was running dead last in a two-horse race.

2

Doc Cummings could smell the aromas while he was still a good stone's throw from the house. No doubt about it, Kate had acquired their mother's knack for southern cooking, the kind that stuck to a man's ribs and left him wishing he could have eaten more. He could tell from the smell alone, and it set his mouth to watering. Reflecting back over the carefree days of their childhood, Doc was suddenly warmed inside by the thought of having Kate so near. She had always been his favorite of the Cummings' brood, and he was immensely pleased that he had been able to finagle a way for her to live in El Paso. Suddenly it occurred to Doc that things were really looking up.

As a widower, he had become used to the heartburn served up in the local greasy spoon, but with Kate in town, it stood to reason he'd get a decent meal occasionally anyway. Perhaps being invited to supper tonight was only the beginning. Maybe if he played his cards right, it would become a regular thing. Whistling a catchy little tune, he entered the Stoudenmire home, beaming like a chessy cat as Kate came to greet him.

When she led him into the living room, Doc's mouth popped open in astonishment. "Great jumpin' jehossafat! Katie what have you done to this place? Why it looks like a palace. A goldang palace!"

Kate flushed, and her eyes took on a little girl sparkle. Considering that she'd had little to work with, she was justly proud of the transformation. That first evening in El Paso she had stood looking at the austere interior of this adobe monstrosity, wondering how in the world she could ever make it appear anything more than a mud hut. But in only three days she had wrought a minor miracle, decorating it with all the frills and foofaraw so dear to a woman's heart.

Each window was now festooned with gay curtains, done

in bright, cheery colors that distracted the eye from the stark
adobe walls. The spartan furniture did little to liven the room,
but somewhere, Kate had found an ornate Persian rug, that
covered nearly the entire floor. Like a peacock amongst a
flock of brown hens, the rug somehow lent beauty to the dull
ugliness of the room itself. Pictures of solemn ancestors and
pastoral landscapes had been hung judiciously along the
walls, and everywhere there was evidence of Kate's remarkable cleverness with crochet and needlepoint. From the native market she had bought great batches of wild flowers and
small boxed plants, which even now were beginning to sprout
tiny blossoms. But the *pièce de résistance* had been reserved
for the mantel over the fireplace. There in somber dignity
hung a strangely lifelike portrait of Kate and Dallas on their
wedding day. Framed in gilded wood with a delicate carved
design, the portrait dominated the room, evoking a degree of
elegance that was curiously foreign to the wattled adobe.

While the Stoudenmire home was located on Magoffin
Avenue in the better district of El Paso, there were few houses
that could match its comfortable atmosphere and simple
grace. Kate had ample reason to be proud, and as she luxuri-
ated in Doc's praise, it somehow seemed right that her brother
was the first outsider to observe the results of her handiwork.

The meal she served was no less impressive than the house
itself, particularly to a widower who had grown accustomed
to the chili pepper and raw spices of local cafes. Spread across
the table in lavish array was fried chicken, mashed potatoes,
cream gravy, blackeyed peas, snap beans, cornbread, and a
huge pitcher of buttermilk. For a crowning touch, she served
a steamy peach cobbler with great gobs of fresh whipped
cream.

Doc Cummings unbuckled his belt and set to with the
gusto of a starved mongrel trailing a gut wagon. Between
mouthfuls he raved incessantly about the food, the house, his
sister's beauty, and his own great fortune in them having chosen El Paso as their home. Watching him, Stoudenmire was
reminded of a gluttonous bear fresh from a winter's hiberna-

tion. And it came to him that with little or no prompting Doc could easily become a steady boarder.

After a particularly effusive compliment on the house, Doc helped himself to another load of potatoes and gravy. "Dallas, you oughta be mighty proud of this gal. It's not every woman that could turn an outsize *jacal* hut into a dazzler like you've got here."

Stoudenmire pretended to consider it a moment, watching Kate out of the corner of his eye. "I expect you're right, Doc. Course, this place might be too fancy for some folks' tastes. Not everybody can get used to being just another ornament in his own house."

"Oh, what gratitude!" Kate's eyes flashed with feminine outrage. "Dallas Stoudenmire, sometimes you drive me to distraction. After I work my fingers to the bone, you have the unmitigated gall to say it's too frilly. Honestly!"

She knew he liked the house from the little things he had said, but it exasperated her no end that he was so close-mouthed with compliments. Still, she should be getting used to it by now. This great bear of a man she had married was no talker, to put it mildly. What he left unsaid about home, job, and his own thoughts would fill volumes. She sometimes had the feeling it was like extracting teeth to get him loosened up for even a pleasant little chat.

Stoudenmire grinned slyly at her obvious indignation. "Doc, I hate to carry tales on your sister, but she's laying it on a little thick. The fact of the matter is, she enjoyed sprucin' this place up so much that I couldn't get her to quit till it was plumb finished. Put me in mind of a speckled pup with a fresh bowl of cream."

"Yeah, her mama was like that." Doc paused with a drumstick in midair, and a mellow look came into his eyes. "Turn her loose cleanin' a house or whippin' up a big meal, and she acted like the Good Lord had just passed out a dipperful of heaven on earth."

"You two should just hear yourselves," Kate exclaimed. "Honest to gracious! It's like you were talking about a doll that just happens to speak passable English. Doc, if mama were alive she'd jerk your britches down and paddle your rump with that drumstick. I swear she would."

The two men couldn't help but laugh, and after a moment, Kate gave in, smiling good-naturedly. But Doc wasn't about to risk spoiling his chances as a steady guest, and he very shrewdly changed the subject.

"Dallas, there's talk around town that Banning is planning something that'll bring both sides of the river up short. Nothin' you can hang your hat on, but the word is out that he means to show everyone just who's runnin' El Paso. You heard anything?"

"Not much. People are still a little leary about where I stand in this deal." Stoudenmire stirred his coffee thoughtfully for a moment. "There's one thing you can bank on, though. Banning will have to act soon. He can't afford for folks to get the idea he's going soft. Which is what'll happen if he lets the Mexicans get away with killin' his men. Just offhand, I'd judge he's giving it some serious thought."

Doc came up for a breather after his second helping of peach cobbler. "Well it's for damn certain he's been too quiet. Especially after you faced him down in the Coliseum the other night. To my way of thinkin', that's a sure sign something big is brewing. But when and where it'll happen is up for grabs. Most of his boys develop lockjaw when anything really salty is hatching."

Stoudenmire's mouth lifted in a tight, sardonic smile. "Just between you and me, we're real lucky he opened his mouth in front of that crowd. I'd been wonderin' how we could stop a mob from crossing the river, and he set it up easy as pie by tryin' to show off. The way things worked out it's a matter of *his* honor at stake. Unless the wind changes, none of the townspeople are gonna get involved, no matter what he does. Now if we can just keep it that way, then maybe folks'll think twice about taking pot shots at one another across the river."

"Oh, I've got no doubt it headed off an open war between us and the greasers. But I'm not so sure I agree with your bracin' Banning the first crack out of the box. Seems to me you might've led up to it slowly. This way he knows you're after his hide even before you've started."

"Doc, there's no easy way to rid yourself of lice. Banning has to be crowded so hard he'll get mad enough to act, and sooner or later he's gonna make the *big* mistake. Think back to when you were a kid, and you'll remember that, once the hounds start snapping at a coon's heels, he doesn't have time to make plans. He has to move fast and hope he doesn't stub his toe along the way. That's why there's more dumb hounds than there are smart coons."

"Maybe you're right." The dubious look on Doc's face belied his words. "I just hope you haven't stirred up a hornets' nest before you're ready to burn 'em out. Now, for example. What've you got in mind if Banning sics his gang on your tail? You know, it's just possible he's got plans to run you out of town. Did you ever think of that?"

"Doc, if I'd let you, I suspect you'd talk the molars right out of my jawbone." Stoudenmire pulled a huge pocket watch from his vest, noting the time as he pushed his chair back. "But I've got evening rounds to make, and Gillette's gonna be champin' at the bit if I keep him waiting. Now you just have another piece of cobbler and don't get yourself in a lather about me and Banning. When he stumbles, I'll be there to dust him off, and it'll likely be all over before you even hear the shoutin'."

The lawman gave Kate a peck on the cheek, then walked from the dining room with Tige at his heels. After a moment, the front door closed with a gentle thud, and the house went still. Brother and sister sat staring at each other, both troubled by the same doubts yet tempted to leave their thoughts unsaid.

3

Throughout the meal Kate had listened silently to the casual exchange between Dallas and Doc, learning more in a few minutes than her husband had told her in three days. Now she felt herself being swamped by an outpouring of fear and downright bafflement about the grim, unyielding man she had married. Suddenly she couldn't hold it in any longer.

"Doc, I'm so worried I don't know what to do. Dallas treats this whole thing so lightly. He won't even talk to me about it. Whenever I bring it up, he just pats my head like I was a child and goes back into his shell. But the way you talk, he's got half the men in El Paso out gunning for him."

Doc made a good try at grinning and clucked sympathetically. "Katie, don't let your imagination run away with you. All of that was mostly talk, nothin' else. Listen, you've got one hellava man there, and he cut his teeth on hardcases like Ed Banning."

"That's something else that bothers me." Kate's words came awkwardly, and she found it difficult to look at him. Somehow her thoughts seemed too terrible to share with anyone, even her brother. "Dallas changes when he starts talking about the law. Almost as though killing another man was some kind of game. It's frightening to say, Doc, but he's like a cat playing with a mouse. Only he's not playing. He's deadly serious, and it's as if he just can't wait for those men to start fighting back." She shook her head numbly. "I just can't understand the change in him. When we're here alone, he's so warm and gentle. Then he puts that badge on, and he becomes someone else, a stranger almost. And that part of him scares me, Doc."

Doc Cummings just looked at her, searching desperately for something to say. But what could a man say to a sister who had blindly married a gunfighter? She hadn't the slightest notion that her husband was a trained killer, the kind that hunts men much as a great cat instinctively hunts animals of prey. How could any woman understand that the man who shared her bed was a specialist at a very dirty game? Dallas Stoudenmire was a professional mankiller, and anyone with a lick of sense never doubted it for a moment.

Doc glanced at her out of the corner of his eye. "Sis, what do you know about Dallas?"

"That's a strange question to ask." Kate gave him a mildly puzzled look, not quite sure what he meant. "I know that his folks, came over from Germany and he was born outside Mineral Wells. He's thirty-three, doesn't drink much, and behaves himself around women. I know lots about him, Doc. Enough that I wanted him to be my husband."

"Sure. But those are things girls're just naturally interested in. What I'm drivin' at is, do you know anything about his life before you met him? What he was doing for thirty years before he turned up in Columbus."

"Well, of course, I do," Kate said indignantly. "I'm not some schoolgirl ninny with stars in her eyes. He was city marshal at Nacogdoches, and before that he was a Texas Ranger, and before that he fought for the Confederacy. Just for your information, he'd never been married before, either."

Doc poured himself another cup of coffee, trying to keep his tone casual. "Didn't that strike you as a little odd? Him being that old and never married, I mean."

Kate shook her head, more puzzled than ever. "Why would it strike me as odd? Lots of men wait till they've sown their wild oats before they settle down. They don't all jump the broomstick with the first thing that comes along in skirts."

"Dallas never seemed to me like a man that'd sowed any wild oats." Doc hesitated, mulling it over, and his next words were those of a man thinking out loud. "Unless I miss my guess, there wasn't much to tell on that score."

"That's ridiculous, Doc. Why should he tell me things like that, anyway?" Kate was growing exasperated with her brother's prying manner. "If you're hinting that Dallas isn't . . . oh, damn, you make me so mad sometimes I could just scream. If you're trying to say that Dallas isn't like other men, then you'd better drink your coffee and go on home."

"Katie, I don't mean it like you think, but in a way, that's what I've been drivin' at. He's not like other men." He faltered for a moment, wracking his brain for a way to open her eyes about the man she had married. "Did he ever tell you that his folks were killed by the Comanche when he was just a kid?"

She stared at him blankly, hardly able to credit her own ears. "Indians?"

"You remember when I came home to visit last year?" Kate bobbed her head, and he went on. "Well I decided to find out about this fella my little sister was stuck on. So I took Dallas out and got him drunk. Leastways as drunk as Dallas can get. Loosened up might be more like it. Just enough so's he would talk some."

"But, Doc, I don't understand. What have his folks getting killed got to do with anything?"

"I'm comin' to that. Just give me time. You see the Civil War was going rough for the South about then, so he ups and enlists. Course, he lied about his age, but the Confederates needed men, and since he was bigger than most already full-growed, they didn't ask any questions. He ended up fightin' with General Joe Johnston. Matter of fact, he was still at it when Lee called it quits at Appomattox."

Kate nodded impatiently, somewhat irritated by his round-about manner. "I know all that. He told me about being in the army."

"Sure, but I'll bet he didn't tell you what it was like." When she failed to answer, he smiled dryly. "Thought so."

There was a pause while Doc collected his thoughts, searching for some way to break it to her gently. "Well now, keep in mind he was only fifteen when he started in at this business of war. Maybe you never thought about it, but that's sort of an early age to get baptized in the ways of killin' men. Fact is, he wasn't but seventeen when the war ended. Those two years had a mighty big effect on him, Katie. Had to. Couldn't have been no other way. There he was, just a kid, watching men being slaughtered like cattle, seeing 'em maimed and going mad with fear. Still, them things was only part of it. More'n likely just a small part. What I'm gettin' around to sayin' is, they took an overgrown kid and taught him to kill, showed him how easy it was. Just pull the trigger and a man falls down. More'n that, though, they taught him there wasn't nothin' wrong with killin'. Not so long as a man's in the right. Don't you see, they wiped away that old buga-boo about 'Thou shalt not kill.' A green kid marched off to war, but an old man came marchin' back. Something had been burned clean out of his soul. Call it feelin', or pity, or whatever you want. Killin' came natural to him now, and he didn't have no more conscience about it than if he was swattin' flies."

Kate stared at him in sheer horror, her eyes wide and glistening wetly. When she spoke her voice was tremulous, shrill. "Doc, are you trying to tell me that the man I married isn't human? That he's some kind of mad-dog killer. If you are, I won't listen to another word. That's sick, to talk like that, and you're no friend of Dallas's to say such wicked things."

Doc winced, stung by her fiery accusation. "Kate, I was your brother before I was his friend. Maybe it's not pretty, and like as not I'm being rash tellin' you all this, but if you don't come to understand the man, your life's gonna be pure hell."

"Understand him? Don't try to play God, Doc. I understand him very well. He's a gentle man underneath all that bluster, and I know it in ways that nobody else could know."

"Is that why he keeps that man-eatin' dog with him all the time? 'Cause he's so gentle." The little merchant's face saddened, and he cursed himself for having ever broached the subject of Stoudenmire's character. "Sis, I'm not tryin' to run Dallas down. I like him, even admire him in a way. Guess I always have. But if I didn't understand him, I'd find him mighty hard to like. Maybe you oughta give that some thought where lovin' him's concerned."

"You're the one I don't understand." Kate appeared bemused, uncertain of her feelings just at that moment. "You tell me all these dreadful things, and in the same breath, you try to convince me that it's for my own good. How, Doc? How is knowing all this going to make my life with Dallas any better?"

"Because there's more to being a man's wife than sleepin' with him. More'n likely, you've already found that out." He studied her for a second, watching the hurt and fear kindle in her eyes, yet he was determined now to see it through. "Kate, this man's whole life is tied up in some funny kind of way with doing what he thinks is right. Upholding the law, destroying the lawless. Sorta like the great god Jehovah visitin' wrath and damnation on the sinners. After the war, he drifted around for a while, then joined the Rangers. First he fought the Indians up north with Jones's company, and considerin' how his folks was killed, I suspect he took few prisoners. Later, he served with McNelly down on the border, and that wasn't no picnic either. Don't you see what I'm gettin' at, Sis? Ever since he was a kid, somebody's been trainin' him to kill and givin' him a license to make it legal. They taught him that killin' is all right so long as it's the sinner that gets killed. That's how he was raised up and that's how he believes."

Then Cummings hesitated, groping for some justification that would absolve the man his sister had married. "Whatever your man is Kate, he's what the people of Texas made him. What they needed, what the times called for. That's all I'm tryin' to say."

Kate regarded him vacantly, her face drained of emotion. "You're saying he kills other men because he has to, because no one ever showed him another way. You don't condemn him, but at the same time, you don't approve. He's the lesser of two evils. A good badman hired to hunt down the common, garden-variety badmen. That's very charitable of you, Doc. Almost Christian."

"Damn, I wish I'd never opened my big mouth." He rubbed his face with both hands, like a man that has sore eyes and a long way yet to go. "Kate, regardless of what you thought I said, I don't believe there's a bad bone in Dallas Stoudenmire's body. Matter of fact, he's about the most decent man I ever met. Otherwise, I'd have raised holy hell before I let you marry him. I'd trust him with my life sooner'n anybody I know, and you damn sure don't put that kind of faith in a man that's not straight. That's what I meant a while ago about him being my friend whatever he is. What he isn't has got nothin' to do with it."

Kate didn't say anything for a few seconds, almost as if she had dismissed the subject from her mind. Then she glanced up with renewed curiosity. "Did Dallas tell you all this the night you got him drunk? Or are you just guessing?"

"Tell you the truth, Seth Hart had him checked out through the governor's office. Most of it came out there. The rest I put together from little things Dallas said. Damn little, I'll admit. He's not the most talkative man I ever met."

"No, he's not that." Kate smiled wanly and sighed. "But deep down he's as good a man as any woman could ask for. And somehow, I'm going to get him out of El Paso and make him forget this horrible life. I don't know how, but I will."

Later, walking back to his room over the store, Doc Cummings had the feeling that he had only made matters worse. He had meant it the right way, for it was plain to see that Kate couldn't go on much longer with the way things were. But then, as parsons were so fond of reminding folks, the road to hell was paved with good intentions. Chalk one up to damn fools and good deeds. Lately they seemed to be a matched pair.

4

They came like ghostly shadows in the night. The moons' golden streamers lighted the compound with a dusky glow, just bright enough for a man to catch his rifle sights when the time was right. Kale placed each man in position, carefully selecting an open field of fire, and by midnight they had the *hacienda* surrounded.

The night riders had split into two parties after Tom Kale personally scouted the layout. The smaller group was to raid the northernmost herd of cattle just as soon as firing broke out in the compound. Leaving nothing to chance, Kale had selected to lead the assault on the *hacienda*. The sole purpose of this raid was to punish the greasers in their own backyard; scare them so badly that they would be posting sentries for a month to come. The cattle herd was strictly a secondary target, and like any guerrilla leader worth his salt, Kale had chosen to direct the main attack himself.

The *hacienda* of Don Miguel Salazar lay some twenty kilometers southwest of Paso del Norte. The aristocratic

hidalgo had inherited a Spanish land grant from his father
and ruled a small kingdom stretching to the headwaters of the
Rio Santa Maria, nearly a hundred kilometers further south.
Located on a tree-sheltered plain alongside a sleepy brook, the
cuadrilla consisted of the master's *casa* and various outbuildings, which included bunkhouses, *jacal* huts, stables,
and storage sheds. The compound was enclosed on three
sides by a low adobe wall with the brook forming the remaining boundary. Don Miguel's large, sprawling home
overlooked the stream just south of the main gate and commanded a view of the entire *rancho* headquarters.

Kale had posted half his men on the far side of the brook
behind trees and the remainder in a grove of giant *maguey*
near the opposite side of the compound. Once the shooting
started, the Mexicans would be caught in a deadly cross
fire, with virtually no chance of mounting a counterattack.
While greatly outnumbered, the Banning night riders had
the element of surprise working in their favor, and their tactical advantage promised to make it a costly night for Don
Salazar's *vaqueros*.

Shortly after midnight, three of Kale's men slithered into
the compound and set fire to a large stable near the west wall.
Within moments the building was engulfed in flames, and
squeals from the terror-stricken horses could be heard a mile
away. *Vaqueros* poured from the buildings in their night-
clothes, forgetting guns, boots, and all else in their rush to
save *el patrón*'s prized breeding stock. Among the first to
reach the blazing stable was Ramón Vazquez, who had served
as Don Salazar's *caporal* for close to five years. Shouting
commands above the raging inferno, Ramón quickly organized a bucket brigade, then led a handpicked crew through
the flames to rescue the panicked horses.

Waiting patiently, like a tawny panther watching a game
trail, Kale bided his time as the crowd thickened around the
stables. Soon every man on the place was frantically engaged
in dousing the fire, and the leaping flames silhouetted their
every movement within the confines of the *cuadrilla*. Observing the rushing figures closely, Kale selected the one

who seemed to be giving all the orders. Carefully aligning his sights on the man's chest, Kale squeezed the trigger and felt the Winchester buck against his shoulder.

Ramón Vazquez would always think back on the night of the fire as a moment of *buena fortuna* for him personally. Had he been standing still he would have been a dead man, *muy muerto*. But at the split second the rifle cracked, he stooped to retrieve a fallen bucket, and the slug ripped through the fleshy part of his arm. Spun around, he dropped to the earth, knowing even as he fell that his people had been skillfully lured into a trap.

Suddenly the night came alive with the yellowish flash of gunfire, and lead hissed across the compound like a swarm of angry wasps. *Vaqueros* fell right and left, clutching their wounds, and those left unscathed after the first volley ran for cover. Rolling beneath a *carreta*, Ramón peered cautiously around the wooden wheel, trying to ignore the dull throb in his left arm. One glance was enough to confirm his suspicions. Their attackers had them neatly scissored in a cross fire, and unless something was done fast, every man in the *cuadrilla* would be snuffed out like defenseless insects.

"¡Dispersad, hombres!" Ramón shouted over the roar of flames and rifle-fire. "Scatter! Run for the buildings! Get your guns and form along the walls. *¡Pronto, hombres! ¡Pronto!"*

The *vaqueros* came off the ground as if electrified by his hoarse command. Scuttling crablike across the open compound, they dodged and weaved in headlong flight toward the adobe structures. The gunfire increased in tempo as they ran, upending an even half dozen before they reached the sanctuary of the buildings. Moments later, they boiled from their *cabañas* like frenzied ants, clutching rifles and bandoliers as they darted toward the walls. Five more of their number jackknifed into the dust as they ran the gauntlet of lead for the second time, but more than forty *vaqueros* made it safely. Within the beat of a heart, their rifles leveled over the walls, and the night was split with a thunderous fusillade as they returned the raiders' fire with a vengeance.

* * *

Three miles to the northeast another deadly engagement was being played out with equally savage results. Ten raiders had infiltrated the cattle herd, moving stealthily through the pale darkness as they waited for the signal. When the ragged sound of shooting drifted in from the *hacienda*, they opened fire on the night guards, presumably killing every man in the first volley. But among the *vaqueros* was an *anciano* of great resourcefulness and daring. The slug meant for him had pulverized his pommel instead, and he very cunningly tumbled from the saddle, squirming off into the brush with the noiseless wrigglings of a chubby snake. From there, he watched silently as the bushwhackers mounted their horses and set about trailing the restless herd in a northerly direction.

But this ancient one wasn't a man who accepted such insult lightly. In his prime, he had been *macho hombre,* and it went against the grain to cower in the brush like a steer with an empty bag. Removing his rowled spurs, he waited until the herd had been lined out and started north. Just as he suspected, one of the *gringo ladrones* fell back to ride drag on the skittish longhorns. With that, the *anciano* exploded from his hiding place, displaying the agility of one half his age as he collared the raider in a bounding leap. Cartwheeling over the horse, they struck the ground, and he scrambled erect as if shot from coiled springs. Balanced catlike on the balls of his feet, the ancient one's heart thudded with the excitement of an old *guerrero* who has forgotten nothing about the deadly games men play. Jerking a battered cap and ball Remington, he clouted the raider upside the head, grunting with satisfaction as the man settled limply into the dust.

¡Caramba! The old fox had lost none of his juices after all. And he, Hector Lizardi, the *vaquero* they had thought to retire to the goat herd, would personally present *el patrón* with this *gringo abominación. ¡Madre de Dios!* It had been a good night indeed for old men.

While Hector Lizardi was gloating over his prisoner, Tom Kale decided it was time to break off the fighting and make a run for the border. Withdrawing his men in small bunches, he managed to keep the *vaqueros* pinned down until everyone was mounted. Moments later the raiders thundered northward, intent on putting distance between themselves and the Salazar *rancho*. Circling back to assign a rear guard, Kale was astounded to find that he hadn't lost a single man in a firefight that had raged for nearly a half-hour. If the cattle raid had come off anywhere near as well, he'd really have something to crow about to the Bannings!

But if Tom Kale was exultant, Ramón Vazquez was seared clean through by a fury unlike any he had ever known. The Salazar *hacienda* was devastated, a burned-out ruin where only an hour before there had been a magnificent ranch. With no one to halt its advance, the stable fire had spread rapidly to other buildings, and the entire *cuadrilla* now lay in smoky rubble. With the exception of Don Miguel's *casa* and a single bunkhouse, every building in the compound had been leveled to the ground.

Still, buildings could be erected again; their loss was but a thing of the moment. Men were something else entirely, and short of *Jesucristo* himself, there was no one with the knack of pumping life back into the dead. With a quick count, Ramón made it eleven dead and twenty-six wounded, some mortally. There would be much wailing in the *vaqueros'* quarters before another dawn, and the thought of his people being shot down like dogs brought a sickening taste to Ramón's mouth. Someone would pay dearly for this slaughter, eye for eye, just as it has been in the old days when they fought Comanches instead of *gringos*.

After seeing to his men, Ramón sought out Don Miguel, who was wandering through the rubble in a numbed daze. *El patrón* had little to say, staring blankly at the carnage and death about them. Ramón tersely explained what must be done, then left him gazing sorrowfully upon a brood mare that had not survived the fire. Ordering horses brought in from the nearby *remuda*, he called on every *vaquero* who could ride to take the saddle. Less than a quarter-hour after the shooting had ceased, the *caporal* led a force of nineteen men toward the Rio Grande.

   With fresh horses under them, the *vaqueros* set a blistering pace, and some ten kilometers from the border, they over-
took the *gringo* column. Kale and his raiders had joined the
tail end of the rustled herd only minutes before and were
hanging back in event the greasers gave pursuit. Upon sighting the Mexicans, Kale ordered the longhorns stampeded toward the river and formed his men to fight a delaying action
until the herd was safely aground on Texas soil.

   Over the next hour, a running battle raged across the countryside. The villagers of Paso del Norte heard the gunfire
and promptly bolted their doors. Those engaged in the fighting seemed to be doing a good job of it, which meant that
only the *estúpido* would venture forth to satisfy their curiosity. Wise men minded their own business, behind locked
doors, leaving other men to attend to such affairs as they
saw fit.

   But the villagers' relutance by no means extended to
Ramón's *vaqueros*. Repeatedly they charged the *gringos*,
only to have their attack blunted by the accurate fire of the
Texans' rifles. Kale kept his men fanned out in a compact
crescent behind the rushing herd, never once allowing them
to bunch together. After losing several men in futile charges,
the Mexicans splintered off, every man for himself in a
ghostly, moonlit duel. But Kale directed the raiders' fire with
telling deadliness, and as the last of the herd was driven into
the river, the *vaqueros* called it quits.

   Drawing to a halt on a rise overlooking the Rio Grande,
Ramón and his men watched helplessly as the raiders swam
the lazy current. On the other side was Texas, and over there
a *vaquero* had one foot in the grave when he stepped from
the water. Better to wait, to make plans, Ramón counseled.
There was always another day, and the *gringos* had departed
owing a debt that would be collected manyfold in time to
come.

   Reining his horse about on the opposite bank, Tom Kale
observed the distant Mexicans with a throaty chuckle. By
God, this was a good night's work well done! He had lost only
two men, and as near as he could count, they had put at least

a dozen of those greaser bastards under for keeps. That's the kind of fighting any man could be proud of!

Thinking on it, he decided he might just hit the Bannings up for a raise.

5

The sun had barely topped the horizon when Don Miguel and Ramón came out to survey the damage from last night's raid. While the *hacienda* itself had suffered only minor damage, the outbuildings were nothing but charred ruins, and a sense of loss hung over the compound like a shroud. Upward of two hundred steers had also been lost in the raid, but among Don Miguel's people, there was a greater sorrow that left no room for smoldering homes or scrubby longhorns.

After the abortive chase to the Rio Grande, there were now fourteen dead *vaqueros*, and the mournful cries of their women was enough to make a strong man lose his breakfast. When Ramón saw the bodies laid out, his guts shriveled into a hard knot, strengthening his resolve that retribution must be swift in coming. There were some things upon which no price could be set, except in blood.

Later in the morning, after the dead and the wounded had been attended to, the captured *norteamericano* was brought forward. Hector Lizardi had become an overnight hero among his people, once again *macho hombre*, proudly leading the barbarian around for everyone to see. The prisoner was a large, fleshy man, towering over his shrunken captor, but a deft tug on the rawhide *reata* around his neck quickly brought him to heel.

When the raider was hauled before Ramón, the *caporal*'s rage centered wholly on him, just as a hawk selects a single dove in flight. This lone man was the one visible symbol of the unspeakable filth that had devastated their homes and murdered their *compañeros*. What he had to say would make interesting listening, and the *vaqueros* gathered closer, eagerly awaiting Ramón's choice of persuasion.

The raider was jerked and shoved across the *cuadrilla*

grounds and roughly bound to a tree near the brook. The
questioning began, but the prisoner proved a stubborn witness. First, he professed no understanding of Spanish, then
when Ramón switched to broken English he simply refused
to speak, sulling up like a paunchy old mule. The night rider
had no illusions about what was coming; he had lived on the
border long enough to know that his fate was sealed. It was
only a matter of what device would be used and how long it
would take. Determined to go under like a man, he clamped
his jaws shut and gave every indication of never opening them
again. These greaser pricks could do whatever they wanted,
but he'd show them the kind of grit a real *hombre* had.

Ramón studied the problem for a moment, then stepped
off a few paces and drew his pistol. Aiming with utmost
care, he squeezed off a shot, and the man's right ear disappeared in a frothy, pink spray. The prisoner banged his head
against the tree as he jerked backwards and a steady stream
of blood trickled down his neck. Ramón waited, giving him
an opportunity to speak, but the Texan merely gritted his
teeth and returned the stare defiantly. The *caporal* raised his
pistol again, and when it exploded, the man's left ear disintegrated in a shower of bloody tissue. The raider groaned, yet
so slightly that only those standing nearby heard it, and spat
a wad of phlegm at Ramón's feet.

Ramón glanced at Don Miguel, who was standing off to
one side, and smiled tightly. This *gringo* promised to be a
tough one; but the day was long, and they had plenty of time.
Perhaps he had greater fear of a slow death than a quick
one, and in that, they could accommodate him easily. The
caporal ordered the prisoner's shirt removed, then looked
slowly around the circle of hard, brown faces. For what he had
in mind, there was one above all others who deserved the
honor, and he selected Hector Lizardi.

"*Abuelo*, it comes to me that your knife needs practice.
This vermin is yours to whittle on, old one. But take care you
do not kill him. The *bárbaro* has much to say before we allow him to die."

The old man's eyes went moist with pride. "*Sí jefe*. I will treat him gently, as if he were merely a child whose manners must be corrected."

Walking forward, Hector Lizardi stopped before the prisoner. With great ceremony, he slipped a long, wicked looking stiletto from its scabbard. Testing its edge with his thumb, he squinted up at the raider, flashing a mouthful of scraggly, brown teeth. "*Amigo*, you are about to witness a miracle. With one swift stroke of the blade, I will reveal how it is possible for you to change from man to *manso*, the tame bull. Have you ever seen a man gelded, my friend? It is an ugly thing, and sad. Very sad. No longer will his pole grow stout, and the women find him a source of much amusement."

Suddenly the narrow blade flicked out and down, slashing the man's belt and pants so that they fell over against his hips. A thin ribbon of blood appeared from his bellybutton to his groin, seeping down over the short, curly hairs that showed above the crotch of his trousers. The raider's buttocks slammed up against the tree as his manhood flinched from the knife. Then he sucked up his nerve and closed his eyes, waiting for the final cut.

But men are unlike cattle, as Hector Lizardi well knew. They die quickly from loss of blood or simply from shock when their *pequeñas rocas* are cut from the sack. Better merely to carve on the *gringo* dog and break his spirit little by little. Suiting action to thought, the old man hefted the stiletto like a surgical instrument and began tracing a pattern of precise slits across the man's belly. When that failed to draw any response, he neatly severed each nipple, watching the exquisite agony on the raider's face as the blade razored through his tender flesh. Still the *ladrón* refused to speak.

Losing patience, the ancient one grasped the Texan's lower lip between thumb and forefinger and gauged an arc from corner to corner with the tip of the stiletto. But as the blade pierced the man's fleshy jowls, Ramón halted Hector Lizardi with a sharp command.

"Enough, grandfather! I see now that this *piojo* is more stubborn than we suspected. Either that, or he is more of a man than his fat belly would lead you to believe. Still there are ways to loosen any man's tongue. Eh, old one? Perhaps we should let him share a moment with the crawling death." Turning to his men, Ramón searched their faces. "What do you say, *caballeros?* Shall we introduce our silent friend to *el culebra?*"

The men roared their approval, flashing curious glances at the prisoner as they nudged one another in the ribs. While the raider hadn't the faintest idea of what was coming next, it seemed fairly clear that it would be worse than what he had already undergone. Bathed in a slime of his own sweat and gore, he sagged against the ropes, thankful for even this brief respite. Galvanized by Ramón's brisk orders, the *vaqueros* set about collecting empty grain sacks and took off in all directions across the parched countryside.

Don Miguel spoke briefly with his *caporal*, nodding occasionally at the prisoner, then walked off toward the *hacienda* What was about to happen wouldn't be pretty to watch, and there were some things that even *el patrón* preferred not to witness. While he saw the necessity, it nonetheless left him revolted. As he knew full well, Ramón and his *vaqueros* had not fought the Apaches and Comanches without learning something about the limits of a man's courage. And the Texan was about to be tested in a way that Don Miguel considered harsh even for a *gringo.*

Shortly the prisoner was marched to a small, open-sided *ramada* and stripped naked. Four ropes were thrown over the rafters and secured to his hands and ankles. Then, before he had time to gather his wits, the man was hoisted aloft in a spread-eagle position. *Vaqueros* strode forward clutching sacks and dumped the contents on the earthen floor of the *ramada.*

The morning stillness instantly came alive with an ungodly buzzing sound, and a dozen furious rattlesnakes coiled to strike. Leaping back, the *vaqueros* grabbed long poles and surrounded the shed, forcing the snakes to remain inside. Being poked and shoved with the sticks infuriated the rattlers even more, and their angry warning swelled to a deafening pitch.

Ramón stepped as close to the shed as he dared and peered up at the helpless raider. "*Gringo*, you can halt this game whenever you feel the urge to speak. From this moment on, whether you live or die is a matter of your own choosing."

Moving back, Ramón barked an order, and the Texan was slowly lowered from the rafters toward the floor. After a moment, the snakes became aware of the new threat and switched their attention from the *vaqueros* to this strange enemy who hovered overhead like a taloned hawk. The raider jerked violently, arching his buttocks high in the air, trying desperately to push himself back up the ropes. But his struggles were in vain, for the lines inexorably lowered him into the viper pit below. As he neared the floor, the snakes poised to strike, and the enraged whir of their rattles came like the call of death itself. Dripping sweat, his eyes bulged out of their sockets, shot through with crazed terror.

Suddenly the man gasped as he spotted one especially large rattler eyeing his dangling manhood. Every fiber in his body strained backwards with inhuman will, for it now became clear that whatever part of him reached the snakes first was exactly what they would strike. Already he could feel the slithering filth gnawing on it, gouging and chomping as they pumped their venom deep within his precious rod. Death came to every man, and once cold, it mattered little how he had gone under. But not like that. *Holy Mother of God, not like that!*

The *vaqueros* watched in frozen awe, wondering if the *yanqui* would hold his tongue until it was too late. Some of his breed were *muy valiente*, brave beyond the measure of other men, and perhaps this fat-gutted barbarian was one. Whatever he was, he would shortly be dog meat unless he opened his mouth soon.

Then, with little more than a yard separating him from the rattlers, the Texan broke. Screaming hysterically, his face etched with mortal fear, he swore to tell all if they would only save him. Ramón ordered him hoisted aloft, but refused to untie him just yet. Drained of the last ounce of courage, the raider hung limply from the ropes, swaying overhead like a

gutted steer. Every muscle in his body quivered uncontrollably, his eyes twitched with spastic madness; like a man
already dead, his bowels flushed in final release.

The questioning began again. This time Ramon was confident that they would come to an understanding, for they
were both reasonable men, and as such, there should be no
secrets between them. But should he prove stubborn with certain answers, of course, they would not hesitate to lower him
again among those who waited below. *¿Comprendes, amigo?
¡Bueno!*

6

Shortly after noon that day, a carriage crossed the Rio Grande
and drove straight to the Paso del Norte jail. There three girls
alighted, their faces wan and solemn, dressed demurely as
befitted housewives. Their driver escorted them into the
calabozo, and as they entered the door, the portly jailer
came forward to meet them. Four *gringos*, three of them
women, was hardly an everyday occurrence in his flea-bitten
lockup, and he instinctively grew wary.

"Buenos días, Mariscal," the driver greeted him in passable Spanish. "These *señoras* are the wives of the prisoners
now in your custody. They humbly request permission to
speak with their men for a few moments. Since it is well
known that their husbands are slated for *rapida ejecución* the
ladies feel honor-bound to look upon them once more."

The jailer sucked up his stomach and sauntered around for
a better look at the ladies. Seldom had he been called marshal, and the title had a heady effect on him in the drowsy
heat. Still one could never be too careful where *gringos* were
concerned. They were a devious race, given to great cunning
and duplicity in their dealings with his people. Yet the man
looked harmless enough, and the women certainly presented
no threat. After all, he, José Flores, was a man of some experience in such matters, not to mention his remarkable
facility for sizing up a person in one glance. Besides, he was
a family man himself, and it was only right that *hombres* who

had an appointment with the firing squad should be granted one last visit with their loved ones. Such a thing would do much for a man on his way to hell.

"*¡Hecho!*" His eyes warmed, and he smiled benevolently. "Consider it done, *señor*. But the ladies will be allowed only ten minutes, and under the circumstances, I fear they will be afforded no privacy."

"*Gracious, Mariscal*. You are very kind." Looking around at the women, the driver related the gist of the conversation, then turned back to the jailer. "The *señoras* thank you and indicate that ten minutes will be more than enough. After the beastly thing these men have done, the ladies wish only to fulfill their wifely duty, and nothing more."

Tipping his hat to the women, the driver turned and walked out the door. José Flores smiled solicitously and ushered the ladies toward the rear of the jail. This was a sad thing, and he felt very *simpático* about these poor, betrayed women. Still, they were exceptionally pretty in that pale, *gringo* way, and doubtless they would have little trouble finding better husbands once this dirty business was finished. He would light a candle and pray to the Virgin that their bereavement not be too incapacitating.

Red and his two cellmates had watched this little charade with mounting interest. They weren't too sure about the play, but there wasn't a doubt in the world that Banning had hatched this scheme personally. The girls were regulars in the Coliseum Saloon, and they wouldn't be here unless the big boss had a hand in this deal. While the prisoners' grasp of greaser talk was limited, they had caught enough of the conversation to understand that the women were posing as their wives. Considering that each of the girls would hump a drunk Indian if the price was right, the three men had all they could do to keep from laughing. Watching the tubby jailer herd them along like lily-pure doves was more than a man could rightly stand with a straight face.

When the girls stopped before the cell, the three Texans crowded against the bars. José Flores thoughtfully backed off a few paces, not wishing to intrude on their tender, yet somehow pitiful, moment. Out of the corner of his eye he saw the men clasp their wives' hands, and the soft murmurings he took to be words of endearment brought a sorrowful frown to his face. *¡Madre mio!* It was indeed a cruel thing that these men had brought such disgrace to their women. The sooner they faced the firing squad the better for everyone concerned!

Suddenly the girls' escort appeared in the doorway and again stepped inside. Instantly alert, the jailer walked toward the front of the room, keeping his hand near the ancient Colt resting on his hip. But the driver seemed peaceful enough, wishing only to inquire if it would be possible to get a cup of coffee. José Flores apologized profusely, for the coffee pot had grown cold since morning. More to the point, he was disgusted with himself at having suspected the man simply because he was a *gringo*. Chattering like an amiable bear, he walked the driver back to the door, and they parted with a warm handshake.

While José Flores was salving his conscience, things in the back of the jail were moving at a furious pace. In a flash the girls hiked their skirts, pulled guns from their underclothes, and passed them to the prisoners. With the jailer's attention thoroughly diverted, it was a simple matter for Red and his partners to stash the guns beneath their mattresses. When the *alguacil* returned, he found everything as serene as a high mass, marred only by an occasional sniffle from one of the women. Again he was struck by the rightness of allowing these doomed men one last glimpse of their wives. Somewhere a man's good deeds were being recorded for that final day of judgment, and his actions here this afternoon would not go unnoticed.

When the girls were ready to leave, he escorted them to the carriage and stood watching as it pulled away. Dabbing at their eyes with delicate hankies, they waved goodbye, and José Flores felt a lump the size of a gourd form in his throat. *¡Madre de Dios!* Such gentle creatures to be married to those filthy *cabrones* back inside.

The day passed uneventfully, and after giving the prisoners their supper, the jailer stepped outside to sit on the front step. Each evening when darkness fell, a freshening breeze drifted in off the river, and it was good to be rid of the heat for another day. The night seemed alive with fireflies and the chirp of crickets, and for the first time in longer than he could remember, José Flores felt at peace with himself. This was a thankless job, one seldom appreciated by the people, but it had its moments. Gazing up at the sky, he watched the moon play hide and seek with the clouds and reflected once again on the skinny beauty of *yanqui* women. *¡Sí!* Today had been one of those moments.

Back in their cell, Red and his cronies stared up at the same moon through a barred window. Yet their thoughts had little to do with cool breezes and pretty women. They would have much preferred a dark night for a jailbreak, but beggars couldn't be choosers. The greasers could easily take it into their heads to march them before a firing squad at any time, and escape might be tonight or never.

They had spent the afternoon planning just how it would be done, and with the village quieted down, there was no reason to wait longer. On signal, two of the men started scuffling, cursing one another in loud, fluent terms. Jerked from his reverie by the commotion, José Flores hurried into the cell block, ordering them to cease fighting. But the tables suddenly turned, and before he suspected what was happening, the jailer found himself staring down the bores of three Colts.

"All right, you greasy tub o' guts," Red snarled. "We'd just as soon kill you as not, so don't fart around or I'll put a slug right through your gizzard. Now get them keys and be damn quick about it."

The jailer wordlessly crossed the room and took a ring of keys from a wall peg. But as he turned back, his offside was hidden for a moment, and his hand stealthily crept toward the gun on his hip. *¡Jesucristo!* If he let these animals escape, the villagers would more than likely decorate a tree with his plump neck. Three to one were bad odds, even for a *pistolero* like himself, but he had to try.

"Hold it!" Red's sharp growl brought him up short. "Listen you fat prick, you're about a hair away from going under.

Savvy, greaseball? Now heist your hands and trot over here
with them keys."

José Flores did as he was told. Even the most fearless *guerrero* knew there was a fine line between bravery and foolishness, and the big, black holes centered on his bellybutton
seemed very persuasive indeed. Besides, he had seven children, who would take it very unkindly if their father suddenly
left them orphaned. Unlocking the cell door, he stepped aside
to let the Texans out.

Without warning Red whacked him over the head with the
heavy Colt. The jailer's knees buckled, but the *gringo*
thumped him twice more before he hit the floor, striking savagely as one would club a fattened steer. José Flores made
no sound as a widening pool of blood puddled up around his
head. Had Red not feared risking a shot, he would have been
a dead man instead of one with a cracked skull.

Easing through the front door of the jail, the Texans stuck
to the shadows and began a cautious approach to the river.
The streets were deserted, and Paso del Norte seemed quiet
as a graveyard. But they took no chances. Moving silently
from building to building in the tawny moonlight, they passed
through the village without arousing a single dog. Though
this struck Red as curious, he chalked it off to an overdue
change in luck and plowed on toward the border.

Minutes later, they reached the river, and the sight of it
made them bolder. Freedom lay on the other side. A land
where there were no lice, ravenous fleas, or firing squads. The
thought alone made them dizzy with relief. Sliding down the
bank in a shower of dust, they plunged into the water and
went splashing across the Rio Grande like frisky yearlings.

But even as they ran, Ramón Vazquez and fifteen *vaqueros* emerged from the treeline bordering Paso del Norte.
Armed with rifles; they watched impassively as the Texans
neared the opposite shore, awaiting their *caporal*'s order.
When it came, the night was rendered with a hollow roar, and
the three renegades pitched forward on the riverbank, dead
even as they hit American soil. The *vaqueros* continued firing until their rifles were empty, shredding the lifeless bod-

ies with a hail of lead. Only when the hammers clicked on empty chambers did they lower their weapons and fade back into the trees.

The debt had been repaid in part. Not fully by any means, and after the savagery of last night, perhaps never. But now there would be no doubt as to the fate of those who violated Mexican women or ravaged the land of their fathers.

CHAPTER FOUR

1

El Paso was alive with talk of last night's brutal slaying of the three Americans. Frank Hollingsworth, the local butcher, happened to be on his way home and had actually witnessed the slaughter, which was the term already being applied to the killings. The townspeople were in a shaky mood, appalled by the savagery of the incident. Though the dead men were generally considered nothing more than common rapists, border scum really, they were human. When the riddled bodies had been carted up to the funeral parlor, word quickly spread that they were as full of holes as a leaky sieve. Such an end was better suited to animals, for whatever else they had been, the men were Texans. The way things were shaping up, no man was safe outside the sanctuary of his own home. Maybe not even in it.

Although the people were unnerved by the Mexicans' savagery, there was also an undercurrent of ill feeling directed toward the Bannings. They had clearly masterminded the escape attempt, and it had been their ranch hands who had stirred up the Mexicans. Though no one could fault them for trying to save their own men, it now became clear that the life of every *anglo* along the river had been placed in jeopardy. The Mexicans meant to fight if pushed, and stirring up a hornets' nest to save three men was hardly the act of a civic benefactor. What had been whispered in the past was now being bandied about openly. Ed Banning was a conniving bloodsucker, and so long as he ended up with all the marbles, he didn't give a tinker's damn for the fate of the town itself.

Tom Kale rode into town late that morning, eager to report the success of his raid. Touching up the brands on the rustled longhorns was taking longer than planned, and he had finally decided it was best to ride on in and let the Bannings know what was happening. Besides, he was a little concerned that Red and his two partners hadn't shown up at the ranch. Assuming the jailbreak came off without a hitch, he had fully expected them to come loping into the home base sometime last night.

Upon entering the office in the Coliseum he found the Bannings sour-tempered and curiously untalkative. The grim scowl on their faces was clear enough to read, and to an old scout like Kale, the sign said to walk lightly.

"Mornin', boss," Kale's voice was neither chipper nor solemn, just sort of neuter in tone. "How's tricks, Sam?"

"Not worth a shit." The burly man's features twisted in a bilious grimace, like he was having gas pains and couldn't break wind. "In case you hadn't heard, somebody just kicked the crapper door off the hinges."

"Yeah? Well maybe I've got a little news that'll cheer you up some." The ramrod wasn't sure what Sam's cryptic observation meant, but where the Bannings were concerned he had found it best not to prod them with questions. "Night before last we whipped the livin' piss out of them greasers and got away with near two hundred beeves. The boys are finishing up the brandin' right now. Sorta puts a new light on things, don't it?"

Ed Banning came erect in his chair. "Kale, you're a day late and a dollar short. Last night your asshole buddies got themselves pumped full of lead. What Sam's trying to tell you is that the greasers let 'em get to this side of the river before they gunned them down. Evidently they got wind of the break somehow and had a whole goddamn regiment lined up along the south bank."

"Sorta like a turkey shoot," Sam growled. "Only your boys didn't have near as good a chance of walkin' away."

"Well I'll be dipped in shit," Kale said, clearly thunder-struck by the news.

"We're all gonna be double-dipped if we don't get things back on an even keel pretty damn quick." The gang leader's waspish comments sizzled with anger. "Instead of busting those three nitwits out of jail and making a fool of Stouden-mire, we've made jackasses out of ourselves twice run-ning. Once more and folks around here are liable to start thinkin' we've gone soft in the head."

"That's for damn sure." Kale shook his head ruefully, still slack-jawed with the turn of events. "Us losin' five men in two days might give the wrong people some big ideas."

"Five men?" Ed Banning snapped. "What the hell are you talkin' about? I only count three."

"Oh, I lost two in the raid the other night. Taylor and Pick-ens. Guess I forgot to mention it."

"Just clean slipped your mind, did it? Like you'd lost a couple of steers out in the brush somewhere. Kale, honest to Christ, sometimes I think your wits are about as sharp as a dull butcher knife."

"Boss, I ain't no dummy, but you plumb lost me." The foreman glanced at Sam for some clue and got only a dour look in return. "We've lost men on raids before. Plenty of times. Where's the difference this go-round?"

"You thickheaded ox. If you had sense enough to pour piss out of a boot, you wouldn't have to ask." Banning's eyes nar-rowed with scorn, and it was all he could do to hold his rage in check. "The greasers got hold of one of your men and made him talk. That oughta be plain enough even for you. Other-wise how would they've known about the jailbreak and had a whole goddamn army waitin' with Winchesters?"

"Well hell, Mr. Banning, I ain't no mind reader. We shot

it out with the greasers the better part of the night, and I just sorta figured them boys went under when I wasn't lookin'."

"That's the trouble with you, Kale. You figure too much. That kind of thing has been known to ruin a man's health."

Banning's surly threat brought the ramrod up short, and he wisely concluded that it was best not to try defending his actions further. Sam was just looking for an excuse to beat the whey out of somebody, and if the elder brother blinked in his direction, he might easily come out on the short end of the stick. Not that he was afraid of Sam one way or the other. It was just that if he had a choice, he'd rather fight a cross-eyed gorilla.

When Kale held his silence, the gang leader cooled down somewhat, sinking back into his chair. "If you'd let me know in time, we could have changed the plan, instead of making asses out of ourselves. But there's no use cryin' over spilt milk. What we've got to think about is that the greasers are holdin' either Taylor or Pickens over there somewhere. And sure as Christ made green apples, he's talking his head off, whichever one it is. If the greasers got cute and handed him over to the Texas Rangers, we'll be hung by our balls on a short string."

Banning's gaze shifted to the ceiling, and his eyes went cloudy, somehow out of focus. Sifting the known from the unknown, and holding it to the light of what urgently needed doing, he slowly came to the only reasonable solution. "Kale, whoever they've got, they're probably holding him at the same hacienda you raided. I want you to make sure he never sets foot off that place except in a box. If you foul this up, you'd better keep right on going."

Kale just nodded, needing no explanation. Once more and he would be playing on borrowed time. That was the message, and he had every certainty that, if he stumbled again, it would be a long fall.

Sam's brutish grunt snapped his thoughts back to the present. "Well I'm damned if I see why we ought to bother about somebody the greasers've got. There's only one man we've got to thank for this whole mess, and it's that shit heel marshal.

I say get rid of him. Once he's out of the way, them bleedin' hearts uptown won't have anybody to hide behind."

"That's the ticket!" Kale agreed brightly, trying to regain lost ground in his deadly race against ill wind and piss-poor luck. "Hell's bells, I'd be willin' to do the job just to see the bastard's face when he got chopped down."

"You two make a pair," Ed Banning observed testily. "Damned if I ever saw anything to beat it. If Stoudenmire turned up dead, everybody in town would know who did it, and there's a limit even in El Paso. That's all the reformers would need. Give 'em a martyr and they'll start poundin' drums all the way back to the statehouse. Now both of you pay attention, 'cause I'm only gonna say this once. Until I give the word, we'll just lay low and keep our eyes open. One way or another, we'll get Stoudenmire, but nobody makes a move till I say the time is ripe."

When neither man seemed inclined to argue the matter, Banning waved his hand dismissively. "Why don't you two trot out and get yourselves a drink. I've got some things to think out."

Sam bobbed his head dumbly and turned toward the door. Kale followed him out, amused by the fickle tides that momentarily put him to rowing with the boss's brother. Over drinks at the bar, they agreed that Ed was a very deep man, hard to understand. But other than this shallow observation, they were unwilling to speculate further about the man they both served so meekly. Some things were just better left unsaid.

2

Shortly before noon, Stoudenmire was crossing the plaza when he met Mayor Porter headed in the opposite direction. Although the two men were on speaking terms, neither was laboring under any illusions about where the other stood. Stoudenmire served but one mistress, the law, while Porter had cast his lot with corruption and personal gain in the form of the Banning machine. Like two battle-scarred old dogs eyeing the same bone, they feinted this it way and that, sparring verbally whenever they met, each seeking some advantage before the fight was joined. Though the marshal respected Porter's skill as a manipulator of men and things, he found the mayor an insufferable bore, not to mention the fact that he was something of a windbag in the bargain. Porter was simply scared witless of the marshal, for after twenty years on a lawless frontier, he had grown accustomed to a certain tolerance where men's misdeeds were concerned. Clearly Stoudenmire couldn't be classed as a tolerant lawman, and it was a bit unsettling to meet a man who had some Jehovah-like concept of himself as the dispenser of justice.

Stoudenmire nodded to the mayor and started to pass on by. But Porter had other ideas. "Marshal, I wonder if you have a moment? As a matter of fact, if you're not too busy, I'd like to buy you a drink."

"Thanks just the same, Mr. Mayor, but I rarely drink before noon." The sarcasm was thinly veiled, just the way Stoudenmire meant it. "Besides, my wife is expecting me home for dinner."

"Well land's sakes, man, she'll keep it hot for you." Porter's tone seemed almost desperate, and he clutched at the marshal's arm with a feeble, birdlike grasp. "This is important. Official business in a manner of speaking, and I'd think that takes precedent over a paltry noon meal."

Stoudenmire sensed some curious change in the politician. Nothing he could put his finger on, but a noticeable crack in the wall nonetheless. "Since you put it that way, Mayor, I'll take you up on the offer. But no drinks, just talk. Suppose we try your office instead of a saloon."

"No. Not city hall," Porter said a bit too quickly. "Let's go to your office. There'll be less . . . ah . . . interruption that way."

Without a word, the marshal turned and began retracing his steps across the plaza. Whatever was on the portly little man's mind, it would prove a hell of a lot more interesting

than Kate's incessant whining about the risks he took. Come
to think of it, there were times a man could get a gutful without ever touching food.

Trotting along at his side, the mayor would have given considerable for a drink right at that moment. Isaac Porter was
a troubled man, more than he cared to admit. He sensed that
the townspeople were growing more and more disgruntled
with the state of affairs that existed along the border. They
had been brought to the brink of outright warfare with the
Mexicans more times than anyone cared to remember;
there was no longer a soul among them who questioned how
far the Mexicans were willing to go to exact retribution. The
fact that the Texans were vastly outnumbered sobered them
even more, and it was hardly surprising that few men expected to come out of it alive if the bloodletting ever started.

More significantly still, word was spreading that the
Bannings, along with their political and business cronies, were
at the root of the trouble. Though this was only partially true,
Porter could see that any further problems could easily bring
about the downfall of the political machine he had helped to
establish. Should that happen there was every likelihood that
some of his more unsavory deals with the Bannings would
come to light, and he had no wish to end up as an ornament on
a telegraph pole. Which was just where this game might
lead if something wasn't done fast. The Bannings weren't
about to look out for anyone but themselves, even if the whole
town was leveled to the ground; so that left it up to him. But
it would be touch and go if Ed Banning ever got wind of what
he had in mind.

When they reached the office, Stoudenmire sent Gillette
to see about his own dinner, and they had the place to themselves. Porter took a chair across from the desk and gave the
room a quick once over, like he expected a barrel of whiskey
to roll out from under the corner bunk. The marshal just sat
and waited, an old hand at the game of "out of the skillet and
into the fire."

Porter had a distinct aversion to silence, as if a moment
uncluttered by words was an opportunity lost forever, and he

soon broke under the lawman's stony gaze. "Marshal, instead of beating around the bush, I'll come straight to the point. El Paso is faced with a crisis. Perhaps the one that could break the camel's back, in a manner of speaking. The killing of those three scoundrels last night has unsettled the people more than any other single incident I can recall. Even the salt war didn't frighten them like this. It's just too close to home."

"Mayor, before you start stretchin' for a second wind, why don't you get down to the point. It's beginning to look like a long day on an empty belly."

"To be sure, Marshal Stoudenmire. To be sure. But let me first impress on you the need for urgency. The Mexican populace on both sides of the river is only one step away from being up in arms. It would take nothing more than some insignificant mishap to put them at our throats."

"Like raping another little girl?" Stoudenmire remarked stiffly.

Overlooking the sarcasm, Porter pulled out a large handkerchief and mopped his face. "Perhaps. Who knows what governs a Mexican's actions. The thing I'm leading up to is this. I believe the citizens of El Paso to be in greater mortal danger at this moment than ever before. The Mexicans lack only a leader to bring them storming across the river by the thousands. While we could put up a stiff fight with the help of the army, I harbor no illusions about the outcome. And unless we move quickly, that day may arrive sooner than anyone suspects."

"I'll have to hand it to you. You're just a sack full of surprises." Stoudenmire scrutinized the politician's face for a long moment before resuming. "Let's get our cards out on the table. You could talk till you were blue in the face, and I still wouldn't believe you're worried about the townspeople. Now suppose you quit making speeches and tell me what all this is about."

"My boy, there are times in a man's life when he must set aside the lessons of the past and deal with the moment on its own merits. Perhaps your cynicism is well founded, but is it so hard to believe that even a politician can want what's best for his community?"

"Maybe. Maybe not. Most times when a politician gets to worrying about the lowly citizen, it's brought about by some threat of his own political survival. If that's what you're sayin', then I reckon I could swallow it."

"Marshal, I won't deny that a certain concern for my own skin prompted me to arrange this discussion." Porter swabbed his face again with the handkerchief, shrewdly appraising his adversary. "Just between us, I would even admit that those who view me as being corrupt are not without cause of a sort. But even if those things are true, a man can still have a genuine feeling for the people."

Stoudenmire snorted contemptuously and gave the older man a flat, uncompromising stare. "Whatever it is you want, why don't you just spit it out? All this hemming and hawing won't change things between you and me one iota."

"Very well. To be perfectly frank about it, I was hoping you would have a talk with the *alcalde* of Paso del Norte. Word is spreading that you have done your best to head off trouble, and I have a feeling the Mexicans would listen to you. They already know what you've done to calm folks over here, and a request from you to hold their own people in check would carry a lot of weight. More than anyone else in this town, you have a strong chance of preventing further bloodshed."

The mayor paused, meeting Stoudenmire's gaze squarely for the first time. "Whatever your opinion of me, I hope you'll believe that I'm sincere in wanting to halt this violence."

"Sure, I believe you. Your kind always gets squeamish when they see blood." The lawman gave him a look that would have raised frost on a brass cannon. "I'll see the headman across the river, but don't think its got anything to do with you. If it was up to me, I'd feed you and your cronies to the Mexicans like dog meat."

After a moment of strained silence, the mayor rose and walked out the door. There was nothing more to say. Stoudenmire would see the Mexicans well enough, but afterwards, he would be right back dogging the Bannings' tracks. And if some of the Banning underlings happened to get caught in the crunch, it wouldn't bother the marshal in the slightest. Thinking back to those cold eyes, it came over the dumpy little politician that Stoudenmire would probably even enjoy it.

Isaac Porter suddenly needed a drink in the worst way. The furies seemed to be gathering, and he had fought enough battles for one day.

3

Later that afternoon Stoudenmire crossed the Rio Grande and inquired directions to the *alcalde's* home. The somnolent village was like a hundred others he had seen along the border while serving with the Rangers, and it occurred to him that time had little effect on the casual pace of these people. Naked, taffy-skinned children rolled in the dirt right alongside mangy dogs, runty pigs, and a motley assortment of bleating goats. Women in sleazy, faded dresses tended the dirt-floored adobes while their men rested in the shade, ever confident that *mañana* would bring about a sharp reversal in their fortunes. They asked little of life, expected less, and somehow struggled along on the lean times that were part and parcel of border living.

Watching them as he rode along the dusty street, Stoudenmire was reminded again that at heart the Mexicans were warm, peace-loving people. They wished only to bask in the mellow sun, to be left alone. Still, even the most gentle creature on earth would turn and fight when driven to the wall. Thinking about it, he recalled that Mexicans weren't exactly disciplined fighters, but they were mean as a barrelful of snakes when it got right down to cut or be cut.

Dismounting before an unusually large adobe, he walked to the door and knocked. Even before the sound of his knuckles faded, the door swung back, revealing an elderly man who somehow appeared taller than he actually was.

"Buenos días, señor," Pedro Vazquez greeted him. "How may I serve you?"

"Buenos días, Alcalde." The lawman flashed that rare smile, which made it seem all the warmer. "I am Dallas Stoudenmire, marshal of El Paso. Pardon this unannounced intrusion, but I come hoping we might speak of matters mutually important to our people."

"Come in out of the heat, Marshal. I am honored that you would call on me and always welcome an exchange of ideas with our *americano* neighbors."

The *alcalde* led him back to a cool, high-ceilinged study and courteously offered refreshments. While they sipped hot chocolate, Vazquez held the conversation to idle small-talk, obviously trying to put the lawman at ease. After an appropriate round of pleasantries, centering on the weather and the merits of Paso wine, the older man sat back in his chair and folded his hands. With formalities out of the way, the serious business could now begin.

"My friend, I have long wanted to talk with a leader from your side of the river." Chuckling, Pedro Vazquez tapped his chest with a deprecating gesture. "But I am an old man given to excesses in speech. Suppose I first listen to what you have to say, for I am sure your errand is of no small consequence."

"Gracias, Alcalde. Your concern is not misplaced, I assure you." Then, without mincing words, Stoudenmire came straight to the point. "I am here seeking some way to bring about peace between our people. Failing that, I would hope to arrange a truce of some sort so that tempers on both sides of the Rio Grande might have time to cool."

The Mexican's brow furrowed in thought as he studied his guest. "This is no small thing you seek. Your countrymen are not noted for their peaceful ways, and unfortunately my people long ago lost faith in the honorable intentions of any *yanqui.*"

Stoudenmire's mouth tightened at the blunt words, but there was no denying the truth behind them. *"Jefe,* your words are harsh, but not without justification. Like most men, Americans come in all shapes and sizes, some good, some bad. Yet it is a curious thing that the bad ones are always more visible; that they somehow seem to lead the good without a struggle, much like a tame bull with a ring in his nose. Still, if those same people are shown a way, they would much prefer to live in peace. Perhaps I reach too high, but should we be content with anything less than our people living as neighbors once more?"

"We also have our bad ones, the *bandidos* in the hills But strangely they prefer to prey on their own kind." The *alcalde* puzzled on this for a moment, wondering why the bandits never dared cross into Texas. It was a thought that would bear examination. "How would you propose to bring about this truce? It is an ambitious undertaking."

"Ambitious perhaps, but not impossible." The lawman searched Vazquez's face for any sign of guile, then decided to go whole hog. "The men responsible for our troubles are mostly Americans. This I admit freely. Already I have taken steps to calm the good ones among my people. Now, I will reveal for your ears alone, that I have taken the trail of the bad ones and hope to have them in jail soon. They are called Banning, and once I bring them to earth, many of our problems will be resolved."

"Yes, I have heard that name. Are these men responsible for the terrible raid of two nights past?" When Stoudenmire nodded, the Mexican came up on the edge of his chair. "This is a good thing you do, Marshal. *Bichos*, vermin like these men, should be stamped out wherever found."

Vazquez had watched his visitor closely, purposely letting him do the talking. Now he was convinced that this large, soft-spoken *gringo* before him was an honorable man. Within the last week, he had heard tales from his people across the river about Stoudenmire's efforts to avert open hostilities, and there appeared every reason to credit them as true. Suddenly a thing he had once said flashed through his mind. *There are times in a man's life when he must blindly trust other men, even* yanquis. Perhaps this was the place to start.

"Marshal, I wonder if you would care to join me in a humble supper? I wish to send for my nephew so that you might speak with him. What he has to say will prove most interesting, you can be sure."

Stoudenmire readily agreed, not quite sure what the *alcalde* had in mind but willing to gamble a few hours to find out. The supper they shared was far from humble, consisting of choice beef, various native dishes, and an unusually fine wine. After working his way through a second helping of everything, it occurred to the lawman that Mexican politicians must eat as high off the hog as their American counterparts. Still, the old man was chock full of amusing stories, and over brandy and cigars it came to Stoudenmire that he wasn't being entertained so lavishly without some purpose in mind. Whatever the game was, the stakes seemed right, and as long as he had taken a seat, he decided to enjoy himself. Listening to the *alcalde* launch into another whopper, he came to the conclusion that the old Mexican might just be a match for Doc Cummings. The two of them in the same room would probably be more than a man could take in one night.

Toward dusk, Ramón Vazquez arrived on a lathered horse and went into a whispered conference with his uncle. He, too, had heard stories concerning this *gringo* lawman and felt there was no harm in discussion. Walking forward, he shook Stoudenmire's hand with a firm grip.

"Our people across the river say you are *simpático* to the Mexican cause. We find this a very strange trait in a *yanqui*, especially one who serves the will of the *ladrones* who rule El Paso."

Stoudenmire was amused yet a little nettled by this shallow test. "You are a foolish young man to judge people so casually. Were I working for the *gringo* thieves, I wouldn't have missed." Jerking his chin, he indicated the arm that Ramón favored with every movement.

"*¿Quien sabe?*" Ramón shrugged, gigged on his own shaft and unable to wriggle free. "Who knows, perhaps there is such a thing as an honest *yanqui*?"

"Perhaps." Stoudenmire's mouth curled in a tight, dry smile. "But if you meet one, I wish you would point him out to me."

The young *caporal* laughed outright, turning to his uncle.

"This hombre bears watching. It comes to me that the man hasn't been born who could order him against his will."

"In your own way, *mi hijo*, you have come to the right conclusion." The *alcalde* had been sitting back watching the exchange with much zest. "Now that you have taken his measure, I suggest you tell him of the matter we agreed upon."

Ramón glanced back at Stoudenmire, less suspicious now, but still not wholly trusting of any *gringo*. "Even if you betray us, I see no harm that can come of it. We are holding one of the raiders prisoner, and he has been persuaded to talk. Other than the details of the jailbreak last night, he has also revealed that one calling himself Ed Banning is the head of these *piojos*. We are still thinking on ways to make use of the one whose tongue has been loosened."

The lawman paced to the window and stood staring out into the night. Here was a chance to put a rope around Banning's neck, and it had been handed to him on a silver platter. Mexican silver at that. But if he was to pull it off, it would take the help of this young firebrand, and that might require some powerful convincing.

Facing the two Mexicans, he thanked them for their trust and asked that they consider what he had to say without judging it too quickly. Then in a terse, businesslike manner, he outlined his plan.

Ramón must accompany him to the Banning's ranch and identify the stolen cattle. As a US marshal, he would then arrest the Bannings and arrange their extradition to Mexico on charges of rustling and murder. With the testimony of the captive raider, they were certain to be convicted. Once they had had their moment before the firing squad, peace would again come to the border. There were many dangers involved, and the plan could easily fail. But as leaders of their two peoples they were obligated to try.

The *alcalde* thought on it for only a moment, then drew Ramón into another guarded conference. There was much risk to the plan, just as the *yanqui* lawman admitted. But then peace was rarely purchased cheaply. Somewhere in the midst

of all this violence and bloodshed, men had to begin trusting
one another. If the men to whom the people looked for leadership were unwilling to try then where would it ever begin?
They must place themselves in the hands of this quiet *tejano*
and pray to the Virgin that their faith had not been misplaced.
How could a *jefe* do less and still look his people in the eye?

The old man and his nephew swung around to find
Stoudenmire watching them closely. Ramón Vazquez stepped
forward and extended his hand. He would appear at the marshal's office in the morning.

4

El Paso was just coming to life when Ramón crossed the river
accompanied by two *vaqueros*. Townspeople blinked the
sleep from their eyes and gaped in astonishment. Considering the temper of the moment, it was most unusual, if not
downright alarming, for armed Mexicans to boldly ford the
Rio Grande. Word raced ahead of them along the street, and
by the time they reached Stoudenmire's office, a small crowd
had gathered on the plaza. Speculation was rife as to their
purpose, for it was indeed baffling to see greasers calling on a
Texas lawman. That was one for the book, no doubt about it!

Then someone recalled seeing the marshal cross to Paso
del Norte just yesterday. Suddenly this strange turn of events
took on even more significance. Yet to what purpose? The
reason for the Mexicans' presence still eluded them despite
a rash of conjecture, and the onlookers were more bewildered than ever.

But if the townspeople were mystified, Ed Banning struggled under no such drawback. One of his men had spotted
the brand on the *vaqueros*' horses, the Salazar Bar Lazy S.
Hotfooting it over to the saloon, he blurted out that it was the
same brand they had doctored on the rustled steers. The ones
grazing contentedly on the Banning ranch right at that moment. Only the new brand was still fresh, and any fool would
take it for exactly what it was. The Bar Lazy S doctored with
a running iron.

Banning was a man who believed in hedging his bet, especially in a game where the stakes included his own neck. After pondering the matter briefly, he sent a rider to warn Kale. Under no circumstances were the Mexicans to reach the ranch alive. Stoudenmire wasn't to be touched, but if the greasers came anywhere near Banning range, they were to be gunned down on the spot. Perhaps they were in town for another reason entirely, stranger things had happened. Still, there was nothing to lose by playing it safe.

When Ramón dismounted before the jail, Stoudenmire stepped outside. "I see you have drawn a crowd, *amigo*. Come inside where we may talk freely."

"*Glacias*, Marshal," the *caporal* replied. "I would be the first to admit that such a pack of *gringos* makes my back itch in a most peculiar way."

The *vaqueros* left their horses ground-reined and followed Stoudenmire through the door. Gillette came forward with a glum smile, and after introductions had been attended to, they got down to the business at hand. Motioning Ramón to a chair, the marshal took his seat behind the desk.

"I am pleased to see that you had no second thoughts about out little venture. Many men would place a greater *precio* on their lives."

"*De nada*." Ramón waved aside the compliment. "It is nothing, I assure you. There are many things a man can live with, but fear makes a jealous companion."

As he spoke, the Mexican glanced uneasily at Tige. The big dog hadn't moved from Stoudenmire's side, and Ramón found it difficult to ignore his cold stare. "This one could teach us both the meaning of courage, I suspect. With such a dog even the darkness holds no secrets for a man. *¿El lobo bajo, eh?*"

"The little wolf?" Stoudenmire gave Tige a rough pat. "Yes, I suppose he would accept that well enough. Yet he was named for the one *vaqueros* have learned to respect above all others. *El tigre*."

"*Sí*, and rightly so. Never have I seen a dog whose manner so closely resembles that of the spotted death. But enough

of such things. We have more important matters to discuss.
How are we to proceed with our own hunt?"

The lawman tilted back in his chair, hands locked behind
his head. "The Banning *rancho* lies something over twenty
kilometers to the northeast. We will ride there and conduct a
quiet search for your cattle. If we can avoid being seen, so
much the better. If not, then we may be forced to fight. Either
way, we will stay until we find what we seek."

"¡Está bueno!" Ramón flashed a pearly grin. "I like your
view of things, *amigo*. We go, we look, and if anyone objects,
we fight. *¡Madre de Dios!* You should have been born a
vaquero."

"Perhaps it is good I wasn't." Stoudenmire smiled lightly.
"One *charro* of your boldness seems to be all Chihuahua can
afford at the moment. Now, let us come to the crucial part of
what we do. Suppose you draw for me the brand used by
Don Salazar. Then we will attempt to determine how these
ladrones might have altered it."

Ramón took the pencil and paper Stoudenmire indicated
and slowly began sketching the Bar Lazy S. Gillette and the
two *vaqueros* moved in closer until the five men were huddled around the desk. Once the drawing was completed, they
began experimenting with various ways it could be changed.
But they had more ideas than pencils, and before long, a lively
debate was raging as to exactly what they should look for
once on Banning land.

Some twenty minutes later, Stoudenmire and Ramón rode
east from El Paso, trailed by the two *vaqueros*. Gillette had
argued to be taken along, but the marshal ordered him to remain behind. Someone had to police the town, and it would
never do for both of them to be gone at the same time. Tige
didn't care much for the arrangement either, and as the four
men rode off, it occurred to the long-faced deputy that they
had been left to hold a fort that hardly rated defending.

After traveling eastward on the main road for some miles,
the horsemen swung north on a narrow, rutted trail. There
wasn't much to see in this desolate land, and Stoudenmire
used the time to get better acquainted with the young *capo-*

ral. The lawman found him a very likeable sort, maybe a
shade too formal for a Texan's tastes, but the kind of man a
fellow wouldn't mind having at his side when push came to
shove. Like many Mexicans, he was a little short-fused, and
there was no doubt that he was headstrong. Too much so. The
way an unbroken stud has a mind all its own. A pound of daring in the same keg with fiery temper made for an explosive
mix, one that could get everyone around it blown sky high if
sparks ever flew the wrong way. Still he was an engaging cuss
when he wanted to be, without a devious bone in his body,
and it was a damn cinch he didn't fear anything this side of
perdition itself. That kind were few and far between, and a
man was lucky if he crossed trails with two or three in an
entire lifetime. Yet Stoudenmire wasn't the sort who committed himself quickly where people were concerned. Ramón
had the stuff to make a good friend, no two ways about it.
Something on the order of Jim Gillette, only a feisty pepper-
ball instead of plodding foxiness. But there was plenty of
time, and thinking about it, he decided to reserve judgment
until they had been back to back a couple of times.

Something over an hour after taking the winding trail, the
riders approached a small chain of sandhills, bordered by an
outcropping of huge boulders and mesquite trees. While there
were no fences or boundary markers, the men knew they
were nearing Banning land, and they became alert for any
sign of cattle. As the road entered a draw, flanked on either
side by higher ground, Stoudenmire felt his hackles come up.

Something was out of kilter, but he couldn't quite put a
name to it.

Before he could react, both sides of the draw came alive
with a sharp crack of Winchesters. The lawman rammed his
spurs home, but his horse needed little urging. The chestnut
hit a gallop in three strides, and Stoudenmire hunched low
over the saddle. Out of the corner of his eye, he saw two of
the Mexican horses falter and go down, then he was out of
the draw and running clear.

Glancing back, he caught a quick glimpse of Ramón and
another *vaquero* returning the fire from behind their downed

horses. The other Mexican was spraddled beside the road, obviously dead. But even as he turned his horse to assist the trapped men, the hills and rocks erupted with flame, slamming Ramón and the *vaquero* to the earth.

Wheeling the chestnut, he cursed himself for a fool and rode north, circling the sandhills. The blood pounded against his temples, and his teeth gritted so hard his jawbone hurt. *Why them and not me*? Did some ungodly specter ride with him that neither he nor his horse had been hit? By what miracle had he come through that hail of lead without so much as a scratch?

Then it came clear. *They hadn't meant to shoot him!* They were after the three Mexicans, and as sure as Christ was spiked to a cross, that stolen cattle herd would be off Banning range before nightfall. For that matter, the bastards might already be trailing the longhorns toward some more remote spot. But with the thought came a vivid kaleidoscope of the murderous fire he had just ridden through, and he knew that every gun on the Banning payroll must have been hidden in that draw.

Suddenly it dawned on him why he had been allowed to live. The Mexicans would blame him for Ramón's death! When violence flared anew, he would be caught squarely in the middle, and he could almost hear the angry chant of the townspeople when they denounced him as a meddling fool.

The chestnut grunted as he raked savagely with his spurs and cut cross-country toward El Paso. The least he could do was get a wagon and return the dead men to their native land.

Then he'd see about settling the Bannings' hash. After today they were past due. Way past due.

5

Shortly after midnight Stoudenmire walked through the doors of the Coliseum with Tige at his heels. Word of the ambush had swept through town like wildfire, and a hush fell over the crowd as he crossed the room. The head barkeep exchanged nervous glances with a pug-nosed bouncer, but neither of them stirred from their tracks. Something about the look on the marshal's face made a man think twice, and it took more nerve than they had between them to try blocking his path. Without bothering to knock, Stoudenmire entered Banning's office and slammed the door behind him.

Ed and Sam Banning were startled by the lawman's sudden appearance, yet they returned his cold stare evenly. Stoudenmire's features were ashen, somehow wooden looking, as though he had just cut the cards with death itself. His hooded eyes gave off a flat sheen, like stained glass in strong sunlight, and every fiber in his body seemed taut as shrunken rawhide.

Ed Banning had seen the killing urge in men's eyes before, but he wasn't particularly intimidated by Stoudenmire's flinty gaze. He had faced many mankillers in his day, and he was still around to tell the tale. Fear was what got a man laid out on a cold slab, while caution was what separated the quick from the dead. The lawman had plainly come looking for trouble, primed to kill—the way a bear thinned by winter noses fresh scent. The gang leader never doubted for a moment that one miscue on his part would trigger a gunfight. But this deal shaped up as a cold deck, and he hadn't the slightest intention of being provoked into a showdown. Stoudenmire's death at their hands would serve no useful purpose, and Banning had already decided to remain calm in the event he forced the issue.

"Evenin', Marshal. Have a seat and rest your feet." Banning's amiable manner was decidedly strained. "Sam, get Marshal Stoudenmire a drink of the good stuff."

When Sam started out of his chair, Tige gathered himself, growling low in his throat. The burly ruffian eyed the dog, then glanced up at the lawman. "Call your hound off or I'll twist a knot in his tail."

"Sonny, you lip off to me and I'm gonna stunt your growth." Stoudenmire's tone was flat, deadly, clearly inviting him to pick up the dare. "Crawl back in your cage or get stomped. Your choice."

"Back off, Sam!" Banning's sharp command froze the

younger brother in his chair. "Just keep your mouth shut and let me do the talking. Now, Marshal, let's get down to brass tacks. Since you're not here on a sociable visit, suppose you just state your business."

"Banning, your string has run out in El Paso. From here on it's devil take the hindmost." The words whipped across the room like pearls of stinging frost. "If you're still around when your number's called, I'll come looking."

The Bannings simply watched him, neither man moving so much as a hair. Stoudenmire remained motionless just inside the door, yet he somehow seemed calmer, even stoic now that he had kicked the lid off. But his unruffled manner was merely the cool shell that settles over an old hand as he steels himself for a fight. His hand hung loose, poised at his side, awaiting some flicker of movement that would send it streaking toward the Colt on his hip. He was ready to kill, and they both knew it.

"Marshal, that's a real pretty speech, but it won't hold water." Banning was very careful with his hands, but his voice was steady and firm. "You're gonna find yourself choppin' tall cotton if you try to run us out of town. And I don't think you've got what it takes to shoot us down in cold blood."

"Banning, you've been drawing aces so long you forgot what it's like to wind up on the short end." Stoudenmire saw they weren't going to fight, but he wasn't ready to call it quits. "Tonight I posted a wanted circular on the Notice Tree. It's got Tom Kale's name on it, and the charge is murder. I'm tempted to save the state the cost of a trial when I run him down. On the other hand, I might just bring him into court and let him put a noose around your neck. Sorta makes your milk curdle, don't it?"

For a moment Ed Banning was too dumbstruck to reply. The Notice Tree in the center of the plaza hadn't been used since Texas won independence. Only in extreme cases was a man's name tacked to the ancient trunk, for it meant he was wanted dead or alive. And few were ever brought in except across the back of a horse.

"Stoudenmire, it appears to me your luck is runnin' a mite thin. I assume you're talkin' about those Mexicans getting killed north of town this morning. But it's gonna be kinda hard to hang a man without witnesses. Course, you're such a smart fellow you might figure out some way to bring them greasers back to life."

The lawman's mouth twisted in a grim smile. "I already have. Leastways one of them is healthy enough to identify your ramrod as one of the bushwhackers. Besides, I was there myself, and I'm not likely to forget Kale's face. Offhand, I'd say my testimony, along with the Mexican's, would just about make him a cinch bet for the scaffold."

This latter statement was sheer bluff. Stoudenmire hadn't seen anything but smoke and gunflashes that morning, and even that had been from the back of a galloping horse. Still there was no one to dispute his claim, and it might just force Kale to come looking for him.

The marshal glanced over at Sam, then back to the older brother. "Banning, I always believe in giving a man an even break. I'll spot you gents a headstart, and we can settle this whole deal right now. Otherwise, I'll crowd you so hard you'll kiss my ass and bark like a fox before we're through."

Ed Banning was tempted, but only for a moment. While one of them might get the lawman, he was damn near certain that the big bastard's first slug would catch him about brisket high. And he hadn't the slightest intention of becoming the late political boss of El Paso.

"Sorry to disappoint you, Marshal, but we'll sit this hand out. And if you're bankin' on that tin star to see you through, you're gonna find out it's nothin' but a damn fine target. When you walk out that door, you'd better keep right on going."

"Banning you can cut your wolves loose anytime you want. Makes no difference to me. I'll still get you."

Stoudenmire turned and walked from the room. When the door slammed shut, the Banning brothers breathed an immense sigh of relief. They had come close, perhaps closer than they had ever been in their lives. For the last few minutes,

Old Scratch had been leaning over their shoulders, and his breath had a hot, fetid smell. Like a bouquet of dead snapdragons.

Crossing the plaza moments later, Stoudenmire cursed the Bannings for a pair of gutless fourflushers. While they wouldn't hesitate to shoot a man in the back, they didn't have the stomach for a face to face showdown, even with two to one odds. The thought touched a raw nerve and his mind drifted back to that afternoon when he had returned to the draw with a wagon.

Already the vultures had gathered, circling ever nearer as the sun warmed their supper. The Mexicans called them *buitres*, and the name fitted like a glove. Filthy scavengers who spent their lives squabbling over rotted carrion in a land that seemed as dead as the flesh they ate. Watching them glide overhead, he had thought that it really didn't matter much one way or the other. When you are dead, a box or a buzzard amounts to about the same thing. Maybe one is a little slower, but no less final.

When he pulled up in the draw, the Mexicans lay just as they had fallen. Walking among them, he again cursed the dirty bastards who had gunned them down so mercilessly. But when he rolled Ramón over, his pulse quickened, and cold beads of sweat popped out on his forehead. Astonishing as it seemed, the young *caporal* still had a spark of life in him. Not much, but a hell of a lot more than Stoudenmire ever expected to find in a man carrying at least four slugs.

Plugging up the holes as best he could, the lawman loaded Ramón in the wagon and raced for El Paso. A doctor worked over him until late evening, pronouncing it an act of the Almighty that the greaser had survived. Somehow none of the slugs had struck a vital organ, and while his days as a *vaquero* were finished, the sawbones gave him a fifty-fifty chance of pulling through.

Leaving Gillette to guard Ramón, the marshal had then returned to the jailhouse to think out his next move. With his blood running cold, the decision wasn't long in coming. *Force the Bannings up against the wall. Make them fight or run.*

But the Bannings seemed disinclined to jump in either direction. They refused to fight, and they showed no signs of making a run for it. Like the *buitres*, they were going to wait and watch, and whatever they had up their sleeves would more than likely come on a dark street when a man least expected it.

Passing the Notice Tree as he headed back to check on Ramón, the lawman had a feeling that El Paso was about to live up to its reputation as the toughest town along the border.

CHAPTER FIVE

—◆—

1

El Paso hadn't exactly returned to normal, but in the two weeks since the bushwhacking, a guarded calm had settled over the town. Like a man holding a stick of dynamite with a sputtering fuse, the townspeople waited for an explosion that seemed dreadfully slow in coming.

Though an inquest into the killings was to be held, it had been delayed until tempers on both sides of the river cooled down. Ed Banning had pulled strings to force an immediate hearing, but when Stoudenmire threatened to expose it as a political fix, the coroner hastily backed off. The local gadflies chalked this up as another point for the marshal and sat back to await results.

Mayor Porter trotted out one lame excuse after another for the postponement, but the real issue behind this political infighting was hardly a secret. Stoudenmire was determined there would be no inquest until his key witness was able to testify. As the sole survivior among the ambushed Mexicans, Ramón Vazquez had much to tell, and the gambling fraternity was laying odds that his testimony would send half the Banning gang scurrying for their holes.

After a week of guarding the *caporal* around the clock, Stoudenmire had secretly moved him to Paso del Norte, figuring he was considerably safer among his own people. Ramón's recovery had been little short of remarkable, considering his wounds; yet he was mending slowly, and the marshal had to curb his impatience as best he could. Until an inquest was held, the wanted circular on Tom Kale was strictly unofficial, and he desperately needed the Mexican's testimony in open court to nail it down tight.

Then, as the uneasy standoff entered its third week, the turning point came. Just before leaving the office for his noon meal, the marshal received word from Pedro Vazquez that Ramón was much improved and anxious to testify. Stoudenmire immediately paid a call on the coroner, who seemed delighted that the troublesome affair was at last coming to a head. When Stoudenmire suggested that the fewer the spectators the better, the nervous little official agreed wholeheartedly and set the inquest for the middle of the week. That way people would have to choose between curiosity and their livelihood, which would hold down the size of the crowd some at any rate. Whether it was enough to maintain order remained to be seen.

Arriving home for dinner, Stoudenmire seemed in a zestful mood for the first time in longer than Kate could remember. As she was serving the table, he playfully swatted her on the rump, something he hadn't done since the day of the ambush.

"Better watch it, missy." Patting her hips again, he gave her figure an appraising look. "Feels like you're putting on a little beef in the wrong places."

Kate shot him an indignant glance and moved around the table to her seat. "How would you know? The last couple of weeks I began to think you had lost interest in things like that."

"Lost interest? Hell, I've just been restin' up." Smearing

butter over a slice of bread, he grinned mischievously. "You pretty near wore me down to a nubbin' there for a while. Course, I'm not complaining, mind you. It's just that I thought I'd married a tabby cat, and it turns out I got myself a lady catamount."

"Oh, that's not fair. You're the one that always starts it." Kate's face turned beet red as she toyed with the food on her plate. "Besides, you said yourself that there's nothing wrong with a woman wanting to please her husband."

Stoudenmire chuckled deep in his throat. "And herself, too. Don't forget, it takes two to ring the bell."

Kate had never seen him so talkative. And playful, like a naughty little boy with some prank in mind. Coming out of a clear blue like this, it left her a bit flustered. "My, but aren't you chattery today. Did the city council give you a raise or something?"

"Better than that." The lawman paused in the midst of spearing another pork chop. "Ramón Vazquez is ready to talk, and we're gonna hold the inquest day after tomorrow. Christmas comes early this year."

She watched his sure hands carve the pork chop, her own food now forgotten. "That means you'll finally get the evidence you've been waiting for."

"Not just evidence, Katie. There's more to it than that. Once Vazquez says his piece, it'll force the Bannings' hand and they'll have to fish or cut bait."

"What you really mean is that they'll have to fight or run. And either way, you'll go after them."

"Sure. What do you think I've been after since we came here? Tom Kale is their foreman, and once he's indicted, it'll smoke the Bannings out in the open. That's what I've really been waiting for. Evidence is all right, I reckon, but the only way to nail the Bannings and make sure they stay nailed is to crowd 'em into a corner."

Stoudenmire's eagerness for this encounter was readily apparent, for he clearly saw it as the most expedient means of putting the Bannings on ice. Seldom was he so enthused about anything, and it was as though the prospect of a good

fight had rekindled his sense of humor. But Kate found it difficult, if not outright impossible, to share his mood. They
had been married less than two months, and she was discovering that the law is a demanding mistress. Stoudenmire
seemed like a man possessed, as if his every waking thought
was devoted to the downfall of the Bannings. That left room
for little else—wives included—and more than ever, she had
begun to question the wisdom of marrying a peace officer.

With some reluctance, she had admitted to herself that she
was jealous of his dedication to the law. This wasn't married
life as she had envisioned it, especially since the gaiety of
their courtship had been replaced with his grim compulsion
to tame El Paso. Still, even that would have been bearable if
she weren't so frightened. This stranger who shared her bed
was plainly more concerned about some piddling inquest
than he was with the shaky state of their marriage. But while
she resented that fiercely, she felt numbed by the thought that
the hearing would place him one step closer to a showdown
with the Bannings. Some inner premonition told her that
he hadn't a prayer of living through the fight that was sure to
follow.

After all, what effect could one man have on a town like
this? He was backed only by Gillette and that ungodly dog,
while the Bannings had a small army at their beck and call.
It wasn't just foolish, it was downright thoughtless! When it
was over, he would be conveniently dead, and she'd be left to
do all the suffering alone. Just thinking about it made her
blood boil, and it came over her that she must have been mad
to marry a selfish little boy who liked dangerous games better than he did a warm bed.

"Dallas, we're going to have this out here and now. You
have no right to go out and get yourself killed. It's just not
fair. Even if you don't care for your own sake, you should be
thinking about me."

Stoudenmire just smiled and shook his head, thoroughly
amused by her petulant little tantrum. The thought of getting
killed had never entered his mind. The likelihood was so farfetched that it was almost laughable. "Kate, you're gettin'

goosebumps where it's not called for. Whenever I start something, I generally manage to finish it."

"Dallas Stoudenmire, don't you dare take that tone with me! I won't be treated like a simpering little schoolgirl, not by you or anyone else. And while we're at it, you might as well know that I didn't get married just to become a grass widow before I've even gotten used to sleeping with a man."

"C'mon, Kate. You're acting like a spoiled brat, yet you want me to treat you like a woman. You know a man can't turn his back on a job and walk off. Not and live with himself."

"You would if you loved me! Don't you understand, Dallas? I want a live husband, not a dead hero. If you loved me, you'd take me away from here this very day, before something terrible happens."

Stoudenmire rubbed his forehead with growing exasperation. "That's what I'm trying to tell you. Nothing's gonna happen. Not to me leastways. Why can't you get that through your head?"

Huge tears welled up in Kate's eyes, and she hid her face in her hands. "Oh, Dallas, please take me away from this horrible town. Please. I just don't know how much more I can stand."

Stoudenmire came around the table and took her in his arms, tenderly consoling her. But the more he talked the harder she cried, and it seemed like a losing proposition. Then a curious thing happened. Irritating as her nagging had become, something about Kate's utter defenselessness aroused him, making his breath come short and fast. Switching tactics, he began to kiss the soft hair at the nape of her neck and, after a moment, started fondling her breasts. At first she lay rigid and unyielding in his arms; then she slowly began to respond, and a hungry little moan escaped her lips.

"Oh, God, it's been so long. I thought I'd just shrivel up and die waiting for you to touch me again."

Stoudenmire kissed her gently, rubbing his hands lightly along her thigh. "I know. I'm a damn fool to get so wrapped up in a job. But everything'll be all right now. You'll see.

There's nothin' at the office that can't wait, and we've got all afternoon to ring those bells any way you want."

Lifting her in his arms, he felt Kate nuzzle softly against his shoulder. Women were strange creatures, so easy to neglect and so damned miserable to live with when they weren't being bedded properly. Maybe an afternoon of diddling every now and then was just what she needed. Certainly it would keep her spirits shored up, and that alone would make it worthwhile. Come to think of it, a matinee here and there wouldn't do him any harm either.

But even as he carried her toward the bedroom, he knew it wouldn't change things for him. The job still had to be done.

2

Ed Banning sipped at the whiskey, only vaguely aware that the henna-haired whore had snuggled closer to his lean body. She had been working on him for nearly an hour without noticeable results, and it seemed apparent she would have to go some to earn her keep tonight. Yet the gang boss made no sign that he wanted her to stop, and the girl never once slackened her efforts. She had seen what happened to other whores who couldn't get it up for Banning, and her instinct for survival was too finely honed to take chances like that. But as her fingers teasingly probed his body, she wished mightily that his rod could become as hard as his face. Around the house, the girls had coined a saying for men like this. *Stone face—soft tool.* And with the exception of a wooden Indian, she couldn't think of anyone who had a better claim to the title than this unresponsive turd sharing her bed at the moment.

Boss Banning was a man with a wide assortment of problems, most of which remained obscured behind an aloof, somewhat haughty manner. The outward, more obvious troubles had to do with the threat to his control of the town. He was a lifelong believer in the process of corruption and deeply suspicious of those who advocated the straight and narrow. From his warped perspective, men were greedy, selfish, lacking in either scruples or anything even remotely akin to brotherhood. While he hadn't invented the rules, he was a master of the game and found it well suited to his ruthless nature. Corruption and fear were the tools of his trade, employed mercilessly in his drive to dominate those around him. The strong ruled the weak, just as it should be; the only part of the earth inherited by the meek was the six feet that marked their passing. And until Dallas Stoudenmire came to town, the essential weakness of other men had served him well.

But on this particular night, Banning's thoughts were focused on a problem that had little to do with politics and forthright lawmen. While he would be the last to admit it, the gang leader was a man of flawed character. The obsession with power that governed his life was merely a manifestation of some inner compulsion; the need to be accepted as a man of substance and stature. His origins were of the dirt poor, beans and sowbelly variety, and within him smoldered the effects of having been born on the wrong side of the blanket. Every facet of his life was tainted by the lowly circumstances of his birth, and from it sprung a bitter resentment of both the haves and the have-nots. He despised the masses for their docile fatalism and hated the wealthy few with the passions of a man reared amidst constant want. The gritty flintstone of his life had chipped and flaked with each blow, leaving a man of choleric malice in the aftermath. As if human warmth had been seared from his being, he was a man devoid of compassion, even for himself. The only emotions he had ever known were a hard fist and a stiff prick. So it was that his life had become a mockery of what other men held sacred, one in which there was neither feeling nor mercy. In Ed Banning's world, force of will alone prevailed, and strength was rarely tempered with selfless motives.

Yet something had gone awry in his relentless pursuit of prominence. The most visible symbol of all he coveted was denied him, and without it he remained but a pale reflection of the man he had set out to become.

Never in his life had he lain with a decent woman.

Well-bred girls wanted nothing to do with a man whose very existence was a blasphemy in itself, and since boyhood, his overtures had been met with the casual disdain reserved for those beneath contempt. Instead of the mansion and genteel wife he had envisioned, he constantly deluded himself in the belief that saloon girls could actually be seduced. When even that became too bothersome, he simply returned to the whorehouses. Strangely, he felt some kinship with these soiled ladies of the night, for his own origins were only one step above the kingdom of whores. And although he detested himself for wallowing in such filth, it was almost as if he had come home each time he returned.

But it was far from a satisfying experience. Amidst frowzy women and stale whiskey, he attempted to elude the furies of his personal hell, only to find that a man can never really outdistance the stench of his own soul. That fickle bitch called fate had allowed him to play with crooked dice well enough but loaded them in her own sly way so that he turned up craps with every roll.

There, sipping whiskey and watching a whore sweat over his intractable body, was where Tom Kale found him. When the knock sounded at the door, the redhead hastily covered them both with a sheet, as if modesty dictated that only her partner of the moment be allowed to gaze upon the merchandise.

"Come on in," Banning called. "We're not bashful."

The door opened, and Kale stepped into the room, peering owlishly through the cider glow of the table lamp. "Howdy, boss. Didn't mean to catch you with your pants down, but I've got to see you *pronto*."

Banning untangled himself from the girl and gave her what passed for a smile. "Sugartit, why don't you run down and get us another bottle. Give me ten minutes, and then we'll pick up where we left off."

The whore scrambled from the bed and into a robe, then headed for the door. She was happy for the respite, no matter how brief. Maybe with a little rest the cold bastard would get some lead back in his pecker. Otherwise, she was in for one long, asshole of a night.

When the door closed behind her, Banning's words came like a slap in the face. "You pinheaded sonovabitch! I oughta have you skinned alive. You've got a lot of nerve showin' up here after you let one of them greasers get out alive."

"Boss, you're treein' the wrong squirrel." Kale moved toward the bed, trying his best to look innocent. "Honest to Christ, them greasers looked deader'n old horse turds. There wasn't no reason to think otherwise, and we was in a hurry to get on back to start trailin' that herd outa there."

"I've told you before, you're not paid to think. You're paid to . . ." Banning bit off the words with a sharp click of his teeth. "What the hell are you doing in town? I thought I sent word for you to lay low."

"Sure, I know. But I got somethin' I figured you wanted to hear."

"Well isn't that dandy? Stoudenmire's got you posted, and you come lollygaggin' into town like school had just let out. You fuckin' dingbat, what if he caught you up here whispering in my ear? You figure to talk us both out of jail?"

"Boss, if you'll quit rawhidin' me, I'll say my piece and get on back to the ranch." The foreman sucked up what backbone he had left and met Banning's stare head-on. "Hell, I wouldn't have come in if it wasn't important."

The gang leader snorted derisively and polished off his drink. "All right, Kale. I'm listening. But you'd better make it damned good."

"It's better'n that." Kale leaned over the brass frame at the foot of the bed, grinning like a skunk in a cabbage patch. "I just had me a little sashay across the river, and I found out where them greasers are holdin' the boy we lost in that raid. They got him locked in a shed close by the *hacienda*, and they feed him once a day, just like he was some kind o' pet dog. I was sorta thinkin' me and the boys would scoot in there some night and bring him back to the fold. That'd really teach them Mex bastards a lesson."

"Your thinkin' is gonna get you killed yet." Banning jabbed his finger in Kale's face, and the ramrod backed away from the bed. "I don't want the sonovabitch rescued. I want him dead! He broke once and he'll break again, even if we get him out. They're planning to spring him on us at the inquest, just as sure as you're standin' there. And if they do, we're gonna be up shit creek without a paddle. Understand, Kale? We'll be swingin' on the wrong side of a long rope."

Kale shook his head with a bewildered frown. "Boss, you're gonna have to run that one by again. How can they lynch us for rustlin' Mexican cattle?"

Banning sighed heavily, staring at the foreman with disgust. "The law calls it corroboration. They've got that greaser you missed, and they've got one of our own men. If those two get up in court and tell the same story, then the fact that we rustled those steers will tie us to the killings. In case it slipped your mind, in Texas they hang people for murder. Even if it was greasers."

Kale nodded dumbly, thoroughly convinced they were in mortal danger. The gang leader poured a shot of whiskey and knocked it down in one gulp. Only then did he look back at the bemused ramrod.

"I don't care how you do it, but I want you to make sure neither of 'em gets to that inquest on his feet. If you miss this time, don't bother coming back. That's my last warning, and you're a dead man if you don't deliver the bacon this trip out."

Kale didn't even bother to argue the point. Banning held the case ace, and only a fool bet into a sure-fire lock. The ramrod simply nodded and walked from the room.

Banning watched him out the door, then settled back against the pillows. No damn wonder he couldn't get up a boner lately, what with Stoudenmire breathing down his neck and numbskulls like Kale stepping in shit everytime they turned around. Thinking about it reminded him of the red-head, and he began listening for her footstep. Maybe the little bitch had thought up a new trick while she was gone. If she knew what was good for her, she had better come up with something. His pole needed greasing, and this goddamn

waiting around for her to get it hard was enough to set a
man's teeth on edge.

3

The day of the inquest was overcast and unusually muggy,
a bad sign according to those who believed in such things.
Tension among the townspeople was thicker than ever, and
as the final hour approached, a crowd began to gather on
the plaza. Stoudenmire's hopes of holding the hearing without a bunch of hotheads jamming the streets were fast dwindling. The people of El Paso had as much at stake as the
Mexicans, maybe more if violence erupted, and they fully
intended to be in on the showdown.

When it became known that a time for the inquest had finally been set, word circulated through town that an army of
Mexicans planned to attend the hearing. Like most rumors,
nobody knew if this one was true or not, but it was enough
to make grown men lay awake at night. The town began to
bristle with armed men, carrying not just pistols but a regular arsenal of rifles and scatterguns that hadn't seen use since
the last Indian scare. The stage was set for a bloody war, one
the Americans couldn't hope to win, and Stoudenmire suddenly awoke to the fact that he desperately needed help.

Bracing Mayor Porter two nights past, he had demanded
official action of some sort. The army had already shown its
reluctance to interfere in civilian matters; and on the face of
it, that left only the Texas Rangers. Porter had no choice but
to approve the marshal's request and promptly fired off a wire
to Austin appealing for reinforcements. Once again, the aging politico found himself unable to guarantee the safety of
his own town. Perhaps Ed Banning would raise hell about
calling in state police, but under the circumstances, their op-
tions seemed severely limited.

After a flurry of telegraph messages between Porter and
the capital, the governor had finally authorized his request.
But there was considerable resentment in Austin about the
whole affair, and Porter was given to understand that he had

better straighten the mess out once and for all, and be damned quick about it. Otherwise, the governor would declare martial law and dump the entire nest of worms right in the army's lap.

The Ranger company had arrived late last night on the evening train. This time they were commanded by no less a veteran than Capt. Frank McCormak, and it was clear that there would be no repetition of the salt war fiasco. Though McCormak and a goodly number of his men were old friends, Stoudenmire found them strangely distant. Their attitude inferred that he, like everyone else in El Paso, had his own bone to pick. With so many factions in contention, the Rangers simply couldn't afford to take sides, and McCormak made it clear that, unless violence broke out, his company would remain in the background.

When Stoudenmire attempted to brief him on the Bannings and the political struggle underlying the conflict with the Mexicans, Capt. McCormak had cut him off short. The Rangers were interested in safeguarding the citizens of El Paso, and nothing more. The political bickering among the town leaders was none of their concern, and Stoudenmire would just have to skin that cat the best way he could. The marshal had turned on his heel and walked off, thoroughly baffled by McCormak's contemptuous manner. So far as he was concerned, the Rangers would be about as much use as a busted paddle, and he had the very distinct feeling that it was going to be all upstream from here on out.

The hour for the inquest was drawing near, and as the crowd on the plaza continued to swell in number, Stoudenmire found himself growing more apprehensive by the moment. This deal had about it everything necessary for the worst massacre since the Alamo, yet there wasn't a damn thing he could do to head it off. Worrying about Kate, and Ramón, and how to nail the Bannings had been enough for any man, not to mention the subtle pressure from Seth Hart and his crowd. But wondering if the Rangers were going to sit on their thumbs until it was too late had hatched a quandary that left him surly and foul-tempered. If the bastards weren't anything more than official observers then they should have stayed in east Texas, where the battles had already been fought. Still, their presence alone might put the damper on a few hotheads, and right now, he would take all the help he could get. Folks always talked about not looking a gift horse in the mouth, and in this instance it seemed to fit.

Abruptly, his sullen mood was broken when yells went up outside that the Mexicans were coming. Stepping to the door, Stoudenmire watched with some amazement as Ramón drove up in a buggy, surrounded by nearly fifty mounted *vaqueros*. The Mexicans presented quite a formidable appearance with their wide brimmed, floppy hats, bandoliers crossed over their chests, and rifles resting on the pommel of each saddle. They plainly meant business, and if anybody was fool enough to try crossing them, there would be a whole batch of new widows in El Paso tonight.

Walking toward the buggy, Stoudenmire gestured at the *caporal's* escort. "*¿Que pasa, Ramón?*" Such a show of force is indeed surprising. I thought we had agreed to keep this affair peaceful."

Ramón was dressed in the traditional short black jacket with large silver coins for buttons, and his pants had a faint silver pattern woven down each side. Despite a slight pallor to his features, he appeared as fiery as ever, and it seemed hard to believe that he was still recuperating from the murderous wounds of a fortnight past. He looked like a young *caballero* on his way to a fiesta, though on closer examination, there was something older and infinitely sadder about his eyes.

Leaning forward, his voice dropped to a near whisper. "*Hombre*, much has happened this day. None of it good. The *gringo* prisoner was to be brought from Don Miguel's *hacienda* to Paso del Norte early this morning. I regret to say that he and his guards were ambushed by *yanquis pistoleros*. He was killed with the first shot, and it goes without saying that he has been silenced forever concerning who is behind the *conspiración* among your people."

"Dirty bastards." Stoudenmire's eyes narrowed, and he

unconsciously glanced in the direction of the Coliseum Saloon.

"*Sí*. That is the least of what they are." Ramón's mouth was set in a tight, thin line. "Without the *gringo*, I fear our cause is hopeless, but I am still willing to testify. As for these *vaqueros*, I had no choice. Don Salazar refused to allow me across the river without a large escort. You would do well to caution your people, for after this morning, these men would gladly spill *gringo* blood."

The lawman was silent for a time, gazing thoughtfully at the armed horsemen. "*Un momento, amigo.* Let me have a word with the Ranger leader."

Turning, he walked toward the Rangers, who were standing in a small knot beside the jail. Capt. McCormak saw him approaching and stepped forward a few paces.

Stoudenmire gave it to him straight, without any frills. "Frank, those *vaqueros* are spoiling for a fight. We can go into the reasons later, if you're interested. Right now, we've got to keep 'em apart from the local hotheads, or we're gonna have more dead bodies around here than you've seen since Shiloh."

McCormak studied the Mexicans for a moment, then looked back at the lawman. "I reckon we can help you that much. I'll put it down in my report as a preventive measure."

Stoudenmire's mouth twisted in a sardonic grin. "You're a real sport, Frank. The next time you see the governor, be sure and tell him I said to kiss my ass."

Wheeling about, he returned to the buggy and helped Ramón to dismount. The Mexican hobbled a bit from his wounds, but he was game as ever, and Stoudenmire led him toward the coroner's office on the north side of the plaza. Mc-Cormak quickly brought the Rangers forward and formed a line separating the *vaqueros* from the townspeople. In a loud, contentious voice, he announced that no one would be allowed inside the hearing room except officials and witnesses. A sullen groan went up from the crowd, but nobody made a move in the direction taken by Stoudenmire and the *caporal*. The Rangers alone would have been enough, but with fifty armed greasers right behind them, it was a little more than anyone cared to tackle on an empty stomach.

Jim Gillette fell in on the other side of Ramón, and as the three men neared the coroner's office, Gus Krempkau, the court interpreter, stepped outside. After being introduced to the witness, Krempkau briefly outlined the inquest procedure, then turned and started back toward the hearing room.

Suddenly a volley of gunfire erupted from the opposite side of the plaza and a storm of lead swept over the four men. Spurts of dust mushroomed off the back of Ramón's jacket, and he staggered on a few steps as if nothing had happened. Then his knees buckled, and he slowly toppled over, dead before he hit the ground. Directly in front of him a few paces, Krempkau clutched his gut, his eyes gone wide and horribly white with shock. The force of the slug had slammed him up against the building, and he very gingerly slid down the wall. But even before he touched the boardwalk, his head lolled over at a crazy angle and he slumped forward in a pool of blood.

With the outbreak of gunfire, the townspeople scattered like fat quail, running for the nearest cover as fast as their legs would pump. Capt. McCormak and his Rangers fanned out in an arc before the *vaqueros*, covering them with cocked Winchesters. While they were outnumbered, the Rangers had the drop on the Mexicans, and for the moment no one seemed inclined to push the matter further.

Stoudenmire and Gillette had instinctively dropped to the ground when Ramón was hit, jerking their sixguns in the same movement. But within a split second, they came up firing, racing across the plaza in a dodging, bobbing run. The bushwhackers had split and run by the time the lawmen reached the opposite corner, presenting them with something of a problem. Then Stoudenmire caught sight of Tom Kale and George Campbell hurrying down a side street and took off at a dead lope. Turning the corner at the end of the block, they saw Kale already mounted and spurring south out of town. Campbell's horse had suddenly gone skittish, rearing and backing away as the former marshal fought to catch a stirrup.

Gillette opened fire on the fleeing Kale, emptying his pistol in a staccato roar. Just then Campbell abandoned his horse and turned to fight, triggering three shots at the lawmen. Stoudenmire's arm came level, and his Colt spouted flame. Deliberately, with precise care, he stitched a pattern of bright red dots across Campbell's shirt front. At each shot, Campbell's body jerked uncontrollably, and he lurched backwards, sinking lower and lower until the last slug pounded him into the dust.

A blue haze of gunsmoke hung in the still air as the lawmen began shucking empties and reloading. Without a word, they came together and turned to stare toward the river. In the distance they saw Tom Kale flogging his horse through the shallow ford, headed southeast into Chihuahua.

4

Stoudenmire and Gillette returned to the plaza only to find themselves confronted with an even graver situation. Townspeople were scurrying about the stores and buildings fronting the square, preparing to defend El Paso. Everyone fully expected the *vaqueros* to begin shooting at any moment, and not a man among them doubted that the Mexicans in Paso del Norte would come running after hearing gunfire. Barricades of trade goods and furniture were being erected on the boardwalk outside a number of stores, and already the plaza seemed encircled by an ominous ring of gun barrels.

The marshal took only a moment to gauge the situation, then turned to his deputy. "Jim, hotfoot it around the plaza and tell those nitwits to get inside and stay there. The man that fires the first shot will answer to me personally. You tell 'em he won't like the way I ask questions, either."

Gillette moved off at a brisk trot, and Stoudenmire headed across the square toward McCormak and his Rangers. But before he had gone ten paces, he heard his name called and turned to find the town leaders bearing down on him like a phalanx of scalded owls. Mayor Porter headed the delegation and close on his heels was the full city council, including Seth Hart and Doc Cummings.

"Marshal Stoudenmire, this madness has gone far enough!" Porter's tone was one of outraged indignation. "You're the one that brought these Mexicans into our town, and I demand that you resolve this dreadful affair immediately. I warn you, sir, we won't stand by and watch our people slaughtered like so many sheep."

Stoudenmire advanced on the jowly politician with a swiftness that rocked him back on his heels. "Porter you're nothing but a conniving old blowhard, and I've had about all of you I'm gonna take. Lip off to me once more, and I'll break your back. That's a promise."

Porter swallowed hard, wilting under the lawman's brutal glare. When Stoudenmire saw that the mayor had run out of juice, he wheeled around and started off. But Seth Hart's gruff rumble again brought him up short.

"Marshal, that won't cut it. We're the elected leaders of this town, and we have a right to know what you're planning. After all, we're not talking about jailing a bunch of rowdy drunks. Man, this whole town could be put to the torch!"

Stoudenmire spun on him, freezing the miller in his tracks with a flinty look. "Mister, you've sorta forgot who's callin' the shots around here. When I took the job, we had the understanding you'd stay off my back. The only conditions were that I run Banning out of town and get the Mexicans cooled off. Maybe it's not as neat and pretty as you'd like it, but that's what I'm doing. Now if you'll just button up your pants and quit dribblin' nonsense, I'll get on about my business."

Doc Cummings stepped forward, grasping the lawman's arm as he turned to leave. "Dallas, don't go off halfcocked like that. These men are only trying to help. They're concerned about the town and trying to figure out what our next move should be. Just slack off and listen to their ideas for a minute. That won't hurt anything."

The marshal shrugged his hand off, scowling at the other

men as if they were worrisome gnats. "Doc, I don't have time to listen to a bunch of politicians blather about if maybe and how come. While they're talking, this whole goddamn deal could blow up in our faces. I know what needs to be done, and as soon as things get quieted down around here, I'll do it. In the meantime, I've got no use for a lot of preachin' from these bullshit artists."

When a crestfallen look came over Cumming's face, Stoudenmire clasped the older man's shoulder. "Listen, Doc, I appreciate what you're trying to do. But if you really want to help, you can go over to the house and keep Kate company. I left Tige with her, and that ought to be enough in case of trouble. But it'd sure take a load off my mind if I knew you were with her."

Cummings just nodded, clearly hurt that he was being elbowed aside like some doddering old man. But Stoudenmire didn't have time to spare his feelings. Out of the corner of his eye, the lawman saw that things were coming to a head between the Mexicans and the Rangers. Without another word, he took off across the plaza at a fast dogtrot.

Though the Rangers still had the upper hand, it was something akin to having a tiger by the tail. Outnumbered as they were, the peace officers wouldn't have a chance if the Mexicans ever went for their guns, and that was exactly what had brought the kettle to boil. As he approached, Stoudenmire heard McCormak arguing with a *vaquero* who appeared to be the spokesman for the Mexicans. When the Marshal came to a halt at the Ranger's elbow, McCormak turned away from the *vaquero* with a troubled frown.

"Dallas, we've got ourselves a real pisscutter. I offered to let these greasers ride out if they'd just lay their guns down, but it's no dice. This bird says they'd as soon die fighting right here as get shot in the back before they reached the river."

Stoudenmire looked from McCormak to the Mexican and back again. "Can't say as I blame him much. In case you hadn't noticed, this town's pretty damn close to being a shootin' gallery."

McCormak glanced around the plaza, and his eyes

squinched up like an old coon. "Maybe so. But we better do somethin' *pronto* or these boys are gonna get tired of pala-verin' and start doing some shootin' of their own."

"Tell you the truth, Frank, I don't know what's holdin' 'em back. If it was me, I'd have shot my way out of here ten min-utes ago." The lawman's gaze again wandered over to the Mexican, who was staring at them with a hostile frown. "Tell you what. Let me have a crack at him. Maybe we talk the same language."

McCormak just shrugged and stepped aside. Stoudenmire turned to face the *vaquero,* gripped by an awareness that what was said in the next few seconds might easily leave El Paso's streets littered with dead. This was the crunch old tim-ers liked to talk about, and it was a damned uneasy spot to be standing in, no matter how big a man's boots were.

"*Está día triste, amigo.* Very sad. We share a great bur-den in the death of your *caporal,* and no one mourns his pass-ing more than I."

"Don't call me friend, *gringo.*" The Mexican spat the words with an angry hiss. "You have a peculiar way of re-maining alive while your friends are being killed."

"Perhaps. But your leader believed me to be *simpático* to your cause, and he was not a man easily fooled." Stouden-mire felt his mouth go dry as he prepared to turn the cor-ner. "Still that is neither here nor there in this thing of the guns. The *tejanos soldados* want only to see you safely across the river, and they will guarantee your lives with their own."

"*¡Válgame Dios!* You must think me *loco.*" The *vaquero* gestured toward the coroner's office, where the bodies of Ramón Vazquez and Gus Krempkau lay as they had fallen. "There is the truth of what comes to those who trust *grin-gos.* We keep our guns! Let us say no more about it. Anyone who tries to take them from us will pay dearly."

The lawman knew a dead end when he saw it and, on the spur of the moment, decided it was whole hog or none. "Let us compromise then, *señor.* You may keep your guns, but the *tejanos* will accompany you to the river. That way we can watch each other. If you are truly the *teniente* of Ramón Vazquez, then you will see the wisdom in what I propose."

The other *vaqueros* had been listening closely to this exchange, and they now edged forward, awaiting some reaction from their new leader. But before the Mexican could answer, Frank McCormak stepped between the two men.

"Stoudenmire, you just hold your horses. Before I take them greasers anywhere, they're gonna give up those guns. There ain't no two ways about it."

"Whatever you say, Frank. It's your tea party." The lawman moved back a pace and waved McCormak toward the Mexicans. "Just walk right in there and collect their rifles. There's only fifty of 'em, and I seem to remember you always did like long odds."

The debate ended right there. Capt. Frank McCormak decided to temporarily join forces with the *vaqueros* and get them the hell out of El Paso. It had been a trying kind of day, and his only regret was that he couldn't leave with them. Chasing bank robbers and horse thieves back on the Pecos was beginning to look like real soft duty.

While Ramón's body was being loaded in the buggy, Stoudenmire pledged to the *vaqueros* that his killer would not go unpunished. They didn't say much, and he let the matter drop there. But he knew the promise would get talked about across the border, and it might just hold the Mexicans in check until Kale could be caught.

When the *vaqueros* were mounted, Stoudenmire and McCormak led the procession across the plaza. Gillette fell in at the rear and the Rangers rode shotgun on either flank. Once out of the center of town, everyone began breathing easier. The real danger was past, and the Rangers were no less relieved than the Mexicans. Moments later, they reached the river without incident, and the *vaqueros* spurred their horses through the shallow stream. Watching them cross to Paso del Norte, Stoudenmire reflected back over the morning and decided it had been a sorry mess for everyone involved. Especially Ramón Vazquez.

Back on the plaza, the townspeople slowly emerged from the buildings under a sky that was curiously chilling to the bones. They still clutched their guns, like little boys playing at being soldiers, and when they spoke, there was a trace of false bravado to their words. The greasers were gone for the moment, well enough, but few believed the trouble would end there. The murder of the Mexican *caporal* was certain to bring reprisals. Maybe not tomorrow, or the day after, or even the day after that. But it would come.

5

Stoudenmire stepped from the courthouse, crossed South Oregon, and headed back toward his office. He had just sworn out a federal warrant for Tom Kale. The next step was to hunt the backshooter down and capture him. Or kill him. That was up to Kale. So far as the lawman was concerned, it made little difference which way it went. If the bastard resisted, Stoudenmire meant to kill him, with no wasted motion. With or without Kale, he would still get the Bannings. Even if he had to call them out in public where they had no choice but to fight or get laughed out of town. Justice could be served in many ways, and when a man started out killing snakes, he couldn't be too squeamish about his methods.

But as he strode along streets that now seemed hauntingly quiet, it came to the marshal that he was letting his temper get the upper hand. Though Kale deserved no more mercy than a rabid dog, there were factors that overshadowed killing him out of sheer revenge. Alive and kicking, he represented a greater threat to the Bannings. On a witness stand in court, the ramrod could put a rope around Ed Banning's neck without batting an eye. It was entirely possible he even had a few juicy tidbits to relate about the political shenanigans going on in town, which was another can of worms that badly needed opening. And nothing would warm the heart quite so much as watching the Bannings accompany Kale to the gallows. That was for damn sure!

Reflecting on it, Stoudenmire decided there was much to

be said for the majesty of the law. Without it, the world would be a dog-eat-dog slaughterpen, with the little guy coming out on the short end of the stick everytime. Not that it wasn't much the same even with the law, but at least the fainthearts had some chance so long as there were courts and men willing to pin on a star. There was even something wholesome about an old fashioned neck-stretching every now and then. Strange as it sounded, folks went away feeling just a little more civilized after seeing a renegade take the long drop. Just knowing that the covenant of an eye for an eye even existed was somehow reassuring, and when a hired killer like Kale tried walking on air, it made a man think twice about flaunting the rights of others. Naturally, if the men who gave the orders, like the Bannings and Isaac Porter, got strung up in the bargain, it made the law seem all the more invincible. Godlike somehow, as if nobody was immune from the rope.

Still, awesome as the formalities of the law might be, there was much to be said for a good, clean bullet just below the brisket. It was neat, saved the state a lot of money and, in the long run, served justice near about as well as a hangman. Folks respected a bullet, too, maybe even more than the rope. And when a fellow started chalking up things like personal satisfaction, there just wasn't anything so deep-down gratifying as putting a slug through some badassed jasper that hadn't gotten the message. Especially a sneaky shitheel like Tom Kale.

Yessir, the law was a good thing. Made people mind their manners and probably converted more heathens into straight-arrow Christians than any Bible-thumper ever thought about. But with snakes like Kale and the Bannings, there was a swifter, more certain law. Which meant that the man wearing the star sort of had to play it by ear. Depending on how the cards fell, some might get hung and some might get shot. Like any sporting proposition, you pays your money and you takes your chances.

Chuckling to himself, Stoudenmire entered the office, noting in the back of his mind that the Rangers had just trooped into a cafe for dinner. The fact that three men had been killed this morning didn't seem to bother their appetites in the slightest. The thought jarred some dim memory of the war, and the lawman remembered how he had always been ravenous as a gaunt wolf after a day on the killing ground. Odd maybe, but nothing startling. Lots of things made men hungry, and if killing happened to whet a man's appetite, that didn't make him some kind of freak. Just different.

Gillette looked up from pouring himself a cup of coffee, his expression just the least bit puzzled. "I sorta figured you'd gone home for dinner. Anything wrong?"

"Nothing that can't be cured I reckon." Stoudenmire eased down in a chair and propped his boots on top the desk. "I'll head home directly. Thought I'd check in with you first."

"Well you needn't have bothered." The deputy took a cautious sip from the steaming mug, then cracked a sly grin. "After you left, I took a little jaunt around town, and it's quiet as a church full of bats. Maybe too much so. But I'll tell you one thing. It's a damn cinch nobody's gonna be visitin' Paso del Norte for a spell."

"If I was you, I wouldn't lay any money on that." Stoudenmire leaned farther back in the chair, locking his hands behind his head. "The way things stand now, I'll be on the other side of the river before nightfall."

"Jesus Christ!" Gillette's startled look was one of sheer bafflement. "What in the raw name of common sense would cause you to do a thing like that?"

"Well, for one thing, I want to have a talk with the *alcalde* over there. See which way he figures his people are gonna jump. For another, I've got it in mind to bring Tom Kale in. Tracking a white man in Mexico won't be hard after what happened here this morning."

Gillette squinted, lifting one eyebrow scornfully. "Dallas, I'm gonna flat-out tell you something. You're out of bounds crossin' the river. Even a US marshal don't have no jurisdiction over the border, and them Rurales are gonna howl like you'd just stuck a hot poker straight up their ass."

The marshall didn't appear too impressed with the argument. "I reckon Ramón's *patrón* will keep the Rurales off my back when he finds out who I'm after."

"In a pig's ass!" Gillette snorted. "Sometimes talkin' to you is like feedin' oats to a dead mule. Even if you run Kale down, the greasers'll likely declare first claim. And to get him back here you're gonna have to fight your way across half of Chihuahua."

"Maybe. Maybe not. But I'm going after him whichever way it works out." Stoudenmire lowered his feet to the floor and began rummaging through the desk drawers. "Ramón got killed because he trusted a *yanqui*, and people over there aren't gonna have any faith in our word until Kale's been measured for a box."

"Pardner, I'm tellin' you for your own good, you'd better chew on this deal for a while. Chances are Mama Stoudenmire's firstborn ain't too popular over there right now. If you keep pushin' your luck, we're liable to have to gather you up with a rake."

The lawman grinned in that cryptic way, like he was thinking of some secret, highly personal joke. "Stranger things have happened. But there's one thing you can't argue. If we're gonna head off a bloodbath along the Rio Grande, then we've got to show that the authorities over here won't condone the killing of Mexicans." Locating a box of shells in a drawer, he paused and began filling the empties in his shell-belt. "Besides, Pedro Vazquez went out on a limb to help me nail the Bannings and lost his nephew in the bargain. I owe the old man, and I mean to pay up."

"Oh, you'll pay all right. Don't fret that." The deputy stared into his coffee mug, as though something profound might be revealed in the dregs. "Trouble is, I've got a feelin' you won't care much for the interest they're gonna ask."

Stoudenmire came around the desk and selected a rifle, then a sawed-off shotgun from the rack on the wall. "Listen, we could sit here jawbonin' till hell freezes over, and it wouldn't change a thing. Unless someone goes after Kale, we might as well shit in one hand and wish in the other. 'Cause he's not coming back this way. Not as long as he's able to talk and get the Bannings fitted out for a rope."

Gillette shook his head slowly, searching the marshal's face for some sign that still eluded him. "Dallas, there's times you act like some kid that's green an' limber an' full of sap. Every now and then I get to watchin' you, and it plumb baffles me where the hell you got off to when the good Lord was handin' out nerves."

"Don't get your bowels in an uproar, Jim. I'll be back before you can say scat. Come to think of it, instead of worrying about me, you oughta light a candle for Mr. Kale."

"Well, you're full growed for a fact, and I reckon your mammy taught you what teeth was for when she weaned you. Just make sure you get first bite."

The two men shook hands, and Stoudenmire walked from the jail. Turning the corner, he headed toward Magoffin Avenue and home, dreading the scene he would face there. After the shootings this morning, the fireworks were sure to go off the minute he walked in the door. But when Kate found out he was riding into Chihuahua alone, she would likely pitch the granddaddy of all screaming fits. Already, he could hear her pleading with him not to go, snuffling and sobbing, harping on those lame-brain premonitions of hers.

Women were damned hard to savvy. When they got married, they prayed to the Almighty that they had gotten themselves harnessed to a real man. Then little by little, they tried to cut his balls off.

CHAPTER SIX

1

Shortly before sundown, Stoudenmire crossed the Rio
Grande. The Winchester was snugged down in a scabbard
beneath his leg, and the shotgun hung from a rawhide thong
over the saddle horn. His chestnut gelding was as frisky as a
colt after two weeks on oats and hay, and behind him trailed
a packhorse loaded with grub. Like any hunter of dangerous
game, the marshal had come prepared.

Running Kale to earth wouldn't be done overnight. The
outlaw had a good lead, more than Stoudenmire cared to admit, and had doubtless swung southwest toward the Sierra
Madres after circling Paso del Norte. Once in the mountains,
he could lose himself for a lifetime, for few there cared if a
man was being hunted. Since the time of the Spaniards, the
Sierra Madres had been a haven for *bandidos* and *insurrectos*
alike; so long as a man tended to his own knitting, there was
no safer hideout within a thousand miles in any direction.

Though the lawman had few qualms about the outcome
of the hunt, he would have felt even more confident with
Tige along. The big dog was like an extra right arm, an

infallible sixth sense that never faltered. Without him, it
was as if Stoudenmire had left part of himself behind, and
it wasn't a good feeling. But where he was headed wasn't a
fit place for a dog, or a man either when it came down to
cases. Before reaching the mountains, he had to cross vast
stretches of desolate wasteland, and just worrying about
himself and the horses was going to be chore enough. Besides, Kate needed some sort of protection around the house,
and next to a double load of buckshot, Tige had few equals
at scaring off uninvited guests.

Right now though, he had other things to worry about.
Riding along Paso del Norte's dusty main street, Stoudenmire
could feel the villagers' hostility all about him, almost as if
their malevolence were alive and breathing deeply of his
loathsome scent. Though they refused to look at him directly,
he sensed their dark eyes boring holes through his back. It
was somewhat the same feeling a stray dog has when he wan-
ders into strange territory, not hunting trouble but pretty
damn certain the neighborhood pack is going to give him a
good chewing just on general principle. When he reined to a
halt before the *alcalde*'s home, the lawman felt a mixture of
surprise and relief. That no one had taken a shot at him wasn't
just remarkable, it was downright astonishing. As he dismounted, it occurred to Stoudenmire that it might be a sign.
A good sign, for a change!

Pedro Vazquez admitted him with the haggard look of a
man who has lost that which he treasures most. The *alcalde*
was a widower, and after Ramón's parents had died in an epi-
demic, he had taken the boy to raise. Through the years,
they had become like father and son, and Pedro couldn't have
been more grief stricken if Ramón had been of his own flesh.
But misery was the companion of all men in Mexico, with
the exception perhaps of the land-wealthy *hidalgos*. Those
who survived learned to bear the pain of life with grace, for
within this stoic fatalism lay their only measure of defense
against the hardships each must endure. Pedro Vazquez had
learned the lesson well over his threescore years, and as he
led Stoudenmire inside, his face was a stony mask. Yet be-

neath this outer serenity, he was a crushed man; it showed in his eyes, vast pools of exquisite sorrow.

Ramón was laid out in the parlor, his face frozen in waxlike tranquillity. The coffin was a simple affair, as unpretentious and as lacking in vanity as the man himself had been. But as Stoudenmire stood over the casket, looking down on the dead man's pallid composure, it struck him that Ramón in death wasn't anything like the fiery young *vaquero* he had grown to admire. Maybe death was the great leveler after all, just like the wise men said. Perhaps when a man went under, he left the bad things behind, all the heartaches and inequities that seemed to dog a fellow's tracks while he was alive and kicking. How else could you account for that petrified smile on Ramón's face? If ever a man crossed over with reason to hate a goodly share of those left behind, it was this young Mexican. And the peaceful calm spread over his features right now was a far cry from the rage he must have felt in those last moments. It was damned strange, more than a man could rightly come to grips with. Like something out of a jumbled-up dream that didn't make much sense but seemed real as hell all the same.

Still, whichever way the dice fell, Ramón was long past caring. The warm climate made it unwise to keep the dead above ground longer than overnight, and by morning he would have a fight of another kind on his hands. Earth to earth and dust to dust, the preachers always said. But the fellow being turned into worm meat might see it a damned sight different. Especially since he was planted six feet deep and couldn't outrun the slimy little bastards.

Villagers filed past the coffin in a steady stream, and a priest was mumbling and waving his hands around like a rainmaker in a dutch oven. Watching them, the lawman wondered who they pitied the most, Ramón or themselves. The young *caporal* would soon be buried and forgotten, but they'd still be trudging along in the same old sea of shit. Before he had time to think that one through, Pedro Vazquez took his arm and guided him toward the study.

After seating Stoudenmire, the *alcalde* went to stand

before the open window. Gazing out into the dusky nightfall, he seemed worn and beaten, a tired old man who had
outlived everything that mattered. His shoulders slumped,
giving him a stooped appearance, as if the burden was simply
too much to carry farther. The lawman regarded him silently,
sharing his remorse to a small degree, yet somehow compli-
mented that the *jefe* would allow him to see beneath the
passive mask. Then the older man's bent figure straightened,
and Stoudenmire realized that it had been only a momentary
lapse. When Pedro Vazquez turned, he was himself again.

"I have often thought that the good die before their time,"
Vazquez said, taking a seat across from the Texan. "After today I am convinced of it."

"In my country we have a saying, *Alcalde*. Only cream
and bastards rise to the top. So it is with death. Sometimes
evil flourishes on the bones of those who least deserve to
go under."

"There is much truth to that. Yet I wonder if it is *mala
suerte* or did God intend it that way? Perhaps the good ones
have merely lost the instinct for survival in this harsh land."

"Perhaps. But that is a question best left to those wiser
than myself." Stoudenmire thumped his head with a deprecating gesture. "I am a practical man, *sin astuto*, and for me
the direct path is the most agreeable. When I see a snake, I
kill it, and in time there will be no snakes where I walk."

Pedro Vazquez gave him an appraising look. "Senor, it
comes to me that there is more than one kind of cunning. I
believe you are attempting to tell me something that resists
words."

The lawman nodded, returning the old man's quizzical
gaze with a solemn frown. "*Jefe*, so long as I remain above
ground. I will blame myself for Ramón's death. Had I been
wiser, he would not be lying in the next room at this moment. But while I live, those who killed him will sleep in fear.
Tonight I begin the search for the one who actually held the
gun."

The *alcalde*'s eyes brightened and he came up on the edge
of his chair. "¡*Madre de Dios!* It is what I had hoped to hear

you say. After this morning, I am convinced that revenge is a good thing. When we heard the *gringo asesino* was riding south, I prayed it would be you who took his trail." Then the old man leaned forward, giving Stoudenmire a fatherly tap on the knee. "But on this other thing, you do yourself an injustice, my friend. Ramón was a man, and he conducted himself as a leader should. What he did was done for our people, and your influence played only a small part. Do not reproach yourself. He died fighting for our cause, and few men go to their grave with such honor."

Before the marshal could answer, a knock sounded at the door, and Don Miguel Salazar stepped into the room. Striding forward he embraced Pedro Vazquez, mumbling condolences in a choked voice. Watching them, Stoudenmire decided it would be a tossup as to which one had loved Ramón the most. Then they separated, and the *alcalde* began talking so fast the lawman could catch only a word here and there. But he heard his name mentioned a couple of times, and when Don Miguel glanced in his direction, it became apparent that their discussion centered on him. After a final exchange, *el patrón* smiled and came forward, offering his hand.

"I have heard much of the *yanqui* whose words are untainted, and I am honored to meet you. Pedro tells me you are going after Ramón's killer, and for this gesture you will be doubly honored among our people."

"*Gracias.* But it is not a gesture, señor. It is a debt owed to a brave man."

"*Sí.* He was that above all else. A man of courage." The *hidalgo's* eyes glistened and he swallowed hurriedly. "But you chose a bad night to ride south, my friend. Chihuahua is no place for an *americano* to be caught alone. Not tonight, perhaps never."

Stoudenmire's expression remained firm. "That is a chance I will have to risk. To delay longer would mean losing the man's trail entirely."

"Yes, I see your point." Don Miguel grew thoughtful for a moment, then suddenly clapped his hands together. "*¡Caramba!* Perhaps there is a way after all. Señor Stoudenmire,

tonight you will be a guest at my *hacienda*. Since it is south
of here, it is in the direction you travel. Tomorrow I will provide you with the one thing that insures success on any hunt.
Regardless of the quarry."

Stoudenmire didn't have the least idea what he was talking about, but there was no reason to refuse. He had to spend
the night somewhere, and so long as it was headed south, one
spot was as good as another. The two Mexicans chatted a few
minutes longer, then *el patrón* indicated it was time they be
on their way.

Pedro Vazquez walked them to the door and took the lawman's big paw between his hands. "Ramón will rest easy
knowing that you ride in his place. *Vaya con Dios, mi hijo.*"

Only after he had mounted and pulled the chestnut abreast
of Don Miguel's stallion did the *alcalde*'s words register on
Stoudenmire. Wasn't that something! That old bugger calling him son. He'd been dubbed lots of things for taking a
man's trail, but usually it was closer to sonovabitch. Maybe
things were looking up after all.

2

Although Jim Gillette hadn't let on to Stoudenmire, he was
just a little put out with the lawman's brash scheme. Maybe
the marshal's plan to sweet-talk the *alcalde* would work. And
maybe it wouldn't. It seemed just as likely that the stubborn
German would get himself killed poking around Paso del
Norte, and that would really tear things. One thing was sure,
the greasers wouldn't be real fond of the man who had gotten Ramón Vazquez killed. Expecially when he was the same
one that had gotten those *vaqueros* perforated in an ambush
only a couple of weeks back. Where Mexicans were concerned there was a time to be tough and a time to be smart.
Some men never lived long enough to learn which was
which. But right now, everybody on the other side of that
river had a mean hair up his ass, and it would have been a
dilly of a time to lay back and play it smart.

Still, there was more at stake here than Stoudenmire's

neck. There was a whole damn town sitting on a short fuse, not to mention a deputy that couldn't hardly work up a good spit. Though he had no qualms about handling roughnecks or diving into a gunfight, this deal was just a bit over his head. The only consolation in the whole sorry mess was that the Rangers were still in town, and if the greasers came storming across the river, he would damn sure dump it square in their laps. But what the hell would he do if they suddenly decided to move on?

While he was ruminating on that unpleasant dilemma, Doc Cummings walked through the door. The storekeeper was just on his way to supper, but he had stopped in on the off chance he could finagle an invitation to one of Kate's meals.

"Evenin', Deputy." He gave the office a quick once over. "Dallas already gone home?"

"Last time I heard, he was headed for points south." Gillette's tone was dry, slightly caustic. "First stop bein' Paso del Norte."

"Paso del Norte!" Cummings parroted incredulously. "What in the name of Christ is he doing over there?"

"Funny. That's the same thing I asked him." The old law-dog grinned like his teeth hurt. "Said he was gonna pour a little honey over their *jefe*, and then he figured to beat the bushes for Tom Kale."

"Well kiss my ass! Doesn't he know a man could get killed that way?"

"Your guess is about as good as mine, I reckon. Dallas is double wolf on guts and savvy, but sometimes I get to wonderin' if he hasn't got more of one than he does the other."

Cummings batted his eyes nervously, thoroughly perplexed by the whole affair. "Damn, I grant you Kale has to be caught, but trailin' him across the border is overdoing it. Dallas oughta know better'n anyone else that he's got no jurisdiction over there."

"He knows, right enough. Just didn't pay it no mind." The deputy spat a black stream of tobacco juice in the general direction of a spittoon. "Thing about Dallas is, he don't like

folks fartin' around in his business. Once they do, he'll chase
'em clean to hell and back. I got an idea Tom Kale is gonna
learn that the hard way."

"Well, everyone wants to see Kale's neck stretched. But
tryin' to take him in Mexico is nothin' but damn foolishness.
Right now those greasers figure any white man is fair game."
The storekeeper dropped into a chair, staring morosely at the
wall. "Besides, it's the Bannings we oughta be worryin'
about. Kale's just hired help."

"I don't know as I'd get all bent out of shape worryin'
about Dallas. Tanglin' with him is sorta like kickin' a porcupine. You generally come away wishin' you hadn't." Gillette
grew silent for a moment, puzzling over something that had
only just now occurred to him. "Course, maybe I was a little
too quick to fault Dallas. Appears to me he figured the Bannings could wait. 'Bout the only thing that's gonna put a
damper on them Mexicans is to get the fellow that actually
done the killin'. Lookin' at it that way, I reckon Kale sorta
comes up with a ring in his nose."

Cummings was becoming testier by the moment. "Well I
don't know as I'd buy that. We're facing a bad situation
here, and Dallas has no business off chasin' around Chihuahua. Brother-in-law or not, he was hired to protect this
community, and his place is in El Paso. All I've got to say is
that his plan better work, or we'll all be out on our ear."

"Mr. Cummings, where I come from, folks used to say
hindsight ain't no better'n hind tit. Dallas did what he thought
was best, and I reckon we'll just have to wait and see how it
pans out. Come to think of it, we haven't got a helluva lot of
choice. Once he gets his mind made up, he's mighty hard to
swing around."

"Damned if that's not the truth. I never met a man so all
fired set in his ways. Now you take this Banning thing, for
instance. We tried to keep him from crowding them so fast.
But no, he had to shove 'em up against the wall. Bang! Bang!
Bang! And now look where it's got us."

The deputy eyed him quizzically, wondering if the man
knew the first thing about bringing law to a border town. And

making it stick. "Just offhand, I'd say that Dallas has got 'em suckin' wind. Every move they've made has turned sour, and if he brings Kale in, their goose is cooked. Course, Dallas would just as soon shoot 'em as send 'em to jail. Can't say as I blame him much."

"Well let me tell you something, deputy. He might not get the chance to do either one." The storekeeper hunched forward, lowering his voice to a conspiratorial whisper. "Seth Hart says he has it on good authority that they're gonna try to kill Dallas just as soon as this Mexican scare eases off. Now, what d'ya think of that?"

Gillette had been a lawman too long to get in a dither over small town rumors. "Seems to me they're going about it bassackwards. Why not just have the city council fire him? Solves the whole problem."

"Not accordin' to Seth Hart, it don't. If they fired him, it'd turn into a political bombshell, and come election time, their boys might just get eased out of city hall. Besides, Dallas is still a US marshal, and gettin' him off the city payroll wouldn't mean a hill of beans."

"Yeah, I can see that. But damned if it don't seem like killin' him would stir up an even bigger political rhubarb. I mean, it ain't like nobody'd have to be told who did it."

Cummings tapped the desk with his finger, grinning like a bloated old cat that had just swallowed the last canary. "There's where you're missin' the boat. People just naturally give a fellow the benefit of the doubt. Even a no-account bastard like Ed Banning. They're too goddamn lazy to get all worked up over something that can't be proved. Especially if there's a chance it might get them shot, too."

The deputy pursed his lips, mulling it over for a moment. "From what you say, it's a matter of who eats who first. That being the case, if I was Dallas, I'd get Banning before he got me. There's all kinds o' ways to egg a feller into a gunfight, you know."

The storekeeper's head jerked around and his eyes widened. "You're talkin' about forcin' a man to fight just so you can use the law to kill. That's a little cold-blooded, isn't it?"

"Why not? You think the sonovabitch is gonna be mannered about it when he has Dallas backshot in some alley?"

"No, I don't suppose he would. But that doesn't excuse using the law to suit your own ends. I've got a strong hunch the respectable people in this town wouldn't condone that kind of thing. Not for a minute."

"Shit fire and save the grease!" Gillette's rubbery mouth twisted in an amused grin. "Man, you've got a lot to learn about the law. It's not what's written down in books. It's what men like Stoudenmire can enforce at the end of a gun. Anytime you don't believe it, you just try pullin' the props out from under the man holdin' that gun. That's the day you'll quit havin' law. *Muy pronto.*"

"Well, that's neither here nor there, is it?" Cummings was on the verge of losing an argument, and he decided to pull in his horns. "All I know is that Dallas acts too hastily sometimes, and one of these days, it's going to be his downfall. Assuming he makes it back from Chihuahua in one piece, tell him I said he'd better watch his step around the Bannings."

"I'll do that very thing." The deputy smiled wryly. "Dallas'll be right proud to know you're lookin' after his welfare."

Cummings saw nothing to be gained by arguing further with the contentious old lawdog. Bidding the deputy good night, he walked from the office and headed uptown. Maybe Dallas Stoudenmire didn't know enough to stay at home where he belonged, but that was no reason to let good food go to waste.

Quickening his pace, the storekeeper hurried toward Magoffin Avenue, savoring the smell of Kate's cooking as if he were already seated at the table.

3

Stoudenmire awoke shortly before sunrise and dressed hurriedly. Through the window, he noted that the dawn sky was metallic, colorless clear to the horizon; to the west he could make out the rugged humps of the Sierra Madres. There was no wind, no sign of rain clouds, nothing to cover a horse's tracks through the parched lands this side of the mountains. A good day for a manhunt.

Moments later, he was striding down the long corridor leading to the center of the house. The lawman had seen many fine homes in his time, but Don Miguel's *casa* was in a class by itself. Though they had arrived late in the night, he could tell that a stranger would do well to have a map if he started roaming these halls alone. The passageways, corridors, and wings would be damned confusing if a man wasn't familiar with the layout. Maybe when things calmed down a little, he would come back with Kate and let the old man give them a guided tour. But right now wasn't the time, not with Kale making dust somewhere ahead.

Stoudenmire's gut rumbled, and his thoughts turned to food. Hopefully he could find the kitchen and get something hot in his belly before riding out. While he would have liked to wait around for a chat with Don Miguel, he just couldn't spare the time. Whatever *el patron* had in mind to help him with the hunt would just have to wait for another day. Every minute lost merely widened a gap that was already pushing twenty-four hours, and that was too big a lead to give any man on the run. Still he was curious about the old *hidalgo's* cryptic offer of last night. *Something that insures success on any hunt.* Damned strange when a man stopped to think about it.

Heading in the general direction of where a kitchen ought to be, he walked through a wide doorway and came to an abrupt halt. Don Miguel was seated at the head of a table big enough for a platoon, calmly working his way through a bowl of fruit. The lawman hadn't figured him to be stirring around at this hour. It was something of a shock to find a *grandee* bright-eyed and bushy-tailed so early in the day.

"What troubles you, my young friend?" The Mexican indicated a chair beside his own. "You appear startled. Is it so remarkable that an *anciano* like myself still rises with first light?"

"De ninguna manera, Patrón." Stoudenmire seated himself as servants began carrying in platters of food. "Not at

all. It is only that I fear your sleep has been disturbed on my account."

"Old men sleep lightly. Particularly when all they hold dear is being destroyed about them. *¡Bastante!* Enough of my troubles. I have ordered the *tejano* breakfast for you, pork and eggs. I hope it meets with your satisfaction."

"Gracias, Don Miguel." The lawman dug in hungrily, bothered not at all that his plate was swimming in grease. "It was kind of you to be concerned with so small a thing."

"No, not kind. *Egoista.*" The *hidalgo* smiled benignly. "But selfishness to a purpose. I want your stomach content and your mind strong for the ride ahead. Even Pedro Vazquez's desire for vengeance pales beside my own."

"That was clear last night, *Patrón.* Only a blind man could have failed to observe your sorrow. I suspect Ramón was as much your son as he was that of the *alcalde's.*"

Don Miguel's eyes clouded over, the bowl of fruit now forgotten. *"Sí. Mi hijo.* He was that and more. When the Comanche killed my wife and children some years ago, I became a man without a soul. Then Ramón came to the *hacienda* as a simple *vaquero.* What a man, even as a boy! He was what I hoped my son would be. And soon that is what he became. *Mi hijo segundo.*"

The old man fell silent, staring at his plate as if some vision from the past had been brought to life on its glossy surface. The moments ticked by in utter stillness, and a tiny smile played at the corners of his mouth. Finally, the mist of what once had been faded from his eyes, and he glanced back at the lawman, blinking sheepishly.

"Usted dispense, amigo. Excuse me for looking back to more pleasant times. Today it seems I have nothing to look forward to but the quick death of the one you seek. Now! Tell me how you would go about trapping this *bárbaro.*"

Stoudenmire pushed his plate away and sat back. "I believe he will attempt to reach the Sierra Madres. Chihuahua to the south has many villages, and it seems unlikely he would ride in that direction. The mountains would appear a safer refuge, and if I am right, I will cross his trail somewhere to the southwest. The man must have food, and wherever he stops he will be remembered."

"Your reasoning is sound. It is obvious you have had much experience with *piojos* of this sort." Don Miguel hesitated, searching for a tactful way to phrase his next question. "But what if he reaches the mountains, my friend? The *bandidos* rule the Sierra Madres like kings. Not even the *rurales* dare to travel there. Should this man ever join the *bandoleros*, he would be safe for as long as he cared to remain in Mexico."

"This is true, Don Miguel. Somehow I must overtake him before he crosses the flatlands this side of the mountains. Speaking of that, I fear I must take leave of your hospitality. The one named Kale is many hours ahead of me, and I must find a way to narrow his lead."

"Now you touch on the heart of the matter. This is precisely why I asked you to be my guest. Come, we are expected outside."

The *hidalgo* pushed back his chair and headed for the door at a fast clip. Stoudenmire tagged along in his wake, still thoroughly puzzled by the old man's air of mystery. When they emerged on the front porch of the *casa* a cluster of *vaqueros* waited at the bottom of the steps. As *el patrón* came to a halt, the men doffed their sombreros, darting hidden glances at the *americano*. The marshal returned their looks with growing curiosity, and in that moment, his eye was drawn toward a man at the rear. Looking closer, Stoudenmire suddenly realized that the man wasn't Mexican. He was a *mestizo*. A half-breed Indian.

Don Miguel motioned with his hand, and the breed edged through the crowd, slowly mounting the steps. When he came to a stop before the old man, the Indian bowed his head, not humbly but proudly as a warrior would honor a king. Watching him, Stoudenmire was struck by the sheer force of the man's physical presence. Unlike the plains Indians he had known, this *mestizo* was remarkably tall, with broad shoulders, a deep bull-chest, and bulging, sinewy legs that looked like gnarled saplings. His hair hung loosely over his shoulders, black as the darkest ebony, and his sharp, angular

features brought to mind images of a fierce, predatory hawk.
Strapped around his waist was a knife distantly related to
a machete, and his clothing consisted solely of breechclout
and moccasins.

But the thing that men remembered most about this *mestizo* were his eyes. They were black and piercing, in the way
fire sears whatever it touches, and among the *vaqueros* it was
said that this strange one could see through other men's souls.
The lawman wouldn't soon forget those eyes either. When the
Indian looked at him, Stoudenmire could think only of Tige.
The same inhuman brilliance, somehow bristling with hunger; the eyes of a beast that had been weaned on raw meat
and warm blood.

Like Tige, the *mestizo* also served but one master, in this
case Don Miguel Salazar. Observing the Indian's manner before *el patrón*, it occurred to Stoudenmire that any one who
messed with the old man was the same as dead. It was a
handy item to keep in mind. While the Texan had never been
bested in a fight, he sensed instinctively that tangling with
this half-breed could get a man killed. Stone-cold—and
sliced to ribbons in the bargain.

Don Miguel waited until they had finished their inspection of one another before he spoke. "Señor Stoudenmire, this
is the man who will guide you in your hunt. His name is
Bajeca. If you were familiar with his tribe, you would know
he is a Yaqui. A race of *guerreros*, descendents of the Incas.
Unfortunately, Porfirio Diaz declared war on them some
years ago, and the Yaqui nation is now scattered across all of
Mexico. When Bajeca came to us, he was near death. But we
nursed him back to health, and he has remained with us ever
since."

Turning, *el patrón* smiled benevolently, and a spark of
warmth flickered and died in the *mestizo*'s eyes. Glancing
back at Stoudenmire, the old man waved his hand toward the
distant countryside. "We only see him occasionally. He lives
out there among the wild things. No one knows where, or
cares to know I would imagine. But when we need him, he
somehow comes to us, and never have we needed him more.

Bejeca can track *el tigre* through running water, and if ever a man lived who can find the *gringo pistolero* in that wilderness, you are gazing upon him at this moment."

"Bejeca," Stoudenmire spoke the name with simple dignity, extending his hand. "I am honored to have a *yaqui guerrero* at my side. Together we will bring this pale-eyed *comadreja* to bay."

The *mestizo* pumped his hand once, then dropped it, staring through him as other men would look past a shadow. "Among the people of *el patrón*, it is said that you are *macho hombre*. When a man sets out on the *jornado del muerto* that is a good thing to be."

"The man we pursue will determine if it becomes a journey of death. If he resists, then he must die. But there are reasons for wanting him taken alive."

The Indian shrugged, inscrutable behind a stony expression. "How had you thought to conduct this hunt?"

The lawman gestured toward the Sierra Madres. "Unlike *el zorro*, this man is not cunning. He will run toward the mountains without bothering to cover his tracks. Somewhere to the southwest we will find his sign."

Bajeca studied him for a moment, watching everything and nothing in the same look. "It comes to me that this *cabrón* you seek was wise to run. If he fears you as greatly as you believe, then we will find his tracks at the village of Los Papalotes. That is the fartherest from the Rio Grande a horse could run without resting."

With that, he turned to Don Miguel, bowed his head slightly, then walked down the steps. The old man looked around at Stoudenmire and smiled. "Bajeca is not a tactful man, but he will never fail you. Give him a free rein, and he will lead you to the *gringo* dog."

Out of the corner of his eye, Stoudenmire noted that the *mestizo* was already mounted and had led his own horses forward. Nodding to Don Miguel, he moved down the steps and climbed aboard the chestnut. Without a word, Bajeca wheeled his scruffy mustang and rode south from the compound.

El patrón clearly wanted Kale brought back in a basket.

Stoudenmire had no doubts on that score. And unless he missed his guess, the breed had been ordered to do the dirty work. The only thing that had him puzzled was what the old *hidalgo* had in mind for a certain *tejano* lawman.

4

The meeting had been called to decide their next move. By now it was common knowledge that the lawman was off hunting Kale, and if he were captured, then the fat was in the fire. Ed Banning laid it out in cold, precise terms. Kale could send them all to jail, probably even get them hung, despite the fact that every judge in town was on their payroll. Should the ramrod be returned to El Paso, their chances were slim indeed, for there was every likelihood they would never live to stand trial. Lynch mobs couldn't be bribed or scared off, and once Kale started squealing, the townspeople might just decide to take matters into their own hands.

Isaac Porter was only about half-stewed, but far enough along to be amused by this little charade. Ed Banning had his mind made up before this meeting was ever called, and to say that they were here to decide a plan of action was like the Almighty asking Moses what should be inscribed on the rocks. It was downright laughable, assuming a man could keep his sense of humor while he was being insulted. They didn't want his advice today anymore than they had in the past. They only wanted to make sure his hands were as dirty as their own. That way they could always toss him to the wolves if and when a mob came pounding on the door. It was the oldest trick in the book. Divert the pack's attention with a juicy bone, and then run like hell.

But on the face of it, there was damn little Isaac Porter could do to protect himself. Though he bitterly resented the Bannings' imperious manner, there was no way he could avoid being used by them. They made the decisions, and it was up to him to perform the political skullduggery. They were always in the background, screened by the simple expedient of staying out of sight. Though everyone knew who pulled the strings, it was the mayor standing stage center who actually danced the jig. And that made him a very vulnerable fellow. People had a way of remembering what they saw rather than what they heard, which meant he was a prime candidate for a lynching bee if things ever came unwound.

Yet if it weren't for the Bannings he would still be scratching out an existence in one grubby scheme or another. They had made him mayor, and like it or not, he was bound to them by a cord that could take a half hitch around his windpipe if he weren't careful. Once a part of their organization, a man did well to toe the mark, even if he didn't care much for their methods. Where the brothers Banning were concerned, loyalty was wisely cultivated. Regardless of how disgusting it might be to play the toady for outright hooligans. Otherwise, a fellow ran the risk of claiming his reward in the hereafter somewhat prematurely.

Whenever he was with them, he felt like a man juggling vials of nitro. Sam was the most dangerous simply because he was the least predictable. He was nothing more than a common thug with a brain the size of a dried prune, someone to be avoided whenever possible. Even Ed had his darker side, though he could be reasoned with if a man had a sound argument. But that made him no less dangerous. Those who crossed him never lived to regret it, no matter how fast they could talk. Generally they just disappeared, buried out in the desert probably, and the message wasn't lost on whoever remained.

Still, a man had to protect himself in the clinches. Even if it meant jabbing Ed in the eye when he wasn't looking. The way things were shaping up, someone was being ticketed for a lengthy stay at Huntsville, maybe even a noose. And it damn sure wasn't going to be Isaac Porter. Listening to Ed rehash their predicament, he decided that a wise man would start hedging his bet. After all, there was no harm done if he put out feelers in the other camp. Not if he played it close to the vest and kept his mouth buttoned when he was drinking.

"Kale is gonna have to be rubbed out." Banning's words came as no surprise to the mayor. This was what the gang boss had been leading up to for the last ten minutes. "If Stoudenmire brings him in, we've got no choice. Maybe he won't talk, but that's a risk we can't afford to take. Better men than him have cracked when they came face to face with a hangman's knot."

"Very true, Ed. Very true indeed." Porter nodded sagely, wondering all the while if Banning's last comment hadn't also been meant for his benefit. "The expedient thing is to silence him. Otherwise, our own necks go on the block."

Banning shot him a curious look. "Isaac, you must be getting smarter in your old age. What happened to all that holier-than-thou bullshit about never resorting to violence?"

The mayor made a game effort at grinning wickedly. "An extreme disease requires an extreme cure. Sometimes a man must forfeit his life so that those about him can carry on the good fight."

"Jesus Christ," Sam growled. "What kinda crock is that? We're gonna kill him 'cause he's got a big mouth. Why don't you just say it straight out?"

"Sam, don't let him get under your skin." Ed cocked an eye in Porter's direction. "When our friend here starts soakin' up the juice, he just naturally can't resist two-dollar words. Isn't that right, Mayor?"

"Ed, you do me a grave injustice. Nothing could be farther from the truth. Why, I'm sober as a judge and twice as circumspect."

"Porky, lemme tell you somethin'. When my brother says you're drunk, you're drunk." Sam jabbed at the pudgy little politician like his finger was a battering ram. "And if you're not careful, I'm gonna give you a fat lip to go along with your fat head."

"All right, that's enough horsin' around. We've got more important things to talk about." Ed's crisp tone stopped both men cold. "That's better. Now whether Stoudenmire brings Kale in dead or we kill him only solves part of the problem. The biggest thing hangin' over our heads is the German himself, and as long as he's kickin', we're not safe. Believe it or not, I've come around to Sam's way of thinkin'. Stoudenmire has got to go. Until he's laid out, we're up to our necks in a bucket of shit."

"Hotdamn! Now you're talkin' my kind of game." Sam swelled up his chest and crowed loud enough to raise the sun. "I'll break that sorry bastard's head in so many pieces he'll look like a junebug in a meat grinder."

Ed glanced around at Porter, again eyeing him in an odd way. "What about you, Mayor? How's your stick float now?"

Porter appeared shaken, though he tried desperately to hide it. The murder of Ramón Vazquez and Gus Krempkau had aroused the townspeople unlike anything in the past. They knew the gang was responsible, and if an innocent bystander like Krempkau could be gunned down, then nobody was safe. What was even more unsettling, they believed the town to be on the verge of a war with the Mexicans simply because the Bannings were out to protect their own hides. Graft and corruption could be tolerated in reasonable doses, but people drew the line when their lives and property were endangered. Just as sure as he was sitting here, the mayor knew that, if Stoudenmire were killed in the wake of yesterday's murders, it might well be the final straw.

"Ed, I'm not sure but what that wouldn't be a mistake. Killing Kale is one thing. Nobody's going to shed any tears over scum like him. But killing Stoudenmire might just be more than the people will stand for."

"Then I reckon that's something we'll have to worry about when it happens. Stoudenmire is more dangerous to us alive than dead, even if it splits this town right down the middle. I'm gonna tell you something, Porter. I think that bastard is crazy as a loon. He means to shovel dirt in our face even if he goes under doing it. When you're up against somebody that likes killin' that much, you'd better get him before he damn well gets you."

Isaac Porter didn't say anything. From where he sat, there was nothing left to say. Banning had clearly made up his mind, and if he talked till doomsday, it wouldn't change things by a hair. They were going to kill Kale, then Stoudenmire; and afterward, the whole goddamn town would come

crashing down around their ears. And when it did, anyone
standing close by was going to be sucked under with them.
If he wasn't sure before, he was now. The time to make a deal
with the opposition was before the worm turned. Which
meant that he would have to move fast, before these lunatics
had a chance to start taking pot shots at the marshal.

Later, reflecting back over the discussion, Ed Banning
came to the conclusion that his political frontman was getting weak-kneed. The signs were all there, and if he was right,
it could be serious. Damn serious if the old reprobate started
talking to the wrong people. Kale was bad enough, but if Porter ever started blabbing, then the Bannings might as well
eat shit and bark at the moon. That's about all that would
be left.

After puzzling over it for a while, he ordered Sam to have
the mayor watched around the clock. It wouldn't hurt anything, and it might just be the shrewdest move he'd made yet.

5

Stoudenmire and Bajeca pulled into Los Papalotes as the red
ball of fire in the sky came directly overhead. They were covered with grit and sweat, and a growing uncertainty. Along
the road south they had stopped at a dozen or more native
huts, only to be told the same story each time.

The *gringo* they sought had not passed this way. On that
the natives were emphatic, for it was a much discussed event
when a lone *yanqui* dared to travel so far from the border.
Had the man they described ridden past, someone would
know, which meant that everyone would have known.

Still the lawman hadn't abandoned hope so easily. This
was a much-traveled road, and a man riding fast might have
gone unnoticed. On the other hand, perhaps Kale was foxier
than he thought. If he had laid up somewhere yesterday and
ridden through the night, then there was little likelihood that
anyone would have spotted him. Had Stoudenmire been on
the run that's what he would have done. And at the moment,
he was damn hopeful that Kale had figured it the same way.

Otherwise they could spend a month crisscrossing the countryside before they picked up the trail.

Stoudenmire waited outside while Bajeca entered Los Papalotes' one general store. Maybe if the *mestizo* was alone, he could get more information. Mexicans down this way certainly made no effort to hide their dislike of white men, and it could be that his presence was putting a quietus on the whole deal. Through the open door he could see the storekeeper nodding and flapping his arms around like a windmill whenever he answered a question. The man's eyes were wide as saucers, and even from a distance it was obvious that he was frightened out of his wits by the fierce-looking breed. After a final volley of excited chatter, the storekeeper jerked a soiled rag and began mopping his face. Without so much as a thank-you, the Indian spun on his heel and walked from the store.

Something about his stride alerted Stoudenmire that they had struck paydirt. The *yaqui* swung into the saddle before looking at the lawman, but his eyes smoldered with a peculiar glint.

"The fat *cochino* inside says he was awakened at dawn by a *gringo* not unlike the one we seek. This man purchased food and an *olla* for water, then departed hastily."

"That is good news, Bajeca." Stoudenmire had the feeling his companion wasn't too keen on sharing all he had learned. "And which direction did this man take upon departing?"

The *mestizo* seemed impatient to be off, but he gestured down the road. "This pig of a merchant says he rode south along the road. Yet he made the *consulta* about a trail across the dry lands."

"Then he is headed toward the mountains as we suspected. Is there such a trail?"

"Only in a man's head and his nose. Even a *gringo* can cross the *arido tierra*, but not without much difficulty."

"*¿Quantos los Sierra Madres?*" The lawman pointed toward the distant mountains. "How far across the bad lands?"

Bajeca shrugged, seemingly bored with the incessant questions. "*Quien sabe. Todo día.* Perhaps a day. Perhaps more. Much depends on the man and the horse he rides."

"And what of the horse our friend rides? Did the *mercante* relate the condition of his mount?"

"*Sí*. The fat one says that the *caballo del gringo* had been ridden hard and would most certainly collapse unless treated gently." The *mestizo* cast Stoudenmire a scornful look. "While we talk, the *yanqui* filth moves farther from our reach. ¡*Andale*! Let us ride before he eludes us forever."

Bajeca jerked his mustang around and kicked him in the ribs. The lawman was only a few strides behind, and they trotted southward in the noonday sun. Thinking back over what they had learned, Stoudenmire estimated that Kale was probably five hours ahead of them. Six at the outside. More to the point, he was riding a jaded horse, and it was a cinch he couldn't push the animal over the wastelands this side of the mountains. Most likely he figured no one was on his trail at this point and wouldn't risk killing his horse. Maybe he would even hole up somewhere during the heat of the day. If they could somehow cut his sign, there was every likelihood they could close the gap by nightfall. The other side of the coin wasn't pleasant to consider. By morning Kale would be in the mountains, and tracking him there was a foolhardy proposition any way a man sliced it.

Once they were out of sight of the store, Bajeca left the road and began casting in ever widening circles over the broken ground to the west. Kale wouldn't have headed for the mountains until he was sure no one could see him, and this was as good a spot to start as any. Within a quarter-hour the *mestizo* found sign and signaled Stoudenmire. The lawman had only to look at the tracks, and he knew they were on the right trail at last. Yesterday, after Kale had spurred out of El Paso, he had inspected the hoofprints carefully. Two caulks had been built up more than usual on the inside of a back shoe, and it left a distinctive imprint. This track matched it perfectly. The road south had been too heavily traveled to make out one hoofprint from another, but there was no doubt in his mind now. He nodded to Bajeca, and they struck out at a steady lope headed due west.

The earth was sandy in most places, with clumps of

stunted mesquite and yucca scattered over the countryside, all of which made tracking fairly simple. There wasn't a tree worthy of the name for miles around, and in the distance they could see the Sierra Madres range climbing skyward from the desert floor. The terrain grew more hostile as the afternoon wore on, and the sun hammered down with a ferocity that was unlike any heat Stoudenmire had ever known. Bajeca took it all in stride, seemingly oblivious to anything save the tracks stretching westward before them. But the lawman felt as though every ounce of sweat in his body had been drained off, leaving him as dry and parched as a weathered slab of rawhide.

Surprisingly, there was no sign that Kale had any intention of halting to rest his mount. The tracks showed that the horse was nearly spent, dragging his hooves through the clutching grip of the sand. Occasionally the rider had dismounted, walking a ways to give the animal a breather, but it was all too clear that Kale meant to cross this desolate wilderness before the day was out. The two hunters held to a grueling pace, taxing the endurance of their own mounts to the limit. They were gaining, and each time the trail showed signs of freshening their spirits climbed. But they couldn't slacken the pace or allow time for even a brief rest. Kale was still running scared, and if he was to be caught, it might just be now or never.

Through the afternoon they trudged on, following tracks that deviated only to skirt stands of giant saguaro, prickly pear, and Spanish bayonet. Rattlesnakes, tiny desert rodents, and a startling variety of lizards were the only life they saw stirring, and along toward sundown it became apparent that there was small likelihood of overtaking the hunted man. As dusk settled over the vast emptinesss surrounding them, the two men decided to call it quits for the night. There was no sense in going on and running the risk of losing Kale's tracks in the dark. Better to wait for first light and put on a final burst of speed in the hope they could close the gap before he reached the sanctuary of the mountains.

They halted to make camp in the foothills bordering the

Sierra Madres. Here the land was a jagged upheaval of deep canyons, arroyos, and treacherous barrancas, all the more reason not to chance traveling at night. Although water was to be found only during the spring rains, their *ollas* were still half-full, and they could at least afford the luxury of quenching their thirst. What remained would go for their horses, to prepare them for the sprint that would come with false dawn.

Stoudenmire had just begun loosening the straps on the pack horse when he heard Bajeca grunt in that odd way Indians use when they run up on something unexpected. Turning, he saw the *mestizo* staring off toward a distant hill at a somewhat higher elevation. Though dusk had fallen there was still a murky half-light in the sky, and he could just make out a stand of gnarled juniper trees on the hillside. There wasn't anything strange in that, and for a moment he thought the breed must be having a bit of fun at his expense. Indians had a peculiar sense of humor, and they weren't above a practical joke on occasion. Then he took a closer look and saw a slight movement among the trees. Rubbing his eyes, he peered into the gloomy twilight, and any doubts fast went by the boards. A wispy tendril of smoke floated skyward through the stand of junipers.

Tom Kale had just played out his string!

Clearly he was on the back slope of the hill and had built a small fire in the belief that there wasn't anything but coyotes and gila monsters within miles of his camp. It wouldn't be easy crossing this nightmarish terrain in the dark, but with any luck at all they would have him trussed up like a yearling steer before the stars came out.

Moving up to stand beside Bajeca, the lawman nodded toward the hill. "It appears the pale-eyed *diablo* has been brought to bay."

The *mestizo*'s eyes remained fastened on the smoke. "An animal being hunted is allowed no mistakes. This one was cursed by a *bruja* even before he started."

"Perhaps it is so." Stoudenmire paused, watching the Indian closely. "Bear in mind, he is to be taken alive unless there is no other way."

Bajeca's stoic features gave no hint of what he was thinking. Without a word he strode to his horse and pulled an ancient Henry repeater from behind the saddle. Stoudenmire thought of saying something else, but gave it up as a waste of breath. Walking to the chestnut, he jerked the scattergun and quickly checked the loads. After a few moments discussion, the two men separated and melted into the darkness. Bajeca would circle in from the south, and the lawman would approach from the north. Once in position, they would sneak up and try to jump the man as he slept.

Working his way through a series of arroyos and rock studded hogbacks, Stoudenmire spent the next hour in a cautious advance. After skinning both knees and a set of knuckles, he was worming his way up the hillside when the dull boom of a pistol shattered the inky stillness. No mistaking it, the shot had come from a Colt and not a Henry repeater. Whatever was happening on the other side of that slope, Kale had gotten in the first lick.

Suddenly the night was split by an ungodly scream of sheer, animal terror. Then just as quickly all went still, and the lawman could feel a vagrant breeze cooling the sweat on his forehead. Wondering if Bajeca had met his match, Stoudenmire scrambled up the hill, trying to make as little noise as possible. Within moments he topped the rise and plowed down the other side, cocking both hammers on the shotgun as he skidded through the dusty soil. Moving cautiously now, he eased through another stand of juniper and tangled underbrush, gliding silently from tree to tree. Abruptly he broke out into a small clearing and froze dead in his tracks.

Beside a crackling little fire sat Bajeca, calmly wiping his knife clean on Kale's shirt. Glancing up, he grinned like a playful wolf and lifted Kale's severed head from the ground.

"A gift for *el patrón*. One *gringo pistolero* who will kill no more."

CHAPTER SEVEN

1

Stoudenmire rode into Paso del Norte just before noon two days later. Since there was no need to push themselves or their horses further, the lawman had set a leisurely pace on the trip back from the mountains. The chase was over, and the bloody sack hanging from Bajeca's saddle horn made it unnecessary to reach El Paso with any haste. Tom Kale's death had turned the clock back almost to where he had started, for without the ramrod's testimony, there wasn't much to be gained by dragging the Bannings into court. The marshal had thought about it plenty in the last couple of days, roundly cursing the way fate sometimes bollixed up a man's best shot. It was a bitter pill to swallow, but there just weren't any witnesses left. First the rustler captured in the raid on Don Miguel's *hacienda*, then Ramón, and now Kale. People who had the goods on the Bannings somehow seemed to wind up stone cold and six feet under. It was a sorry goddamn mess, no two ways about it.

When Stoudenmire and the *mestizo* had ridden into the *rancho* the evening before, Don Miguel insisted he spend the night. They had much to celebrate, *el patrón* announced, and he promptly ordered a royal *banquete* in honor of the successful hunt. After presenting his gory trophy, Bajeca had quietly disappeared. Clearly he preferred the solitude of the wilderness to a Mexican shindig, and Stoudenmire couldn't fault him there. The lawman wasn't in a particularly festive mood himself, what with being fresh out of witnesses. But he had little choice in the matter since everyone on the place took to addressing him as *compadre*.

Damned if a man could figure these people out. Only a few days ago, the *alcalde* started calling him son, and now he had been appointed sidekick to a whole crew of Mex cowhands. That was heady stuff, and he could see how the *hidalgos* had made a good thing for themselves by playing on the herd instinct of their people.

Kale's head was mounted on a pole in the courtyard and anyone who could still fog a mirror filed past to have a look, women and kids included. The *vaqueros* swarmed around Stoudenmire throughout the entire night, pumping his hand till it was sore. He was *macho hombre*, the man who had avenged the murder of their young *caporal*, and from this night forward, his name would be honored among the people of Don Miguel. Somehow Stoudenmire took it all in stride, and even managed to loosen up a bit after a few shots of tequila. But Kale's swollen eyes staring down on the festivities played hell with a man's appetite, no matter how much firewater he downed. The lawman ignored the food and stuck to drinking, all the while wishing there were some way to wind that head up and let it speak its piece in a courtroom.

Thinking back on it as he reined to a stop before the *alcalde*'s house, Stoudenmire seemed to recall having held a conversation with the head sometime during the night. But it was all a little muddled, and he couldn't remember exactly what Kale had said. If anything. That tequila was wicked stuff, probably the very drink people had in mind when they started talking about popskull. Anytime it made a stray head start popping its jaws, there was damn sure more to it than a fellow might suspect. But what the hell, he was among friends. And near as he could recollect, they had listened to the conversation like a flock of stewed owls anyway.

Pedro Vazquez threw open the door at his knock and embraced him with a great show of affection. The *alcalde* had already heard about the outcome of the manhunt, as had everyone in Paso del Norte. Ramón's killer had been tracked down and executed, which was the kind of justice people understood best; and so far as the old man was concerned, Stoudenmire wasn't far shy from walking on water.

Vazquez ordered a lavish meal in his honor, then made him sit down and relate every detail of the chase. When the lawman came to the part about finding Bajeca with Kale's severed head, the *alcalde*'s eyes glistened brightly, and for a minute Stoudenmire thought he was going to jump up and shout *¡Ole!* But the aging politico merely nodded with vast approval and listened attentively as the Texan concluded with the highlights of Don Salazar's impromptu fiesta. When he finished, Vazquez chuckled happily and slapped his knee.

"*¡Madre mio!* I would have given much to see that *monfeta*'s head on a pole." Then he darted a sheepish glance at the lawman. "Do not be offended by our barbaric ways, *amigo*. We Mexicans are a peaceful race, but even the *santos* might become bloodthirsty if their loved ones were being slaughtered like mad dogs."

"My only regret, *jefe*, is that the head belonged to Kale instead of the man named Banning. But that is a problem I will face tomorrow. Tell me now of what happens between our people during my absence."

"Absolutely nothing, my friend." The old man scratched his head as if studying an unusually complicated riddle. "Trade has come to a standstill, but other than that there have been no *incidentes*. Not even one. It surpasses all understanding."

Stoudenmire found it equally bewildering, even unsettling in some curious way. "That is more than I had hoped for. I expected the pursuit of Ramón's killer to calm the more reasonable among our people, but there are many hotheads on both sides of the river. Perhaps the *salvajes* among us tire of fighting after all."

"Perhaps. Yet it is known that a stillness always moves ahead of the storm. Pardon an old man's *cinismo*, but I fear that even a slight rupture would once again set the people at one another's throats."

"*Sí*, there is truth in that. Though the one who must enforce the law sometimes finds himself wishing it were not so."

"You are a young man, and it is only natural that you would wish away the bad. I have lived much too long for such things. Occasionally I can deceive myself into believing that the human race is human after all, but only for a moment. Late at night when I face my God and myself, I must admit that brotherhood is a false dream echoed by false prophets.

"You paint a bleak picture, *anciano*." Stoudenmire tapped the star pinned on his shirt. "Perhaps if men like myself kill enough of the evil ones, there will one day be peace over this land."

The *alcalde* chortled skeptically. "You had best start with the women, my friend. Only when there are none left to bear sons will we eliminate the greed that drives men to kill. The Spaniards took this land from the *indios*. The *juaristas* took it from the *españols*. And now the *gringos* would take it from my people. There is no end. Only change."

"You are no doubt correct, *jefe*. Still there are many who would prefer to live in peace. Otherwise, they would not hire men like me to rid the world of lice. Perhaps the day will yet come when the good ones can set their *diferencias* aside and live in harmony."

"Only a foolish man would cease to pray for such things. To abandon all hope is to renounce *Jesucristo* in the same breath." Pedro Vazquez's deadened eyes belied his words, and it occurred to the lawman that Ramon's death had turned the old man into a devout cynic.

"I am not a religious man, but in my own way I help *Padrenuestro* along." Stoudenmire rose and settled his gunbelt in place. "Now I must leave you. There are those across the river who grow anxious for my return."

Vazquez came erect and shook his hand warmly. "What will you do now, *mi hijo?* All who could have helped you have been silenced forever."

The lawman grinned. "I will do what it is that I do best, *jefe*. Kill a few more of the evil ones."

"Excelente! There is always room in the graveyards for those who prey on the weak. *Buena fortuna*, my young friend. Walk lightly and *vaya con Dios*." The *alcalde's* eyes twinkled and a sardonic smile spread over his brown features. *"Y el diablo* if need be."

Ten minutes later Stoudenmire nudged the gelding into the water and forded the Rio Grande. For no particular reason it passed through his mind that Pedro Vazquez was a man who had lost his grip on his own soul. The old Mexican no longer believed in anything, least of all himself. Losing faith in God was one thing, that happened to lots of men who still somehow managed to toe the mark. But when a man lost faith in himself, he was treading on a real hellish piece of quicksand.

The marshal's hand lightly brushed over the holstered Colt, finding curious reassurance in the cold metal. There were some things a man never lost faith in, no matter how troublesome times became.

2

People along San Antonio Street stopped to stare as the lawman rode past. Behind him Stoudenmire could hear their excited chattering, and as he neared the plaza, a small crowd had formed in his wake. They appeared neither pleased nor distressed by his return; their attention centered solely on the fate of Tom Kale. Everyone knew the marshal would come back, and seeing him in the flesh only piqued their curiosity all the more. What they really wanted to know were the particulars of his widely discussed manhunt in Old Mexico.

Presumably Stoudenmire had caught up with Kale; that much was taken for granted. But the wanted man wasn't strapped across the marshal's packhorse, and that raised questions of an even more intriguing nature. Had he killed the Banning ramrod and buried him across the border? Or had Kale somehow outwitted him, maybe even outshot him, and reached the interior safely? Both possibilities had an appeal all their own, and the crowd batted them back and forth as if Stoudenmire weren't anywhere within spitting distance.

The lawman wasn't especially interested one way or the other, and he simply ignored them, reining the chestnut catty-cornered across the plaza. He was so tired he felt like he had been run through an ore crusher; over two hundred miles in less than three days was enough to wear any man's tailbone down to the nubbin. Yet physical weariness was only part of the dull ache that rode with him. Tom Kale's death had been a bitter disappointment and returning without a witness against the Bannings only rubbed salt in an already festered sore. Maybe if it had been he who killed Kale, it wouldn't have galled so much. But he felt like he had just been along for the ride, and the scenery damn sure wasn't anything to write home about.

The crowd was still hard on his heels, and their curiosity had been whetted to the point that one man finally worked up the gumption to address Stoudenmire directly. "Marshal, if it ain't too much trouble, we'd be obliged to know what happened over there."

"Mr. Kale won't be coming back." Stoudenmire didn't bother looking at them. Instead, he kicked the chestnut into a trot and left the crowd gawking at his broad back.

But his cryptic answer was clear enough, if somewhat short on details. *Tom Kale had gone under!* How or where wasn't all that important, not at the moment. The thing that mattered was that Stoudenmire had returned, and the wanted man was dog meat. The news swept through El Paso like wildfire, cresting from building to building as if fanned by a hot wind. *Dallas Stoudenmire had pickled the fastest gun in town, and the Bannings were next!*

The marshal didn't give a good goddamn what they thought. By tonight it would be all over town how Kale had actually died, and that would really give them something to talk about. Maybe it would even put the fear of God in some of Banning's cutthroats and set them to making tracks for parts unknown. As for the Bannings themselves, they might just drop around to shake his hand. Kale's death had damn sure gotten them off the hook, and unless he missed his guess, the Coliseum would start serving drinks on the house in about ten minutes. Cursing under his breath, Stoudenmire dismounted in front of the jail and looked up to see Gillette hurrying across the plaza.

The lanky deputy ambled to a halt and eyed him critically. "Well I see you made it back. But damned if you don't look like somebody rolled you over a cliff in a gunnysack."

Stoudenmire tied the horses to a hitch rack and smiled tightly. "Jim, that's pretty much how I feel. Either I'm not used to sittin' a saddle three days straight, or else my rump's gone soft with city living."

"Probably a little bit of both." Gillette craned his long neck around and gave the packhorse a quick once over. "See you didn't bring Kale back after all. Don't tell me now, lemme guess. The Rurales have got him, and they've done thrown away the key."

"Matter of fact, I didn't see a Rurale the whole time I was gone." The lawman grunted as Gillette's wiseass grin evaporated. "C'mon, let's get in out of the heat, and I'll tell you all about a sneaky half-breed I've been keepin' company with."

Once inside, Stoudenmire got himself a cup of coffee, then settled down behind the desk. Skipping minor details, he briefly sketched out what had happened across the river, winding it up with a step by step account of the manhunt's grisly finish. Gillette appeared speechless for a moment, and the lawman chuckled to himself. Anything that could silence this old turkey-gobbler must be hair-raising enough for the best of them.

"Jeeesus Christ!" The deputy looked like a man with a harelip trying to quote scripture. "That's the god-damnedest thing I ever heard tell of. Them bastards sorta play for keeps, don't they?"

"Yeah, I reckon you could say that. They sure as hell snuffed out our last witness against the Bannings, and that's about as permanent as you can get. Looks to me like we're right back where we started."

"Noooo. Not just exactly, that is." Gillette rubbed the back of his neck, and his forehead wrinkled in a frown. "Way I hear it, the Bannings are about half-froze to lift your scalp. So it's just likely you might've smoked 'em out in the open after all."

Stoudenmire's mouth cracked in a tight smile, and the weariness seemed to drain out of his face. "Well now, that's a horse of another color, sure enough. Did you happen to hear when they would make a try, or how they'd go about it?"

"Nope. Just heard that Ed Banning's been kickin' up dust like a pony going off in four directions. Don't take much savvy to figure out how they'll try it, though. Their kind always comes at a man from behind."

"I expect you're right. But it doesn't make much difference one way or the other. Just so long as we can force 'em to show their hand, I won't be too particular. Where'd you run across a juicy tidbit like that, anyway?"

"Well it starts to get a little dicey right about there." Gillette absently twirled the ends of his mustache and cocked one eye. "Doc Cummings got it from Seth Hart who got it from somewheres else. Accordin' to Doc it came straight from the horse's mouth, or pretty damn close thereabouts."

The lawman grimaced and shook his head skeptically. "Hell, I thought you'd got it from one of those unimpeachable sources the newspapers are always carryin' on about. Listening to Doc talk is like pourin' shit through a tin horn. No matter how it comes out, there's not a clear note in the bunch."

"Maybe. But I've been hearin' the same story all over town. The word's around that Banning's not just bowed up anymore. You got him plumb spooked and from where he sits, it's you or them. Folks allow that he don't mean to leave any loose ends this time, either."

"Jim, it sounds to me like someone just made an educated guess and started themselves a fair-sized rumor. Hart and

Cummings can speculate all they want, but that's not gonna get the Bannings off their duff and into the street."

The old lawdog splattered the spittoon with a brown wad and licked his mustache. "When it comes to hardheaded, you could spot a jackass a city block and win going away."

Stoudenmire blew steam off his coffee and mulled it over for a minute. "I'm not sayin' it won't happen. Where there's smoke, there's always fire. Even if it's only a little one. I just don't happen to think the Bannings are rattled enough to start doing their own dirty work. Not yet, at any rate. If they try anything, it'll come from one of those knuckleheads on their payroll."

"Damnation, that's all I've been tryin' to say! Somebody's gonna be layin' to kill you. What the hell difference does it make who it is?"

"None, I suppose. Except that the only way we're gonna get the Bannings is to rawhide 'em into a gunfight." The marshal considered that at some length before he looked back at Gillette. "What about Hart and his crowd? How are they taking all this?"

The deputy's mouth split in a big, horsey grin. "Well, I'll tell you. 'Pears to me they don't know whether to shit or go blind. First they got a case of the hives 'cause you lit out after Kale. Then they started bendin' my ear about Banning plannin' to catch you in a dark alley. Sometimes I get to wonderin' if they've still got to have a light when they get tucked in every night."

Before Stoudenmire could frame an answer, Kate burst through the door and ran around the desk. With a tiny cry of delight she threw herself into his arms and began smearing his face with wet, sticky kisses. Gillette guffawed behind his hand, watching the lawman turn beet red with embarrassment as he tried to fend Kate off.

"Slow down, girl. I've only been gone three days."

Ignoring him completely, she smoothed back his hair and settled more securely into his lap. "Oh, it's so good to have you back. It seems like you've been gone forever, and I promise I'll never be cross again. I was over in Doc's store, and when I heard you were back, I said to myself, the very first thing I'm going to say is that I'm sorry. Well, I'm sorry. So don't you dare act grumpy." Clutching him around the neck, she gave him a big kiss square on the mouth.

Stoudenmire lifted her easily and set her feet on the floor. Rising, he gave Gillette a helpless look. "Jim, how about taking care of my horses. I can see we're not gonna get much work done around here today."

With an arm around Kate's waist, he headed for the door, and she snuggled hungrily against his chest. Just as they disappeared through the door, he turned and called over his shoulder. "Mind the store, deputy. I just decided to take the night off."

3

After checking in with Gillette next morning, Stoudenmire strolled over to the mayor's office. Overnight a scheme had occurred to him that could easily drive another nail into the Bannings' coffin. Whether it worked out or not, he had nothing to lose except a little conversation. Talk was cheap enough, and he might just wind up with a songbird who knew where all the skeletons were buried.

After Kate finally fell asleep in his arms, he had lain awake far into the night sorting through the alternatives that remained. There were many ways to make a gang run for cover. The quickest was to force their boss into a gunfight, but Ed Banning showed a decided reluctance to accept the challenge. Some men preferred to hire others to do their killing for them, and the weasel-faced saloon owner was plainly of that stripe. Whatever it was that would make him stand and fight hadn't come clear as yet, so the lawman set that tactic aside until he could get a better handle on what made Banning tick.

Another method was to whittle away at the lesser gang members, undermining confidence in the boss as his flunkeys were fed to the meat grinder one by one. This was the tack he had followed from the start, yet he had to admit that the

score seemed a bit lopsided. Campbell and Kale had gone under to be sure, but at a cost of Ramón, a court official, and
two *vaqueros*. Somehow it seemed like a damned poor trade,
even though Banning had lost four men in the rhubarb over
the young Mexican girl. Besides, taking a bit here and there
was the slow way to get results, and he needed something to
speed this deal up.

Staring at the ceiling, he had wracked his brain for some
foolproof way to clobber the Bannings once and for all. Just
when he was about to chuck the whole mess and get some
sleep, he remembered the old saw about divide and conquer.
Look for the weakest link in the chain and twist till it broke.
Once it snapped, Ed Banning would never get it spliced in
time to save his own neck. With his grip on the town loosened,
both the political machine and the gang itself would come
apart at the seams. The more Stoudenmire thought about it the
better he liked the idea. And unless he had lost the knack of
sizing up men, Mayor Isaac Porter was the weak link.

Stoudenmire found the politician alone in his office, seated
behind a desk staring listlessly at a stack of ledgers. His heavy
tread brought Porter's head around, and the marshal sensed
that this wasn't the same man who had berated him the
morning of Ramón's death. Something about his eyes had
changed. Nothing a man could put a name to, but it was there
just the same. Like a gopher when it's cut off from its hole
and no place to run. Suddenly his plan took on a new dimen-
sion, for the easiest man to buffalo was the one that had
already scared himself.

"Morning, Mr. Mayor," he said, nodding at the ledgers.
"How goes the fight?"

Porter darted a nervous glance at the gray-bound records.
"Oh, these. Nothing really. The city fiscal year is upon us, and
I was just going over the books."

Stoudenmire was well aware that such matters were generally left to accountants, but he let it pass. "Well that's a little
out of my bailiwick. Never was much of a hand with figures.
If you can spare a minute, I thought I'd fill you in on my trip
south."

"No, no. That's quite all right, Marshal." His eyes widened, flashing an unnatural amount of white. "We can dispense with your report. The story's all over town. As a matter of fact, people aren't talking about much else."

"Yeah, something like that would just naturally get people to beatin' their gums." The lawman dropped into a chair and crossed his long legs. "Course, I'd better give you the lowdown anyway. Folks have a way of twistin' things out of shape, and you might've heard the wrong version."

The mayor sighed and slumped back in his chair with an acute look of resignation. "If you insist. But keep it to official matters. I've already heard the gory details."

"You mean about Kale?" Stoudenmire's expression was deceptively bland, but when Porter stiffened at his words, he knew he was on the right track. "Damned if that didn't beat anything I ever saw."

"Please, Marshal." The politician squirmed uneasily and a nervous tic surfaced beneath his left eye. "Just hold it to the facts, if you don't mind."

"Well, Mayor, I reckon the way a wanted man goes under is part of the facts. Come to think of it, not much else matters when it comes down to an official report. Wouldn't you say?"

Porter opened his mouth to reply, but the lawman plowed dead ahead, waving aside his sputtering objections. "You see, it was like this. I was teamed up with this breed, and we had trailed Kale to the foothills this side of the Sierra Madres. That night we separated with the idea of sneakin into his camp and taking him alive. Well wouldn't you know that damned Injun got there before me. I came wormin' through the brush, and there he sat. Holdin' Kale's head up like he was huntin' for fleas. The sonovabitch had whacked it off the way a man would split a fresh melon."

Stoudenmire flicked his hand across his throat in a slicing motion, and beads of sweat popped out on the mayor's forehead. For a moment the lawman thought Porter was going to swoon dead away, but he somehow got a grip on himself and straightened in his seat. "That will do, Marshal.

I'm not a violent man, and I see no need to belabor how Tom Kale died."

"Why hell, Mayor. How he died is only half the story. What happened the next night was the real gutbuster." Stoudenmire hitched his chair around and leaned forward, eyeball to eyeball with the little man. "Them Mexicans got a fiesta going and the guest of honor was none other than old Tom Kale himself. The bastards stuck his head on a pole and spent the whole goddamn night dancin' around it like a bunch of wild Apaches. Course, I'll have to admit that it smelled a little rank by then, and those eyes bulging out of their sockets was enough to gag a dog off a gut wagon. But it was purely something to see. Just think of it! Jammed up on a pole and grinnin' like a jack-o'-lantern."

Porter's face turned green, and the lawman scooted back, certain the mayor was going to puke at any moment. The politician jerked a handkerchief and clapped it over his mouth, breathing heavily. Then he fell back in his chair and closed his eyes, taking short, fast gasps like a man trying to clear his head of a sickening stench. After a brief struggle to hold down his breakfast, his color returned, and he slowly opened his eyes.

Stoudenmire poured him a glass of water from a beaker on the desk, then let him have it right below the gizzard. "Porter, I told you that little story just to give you an idea of what's in store for anybody that stands in my way. I intend to scuttle the Bannings and all their cronies, even if it means fighting dirty in the clinches. And when I said *all* their cronies, I meant you especially, Mister Mayor. Course, I don't need to paint you a picture. You're smart enough to figure who's gonna be left holdin' the bag when the rats start scurrying for safety."

Isaac Porter blanched, and he suddenly felt sick in a different way. Stoudenmire's last statement jibed perfectly with his own estimate of what would happen when the Bannings were finally put to flight. Someone would be left behind as a sacrificial goat, and he had a pretty fair idea of who that *someone* would be. But that didn't shake him nearly as much as

the knowledge that the coldblooded bastard seated across
from him would be right there waiting. Ready, willing, and
able to supply the noose that would stretch his plump neck.

The mayor wanted desperately to talk to someone; to un-
burden himself and erase the sense of doom that was with
him constantly now. Yet there was one unknown in this whole
ghastly mess. *Could he trust Stoudenmire?* Or should he go to
Seth Hart? Maybe even the governor. It was a critical decision,
and a man in his position couldn't afford even one mistake.

Glancing back at the lawman, he spoke with a bravado that
seemed curiously out of character. "You're just trying to
frighten me. But you'll find I don't fold so easily, Mr. Stoudenmire."

The marshal regarded him with mild disgust. "Porter, I'll
make it easy for you. Swap sides now and testify against the
Bannings, and you can walk away a free man. Otherwise
you'll swing with the rest of 'em. The offer's good for forty-
eight hours. No longer."

Stoudenmire rose and walked to the door. Then he turned
as though an afterthought had suddenly occurred to him.
"Something you oughta keep in mind while you're thinking
it over. I can protect you from the Bannings. But the Banning's
can't protect you from me."

The door opened and closed, leaving Isaac Porter alone
with his fear.

Crossing the plaza, Stoudenmire wondered if he really
could deliver on that last statement. He damn sure hadn't had
much luck protecting people from the Bannings so far. But,
what the hell! There was plenty of time to start worrying
about a grubby politician if and when he decided to switch
horses. The thing to do now was to take up the slack and see
if a little judicious pressure wouldn't pop that weak link right
under the Bannings' nose.

4

The Bannings were involved in working out a scheme of their
own. Late that afternoon Ed and Sam came together in the

backroom office to discuss how it should be handled. Stoudenmire had to be snuffed out, on that they were agreed. The
sooner the better for everyone concerned, particularly themselves. The marshal's bulldog tenacity showed no signs of
weakening, and by his own word he wouldn't slack off until
they had been plowed under. Even if they were disposed to let
things rock along for a while, the surly bastard seemed determined to force their hand. Each day he lived, he became a
greater threat, that was plain enough for anyone to see. And
only a fool greenhorn let another man pick the time and place
for a fight.

Whatever remnants of the code duello that remained after the war hadn't taken root in El Paso. Here the only recognized code was survival, and whoever struck first was
generally thought to have something besides beeswax between his ears. The logic was really quite simple, profoundly
earthy in its own way. Stoudenmire had poked his nose where
it didn't belong, which was the kind of thing a man could
overlook only so long. The German clearly didn't know when
to let well enough alone, therefore he had to be killed. That
was the only kind of language some people understood, especially hard-nosed lawdogs.

But Ed Banning was of the opinion that it had to be handled discreetly, in a manner that could never be traced back
to them. Although elections were still more than a year away,
they couldn't afford to take any chances. Voters had a long
memory when it could be proved that a town's political boss
was playing dirty pool, which meant that the Banning name
had to be kept out of it at all costs. And right there was where
Sam bowed his neck.

"Dammit, Ed, that's not fair." Sam was just dense enough
to think it should be kept in the family. "I've got a personal
score to settle with that shithead, and you got no right to let
somebody else do the job."

The elder Banning shook his head wearily, as though involved in a senseless argument with a slow child. "Brother,
I'm tellin' you, it's not worth the risk. You can get your jollies
off just as well watchin' somebody else do it."

"Ah, horse apples!" The burly ruffian slunk down in his chair and petulantly slewed his eyes around the room. "That's like sayin' I'd get my load off watchin' some jasper fuck my best girl."

"Now there you go again," Ed snapped. "Making dumb comparisons that you can't back up. You know goddamned well those things have nothing to do with each other. This is business." He sighed heavily, glancing sideways at the younger man. "Besides, you don't even have a best girl."

"Now look who's harpin' the same old tune. One of these days I'm gonna get tired of you raggin' me about girls. You just wait and see. I know a few stories about you that ain't been told. Don't think I don't."

Ed's eyes scrunched up at the corners, and he regarded his brother with a wary gaze. "Is that a fact? Well suppose you just tell me what you know if it's so goddamn earth-shattering."

Sam darted a secretive look at him. "Oh, I know something. Don't you worry about that. Them girls over at Lizzie Pride's do a lot of talkin', and I got big ears."

"No shit? Up beside a jackass I'd never have known. Now suppose you quit playin' ring-around-the-rosie and tell me what the hell you've heard."

Sam's mouth twisted in a juvenile smirk, and he giggled nervously, not unlike a schoolboy telling his first dirty joke. "They say you can't get it up. They're all the time laughin' and carrying on about it when they think nobody's around. That redhead swears up and down you couldn't stick your pecker in a pail of soft lard."

Ed Banning's features went red as ox blood, and he half rose from his chair. "That rotten little bitch! I'll cut her tits off and stuff 'em down her gullet. Then we'll see how much talkin' she does." The rage slowly drained out of his face, leaving it a mottled purple. After a moment he settled back, raking his brother with a furious scowl. "And you better keep your mouth shut, too. If I ever get wind of you talkin' out of turn, I'll crack your balls good. Savvy?"

"Sure, Ed. Whatever you say." Sam clamped his legs shut,

dimly wondering why a sharp pain had suddenly pulsed through his seeds. "I was just funnin.' You know I didn't mean no harm."

Ed drew a deep breath and released it slowly, forcing his mind back to the more immediate problem. "All right, let's drop it and start thinkin' about Stoudenmire. You're not gonna do it, and that's final, so don't give me any lip. The way I've got it figured, we need ourselves a stalking horse."

When Sam gave him a baffled look, the gang leader broke it down into two-bit words. "That's someone who has reason to want the German six feet under. Then everybody'll think he had a personal motive, and we won't be connected to it. He does the killin,' and our hands are clean. Sort of like havin' your cake and eatin' it too."

Sam digested his brother's scheme in an unhurried way, and a brightness slowly kindled in his eyes. "Yeah, that's real smart. Maybe we could even hire us a greaser to do it. Folks around here think greasers are dumb enough to do anything."

"No, we don't have time to go scoutin' up some Mex pigsticker. We need somebody that's handy, and it's got to be a man with a first class grudge against Stoudenmire. I've been giving it a lot of thought, and I think I know just the man."

"Well hell, there's your answer, slicker'n rat shit. Who is he?"

"Bill Johnson."

"*Bill Johnson?*" Sam parroted the words with gaping disbelief. "That goddamn alky couldn't hold a gun steady enough to hit a bull in the ass across a fence."

"That's the whole point. We're gonna get him stiffer'n a board. Then we'll start talkin' about Stoudenmire. How he fired Johnson and booted his ass out the door. How he killed George Campbell, the only friend Johnson had in his whole miserable life. Before you know it, we'll have him foamin' at the mouth like a blind dog in a butcher shop. Then we'll open the back door and turn him loose. Everybody in town'll figure he had a shitpot full of reasons to kill the German."

"You know somethin', Ed? You're nothin' but a goddamn wizard." Sam nodded sagely for a moment, then blinked as though some part of the riddle remained unanswered. "Say, I just now thought of somethin'. You never did tell me if it was true."

Ed was still preoccupied with engineering the marshal's sudden demise. "If what was true?"

"What them girls said. That you couldn't get a hard-on no more."

Banning came up out of his chair. "Get your ass out of here! Go find Johnson and tell him I want to see him tonight. And you'd better listen to me close, little brother. Don't you ever again start runnin' your tongue about what those girls said. Not unless you want me to cut it out."

Sam backed slowly across the room, easing through the door without once meeting his brother's smoky glare. When he was gone, it passed through Ed's mind that he looked like a little boy who had just had his wrists slapped. The hell of it was that the dumb brute would always look like that. If he lived to be a hundred, he'd still be a half-grown kid masquerading as a man. And big brother would still be giving him a sugartit to suck instead of letting him fend for himself. Shit!

Later that night Sam returned with Bill Johnson in tow. But as it turned out, they didn't have much of a chore getting Johnson squiffed. The former deputy had installed himself as the reigning town drunk, and he was generally able to cadge enough drinks to stay half-crocked around the clock. When he came through the door, he was already walking on his heels, and within an hour Ed had floated his gizzard with a liberal dose of forty-rod.

Things went pretty much as Banning had predicted. Once they had Johnson cross-eyed, the gang leader started baiting him. *Hadn't Stoudenmire fired him, made a fool out of him in front of the whole town? Hadn't the marshal also killed his best friend, shot him down in cold blood? No real man would take something like that flat on his back. Anybody with any guts would make sure that the sonovabitch was laid out stone-cold dead. The sooner the better!*

Johnson responded to the goad more readily than Banning had expected. Staggering about the room in an alcoholic rage, he swore he would settle Stoudenmire's hash that very night. Before he could have any second thoughts, Banning thrust a shotgun into his hands and shoved him out the back door. Get him when he makes his night rounds, the gang leader whispered, down by the old church on Texas Street, Johnson nodded drunkenly and reeled off into the darkness, mumbling to himself. Banning watched for a moment to make sure he was headed in the right direction, then stepped back inside.

Sam was grinning like a short-fanged hyena. "Ed, it's just like I said. You're a fuckin' wizard."

Banning's eyes swung around, boring holes clean through him. "Listen close you big ox, 'cause I've only got time to say this once. Stick on Johnson's trail like a leech. If he gets it when the fireworks go off, then we've got no problem. But if he's still kickin' after he gets Stoudenmire, then you kill him on the spot. Got that? Blast him before he moves out of his tracks. Make it look like the German got him. The one thing we sure as shit don't need is another witness. Now vamoose. And mind what I told you."

Shooting clay pigeons was old hat to Sam, and he took off like the dinner bell had just caught him out in the north forty. When the door closed, Ed Banning settled into his chair, pouring himself a long, tall drink. It had been a grueling night, but for the first time in weeks he felt like a man holding all the cards.

Then he chuckled. After tonight he'd be the *only* man holding the cards.

5

Doc Cummings came through the jail door shortly after eight that evening. His face was furrowed with solemnity and concern, the way an undertaker looks at an expensive funeral. The storekeeper had purposely avoided Stoudenmire's house for this discussion since he didn't want to upset Kate needlessly. Tonight he meant to talk some sense into his brother-in-law's thick head, and the kind of language he had in mind wasn't exactly suited to a lady's ears.

The marshal was seated behind the desk paring his fingernails. When Cummings entered, he glanced up, then casually went back to work with the jackknife. "Evenin', Doc. How's tricks?"

Somehow Stoudenmire's unruffled composure grated on the little merchant. It put him in mind of a big cat calmly cleaning its paws as the hunters closed in for the kill. His eyes darted about the office, noting that the lawman was alone. "Where's Gillette, out makin' rounds?"

"No, I gave him the night off." Stoudenmire met the older man's stare, then grinned furtively. "He was overdue, and tonight seemed as good as any."

Cummings couldn't speak for a moment; couldn't bring himself to believe that anyone would be that calculating. Then it came to him that the man his sister had married was just cold-blooded enough to do it.

"Jesus H. Christ. You let him have the night off just to bait somebody into takin' a shot at you. Didn't you?" When Stoudenmire didn't answer, the storekeeper dropped into a chair, now thoroughly exasperated. "Dallas, I'll swear to God, sometimes I get to thinkin' you're on a steady diet of loco weed."

"Doc, you're a born worrier." The lawman chuckled and went right on scraping his thumbnail with the big knife. The abrasive sound sent a chill down Cumming's spine, like chalk screeching across a blackboard. Without looking up, Stoudenmire commented, "The town's peaceful as a church social and I just figured Gillette could use a good night's sleep. Quit your frettin'. Nothin' is gonna happen that I can't handle."

The marshal had a point, and Cummings about halfway believed him. El Paso seemed to have recovered from the shock of the recent killings, or perhaps folks were just learning to take such things in stride. They had damn sure had plenty of practice in the last month or so, enough to last any sane man a couple of lifetimes. But whichever way a fellow looked at it, there was no disputing that the fear of bloodshed had subsided noticeably. Word had gotten around about Stoudenmire's peace talks with Pedro Vazquez, and the

townspeople were convinced that they at last had a lawman
worth his salt. Still, there was more to it than a bunch of
grubby Mexicans. A hell of a lot more where the marshal was
concerned.

Cummings made a church with his hands, then flexed his
fingers into a steeple. Although Stoudenmire's concentration
centered wholly on his fingernails, the storekeeper knew
damn well he was watching out of the corner of his eye. Since
shouting would obviously accomplish nothing, Cummings
decided instead to play it cool and devastate the stubborn
German with sheer logic.

"Dallas, I've just come from a meeting with Seth Hart and
the rest of the boys. Since you're so all-fired touchy, they
asked me to pass along their thoughts and see if we couldn't
come to some sort of understanding."

"You mean Hart asked you to pass along his thoughts,
don't you? I recollect that he does the talkin' and the rest of
your crowd does all the listenin'."

The merchant reddened slightly, but kept his tone lowkey.
"Seth's smarter'n you give him credit for, Dallas. While
everybody else is runnin' around poppin' off at the mouth,
he sits back and figures which way the frog is gonna jump."

"You're readin' the cards wrong, Doc. I'm not sayin' he
isn't smart. I just don't want him meddling in my game. He's
got his own ax to grind, and I'm not real sure I want any part
of it. Not just yet, at any rate."

"For the life of me, I can't figure you out. Seth Hart is
probably the most honorable man in this town, bar none. The
only thing he wants is to get El Paso back in the hands of the
people. Can't you see that, or is it that you just don't trust anybody?"

"Sure, I trust lots of folks. Just not all at once." The lawman
left off paring his nails and pointed the blade in Cummings'
direction. "You're the one that's got a lot to learn about who to
trust. Nobody does nothin' out of Christian charity. Seth
Hart included. Saintliness went out of style when they started
feedin' people to the lions."

"Is that a fact?" The storekeeper's words came out a little

waspish in spite of himself. "Well suppose you just tell me what Seth's got up his sleeve."

"Can't say as I've given it much thought, what with one thing and another. But just for openers, let's suppose I've gotten rid of Banning, and the political goodies are up for grabs. Who do you think is gonna step in and fill his shoes?"

"Why Seth Hart, naturally. Every respectable person in El Paso looks to him for leadership. But that's no reason to suspect him. Good Lord, somebody has to run things. A town just doesn't run itself, you know."

"Nope, I guess not. Leastways there's generally plenty of people willing to take on the job." Stoudenmire regarded his nails critically for a moment, then snapped the knife shut. "Maybe Hart's everything you make him out to be. I'm not sayin' yay or nay. We'll more'n likely find out soon enough, and until then I'll just keep on playing 'em close to the vest."

Cummings bounded out of his chair and paced across the room, flailing the air with his arms. "Damnation! That beats anything I ever heard of. Do you want to know why Seth Hart called that meeting tonight?" Whirling, he advanced on the lawman. "Because he's worried about you, Mr. Doubting Thomas."

"Me?" Stoudenmire echoed skeptically.

"That's right, you. He believes you're in danger, and he means to do something about it."

Cummings' terse statement neatly skirted what had actually been said in the meeting. For over an hour Seth Hart had lectured his political cronies, building as always toward a predetermined and entirely logical conclusion. The Bannings were boxed in, damned if they did and damned if they didn't. Marshal Stoudenmire had become too popular with the townspeople for the city council to fire him, yet he was daily drawing closer to fitting the Bannings for a noose. They had no choice but to kill him. That or run. And the Bannings weren't the type to just fold camp and sneak off into the night. Still, one man wasn't a match for an entire gang. He could flush them, but when it came down to a shooting war, he

couldn't stand alone. The conclusion was obvious. Stoudenmire needed help.

"Dallas, we've discussed this matter thoroughly and the
solution is as plain as a bump on a log." Cummings met the
lawman's gaze squarely. "What El Paso needs is a vigilance committee."

"Not on your tintype!" Stoudenmire's hoarse growl buf-
feted the storekeeper back on his heels. "The first sonovabitch
that takes the law into his own hands is gonna get his ass
handed to him on a platter. And I don't draw the line at anybody, Doc. Not even you."

"Man, stop and think for a minute. You're bucking impossible odds. The Bannings have to be made aware that this
town won't abide further killing. Otherwise, you'll wind up
trying to kick the slats out of a pine box. What we need is a
group of armed citizens willing to back your play. That's
what'll turn the trick, and once the Bannings see the town's
behind you, we can end this dirty business."

"No dice. When a town resorts to vigilantes, they've the
same as admitted that the law won't work. I'm tellin' you
right now, Doc, that won't happen while I'm wearin' this
star."

"But, Jesus Christ, you haven't got the chance of a snowball in Hades. Are you so pigheaded you can't see that? Or
are you just set on gettin' yourself killed?"

Stoudenmire ignored the merchant's nasty tone. "Doc, I
appreciate the gesture, but I'll have to finish this job my own
way. I was hired with no strings attached, and that's how
we're gonna play it out. Worryin' about a bunch of amateur
gunslingers would just slow me down, and right now I need
to keep movin'."

Cummings started to object, but the lawman stilled him
with an upraised hand. "Now let me tell you something for
your own good, Doc. What would happen if Hart formed the
vigilantes and I still ended up in a basket? Think about that,
real hard. You might be trading one political kingfish for another. Maybe I'm pigheaded, but I reckon I'll take my
chances without Hart standin' behind me with a gun."

When the storekeeper seemed inclined to argue, Stoudenmire decided it was time to make the evening rounds. But Cummings wasn't about to be put off by that old dodge. Like a feisty dog worrying a bone, he tagged along, talking a blue streak. Crossing the plaza, he extolled the many virtues of Seth Hart, lambasting Stoudenmire for being overly suspicious of the very people who could save his hide. When the marshal merely grunted and kept on walking, Cummings forgot about logic and launched into a harangue about the folly of pride and rockbound stubbornness. Turning off the plaza onto Oregon Street, the lawman headed for the southside, trying his best not to listen as Cummings haughtily pronounced him a brute for punishment.

Short of jailing his own brother-in-law, there seemed no way to end it, so Stoudenmire just plowed on, nodding every now and then to let the little storekeeper know he wasn't talking to himself. The southside dives seemed no more rowdy than usual, and the pair made quick time as they strolled through the quarter. Apparently the saloons and dancehalls had been able to handle their own troubles, and for once it appeared that Stoudenmire would get through a tour without making a single arrest. Still, the night was young and anything could happen. As a matter of fact, it usually did. On the southside every night was the same, some more so than others, and long before closing time the jail was generally packed to the gunnels with a motley assortment of belligerent drunks and weepy rumdums.

Nearing the end of Texas Street, the lawman was only vaguely aware that Cummings was still rambling on about the need for a vigilance committee. Leaving the boardwalk, he took to the street and headed for the far corner, figuring to shuck Doc for the night once they again reached the plaza. Suddenly there was a deafening explosion only yards behind them, and a load of buckshot kicked up dust at their feet. Cummings howled and grabbed at his leg, crow-hopping forward a few steps before he toppled over.

Staggering drunk, Bill Johnson wobbled from behind a stone pillar of an old mission and raised his scattergun for a

better shot. But the lawman made a hellishly poor target.
With the first report, he had hit the ground, rolled sideways,
then reversed himself in the middle of a roll. Even as Johnson
pressed the trigger, he swung around on his belly with his
pistol out and cocked. The Colt roared a fraction ahead of the
shotgun's hollow boom, and Johnson stumbled backwards
into the crumbling pillar.

The buckshot tore a sign loose over a store on the other
side of the street, and even as it fell, Stoudenmire dusted the
former deputy with three quick shots. Johnson hung against
the pillar, jerking with the impact of each slug, then pitched
face down in the street.

Stoudenmire came to his feet just in time to glimpse a man
dart from the shadows and take off running down Stanton
Street. Hurriedly, he snapped off two shots as the dim figure
disappeared around a corner, knowing even as he fired that
he had missed. There was no sense in giving chase with an
empty gun, and he turned back to see what could be done for
Cummings. But the storekeeper was already up and hobbling
toward the fallen bushwhacker, gripped by a curiosity that for
the moment overshadowed the pain in his leg. Both men
reached the body at the same time, and Stoudenmire toed it
over with the point of his boot. In the faint starlight, the dead
man's glassy eyes shone like cloudy agates.

"Well I'll be double-dipped," Cummings croaked. "It's old
Bill Johnson. Who'd have thought that miserable bastard
would've had the guts for it."

Stoudenmire started kicking out empties and reloading.

"They've all got the guts for it when they're shootin' at
your back."

Holstering the Colt, he draped Cummings arm around his
shoulders and took off at a slow walk. After a few steps he
nodded down at the storekeeper's bloody leg. "That's the very
reason I didn't want your vigilantes roaming the streets. Amateurs always end up gettin' shot."

CHAPTER EIGHT

1

Early next morning Stoudenmire sent word to Seth Hart calling for a meeting. Things were coming apart at the seams, and unless they did something fast, the whole damn town was going to look like a shooting gallery.

Johnson's assassination attempt had fooled no one, least of all the respectable element. The Bannings were behind the bushwhacking just like they were behind every other dirty thing in El Paso, and trying to gun down a peace officer was the last straw. The town had split right down the middle, the southside scum against the decent folks, and battle lines were already being drawn. Word about the proposed vigilance committee had somehow leaked out, and knots of men were even then gathering on the plaza, bolstering one another's courage with loud talk and cheap whiskey. The general feeling seemed to be that Stoudenmire needed a hand in ridding the town of its undesirables, and for the first time, the people of El Paso were openly declaring their opposition to Boss Banning.

Stoudenmire wasn't too keen on meeting with the Hart

faction, but he saw no alternative. The townspeople had to be headed off before armed mobs took to the streets, and much as he hated to admit it, that was something he couldn't handle alone. Hart and his cronies had started this crazy business about vigilantes, and they were the only ones who could quell the hotheads gathering on the plaza. The important thing now was to get the leaders talking against mob action, and damned quickly. Otherwise, good men were going to die needlessly.

Although he would have been the last to admit it, the marshal could have used a little breather himself. Getting bushwhacked hadn't bothered him so much, but things were getting pretty fierce around the house. Kate had given him the roughest night yet, railing at him for getting Doc shot, then blistering him in the next breath for being so careless with his own life. Stoudenmire couldn't tell which had infuriated her more; she had skipped from one to the other for the better part of two hours. Finally he had stalked out of the house and returned to the office, leaving her to stew in her own juices. Women were damn strange creatures, temperamental as a mare in heat and about as predictable as a landslide.

Still, taking the shooting back to back with Kate's tantrum didn't gall him nearly as much as this meeting with Hart. The plain fact was that he would have to ask for their help, and it curried him the wrong way to be forced into that position. Seth Hart was a horsetrader from way back, and an exchange of some kind would have to be made before the lard-faced politician agreed to back off. But Stoudenmire didn't have a hell of a lot to bargain with. Except maybe to reveal the next step in his war on the Bannings. And that really grated on the bone! So far no one knew what he was going to do until he did it, and that was the biggest edge a lawman could ask for. Once somebody else was made privy to his plans, the cheese could get binding, real fast. Yet it was sort of like the fellow caught in a blizzard with only the shithouse in sight. He had damned little choice.

The morning passed uneventfully enough, but a hard core of troublemakers were still congregated on the plaza.

Stoudenmire resisted the temptation to send them packing; they would only gather somewhere else, and as long as they remained on the square, he at least had them in sight. The time to start worrying was when he couldn't see them. With the way things were breaking, that'd be the time some spell-binder would get them all fired up and start a march on the southside. Crossing the plaza on his way to the meeting, it occurred to the lawman that El Paso was a town that seemed damned set on getting itself leveled to the ground. Oddly enough, some folks had the quaint notion that the only way to bring about change was to burn everything down and start all over. And unless Seth Hart got off his ass, the hammer-heads in town might just get their way.

Upon arriving at Hart's home back of the mill, he found the clique assembled and waiting. Looking them over as Hart led him into the room, the lawman was struck by a certain sameness about their appearance. Then it came to him. They were seated in exactly the same chairs as on his first visit to this house. Each man probably had squatter's rights on his chair by now, and doubtless there was some hierarchy in-volved that made the whole thing seem vastly important to them. *Little men playing for big stakes.* That's what it all boiled down to, whichever way a man came at it.

Doc Cummings was the only one who greeted him by name. Horace Adair merely nodded, letting the lawman know that he hadn't forgotten their last encounter. John Simmons and Nate Hobart ran a dead heat to see who could cake the most ice around the word *marshal*, and curiously enough, they both won. So far as Stoudenmire was concerned, the whole damn room was swathed in frost, and he had the dis-tinct feeling it was going to be all uphill in the next few min-utes. Hart waved him to a chair, then took his own seat and sat back with his hands folded over his ample stomach. Watching him, Stoudenmire was reminded of an old bullfrog hunkered down on a lily pad flicking his tongue at passing flies. The trouble being that he seemed to be the only fly in sight.

Hart purposely let the silence build for a moment, then

looked over at the lawman with a gloating smile, "Marshal, I'll have to admit you've got us curious. Doc relayed your feelings about a vigilance committee, and I suspect he toned them down for our benefit. Be that as it may, you called this meeting, and we'll listen to whatever you've got on your mind."

Stoudenmire didn't even bother looking at the other men. They reflected Hart's mood like images on still water, and he addressed himself directly to the miller. "Mr. Hart, I'm gonna give you some cold facts. What you do with 'em is your own affair. But I'm warnin' you straight out, if you jump the wrong way, you'll wind up getting a lot of people killed."

"Like I said, Marshal, we'll listen." Hart's eyes roved around the table, and the other men nodded hastily. "I can't promise any more than that."

"Suit yourself. I'm just hired to keep the peace. Whichever way it goes, it won't be any skin off my nose." Horace Adair's jaw popped open, but Hart stilled him with a sharp glance. The lawman went on as if the Irishman didn't even exist. "Let's take first things first, just to clear the air. You're out to form a vigilance committee, and I mean to stop you. If I have to, I'll toss every man here into the hoosegow and forget where I hid the key."

"That's pretty strong talk for a hired hand." Adair broke in before Hart could silence him.

"Nothin' I can't back up, Mr. Adair. But unless I'm pushed, I'd prefer to handle it another way. Right now it's between the Bannings and me. That's the way I'd like to keep it. If you fellas organize the vigilantes, that means Banning will have to muster his own army on the south-side. Since he controls the vice district, it wouldn't be any sweat to raise more guns than you could count. Once your vigilantes cross the line, it'll mean open warfare in the streets, and nobody knows where that'll end. Not even Mr. Hart, here."

Seth Hart moved his hand in a dismissive gesture. "We're not the amateurs you think, Marshal. These same thoughts have occurred to us. But we figure to raise enough men to counter anything Banning could scrounge up."

"What kind of men? Clerks and bank tellers." Stouden-mire's lips curled back from his teeth in a grin that was more like a grimace. "Maybe you men can run a business, but when it comes to killin', you haven't got sense enough to wad a bird-gun load. Those hardcases on the southside would eat you alive and spit out the seeds. But that's not what troubles me."

"Well now, that's a damn curious thing for a lawman to say," Hart rumbled. "Just exactly what is it that troubles you, Mr. Stoudenmire?"

"Anybody that goes huntin' trouble deserves what he gets, no matter which side of town he's from. But if you turn the vigilantes loose, a lot of innocent people are gonna get killed in the bargain. I've seen mobs before, and once they get a taste for blood, there's no telling where it'll stop. You people have just missed a couple of showdowns with the Mexicans by the skin of your teeth. Seems to me it'd be damned fool-ish to start a war among yourselves that could be just as bad. Maybe worse."

Horace Adair snorted derisively and slapped the table with his open palm. "By God, Stoudenmire, for sheer gall you take the cake. You haven't got any evidence, your witnesses have all been murdered, and the Bannings are still running El Paso like they had a patent. But you have the audacity to come in here and ask us to hold back. Hell man, you haven't done the job you were hired to do. It's time somebody else took a crack at it."

Stoudenmire's flinty gaze swung around and settled over the Irishman like a cold mist. "Mister, I'm tryin' to overlook your bad manners, but it's gettin' to be a chore. Don't press your luck."

"All right, boys," Hart said, "let's not fly off the handle. Suppose everybody just calms down and tries using a little reason for a change."

"Seth, I'm all for reason, but it seems to me that Horace has a point." Nate Hobart rarely said anything, and his unex-pected comment brought the other men's heads around. "Just think about it for a minute. The Bannings are so deeply en-trenched in politics that we'll never get any evidence of corruption. All the witnesses that could link them to these killings are dead, so there's no way we can legally bring them to justice on that. Now the marshal tells us they're too well organized for vigilantes to be of any use. If that's the case, then just what is it he's suggesting?"

There was a moment of profound silence. The normally laconic hotel owner had deftly hit the nail right on the head. *Just what the hell did Stoudenmire have in mind?* Doc Cummings had held back up to this point, not wanting to put his own brother-in-law on the spot. But he could see Adair priming himself, and he decided to jump in before the meeting disintegrated into a real donny-brook.

"Dallas, don't get your hackles up. John's question seems like a fair one to me. If you want us to keep sittin' on our thumbs, then you've got to give us a reason. Have you got an ace in the hole, or are you just giving the Bannings more rope in the hopes they'll hang themselves?"

The lawman looked around the table, fixing each man in turn with a probing stare. Finally he spoke, not to anyone in particular but to the five men as a whole. "I'm not in the habit of tellin' people my plans. The fewer that know, the less chance of a leak. You figure you've got a right to hear it, so I'll tell you. But if it gets out, I'll know where to come lookin'."

Stoudenmire's cold eyes again traveled around the table, and the men felt their innards shrivel under his gaze. The threat was only thinly veiled, and not one among them doubted that he would kill the first man who opened his mouth in the wrong place. Like he said, they wanted to hear, and with it they accepted the responsibility of keeping their traps shut.

"The Bannings are vulnerable in three spots." The marshal selected three poker chips from a rack in the center of the table and stood them on edge, side-by-side as he spoke. "Their rustling operation, their corrupt deals with city officials, and the protection racket they run in the vice district. Starting tomorrow, I'll be probing for the weak links in each of these operations. What I'm after is hard evidence that'll stand up in court. It's a gamble, I grant you, but keep in mind that it

only takes one informer to topple the whole shootin' match."
Stoudenmire flicked one of the chips with his finger, and it
fell sideways, toppling the others in turn. "With a little luck
I might just have a songbird in the bag within a couple of
days. But even if that peters out, we'll still be giving Banning
the cold nose every time he squats."

Seth Hart nodded solemnly, studying the top of the table
for a moment. Then he looked up. "Marshal, we want shed
of the Bannings, but by the same token we don't want you
killed. Quite frankly, I'm not sure you can pull it off by yourself."

Stoudenmire's mouth quirked a little at the corners. "Well
if it doesn't pan out, you can always storm the Coliseum.
I might even go along with you."

Hart's belly rumbled, and his mouth parted in a wet
chuckle. The decision had been made. Stoudenmire would
have his chance, but the vigilantes would be held in reserve.
Just in case.

2

When the train pulled in next morning, a swarthy, dark-haired
man stepped off onto the platform and stretched his arms,
like a great black cat warming itself in the mellow sun. The
only baggage he carried was strapped to his hips, twin Colts
with darkened walnut grips and as deadly looking as the man
himself. There was nothing fancy about his hardware, just
tools of the trade, weathered, well oiled, and always close at
hand. But two guns singled a man out, even in a border town,
and it didn't take a swami to come up with his profession.

Still, guns and all, the thing that made people stare after
this man were his eyes. Sort of dark and impassive, like thin
ice on a winter pond. The kind of eyes a fellow didn't forget
and, more often than not, went out of his way to avoid meeting directly. They weren't cruel eyes, or even pitiless, they
were just black orbs that looked at nothing, yet saw everything, and registered absolutely no emotion whatsoever.

Somehow he put most folks in mind of a sleek carnivore

stalking its supper, moving sort of soft and lithe like he was walking on padded feet. And if he came scratching at the door some dark night, a smart man would have blown out the lamp and thrown the bolt.

After working the kinks out of his back, the man ambled off toward the vice district. There was a certain arrogance to his walk, like maybe he had just foreclosed on the sidewalk, and even burly, ham-fisted teamsters gave him a wide berth. Though his gaze touched on everything and everyone along the street, there was no sign on his face of either like, dislike, or even passing curiosity. Just a stoic disinterest that looked through and past whatever happened to cross his path. Which wasn't a hell of a lot. Most people just naturally got out of his way and left well enough alone.

Ten minutes later he walked into the Coliseum Saloon and planted his foot on the brass rail. When the bartender meandered over, the man nodded just once, as though he was conserving his strength. "Where can I find Ed Banning?"

The stranger's slow, guttural words put the barkeep in mind of a mission-schooled Kiowa he had once known. But something about the man warned him that this was one pilgrim who wouldn't take kindly to questions. Jerking his thumb toward the rear of the room, the barkeep said, "That's his office back there. Best knock before you go in."

The man didn't even acknowledge that he had heard. Moving away from the bar, he crossed the room, rapped once on the door, and entered. The bartender shook his head in a mild quandary and went back to polishing glasses. Some minutes later the door opened again, and the stranger came out, trailed closely by Ed and Sam Banning. The men bellied up at the end of the bar, with the soft-spoken jasper between the two brothers. Ed Banning signaled for drinks, and the barkeep hustled forward with a bottle, growing more puzzled by the moment. The boss looked fidgety as a whore in church, and that was one for the books. Up till now he had always thought the skinny bastard didn't have any more nerves than a gorged snake.

"Jack, let's have some of the good stuff," Banning ordered.

Looking about the saloon, he called out to a scattering of early morning patrons. "Boys, the drinks are on the house! Step up and name your pleasure."

The men sitting about the room exchanged startled glances, them made a rush for the bar. Ed Banning wasn't especially noted for his generosity, and everybody figured they had best get to drinking before he recovered his senses. The hubbub gradually died down after the men got their drinks, but Banning waited till everyone was swilling contentedly before he let them in on the reason for the celebration.

"Boys, in case you're wonderin' who this gent is, I'd like you to meet Choctaw Tyler." Banning placed his hand on the man's shoulder, then pulled it back like he had touched a hot stove. "From now on he's gonna be my right-hand man. Next to Sam here, of course."

There was a sudden stir of interest from the men crowding the bar. The name was known and feared, at least by anyone with sense enough to pour piss out of a boot. Choctaw Tyler, the scourge of Indian Territory, deadlier than smallpox and scarlet fever back to back.

Although facts were sketchy, he was reputed to have killed a dozen men in gunfights, maybe even twice that number. No one knew for sure. They only knew that, next to Doc Holliday and Wes Hardin, he was the most feared gun in the west. Perhaps the most deadly of all according to some folks, for it was a well known fact that gut-eaters placed no value whatever on human life, their own or anyone else's. And a man had only to look at him to know that Choctaw Tyler was a full blood, just a hop and a skip from carrying a scalping knife instead of a six-gun. Even the US marshals working out of Ft. Smith steered clear of him, and with good reason. Word out of the Nations had it that he was tougher'n boiled owl, and some even swore that wherever he spit, nothing ever again grew on that spot.

Now he was standing right before their eyes in the flesh, and he looked just about as mean as his reputation claimed. And the Bannings had imported him all the way from Indian Territory! By Christ, that would make folks sit up and talk,

sure enough. But not a man at the bar needed to ask why
Choctaw Tyler had been brought to El Paso. They knew. Just
as sure as they knew their own names.

After a couple of drinks, the Bannings and their new hired
gun returned to the office. The little charade at the bar had
been nothing more than a means of letting everyone know
that the Indian was in town. Word would spread through El
Paso like a dose of clap in a whorehouse, and by noon folks
wouldn't be talking about anything else. Maybe the uptown
crowd wouldn't like it, but they'd wait around to see how it
came out. Even Bible-thumpers had a certain morbid curiosity about such things.

Once they were seated in the office, Ed Banning briefly
related the events leading to the present stalemate with
Stoudenmire. Choctaw Tyler sat and listened, making no
comment one way or the other about the killings, the political maneuverings, or the near misses. When the gang leader
finally wound down, Tyler just looked at him, like he was
watching a talking dog and waiting for the next trick.

"Right now we've got ourselves a Mexican standoff,"
Banning declared, slightly unsettled by the Indian's fishy
stare. "But sooner or later, there'll be a showdown. Stoudenmire will either come lookin' for us, or else the vigilantes'll
suck up their balls and start a free-for-all. Whichever way
it falls, we want your gun backing our play."

"Money talks." Tyler's dark eyes hooded, revealing nothing. "Five hundred now. Another five when it's done. Sundays extra, and I buy my own shells."

Banning wasn't sure if the inscrutable sonovabitch was
pulling his leg or not, but he let it pass. "Fair enough. We've
got no gripes about payin' top dollar. This shitheel marshal
has got the whole town walkin' on eggshells, and it'll be
worth every penny of it to watch him eat dust."

Choctaw Tyler's mouth set in an ugly grin, like a skull-
head covered with burnt rawhide. "Just pick a spot. I'll drop
your hick lawdog like a load of bricks. They all go down when
Tai-me rattles the bones."

Banning didn't have the least idea who *Tai-me* was, but

he had a notion that the fullblood seated across from him would tackle a turpentined catamount if the price was right. While he started counting out five hundred in greenbacks, Sam got busy pouring another round of drinks. Maybe their celebration was jumping the gun a little, but what the hell! Choctaw Tyler had just signed on for the duration.

3

Seth Hart was as good as his word. Along with Doc Cummings and his other cronies, the miller had circulated around the plaza talking his own brand of horse sense. The time wasn't right, he cautioned the men standing on street corners and crowding the boardwalks. The Bannings knew every move they were making, and the only way to invade the southside without needless killing was to take them by surprise. Wait, he told them, stand ready. Vigilantes may yet be needed, and when the right moment came, he would put out the call. Until then, everyone was to go about their business just as usual and avoid trouble with the Banning crowd.

When a handful of hotheads tried to argue the point, Hart gave it to them straight. Lay off or get your ears pinned back, he growled. Any man who started trouble today would find hard times camping on his doorstep. The warning had its effect. Once the Bannings were gone, Seth Hart would be the most influential man in El Paso, and everyone knew it. Crossing him now would only make for lean pickings farther down the road. The miller would eventually wield the power in the basin, and the man who got on his wrong side might just find himself starved out of town.

But Hart was too good a politician to send them away disgruntled. He had given his word to the marshal that the townspeople would hold off until the law had had its chance. That meant that the vigilantes would probably be needed after all, since Stoudenmire was fast working himself into a corner. Keep it confidential, he told them, but sleep light and have your guns handy. The call could come at any time.

Seth Hart had few illusions about his fellow townsmen.

They would keep it about as confidential as a medicine man hawking elixir water. By nightfall what he had said would be all over El Paso, in ten different versions. But it had gotten them off the streets, and as long as they had some burgeoning conspiracy to occupy their minds, they wouldn't be out hunting trouble.

Stoudenmire and Gillette watched Hart's performance from the door of the jail. While the fat man wasn't exactly their cup of tea, they grudgingly admitted that he was a slick operator. The crowd had been manipulated without even knowing it, which was the mark of a true bunco artist. Maybe Hart called himself a politician, but he was a kissing cousin to a con man, and the two peace officers found the knowledge a little unsettling. Still, the mob had been dispersed, and for the moment that was the only thing that counted.

The lawmen stepped back inside the jail and started tussling with their own problems. Stoudenmire had purposely held off discussing the next step in their campaign against the Bannings until they could get more information on the latest development. Namely, Choctaw Tyler.

Word of the redskin gunfighter had spread through town at a dizzying pace, and rumors were flying thick and fast. The Indian was here, that much they knew, and everyone suspected why he had been imported. After that it was pure speculation as to how the Bannings intended to use him.

Stoudenmire had his own ideas on the subject, but right now he was more concerned with other matters. Tilted back in his chair, he spoke absently, as though trying to flush his mind of distractions and focus only on the job ahead. "Jim, we've been losin' ground fast in this deal, and it appears to me we've got to play hurry up and catch up. Everybody in this town seems bent on givin' us the fast shuffle, including the ones that're supposed to be on our side."

"Ain't that the godawful truth," Gillette agreed sourly. "I never seen people so damn set on gettin' their brains blowed out. Seems like they're bound to get in a fight with somebody. Now that you put a damper on the greasers, they're half froze to start cuttin' on one another. Beatenest thing I ever run across."

"Well in a way it is, and in another way it's not." The marshal flipped his hat on the desk and locked his hands behind his head. "Most folks'll live and let live if they're left alone. Hell, wolves and cougars live right alongside one another, and they hardly ever tangle. People are the same way. They figure every man has a right to his own game, whether it's crooked or straight, so long as he don't step on their toes."

Gillette ran a hand through his unruly shock of hair, and his forehead wrinkled in a bemused way. "Pard, you just lost me on the turn. People ain't much different than the beasties, I grant you. But what the hell's that got to do with live and let live?"

"Why, I reckon I'm tryin' to say that, whether it's man or beast, they just naturally don't go huntin' trouble. Now you take wolves, for instance. Sometimes an old stud wolf'll get the hots for another outfit's territory. Before you know it, he'll start a battle royal and get his whole pack chewed to shreds just because he wants what the other fellow's got. Same thing happens with people. They let some sorry bastard get 'em all riled up, and before anybody takes the time to think it through, they're squared off lookin' for the other fellow's jugular."

"You're sayin' it's the leaders that cause the trouble. If the people was left to their own hook they'd figure out some way to get by without all this fightin'." The deputy scratched his head and mulled it over, unmindful of the shower of dandruff that flaked down over his vest. "Well, it's somethin' to think about. Don't know's I ever heard it put just that way."

"No other way to put it," Stoudenmire commented. "Just take a look around you. Ed Banning's got this town locked up tighter'n a drum, and Seth Hart figures he oughta be king of the hill. Between 'em they're liable to get half the people in El Paso laid out with their toes curled backwards. What folks oughta do is let those two fight it out man to man and then hang the winner. That'd solve most of the probems this town's got."

"Well you sorta set Hart back on his haunches for the time bein'. Leastways he called off the vigilantes."

"Not for long. He's only giving us enough time to make himself look good. If we don't come up with something fast, he's gonna have that mob back on the street yellin' for blood."

"You wanna know somethin,' Dallas? If I didn't know you better, I'd think you had rocks in your head. You got a hired *pistolero* sniffin' your trail, and you sit around worryin' about what's gonna happen to the little folks when the big dogs finally tangle. That's some kinda nervy, but I ain't sure it's too bright."

The lawman just chuckled, more amused than offended by Gillette's tone. This crotchety old fart was the only man on earth who could talk to him like that, and they both knew it. In some curious way, that made it all right. Perhaps everybody needed their own personal devil's advocate, someone who constantly looked on the dark side simply because they were too damned cantankerous to play it any other way. Oddly enough, it helped to keep things in perspective, and he always felt uneasy when Gillette wasn't around to nettle him with testy remarks.

"Jim, the way I see it, Choctaw Tyler's the least of our worries. The Bannings can't use him openly 'cause it would ruin 'em politically. Course, they could have him bushwhack me, but I sorta doubt that, too. I've got an idea they brought him in as a bodyguard more'n anything else. Like as not, the only time I'd trade lead with him is if I went lookin' for the Bannings."

"Jesus Pesus!" the deputy woofed. "You make it sound like a shootout with him wouldn't be no more'n a friendly game of mumblety-peg. You better check your paint pots again, *amigo.* I hear tell that gut-eater has already filled a couple of graveyards all by his lonesome."

Like most peace officers, Gillette and Stoudenmire kept themselves fairly well informed on the activities of the West's more publicized bad men. Even now they knew that Wyatt Earp and Doc Holliday were involved in a fracas out in Tombstone. Luke Short was still in Dodge, and Billy the Kid had recently gone under at old Ft. Sumner. Wes Hardin was serving twenty-five years at Huntsville, of course. And incredible as it seemed, Ben Thompson had been elected city marshal of Austin. There was just no explaining some people's taste in lawmen. Then there was Choctaw Tyler. Never been indicted, much less in jail, and reportedly as sudden as a snake with either hand.

Stoudenmire slowly unfolded from his chair, then crossed to the stove and poured himself a cup of coffee. Turning, he gave Gillette a searching look. "Jim, think back to all the gunslingers we've run across in our time. Every one of 'em had a reputation about a mile long and a yard wide. But when it got down to cases, their rep assayed out to one part fact and nine parts bullshit. Seems to me they trade on the fact that people are scared of 'em, sorta bluff their way through just because folks have heard they're sudden death. When it comes to shootin' at somebody that's gonna shoot back, they head for the hills. *Muy pronto.* I'm bettin' Choctaw Tyler's not any different. Just more so."

"I can't argue it. Likely as not you're right." Gillette returned his look levelly. "But I still say it's a piss-poor bet. What we oughta do is come up on either side of that knothead and throw his ass in the can."

Before Stoudenmire could reply Doc Cummings popped through the door. The little merchant's bearing was square-shouldered and somewhat martial, like he had just led the Light Brigade through the Valley of Death. Halting before the marshal's desk, he stuck his thumb in his vest pocket and puffed out his chest.

"Well gents, we've disbanded the troops and sent 'em home. But all you have to do is say the word, and we'll have 'em formed and ready to march before you can bat an eye."

Gillette and Stoudenmire exchanged sardonic looks. After a moment, the marshal returned to his chair and glanced up at Cummings, who seemed frozen in his pose. "Relax, Doc. Have a seat. I was just getting ready to fill Jim in on what we discussed at the meeting. Maybe you could give us some advice."

Stoudenmire saw Gillette cover his mouth to hide a grin, but Cummings didn't tumble to the joke. The storekeeper dragged up a chair and plopped down, immensely gratified that his expertise in such matters had at last been recognized. "Fire away, Dallas. I won't interrupt unless I see something that's out of kilter."

"Thank you, Doc. I appreciate your help." The lawman cocked an eye in Gillette's direction and stifled a smile. "Now here's what I've got in mind. Jim, I want you to rent a pack-horse, lay in some supplies, and go find yourself a spot where you can spy on the Banning ranch. What I'm hopin' is that they figure it's safe to start rustlin' again. If so, you trail 'em and spot the outfit they hit. Assuming it works, we'll call in the Rangers, get the Mexican rancher over here to identify the cattle, and sack the Bannings with a federal warrant."

"Sounds fair enough to me," Gillette observed. "But what if they've retired from the rustlin' business?"

"Good question," Doc interjected soberly. "That leaves us out in the cold."

"Not exactly," Stoudenmire noted. "While Jim's gone, I'm gonna visit every dive in town and put the pressure on 'em for evidence of kickbacks to the Bannings. Along with that, I'll also be nosin' around to see if we can turn up any political payoffs. Like that waterworks contract to Pud Brown's brother. We'll be hittin' 'em from three sides at once, and all we need is one good lick to bring them to their knees."

"Yeah, it might work," Gillette allowed. "But if it don't, they'll suck their ass up so tight we'll never get a hold on 'em."

"We'll cross that bridge when we come to it." The marshal paused, watching the other two men intently for a moment. "If we come up between a rock and a hard place, I've still got an ace in the hole. I had a meeting with the mayor after I left Hart's this morning. The second meeting, as a matter of fact. He's scared shitless, and I've about got him sold on testifying against the Bannings. The only thing holding him back is that he wants another witness to back up his story. He's afraid we won't get an indictment otherwise." Again he hesitated, looking them both squarely in the eye. "I don't have to tell you to keep this under your hats. And, Doc, that includes Seth Hart. If this ever got out, Isaac Porter is cold meat. Savvy?"

Both men nodded solemnly, and Cummings came up on the edge of his seat. "Dallas, I just volunteered to help you. By God, if anybody knows what's happening in this town, it's me, and I'll betcha I can turn up a wagonload of evidence on corruption and bribes."

"Doc, I appreciate the offer, but I'll have to turn you down. The stakes are just too damn high. Banning and his crowd play for keeps, and they'd kill you dead as hell if they caught you diggin' for skeletons. This is a rough game, and there's no room in it for eager beavers."

Cumming's face purpled with indignation, and they argued briefly, but Stoudenmire was adamant. Under no circumstances was the storekeeper to get involved, and that was final. If he did, he'd find himself locked in a cell under protective custody. With that, Cummings kicked back his chair and marched out with his nose in the air. As he went through the door, they heard him muttering to himself. "By Christ, it's a sorry goddamn mess when your own brother-in-law treats you like a snot-nosed kid. Believe you me, Kate's going to hear about this."

Stoudenmire just grinned and went back for a refill on coffee. Some folks just didn't know when they were well off. Especially storekeepers trying to convince themselves that they didn't belong among the fainthearted.

4

Overnight some disturbing rumors had drifted back to Ed Banning. Stoudenmire was making the rounds of various gaming dives and whorehouses on the southside. The message he carried was blunt and to the point. Cooperate in greasing the skids for the Bannings, or else. The latter part of his threat wasn't spelled out, but it was plain enough. Those who refused would be hauled down and trampled in the shitstorm that was sure to follow. Clearly the marshal had begun a war of nerves with the madams and gamblers in the vice district, and he damn sure wasn't pulling any punches about what he had in mind.

That in itself didn't disturb Banning. The trick was as old as the hills, and every highroller and whore on the southside knew what would happen if they opened their mouths. What really bothered him was the fact that only two dive owners had reported the incident. That meant the sporting crowd was spooked, uncertain who would win in the end; otherwise they would have come running to him the moment they were contacted. Sam's bullying tactics had kept them in line in the past, true enough, but in a deal like this, nothing could be taken for granted. Even the threat of Choctaw Tyler couldn't be counted on now that Stoudenmire was out cracking knuckles. Some dunghead might get a case of the shakes and decide to hedge his bet. It only took one loose tongue to start the ball rolling, and it might just turn into a goddamn avalanche if something wasn't done fast.

Then, along about his third cup of coffee, Banning's morning turned even darker. One of the boys brought in word that Deputy Gillette had ridden out of town shortly after dawn leading a packhorse. The stablehand who had passed the information along didn't know Gillette's destination, but any numbskull could figure that out. Even Sam had tumbled fast enough. The old lawdog was headed for the ranch, only it was a cinch he wouldn't be paying a social visit. Once he got into the hills back of the spread, even a bloodhound couldn't track him down, and with a spyglass he could count the whiskers on everything that moved down below. The rustling operation would have to be shut down tight as a drum. Banning sent a rider pounding out of town with a terse message. Until he gave the word, nothing moved!

Ten minutes later Banning began wishing he had stayed in bed. One of his men from city hall came tapping at the back door and damn near wet down his leg while he was trying to spit out the story. These political hacks were all alike; they never made a move without mulling it over for at least a day, and even then you couldn't be sure they weren't playing both ends against the middle. Still, this one had finally decided his bread was best smeared with Banning butter, and the story he had to tell was the worst news yet.

Yesterday Stoudenmire had paid a call on the mayor, and they had holed up in the politico's office for the better part of a half-hour. Although the man didn't know what they had talked about, Isaac Porter appeared visibly shaken when the marshal left, and it seemed pretty certain they hadn't been discussing official business. Banning gave the man a good tongue lashing for not reporting sooner, then booted his ass out the back door.

Turning back to Sam and Choctaw Tyler, he had the look of a man who had just been served fried dog turds for breakfast. "Well you have to hand it to that goddamn German. When he cuts the wolves loose, he goes all the way. The bastard's kickin' over rocks in every direction."

"Yeah, but what's it mean?" Sam frowned, now thoroughly baffled by the morning's rash of problems. "Is Porter talkin', or did Stoudenmire just brace him the way he did everybody down here?"

"I don't know," Banning pondered aloud. "After all we've done for him, I'd hate to think the mayor would double-cross us. On the other hand, I'm damned if I'd put it past him." Then he blinked, glancing around at his brother. "But I'll tell you one thing. Porter could be real trouble. He knows enough to put us all away, and if he ever got on a witness stand, we're lookin' at a jail cell. Maybe even a neck stretchin'."

Sam's bemused look suddenly turned to anger. "Goddamnit, it's just like I been sayin' from the start. We gotta get rid of that fuckin' marshal once and for all."

"Don't worry, little brother. We're gonna dig his hole real soon. But we have to pick the time and the place, and it's gotta look right. Otherwise, the reformers'll start beatin' drums all over town."

Choctaw Tyler grunted and smiled like a cat with a mouthful of feathers. "Anytime you say, suits me. Sooner I earn my money, the sooner I can hit the road."

Banning darted a glance at the Indian. "I'll tell you when.

And you can bet your boots it won't be long in comin'." He seemed on the verge of saying something else, then fell silent, and after a moment looked over at Sam. "What we need is to buy a little time, and it occurs to me there's a trick we haven't tried. Send the swamper over to Stoudenmire's office. Tell him I've got something to say that he'll be real interested in hearin'. But only over here. Nowhere else."

Sam's mouth popped open, but he never got a chance to speak. Banning shot him a withering look, and the burly ruffian obediently made tracks for the door. Choctaw Tyler just smiled and pulled out the makings. Watching him, Banning decided that the gut-eater would be hard to take as a steady diet. All he did was look at you with that shiteatin' smile and stink up the place with his goddamn Bull Durham.

Sam returned shortly, and they all sat around looking at one another in deadened silence. Twenty minutes later Stoudenmire walked through the door, and it escaped no one's attention that Tige padded along at his side. The brute looked meaner than ever if such a thing were possible, and it was clear that he hadn't forgotten his trip to this room. It was equally clear that the lawman had come loaded for bear. If the gang leader wanted trouble, he figured that between Tige and himself they could dish out enough to go around.

Stoudenmire ignored the Indian as though he didn't exist, leveling down instead on Banning. "Whatever you've got to say, get it said. I haven't got all day."

Banning smiled, but only with great effort. "I don't think your time will be wasted, Marshal. But first I'd like to ask you a question. Just what do you hope to gain by badgering my people down here? They're not gonna spill their guts to you in a month of Sundays."

"Banning, you'd be surprised what folks'll spill when they see the writing on the wall." The lawman saw the other man's eyes narrow, and he drove the needle a little deeper. "Your outfit's got more leaks'n a rusty sieve. Damned interestin' the way people'll talk when they know the string's about played out."

Ed Banning's thin blade of a face suddenly lost its smile. "You oughta've been a poker player instead of a lawman. With a bluff like that you could've made a fortune."

Stoudenmire's chuckle had a mocking ring to it. "The only way to find out is to call the bet. Course, when you take another peek at your hole card, you're gonna discover I've got you by the short hairs."

"One hand don't make a game. Not the way I play." Banning dismissed the subject with a wave of his hand, plastering another shallow smile across his face. "Look, I didn't call you over here to trade insults. I've got a proposition to make, and I'll give it to you straight out. You're not gonna turn up anything I can't handle, but you are sort of a nuisance. Not that it bothers me all that much, you understand. Just takes my mind off more important matters. Suppose I was to open the safe and count out . . . say three thousand dollars. Hell, I might even go as high as five thousand. Don't you reckon that'd get your mind back on your own business?"

Stoudenmire felt his pulse quicken. The bastard was running scared! One more push and he might just crack. "Banning, I've got a better idea. Why don't you stuff that money up your ass and set a match to it. That's about the only way you'll get me off your back."

Sam started out of his chair, but the gang leader stayed him with a short, chopping motion of his hand. Then Banning leaned forward and nodded toward the Indian. "Marshal, I don't think you've met Choctaw Tyler. He's been hearin' about the big *pistolero* we've got for a lawman, so we brought him down to have a look-see for himself."

Stoudenmire gave the gunslinger a slow, appraising look. For a moment Choctaw Tyler just puffed on his cigarette, seemingly absorbed in the aimless drift of the smoke. Finally he turned and met the marshal's stare with an insolent smirk. His mouth was like a hard slit that had been traced across his face with a razor, and when he spoke, his words came out a soft, guttural hiss.

"Mister, you'd best listen to reason. Else you're gonna end

up on the short end of the stick. Shit, he's offerin' you more money to stay alive than he's givin' me to kill you. Take it, 'fore I decide to do the job for free."

The lawman's pale eyes riveted into the full blood, and his voice was gritty as ground glass. "Tyler, I'm gonna give you some advice, maybe the best you ever got. Start makin' tracks out of here and don't look back. If you do, you're liable to lose an eye."

Choctaw Tyler tensed, ready to come up out of his chair, but Banning stopped him cold. "Choctaw, leave it be! He's just tryin' to get you riled up, and we can't afford a shootout in here."

When Tyler eased off, the gang leader looked back at Stoudenmire. "Marshal, I reckon we know how everybody stands, so let's just play the cards as they fall. Only don't ever say I didn't warn you that you're playin' with a cold deck."

"That's real white of you, Banning. I'll remember it when I put a noose around your neck."

Stoudenmire walked from the room with Tige bringing up the rear. Sam jumped out of his chair and spat a wad of phlegm at the door as it closed. Banning and Choctaw Tyler exchanged disgusted looks and watched silently as the spittle slowly wormed its way toward the floor. There wasn't much left to say, and besides, it had been one turd-knocker of a morning, start to finish.

5

That evening Banning sent for Isaac Porter. Things were at a point that he couldn't afford another miscue, and one way or the other he had to find out if the mayor was going soft in the guts. Something was boogering the old scoundrel, that was for damn sure. Over the past few weeks he had steadily grown more jumpy, almost choleric in his drunken fits of gloom. That was another thing, his drinking. Since becoming mayor, he had religiously avoided the booze, finding solace instead at the gaming tables around town. But lately he had been soaking up whiskey like a sponge, and so far he hadn't shown any signs of slackening off. Having a rummy as a frontman was a risky proposition, particularly in a business where corruption and graft were the order of the day. The cause of Porter's dismal moods was easily traced. In a word, Stoudenmire.

Until the German came to town, Isaac Porter had been a glad-handing, back-slapping, bon vivant. The rotund, rosy-cheeked, little charmer that everyone liked to think typified the warmth and casual hospitality that made El Paso what it was. This jocular, ever sprightly disposition was the big factor in getting Porter elected, and it had made him a perfect show-horse for Banning's political machine. But with Stoudenmire's arrival, a gradual transformation had taken place, almost as though Porter had been sapped of his vitality and amiable wit. Banning didn't give a tinker's damn for the dissolution of the man himself, but when it endangered the organization, that was a different ball of wax altogether. And if Porter had any notions of talking out of school, he would become expendable faster than a bat fart in a windstorm.

When the mayor arrived, he looked like a man with a mild touch of St. Vitus's dance. His face was pale and drawn, and he couldn't seem to sit still, squirming nervously in the chair like his chubby rump was stuck to a hot griddle. Around the Bannings he was normally as docile as a circus elephant, accepting their sarcasm and biting remarks with quiet good humor. But tonight he had a real case of the shakes, and Choctaw Tyler's flat stare did little to settle his nerves. Obviously he had spent the afternoon in company with John Barleycorn, for he reeked of stale whiskey, and his eyes were a watery shade of red. Yet even the whiskey had had no apparent effect on his frayed spirits. He was a bundle of raw, suppurating nerves, and whatever rode astraddle his shoulders had raked him bloody with fear and uncertainty. A man had only to look to see it gnawing on him, and none saw it more clearly than Ed Banning.

The gang leader worked up what passed for a smile. "Well, Isaac, what's new over at city hall? We haven't seen you much lately. Thought maybe you'd forgotten old friends."

"No, no. Nothing like that, Ed." Porter's eyes flicked
around the room, like timorous sparrows unable to find a
perch. "Just closing the books on the fiscal year and preparing the new city budget. Have to keep burning the midnight
oil, you know."

"Sure," Banning agreed congenially. "Running this town
is a big job. And we're damned lucky to have a man like you
to shoulder the load. Being mayor's not all rose water and kis-
sin' babies, is it?"

Porter dredged up a spastic smile, trying to ape the gang
leader's easy manner. "That's right, Ed. It's more of a burden than folks suspect. Carries a great responsibility, and
sometimes it gets to weighing on a man."

"Now it's funny you mention that, Isaac." Banning motioned over at Sam and Choctaw Tyler, who looked like a
couple of men watching a snake mesmerize a plump field
mouse. "I was just telling the boys today that we've been
workin' you too hard. By God, overseeing this operation is
no soft touch. Man needs a little time off every now and
then. Fact is, I was thinkin' of treating you to a vacation.
St. Louis maybe, or Kansas City. That wouldn't be too hard
to take, would it?"

The mayor's rubbery features brightened with surprise.
"Why no, that wouldn't be hard to take at all. Tell you the
truth, I have been off my feed a bit here lately."

Banning lit a cigar and casually drifted into a long mono-
logue on the merits of various eastern cities, making it clear
that he considered Chicago the best watering hole east of the
Big Muddy. Isaac Porter listened and nodded like an eager
schoolboy as the gang leader spoke. Slowly he began to relax, inwardly deriding himself for the groundless fears he had
conjured up about this meeting. Banning just wanted to chat,
deliver one of those rambling, disconnected lectures he was
so fond of on occasion. Porter slouched back in his chair with
renewed confidence. Hell, he wasn't in any danger! Banning
had himself a captive audience, and he was going to make
the most of it. And if Mother Porter's youngest son played
his cards right, he might just get a ticket east. A one way

ticket! Where didn't matter, just so he never had to return to this murderous hell-hole.

Porter was jarred out of his reverie as Banning neatly switched directions. "Say, Isaac, before I forget it. Stoudenmire has been down here bracing my people with threats. The knothead actually thinks somebody's gonna rat on me. Heard anything about it uptown?"

The mayor felt cold beads of sweat pop out on his forehead. Should he jeopardize this trip back east by telling the truth, or would it be better to play dumb? It was a knotty question, but he hesitated only a moment. "No, not a thing. You mean to say he's actually making threats against the people down here?"

"Worse than that. He's telling 'em that the only way they'll save their own hides is to swap sides and testify against me. Matter of fact, a little bird told me he'd even paid you a call."

Porter was taken completely off guard, and he suddenly had the look of a trapped animal. He was sweating profusely now, fighting desperately to keep his hands from shaking. "You mean yesterday? Oh, yes, he dropped by for a few minutes. Completely slipped my mind till you mentioned it. Just wanted to tell me that he'd taken steps to put the quietus on this vigilante scare. Nothing really. Nothing at all."

The mayor's voice had cracked only once during his short recital, but he had lied poorly, unconvincingly, and even now his face had the look of a constipated warthog. Banning betrayed nothing of what he was thinking, nodding absently as if the subject had been only of passing interest. The gang leader easily returned to events of a lighter nature, smiling and poking fun in his usual caustic manner. Porter once again relaxed, congratulating himself for having brought it off so smoothly. *By damn, when it came to tricky dodges, it took more than these louts to outfox an old con-man like Isaac Porter.*

Shortly the gang leader's banter wound down, and he allowed as how it was time to get back to business. If the mayor wouldn't mind, he had some things to talk over with Sam and Tyler. They'd get together again soon, real soon, and work out

the details for his trip east. Porter's spunk and jaunty disposition were again restored, and he took his leave appearing
vastly relieved. Easing through the door, he cocked his hat
at a rakish angle and got busy planning a real rip-snorter to
celebrate his own devilish cleverness.

When the door swung shut behind the old politico, Ed
Banning put it to a vote. Not that his outfit was anything even
mildly related to a democracy, but he just wanted a sounding
board for his own opinion. Sam and Choctaw Tyler both
agreed. *Porter had been lying.*

Banning tilted back in his chair and considered the matter at some length. The minutes ticked by, and the other two
men began to wonder if he had gone to sleep. After a while
his eyes opened, and he came back to the present, outlining
in clipped, brutal words how it would be handled. They had
no recourse but to kill Porter before he spilled his guts to the
law. Tyler was to shadow him and wait until he headed home
for the night. When he caught the mayor alone on some dark
street, he was to finish him off. But it had to be done with a
knife. Make it look like the old prick had been robbed and
killed by some drunk greaser. That way the townspeople
would have something to piss and moan about besides the
Bannings.

Choctaw Tyler found the idea of using a knife vastly appealing. Somehow when a man felt it slip home, grating on
bone, rending flesh, there was a greater sense of accomplish-
ment; then, too, the smell of warm, fresh blood had always
aroused him in some strange way, and that made it all the
better. Happy to be functioning at last, he nodded to Banning
and slipped out the back door.

Some three hours later Isaac Porter was weaving along a side-
street when the Indian caught up with him. The mayor was
carrying a heavy load, but when he saw the knife, his deadened senses surged back with alacrity. Still, it was a short and
savagely unequal struggle. Porter managed only one bleating
cry before Choctaw Tyler sunk the knife up to the hilt beneath his breastbone. The politician shuddered like a bolt of

lightning had just fired up his rectum, then collapsed at the knees, and folded to the ground. Hunkering down beside the dead man, Tyler wiped his knife clean, then expertly went over the body for wallet, watch, and other valuables. Just as he finished, he heard the crunch of a footstep in loose soil.

Someone was standing directly behind him, and from the nearness of the sound, he wasn't more than ten feet away.

"Don't move!" the deadly click of a Colt hammer being eared back had a logic all its own. "Stand up slow and get your hands over your head. Then turn around."

The Indian obeyed, and when he came about, he found himself facing a Peacemaker in the hand of Dallas Stoudenmire. *Tai-me* was indeed a god of strange whims. Grinning, he jerked a thumb back at Porter's body. "Marshal, you're trickier than I thought. Looks like the fat man wasn't the only one being followed tonight."

Stoudenmire felt his guts constrict into a hard knot. The mayor hadn't been much, but he deserved better than this. "Tyler, I sure wish I had been on your tail. From the looks of things, I should've been. But just between you and me, I was makin' night rounds when I heard the ruckus. Course, it's not like I came up empty-handed, is it?"

Choctaw Tyler's guttural chuckle sounded softly in the narrow street. "Tell you what, Marshal. There's just you and me here. Why don't you poke that Colt back in the holster and give me an even break. If you don't, we never are gonna find out who's the fastest."

Stoudenmire just shook his head, his eyes cold and hard as hailstones. "No dice. I want you alive. The only choice you've got is between hangin' or doing some tall talkin' about who set this deal up. Course, if you're stupid you could go for your gun. But that'd just get you dead." The Colt moved slightly in a sideways motion. "Unbuckle your gunbelt and be real careful."

The Indian shrugged, a look of stoic resignation coming over his face. His left hand moved toward the belt buckle, but in the same instant his right hand snaked down and swept up with a six-gun. It was the old magician's trick with a deadly twist; distract the eye with one hand and work your magic with the other.

But as his pistol cleared leather, Stoudenmire Colt belched flame in a blinding roar. Three bright dots appeared on Choctaw Tyler's shirtpocket, and he stumbled backwards, tripping over the mayor's body. Dead even as he fell, he hit the ground with a dusty thud.

Stoudenmire walked forward and stood for a moment inspecting the Indian's spread-eagled form. Satisifed that the man was dead, he turned and headed toward the plaza, shucking empties and reloading as he walked.

Killing men was one thing, but he never could stand the stench when death released its grip on their bowels.

CHAPTER NINE

1

Jim Gillette awakened only moments after the dusky glow of false dawn erased the darkened sky. The stars that hung suspended in the heavens each night, all cold silver and iced blue, had disappeared, and he shivered in the chill morning air. The resinous, piney odor from the embers of his fire had a sharp bite, and through the cobwebs of his drowsiness came images of a cherry blaze and a coffee pot perking delicious aromas. His camp was high on a mesa overlooking the Banning ranch in the valley below. These huge orange and golden buttes jutted skyward from the flatlands, forming sheer palisades that dominated the countryside in every direction. Above the escarpment there was an expanse as level as a billiard table, as though the gods had cleaved the top away in a moment of petulance and outrage. Over this barren, windswept rock-pile nothing grew save a profusion of piñon trees, gnarled and deformed by time and altitude into a stunted mockery of green things. Yet even atop these grotesque battlements, a man always had the taste of grit in his mouth, as though powdery granules of some tasteless filth were forever lodged between his teeth.

The deputy curled up into a tight ball, drawing his blanket closer against the damp cold. Something had roused him, and he tried to push back the fuzziness that clouded his brain, but for a moment his wits slogged along like a crippled mule. Then it hit him. What he heard was the pounding of hooves, and it was coming from the valley below. Not just horses either but cattle, lots of cattle. *Great smokin' Jesus! The gang must have ridden out during the night without him hearing them. But how the hell could that be?*

Whipping the blanket off, Gillette scrambled to his feet and ran toward the forward edge of the mesa. Taking cover behind a huge rock, he eased down on his belly and peered over the cliff. Suddenly he went slack-jawed with astonishment, rocked back on his haunches as though someone had dashed him in the face with a pan of cold water.

The Mexicans were raiding the Banning ranch! Goddammit, it just couldn't be possible.

Unable to believe what he had seen, he rubbed his eyes and took another look. This time there was no mistaking what he saw. Maybe it wasn't possible, but it was sure as hell a fact. The greasers were rustling Banning's cattle herd, and from up there, it looked like they were flat going to clean him out.

Gillette was staggered, his mind reeling with this quirky turn of events. Christ almighty, what Stoudenmire wouldn't give to be here right now! Although it was the last thing they would have imagined when he set out to scout the Banning ranch, it was damn sure a fine joke on those meatheads down below. The best joke he had ever heard, in fact. The rustlers getting rustled! Jesus, that was rich.

Evidently, Don Miguel Salazar figured it was time the *gringos* had a taste of their own medicine. Banning's night riders had sure as shit driven off enough of his stock, and the turnabout was long overdue, no two ways about it. Hell, the Mexicans could raid Banning every night for the next year, and they would probably still come out with a hole in their pockets. Not to mention the number of men they had had killed trying to protect their own herds. *¡Bueno!* Now maybe the pack of scutters working for Banning would hit leather and keep on riding until they found a place where folks weren't so all-fired persnickity about a bunch of cows.

Though it tickled his funnybone to see the Mexicans raiding Banning, the old lawdog would have much preferred it the other way around. That way he could have stuck to the plan and maybe come up with some hard evidence that would carry a little clout in a court of law. But at least something was happening, even if it wasn't what the marshal had set his sights on.

Gillette had been perched atop this windswept mesa for two nights now, and he was growing dismally bored with the whole deal. The gang had done nothing but loaf around all day and drink whiskey far into the night ever since he arrived. They had no apparent concern for the operation of the ranch itself, and quite obviously weren't planning a raid any time soon. Things were so peaceful, downright stultifying as a matter of fact, that he had intended returning to El Paso that very morning. It was a waste of time watching rustlers who for all intents and purposes had retired from the rustling business. Broiling under a hot ball of fire during the day and freezing his ass off at night wasn't exactly calculated to improve a man's frame of mind. Especially when those sapsuckers down in the valley had all the whiskey.

But all that had suddenly changed. Maybe the Mexicans had thrown a monkey wrench into his plans, but they had sure as hell livened things up. Even now they were driving the Banning herd right past him as they pushed south toward the river. In the faint glow from the sky, Gillette could see the *vaqueros* using their *reatas* as whips, hazing the longhorns into a ground-eating lope that shook the earth with a dull rumble. They had a ways to go, near-about twenty miles before they hit the border, and it looked like the Mexicans figured to stampede the stolen cattle every foot of the way. Watching them, the deputy couldn't help but think that they were real greenhorns at this rustling game. They should have hit just after midnight; that way they would have been across the border long before first light. The way things were shaping up, they would be damned lucky to get that herd into Mexico much before dinner time.

Out of the corner of his eye, he suddenly picked up movement around the ranch house. Changing positions for a better view, he saw men running helter-skelter across the compound, shouting and waving their arms toward the fast disappearing herd. Then they turned and raced for the corral, grabbing any horse that came to hand in their haste to get mounted. Within moments they were saddled and pounding out the gate, clearly intent on carrying the fight to the Mexicans.

While the *vaqueros* could save themselves by making a run for it, Gillette saw it as a profound injustice that they should lose the cattle. That presented him with a thorny problem, one which he couldn't debate overly long, for the Banning gang was riding fresh horses, and they would close the gap in a matter of minutes.

Should he side with the Mexicans or remain strictly an observer?

His instinctive reaction was to stick with his own countrymen even though they were outlaws, nothing more than border scum when a man got down to cases. Simply by doing nothing he would be taking their side, and no matter how it was sliced, it wasn't any of his business to start with. The smart move was to just sit back and play like a spectator; let them fight it out amongst themselves and devil take the hindmost. But then nobody had ever accused him of being smart, or even bright for that matter. Besides, he felt a nagging sense of loyalty to something greater than those two-bit desperados, whether they were American or not. Like Stoudenmire always said, personal feelings shouldn't get between a man and what's right, especially if it's got to do with the law.

Just then a small band of *vaqueros* fell back to fight a rear-guard action, and his debate came to a skidding halt.

Grabbing his rifle, Gillette jacked a shell into the chamber and steadied himself against the boulder. Yet even with the decision made, he couldn't bring himself to ambush the no-account bastards. Waiting until they passed beneath his hideout, the deputy drew a bead on the lead horse and squeezed off a shot. When the rider pitched headlong to the ground, the rest of the gang reined up short and milled around him in swirling confusion. Methodically, Gillette aimed and fired, dropping their horses from beneath them like cattle in a slaughterhouse chute. With each report another animal fell, thrashing and squealing in blind terror, and before he could empty the rifle, the gang had scattered over the countryside, running for their very lives.

The Mexicans were no less astounded than the Texans themselves, but only a fool would stop to question divine intervention such as this. Waving their rifles in salute, they wheeled their mounts and thundered off after the herd. Whoever the *hombre* was up on that cliff, he was a great artist with a rifle, and he wouldn't be forgotten in their prayers tonight.

Gillette wasted no time gloating over his handiwork. Striding back to his camp, he quickly packed his gear and saddled up. Ten minutes later he was riding down the narrow trail on the backside of the buttes and damned glad to be on his way. This deal had been a washout from the start, and it was high time to get his skinny rump on back to El Paso.

Suddenly he wondered what Stoudenmire would have to say about this little fracas. Probably wouldn't be too amused, but he'd be damn hard put to fault it. Compromise wasn't the marshal's way of doing things. He'd doubtless have shot the men instead of the horses. Still, all things considered, Gillette felt like it had been a pretty good morning.

2

Stoudenmire was discovering that there was more to catching fish than baiting the hook. The murder of Isaac Porter had silenced the sporting crowd as if a steel trap had clamped shut. Since he had caught Choctaw Tyler with knife in hand, there wasn't much doubt about who had ordered the killing. But knowing it and proving it was sort of like spreading horseshit on a soda cracker. Everybody admitted it looked good, but nobody wanted to take the first bite. Rightly enough, the marshal figured that the Bannings had somehow tumbled to his deal with Porter, yet the knowledge did little except add to his already sullen disposition.

Porter's death had soured his mood enough for one night, but Kate had really finished the job off. After rousing the undertaker and getting the bodies attended to, he had gone home prepared for another bitter argument. But Kate had already heard the whole story from Doc, and she didn't care to discuss the matter further. As it turned out, she didn't care to discuss anything. She had decided that if yelling and screaming couldn't sway him, then maybe the silent treatment would get better results. Not only was she silent, she was downright aloof, even to the extent of turning her back on him when they crawled into bed. While it was a childish thing to do, and damned irritating coming on top of everything else, Stoudenmire found it to be a grimly humorous joke on her. His tallywhacker wouldn't have stood on end right then if a whole troop of vestal virgins had swarmed over him buck-assed naked.

Somehow killing took its toll on a man in a way that he had never fully understood. After the shooting was over and the other man lay dead, it was like the hot juices inside him had all been drained away. Often during the war he could have laid down and slept for a whole week after an especially busy day on the killing ground. It had always puzzled him, even disturbed him in a way, for it was as though killing sucked him dry of passion and left his twig as limber and lifeless as a doddering old man's. Over the years he had finally come to accept it for what it was. Killing just plain wore him out, and there wasn't anything to be done about it. But he often wondered if it had the same effect on other men. It wasn't rightly something a man would talk about, and he had never felt close enough to anyone to ask. Not even Jim Gillette.

Staring into the darkness last night, listening to Kate pretend she was asleep, it came to him that the joke was really on her. She thought she was punishing him by cutting him off, when all the time, he had about the same urges as a gelded hog. Still, wanting it or not, her peevish little contrivance had left him with a foul taste in his mouth.

The chilly atmosphere around the southside this morning hadn't done much to improve his mood either. The Bannings hadn't wasted any time circulating the word, and overnight it became known that the mayor had met the same fate that awaited any double-crosser. The warning didn't pass unheeded, and Stoudenmire had been rebuffed at every turn on an early morning jaunt through the vice district. Those who had considered talking yesterday now wouldn't even give him the correct time. Maybe he would end up putting them in jail, they conceded, that remained to be seen. But if they spoke out of turn, Ed Banning would put them in a box, and dead was a damnsight more permanent than a visit to the pokey.

Yet there was one aftereffect the Bannings hadn't counted on. Although Porter was generally regarded as a corrupt politician, the townspeople took a dim view of anyone murdering their mayor. Even if he was a crook. More than ever before, the people of El Paso closed ranks against the Bannings. There was even talk of forming a coalition ticket to defeat them in the forthcoming elections. Reflecting back over the vigilante scare, Stoudenmire was pleased to see that folks were thinking in terms of ballots rather than bullets. Once they were united against gang rule, they wouldn't have much trouble ridding city hall of its resident scoundrels.

But simply defeating the Bannings at the polls wasn't enough for the lawman. He wanted their hides nailed to the wall, and he had no intention of slackening the pressure. Gillette might return at any moment with evidence of rustling, and he had already made arrangements with the banks to inspect the records of various politicians. Still, he was going to need a witness, someone who knew all the details behind the Bannings' skulduggery. Gamblers, saloonkeepers, and madams had met his most recent overtures with stony silence, and obtaining proof of protection kickbacks now seemed highly unlikely. That left official corruption, and with nothing much to lose, Stoudenmire decided to brace the second most powerful cog in the Banning machine.

Judge Marcus Hamer was an imposing figure of a man. He was tall, stoutly built, with a mane of white, wavy hair, and he had the disconcerting habit of staring a man straight in the eye whenever he spoke. Moreover, he was a man of some refinement, cultured in his ways, highly educated, and obviously from a background of considerable breeding. Though it was common knowledge that his family had once ruled Atlanta society, not even his closest friends knew what quirk of fate had brought him west. Local gossip attributed it to a family scandal of some sort, but the only thing known for certain was that he had chosen El Paso for reasons of his own and, having done so, quickly aligned himself with the Bannings. He owed both his soul and his position as circuit judge to the machine, yet he gave every impression of being his own man. One who didn't flinch when the political waters got choppy.

Stoudenmire found him affable, somewhat amused by the Bannings' bumbling peccadillos, and quite willing to talk. But strictly off the record. After offering the lawman a chair, he lighted a thin cheroot much favored by southern gentlemen, then settled back with a patronizing smile.

"Well, Marshal, I presume you're here to offer me immunity from justice. Frankly, I'm just the least bit affronted that it took you so long to get around to me. I understand you have been all over town extending the same inducement to the more scurrilous element."

Stoudenmire missed some of the words, but not the tone. This man was an old campaigner, and he might just be the toughest nut to crack in the whole organization. "Judge, I won't waste your time beatin' around the bushes You know I'm after the Bannings, and I suspect you know I'll get 'em. What I'm offering you is a chance to come out on the winning side. It's as simple as that."

Hamer smiled wryly and exhaled a thick cloud of smoke

through his nostrils. "My boy, an Englishmen by the name of Spencer once said that the ultimate result of shielding men from the effects of folly is to fill the world with fools. Now by no means am I inferring that you're a fool. But I do believe that you are perpetuating a folly. If it won't offend you, I would be happy to explain why."

"Fire away." Stoudenmire returned the smile, finding himself liking the old reprobate even if he was a thief. "I've got a thick skin."

"So I've heard." The judge flicked ashes from his cheroot and glanced around slyly. "But it will take more than that to bring Ed Banning to earth. Quite candidly, Marshal, you put me in mind of a man trying to shovel quicksand. The faster you shovel the deeper you sink, and the only way it ends is when you have sunk into obscurity. Now, as a case in point. You've been flitting about town trying to drum up a chink in Banning's armor. But there's not a man in El Paso who would dare to speak openly. Isaac Porter's death was a deplorable thing, but most effective, you'll have to admit. The denizens of our vice district have had their lips sealed forever. Whoever talked would be killed even though the Bannings went to jail, and that rather salient fact hasn't gone unnoted. Your folly, my friend, is that whoever deals with you ends up dead. I might also add that it is a folly that has now been exposed fully in a most impressive manner."

"What you're trying to tell me is that I've played out my string. That there's no way to get the Bannings."

"Precisely. By election time this whole affair will have blown over. I regret to say that most people live out their lives in thimbles. The dolts that populate El Paso are no different. They will gladly take the path of least resistance and be quite content to return to their humdrum existence."

Hamer chuckled to himself, as if amused by the profundity of his own statement. "Ofttimes, to win us to our harm, the instruments of darkness tell us truths. You and I, Marshal, must suffer under the knowledge that nothing ever changes. Politicians and lawmen come and go, but corruption never

falters. It feeds on itself as well as the people, and in our
benevolent form of government, it is the only constancy that
remains."

Stoudenmire's eyes narrowed, regarding the older man
speculatively. "What about you, Judge? Haven't you ever had
an urge to make it work better? Could be El Paso is the place
to start."

Hamer blinked and gave him a wry look. "My boy, it
occurs to me that you are considerably smarter than Ed
Banning gives you credit for. But don't waste your energies
trying to lure an old curmudgeon like myself into your
schemes. I no longer feel a young man's compulsion to wager against time and life. Like the apathetic masses, I am
content to exist."

Later, after having left the judge's office, Stoudenmire
crossed the plaza under a cloud of foreboding. Maybe the
high-toned old bastard was right. Everywhere he turned
he found nothing but blank walls. And damned if each one
didn't seem to be constructed of solid granite.

3

Kate had suddenly found her voice again. That evening when
Stoudenmire came home for supper, she was primed and raring to go. The moment he walked in the door the lawman
knew she was out for blood; even Tige crawled off in a corner and played possum. Her eyes crackled with a smoky brilliance that put him in mind of a treed wildcat, and he knew
it was only a matter of time until her claws came unsheathed.
Watching her bustle back and forth between the kitchen,
clanging pots, slamming dishes down on the table, he thought
again how complex and outright bewildering females became
once they got married. Evidently a wedding band wrought
some powerful change inside their skulls, and what it did to
their tongues was an absolute marvel. Not the good kind, or
even pleasant, just damned baffling and more than a man
could handle on an empty stomach.

Maybe it had something to do with the moon. Hell, everybody knew what wild things went squirrely at certain times of the month, and the longer he was married the more certain he became that women weren't anywhere near as tame as folks made out. Leastways the one he slept with wasn't, and by Christ, now that he stopped to think about it, he had the scars to prove it.

After they were seated at the table, the silence lasted only as far as the mashed potatoes. Kate let him get a big glop piled up on his plate, but when he reached for the gravy, she came out swinging. "Dallas, there's something we have to discuss. Things have gone far enough, and I think it's about time we started being honest with each other."

"Goddamn, Kate, can't you pick some place besides the supper table to start these squabbles? Let me at least eat my meals in peace."

"Please don't blaspheme my house with your crude language." She got that prim look on her face, like she had just led a prayer meeting in scripture reading. "Just for your information, the only time I ever see you is when you get hungry. You're so busy being a rootin'-tootin' lawman that you've forgotten you're also a husband. You've even gotten to where you come home at night and flop down in bed like I was some kind of wooden Indian not worth talking to."

"Me!" Stoudenmire almost choked on a mouthful of corn bread. "Now, by God, that takes the cake. Last night you acted like somebody had hemstitched your mouth shut. You've sure got a lot of room to rake somebody over the coals for not talkin'."

"Well I had every right," Kate replied indignantly. "You can't come tromping in after killing another man and expect me to be a cuddly little furball."

"Why not, for Chrissakes?" the lawman grated out. "The sonovabitch was trying to kill me! What should I have done, took off runnin' and let him pump my ass full of lead?"

"Dallas, I'm going to leave the table if you can't talk civil."

Stoudenmire almost laughed in spite of himself. She was like a spoiled little girl trying to play the great lady. So proper and chock full of decorum. Except in bed. By Jesus, she wasn't any lady then. After a moment he became aware that she was waiting for him to say something. "Kate, I'm damned if I can figure out what's got you riled up. Are you worried about me getting killed? Or is it the fact that I have to use a gun on other men every now and then?"

"Oh, what a horrible thing to say." Her face squinched up tight, and she looked on the verge of tears. "Dallas Stoudenmire, you ought to be ashamed of yourself. Every time you walk out that door, I die a little inside thinking you won't come back." Yet that was only part of the truth, she thought to herself. For she found it increasingly difficult to sleep with a man who killed so callously, almost as if he considered it his calling, maybe even enjoyed it. Still those were fears she was barely able to admit to herself. Never to him. "Of course it's you I worry about. With half the people in this town wanting to kill you, I'm almost out of my mind with fear."

"C'mon now. You're paintin' it darker than it is." He smiled, letting a joshing tone creep into his voice. "Besides, the other half's on my side. So that sorta evens things out."

"Very funny. But it's not a joking matter. You've risked your life enough for this dirty town. After all, only so much can be expected of one man, and it's time these people took a hand in their own troubles."

"That's what they pay me for. If people were willing to weed their own garden, then there wouldn't be any need for men like me."

"But that's no reason for you to keep on doing it," Kate insisted angrily. "They've stood by and watched it happen for years, and whatever El Paso is, it's just what they deserve. It's their fight, Dallas, not yours. If you can't see that, then you're either bullheaded or blind as a bat."

"Maybe. But I'm a lawman, and you'd better get used to the idea, missy. That's what I was when we got married, and that's what I'm gonna stay. So you just might as well quit flouncin' around with your tailgate up in the air and learn to live with it."

Stoudenmire sighed wearily, noting the wounded look on her face. "Let's talk about something else. I've got a meeting, and I'd like to get through it without belchin' up this meal all night."

Later, walking toward Hart's mill, the marshal thought back to Kate's last stinging comment. *Bullheaded or blind as a bat.* Damned if he didn't know but what he agreed with her. The way things had worked out a man had to be one or the other just to keep on going.

After inspecting the bank records of various politicians that afternoon, he had reached the conculsion that crooks must bury their money in tin cans. Despite his time and effort, the idea was simply another in a long row of washouts. Then Gillette had ridden in shortly afterwards with an astonishing report. The rustlers not only weren't stirring from the ranch, they were now being raided by the Mexicans! Even if the Banning gang was caught crossing the river with a whole goddamn herd, it probably wouldn't stand up in court after this. What judge was going to sign extradition papers against men who were merely retaliating against Mexican *bandidos*?

Jesus, it was enough to give a man the blue swivets. And the hell of it was, he couldn't think of a damn thing to do to get things straightened out. It was like old Judge Hamer had said. He had shoveled himself ass-deep in quicksand, and nobody seemed to have a rope handy. Maybe somebody was getting their shits and giggles out of this sorry mess, but it sure hadn't given him any laughs lately.

Stoudenmire found Seth Hart and his cohorts in their usual chairs. As he took his seat, it passed through his mind that he was getting to be a regular member of this little conclave. But it was a damned disquieting thought. Still, these men had brought him to El Paso, and he owed them an explanation, if nothing else.

Looking around the table at their silent faces, he found that the words came hard. "Gents, I'll make it short and sweet. What I've got to say speaks for itself."

The grave tone hardly seemed necessary, for the businessmen could tell from the look on the marshal's face that the news wasn't good. Briefly, he outlined the latest setbacks in their war on the Bannings. The rustling operation had been brought to a standstill. There wasn't a solitary soul in the vice district who would consider turning on the gang. The political hacks absolutely refused to cooperate in exposing corruption, even if granted immunity. Ed Banning had everyone in town scared shitless, and without hard evidence, the law was running dead last. Shrugging his shoulders with a futile gesture, Stoudenmire observed that it was a Mexican standoff. Short of forcing the Bannings into a gunfight, he didn't know where to turn.

When he finished, the businessmen merely stared at him in stony silence. What they were thinking was best left unsaid, and much as they hated to admit it, none of them had any worthwhile ideas anyhow. Seth Hart finally broke the uncomfortable lull. "Well, it's not like we haven't gained something out of all this. The people are fed up with the Bannings and their methods, and by election time we might just put a reform ticket across. One thing's for sure, Ed Banning will never again exert the influence he has in the past."

"Horseshit!" Everyone turned to look at Horace Adair, startled that he would dispute the old miller so openly. "Elections are more than a year off, Seth, and you're just kidding yourself if you think Banning won't have the town weighed and sacked by then. Goddammit, what we need are the vigilantes! I've said it all along, and I still contend it's the only way we'll ever rid ourselves of those bastards."

"Horace, you might have a point there." Hart studied the Irishman for a moment, then turned to Stoudenmire. "I seem to recall that the marshal said if his way didn't work, he'd be glad to lead the first charge on the southside."

The lawman's face was wooden, clearly the look of a man absorbed in reflections all his own. "Mr. Hart, I reckon that's one charge you'll have to lead yourself. I don't believe in mob law, and I won't have any part of it. If that's what you decide, then I'll resign and leave you to do what seems best. Otherwise I'll keep right on till I find some way to put Banning under."

"That's all very commendable, Marshal," Hart said. "But

it appears to me you're fresh out of ideas. What's left to do that you haven't already done?"

Every man at the table regarded him with somber gravity, and a deep stillness settled over the room. The moments ticked by with excruciating slowness while the lawman considered. When he spoke, his words were as cryptic as his expression. "I don't know. Maybe nothing. Maybe more of the same. Whatever it is, it'll separate the men from the boys."

Seth Hart just nodded, then suggested they all think it over and meet again the next evening. There was a quick murmur of agreement, almost as though each of the men wanted to escape the tension that hung between them. Dispirited, they trooped from the mill and walked off into the darkening night. They had much to reflect on before the harsh light of day brought them face to face with themselves, and a man was best left to his own devices when he crawled away to lick his wounds.

4

Doc Cummings trailed along with Stoudenmire when they left the meeting. Not saying much, they crossed Santa Fe Street and headed uptown, each man lost in his own thoughts. The little storekeeper had remained silent during the brief exchange between Hart and the lawman. As far back as he could remember, it was the first time he had ever been at a loss for words. But how could a man speak up when he knew that every word out of his mouth would only add to a friend's already grinding misery? Stoudenmire had been brought to El Paso on his say-so, which sort of left him betwixt and between. Anything he said now would have the ring of sour grapes, and he wasn't about to badger the marshal like some old fishwife, particularly when recriminations would serve no useful purpose. Stoudenmire had failed and the less said the better. The whys and wherefores of that failure now seemed meaningless, something that required neither explanation nor discussion. They knew, and that was enough. Even Hart and the boys hadn't been too rough on the lawman, and Cummings was thankful for that. The man was being devoured whole by furies of his own, and he damn sure didn't need anyone to tell him that he'd fallen flat on his ass. He knew, and whatever he was saying to himself right at this moment was a damn sight worse than anything Seth Hart's crowd might be thinking.

Reflecting back over the past month or so, that first night flashed through Cumming's mind. The night Stoudenmire had come to El Paso to discuss cleaning up the town. He had seemed so sure of himself, cocky almost, and if ever a man looked the part of a town tamer it was Dallas Stoudenmire. *Town tamer.* That was the term John Simmons had used, and everyone readily agreed that such a man was exactly what they needed. Then, when Stoudenmire had walked into the room, they knew that this was the man for the job, sensed it somehow, like when a fellow gets a hunch at the faro table and goes whole hog. Whatever kind of inner steel that it took to belt other men in the head, intimidate them, shoot them if necessary, Stoudenmire had it. When he left that night to catch the train back east, they had laughed and carried on like kids. Slapping one another on the back, they had congratulated themselves on picking a real stem-winder, even drinking numerous ribald toasts to Ed Banning's early demise.

Now that night seemed long ago, as though each week had been a year in itself, and he felt like he had aged just about that much waiting for Banning to fall. Seth Hart always said that a man had to think big if he wanted to make his mark. What he forgot to add was that anyone who reached for the sun was just naturally bound to get blisters. *Blisters!* Hell, they had gotten enough to make them look like they had been scalded in boiling oil. Enough to make fools of them all.

Still, Stoudenmire's tenure as marshal hadn't been a complete loss. He had put the quietus on the Mexican trouble, and there was some solace in that. Not much, but you had to give the man credit. They had hired him to put the damper on the greasers as well as get rid of the Bannings, and he had done half the job anyway. But with the Mexicans peaceful again, everyone tended to ignore that and remember only that he hadn't axed Ed Banning's skinny neck. Christ, it was a grudging world. Full of fat old men who paid others to do their fighting and then bellyached like foundered mules when the hired gun didn't get himself killed just on cue.

Suddenly a very curious thought raced through Cumming's head. What if Dallas had been right all along? Maybe Seth Hart was another Ed Banning after all. Not so cold and deadly perhaps, but a man of ruthless ambition nonetheless, one who merely clothed it under the guise of civic benevolence. The more he thought about it, the better sense it made. Hart had never been overly concerned about the Mexicans, not even at the start. It was always the Bannings he harped on, and it stood to reason that he had engineered this whole deal just to rid himself of a troublesome obstacle. Namely, Ed Banning.

Even now the old devil was laying the groundwork to sack Stoudenmire as marshal. That benign little speech he made tonight was only so much crap. *Let's think it over and meet again tomorrow night.* Bullshit! He had seen Hart use that gambit a hundred times. Let the other man stew in his own juices for a day and then chop his head off with a few kindly, well chosen words. Stoudenmire wasn't going to get another shot at the Bannings. He was on his way out. Then, after things had returned to normal, Hart would recruit another fast gun and start the whole bloody business all over again.

Before Cummings could carry the thought further, he realized the lawman had said something. "Sorry, Dallas, I didn't hear you. My mind was a thousand miles off."

Stoudenmire jerked his head toward a sleezy cantina at the side of the street. "Just said I feel like a drink. Wanta join me?"

"Sure. I could stand a little fortifying myself, come to think of it." The storekeeper looked away, fearing his face would somehow betray the surprise he felt. Things must really be bad. Never had he known Stoudenmire to take a drink while on duty. The man was like a monk, spartan in his habits, limiting the pleasures other men took for granted to within the four walls of his own home.

Without another word Stoudenmire led the way into the cantina and took a seat at a table along the far wall. The men ranged around the room were mostly Mexican, and they studiously avoided any show of curiosity. *Gringos* seldom frequented this place, but if *el hombre* wanted to drink here, then who were they to object. Presently a barmaid materialized at their table, and the marshal ordered tequila.

When the girl returned with a bottle and two glasses, Stoudenmire calmly poured both brimful. Sprinkling salt over the web of flesh beside his thumb, he licked sparingly and tossed the drink off in one gulp. The tequila hit his gut like molten lead and bounced dangerously, but he held it down. Breathing deeply, he shuddered like a wet dog, then glanced over at the storekeeper.

"Doc, get that stupid look off your face. You've seen grown men drink before. What's so strange about that?"

Cummings still hadn't touched his glass. "Nothing, Dallas. Nothing at all. Except that you're going about it for the wrong reasons. Hell, tomorrow things won't look half so bad, and I'm layin' odds you'll figure a way out of this deal yet."

"Thanks for those kind words, brother-in-law." The lawman refilled his glass and stared at it listlessly. "But you and I both know that Big Daddy Hart is gonna give me the gate tomorrow night. So if I was you, I wouldn't be coverin' any bets."

The storekeeper started to say something, then tossed off his own drink and gasped when it hit bottom. After a moment he looked up. "Much as I hate to admit it, you've been right about a lot of things. Looks like old friend Seth is out to crown himself king, and near as I can figure, you're not arranging the coronation as fast as he'd like it."

Stoudenmire grinned wryly. "You figure pretty good, Doc. The old fart is gonna get rid of the Bannings even if he has to raise the vigilantes. That hogwash he was dishin' out tonight didn't mean a damn thing. Just as soon as he ties a can to my tail, there won't be anyone to stop him, and he'll put this whole goddamn town to the torch if that's what it takes."

"Yeah, but you're still US marshal. Don't forget that. You could stop him no matter what."

"Maybe. If I want to get myself killed facin' down a mob. I'm not real sure El Paso's worth it. The only other way is to send for the Rangers, and I doubt they could get here in time to head off what he's got in mind."

"Well hell, there's more'n one way to skin a cat." Cummings leaned over the table and tapped the lawman's arm. "Listen, there's plenty of good people in this town that won't hold still for that kind of crap. Why, I bet I could round up twenty, thirty men who'd stand with you when the time came."

Stoudenmire jiggled his glass, watching the tequila swirl around in tiny circles. "What good would it do gettin' them killed? It's like I told you before, Doc. When you've got two men who figure that there's room for only one kingfish, it's the folks in the middle who end up gettin' hurt. Maybe that's not how the Good Lord intended it, but that's damn sure how she works out."

Cummings nodded absently, staring into his empty glass. "Funny. When we were walkin' over here, I had it all figured out that Hart wanted to can you so he could hire another fast gun. Never occurred to me that the tricky bastard was just workin' up to an excuse for calling out the vigilantes." His voice faltered, as though the thought had touched a raw nerve. "Shitfire, let's have another drink. Maybe the sonsabitches'll kill each other off and we can start this town off right, the way it should've been."

Stoudenmire regarded the older man for a moment, then shook his head. "Guess I didn't want a drink as bad as I thought. Like the fella said, answers come sorta hard at the bottom of a bottle. Think I'll call it a night, Doc. Maybe tomorrow we'll wake up and find out we're both just a couple'a damn fools."

He tossed a coin on the table and headed for the door. They parted outside, and Cummings watched him walk off into the night, a deeply troubled man. Musing on it for a

moment, the little merchant hoped that Kate didn't give him
too hard a time tonight. Whatever else he was, Dallas Stoudenmire wasn't a quitter. But right now he was feeling mighty
close to being one. He would need all the understanding Kate
could give him, and then some.

Cummings wandered aimlessly for a while, then struck off
toward the plaza and his store. After entering through the
back door, he lit a lamp, broke open a fresh bottle, and sat
down to do some serious thinking of his own. If Stoudenmire
couldn't rid El Paso of the Bannings and hold Seth Hart in
check, then what the hell was left? The question disturbed
him, but the lack of an answer was downright chilling.

Puzzling over it, Cummings realized that the marshal was
essentially a man of action, one who always chose the most
direct solution to a problem. He wasn't a devious man, a
schemer, the kind who could employ subterfuge or guile to
put an opponent under. Moreover, he believed in the sanctity
of the law, respected it fiercely. He wouldn't bat an eye at facing another man's gun, but it would never occur to him to
acquire evidence in an illegal manner.

Like stealing the Bannings' records!

The thought came to him like a bolt from the blue, and
with it the gut reaction that it was the solution to their dilemma. The Bannings must keep records. They couldn't run
an organization without books of some sort. Whatever dirty
work had gone on in this town and whoever had gotten paid
off would be in those books. He knew it just as sure as he
knew his own name, instinctively and without a doubt in the
world. And the first place to look was the safe in Ed Banning's
office.

The storekeeper had another drink and mulled it over. He
wasn't a particularly brave man even by his own standards,
but by Christ, he wasn't a coward either. It would be risky,
and he'd have to be slicker than greased owlshit to pull it
off. But he owed it to the town to try. And to Stoudenmire.
Goddammit, that's what it all boiled down to! He owed it
to Stoudenmire more than any of those mealy-mouthed bas-

tards who sat around waiting for someone to save them from their own gutless palpitations.

By damn, he would drink to that. And to his first little sortie as a burglar. Down with Ed Banning and up Seth Hart's fat ass! Sonovabitch, that had a good ring to it, and if anybody could pull it off, it was that sneaky little shit by the name of Doc Cummings.

Late that night, after the southside dives had closed, Cummings gingerly stalked through the alley behind the Coliseum. He had downed the better part of a quart, just to steady his nerves, he told himself. Still, he wasn't feeling any pain, and his step was about as light as a bull elephant. After looking up and down the alley, he forced the lock on the rear door of Banning's office and scuttled inside. There he found himself confronted by what seemed the biggest goddamned safe in Christendom. It was an ugly, black brute that towered over him like a barge, but he had to snicker in spite of himself. In the dark its round, shiny dial looked like Cyclop's beady eye watching his every movement, and somehow that struck him as damned humorous, hilarious almost. Shushing himself he went to work.

Although he was a fledgling thief, he knew how to use a crowbar, and he tackled the job with all the finesse of an ore-crusher. Gouging and prying, he went to work on the safe's doors.

But as he heaved and sweated over the cold steel, he failed to see the door knob slowly turning. In his fuzzy euphoria, the storekeeper had forgotten one salient detail. Sam Banning didn't live at the Parker House with his brother. He kept a room upstairs.

The door suddenly flew open, and Sam leaped into the office, covering him with a cocked six-gun. Cummings didn't cower or beg for mercy. He was looking the grim reaper straight in the eye, and it wasn't exactly the moment to go fainthearted. Whirling, he threw the crowbar with all his strength and jumped for the back door. But he never made it.

The Colt roared twice, and the game little merchant crashed to the floor dead.

Lighting a lamp, Sam turned the body over and stared in slack-jawed bewilderment. *Doc Cummings!* He lumbered back a step, head spinning in a witless stupor, and for a moment he went cold with sweat. Then he slammed the lamp down on the desk and raced out the back door. Whatever had happened here was over his head, and right now the only thing he wanted was to get his big brother.

By Jesus, that was the ticket. Let Ed figure it out!

5

Early next morning Jim Gillette knocked on Stoudenmire's door. The deputy was filled with a sense of dread; unable to shake the feeling that he had unwittingly become a messenger of death. Last night he had restrained himself with no little effort from awakening the marshal, knowing full well what would happen if he did so. Instead, he had downed a pot of coffee and waited for the first, golden streamers of sunrise, telling himself that Stoudenmire would be more reasonable with Cumming's body already laid out in the undertaking parlor.

From years of watching men kick out their lives on saloon floors and dusty cowtown streets, he knew that time often worked a curious change on the dead man's friends and family. Those who were notified immediately experienced a mixture of shock, sorrowful bereavement for their loved one, and blind rage for the man who had killed him. But if they found out about it later, often even as little as a few hours, their pain and mindless fury was mitigated in a quirky sort of way. Somehow the hurt faded almost as fast as it began, and instead of mourning the dead man, they felt sorry for themselves. It was as if they regretted the poor fellow's death not nearly so much as they resented him leaving them in the lurch on such short notice.

Gillette had always thought it was damned odd, but then most folks were sort of queer in the head anyway if a fellow stood off and watched the numbskull things they did. Like trying to crack Banning's safe with a crowbar. Jesus!

Still that was over and done with, and there was no way to bring the dead back. Right now he had to face the living, and whatever gods were watching, he sure as hell hoped they would lend a hand in putting the damper on Stoudenmire's temper.

When the lawman opened the door, he knew immediately that something was bad wrong. "C'mon in, Jim. You look like a man carrying a heavy load."

Gillette stepped inside and pulled his hat off, twisting it nervously between his fingers. "Dallas, I wish to Christ I wasn't the one that had to tell you, but there ain't no other way. Doc Cummings is dead."

Stoudenmire just stared at him, showing nothing. "Who got him?"

"Sam Banning." The deputy knew what was coming and he added hurriedly, "But it ain't like it sounds."

Stoudenmire's face went ashen, and every muscle in his body seemed taut as strung catgut. "Tell me."

"Doc broke into Banning's office and tried to crack the safe. Hadn't no more'n got started when Sam caught him." Gillette's voice faltered then, and he looked down at the floor. "Doc heaved a crowbar and took off runnin'. Sam drilled him twice goin' away."

"What about witnesses?"

"Nary a one. Just the two of 'em involved. The sign's all there to read though. Sam went over and rousted Banning out of bed, and then they come and got me. I went over it real careful, and it's just like I said."

The marshal's color had returned, but his eyes were like death warmed over. "When did it happen?"

"Somewheres after two this mornin'." Gillette hawked and cleared his throat. "I had Doc taken over to Pritchard's funeral parlor."

Stoudenmire nodded vaguely, suddenly aware that Kate would have to be told. Then he glanced back at Gillette, and his gaze hardened. "What'd you do with Sam Banning?"

The deputy shifted his cud of tobacco and swallowed heavily. Now came the hairy part. "Nothin.' There ain't no way we can touch him legally. Doc was caught in the act, and every man's got the right to defend his own property. Even if his name's Banning."

Some moments passed as the lawman digested that. Then he grunted skeptically. "That sounds like something Ed Banning would say."

"Matter of fact, he did. Just used more words, that's all." Gillette took a hitch at his belt and met the younger man's look head-on. "Dallas, I got an idea what you're thinkin', but it won't wash. Whatever Doc was lookin' for in that safe, he was out of line. There ain't nothin' we can do to the Bannings, and you'd best set your mind to it."

"What's that about Doc and the Bannings?" Kate's voice came from the kitchen doorway. Turning, they found her staring at them with mild alarm. Gillette was reminded of a young doe, all wide-eyed and nervously alert at some strange sound, and he suddenly wanted very much to be somewhere else.

Stoudenmire spoke without looking around. "Jim, you'd better get on back to the office. I'll be down a little later."

The deputy shot a glance at Kate, seeing her tense, then ducked out the door. Stoudenmire was left with the dirtiest job of all, but he was damn glad the lawman had let him off the hook. Relieved was more like it, as though somebody had just pulled him clear of a load of granite. Telling people their kinfolks had gone under was a messy business, and no matter how many times a man did it, he always walked away feeling soiled and kind of rotten at the core.

When he went through the gate, it came just about like he expected it would. First the stifled cry, then a scream of shock and disbelief, and finally the wretched, sobbing moan that was enough to tear a man's heart out by its roots. The wail of Indian women was worse, but not a hell of a lot. Whatever kind of female it was, animal or human, the sound stuck with a man for days, and even worse sometimes in the night when he couldn't chase it away. Lengthening his stride, the old lawdog struck out for the plaza, not the least bit shamed that it was Stoudenmire back there instead of him.

When Gillette reached the office, men slowly began drifting in to discuss this latest calamity. They cursed and grumbled, drank coffee, swilled whiskey out of pint bottles, and talked incessantly of raising the vigilantes. Seth Hart waddled in before long with his somber-faced cronies, and the crowd swarmed around him demanding some action be taken against the Bannings. The miller talked a hell of a lot without saying anything one way or the other, and the morning ground on with deadly slowness. Listening to them jabber on and on, it passed through Gillette's mind that, if a man was to put their brains in a jaybird, the sonovabitch would probably fly backwards.

Then, shortly before noon, Stoudenmire walked through the door. Tige was at his side, and for a moment the two of them regarded the crowded room with a hollow stare. The lawman's face was grim as weathered tombstone, and it was obvious that he had just come from a house where death now resided.

Seth Hart stepped forward and extended his hand. "Marshal, we all want you to know how sorry we are, and we'd be beholden if you would pass along our condolences to Mrs. Stoudenmire. Doc was a fine man, a friend to every decent person in this town, and he'll be missed around here."

The lawman's face remained blank, and he dropped the politician's hand after a perfunctory shake. "Thanks. My wife'll be glad to know he had so many friends."

Hart glanced around uncomfortably, wondering if the others had caught the marshal's sardonic tone. But he came right back, blustering with authority and purpose. "I might add that his friends mean to do something about this cowardly act, Marshal. The boys have been talking it over, and we think it's high time to call out the vigilantes. The Bannings absolutely can't be allowed to go any further. Naturally, we'd prefer it if you'd deputize everyone and make it legal and above board."

"Naturally." Stoudenmire's reply was clipped, with just the

faintest trace of insolence. "Tell you what, Hart. It's gettin'
along toward dinner time so why don't you get these boys fed
and meet back here in a couple of hours. By then we oughta
know what's what."

Seth Hart got a funny expression on his face, like he had
heard it but he couldn't quite believe it. There was something
more to this than met the eye, and he had the distinct feeling
that the marshal had just snookered him into a corner. But
he couldn't very well refuse, and it would look fishy if he demanded they march now. Stoudenmire's suggestion seemed
very practical and everyone knew it. Hell, nobody wanted to
fight on an empty stomach.

The men filed out with Hart in the lead, and within moments Stoudenmire and Gillette had the place to themselves. Gillette was more than a little thunderstruck himself
by this sudden turn of events but he just waited for whatever
was coming next. The lawman had something up his sleeve,
and knowing him, it would probably be a real ball-buster.

After a moment the marshal sat down at his desk, took out
pen and paper, and began writing. Finished, he unpinned his
badge and tossed it on the desk. Then he handed Gillette the
note. "Jim, that's my resignation. As of right now, you're marshal of El Paso."

Gillette studied the paper for a moment, then looked up.
"I reckon you mean to call the Bannings out."

"That's about the size of it," Stoudenmire observed.

"And you just suckered Hart into gettin' the vigilantes out
of your hair so you could do it all by your lonesome."

"You're a foxy old buzzard." Stoudenmire gave him a wry
look. "Didn't figure I had you fooled."

Gillette dropped the note on the desk. "You didn't have
Hart fooled neither. But that's nothin' one way or the other.
What's important is that you're settin' out to do something
that goes against everything you ever stood for. Call the
Bannings out and you're gonna be spittin' in the teeth of the
law you've sworn to uphold. Now you tell me how that differs
from the vigilantes marchin' over there and lynching 'em?"

Stoudenmire's mouth set in a hard line. "Jim, I'm fresh out

of answers. Maybe there's times when the law's just not enough. The Bannings toe-dance around it and make it bend to suit themselves. I couldn't stop 'em, and Doc got himself killed trying to help me. I reckon if I had put 'em under when I should've that wouldn't have happened."

He paused, staring at his scrawled resignation for a moment. "I failed as marshal, but I'm not gonna fail Doc. Sometimes a man has to fight just because he couldn't live with himself if he walked away. Right or wrong, that's how my stick floats."

Their eyes met and Stoudenmire flashed his old grin. Then the moment passed, and he came up out of the chair, heading for the door. "Look after yourself, pardner."

Gillette moved to block his path. "Listen goddammit, there ain't no law that says you get to have all the fun. I'd sorta like a whack at them pricks myself, so just count me in."

"Thanks, Jim, but it's no go. This is personal. Besides, this town's got to have some law even if it's a crotchety old coot like you."

Smiling tightly, Stoudenmire brushed past him and walked out with Tige at his heels. Crossing the plaza, he felt a strange numbness settle over him. He had lived with danger all his life; sometimes it seemed as though he had no memory back beyond those first bloody days on the killing ground. But this was different. There was a cold, icy feeling in his spine, like death's ugly, fleshless hand was squeezing down on his backbone. Maybe it was a sign. Something warning him of what was to come. Then he chuckled. There weren't any signs. Just fast men and slow men. The quick and the dead.

Absently he noted the shops and people on the streets as he walked along. Curiously, it was as if he were seeing it all for the first time. Again he chuckled to himself. Or maybe for the last time. Then it came to him that first, last, or never, it really didn't make a damn. The only friends he had in this town was the one he had just left behind and the dog padding along at his side. Come to think of it, they were the only friends he had in the world. Whatever the reason, he just naturally couldn't take people except in small doses. But what the hell, a man in his game needed allies, not friends. After all, the friends you didn't have couldn't weasel out when the shooting started. That was the nice thing about Tige. The surly sonovabitch wouldn't back off from a bull alligator if he was hamstrung and blind in both eyes. Which was a hell of a lot more than you could say for most men. Even the best of them.

Without realizing it, he found himself standing in front of the Coliseum. The icy feeling was still with him, but he felt calm now, loose and easy inside where it counted. Then he knew that it was all right. Once the tightness drained away, everything else fell into place, and he didn't even have to think. Just react.

The moment he pushed through the bat-wing doors, he sensed that the Bannings had known he would come. Ed stood at the bar, while Sam casually studied a shot on the billiard table across from the door. They had him in a cross fire, no matter who drew first. But even so, he liked the odds. Somehow it made the game sweeter, more inviting, just the way he would have wanted it.

Glancing from one to the other, he decided to take Sam first. The overgrown crock of shit deserved it, and besides, Doc would have liked it that way. Watching Sam out of the corner of his eye, he laid it out for Banning.

"Banning, I've come to punch your ticket. Maybe you recollect I warned you once not to be around when your number was called."

Banning turned from the bar, brushing his coat back over the handle of his pistol. "Stoudenmire, you'd better turn around and walk out of here. Cummings got what was coming to him, and we've got the law on our side. Don't push it."

Stoudenmire's pale eyes went cold as chilled stone. "Shit, there's no law here. There's just you and me and your dumbass brother. Make your fight, mister. You're about to get killed."

Sam Banning's nerve suddenly broke, and he clawed at the pistol on his hip. Stoudenmire's arm moved in a blurred motion, and a Colt appeared in his fist. The gun bucked, and Sam was thrown across the billiard table, dusted front and back.

Crouching, Stoudenmire spun around, noting that Ed was no slouch with a gun. The gang leader had fired even as Sam died, but Tige was leaping for his throat, and the big dog took the ball straight through his spine. Banning thumbed off another shot as Tige dropped at his feet, and the slug caught Stoudenmire in the chest. Hurled backwards, he crashed into the wall and felt his knees start to buckle. Banning's mouth tightened in an evil grin, and he popped off a third shot. But he had rushed it, overanxious for the kill, and the window at Stoudenmire's side exploded in a shower of glass.

Steadying himself against the wall, Stoudenmire raised the Colt very deliberately, as if he had all the time in the world. When it jumped in his hand a small fountain of blood spurted out over Banning's shirtfront. Drunkenly, he staggered away from the bar and began to sag, groping blindly with his hands like a man trying to break a fall.

Extending his gun arm, Stoudenmire drew a fine bead and gut-shot Banning just as his rump hit the floor. The gang boss jerked upright, as if he were rowing a boat, his eyes bursting with pain and shock. Then the stench came as death loosed his bowels, and he settled to the floor. His leg jumped once, then stiffened, and he lay very still.

Stoudenmire's eyes glazed over, and he wiped his hand across his face. When his vision cleared, he looked down on the dead men for a moment, then shoved away from the wall. Willing himself to stand, to walk, to remain erect, he lurched across the room and pushed out through the doors. Gillette was there, and he rushed forward, eyes glistening wetly without shame.

Stoudenmire looked up through a bright haze of pain and grunted hoarsely. "Jim, you'd better call the undertaker. They killed Tige."

Then the Colt dropped from his hand, and he fell into Gillette's arms.

EPILOGUE

Stoudenmire stepped to the door, then paused to kiss Kate once more. Her arms encircled his neck, and she planted one square on his mouth, long and slow with a naughty little probing just for good measure. The kind of kiss nice girls weren't supposed to know about. The lawman squeezed her in a bearish grip, feeling the soft flesh yield and melt against him.

Christ! She was a shameless hussy about some things. Putting a kiss like that on him, right in the doorway where all the neighbors could get a real eyeful. But who the hell cared what other people thought? They didn't know about the wildcat that crawled into his bed every night, and by God, if she wanted a little kiss every now and then, he was damn sure going to oblige her.

Kate's soft lips curved in a teasing smile, and she stepped back, straightening his coat lapel. "There now. That ought to hold you till suppertime anyway. You just make sure you don't wear yourself out jayhawking around town."

"Lady, you oughta be arrested for carryin' dangerous weapons." He spun her about and swatted her on the bottom. "And don't be givin' people advice about getting their rest. It's not me that yells uncle in the clinches."

"Oh, what conceit!" Her mouth curled in a tiny pout. "Run along, Mr. Stoudenmire. Go on downtown and let everyone gawk at the big bad lawman. You'll get your comeuppance tonight."

Stoudenmire chuckled, then turned and hobbled off down the walk. "Is that a promise or a threat?"

"Both. But I'll let you take it out in trade." Kate giggled wickedly and slammed the door shut when he looked back.

The lawman went through the gate chortling to himself. Damned if things didn't have a way of doing a bellyflop just when a man least expected it.

The last couple of months had brought a warm glow of discovery in the Stoudenmire household. Doc Cummings' death and the subsequent shootout with the Bannings had wrought a startling transformation in Kate. Somehow she had sifted it out for herself and come to the conclusion that certain men just weren't meant to be gelded. Once that dawned on her, and she came to grips with it, her entire attitude had changed. Now she made jokes about other women and their henpecked husbands, laughingly dubbing them *mansos*, the tame bulls, a term she had picked up from her Mexican housekeeper. Though Kate never said anything openly, she had become fiercely proud of her man, and quietly confident that he could handle anything that came down the pike. When she looked at other women nowadays, she felt something akin to pity, or perhaps merely compassion, for they would have to live out their lives never knowing what it was to take a real man to bed. And under the Stoudenmire roof, there was no longer the slightest doubt who ruled the roost.

Kate had become a woman, and she reveled in the sheer joy of using feminine wiles to get her way. Dallas Stoudenmire was just a big, lumbering teddy-bear now that she had figured him out, and Mrs. Stoudenmire had his number anytime she wanted to punch it.

The lawman himself had spent considerable time reflecting on this volatile and highly mercurial creature who now shared his life. But he still wasn't sure that he understood her, or for that matter that he ever would. Maybe the fact that he had broken with his own code to avenge Doc had triggered the change in her. Though she had never said one way or the other, he sensed that a bond of some sort had taken root between them the day he killed the Bannings. Love. Venegeance. An eye for an eye. Simple gratitude for not letting her brother go to his grave with the debt unsettled. Damned if he knew what made her tick, and somehow it didn't seem so important anymore that he try and decipher it. She had turned out to be the kind of woman he had always wanted, the loving, gutsy, spitfire who was "root hog or die" all the way. And that was enough.

Still, he had to laugh sometimes when he saw that sparkle come into her eye, and she started wheedling and conniving. Women just weren't happy unless they had some little plot going; scheming and finagling new ways to twist a man's ying-yang so he'd sit up and bark like a lap dog. But what the hell! Long as a man didn't lose his balls in the bargain, it was a pretty comfortable arrangement.

Strolling along the street, he greeted merchants and townspeople with an easy smile as they inquired after his health. The briskness of winter had settled over the basin, and it was good to be walking again, even though he felt slightly ridiculous using a cane. The crisp air made him forget the dull throb in his chest, and the sight of snowcapped mountains in the distance brought new strength to the rubbery joints in his knees. His recuperation had been slow and painful, and damned uncertain at times. But he was back on the job, part way anyhow. And that was what counted most.

After circling the plaza, he entered the office to find Gillette catnapping. The old lawdog roused himself with a lazy stretch and started grumbling right off. "Dallas, we gotta do something to stir up a little excitement around here. This goddamn town's so peaceful it's downright mortifying."

Stoudenmire hobbled around the desk and eased down in his chair. "Pardner, you name it and we'll do it. What'd you have in mind? A little mumblety-peg. Rackin' up some horseshoes. Maybe a fast game of marbles?"

"Aw, quit your joshin'." Gillette opened the door on the

little pot-bellied stove and tossed in a load of wood. "You know what I'm talkin' about. Maybe we oughta pull up stakes and find us a town that ain't had a dose of law yet."

"Christ almighty," the lawman snorted. "We've just got started in El Paso. As long as there's whorehouses and gambling dives, some bonehead is gonna try to get his meathooks on the whole box of goodies. The game's the same, Jimbo. Only the faces change."

"Like Seth Hart, maybe?" The deputy cocked one eye with a sly smirk.

"Maybe, Maybe not. Looks like the old devil might just run for mayor." Stoudenmire explored the thought for a moment before resuming. "Which means he'd have to play it strictly on the up and up, leastways if he wants the reformers' vote. But that doesn't change nothin'. If it's not him, someone else'll come along. There's always somebody that wants to sandbag the bets and skim off the cream."

"Damn me, if you ain't right. Matter of fact, it looks like that particular ailment is goin' around like measles." Gillette pulled a newspaper off his cot and tossed it on the desk. "Accordin' to that, the Earp boys just had 'emselves a turkey shoot over in Tombstone. Caught a bunch of the opposition in some corral and just flat plowed 'em under. You reckon Wyatt's tryin' to do the same thing over there that Banning done here?"

Stoudenmire studied the newspaper article, nodding to himself. Some moments passed before he looked up. "From what I saw of Earp in Dodge, I wouldn't put it past him. Course, you never can tell. Some towns need more law than others. Hell'sfire, there's even times when the law itself has to have its neck jerked back in joint."

"Well, much as I hate to say it, I don't look for no more trouble in this burg." The deputy wagged his head ruefully and squirted the stove with tobacco juice. "Folks've just naturally got the idea you're half-bear and half-alligator, and they don't want no part of it."

The marshal let that pass. Everybody in town had been goggling over him like he was some circus freak, and it was growing a bit wearisome. "I'll tell you something, Jim. It's the elections that are gonna tell the tale in El Paso. People have got a right to choose whatever kind of leaders they want, and they generally get just what they deserve. But whichever way it works out, lawmen can't take sides. We're sorta like spectators at a cock fight. The best we can do is try to keep the lid on and make sure the good ones don't die for nothin'."

"Like Doc Cummings?" Gillette observed.

There was a momentary lull, and even the pot-bellied stove seemed to be thinking it over, holding its angry crackling to a simmering whisper.

Gilette quickly shifted the conversation around to routine matters of policing the town, and after a while Stoudenmire decided he would call it a day. Cane in hand, he hobbled out the door and headed back uptown. He still tired easily, and he had begun to look forward to his afternoon naps.

Moving slowly along the street, it occurred to him how much he missed Tige trotting along at his side. Maybe this afternoon he would take a stroll over to the big dog's grave. They had buried him back close to Commanche Peak where the wild things still ran free. Tige would have liked that, being out there among his own kind. *El lobo hambre*, the Mexican kids had called him that first day in town. Well, hell, he never was what a man would rightly call civilized. Never wanted to be either, just like his master.

Stoudenmire chuckled to himself. Damn, they'd made a pair, sure enough. Maybe they would cut trails again when it came his time to cross over. The thought brought a warm glow deep down in his belly, and just a touch of the old cockiness crept back into his stride.

Hefting the cane, he slung it into the middle of the road and struck off at a fast limp toward home.